Th

Side of Morning

By
Loretta Wade

For My Family,
Jamie, Kurt, Kaylee, Nikki and Joseph
With Love

Jazzman

Carol King

Lift me, won't you lift me above the old routine?
Make it nice, play it clean, Jazzman
When the Jazzman's testifyin' a faithless man believes
He can sing you into paradise or bring you to your knees
It's a gospel kind of feelin', a touch of Georgia slide
A song of pure revival and a style that's sanctified
Jazzman, take my blues away
Make my pain the same as yours with every change you play
Jazzman, oh Jazzman
When the Jazzman's signifyin' and the band is windin' low
It's the late night side of morning in the darkness of his soul
He can fill a room with sadness as he fills his horn with tears
He can cry like a fallen Angel when the risin' time is near
Jazzman, take my blues away
Make my pain the same as yours with every change you play
Jazzman, oh Jazzman
Oh lift me, won't you lift me with every turn around?
Play it sweetly, take me down, oh Jazzman

Acknowledgements

This novel was inspired by an ancestor (Dr. 'Doc' William May) who suffered death at the hands of his forty-year-old suitor's (Andrew Sheffield) father, Col. James L. Sheffield in 1890. Andrew Sheffield's story is written in John S. Hughes *The Letters of a Victorian Madwoman*.

I must mention my parents, James and Ora Freeman May, for giving me a carefree country childhood in the Thompson Falls community of Marshall County, Alabama which is still listed by its old name on the county map as Ben Johnson Ridge.

There are so many to thank for the completion of this novel, I fear it impossible to list each and everyone. Let me begin with childhood friends and neighbors that inspired my rich and relevant characters. My dearest friend since first grade, Rebecca 'Becky' Reynolds, who shares her family with me to this day, and who gave me my fondest characters *Minnie Mama, Willene, Billy and Bonzie*.

I am deeply grateful to friends Debbie Reynolds Clayburg and Ramona Butler Harris for the hours of time spent exploring my story and their invaluable contributions to characters and plot. Billy Skidmore deserves a huge thank you for editing and suggestions, as does Tammy Eudy Noble for her hours of photography. And many, many thanks to Brian Myers, who waited and waited for the completed manuscript. Mere words could never express the gratitude I feel.

Author's website photo courtesy of:

The Late Night Side of Morning

By

Loretta Wade

Summary

Rosie Moon is a sixteen year old farm girl growing up in the southernmost foothills of Appalachia in Northwest Alabama. Her story begins in the summer of 1969 when relatives come to spend the summer in her small mountain community of Ben Johnson Ridge. She takes a special interest in her youngest cousin, a ten year old girl named Janie Noble; a child filled with grief, anger and guilt after witnessing her father's suicide.

During that passionate season of free love Rosie and Janie become almost inseparable as tragedy and danger force them into a family bond of survival when a mostly benevolent ancestral ghost is unleashed into their lives. This long-dead ancestor reveals himself as a medical doctor who practiced after the Civil War, and leads them on a precarious treasure hunt.

The girls are forced to seek refuge and embark on an adventurous journey in the summer of 1970, where they learn no good deed goes unpunished, yet erudition eludes the lesson. As one good deed follows another, the girls become entangled in legalities, finding their actions potentially libel, with possible criminal prosecution, all the while still facing Doc Campbell in vividly detailed dreams during the late night side of morning.

Chapter One
Beaches and Mountains

June 1969 - Gulf Port, Mississippi

The morning sun glared through the dingy window panes arousing ten year-old Janie from her Saturday morning slumber. She quietly left the room she shared with her seventeen year-old sister, Shelley. A refreshing gulf breeze floated through the opened window as Janie peered out to watch the sea gulls sail through the blue cloudless sky above the aqua green water of the Mississippi gulf. The waves caressed the sandy shore lazily, before rolling back into the surf leaving the sand dark with moisture. Janie stopped in front of the dresser and peered into the old mirror, fogged with age. Her unruly brown hair sprang about her face. Taking up the hairbrush, she made a half hearted effort to tame the frizzy locks. At last the task was completed by using a wide clasp to create a flattened ponytail.

There was an unusual quietness to the house as she made her way to the kitchen of the two bedroom apartment that sat above the bait shop her father owned. Trying to be completely silent, and not awake her grumpy teenage sister, she stepped lightly. Finding her father sitting at the kitchen table quietly smoking a cigarette in the morning lull was nothing unusual, and the solemn look on his face kept her mute. It seemed that every soldier who had returned from Vietnam suffered from what her mother called 'the blues'.

She took the box of *Rice Crispy* cereal from the pantry, and quietly prepared her breakfast. Occasionally, she would give her father a silent gaze as he sat staring out the kitchen window at the empty beach. Something about the way Tom Noble clenched his cigarette between his teeth told Janie that her father was distressed, and she worried he might have another flashback.

The absence of the old station wagon from the driveway made Janie aware that her mother wasn't home. Anxiety began to creep into the child as she watched her father snuff out a cigarette just to light up another. A salty ocean breeze floated in through the open windows with the sounds of surf and seagulls, suggesting a beautiful day ahead.

While returning the milk to the refrigerator, Janie stood for a moment gazing at the back of her father's head. Behind him on the kitchen wall was a framed photo of President John F. Kennedy sitting at his desk in the oval office. Directly beneath it was an enlargement of a black and white snapshot of himself with some army buddies taken while deployed overseas. An army soldier's helmet hung next to the photo, a hole blasted through it from sniper fire. Janie knew the story of how her father had survived that awful experience in the bloody conflict called a *Police Action*.

A small black and white television sat temptingly in the living room. The best thing about Saturday mornings was cartoons. As she leaned down to listen to the popping sound of the rice cereal a thunderous noise rocked the quite house. The bowl crashed to the floor as she whirled to see her father, now slumped and lifeless. Blood spread across the stained oak table, flowing around a green pack of cigarettes as if it were an island in a crimson tide. A small handgun lay in the floor, mockingly.

Panicked screams infused the atmosphere. Darkness closed in, and the cries were deafening. Someone was shaking her. Janie realized it was herself that was screaming as she focused on her sister's face, pale and terrified. Shelley grabbed her little sister and pushed her back into the bedroom. With a closed door, Janie crawled into her bed and sat there alone. For long quiet minutes that turned to hours, she stared at the tiny pink roses in the wallpaper.

The following days were a blur. Gulf Port neighbors came to the family's aid. The blood was washed from the kitchen table, and people came to the bait shop offering condolences. Neighbors prepared food and sat about drinking coffee with more neighbors, making polite conversation. An occasional joke would bring chuckles of laughter that ran through Janie like jolts of electricity. She was on her own, for her mother was bedridden with grief, and her sister was simply indifferent. When her grandparents arrived from Alabama, Janie fell into her grandmother's arms crying, "G-Mama! How can those people laugh in this house? They should be sad, but hear them? They laugh!"

"Don't fret over little things like that, child." Maggie Campbell said as she stroked her granddaughter's hair. "When people get older they get used to death. That's why they don't seem to be sad."

Maggie released her granddaughter and hurried to the bedside of her own child, Elizabeth. Janie sank into the chair left empty by her grandmother's departure and succumbed to heart wrenching sobs. Someone put arms around her and pulled her into a warm embrace. It was the familiar smell of *Old Spice* cologne that told her she was in the arms of her grandfather. She composed herself and pulled away. Albert Campbell smiled from his knees and wiped her face with a clean handkerchief. "My sweet girl," he said. "No one deserves what you've been given. I wish with all my heart I could change things. I would have done anything to save your daddy."

The child's sobs only intensified. Bert rose from his knees and pulled her to her feet. "We're going for a ride. It will do us good."

Outside her sister and cousin, Kid Campbell, were waiting. Kid was a cousin they rarely got to see, because he lived in Detroit, Michigan. Everyone in the family knew that Kid was Janie's favorite cousin. Just seeing him lifted her spirits. "Hey, Kid! I didn't know you were here," she called as she ran into his outstretched arms. He lifted her off the ground, and whirled her around in a flying circle.

"I've been trying to stay out of the way. It's a little crowded in there," he said, pointing at the apartment above the bait shop.

"Are Uncle James and Aunt Joyce here, too?" Janie asked.

He shook his head no. "Dad couldn't get away from the plant. The foreman has been threatening the workers to work overtime or get fired, so the old man works. Mom has to take care of him, so she couldn't come either, but she sends her love." Smiling down at Janie, he clasped his hands together, "Now, about that ride, maybe we should take my car. Want to see it?"

"Yes!" exclaimed Janie.

They walked around the bait shop where several cars were parked. "Okay, guess which one it is?" teased Kid.

Janie recognized all the cars, but one. "It's the convertible!"

"It's so cool!" Shelley exclaimed. She was already looking at the white leather interior of the cherry red convertible. "A Lincoln," she cooed in admiration. Running her hand across it she teased her cousin, "Bet you get lots of girls with this thing."

"I don't need a car to get girls," he declared defensively. "All they got to do is hear me sing, and they fall madly in love!"

"You leave them loose girls alone, boy!" Bert warned his grandson, "You'll get something that'll make your pecker fall off!"

All four of them laughed out loud. "Yeah," Janie interjected. "Then you'll have to sit down to pee."

With a look of disgust Shelley said, "Let's ride!" Turning to her handsome cousin with the shining blonde hair and dark blue eyes she asked, "Ready?"

"Let's roll!" Kid held out his hand with the keys dangling from his fingers.

Bert acted scared, "You gonna let a girl drive us around in this thing? Have you lost your mind boy? Folks will think we're drunk or crazy!"

Grabbing the keys Shelley said, "I'm not letting you change your mind." She slid beneath the steering wheel and called, "Get in!"

"I never did like riding with a female driver," Bert teased. "They slam on the brakes for squirrels, sticks and big leaves."

Janie called from the back seat, "Sit with me G-Daddy!"

Bert gave her a narrowed look and smiled, "Well, I guess I can do that."

Shelley drove through town like a tour guide, showing Kid the noteworthy sights of Gulf Port. It was a typical midsummer day on the beach. The cloudless sky blazed a hot sun down onto the travelers in the convertible. Soon, they were strolling languidly on the beach where waves rolled inland, spreading leisurely across the sand. Shelley and Janie slipped off their sandals and walked beside their grandfather, kicking sand with bare toes. Kid trailed along behind and sometimes walked ahead. It was a healing time.

On the drive back, Shelley sat with Janie in the backseat. The wind from the open topped car was playing havoc with Shelly's hair. She sat side ways, and held it clenched into a fisted ponytail. Janie had her own hair pulled back with a red ribbon. Upon noticing her sister's plight, she pulled the ribbon from her hair and offered it to her sister. "Here, Shelley. Take my ribbon for your hair," Janie said sweetly.

Shelley narrowed her eyes at the kid sister she detested, and slapped her hand away. "Oh, don't be stupid! I don't want that ugly thing."

Janie frowned in hurt disappointment. Kid watched the sisters in his rearview mirror taking note of Shelley's hideous behavior. Hoping to annoy her sister, Janie lifted her arm high above her head and let the ribbon flutter in the wind noisily, like the tail of a kite in a hurricane. Catching Kid's gaze in the mirror, she made a bittersweet request. "Kid, will you play a song on your guitar at Daddy's funeral tomorrow?"

Ben Johnson Ridge, Alabama

The early morning sun was quickly heating up the June day as Rosie toiled to fill her pail with the blackberries growing wild along the mountaintop. The day was humid. A few dark clouds mingled with downy white puffs high in the atmosphere, suggesting a hint of possible rain. Occasionally, she could hear the engine of a motor boat echo up the cliffs from the lake below. Just a few miles north ran the Tennessee River with the dam that kept the lake level, and supplied electricity for nearby towns.

The beetles seemed to want the blackberries as much as she did, yet showed a preference for the rotting fruit, which suited her very well. Now and then, she would plop a succulent berry into her mouth, and savor the sweet sun ripened flavor. The old cotton dress she wore was stained by the juice of overripe berries she brushed against, while reaching for the preferred outgrowth almost out of reach. The tall black wading boots did nothing to protect her knees from the briars that furiously snagged her flesh. Mosquitoes buzzed relentlessly, and perspiration left a visible damp spot on her bodice.

The sound of a pickup truck approaching took her mind momentarily off the chore at hand. She stepped from the brier bushes to see who was in her pasture. The familiar old blue truck bounced and swayed as it topped the terrace rows, and rolled hesitantly over them. A golden haired teenage boy and his younger sister laughed as they bounced about inside the truck cab. Rosie waved a greeting to her neighbors, Lewis Shirey and his younger sister, Angel.

Lewis parked with the front of the truck imbedded into the brier bushes. Angel jumped out and ran to Rosie, her long blonde hair hanging straight with bangs across the brow, was tangled from driving with open windows. "How much jam are you planning on making, Rosie? You've been out here every day this whole month!"

"It's not just for jam, Angel. There's jelly and cobblers, and don't tell nobody, but I think Daddy's making some wine, too. But today's pick is for Willene to make Minnie Mama a cobbler."

Getting out of the truck and leaving the door open, Lewis jumped onto the hood. "I thought I'd help you get those berries that grow up high on the bush." Then he proceeded to pick a few sun sweetened berries, and pop them into his mouth with a sly grin.

"Oh, I can see you're going to be a lot of help!" she teased with a flirtatious smile. Lewis and Rosie were the same age, anticipating their senior year in the fall, and Angel was only ten. Living on connecting farms and riding the school bus together, they had become good friends. She had been helplessly in love with their older brother, Ed. But, when he broke off the relationship to pursue a girl three years older than himself, Rosie was emotionally crushed. Even though, she never stopped caring for Ed, and cried when he was drafted.

"Hey! Angel! Try to get some music out of that busted up old radio." Lewis instructed his sister, "Anything, but Bluegrass. I practiced with the Mountaineers for three hours yesterday, and just about every other song we played was Bluegrass. But, we have to practice if we're going to have a chance at winning the five hundred dollar prize for the battle of the bands the city is giving on Independence Day."

Angel set about twisting the knobs on the dashboard radio. The static from the speakers filled the air as Rosie joined Lewis on the hood, and continued filling her pail. Standing near him in the heated sunshine she could smell the soap he'd used in his morning shower. At the same time they both reached for a cluster of berries, brushing their arms together, and invading personal space. Bobby Goldsboro's *Honey* filled the atmosphere with sad sweet music, giving her a chance to break the intense silence that suddenly overcame them.

"Oh God!" she moaned. "That song always makes me cry."

"Oh, boohoo little baby. Let me wipe your tears away," he teased. "Hey, did you see yesterday's *Dark Shadows*? Barnabas is still in the year 1897, and Jamison dreamed of David's death that's happening now in 1969."

"How did Quinton become a werewolf? I don't get to see it very often; I have so many chores to do. Hell, I only saw a few seconds of the lunar landing on the evening news! Today, I have to weed the vegetable garden and do laundry. My stepmother never does any of the household chores. I really hate her!" Rosie wailed.

Angel exclaimed, "Don't go back home today! Stay out with me and Lewis. We're going down to the lake after lunch. I'm going to wade in the water while Lewie fishes."

"No, you are not getting in the water. That scares the fish away. Don't you know anything?" protested her brother.

Surprised, Rosie asked, "You mean your grandfather lets you drive the truck to the lake?"

Angel interjected, "What Granddaddy don't know won't hurt us!"

Rosie said, "I wish I could go to the lake. But, I still have chores to do."

"Okay, then! This is what we will do," Angel brainstormed. "We'll all go back to your house, and finish your chores. Then we'll sneak away. If the step-monster asks where you went, all you have to say is that you went back out to pick more berries."

Rosie looked at Lewis and said, "Sounds good to me, what do you think?"

"Let's go! Your pail is full now, anyway," he said tossing a handful of berries on top of her harvest.

They drove the old truck through the field and parked it out of sight. While she hurried to store the blackberries in the refrigerator, Lewis and Angel got the hoes from the garden shed and began weeding the garden. As usual, loud television sound came from the living room as a talk show played.

Eva heard Rosie putting the laundry in the washing machine and called out, "Rosie! Make me some iced tea. I just got the last that was in the fridge." Wispy clouds of cigarette smoke trailed through the air and permeated into the kitchen.

She could feel her ire rise as she imagined her lazy stepmother propped back on the sofa with a creepy long cigarette dangling from her severely thin lips. She called back, "Okay," and pulled a pan from the cupboard. After filling it with water, she placed it on the electric stove. As fast as she could, she gathered the laundry and stuffed it into the washing machine. Snatching her swimsuit and towel, she took it with her to the kitchen. "Eva, the tea is in the fridge. I'm going to hang out the laundry now."

From the living room Eva yelled, "Okay! Okay! I'm watching TV. Can't you be quiet?"

Quickly, she hung the wet linens then joined her friends in the garden. "Okay, you guys, let's go!"

Lewis had parked the truck on a hill so he could let it roll off quietly. They drove to the Shirey farmhouse where Lewis and Angel lived with their grandparents. Mamie had lunch on the kitchen table for them, greeting Rosie warmly when she entered. "Rosie! How nice to see you. I hope you're having lunch with us. It's nothing fancy, just some garden vegetables and cornbread."

Mamie Shirey was one of Rosie's favorite people in the whole world, as she left an open invitation for Rosie to join her family for church each and every Sunday. The Shirey family was the music of the church. Mamie played piano, while Robert and Lewis played piano and guitar. Lewis had been learning music since childhood, and was often the main attraction at revivals for his beautiful singing voice.

After washing hands in the crowded bathroom sink with Lewis and Angel, Rosie joined them at the table with Mamie. Two empty chairs sat without place settings. She was painfully aware of the absence of Ed, and felt a need to bring up the tender void. "When was the last time you heard from Ed?"

Mamie looked softly at Rosie as if she understood the pain Ed had caused her. "We got a letter last week. He's hoping to be home at the end of the summer or early fall."

With a smile and a polite nod of her head Rosie expressed a kindly hope as she commented, "I look forward to seeing him, again." She asked lightly, "What's Mr. Shirey doing today?"

"Rob is out with Charlie at the stockyard." The older woman frowned, "I hope they don't bring home another wild bull that we can't keep pastured."

Rosie said lightheartedly, "That Charlie Brown is such a character! Whenever I see him out he always grabs at my nose and says 'I dot ewe nose!'"

Mamie laughed, "Bless his old sweet heart. Poor Charlie was born with that speech defect, and I guess he'll take it with him to the grave."

Lunch with the Shireys was a pleasant event for Rosie. Her days were always filled with chores and boredom. Mamie's fried green tomatoes were wonderful, especially served with her chow-chow, a relish made with green tomatoes, onions and red peppers. After lunch, the young folks made a premise of adventuring into the woods to fish for crawdads.

Again, Lewis let the old truck roll down the hill for a silent get away. They drove down dusty dirt roads winding around the mountain, lush and fragrant with thick blooming honeysuckle. While the girls splashed in the cool mountain lake, he took his cane fishing pole and can of red worms, then walked to a calm place on the lake where milfoil grew and fish gathered in the heat of the day.

The cool water was a delicious pleasure. The two girls bravely ducked underwater, stirring up the red clay of the river bottom. Angel paddled about keeping her head above water looking very much like a turtle. "Can you dog paddle?"

"No, I can only sink like a rock!" replied Rosie. "But, Miss Willene did try to give me some lessons last summer at the community pool. I guess I'm just not a natural born swimmer."

"Miss Willene is my grandma's best friend. We spend a lot of time with her and Minnie Mama. Grandma visits her every Saturday afternoon, and they watch the *Lawrence Welk Show* together," Angel explained. "Since Minnie Mama had that stroke Miss Willene can't leave her alone. I miss having her in the school cafeteria. But, she makes those chocolate oatmeal cookies every Saturday. I think she does that just to bribe me into coming over."

Angel walked out of the water and headed for a large old oak that had fallen into the lake. It stretched outward with its large limbs mostly submerged beneath the murky green water. The aged oak was anchored to the earth by roots still embedded into the red clay, while the roots that had been ripped away jutted skyward. She began walking down the length of the trunk sending shards of the rough decaying bark into the water, holding her arms out for balance.

"Careful Angel, the water looks deep beneath that tree," cautioned Rosie.

Angel looked over her shoulder and replied mockingly, "Don't worry." She leaned back on a thick branch folding her arms across her chest. "Rock-a-bye baby," she began to sing. A moaning snap of the branch was followed with a startled look of trepidation. She tumbled backward with the broken branch creating a sudden loud splash. Screaming Angel's name, Rosie ran onto the fallen tree. Angel surfaced the water and thrashed about violently. Rosie looked for Lewis, but he was nowhere in sight.

"Lewis!" Rosie screamed, "Lewis, help!" She lay down flat on the tree and stretched out her hand, but the tree was too high above the water. Angel surfaced the water again and again, but could not reach Rosie's hand. With one final scream for Lewis, she jumped into the water, hoping to touch the lake bottom.

Rosie did feel the lake bottom and pushed up, guessing the water was only a few inches over her head, but when she surfaced the water a panic stricken Angel grabbed her around the neck and forced her back under. Grasping a hold of Angel's waist, Rosie pushed her toward the surface, hoping she would grab onto the fallen tree. But, Angel only clung to her with every effort made. Unable to get a breath of air, Rosie herself began to panic. In only a few moments of oxygen deprivation, she began to grow weak. In desperation she silently prayed for Angel's life to be spared.

From the red clay river bottom a brilliant light surrounded her. The white light circled her with warmth and calmness, and she wondered where it was coming from. The area where she and Angel had been wading was shaded by tall pines. A soft sense of peace overcame her, and her fear was washed away in the pallid radiance.

Chapter Two
Fly Away

The small red brick church was filled with people who had gathered to pay final respects to Thomas Ray Noble. Fragrant flowers were nauseatingly oppressive, enhanced by the afternoon humidity. Opened windows without screens invited honeybees and other buzzing insects inside for a chance at the heady perfume of funeral blossoms. Electric fans whirred in all four corners of the chapel in an attempt to comfort the mourners.

Pasty faced women sat in the choir. Some held damp handkerchiefs to the nape of their neck, and some fanned themselves passionately with cardboard fans adorned with a picture of Jesus praying in the garden. Elizabeth Campbell Noble seemed oblivious to her two heartbroken children, leaving their care to her father as she leaned on her mother for guidance and comfort. The worn black skirt she wore had a snagged thread at the hem that she picked at obsessively.

Speaking the sermon, a Baptist preacher wiped sweat from his balding head while beseeching mourners to find the righteous path of God before it was too late, and they would have to face the sting of death without the Lord's redemption. His occasional passionate shout would startle the grief stricken Elizabeth, while the one most injured by Tom's passing heard the preacher through ringing ears, as if the gunfire had only just happened. After the pinched faced women sang their mournful rendition of *Amazing Grace* and *Precious Memories,* their clammy faces held a look of surprise as Kid strode to the pulpit with guitar in hand.

"Yesterday, my little cousin, Janie, asked if I would play a song for her daddy's funeral. Therefore, I'd like to play *I'll Fly Away.*" He strummed the melancholy melody on his guitar in a fast almost rock and roll beat, and no one moved. Even the babies stopped fretting in the heat. His voice rose in an impassioned rhythm as he went through the lyrics.

Tapping feet began throughout the congregation as rhythm overtook the solemn mood. A pleasing approval of the music's style spread like inspiration, and several of the choir members couldn't help but to sing along at appropriate intervals.

Later, as they sat beneath the tent casting shade over the gravesite, the family listened to the final words of the minister. While the flag covering the casket fluttered from an occasional breeze as it sat resting on the buttress above the opened earth, the minister spoke a final prayer. Two uniformed soldiers stepped forth and began folding the flag as another soldier, who stood out of sight, played a mournful rendition of *Taps* on trumpet. Elizabeth's composure crumbled as she was given the folded flag. She covered her face with the esteemed banner, and wept uncontrollably.

When the minister asked the family to step aside while the workers placed the coffin and covered the grave, she broke down sobbing. Elizabeth begged for the men not to place her husband in the tomb, and Bert, with the help of Tom's brother-in-law, took her physically from the grave. Maggie was overwrought by her daughter's grief, and brushed past her weeping granddaughters to comfort Elizabeth.

Janie clung to Kid as she cried her heartache into his shoulder, while Shelley was comforted by an Aunt related on her father's side of the family. He pulled Janie into his arms and carried her to the shade of three lofty pines that grew together near the roadway. By the time they reached the shade Janie had stopped crying. Her features were swollen and pink, and his heart ached for the child.

From his stance beneath the trees he watched Shelley crawl into the backseat of a large white Oldsmobile, and drive away from the cemetery. He stared incredulously about. Even his grandparents had gone. But he felt especially angry at Shelley. How could she overlook her little sister at such a time of great need? Kneeling beside the pale faced girl with glazed blue eyes he asked, "Do you want to walk back up and look at all the pretty flowers, or do you want to go home?"

With an emotionless voice she answered, "I never want to go home."

Stunned by her admission, Kid took her by the hand and walked back to the tent covered grave, now completely filled in with soil, and swathed in floral arrangements. When Janie took a seat in one of the folding metal chairs he sat down next to her. The heat of the Mississippi Delta penetrated the canvas while buzzing insects alighted on the flowers, lured by the promise of rich nectar.

Janie watched as a bumble bee crawled across a long streaming yellow ribbon embellished with silver glitter spelling the word *Father.* Occasionally, a few mourners who hung about the cemetery would approach the twosome and murmur soft condolences. Impatience encroached as the sweat soaked Kid's white dress shirt, and the Gulf offered no hint of a cooling breeze. He pulled the tie from his neck and watched Janie sit motionless looking upon the wilting petals, vibrant and perfumed.

Leaning toward her he asked, "Are you hungry? Maybe you would like to go with me for a burger and a milkshake?"

"I'd like that," she replied softly. "No one has ever been nicer to me than you are. Not even my own sister." With a resigned sigh Janie confessed a dark secret, "She hates me you know."

Still stinging from the fact that Shelley had left without showing any concern for Janie he said, "I don't think she hates you."

Without emotion showing she coolly remarked, "No, she hates me." Pulling her sleeve up over her left arm she said, "See this? Shelley did this."

A pink jagged scar spanned across her upper arm. "Dang!" he exclaimed; then asked, "Did you have stitches?"

Sliding her sleeve back over the offending disfigurement she answered frankly, "Oh, yeah."

Incredulously he asked, "What happened?"

With her gaze still focused on the embellished ribbon hanging from the wreath of funeral flowers Janie answered, "I told you. Shelley did it."

Shaking his head, Kid probed the little girl for more information, "How?"

Taking her gaze from the ribbon that proclaimed for all to see that the person buried beneath the mound was someone's father, Janie looked at him squarely. "She slashed me with a pair of scissors."

"Why on earth would she do such a thing? Was it an accident?"

Janie inhaled slowly, "No, it was on purpose."

Astounded with the belief that Janie thought her sister would deliberately harm her in such a savage way he asked, "Well, what provoked her to do that to you?"

"We were arguing over the television set. I wanted to watch *Captain Kangaroo* and she wanted to watch a rerun of *Gilligan's Island*. She told me she would cut me, but I didn't believe it. As you can see, I was wrong." Janie was aware that no one wanted to believe Shelley deliberately hurt her, so she continued talking. "Of course she said I ran into the scissors. But the truth is that I was standing still, and she slashed me with them. Everyone believed her. Mommy and Daddy just thought I was telling a fib, because I was mad at getting hurt."

Uncertain about the tale she was spinning, but certain that no one, not even her own mother was looking out for her this day, he took Janie by the hand and said, "Come on. Let's get something good to eat." And, she followed him to his car.

When they returned to the apartment only a few relatives were still there enjoying the food and coffee that neighbors had brought. Janie walked slowly past the kitchen not looking toward it or the dining table. Her curiosity peaked when she noticed suitcases and boxes stacked in the living room. "Are we leaving?" she asked to no one in particular.

Bert picked up an arm full of the stuff and said, "You and your sister will be spending the rest of the summer in Alabama with your grandmother and me." He looked at Kid and commanded, "Don't just stand there, boy. Help an old man out!"

Obligingly, Kid picked up a box filled with things for Janie. A large pink rabbit protruded from the top. He looked down at Janie saying, "Well, this is cool, huh? You'll be spending time in Alabama on G-Daddy's farm. You'll have fun, don't you think?"

Poking through boxes she answered, "Yeah."

The sound of Shelley's voice sounded behind them, giving Janie a start. "Listen, Twerp! That box has my stuff in it. So keep your hands off!" She reached down and snatched the box from Janie.

Kid couldn't refrain from speaking his mind to the rude older sister. "You're being a little rough on the kid, don't you think? She's suffered just as much as you have, so have compassion for her already."

Shelley's face softened, and with an intent look she answered, "Gee, I'm sorry, Kid."

He continued stacking boxes and snapped tersely, "It's not me you should be apologizing too." He walked away peering over the boxes he carried. Janie ran after him and held the door. Bert's trunk was full, and they began placing what they could in the floorboard of the back seat.

"We can put some of this stuff in my car," Kid offered.

An idea struck Janie, "Can you get my bicycle in the trunk of your car, Kid?"

He tousled her hair and answered, "Well, let's give it a try. If it fits, it rides!"

Later, as Kid worked alongside of his grandfather, when no one else was around he said, "Whatever you do, make sure you leave enough room in the back seat for Shelley. I'll take Janie with me, but I've already had enough of Shelley."

Bert wiped the perspiration from his forehead with a handkerchief. The afternoon sun was slowing giving up the day, and the sound of the surf seemed to intensify the solemn mood clinging to the members of his family. "Okay," he agreed. "But, can you tell me what she's done to eat at you?"

Choosing his words carefully he murmured, "I don't like the way she treats Janie, that's all."

Bert gazed at his grandson's handsome young face, tanned from the summer sun, and said, "Fine. We'll ride back like you want. I just want you to follow behind me at a reasonable speed. We ain't in any hurry. Got it?"

Sliding the bicycle into the trunk Kid affirmed, "Got it."

When they went back to the apartment Maggie was fretting with her daughter, Elizabeth. Imploring her to close the shop, and come home with them for the last few weeks of summer. Elizabeth sat pale and serene at the kitchen table where her husband had lived his last moments, looking out the window. She leaned her head over into her mother's bosom, and pleaded for Maggie to not worry about her.

As the Campbell family headed to the loaded cars for the long trip home, Elizabeth did make a final request of her family. "Oh, wait just one moment. I'll be right back!" She rushed up the wooden stairs that ran on a vertical slant up the side of the building, and came back with an elegant garment box. "Mother, please find a place in the attic for my wedding dress. I just have so little room here in the apartment." As Maggie reached for the box she noticed four framed photos, and a photo album.

With a bewildered look Maggie asked, "Don't you have room for your pictures either?"

With anguish returning she answered, "Yes, but I don't know if I can ever bear to look at them again."

Maggie asked Kid, "Do you have some room in your backseat for this, dear?"

Approaching his grandmother he took the carton, "I'll make room, G-Mama." Then looking down at the family portrait that had been taken when Janie was still a baby, and Tom hadn't yet been to war, a hard lump rose in his throat. He said to his aunt in a shaky voice, "Don't worry. I'll be careful with this."

Stepping next to him Shelley asserted, "I'm riding with you, Kid."

The memory of how cruel she'd treated Janie was still fresh, and he said frostily, "Sorry, Janie's riding with me."

A repugnant look crossed her face at the thought of it. "Okay, we'll both ride with you."

He said, "No, Shelley. Janie's riding with me, and you're riding with G-Daddy. That's all there is to it."

Shelly demanded, "Why, Kid? Why don't you want me to ride with you?"

Losing patience he snapped, "Cause, I don't want you to!"

Appearing hurt she asked, "Gee, Kid. What did I ever do to you?"

Speaking across the white canvas top he said to his indecorous cousin, "It's not got anything to do with me. I've noticed the way you treat your little sister. And, I'm standing here to tell you I not only think it's wrong, I think it's downright low. How old are you, Shelley? Seventeen right? But you act like a spoiled little baby with no feeling for anybody but yourself." He pointed his finger at her, and narrowed his eyes, "Well, I'm going to be around for the next couple of weeks, and if I see you mistreat that little girl don't think I won't do something about it."

Faltering for the last word she stammered, "Don't think I'm afraid of you!" and stomped away. Without giving her mother a final kiss goodbye, Shelley crawled into the backseat of Bert's sedan.

Janie clung to her mother, and begged for Elizabeth to call her at the farm in Alabama. Bert had to pull the child from her mother's waist and settle her into the front seat of Kid's car. They drove away with Janie calling tearfully, "I love you, Mama!"

The setting sun hung low over the horizon, bathing the highway in soft golden light. Kid reached behind the seat, pulled the pink bunny from the box, and placed it in Janie's arms. She hugged the toy close, and silently rode long miles until she fell asleep with the pink rabbit pillowing her head against the car door.

Rosie awoke with a gut wrenching cough. She was lying on her left side when her eyes focused on what appeared to be her own puddle of vomit. Rolling onto her back, she looked skyward into the towering branches of Maples and Oaks that blocked the torturous rays of midday summer sun. Someone was crying, and speaking her name softly. When she took her gaze from the leafy solitude of the sky, she saw Lewis kneeling over her, his face contorted with fear. "Rosie? Rosie? Can you hear me?"

Becoming fully conscious she spoke with startled agitation, "Angel! Help her!"

"Angel's right her," Lewis soothed, "You saved her."

Angel picked up Rosie's hand and cried, "Oh! Rosie! Thank God! You're okay now!"

Rosie sat up suddenly, the motion made her dizzy, and nausea overcame her. She lurched to her knees and vomited. Embarrassment filled her. A sudden swell of emotion overtook her senses, and she began to cry. Lewis pulled her from her knees, embracing her tightly. Angel wrapped her arms around her brother and friend, and they all shed tears of relief together.

After having changed into their dry clothing, the young people began their journey back up the mountainside. The dry summer dust clung to the heated still air like fog as the old pickup truck labored back up the mountain road. A surreal sense clung to Rosie's brain, like a haunting. The once fragrant honeysuckle impeded the cab of the truck with a nauseating memory of funeral flowers. With a horrified gasp she put her hand over her heart.

"What's wrong?" asked Lewis.

"I just remembered that my cousin's father is being buried today, Uncle Bert and Aunt Maggie's son-in-law. They are there now in Mississippi for the funeral, and I almost gave them another funeral to come back too."

The threesome fell silent as they leaned one upon the other while the pickup rolled over the bumpy dirt road. Large groves of maple trees grew along a long stretch of the road leaving the well traveled thoroughfare darkened in a tunnel of cooling shade. Braced one upon the other they rode in silence until the main road appeared. As the gears were wound out, and the battered old truck gained speed, the air cleared in the dusty truck cab. Straws of hay began flying about for Angel to slap away. Suddenly an idea occurred to Rosie, and she asked Lewis, "Would you teach me to drive a stick shift?"

He smiled, "Love too! But first I'm gonna teach you how to swim."

The next morning, Rosie worked in the garden to escape Eva and her visitor only to be surprised by a visit from Lewis. He rode his bicycle into the garden, and dismounted, taking time to put down the kickstand. She knelt beside the strawberry plants, thinning the patch. He stared down at her with his gaze resting on the bodice of her dress as though he noticed the strain on the buttons.

"Lewis! How nice to see you," she said sweetly.

"You, too," he replied taking his gaze from her bodice to her soft brown eyes. "Whose car is that in the driveway?"

With a wrinkled brow she replied, "I don't know, and I don't want to know. What are you up to today?" She gathered up the strawberry vines that she had clipped away.

Looking at the tops of her breasts round and firm, he felt the heat within him stir. Shaking the vision from sight he cleared his throat and explained, "I came to take you swimming. Remember? I told you I wanted to teach you to swim."

"What about Angel? Didn't she want to swim?"

Taking the pruned vines he answered, "She's out shopping with my Grandmother today, and besides I've been trying to teach her to swim her whole life. She's not a very good student."

Standing with her back to the sun, Rosie drank in the beauty of her young friend's face. "Do you know who you look like?"

Looking at her sheepishly as though maybe he didn't want to hear her opinion, he smiled and asked, "Who?"

She turned and led the way from the garden to the compost heap. Looking over her shoulder to make sure he was following she answered, "The guy who plays that character on *Dark Shadows*, Willie Loomis. You know who I'm talking about, John Karlen." After pausing a moment to see his expression from her comment, she reached out and took the vines, tossing them onto the compost heap. "I think Willie is the cutest guy on that show."

He reached out and took her hands, turning them over to observe the rubbed in dirt. "So, you think I'm cute?"

"I think you are the cutest boy in this whole world!"

Fighting an impulse to kiss her, he rocked back on his heels and sighed heavily. "Okay. So, you want to go swimming or what?"

She reached out and traced her index finger down his forearm sending shivers into both their bodies. "Where are you taking me swimming, not the lake again?"

"Bert built a new pond this summer. Let's use it before the cattle do."

Her eyes sparkled at the notion, "Yes! That's a great idea."

They retrieved the bicycle from the garden, and she climbed into her bedroom through the window to avoid Eva and her friend. After donning her swimsuit, she pulled the dress that was a size too small back over her head, before climbing back out the window. Lewis mounted the bike and motioned for her to get aboard.

She looked at him suspiciously, "You want me to ride on the handle bars?"

"Look, it's not that far, just about a mile. Sit your bottom right here, and it'll only take a few minutes to get there."

"Okay, here goes," she giggled and hoisted herself into place.

"Now, lean back against me."

"Are you sure this will work?" she asked, grasping the handlebars.

"I ride Angel like this all the time. Of course it will work," he reassured her.

They began rolling smoothly along the blacktop with her snuggled against him. The morning sun warmed the asphalt, ricocheting a cloud of humid heat. Rosie could feel the warmth of his body, and soon the sweat was penetrating his shirt and seeping into the back of her dress. They glided through the shadows casts by the tall pines and hardwoods lining the quiet country road. Frogs croaked as they passed by a slime covered pond. Horses stopped grazing to watch them sail by. Contented by just being in his embrace, Rosie relished the final moments of the bumpy ride. They came to a stop at her uncle's front porch, and Rosie pushed herself from the handle bars.

The residence was quiet as she knocked on the door. "No one's at home," she observed. "Bert won't mind, anyway. Let's go!"

The pond was murky, but the water was clean and cool in the shade of the woods. A large rock protruded near the edge. Holding her afloat at the waist as he instructed her in swimming, Lewis stressed relaxation and controlled breathing. The lesson ended with floating. The pond was peaceful with only the forlorn sound of a lonesome crow cawing in the distance. After exhausting himself by swimming back and forth across the pond, Lewis joined her on the rock.

"Let's just sit here in the sun and dry off a bit, before we start home."

"You know I need to do something nice to repay you for your swim lesson today. Heather is coming over tonight. Eva and Daddy are going out to play poker, so why don't you come over and join us after they leave?" Seeing the uncertain look on his face, she continued, "Heather has one of those Ouija boards, and she wants to perform a séance. I think she's been watching too much *Dark Shadows*."

"You know, our preacher has talked about those things being instruments of the Devil. He says you can invite demons into your house with them. It sounds a little dangerous."

"She's bringing pot to make brownies," Rosie added in a sing-song voice.

A brilliant white smile appeared between his parted lips, "Oh, yeah. I'll be there. I hope it's some more of that Acapulco Gold like she had last week."

"Lewis, can I ask you a personal question?"

With a look of apprehension he asked, "Like, how personal is it?"

"How do you keep your teeth so white?"

"I read this thing in an old magazine that Mamie has lying around. It said to use strawberries to brush your teeth. There's some kind of acid in them that makes your teeth white. So, I guess it works, huh."

"Yeah, it really does.

It seemed that all of Rosie's clothing was too small for her. The two piece swimsuit she wore threatened to spill her breasts, and her rounded buttocks fell from the sides of flimsy fabric. Aroused and irritated by it Lewis asked a bit harshly, "Why do you wear clothes too small for you?"

It was impossible to hide her embarrassment. "I need new clothes. But my dad just doesn't earn much money. I've been making enough on my homegrown to buy school clothes for the past three years. I expect I'll earn enough to do the same this year. But, swimsuits just aren't a priority for school, you know."

"Well, like Mamie always says, God will provide. So this Sunday I'll ask him to send you a new swimsuit," he said with a sardonic smile which sent a blush across her cheeks. Together they stood and made their way back. Walking side by side, he with his jeans slung over his left shoulder, and she with her tired threadbare dress draped over her arm.

"Hey! You two been trespassing?" Bert's voice came from the front porch and startled the teenagers. He laughed at the anxious looks on their faces. "Well, Lewis! I see you've been swimming in my pond again. You didn't see any water snakes around down there did you?"

Smiling brightly he answered, "No sir. Not a one."

Bert looked at Rosie, "What about you, young Sunshine? How are you today?"

She smiled at her mother's cousin. He always called her by her first name, Sunshine. Her mother had called her Sunny, but her father preferred to call her Rosie, a play off her middle name of Rose. "Uncle Bert! You're back from Mississippi already? How is everyone?"

"I brought everyone back with me. They're all inside, my granddaughters, Shelley and Janie. My grandson, Kid, came all the way from Detroit for the funeral. He's inside too. We just got home. The trip got to be too much for Maggie, so we stopped off and got a room to spend the night just this side of Wetumka. We just got in a few minutes ago. Come on in and say hello to your cousins," he said while motioning for them to follow.

Quickly, Rosie pulled the dress over her head while Lewis stepped into his jeans. Together they followed Bert into his house. A flurry of activity greeted them. The two sisters were unpacking a summer's worth of articles brought from their home in Mississippi. Bert called to Maggie and she hurried from the kitchen.

"Oh sweetheart, it's so good to see you," Maggie said to Rosie. "You've got to see your cousins. It's been so long since you were all together. Shelley! Janie! Kid! Come here kids, hurry!" called Maggie to her grandchildren.

Trepidation rushed through Rosie. Shelley had always treated her with a distant coldness, and now in light of her present situation, she wondered how Shelley would treat her. Janie raced into the living room and threw her arms around Rosie. "Rosie! Can you stay all day and play with me?" Janie pulled back and looked up into Rosie's kind brown eyes saying, "My Daddy is dead. We buried him back home in Mississippi, and my Mommy is all alone taking care of the store. She wouldn't come with us."

Shelley emerged from the hallway just in time to hear Rosie reply, "I wish I could stay all day with you, but I have to go home, and finish my work. We'll make plans to spend an entire day together soon. We'll have a picnic at the lake, okay?"

"What fun that'll be," snorted Shelley sarcastically.

With genuine sympathy, Rosie looked at her cousin with the boney frame, flat chest, light brown frizzy hair and crooked nose. The old dislike she felt for her was overshadowed by pity. "How are you, Shelley?"

An exaggerated roll of the eyes answered the question. Leaning heavily against the wall with her head looking up at the ceiling, she responded bitterly, "How do you think?"

Rosie's attention was drawn to the ceiling, as though there was something there worth looking at. Lewis stepped next to her saying, "Sorry to hear about your dad's passing."

Shelley's gaze fell from the ceiling. "Lewis! It's been so long since I've seen you." She raced across the room and threw her arms around his neck hugging him tightly against her thin body. Caught up in confusion by her amorous behavior, he stiffened his stance while his arms hung limply, declining to return the sentiment.

A masculine voice pulled everyone's attention to the kitchen doorway. "Try not to suffocate the poor boy, cousin." A tall lean young man with chin length blonde hair and a thin blonde mustache stood with his arms above his head as he held to the doorframe. Taking notice of Rosie he exclaimed, "Sunshine! It's been a long, long time since I've seen you. Do you even remember me?"

Maggie had kept Rosie proudly informed of Kid's achievements over the years. "Well, I would never have recognized you, Kid," she admitted with a smile. "How are you, and the folks back home?"

"Oh, everybody's doing good back home. I still play with the band, and I'll enter my third year of university this fall." Stepping closer he reached out to touch her hair. She could smell his expensive cologne. "Have you been swimming?" He pulled on a damp tendril of dark hair, and then pushed it back behind her shoulder.

Her pulse quickened. Kid Campbell was Albert's grandson, her grandmother's cousin's grandson. He was extremely handsome and well dressed. Nervously she stepped back and stammered, "Well, yes. We, Lewis and I . . . were swimming. Uh, out back in Uncle Bert's pond."

"Can I go, too?" asked Janie.

"Be careful not to step on a snake out there!" Maggie declared.

Shelley wedged a place between Kid and Lewis, "Well, what fun! Swimming in a cow pond! What will we think of next?"

Bert interjected, "Yes, dear girl, when you were Janie's age you, too, had fun swimming in my cow pond."

"Is anyone thirsty? I can make some lemonade," Maggie suggested.

Taking a step toward the door, Lewis hastily said, "None for me thanks. I've got to be getting home."

Promptly, Rosie agreed, "Thanks, Aunt Maggie. But, I've got to be going, too."

"Wait now," Bert said. "I noticed you rode a bicycle down here. Let Kid drive you home. You can put your bike on the back of my truck."

Rosie looked to Lewis who nodded his head and said, "Okay, sure." "Can I go, too?" asked Janie.

Bert answered quickly, "No! You and your sister have a lot to do around here, so get busy doing what you're supposed to be doing. I'll take you visiting later."

Shelley rushed forward and hugged Lewis again, "See you soon, Lewis. Okay?"

His discomfort was painfully apparent. "Okay," he said through gritted teeth.

Kid followed the young people outside where Lewis was walking his bike to Bert's pickup. Pointing at his car with the convertible top down, he said, "Hey, Rosie, maybe later, before I leave to go home, you can take a ride with me in my car and show me the lake."

The sound of his suggestion did not sit well with Lewis, and he looked at Rosie with narrowed eyes. Taking note she replied, "Gee, I don't know about that, Kid. My Dad is really strict. He keeps me on a short leash, if you know what I mean. I don't get to go out much."

Kid laughed, "It's not 'going out' Rosie. It's just a ride around the lake. Let me talk to the old man. He'll let you show me around, I promise."

Slamming the tailgate shut, Lewis slid in next to Rosie with his arm leaning out the passenger window.

During the drive Kid talked about the beauty of the mountains and farmland of North Alabama. When he suggested driving Lewis home first, Lewis unconsciously clenched his right fist and release it again and again as he rested his arm halfway out the window. Noticing his agitation, Rosie took him by the left hand and said sweetly, "Thank you, Lewis, for the swimming lesson today. I look forward to another."

His hand tensed in hers when Kid said, "I can teach you to swim, Sunshine. When we go to the lake, just bring your swimsuit."

Silence fell over the threesome until it was time to pull into the drive at the Shirey farmhouse. Kid spoke first. "Nice spread."

Lewis answered, "This is my grandfather's farm." Then he exited the cab leaving the door open, to remove the bicycle. Leaning into the passenger side he said, "Thanks, for the ride."

"Anytime," replied Kid, adding, "I'll be seeing you around."

"Yeah, guess so," Lewis answered, before turning his attention to the soft doe eyes that could provoke him to lunacy. "Thanks for going swimming with me, Rosie. We've got to do this again, soon." And, without giving her time to answer, he leaned in a planted a moist kiss upon her lips.

When he pulled back she said breathlessly, "Yeah, I can't wait."

He stepped aside and closed the truck door. Pounding lightly on the hood he gave a final farewell wave, then turned and walked into the house without looking back.

"He seems like a nice guy," Kid said. "Are you two going together?"

Rosie answered, "No, just friends."

The distance between the Shirey and Moon farms was short. Within only a minute of letting Lewis off, Kid was pulling into the driveway at her house. "Thanks for the ride home. It'll probably be a long time before I see you again. You more than likely don't get down here too often, only for funerals and stuff."

He laughed, "Well! Let's hope it's a long time before we have another funeral."

"Yeah, let's hope," she agreed.

"Hey, is there like anything to do for entertainment around here?"

A soft smile swelled her lips, and her voice held honest disappointment, "Not much, sorry."

"Well, do you have any girlfriends you'd like to introduce me to?"

Relaxing against the truck seat she said, "Well, I do have one girlfriend coming over for the night. Would you like to meet her?"

Considering the invitation, he licked his lips and candidly asked, "Is she as pretty as you?"

Getting out of the truck she closed the door gently. "Just come over after dark." With the sun shining full upon her face, she tilted her face toward the golden rays, and said with closed eyes, "We're gonna have a séance."

He deliberated the invitation, "Who else is coming?"

Her gaze dropped to the grass that tickled her bare feet. "I asked Lewis, but I had to bribe him with brownies."

Wrinkling his nose he asked, "What's so great about brownies?"

With a devilish little giggle she began walking away, and called over her shoulder, "My secret ingredient, that's what."

Chapter Three
Séance and Gunpowder

Heather arrived before Rosie's parents had left the house. Her glossy raven hair was pulled into a smooth ponytail held by an elastic cloth band, and she wore a loose fitting tan sun dress with shabby brown leather sandals. Charcoal eyeliner accentuated her dark Native American eyes, and turquoise earrings dangled from her earlobes. "Only my grandma does more canning than you do, Rosie."

Amused, Rosie said, "I do this every summer. It's how we save money on the grocery bill during the winter."

Heather sidled close to Rosie as she stood elbow deep in hot, sudsy dishwater. "Don't you ever wonder what your Dad does with his money?"

With a furrowed brow she answered, "What do you mean? He pays the bills, and Eva's car payment. He just doesn't make that much money working for the highway department."

Heather replied incredulously, "Oh, really? Well Tabitha Fletcher's dad works with your dad, and they have two cars and take vacations."

"Well, I think Tabitha's grandparents help them out a lot, too. And, have you noticed? We don't have grandparents around this house."

Snooping around the kitchen, Heather poked at vegetables Rosie had gathered from the garden. "Sorry, if I sound suspicious."

Rosie shushed Heather as Sturgill and Eva sauntered through the kitchen on their way out. Eva's slumped shoulders, along with the long cigarette that hung on her lower lip, gave her the appearance of a cartoon caricature. They exited the back door without speaking a word to the two girls.

"Come on! Let's get ready for the party," Heather said as she pulled forth a plastic bag with finely ground marijuana.

Taking the chocolate mixture she had waiting in the refrigerator, Rosie added the substance while blending it with a spatula. Heather pulled the baking pan that she had already greased from the oven, before turning the heat on. Rosie poured the batter into the pan, and then Heather slid it into the oven.

While rinsing the bowl, Rosie said, "We've got to get a candle for the séance from dad's room. Come with me."

The girls entered the closed room, and began fumbling around for the candles Eva kept for power outages. Heather began poking around in the dresser drawers while Rosie located the long box of tapers on the closet shelf. "I've got it!"

Heather answered, "Uh, oh, so do I."

Coming to stand beside Heather, Rosie peered into the open drawer to see what had been found. "What?"

Pulling out a clear plastic bag filled with plastic objects she asked, "Don't you know what these are?"

Reading the package Rosie asked with confusion, "Insulin syringes? What are those doing here? Nobody in this house has diabetes."

Shoving the bag back into the drawer Heather said, "I think this solves the mystery of why your dad never has any cash."

Shaking her head in disbelief, Rosie whispered, "It can't be. I would know, wouldn't I?"

Heather reached out and took the candle from Rosie. "You do know, now." Studying the candle she frowned, "Shit! It's bad karma to use a red candle for a séance. They attract victims of violent deaths. Those are the ones that want to kill you."

Stunned by Heather's discovery, Rosie softly requested her friend's confidentiality, "Hey, don't tell anyone about those things we found, okay."

Holding the candle horizontally in front of her face Heather said, "We didn't find anything worth talking about here, Rosie. Trust me." Then she protruded her tongue in an obscene way and licked the candle from bottom to top. With narrowed eyes she explained, "I heard my mom and one of her friends talking about some spinster lady masturbating with candles."

Rosie inhaled sharply, "I really didn't need to hear that!"

With the tip of her tongue clenched between her teeth, Heather stared wickedly at the candle. "It does sort of look like one, doesn't it?"

Grasping Heather by the shoulders, she turned her friend toward the door, and gave her a push. "We don't need candles. We have real men coming over."

A suspicious look clouded Heather's face. "It better not be that geek face Zeke Tidmore! Zeke the geek has crushed on me since first grade."

Speaking in a voice that sounded more like the purr of a kitten, Rosie answered, "No geeks welcomed here." The sound of a car's engine and flashing headlights signaled that someone had arrived. "You get the door while I check the brownies."

She could hear Heather greeting Kid at the living room door as she stuck a tooth pick into the brownies. The sound of two young people introducing themselves carried through the house as they walked together into the kitchen where Rosie stood holding the pan of brownies with oven mitts covering her hands. She exclaimed, "Ha! Look who's just in time for brownies."

Shaking his head in confusion he asked, "What's the big deal about brownies with you girls?"

Heather pulled a chair away from the table and motioned for him to take a seat. The Ouija board sat upon a crisp white table cloth. Using the butane lighter from the coffee table, Heather melted the bottom of the candle, before adhering it to a small white saucer. "Prepare to be spooked, Mr. Campbell," she said with an impersonated gypsy accent.

Placing the brownies on the table, Rosie asked, "What shall we wash these down with, how about some whiskey-lemonade?"

"Oh, that sounds good, but I've never heard of it before," said Heather.

Removing a pitcher from the refrigerator Rosie asked, "Straight or on the rocks?"

"Rocks for me, please," answered Heather as she flirted shamelessly with Kid.

Lewis appeared at the back door and asked, "Have I missed anything, spooks, ghouls or vampires?"

"Sit down, Lewis. We must partake before we begin the process," instructed Heather.

He sipped the beverage and exclaimed, "Wow, this stuff bites! What's in it?"

"Just a little *Jim Beam* I snitched from Eva," Rosie answered. Then she turned on a local radio station, and joined her friends at the table.

Heather spoke with her mouth full of brownie, "You know," then pausing to swallow she continued, "There are a few exercises we must do to get the psychic juices flowing."

"Psychic juices, is that what you call it?" teased Rosie.

Flashing her friend a dirty look, Heather continued explaining. "After our snack we should all go into the living room where we have more space to stretch out and warm up our spiritual energy."

Lewis shoved a brownie into his mouth, and grinned through clenched teeth when he saw the raised eyebrow look Heather gave him. "Gee, Lew? Don't you even chew?"

Rosie leapt to her hero's defense, "Don't be mean to Lewis! He saved me from drowning yesterday."

Nibbling at the brownie he held on a paper napkin Kid asked, "Were you really drowning?"

"If it weren't for Lewis I might be the dead spirit you conjure up tonight," Rosie answered sincerely.

Heather leaned over and slapped Lewis on the knee, "Dang! I didn't realize we had a hero in our company!"

Throwing up both hands he asked, "Can we just change the subject?"

"Okay," Heather agreed adding, "Kid, you have to eat more than one brownie." She shoved the pan at him.

Sipping the bitter lemonade Kid acknowledged, "Sorry, but they're a little dry."

The others laughed. Rosie explained, "That's because of the secret ingredient."

Heather stood and said, "Bring your drinks. It's time to go into the living room for the extrasensory exercise." Pushing the coffee table to the wall she said, "I'll need a volunteer. Let's use you, Kid. You look like the heaviest one of us."

Looking skeptically at Heather he responded, "Are you sure? Maybe we should bring out the bathroom scales. You don't look all that light yourself."

Heather feigned insult.

Kid laughed and said, "Okay, okay. I volunteer, but for what?"

Pointing to the floor Heather said, "You have to lie down there."

With a look of suspicion on his face he stretched out onto the ragged rug that covered the wooden floor, placing his hands behind his head.

"Oh, no, your arms have to be down at your side." Heather instructed as she knelt on her knees beside him. "Rosie you come over beside me and Lewis you get on his other side." When they were situated, Heather instructed, "Now everybody place two fingers on each hand beneath Kid."

"No tickling," Kid warned.

Rosie slid her fingers beneath him, and asked, "Okay, now what?"

Heather looked to make sure everyone was in place then she stepped to the switch plate and flip off the overhead lights. Resuming her position she began, "Okay, now everyone clear your mind, and listen only to the sound of my voice. Kid, you must pay close attention to every word I say."

Silence fell over the room, and Heather began spinning a story in a low monotonous voice. "Everyone close your eyes and imagine a black dot on a white piece of paper. Stare at the black dot. Don't look away. Now watch the black dot get larger and larger. Now, all you can see is black. Kid, you've had a long hard day, and you just want to rest. You are driving along a dark, rainy, wet road. You're driving too fast, because you want to get home, so you can sleep. You are so tired. You can't hold your eyes open. You're falling asleep. You are asleep. You are asleep, and you are dead. You just crashed into a tree. You're becoming stiff with death. You are dead, cold and stiff. You are getting colder, and stiffer. Rigor mortis begins to set in upon your dead, cold body, and you are growing stiffer, and stiffer. You are as stiff as a board. You're dead, cold and stiff. You begin to feel as light as a feather, and stiff as a board."

Heather began chanting, "You're dead. You're dead. You're dead, dead, dead. You're dead, you're dead. You're dead, dead, dead."

They all joined in with the chanting. "You're dead, you're dead. You're dead, dead, dead."

While Rosie and Lewis chanted, Heather began a different chant. "You're light as a feather and stiff as a board, light as a feather, stiff as a board, light as a feather, stiff as a board."

Without realizing what was happening, Kid's body became rigid. Heather, Rosie and Lewis began lifting him slowly off the floor with two fingers of each hand and continued chanting. A sensation of floating rushed through him, yet he was unaware that he was being lifted up. He opened his eyes when the chanting stopped, and the spell was broken. Suddenly, he fell back to the hard floor. "Hey!" He complained, "What the hell did you just do to me?"

Heather apologized, "Oops! Sorry about that, Kid. You were levitating, and I just didn't know how to get you back down without bringing you out of the trance. That's something we're going to have to work on next time we try this."

Not amused he snapped, "Trance, my ass! I wasn't in a trance."

But, Rosie and Lewis were stunned by the event. Lewis alleged, "Okay, so you weren't in a trance. But you damn sure were floating on air."

With his remark being made, the three burst into giggles as Kid sat dumbfounded on the floor. "You are all just shitting me," he assumed out loud and struggled to stand. Taking a clumsy step backward, he rubbed a hand across his face, "I feel a little dizzy, though."

Heather grinned, "Yeah, me too. The brownies are taking effect. Anybody else feel the buzz?"

"I do," Rosie and Lewis synchronized. Then they pointed to one another and again said in spontaneous harmony, "Pinch, poke, you owe me a coke!"

With fuzzy perception, Kid stared at Heather and asked with a voice enchanted by misapprehension, "What was in those brownies?"

Reaching a guiding arm around him Heather guided him back into the kitchen explaining in a soothing voice, "Don't fret, city boy, just a little Acapulco Gold, nothing at all to freak out over. Unlike the Aztec Ceremonial Trip Weed I had last week. That stuff would put you into a cannabis coma!"

His mouth fell open with enlightened awe and his eyes danced about as questions, answers and a plethora of emotions traversed, beginning to end, in his adulterated thoughts. Finally, Kid whispered through a perceptive smile, "And, I thought you *country* people didn't know how to have fun."

The leftover brownies were brought back to the table and they each helped themselves to another. "More lemonade, anyone?" asked Rosie while dividing the remaining beverage to everyone's upheld glass.

After the brownies were devoured, Heather finished her drink and said, "Okay, now this is the time to get serious. When you utilize the Ouija board, you don't actually touch the pointer, okay. You just hold your finger tips above it. The energy of your psychic authority is what causes the planchette to spell out messages from the spirits you contact. No matter what we do, we will not give any spirit permission to come into our world. This is very important, because demonic spirits will pretend to be benevolent to gain your trust."

Sitting back uneasily Kid inquired, "I thought this was just a game. What are you talking about, rules, clues, missions?"

Heather coached, "Everyone place your fingertips just above the pointer, and clear your minds."

Lewis flipped off the light switch, and turned off the radio as Kid lit the candle. When everyone had their finger tips in place Heather continued, "When the pointer moves, be careful to follow it. If you remove your hand the energy will be lost."

Silence settled upon the group as Heather began her spiritual directives, "We summon the lost souls who have passed over for answers to the questions we have. We ask for a nearby spirit to speak with us tonight through the power of Ouija."

The four sat holding their hands in place for a long silent moment before Heather continued her summons. "Spirits of the dead come speak with us through Ouija. Tell us what you would have us know about business you left unfinished upon this earth."

The candle flickered from the breath of the four participants as they sat with elbows in midair holding the uncomfortable pose for the Ouija board. Long silent moments passed as the candle put forth heat from its flame, and melted wax oozed beaded rivulets down its tapered sides.

Heather commanded, "We seek the repressed spirits who need to tell the living the secrets of their desire. Come forth with your message from beyond. We beseech you to confess that which you wish us to know."

With that request an unseen energy peeled away the dark shadows dancing upon the kitchen walls. The pointer moved in a slow circle then at a snail's pace moved to the letter M. It moved so slowly, that at times Rosie believed it had exhausted its energy. But, with painstaking slowness it eventually spelled M-U-R-D-E-R. After this one word was spelled the plastic game piece stopped moving.

Heather continued probing the spirit who wanted to speak. "Come into our realm, and give us the knowledge you wish for us to have. Step forth, and speak with the living. We want to help put your worries to rest. Tell us the secrets, let us help you."

With everyone holding the position of finger tips above the pointer a strong oppressive odor filled the room. Sticky moisture seemed to attach itself to the flesh, and a low moaning wind whisked about the outside windows. Fear marred the faces of all four.

Heather's voice grew stern, "Speak to us now, or leave us alone!"

The planchette beneath their fingertips flew out of their reach and clattered upon the floor. The shadows that had clung to the walls danced away from the fortification, toward the young foursome seated at the table. An oppressive force arrested Kid's consciousness, and he slumped across the table, almost knocking the candle over. Rosie jumped to his aid. Pulling him upright, she leaned him back against the chair. In the dimly lit room she could see that his eyes were wide, and instead of the blue iris, his were now a deep brown like her own.

Heather shouted, "Speak to us spirit!"

His lips trembled, and a frosty breath escaped, but there was no sound. Finally, a low audible swishing whisper came from his mouth, but it was not his voice. It was the disembodied voice of a spirit. A faint despondent sobbing began, as though the phantom used Kid's body to express unalleviated grief.

There came a sound of air being expelled from an unknown source, and the shadows that had once clung to the walls gathered about him, moving in a circular motion, as would leaves in a cyclone, and a desiccated, smoky aroma coasted into the room. No one took their fixated gaze from the ashen faced Kid as he sat statue like, with his eyes gazing upward in unblinking mania. A slow mournful cry began from the cold unmoving lips, and became a loud emotional scream as he wrenched himself from the mystery and leapt to his feet, his heart pounding in his ears. "Ah! What the hell did you do to me? I was having a nightmare from hell, man! Someone," he stammered as his eyes darted madly while trying to logically explain, "someone dead, who had been murdered, was trying to tell me who killed them, but I wouldn't listen! I refused to hear!"

The flickering candle flame sent diminutive stalks of liquefied beeswax descending the tapers like crimson ivy, capturing Heather's perception and prompting her to say, "I knew we shouldn't have used that red candle."

Awestruck, Lewis asked, "What about that smell? Did you recognize it? It's like a mixture of smoke and sulfur. What kind of smell was it? Gunpowder I think."

Rosie gawked at Kid, her eyes feral. "Your eyes changed color! And, you spoke with a different voice. What can you remember about that dream? Please, please try to remember!"

Pacing the kitchen like a confined animal Kid advised, "Let's just get out of here! Come on everybody. Let's take a ride to the lake or something."

Disintegrating into acidic tears Rosie wailed, "Oh! Why did we do this?"

Stabbing at an explanation, Kid shook his head slowly, "I didn't see a person in my dream. I only saw these dark eyes. There was no face or body to it. Just the eyes and a soft rasping voice begging me to listen to the name of the killer." He looked around at the others with liquid filled eyes and said, "I didn't want to know who the guilty person was. I was afraid to hear the name. I fought so hard to wake up and get away from those eyes, and that sad voice!"

"Okay, I agree with Kid. Let's just get out of here," said Lewis as he followed Heather out of the kitchen.

Moistening her lips with the tip of her tongue, Rosie said to Kid, "Before you leave next week, I'd like to talk with you about how well you remember my mother."

He nodded his head in agreement, and she quickly held up her hand to hold back anything he might want to say. "Don't tell me anything now, but later. Okay?"

They walked from the house and onto the front porch. The night air held a mystic summer scent as the fire flies darted about in the velvety darkness. Rosie took a deep breath and declared, "I smell rain!"

Lewis replied, "Rain would be good."

They stepped into the velvety darkness of the night amid nocturnal sounds and sights. The scent of rain clung to the air, but the sky was cloudless, and sparkled with astral jewels. A quarter moon gleamed with gracious candor, and the still darkness exuded tranquility. No one spoke as the car glided along the roadway following the path of headlamps, and the radio remained off.

Rosie was captivated by one single star that shone brighter than the others and she watched it sparkle with brilliance as they drove along the quiet country road. Without reason, the watched star fell from the sky leaving a long streak of radiance in its wake. The last dying embers vanished as would ashes from a bottle rocket. The spectacle enthralled her, causing her to inhale a sharp breath of surprise. Suddenly she and Lewis looked at one another. It was reassuring to know that he, too, had witnessed the stellar demise.

Saturday morning dawned and Rosie awoke from a dreamless sleep. Heather lay next to her, still sleeping. She tried to leave the bed without disturbing her friend, but as she placed one foot on the floor, Heather rolled over and asked, "What time is it? I've got to call my Mom. We're going to visit an aunt in the nursing home today."

"It's eight fifteen. Sorry I woke you. I was trying not to."

Heather stretched and yawned, "Yeah, well, you were trying too hard." As she watched a fly crawl insidiously across the ceiling she said, "My mom has a friend that can help us understand what happened to Kid last night."

Picking up the clothes she would wear for the day Rosie said, "Hold that thought. I'll be right back after a quick shower."

When she returned, Heather was waiting for her mother. "I think I have an idea," Heather said. "Find out from your family all you can about who lived in this house, and how they died. If you come across any stories of a murder, then we can bring in my mom's friend to do a psychic reading."

A long silence fell over them, as neither had an appetite to dissect the events of the evening past. The sound of tires crunching gravel told Heather it was time to go. She stood and gathered her belongings. Standing at the bedroom door to exit, seemingly at a loss for words she said, "Call me." Then opened the door, and departed.

The day progressed as a usual Saturday. Rosie and her father took the yellow VW bug from the car shed, and drove into Byron Town for grocery shopping. After having parked beneath a large tree to shade the car from the hot sun at the far corner of the parking lot, she left her father reading a newspaper to do the shopping for the week's grocery supplies. A crowd had gathered close to the main road as people milled about a large yard sale. Rosie poked her head back into the car via the passenger side window and said to her father, "Got any yard sale money?"

Sturgill looked at his daughter tiredly, stretched out his leg and reached into his pocket. He retrieved a handful of change and dropped it into her hand.

Yard sales were one of her passions, and it was exciting to see that one of the hosting ladies was a member of the same church the Shirey's attended. Evelyn Edwards greeted Rosie warmly and pointed out some clothing that her own daughter had outgrown. A lovely summer dress for church was the first thing she chose. Then a pair of shorts for PE and a pair of sandals, but she only had a few cents left when she came across a pair of jeans that would fit better than the ones she owned.

"I think those would fit you nicely."

Rosie turned to face Evelyn. "I know, but I don't have enough money left."

"Yes you do. How much money is that in your hand?"

She opened her hand to reveal the two nickels and six pennies in her palm, "Sixteen cents."

Evelyn scooped up the coins saying, "Well, you do so have enough money," and deposited the coins into her apron pocket. "Will I see you in church tomorrow, dear?"

"Yes, I'll be there."

Evelyn smiled, and gave Rosie a tender hug. There seemed to be something else Evelyn desired to say, but she didn't. Rosie took her new things to the car, and left them on the backseat while she did the grocery shopping.

As was her usual routine, she stepped out to the curb while the cashier rang up her purchases. After motioning for her father to bring the car around, she stepped back inside. Momentarily, Sturgill entered the store and approached the check out register with wallet in hand. The cashier finished the process and the bag boy put all the things carefully into brown paper bags. The cashier, whom Rosie knew as Doris, looked up from her completed task and announced the total to Sturgill, "Twenty-seven sixty-two."

Sturgill looked at Rosie with surprise. The grocery bill was never more than twenty dollars. "What the blazes did you buy?"

Taking note of the concern on his face she answered, "I had to buy some extra things for Eva's Tupperware party. Is something wrong?"

Sturgill looked uncomfortably at Doris, "Oh, dear. I just didn't bring enough cash with me." Then looking to his daughter he said in an apologetic tone. "Well, just put some of those things back. Eva can pick those up later."

Doris smiled, "Not a problem. What shall we take off?"

Sturgill handed Rosie twenty-three dollars, and went back to the car. She began by removing the paper napkins, plates and plastic cutlery Eva had instructed her to buy. She also put back the dish detergent and True Confessions magazine. Doris subtracted the items and reversed the total to twenty-four dollars and eight cents. Rosie stood indecisive. As a last resort she took the box of sanitary napkins, and placed them back on the counter for Doris to subtract. Feeling humiliated as the young pimple faced bag boy watched the process impatiently, Rosie expressed her appreciation for the clerk's help, took the receipt offered with change, then followed the boy with the bags out the door.

As soon as Rosie and her father returned home an explosive argument ensued. Sturgill began berating Eva for hosting a silly Tupperware party that the family couldn't afford. Eva had been nipping on whiskey, and threw back hurtful words regarding Sturgill's lack of education and salary.

When Sturgill fumed that most of her party accessories had been left at the store Eva became furious. She faced Rosie and demanded to know what Sturgill was speaking of. Explaining how she had to sacrifice the paper goods for the party, she attempted to calm her stepmother by saying they could borrow linen napkins from Mamie Shirey. After all, Rosie reminded, they were borrowing Mamie's punch bowl anyway. Eva sat puffing on a long slender cigarette and suddenly noticed that something from her shopping list was missing among the items.

"Hey!" Eva expressed indignantly inebriated, "You didn't get my magazine!"

"I was going too, but that was one of the items I had to put back."

The stepmother's eyes narrowed and her face darkened like Cinderella's evil guardian. She stood and drew her hand back sending a loud slap across Rosie's face. Rosie gasped a startled scream and put a hand to her stinging cheek. In a half moment Sturgill was back in the room. He could tell by looking at his daughter's tear filled eyes and reddened face that she had been assaulted.

Grabbing Eva by the arm he screamed, "I've told you for the last time, woman. Keep your filthy hands off my kid!" Snatching her by the back of her neck he flung her forcefully down on the floor.

Catching her father by the arm Rosie pleaded, "Daddy, don't! You'll only wind up in jail!"

Leaning down, he grabbed his wife by the arm saying, "Get your sorry ass out of this kitchen! You never do any work in here anyway!"

The argument escalated, and could be heard from the living room as Rosie continued her work. Hot, bitter tears streamed down her face as she finished putting the groceries away. She took the yard sale clothing to her room, and placed them on the shelf in her closet. Eva could be heard begging for forgiveness as Sturgill threatened to put her out of the house. Their arguments were always the same, and Eva always won him over with her pleas and promises.

Rosie's days were spent harvesting vegetables, and collecting fruit from the wild vines that grew along Ben Johnson Ridge. The evenings were spent processing her day's labor into jellies, and canned produce that would be used during the upcoming winter. Her father toiled his days away for wages with the Alabama Department of Transportation, doing manual labor on bridges and roads.

Eva's days were spent lazing on the sofa in front of the television, watching soap operas and game shows, as she smoked one cigarette after another. It was Rosie who did all the work in the house and in the yard, keeping the lawn cut clean and raked. Even the meals were prepared by Rosie. Each evening her father came home to fresh garden vegetables and cornbread, served with fresh cow's milk strained of its cream and chilled.

After his meal with a tall glass of milk, her father would disappear into his bedroom. Having spent some time behind the closed door of his room, he would retire to a worn spot on the sofa where he would watch TV, and doze with his chin resting upon his chest.

Some evenings after the kitchen was cleaned from the evening meal, she would spend late night hours snapping beans, peeling tomatoes or cutting corn from the cob. Occasionally, her work would be noisily hindered by the arguments coming from the living room. The loud exchanges were embarrassing, and Rosie was thankful no one lived close enough to hear. She attempted to keep harmony by ensuring the chores were completed, and the food was pleasant. Rosie baked breads, cakes and cookies to satisfy her father's sweet tooth; even seeing that there were plenty of baked goods, and sweet tea for Eva to entertain her friends who came to call during the day.

On occasion, she would come home from the fields before a man friend of Eva's had left the house. Once she found a man tying his shoe laces while sitting in the kitchen, with a bottle of liquor missing a bit of its contents atop the table. When Eva drank too much with her friends it made her sadistic. Pent up wrath was expelled on Rosie, when her father wasn't around.

On the days Eva was drinking, Rosie would grab a sandwich and head for the woods, spending the day walking barefoot in cold mountain streams, and play acting on large boulders that she pretended was a stage. She would sing passionately to entertain the imagery audience. Other times, she would sit in the sun to read large thick novels borrowed from the library.

Picking up a tattered straw gardening hat, she left the house to find solitude in the garden. The day was hot and hazy as clouds gathered in the sky. Hot winds blew across the meadow with a slight threat of rain. As she calculated the maturation of her corn and butter beans, her attention was drawn to the driveway by the sound of an automobile. Looking up, she saw Kid emerge from his convertible. Raising her right arm high above her head she waved to catch his attention.

"Hey, what 'cha doing?" he asked as her got near. His blonde hair shone almost translucent in the light of day. "Do you think you could get away from your work long enough to grab a soda with me?"

Standing straight, she lifted her hair, allowing the warm breeze to hit the back of her neck. Noticing this, he stepped closer and blew a cooling puff of breath onto her neck, sending shivers down her spine. She found herself dumfounded as to why he excited her so. Staring into his blue eyes, she took note of the sapphire particles that swam within the azure irises. "I can't ask for any privileges now. My dad and Eva just had a knock down drag out fight, because of me."

"Because of you?"

"Don't even ask," she moaned, "it's just too embarrassing."

They strolled through the garden, and walked across the lawn. A rickety old chair sat near the shed, and Kid took a seat in it. Sinking to the ground, she sat facing him. "I'm glad you stopped by," she began softly. "I want to know what you remember of my mother."

Leaning toward her, he inhaled the perfume of her scent mingled with a nearby rose bush before responding. "Well, I remember playing in a sprinkler right here in this yard. We both stripped down to our underwear, but somehow yours got lost." With a devilish gleam in his eyes he asked, "Hey! You want to do that now?"

A blush crept across her cheeks, "No, thank you. I've learned to keep my clothes on." She giggled as Kid feigned disappointment. "What else do you remember?" Aching to hear something poetic, and beautiful about the woman who bore her into the world, she yearned for confirmation that her mother had loved her, adored her, and dreamed wild successes for her.

Sitting back, he appeared to get lost in a far away memory. "I can remember one time when you stepped on a honey bee. You were screaming bloody murder, and Aunt Dorothy very calmly scraped the stinger out of your foot with her fingernail. Then she made a poultice from some of Charlie Brown's snuff, and smeared it onto the bee sting. In only a few minutes you were back running barefoot through the clover." Suddenly, he grew thoughtful, "I know your mother wasn't actually my aunt. She was my grandfather's cousin's daughter. But I always called her Aunt Dorothy."

"Yes, I know that." The disappointment was impossible to conceal. Rosie's dismal conclusion was that he could not burrow into the twilight memory of his childhood to produce evidence of a mother's love for her daughter that was so binding it could reach beyond logical reason. A deep desire for tangible proof of a mother's devotion so strong it could descend from heaven, and reach back to earth filled her with a hunger to simply know.

Silence overtook the two of them as they sat in the shade of the garden shed. Bumble bees provided a contented harmonious song, as they buzzed about the bending rose bushes in the garden, strained from the burden of their blossoms. Impulsively, he leaned over and pulled a long tendril of hair from her shoulder. Caressing it gently beneath his finger tips he said in a voice softer than a whisper, "Sunshine, we don't have girls like you in Detroit."

Sweetly, she smiled, "Well, maybe that's because you only find farm girls on farms, not in big cities."

Seriously he asked, "How serious is this thing between you and Lewis?"

Honestly she answered, "Lewis is my best friend in this whole world. I love him!"

His eyes widened, "Love?"

Attempting to be transparent she explained simply, "It's an innocent relationship. His family has practically adopted me." How could she make her cousin understand the loneliness of her life; void of a caring mother, and burdened by an inept father. With a soft sigh she confessed, "And, I guess I should go ahead and be honest enough to tell you that I was at one time completely head over heels in love with his older brother, Ed." She smiled and admitted, "It was crushing when he found a girl he liked better, but" she paused a moment to engage his attention, "I'm over him now."

He clenched his fingers into a fist, as though to keep them from reaching out to touch her again. "Is he over you, too?"

"I'm sure he is. Anyway, he's in Vietnam. The Shirey's are hoping to have him home at the end of summer." The quiet calm of the house seeped into the backyard, and she wondered what she would find if she ventured inside. Rising from her knees, she said "I'll go with you for a soda. I'll meet you at the car in just a few seconds."

His face softened as a sugary smile curved his lips, "Okay."

Television noise carried through the house as she entered the back door. Carefully she avoided the living room, and taking the jeans she had purchased earlier from the yard sale, she slipped them on. After pulling on a white t-shirt, crawled out her bedroom window, and hurried to the car where Kid was waiting.

You always crawl out your bedroom window like that?"

She giggled, "Only when I want to avoid my parents." It wasn't necessary to tell her handsome relation about the complete dysfunction of her family. She knew he could never understand the life of a farm girl orphaned by the death of one parent, and the drug addiction of another.

They drove to the nearest store and purchased Coca-Cola in six ounce bottles. Directing him along winding country roads where farms lay next to one another and farmhouses sparsely populated the landscape, she told him to pull off the roadway onto a single lane dirt road. They parked beneath a towering oak tree, and continued walking along the rutted road. The sound of a waterfall became evident as they neared Rocky Falls. The view of turbulent water rushing over treacherous jagged rocks, framed by stone cliffs enthralled Kid, bringing nostalgic memories of summer visits as a child. They removed their dusty canvas sneakers, and with rolled up jeans strolled into the cold pristine mountain water. The sun disappeared behind gray fluffy clouds, and a brisk breeze ruffled the leaves among the trees. They climbed back up the path along the embankment and took a seat on the bridge that stretched across the creek, connecting two public roads above the waterfall.

There they sat side by side and watched the water flow to the precipice of the cascading stream. The breeze picked up strength and the sky grew darker. The sound of distant thunder was muffled by the reverberation of crashing water against stone cliffs. The wind strengthened, twisting branches until the leaves lay sadly upside down. Shouting to be heard, she motioned for him to follow. Together, they started back to the car.

Chapter Four
Laughter in the Rain

The climb up the rutted roadway was strenuous. They were out of breath before reaching the car. Just as they entered the clearing fat drops of rain began to fall, sending stinging droplets against them. Together they ran toward the car, but were completely caught in the downpour.

Throwing up her arms in defeat, Rosie laughed wildly. Her drenched t-shirt clung like skin, revealing what the cotton bra underneath struggled to contain. Upon noticing her fun, he stopped. With her arms flung wide, twirling around and around in the downpour he caught her up impulsively, pulling her close. Her pulse quickened, for she fully expected him to kiss her. But he didn't. Taking a step back, he caught her hand in his and drew her along the path.

The leafy boughs of the great oak shielded them from the punishing rain once they reached the car. Opening the passenger door, he thrust her inside, then ran around and entered at the driver's door. Inside the car they sat panting for breath. Popping open the glove compartment, Kid pulled out a stack of paper napkins from a fast food restaurant. Dividing the stack he handed some to her, and the other he used to dry his face. When the rain saturated the Oak branches, and began to infiltrate the open windows of the car, they rolled the glass up on the doors.

"I knew I smelled rain in the air last night," sighed Rosie. Unable to suppress the question she blurted it freely, "Why didn't you kiss me? I know you wanted, too."

He smiled and answered lazily, "Well, a man would have to be blind, crazy or gay if he didn't want to kiss a pretty girl like you."

"So, you're telling me you're gay?" she teased.

Shrugging his shoulders he replied, "Just because I'm in Alabama doesn't mean I can go around kissing my cousins."

Suppressing a chortle she said, "We aren't true cousins, you know."

Breathing in sharply he teased, "You really do want to kiss me bad, don't you?"

Playfully she slapped him on the shoulder. "You conceited ass!"

For a long minute they sat in stillness and watched the rain fall against the windshield. Distant thunder rumbled through the valley, and the windows began to fog from the warmth of their breath. Kid straightened up, and using one of the soggy napkins wiped a circle of fog from the windshield. "I guess it's time to get you back home. We don't need you getting in trouble today, do we?"

"No, we don't need to do that," she remarked, remembering the harsh slap across her face.

When they arrived at her house the rain had lightened to a mist. She was about to push the door open when he put out a hand to stop her. "Hey, wait! Do you want to do something with me tonight, something that doesn't include Lewis, or séances?"

Her heart lightened, "Of course! I'd love too. You know Heather that you met last night? She's camping overnight at the dam with some friends. We could crash their party." She added as a tease "Maybe you'd like to give her a kiss?"

Nodding his head as though in agreement he said, "Yeah, maybe. So what time do you want to go?"

She answered thoughtfully, "I don't want Daddy to give me a hard time, so wait until after dark. See that old barn across the road there? Meet me there just a little before eight, when it's dusky dark."

"What's your dad going to do if he catches us sneaking around?"

"I don't want to think about it!" She blew him a kiss as one last taunt, "Don't be late!"

Crawling back through her window, she changed out of the wet clothes. Taking the red leather diary from beneath her mattress, she stretched across her bed, and began putting her affection for Kid into words.

The afternoon rain had washed the air clean, leaving coolness in its wake. That evening tree frogs sang a familiar summertime song and the fire flies illuminated their flight along Ben Johnson Ridge. Sturgill kissed Rosie on the cheek and thanked her for cooking his super as he always did, before he disappeared into his bedroom for the nightly ritual that made him groggy and giggly while he sat beside Eva watching television.

After showering, Rosie towel dried her hair while looking for something to wear to her clandestine meeting. Settling for tattered jeans, she slipped on a faded blue blouse with fluttery sleeves, and a tired lace bodice. When her hair had almost dried, she pulled it into a ponytail high off the nape of her neck. A rubber band and a white satin ribbon secured the thick tresses. Extinguishing the overhead light, she left via the window.

The clouds had cleared and the stars twinkled around a sallow quarter moon. The night air was fragranced with a rain washed scent of Magnolia blooms carried on a light breeze as Rosie walked the path to Mr. Reyes' barn. Once inside, she clicked her tongue to announce her presence to the horses, Sugar and Spice. They welcomed her with a soft raspberry sound, and she took turns going from one stall to the next, patting their velvety muzzles. Dimmed headlights swept across the pasture as Kid arrived in his car. She waited inside the barn until the headlamps were dimmed to parking lights. Then she raced to the car, and jumped inside enthusiastically.

He was directed along the back roads that would lead them to the Byron Town dam in the shortest amount of time. The short cut took them through an undeveloped stretch of land used as a game preserve, and managed by the Tennessee Valley Authority. They had to slow their speed considerably to safely cross a one lane concrete bridge spanning a wide creek. Approaching the bridge, Rosie expressed sadness at the sight of a dead puppy lying on the road. She squealed for him to stop when she caught sight of another pup evading the glare. Kid pulled over and leapt from the car to snatch the frightened puppy.

Putting her cheek to the furry little black face that sported a brown spot above each eye she smiled, "I just love puppy-breath!"

"What are you going to tell your dad about the pup?"

She exclaimed, "I can't take him home with me!" Seeing his confused look she explained, "It's simple. The puppy will be on Bert's porch in the morning, and Janie will have a fit to keep him."

Putting the car in gear, Kid crossed the bridge. Rosie peered into the darkness for a glimpse of the dead puppy saying wistfully, "I wish we could have saved the other one, too."

He remarked, "Well, darling. You just can't save the world."

The road to the Byron Town dam took them down a steep mountain road with lots of curves. When they drove into the parking area they saw the night lit up with electric light, and lots of camping activity. The smell of food cooking over charcoal wafted through the air, causing the hungry pup to stir.

They drove into the primitive camping area, and parked under bright street lamps. Tents were strewn about and bonfires lit the night sky. People milled about drinking beer as a group of young musicians entertained them. Rosie was thrilled to see that Heather was one of the musicians producing the tunes. They arrived to hear her singing a duet with a nice looking young man with long, silky brown hair. When the song was finished Rosie called out, "Great job, Heather!" And, she joined in the applause.

The raven haired girl looked up to see her friend from school, and stood to greet her. Heather was tall and plump, with a pear shaped body. She was from Native American decent, her face was pretty, oval shaped, dark lashed and clear of complexion. The soft denim shirt she wore with rolled up sleeves was adorned with a fringed buckskin vest, which enhanced the appearance of her heritage. "Hey! You didn't tell me you were coming tonight."

Holding the puppy, Rosie answered, "It was a last minute idea."

Kid asked to see her guitar. Heather handed it to him, and then instinctively reached for the puppy. "Where did you get the rug rat?"

"We rescued him. I think he's hungry, have you got something we could feed him?" asked Rosie.

Walking in the direction of her tent Heather replied, "Gee, I don't know. You think he would eat some cereal?"

As they followed Heather to the tent Kid began picking a tune on her guitar. "Hey! You finger pick nice. Want to do a song later? I'll get you a beer for your efforts."

He smiled, "You know I do, girl!"

Heather poured some cereal and milk into a bowl. She placed the bowl onto a towel, and sat the puppy inside the tent, before zipping the tent flap closed saying, "There, he'll be safe. Now, let's go play some tunes."

Heather introduced Kid as Rosie's cousin from Michigan, and the music makers welcomed him. It took a few minutes of regrouping, but Kid came up front and did a rendition of the Blood Sweat and Tears hit song *Spinning Wheel*. His voice was strong like that of the singer David Clayton-Thomas, and the crowd was pleased with his performance. He returned Heather her guitar just in time to make his hands free for the two beers thrust at him by men in the crowd.

Mesmerized by Kid, Heather held a ravenous look as she gazed at him. She asked, "Hey, you guys want to drop some Owsley?"

Kid's eyes grew big. "Are you kidding? What about you, Sunny? Want to drop some acid, take a little trip?"

With apprehension she answered, "I've never done acid before, maybe I shouldn't."

He pulled her close. "Trust me, will ya? It'll be a blast and I'll take care of you."

Heather said, "Follow me to wonderland."

Kid smiled brightly, "Let's go, Alice!"

Heather led them to a van in the parking lot under the street lamps. She took an aspirin bottle from a hobo bag, and slid open the side door motioning for Kid and Rosie to get inside where she joined them. "I've already promised Barron half a tab, so you guys are going to have to share one. It'll still be fun. I usually only do a half anyway."

Rosie asked, "Is this Barron's van?"

Taking up a fifth of Tequila, Heather unscrewed the lid and took a drink. She answered Rosie's question as she handed Kid the bottle, "Yeah. Here you go, wash that stuff down with a gulp of this cactus juice." To Kid she explained, "Did you notice the dude I was singing with? That's Barron."

Taking a small sip, Rosie winced as it burned her throat. "Let's go back to the campfire. This van smells like dead fish and lemon soap."

Later, while she sat away from the fire that ebbed into slow flickering flames, Rosie began to feel the effect of the drug. Comical antics seemed to be happening all around. She laughed hysterically when a girl lit the wrong end of her cigarette, and howled when a young man went to sit in a folding lawn chair, and it slipped from beneath him, sending him onto the ground with a jolting thud. The amusement was unending, and people began dancing as Heather and Kid sang upbeat tunes together. Rosie was getting attention from young men that she neither desired nor asked for. But, there was something in the Owsley that made her oblivious to all the irritations that usually perturbed her.

The drug wasn't overpowering as she had feared, but rather enlightening. It seemed that perplexing questions now held such simple answers. Life was simple indeed, when mind altering drugs guided your inner wisdom. When she saw that dawn was about to break, she pulled Kid from the crowd, and asked him to walk to the water's edge. They sat together on huge rocks as the water lapped lazily at the river's bank. An occasional shadow of a river rat would catch in her peripheral vision, expanding into a wonderment of the nocturnal creatures. When the sun broke the horizon and the rays gleamed golden across the sky, Kid inhaled sharply. The river reflected the dawning rays, cascading rich golden hues across the rippling waves.

"I wish we never had to leave here. This moment is just so perfect," he whispered. Then he said matter-of-factly, "I'm not leaving here next week. I'm staying till the end of summer. Right here, with you."

"With me?" she asked, astonished.

"I'm staying so I can convince you to come back to Detroit with me. You'd love the neighborhood where I grew up, and you can finish your last year of school at the same high school I graduated from."

Light hearted laughter ripped through the serenity of the morning. "You're stoned out of your head, Kid Campbell! Why would I want to do such a crazy thing?"

Without thinking he pulled her close to him, "Because, I'm crazy in love with you!"

He attempted to kiss her, but she pulled away laughing, "I'm only sixteen!"

"Seventeen, next month," he interjected. The surprise showed in her eyes, prompting him to explain, "G-Dad has mentioned that your birthday was in July."

With a sweet smile she tugged at his hand leading him along the river bank to Heather's tent, and the smell of coffee. Wanting to make certain that she understood completely, he repeated, "There's no way I'm going home next week. I'm spending the rest of the summer right here with you."

Janie awoke early in the room she was given at her Grandparents home. The morning sun poured golden light through the sheer curtains that covered her bedroom windows. Tossing aside her bedcovers, she removed her nightgown to dress for the day. She found a pair of yellow shorts and a mint green t-shirt. Looking about for some shoes she slipped on a pair of blue thongs, and exited her room without making the bed. It was early, and Maggie was just beginning breakfast. Janie joined her in the kitchen, offering to help. Maggie was having a hard time keeping Janie out of her way when Bert made his morning entrance, heading straight to the coffee pot. As he slid into place at the kitchen table he gazed out the window, and noticed Kid's car was not in the driveway.

"Damn that boy," he grumbled to Maggie. "He stayed out all night. Makes you wonder what in hell there is to do out there that can keep you up all night." He sipped his hot coffee with small slurping swallows.

Maggie frowned, "Well, let us not discuss those kinds of things right now."

Janie talked incessantly, "G-Daddy? Do you think we could go fishing at the lake today? Maybe we could take a picnic, and ask Rosie along? I love Rosie, she always plays dolls with me, and sings me songs, and reads me stories." Janie's childish exuberance revealed that her depression had been left in the dark crevices of memory for the moment.

Bert shook his head and said, "I don't know right now, Janie. You've got to let me wake up, and think about what all I've got to get done today." He drank his coffee contemplating which young girl in the community had kept his grandson out all the night long.

"Well, maybe the two of you could take a walk outside while the biscuits are baking. I'll be sure to call you as soon as the gravy is ready." Maggie urged hoping to get them out of the small kitchen for a few minutes.

Bert realized the problem little Janie was being to her grandmother, and picked up his cup of coffee. He spoke down to the child sitting next to him. "Come on with me, squirt. Let's see if the chickens are hungry.

"Can I feed them G-Daddy? I know how to feed chickens."

Bert winked at his wife, and responded gruffly to Janie, "Well, come on then!" The two left the kitchen for the backyard pens. Summer dew clung to the grass, and the insects buzzed frantically. The time was coming up on eight o'clock when Maggie called them inside for breakfast. Bert cautioned Janie to wash her hands, or wind up with a chicken disease. Janie wrinkled her nose in disbelief, but washed her hands anyway.

Bert and Maggie were being thoroughly entertained by Janie as breakfast was coming to a finish, when there was a soft knock at the back door. Bert stood to open the door and saw that it was Robert Shirey's grandson who had come to call. "Well, come on in, Lewis!" Bert called through the door. When Lewis stepped inside Bert suggested with hospitality, "Have a cup of coffee with us. Have you had breakfast yet?"

He declined while explaining his visit, "I thought Charlie Brown might be here with you. I couldn't find him at his cabin."

Bert nodded in understanding. Charlie Brown had lived on Bert's land in a small cabin they built together more than twenty years ago. Bert had become somewhat of a guardian for Charlie since most of Charlie's family had passed on. Charlie was a mentally challenged friend from childhood, who often earned money by helping other farmers with field work.

"Does Rob have some work for him?"

Lewis shook his head, "No, Charlie said he would teach me how to track the honeybees to their hives. I've been promising Mamie that I would fetch her some wild honey. I woke up early today, and thought I might talk Charlie into a honey hunting spree after church."

Maggie smiled, "Well, we can tell him you came by."

Lewis shook his head. "I'll catch up with him later." He looked over at Janie scraping gravy into a spoon. "Is your sister still sleeping?" He asked just to make polite conversation with the little girl.

"Yeah, she always sleeps till noon. I want G-Daddy to call Rosie up and ask her to go fishing with us today. Shelley's never any fun, Rosie's always fun."

"Well, when I see her today at church, I'll let her know that you really want to spend some time with her, how's that?"

"Tell her to hurry, I'm bored," Janie interjected.

Looking at Bert, he asked, "Has Kid already gone back home? I didn't see his car in the driveway."

Janie said, "He stayed out all night, and G-Daddy's not happy about it."

Bert narrowed his eyes at Janie and said, "Okay, blabber mouth! Lewis was talking to me."

With a furrowed brow Janie said to her grandfather, "Oh, sorry 'bout that."

"Well, I need to be going." Lewis had an idea, "Maybe I should bring my little sister to meet you. She likes to go swimming at the lake. Would you like to go swimming at the lake with us sometime?"

"Yeah," Janie's eyes brightened with excitement at the thought of a playmate. "What's her name?"

"Angel," he answered, as his attention was pulled away by the sound of a car engine pulling into the drive way. "Hey, I got to be going. I'll see you all real soon. Bye!" And he exited as he had entered, through the back door.

Janie excused herself and wandered into the living room. The television didn't interest her, but the radio did. She walked to it and stopped just short of turning it on, for fear of waking her sister. Janie didn't want to have to deal with Shelley any sooner than was necessary. The shadow of a figure walking past the front porch caused her to go to the window. She saw Kid stepping off the far corner of the porch.

Kid placed the puppy at an opening that led beneath his grandfather's house. The puppy scampered into a dark corner. He looked around with sad eyes, before lying down and producing a tired sigh. Just as Kid stepped up onto the porch he was stopped by the sound of someone calling to him.

"Hey, Kid! Got a minute?"

Not happy to see his rival for Rosie's affection, he answered, "Sure," and walked over to the porch swing. "Want to have a seat?" He motioned to the space next to him.

"No, thanks, I was just wondering where you've been all night?"

Kid's face darkened, "Why, were you worried about me?"

Lewis responded casually, "Just curious."

Kid growled, "I'm not in the mood for an inquisition."

With a nod of the head Lewis stood straight and excused himself, "Fine. Sorry I bothered you."

Stepping from the swing Kid said, "I don't suppose there's any reason I can't tell you about hanging out with Heather and her friends at the dam."

"Yeah, Barron asked me to come down, but I had some other things to do." Turning as if to leave Lewis asked, "So that's where Rosie was last night, right?"

Laughing mockingly, Kid asked, "Tell me what you're trying to say straight up."

With his right hand over his heart, Lewis said, "There's nothing to tell." Then he stepped back another step, and replied, "Yet."

Standing from the swing abruptly, Kid said arrogantly, "You've nothing to tell, yet. But, I do." He crossed his arms over his chest saying, "I'm taking Sunny back to Detroit with me."

"You've lost your marbles, dude!" Lewis said with a little laugh.

Lurching toward him Kid asked, "Are you trying to start something?"

Shelley stepped from the entrance. "Lewis! I thought I heard your voice out here! I am so glad you came to see me. Just give me a moment to get dressed." She continued gushing as she turned to hurry back inside, "We have so much to talk about!"

Kid chuckled, "Ha! At least someone is glad to see you." He then turned and followed his cousin into their grandfather's house.

When he stepped into the living room Janie stepped from the window. He looked at her and smiled, "Umm! I smell G-Mama's biscuits."

"They're yummy. I already ate."

Holding out his hand, he asked, "Will you sit with me while I eat?" A warm smile softened his face when she slipped her hand into his.

Lewis paced the front porch, feeling foolish for his entanglement. He rubbed his face with both hands, and an idea hit him. When Shelley emerged a short while later, he cleverly asked, "So, would you like to hang with me, my little sister and Janie this afternoon? I offered to take the girls to the lake."

Shelley answered with a phony smile, "Oh, sure. A day at the lake with the younger girls sounds like fun."

Chapter Five
Kissing Cousins

Lewis escaped the attentions of Shelley, and hurried away in his grandfather's old farm truck. Along the way, he stopped in to see Rosie. She was puttering about the kitchen, flipping pancakes and stirring sizzling sausage in a cast iron skillet. The aroma of fresh coffee was inviting, and he helped himself.

It was not surprising to see Lewis up and about at such an early hour. He often popped in on his way out to do a task for his grandparents. Rosie offered him breakfast, and he took a plate with two pancakes and a sausage patty. He helped himself to her homemade blackberry syrup, and moaned his appreciation for the delectable fare. She joined him at the table.

Trying to explain his early morning visit, he said, "I went looking for old Charlie, and thought I would stop in to see if you wanted to go with us to church today? I forgot to ask you Friday night." His voice faltered at the memory of the sinister events that had occurred at the very place he now sat.

Sensing his uneasiness, she didn't mention the experience. "Oh, yes. Thank you." She had not slept in twenty-four hours, and the effects of the drug had faded.

"I'll pick you up around nine-thirty?"

When it was time to go, Rosie stepped to the kitchen to announce her departure as her parents sat breakfasting. An automobile pulling into the driveway snatched her attention. Saying a quick good-bye, she hurried along. It was surprising to see that the automobile was none other than Rob Shirey's pickup that he used for farm work. Lewis was sitting alone in the cab. Smoothing the dress she had purchased the day before at Mrs. Edward's yard sale, she entered the battered and reliable old truck.

"Is the rest of your family going to church today?" she asked while settling on the lumpy seat.

He looked at her sweetly. Her pinned hair had loosened, and some wispy strands fluttered about her face in the morning breeze. The white summer dress she wore fit her maturing body. Clearing his mind, he answered, "Yeah, they're coming. I thought we could skip Sunday school this morning, and just attend the sermon."

"Okay, so why are we leaving this early?" she asked, wilting against the seat.

"There's a place I want to show you." He fell quiet for a long moment, and then said, "That séance must have done something to me. I can't seem to stop thinking about you."

Her eyes were heavy with fatigue, "How sweet."

They drove into a neighboring county, leaving the highway for a narrow back road. He pulled into a wooded grove, and from there they walked hand-in-hand along the road. Rounding a curve, they were welcomed by a historic covered bridge spanning a wide creek flowing across a rock strewn bottom of limestone and smooth pebbles. The massive wooden structure stood like a sentinel of time.

She ran ahead, and stepped onto the wood covered roadway that sat tunneled in the darkness of shadowed sunlight. Small windows invited rays of sunshine into the darkened abyss of the bridge.

He stood admiring her dark almond shaped eyes, shinning soft and awestruck in the dim light. She radiated brilliance in the white eyelet summer dress with one strap sliding off her shoulder. Soft dewy perspiration glistened across her forehead, and he longed to kiss her. She stepped closer, placing a soft feathery kiss on the corner of his mouth. "It's such a beautiful, quiet, serene," her voice trailed off.

"Romantic kind of place," he finished.

"You're finishing my sentences now?" Tenderly, she brushed back his bangs, admiring his young, handsome face.

He stirred restlessly, and catching her hand in his, yelled into the wooden tunnel, "I love you, Rosie!"

While the echoes reverberated she whispered, "You love me?"

With his heart pounding, he admitted, "Yes, I do."

Dizzy emotion weakened her intellect, and she staggered saying, "I really don't know what to say. This all," motioning with her hands, "just caught me by surprise."

With a weighted sigh of disappointment he declared, "If we don't go now we'll be late for service." Gently, he tugged her away, leaving behind the spell of romance, real or imagined, floating among the singular rays of sunbeams and perpetual echoes of endearment.

The church was stifling. Cardboard fans fluttered in pasty hands, and ceiling fans whirred on high speed. A sweet emotion filled Rosie as she relived the events at the covered bridge. Lack of sleep left her in a surreal state, and each time she closed her eyes she could visualize the tranquil water flowing beneath the bridge. With closed eyes the memories became a dream state as she drifted into sleep, dosing silently against Lewis' shoulder. Roused when he stood for hymns, she strained bleary eyes to follow along with the hymnbook. Finally, the minister said the dismissal prayer, and the congregation milled about to exit the oppressive heat of the little rock church.

Evelyn Edwards caught up with Rosie as she stood in the shade of some pine trees, waiting for Lewis. "Rosie, it's so good to see you today. How did the things fit, that you got yesterday?"

"Perfectly, see, this is the dress." She turned in a full circle.

Evelyn smiled, "Oh! That does look good on you. I don't think Sandy even wore it more than three times." She wet her lips and continued, "Rosie, I wanted to ask you something, and don't worry about hurting my feelings. But, I had a few things of Sandy's left over from the sale, and I wondered if you might like to have them. Whatever you don't want, you can just drop off at the Salvation Army." Mrs. Edwards was so gentle with her words, trying desperately not to offend the young girl.

With a grateful grin, Rosie told Evelyn in an assuring manner that she would be honored to take the offering. Evelyn led Rosie to her car, where she produced a box from the trunk. With one last tender hug, Evelyn sent the teen on her way. Placing the box in the back of Robert Shirey's pickup truck, Rosie wandered off to find Lewis. He was gathered with a group of men telling a joke, and she walked up just in time to hear the punch line.

Lewis smiled triumphantly when the older men burst into good natured laughter. He caught sight of Rosie standing back, listening to his joke. "I'll see you all next Sunday, if not sooner." Lewis broke from the group, and joined her. "Sorry to keep you waiting."

She pointed to the box and said, "See how nice Mrs. Edwards is? She brought me some clothing that Sandy outgrew."

For a moment, she thought she detected a hint of pity in his expression, but he only said, "Mrs. Edwards is the kindest lady I know, and she can't stand to see anything go to waste." Opening the truck door in an exaggerated gentlemanly manner, he motioned for her to enter. After closing the door, he pulled on it to ensure that the aged mechanisms held it shut.

As usual, Eva and Sturgill sat like stone images in front of the black and white television set when Rosie returned with Lewis carrying the box from Mrs. Edwards. Sturgill greeted Lewis, asking about his parents and grandparents, then Edward. Responding with hopeful words, Lewis explained that the Shirey family expected his brother would be coming home in August or September.

Sturgill sighed deeply saying, "This damn war has gone on way long enough. If Nixon doesn't bring our boys home soon, this nation is going to explode!"

Taking up the box Rosie said tiredly, "Thanks, Lewis," and, giving him a sweet smile she continued in coded words, "for everything. I'll see you later. Don't forget me when you and Charlie go raiding the honey tree." She disappeared into her room.

Removing her dress, she sprawled across the bed. But, curiosity about the box of clothes overwhelmed the call of sleep, and she opened it. Mrs. Edward's had folded each item neatly, but Rosie dumped the entire contents onto her bed, and began rummaging through them. She found two dresses, four blouses, a skirt, dress slacks, jeans, denim jacket, and a one piece swimsuit with a ruffled rear. Delighted by the articles, she hung each piece carefully. Stretching across her bed, she slept.

Rosie awoke with someone nudging her gently. She opened heavy lidded eyes to see Kid sitting on the edge of her bed, smirking at her. Sleepily she sat up and saw that the time was three in the afternoon. She asked with a graveled voice, "What are you doing? I was asleep." She lay back down, closing her eyes.

Putting his head down next to hers he spoke tenderly against her ear, "Come with me to the lake. I've already asked your dad, and he gave his permission." He leaned in closer and inhaled the perfume of her shampooed hair. "Don't disappoint me, darling."

Her eyes fluttered open with surprise. She rolled onto her back, and stared at him through sleep stained eyes. He was handsome with his shirt unbuttoned, and the gold chain gleaming against his tanned skin. He invigorated her. She smiled and stretched her body, pushing away the call of sleep. "Okay, darling!" she mimicked. "Get out so I can get dressed."

Minutes later, they were rolling along the familiar roadways. The top was up on the convertible, shielding them from the sun. "Lake Byron is a big lake," Rosie announced. "There are places with cliffs, and places with man-made beaches. What are you up for?"

Kid knew where he was going, but asked, "Where do you go swimming with Lewis and his little sister?"

Not finding the question odd, she directed him to the area of lake on TVA property where cattle grazed the meadows. It had been nicknamed The Cow Pasture, and many parties had been enjoyed by teenagers there. To Rosie's surprise, she saw Rob Shirey's battered old pickup. Seeing the expression of surprise he said, "Oh, I guess this is where Lewis brought Shelley."

Rosie was dumbfounded. He hadn't mentioned anything about taking Shelley to the lake that morning, before or after church. Her heart began to race. Kid parked next to the truck chatting about having brought along drinks, towels and some inflatable things. She could hardly pay attention to his conversation, because her pulse pounded wildly.

The laughter of young girls greeted their arrival. As they came upon the group of swimmers, a familiar voice cried out, "Hey, here's Kid and Rosie!" Janie splashed from the water and ran to Rosie giving her a wet embrace. "I'm so glad you're here, Rosie!"

Putting his cooler aside, Kid said to Janie, "I've got something for you," and pulled a plastic wrapped item from the bag.

Holding it into the air, she shouted to Angel, "It's a Donald Duck float!" She tore open the package and pulled the plastic toy out, putting the valve to her lips. She blew a few puffs of air into the deflated duck before she asked, "Kid, will you blow this up for me?"

With a grin he answered, "Have your sister blow it up. She's the one full of hot air."

When Janie had stepped away Rosie said to Kid, "You knew they were here, didn't you?"

With a shrug he answered, "I'm not going to lie about it. I overheard Lewis asking Shelley this morning, and I wanted to expose him for the two-timer he is."

Anger crept over her as she stared at her handsome cousin, "He's no two-timer, Kid! He's just being nice."

With a skeptical smile, he replied, "Yeah, whatever."

Lewis emerged from the water with Shelley at his side, and knelt on the blanket, where Rosie sat inflating the flotation device with big hot puffs of irritated breath. Her eyes were drawn upward as his shadow fell across the coverlet. Removing the valve from her lips, she calmly said, "Hi, Lewis. Great day for a swim, don't you think?"

"Nice swim suit. Must be new," Lewis said as his eyes devoured her shapely body in the appealing attire.

"Thank you. Yes, at least it is new to me. It's a hand-me-down from Mrs. Edwards. It's much better than my old suit, don't you think?"

"Much better," he agreed. "Now what is it Mamie always says?"

Rosie responded with a smile.

Looking to Kid, Lewis said, "Well, I think you'll be impressed with our lake. It's cold, deep and clean. I know how rivers sometimes catch on fire up there where you come from."

Kid smirked at the muddy water, "Oh, it looks crystal clear!"

Lewis tried to act contrite by saying to Rosie, "I should have invited you to come with us this morning, but you seemed to be so tired."

Empting out the bag he had brought, Kid instructed Angel to help herself to the inflatable toys and handed the mattress he had inflated to Shelley. Then, taking Rosie by the hand he led her into the water. Rosie was aware of being watched, and was careful not to appear too familiar with Kid. She mounted the air mattress, and lying on her stomach, paddled herself across the water as Kid swam out into the lake. The sun was relentless, so she paddled toward the fallen tree, and grasping hold of a skinny branch protruding into the water, she held herself afloat in the shade. Sleep summoned her, and she succumbed.

She was awakened by Kid grasping her foot. He had tied a slender rope around her ankle. "What are you doing to me?"

Taking the other end of the rope, he tied it to the skinny branch that she had been grasping. "I'm keeping you from floating to Chattanooga."

Closing her eyes she said, "Oh, okay." The warm summer day hummed activity around her. But, the tug of sleep was too much to resist, and she slept as she bobbed lazily on the lake among sounds of ski boats and laughter.

Kid left the water, and retrieving a towel, walked along the giant fallen tree. After spreading out the towel, he lay down upon his stomach, and stared at the lovely Rosie as she slept. He thought of her standing in the pouring rain the day before, and remembered the sweetness of her laughter just after dawn. Rosie had become a summer conquest, and his mind raced as he dreamed of ways to seduce her.

The afternoon sun was relentless with its burning rays. Lewis called out to Angel, "Better use that lotion, or you'll get burned."

The two younger girls smeared the suntan cream on one another, giggling at the picture on the bottle of a dog pulling down the little girl's swimsuit, revealing her butt crack. While the younger girls entertained themselves, Shelley slid closer to Lewis. "You know, Lewis. I'll be going home at the end of summer, and I would really like to have some fun before I leave."

"Okay?"

She bravely spoke up, "I think maybe you should know that I'm a lot more experienced than little Sunshine."

Gazing at his little sister splashing in the lake near the fallen tree where Rosie had risked her own life for the child, he looked blankly at Shelley and said, "Look, Rosie and I are like family. We're close."

Swimming around the floating air mattress, she boldly put her hand on his leg protruding from the cut off jeans he wore. "Good, then. That means there won't be any reason for you and me not to get to know one another better." She expertly rubbed her hand upward toward the sensational place that would ensure his complete attention.

Lewis squirmed and brushed her hand away, mumbling, "Let's get out of the water."

He left her with the floating air mattress, and swam out. Shelley followed, dragging the float with her. Tossing the air mattress aside, she returned to the blanket they shared. The attention Rosie was getting from Lewis and Kid completely irritated her, and she resolved that Lewis would overcome his feelings for the shapely young Sunshine Rose, soon.

Awakened by the girls splashing through the water, Rosie heard Janie call, "Rosie, will you tell us a story?" She held to her floating duck, occasionally squeezing the head, sporting a little blue sailor's hat, to make an irksome squeal.

Grimacing at the sound, Rosie roused. "Okay, but you've got to untie me."

Angel giggled and hurried to her rescue, "Why did you do this? We would never let you float away."

Janie suggested Rosie sing a song for them, and Rosie recommended a poem instead. Janie's eyes widened, and her face flashed an enthusiastic smile, "Okay, but not a little kid's poem."

Very seriously she said, "I was thinking of *The Owl and the Pussycat.*"

Janie looked to Angel, "I've never heard of *The Owl and the Pussycat.*"

"Go ahead Rosie, tell it," implored Angel.

Looking up into the fallen tree, she saw Kid staring intently at her, as though he wanted to hear the tale himself. So Rosie began with a flourish of flamboyance, "*The owl and the pussycat went to sea in a beautiful pea green boat. They took some honey, and plenty of money wrapped up in a five pound note.*"

"What's a five pound note?" interrupted Janie.

Angel explained, "It's English money."

Janie was confused, "But aren't we English?"

Getting angry with her persistent interruptions, Angel queried, "Are you dumb? We're American!"

Janie accepted that as fact and simply said, "Oh, yeah."

Rosie continued, "*The owl played on his small guitar, and sang to the stars above. 'Oh Pussy my love, what a wonderful Pussy you are, you are, you are. What a wonderful Pussy you are.*"

This phrase struck Janie as funny and she burst into giggles. Kid giggled along with her, and stirred himself into a sitting position on the fallen tree.

Angel jumped to Rosie's rescue, "Don't mind them! They're just juvenile. You're doing a great job, continue."

Taking a deep breath she continued, "*So they sailed away for a year and a day, to the land where the bong tree grows.*"

Kid interjected, "Bong tree! That's where I want to be."

Sliding off her float, Rosie began dragging it and the two girls toward shore while continuing the poem, "*And, there in the wood, a piggy wig stood, with a ring at the end of his nose, his nose, his nose, with a ring at the end of his nose.*"

"What's a piggy wig?" asked Janie.

Angel slapped water at her and exclaimed, "You don't even know what a dad blame pig is!"

Janie furrowed her brows in wounded pride, "I know what a pig is. I just didn't know what a piggy wig is!" She slapped water back at Angel.

Soon the girls were splashing water at one another, and Rosie was caught in the middle. Abandoning the float, she left the girls holding to it splashing violently in the shallow water, but stopped as she noticed Lewis and Shelley sitting together on the blanket. Approaching slowly, she made eye contact with Lewis and said, "You know, Lew, even if you had asked me to come to the lake with you, I would have said I was too busy. So, don't think I'm sore at you or anything."

Taking note that Kid was walking up behind Rosie he answered without smiling, "Gee, I really wasn't planning on coming out here today, it just kind of happened. Like with you and Kid, huh?"

The gleeful look Shelley held on her face did not go unnoticed. Shelley had always been rude. Throughout the years of family gatherings and reunions, she had gone out of her way to persecute Rosie. Kid stepped close, "Are you ready to go back up the mountain?" He spread his damp towel across her shoulders. "You're getting a little pink, sweetheart."

Snatching the sentiment Shelley remarked, "Sweetheart! What have we got here, kissing cousins? Oh, tsk, tsk, tsk! What scandalous behavior, Kid. Your father will not understand," she wagged her finger in the air.

Smiling boyishly he retorted, "Haven't you heard? I am scandalous!" And, to prove his point, he grasped himself in the crouch, mimicking a look of ecstasy.

Shelley laughed wickedly. Rosie said, "I do need to get home." She turned to take the air mattress from Angel as she dragged it across the grass.

Popping open the valve, Rosie began squeezing the air from the floatation device, and the two little girls did likewise. As she started walking toward the car, Janie called, "Hey! Can me and Angel ride back home with you?"

Smiling at the little girl as she placed her towel over the car seat, she said, "It's 'Can Angel and I'."

Correcting her sentence, she restated, "Can Angel and I ride home with you?"

Angel came up beside Janie, "You go ahead. I've got to stay with Lewis." She looked over her shoulder at her big brother and added slyly, "I think he needs protection from your sister!"

When they arrived at Rosie's house, Janie leaped from the car and rushed inside to announce their arrival. Sturgill was his usual groggy Sunday afternoon self. Eva responded to the little girl with polite inquiries. Kid and Rosie entered just as Janie finished her summary of their afternoon at the lake.

Sturgill spoke to Kid warmly, "Good to see you, son!"

Pushing her father aside, Rosie perched upon the sofa arm and spoke to her companions, "Would you like to stay and eat with us?"

Sturgill said, "Oh, listen? If you haven't had any of Rosie's fried chicken, you haven't lived. This girl is magic in the kitchen."

Janie responded, "Oh, yes! I'd love to stay and eat. Rosie, can I help you do the cooking? I know how to do a lot of stuff in the kitchen, you know." She abruptly stopped talking when Kid covered her mouth with his hand as a way of halting her incessant chatter.

"I think we have to get someone else's permission first," he told her. Then he said, "If G-Daddy and G-Mama don't mind, we'll be back." Then, without removing his hand, he said to Janie, "Okay?" She nodded her head up and down in agreement.

At six o'clock, she had dinner prepared, and the table set for five people. She dressed in a pair of slacks and blouse that Evelyn had given her. Her long dark brown tresses were pulled back into a ponytail, with her favorite white ribbon. Kid and Janie arrived shortly thereafter, and everyone gathered around the table for Sunday dinner at the Moon household. Rosie poured glasses of iced lemonade made with fresh lemons. Sturgill took a sip of the beverage, grunting appreciation.

"This ain't lemonade!" he declared. "This is nectar of the gods. What did you do different, Rosie?"

"I used half sugar, and half honey to sweeten it," Rosie replied. "And, I used a secret ingredient." She looked at her father over the rim of her own glass with a smile.

Sturgill's smile fell from his face, "You didn't make this with that spring water?"

"Now, Daddy, that water is perfectly fine, but just because you told me to, I boiled it."

Kid and Janie looked at one another dumbfounded. "Why do you have to boil water for lemonade, Rosie?" asked Janie.

"Daddy thinks that spring water gets contaminated with stuff."

Again, Kid and Janie looked at one another, and this time he asked, "What kind of stuff?"

Rolling her eyes heavenward, she explained, "My father thinks that micro organisms get into spring water that can cause illness, like diarrhea." Then she smiled sarcastically, "Which probably would do a constipated old man some good."

Janie burst into giggles and Sturgill blurted, "Do I smell cake?"

"The cake is for Eva's party," answered Rosie. "But I did make you a cupcake!" She sprang up from the table, and brought back a plate with six frosted cupcakes.

Sturgill waved both hands in the air with a delighted gesture, "I don't just have a daughter I have an angel!"

After dinner Sturgill said, "Rosie, you take your company for a walk, Eva will clean up." Then he gave Eva a sly wink when he saw the disgruntled looked she flashed him.

Rosie agreed, asking Kid and Janie if they were in the mood for a walk. Janie jumped to her feet eager for activity. Kid rose from the table, and rubbed a hand across his stomach groaning, "Yeah, sure, but, not too far. I think I ate too much."

They crossed through a pasture that was grazed short, and followed along a stream. During the leisurely walk Rosie asked Janie, "Didn't you find a puppy at Bert's house?"

"I didn't, but old Charlie did. He took it home with him," answered Janie while staring intently at the stream pool of sky reflected light through a moving paint brush of young summer leaves. Tired of the scenery, she looped her arm into Rosie's and chattered, "I wish you were my sister instead of Shelley. She's so mean to me." They began walking away from the pool, as Janie explained all the horrors of living with the skinny older sister. Kid walked along behind her, mimicking her chatter by holding his hand like a pantomiming puppet.

Thoroughly entertained by the both of them, Rosie recommended they go across the street to check on Mr. Reyes' horses. The mention of horses swept Janie into a completely different dialogue that kept her talking until they reached the barn.

Dusk was gathering along Ben Johnson Ridge as Rosie and her companions entered the dimly lit barn. Pointing to the beautiful pink colored sky, Kid exclaimed, "There it is, my favorite color, sky blue-pink."

They stayed at the barn until dusk settled over the mountain, then Rosie led the way back to her house with yellow windows gleaming electric light. Janie moaned, "I want to stay the night with you, Rosie."

Reassuringly, Rosie said she was welcome to stay with her any time. Janie reluctantly climbed into Kid's car, and waited patiently for him to drive her home.

Stepping to the driver's side Kid asked Rosie, "So, what are we doing tomorrow?"

A soft laugh of amazement blurted forth as she asked, "What am I, the entertainment committee?" Once he was inside with the door shut tight, she leaned down and said, "I have a lot of work to do tomorrow, and Eva's having that Tupperware party tomorrow evening. I don't know that I'll have time to do anything with you, Kid."

"You know, I haven't been to a Tupperware party in a long time. What time do you want me here?" He turned the key in the ignition, smiling mischievously.

Rosie grinned, "Six-thirty. And, wear your prettiest dress."

She entered her house with the usual scene playing out. Eva and a drowsy Sturgill sat before the television. Rosie went to her room, and retrieving her diary, began to write about her day. She wrote of the beautiful covered bridge that Lewis had taken her to, and his shocking remarks echoed into the wooden tunnel. She wrote of the jealousy she felt over his attentions to Shelly, and the bliss of Kid's affection. Once finished journaling, she retired to bed, and sleep came easily. But, haunting dreams disturbed her rest with strange disquieting images. Swelling tides of panic invaded her slumber. Sinister memories of foreboding dreams occupied her thoughts when she awoke the next morning, triggering a tension headache.

Chapter Six
Puppy Love and Honey Bees

Monday morning dawned, illuminating the mountain with delicate golden hues. Rosie went about her usual routine, as the disturbing dreams followed her into the daylight. The dreams were dark and haunting, with a lingering remembrance of terror, but just out of reach of complete recall. While Sturgill ate breakfast, she packed his lunch pail. He chatted lightly with his daughter as he had breakfast. "Has Kid ever mentioned the fact that his daddy doesn't like me very much?"

She frowned, "No. Why doesn't Uncle James like you?"

Sturgill snickered slightly and said, "Well, it's a long story, and I wish you wouldn't call that man 'uncle.' He's no more your 'uncle' than he is mine!" Seeing the curiosity he had stirred in his daughter, Sturgill continued, "Well, I was working in Detroit with James, at the Ford plant. And, it just happens that he and Eva were having a little romance on the side. You know, without his wife knowing about it." Pushing his coffee cup to her for refill while he continued, "When Dorothy died, I decided I wanted Eva for myself." At this point of his story he gave a dry little laugh, "There wasn't much James could do about it, since he didn't want his old lady to find out about his cattin' around. And, Eva was glad to dump him for me anyway."

Flabbergasted by this information she asked, "You took Eva away from Uncle - I mean Kid's father? What a story!"

"Well don't you go telling him anything about it. No sense in causing trouble between his folks fourteen years after the crime, is there?" The blast of a car horn from the driveway caused Sturgill to gather his hard hat and lunch pail. "I thought you should know that little fact, just in case you ever need to know."

Rosie stood on tiptoes and kissed her father's cheek, "Don't worry, Dad, I won't tell."

For the rest of the morning, she worked preparing her vegetables for the canning process. While returning jars of spices to the pantry, she became aware of an unusual coldness that lingered around the shelf holding the assortment of spices. For a long moment she stood placing her hand in and out of the eerie coolness. It was while she was placing towels around her steaming hot pint jars of canned squash that Lewis came pecking at the back door. "Come in," she called.

Fanning himself with one of Eva's *True Confessions* magazines he muttered, "Whew! You've got it hot in here."

Self conscious by the ragged clothes she had been puttering around in, Rosie lied, "Yeah, well I was just about to get dressed and get out of here."

"Do you want to come with me and Charlie? You said you wanted to raid the honey tree with us. He's outside in his truck waiting for us to go."

"I'll be out in just a minute." Quickly she changed clothes, and hurried from the house. She placed a basket alongside some other equipment on the back of the truck, and slid in between Lewis and Charlie. "Hello, Charlie! How are you today?" she asked before noticing the black and tan pup he held in his lap. "Oh! Who do you have here?"

Charlie cranked his old truck, and answered in his impeded dialogue, "Dat dere is Teddy." He said, smiling broadly, "I named him Teddy 'tause he 'ooks 'ike a Teddy Bear I had when I was a tid. I find him at Bert's house, and Bert don't 'ike dogs. So, I took him to my tabin. He 'ikes me, and I ike him."

Stroking the puppy, Lewis said, "Well, he looks like he'll make a fine dog, Charlie. He's got little paws. That means he won't get real big. It looks like he's got some Cocker Spaniel in him. Maybe the good Lord sent him to you, Charlie. Looks to me like you two need each other."

Charlie agreed, "Yep, yep. He's a dandy!" He maneuvered the truck along the road until it was time to turn off and drive across a field of freshly cut hay. The truck bobbed and swayed over the terrace rows until they came to some woods. Charlie parked the truck, then he and Lewis gathered supplies. They headed off deep into the forest, with the puppy chasing at their feet. Charlie led the group to a stand of Black Locust trees, and pointed to a particular tall tree with thorny branches and rough bark where humming bees darted about.

"'Dat de honey tee," Charlie announced proudly.

Rosie gazed at the ancient branches with wilting blossoms hanging like melting clumps of dingy snow. The curling long tendrils of dried fruit pods clung to the tired blooms of the Black Locust, like sinister creatures threatening all to stay away. Small round leaves hung clustered onto the stems like fragile green coins.

Lewis and Charlie donned bee keeper hats and gloves. They put on long sleeved shirts and stuffed the net from the hat down into the collar. Charlie operated the smoker, a battered antique appliance that must have seen many honey raids. With Lewis holding a large dish pan, they slowly approached the bee tree.

Holding the puppy back, Rosie watched the men carefully drug the bees with the smoke. Slowly, they reached in and pulled out large chucks of honey comb, dripping with translucent gold sweetness. Some of the lazy bees recovered from the intoxicating smoke, and buzzed about as they made off with the bounty. When they had reached the truck, Rosie reached to grasp the pan from Lewis and unknowingly placed her little finger against a hostile hitch-hiker. The stinger sank deep into her flesh, and she drew back as though she had touched a hot coal. Tears sprang to her eyes from the shock of the pain. Sitting the pan in the truck bed, he grasped her injured hand. Seeing the stinger still embedded in her flesh, he took his pocket knife and flicked a blade out. Her eyes grew large as she watched him approach her stinging finger with the sharp edge.

Noticing her apprehension he softly explained, "You have to be careful how you remove the stinger, or you could inject more venom into the bloodstream." He used the tip of the blade to scrape away the stinger.

She put the burning finger to her lips, "Dang! That smarts."

Later, at the Shirey farm, Lewis and Rosie took the pan full of honey into Mamie's kitchen to ladle into jars for storage. Mamie and Angel were helpful in the process, and allowed Rosie to sit aside due to her injury. When he announced that he would deliver Charlie's honey later in the day, Rosie couldn't help but wince at the idea of him being in such close proximity to Shelley. Her spirits were lifted when Mamie announced that she was dropping Angel off to play with Janie on her way to town, and would gladly drop by Charlie's with his share of honey.

Angel teased Rosie by poking her and saying, "Buzzt!" and broke into good hearted laughter when Rosie flinched.

When Mamie and Angel had left, Rosie and Lewis were left alone in the large old farmhouse. He gathered her hair up as he stood behind her chair. The caress was a tickling sensation, and she gasped as he leaned down, and placed a soft kiss on the back of her neck. His brash action gave her the courage to ask, "Lewis, are you interested in Shelley?"

"The only girl who interests me is you, Rosie. I told you yesterday how I feel about you, and I meant it."

Not wanting to minimize his statement she remained silent for a long moment. "Do you want to come over tonight, and watch a late movie with me and Heather?"

"I'm going to be practicing music with some of the guys. We're trying to get ready for the Fourth of July festival." Seeing her disappointment he added, "We'll watch another movie together, soon. You want to listen to some music?"

Wanting nothing more than to spend time alone with him, she had chores at home that nagged her. "I do, but I have to get ready for Eva's party." She stopped, and thinking it over quickly added, "Okay. But just for a few minutes."

Lewis had a bookshelf full of record albums. They listened to The Doors, The Rolling Stones and The Beatles. Rosie fell in love with a song from a Dusty Springfield album. As she was browsing through the collection of music, she noticed a corner of paper sticking from between two albums. She gently tugged on the page, and it slid easily out. The page was from a sketch book, and the drawing fascinated her. "Is this a self portrait?"

"Well, yeah. It is, sort of."

Letting her fingers play across the sketch, she traced the tattoos on each broad shoulder. The man was depicted with his back to the artist, his chin in hand, and muscles flexed from the effort. On his left shoulder was the tattooed art of an arch angel while the right bore an evil demon. "What does this symbolize, a battle?"

"Yes, a battle between good and evil. I plan to get tats just like these." He emphasized his statement by flipping the page with his index finger. "I've always had the little angel on my left shoulder telling me what to do that was right. Then on my right shoulder is the little devil telling me how much fun it would be to do the wrong thing. I've always been stuck in the middle."

She sighed, "I'm like that, Lewis. So, does that mean I'm stuck in the middle, too?"

"We've got heaven above, and hell below. We here on earth are all stuck in the middle."

"You're a very old soul, Lewis Shirey," she breathed astutely.

Later, Lewis walked Rosie home carrying the basket of honey jars. The day had begun hazy and dark clouds loomed with the threat of rain. They talked about their final year of high school, and after graduation plans. Rosie held fast to her desire to become a nurse as her mother had been, and he only had dreams of making music. As he told one joke after another, her laughter rang out like music that echoed up into the branches of the towering trees they passed under. The exuberance of youth was enchanting, and they were spellbound. When they reached her doorsteps, she took the basket saying, "Thank you, Lewis. I enjoyed today's adventure."

"How about a driving lesson tomorrow?" he asked. "I'll have Granddaddy's truck. You can go with me to pick up some chicken feed at the Co-op."

"Yeah, I really need to learn to drive the stick. The bug isn't automatic, and I can't drive it until I learn how."

"Okay, so let's get an early start. How about eight o'clock?" He asked as he began walking away from her in slow backward steps.

She hated to see him go. "Eight will be perfect."

He turned and started his walk home. Shielding her eyes, she looked skyward. A breeze picked up and tossing her hair carelessly. Dark clouds gathered and distant thunder rumbled.

Ernest T. Bass was up to his silly shenanigans on a midday rerun of the *Andy Griffith Show* when Rosie stepped through the front door. Eva was drinking gin and giggling, because some man was trying to shove his hand up her skirt. At the sound of the slamming door, she turned quickly and faced a cross Rosie.

Pulling her skirt down to her knee, she put aside her glass and asked, "Rosie, why aren't you out working?"

Holding the basked aloft, she announced, "I've got honey." Seeing that Eva wasn't impressed she added informatively, "Black Locust honey." Then she turned and left Eva with her hankering friend alone on the sofa.

By the time Sturgill returned home from work, Rosie had dinner for the family ready, as well as the food for the social gathering. Sturgill was sullen. He grumbled about driving to Hank Tanner's house to be out of the way for Eva's event, and boasted shamelessly on Rosie's honey find. A dark scowl crawled across Eva's face while Sturgill spoke his admiration for his daughter's talents.

Noting Eva's resentment fueled his praise, he delivered the most insulting remark possible. He suggested the hostess gift be bestowed upon his daughter for her hard work, not his lazy wife. By the time dinner was finished, Eva was sullen. When Sturgill left the house, he didn't bother saying good bye to his wife, but did place a quick kiss on his daughter's cheek.

After his departure, Eva rose from the table saying haughtily, "Well, since you're so talented and hard working, I'm sure you won't need my help here." Quickly, she slid a long cigarette from the package and lit it with a wooden match. Extinguishing the flame with a harsh breath she dropped it dramatically on a dinner plate. The crooked stem of smoke ascended from the burnt match eerily as Eva stomped from the room.

For the party, Eva dressed in a pretty yellow summer dress, and brushed her hair into an attractive style. The arriving ladies complimented her appearance. But, Rosie garnered the most attention as they asked for tips on gardening and canning.

Ester Thompson asked, "Rosie, what can I do to make my pickles crisper?"

"I soak my vegetables overnight in a pickling lime and iced water solution."

Vera Hobbs exclaimed, "Vegetables! I only pickle cucumbers."

Rising from her chair, Rosie slipped past the lady preparing her display. She returned with a jar of mixed vegetables pickled in sweet brine holding a plate with several forks.

"Who would have ever thought of pickling onions and cauliflower?" asked Ester.

Eva sat quietly in her corner of the sofa as the ladies raved over the pickles. As Maggie and Shelley arrived, the demonstrator of plastic kitchen items asked if she could begin her demonstration. Rosie was just about to take a seat when Kid opened the screen door. A hush fell over the chattering ladies.

Radiating in the spotlight of attention, he took a slight bow while holding out his guitar case. "Hello, ladies."

Rosie said to the guests, "My cousin is wonderful with his guitar. I promised him punch and cake if he would do a song for us this evening."

The ladies twittered with giggles. Savoring the interest, Kid swaggered a bit with his guitar and said in a deep voice, "Hello, I'm Johnny Cash." He then proceeded to pick the beginning chords of *Folsom Prison Blues*. The women were delighted.

When Kid took the chair that Rosie offered him and began to pick a complicated melody, a solemn mood fell upon his audience, and he captured their unwavering attention. The ladies tapped their feet, keeping rhythm with the music. When he finished with a flourish of strumming strings, a burst of applause demonstrated appreciation for his talent.

He proved to be even more entertaining as he flirted shamelessly with the married women. With unabashed boldness, he complimented Vera on her shapely legs, and Eva's voluptuous breasts. The ladies were pink cheeked, and pleased by his candid comments. Shelley was quick to make some scandalous remarks of her own as she observed her cousin's flirtations. But, Maggie was quick to chastise her granddaughter whereas she said nothing to her handsome grandson, who held the affection of every woman in the room. When the demonstration was finished, and booklets were passed around for orders to be made, Kid knitted his brows together when he wasn't given one.

"Excuse me," he said to the Tupperware lady. "But I'd like to buy something." When he took note of the surprised expression on her face he added, "That is if there's no rules against men buying Tupperware."

The lady quickly handed him a booklet and order form. Rosie gave him a pleased look then stood and said, "When you ladies-" quickly she corrected herself. "When you *all* are finished placing your orders, please come into the kitchen for refreshments."

While standing at the punch bowl stirring the frozen juice into slush, Rosie felt the sensation of someone breathing down her neck. Without looking, she asked, "What took you so long?"

Stepping around to face her, Kid asked, "How did you know it was me?"

"You're very good at seducing women, aren't you?"

His face fell in a mock look of abashment. "Why, Sunshine what do you mean? Are you calling *me* a Cad?" He inhaled sharply and said, "Damn, girl! You look good in those jeans." Then to emphasize his remark he licked the salt from his lips.

Tilting her head back, she laughed, "You're good Kid, real good. But I'm not an old married lady who can be flustered with some half hearted sweet talk."

Reaching out with the intent to grab her in a forceful acknowledgement of his sincerity, he was abruptly forced to abandon his plan when the kitchen filled with chatting ladies eager to see what Rosie had prepared. Reba Holland was the first to enter and declared, "Oh, look girls! Kid has beaten us to the punch."

Tillie Smith declared, "Who can blame him? Rosie can win any man over with her cooking." Then she added, "Can I get that pickle recipe, dear?"

"Are you sure it's her cooking?" asked Shelley giving Rosie a scathing look that went up and down the entire length of her body.

Vera interjected, "Well, if those pickles are any indication of her talent I would say she has her pick of any eligible man."

As the ladies headed back to the living room with their overflowing plates, Kid lounged against the door frame refusing to leave Rosie's side. "Why on earth would you want any other man when you could have me?" He beamed wit when she giggled at his remark.

Heather came in the back door. "Hidey-ho!" she sang as she entered. "Sorry I didn't get here in time for the party." She brushed past Kid, reaching for the chips, "Hey, Kid. How's it hanging?" Then she burst into snickers of laughter when he made a vulgar motion toward his crotch.

Rosie said, "Please don't encourage him. He's been on very bad behavior with the ladies tonight."

Heather raised her eyebrows, "Are you serious?" Then she pushed a dip covered chip into her mouth, and reached for the punch bowl ladle.

Rosie kept her eyes on Kid as she continued talking. "Yeah, but get this." She waved her arm for effect and said, "They *love* him."

He pouted, "Hey! *Him* is standing right here listening to you talk mean about him." Then he nuzzled closer to Heather and whispered something in her ear that made her blurt forth unbridled laughter.

When Heather got control of herself, she said to Kid, "Hey, you want to stick around and watch the late movie with Rosie and me?"

Finishing his cup of punch he joked, "Now, come on girls. You know we can think of something more fun to do than a late movie." He stepped between the girls and putting an arm around each of them pulled them close.

Tugging his arm from around her neck Rosie commented, "Kid, you've just got to face the fact that not every women in this world wants to take her clothes off for you."

Heather looked up into his face and said, "She's just speaking for herself. I'll talk about what else we can do that's more fun than a movie."

"Heather, you wouldn't!" exclaimed Rosie as she turned and left the kitchen to rejoin the party.

The Tupperware lady had packed her plastics into her large vinyl bag and was calculating the amount of sales from the party. "Congratulations, Eva," she said to the hostess. "You sold enough to earn the hostess gift you wanted. I can deliver your luggage with your order next week."

"Oh, that's wonderful!" exclaimed Eva.

The ladies were leaving, expressing their gratitude and good nights. As Maggie and Shelley were going, Eva asked Shelley to stay and watch the late movie with Rosie and Heather. Gleefully, Shelley watched Rosie for her reaction when she announced, "No, Lewis is expecting me for practice. I'm performing with his band at the festival."

This information stunned Rosie. Jealousy flooded her emotions, and left her nauseous.

Later, she confessed her displeasure over Shelley spending time with Lewis, as she prepared popcorn. Heather agreed by saying, "Cindy Thompson swears that her brother had Shelley last Sunday in the back seat of her parent's car out in the church parking lot. The two of 'em snuck out during the sermon."

Kid sat at the kitchen table picking softly on his guitar, "Oh, yeah, she's a slut alright. But, it takes two to tango."

Rosie slammed the hot pan filled with popcorn against the bowl as she emptied it. "Okay! No more talk about Shelley." She took up the bowl of popcorn, and exited the kitchen with Heather following behind her with two glasses of soda. Taking up his glass, Kid slowly made his way to the living room.

Heather slid to the far end of the sofa, and patted a place in the middle for Kid to sit. "Rosie," she soothed, "don't worry about Lewis with Shelley. You know he's not the kind of guy who would jump at a chance for an easy lay." She regretted her words the instant she caught sight of the hurt and insecure look on her friend's face.

As the young people sat before the television screen awaiting the movie, they munched on popcorn, and became mesmerized by a cigarette commercial. The beautiful blonde girl strolled along a beach wearing a one piece swim suit. As the lovely lady pulls forth a cigarette a handsome man emerges from the shadows to light her smoke.

Kid exhaled a wolfish whistle to express his lustful pleasure to see the swimsuit clad model walk away from the camera. Rosie observed him humorously, until her attention fell onto the television as the movie began. When the movie title rolled it read, *Gentlemen Prefer Blondes*. Turning her head from the direction of the TV to look at Heather she said, "I thought you said this was *How to Marry a Millionaire*. I've seen this already."

Kid sat straight and asked factiously, "Oh! Is someone cranky, maybe because Lewis is making music with someone else tonight?"

To show Kid her nonchalance on the subject, Rosie snuggled back on the sofa with her legs drawn beneath her. He followed suit, and crossed his legs beneath him. The movie held them attentive until commercials broke the interest.

While Kid and Heather raided the kitchen for more snacks, her thoughts wandered to Curtis Vaughn's barn. She imagined Shelley and Lewis singing together, and falling in love with one another. These nagging thoughts played on her nerves, wrenching her heart. Hot tears played at the corner of her eyelids. Kid and Heather sauntered back into the living room laughing lightly at the small talk they had made.

Kid sat down in the middle of the sofa and took a long look at Rosie. "Why the sad look, Sunshine?" He sat back and turned his attention on Heather. In a feminine manner he waved his hand through the air and said, "Something is wrong with our little Sunshine Cookie! What are we to do about it?"

"I know," she exclaimed, "dog pile!" She pushed Kid over on top of Rosie, and she slung herself on top of the heap.

Rosie giggled and squirmed beneath the arms and legs that twitched above her. Begging for release, Heather slid off of Kid's back, and he slowly pushed his way off. Being on the bottom of a dog pile did indeed lighten her spirit. Rosie had great fun mimicking Marilyn Monroe's voice and wiggly walk.

During a commercial break, Kid took his wallet from his back pocket and removed his driver's license. Handing it to Rosie, he said, "Take a good look at this and tell me what we share in common."

She studied the license. "Well, gee Kid! You have blonde hair, and I have brown. We don't even live in the same state. I don't see what you're talking about."

He leaned forward and pointed his finger in her face. "If you don't figure it out in five seconds, I'm going to put you across my knee and spank you like it's your birthday."

"Your birthday is the same as mine!"

He flashed a smile, "Let's plan something outrageous for our birthdays. Hey, Heather you want to celebrate with us?"

Heather responded, "For sure."

As the movie ended, Heather stood in front of the set and began singing *Two Little Girls from Little Rock.* Rosie smiled and chimed in on lyrics she could barely remember. Encouraged by Kid, she stood with Heather and side stepped an improvised dance while singing with her best Marilyn Monroe voice, *"So you should marry a guy who's shy or bold, or young or old."*

Heather chimed in and they concluded, "*As long as he's a millionaire*!"

Kid expressed his affectionate appreciation by air clapping and making noise to resemble the sound of a distant cheering crowd. He said to Heather, "Let's go, Songbird. Time to leave," and opened the door for her to exit. Before leaving, he stepped to Rosie, kissed her cheek and whispered, "Night, night."

Standing on the front porch, Rosie waved goodbye. She lightly brushed her fingers across her cheek where Kid had left his kiss, and as she turned to go inside, something caught her attention. Turning completely back around, she noted that an old wooden porch rocker, splintered and peeling faded paint, was actually rocking slowly. She lifted her face in the direction of the wind. There was no breeze strong enough to push the heavy chair. Stepping inside, she latched the door and went to bed.

A restless exhaustion seemed to consume her with a torturous inability to sleep. She remembered every moment of the honey hunt, and savored each second's memory of listening to the music with Lewis in his room. Sleep eventually came, and took her scattered memories into a peaceful dream of flower strewn meadows, basking beneath a summer sun with puppies, rabbits and honey bees playing nature's game. Her pleasant dream turned dark as storm clouds rolled in over the horizon. The rabbits scampered to safety, the honey bees disappeared and the puppies gathered close around her. She found shelter in a dark house in the woods, but when she called for the puppies they huddled together in the rain, refusing to enter the house. Lightning and thunder deafened her, and the blowing rain forced her to close the door against the storm, leaving the puppies outside. The house was solid, and kept the noise of the storm quieted. As she wandered across the dark wooden floor, she could hear someone whispering a zealous message. Intent on hearing the words, she called out, "What?" When there was no response she asked again, "What did you say?"

The whispering came closer and spoke louder. An evil force seemed to be distorting the sound in a way to make the voice unintelligible. Her desire to listen to the omen was so intense that she strained with every fiber of her being to hear the words. The storm had intensified. The flashes of lightening illuminated the room, exposing no shadowy figures that could be responsible for the whispering voice. "What did you say?" Anxiety compelled her to hear the whispering voice with clarity. Heavy booms of thunder followed intense flashes of lightening, and the voice continued to fade. She awoke sitting up in bed calling out, "What? What did you say?"

Pale moonlight streamed through the opened curtains at her window. The storm had been left behind in her nightmare, but the desire to learn the message of the whisper still lingered. The experience of the dream kept her awake and pondering it. Could it be like Lewis said, heaven is above us and hell is below. Leaving those on earth stuck in the middle. The slumbered prophecy haunted Rosie as she tried to return to sleep. Did she, too, have an angel fighting the devil for her soul?

Chapter Seven
Rescuing Lewis

The mild June sun streamed through the thick needles of a tall pine that Lewis had parked under. Rosie clutched the steering wheel of the old farm truck as he explained the gears, stressing the importance of letting the clutch out with a smooth, slow motion. The morning sun extended the promise of a beautiful day, perfect for driving. Assuring him that she was ready to drive, she promptly released the clutch too fast, which sent the truck into a jerking convulsion that killed the engine. Pointing a finger he said sternly, "Use your heel, like I said."

She released the clutch using the middle of her foot for control. The truck engine whined, and began rolling. Changing gears unnerved her, and Lewis kept making her stop just to start again. She drove to the Co-op, where they bought animal feed for the Shirey farm. Driving back toward the farm, he suggested they go to Rocky Falls for a morning adventure. Rosie made the slow painstaking drive along the single lane, bumpy dirt road, and parked underneath the same tree she had spent that rainy afternoon with Kid. "How did I do?"

Getting out of the truck he confessed, "Better than I expected, but still you have a lot of work to do." The disappointed look on her face scolded him. "Lighten up, Sunshine Rose. It's a bright beautiful day, and guess who's coming home next week?"

He smiled easily as Rosie cried out the answer, "Ed Shirey! Your folks must be thrilled!"

"Yeah, well I was a little worried that you would be thrilled, too."

With cautious words she replied, "Oh, I am. But not because I'm still crazy in love with him." With a sideways glance she continued, "Your brother hurt me really bad when he dumped me for Sharon. And, what goes around comes around."

Long quite moments passed before he spoke. "No one would blame you for hating him, you know."

"I'll admit there was a time when I thought I couldn't live without him. But you know something? When someone betrays you, and makes a mockery of your love," she inhaled deeply before finishing her thought. "It makes you stronger."

Giving her hand a soft squeeze, he said, "He was a fool, and nobody knows better than me what an asshole he can be." Then he said with a smile, "I can only promise you that I will never make his mistakes."

The cooler temperature of the deep woods was welcoming. They walked hand in hand along wooded trails to the falls. Mist from the falling water left dewy moisture on their skin, and they had to shout above the din of the roaring water to be heard. Their attention was captivated at the sight of a crashed car crumpled in the gully of rocks. In leisure time they made their way to the bridge spanning the creek. Rosie lay back on the bridge, and stared into the leaf filtered blue sky above her. In the distance, a truck could be heard approaching from the bottom of Rocky Falls.

Janie sat between Charlie and her grandfather, as Charlie drove his four wheel drive truck over the rutted and washed roadway leading up the ridge line of the falls. In the floor board at Bert's feet sat the curly haired puppy. She found it exciting to ride in the bumpy truck as it lurched and stalled along the pitted road. When they reached a certain point, Charlie stopped the truck and switched off the ignition. He opened the driver's side door and began to get out when Bert asked casually, "Is this it?"

Charlie closed his door and leaned back in to motion at Bert, "Det out!"

Sliding out just as quickly as her grandfather was out of her way, Janie reached back for the puppy, which she promptly dropped to the ground. Teddy followed her with a quick moving trot, stopping here and there to sniff. A roar of rushing water greeted them, along with misty air. Downstream, a pink 1968 Cadillac convertible rested upside down in the flowing creek. White wall tires sparkled in the dappled sunlight, and polished chrome glinted reflections of the passing ripples. The soft pink enamel was starkly overpowered by the dark undercarriage, lying exposed like a steel skeleton.

Bert declared, "That looks like a brand new car!" With a wide smile, he nudged Janie, "Well, squirt. If the insurance company plays nice I'll have me a parts car."

With her incessant need for knowledge, Janie asked, "Why did this happen to the car? How did it get down there?"

While waiting for an answer, a black fly buzzed about her face. Swatting the fly away, she noticed a green fly buzzing in the tall grass. With a new question on her lips she asked, "G-Daddy, why are some flies black, and some are green?" She peered up into the wrinkles softly surrounding her grandfather's blue eyes, expecting to hear a scientific explanation.

Bert answered with hardly any hesitation, "Because the green flies eat more shit than the black flies." Bert's statement did not go unnoticed or unappreciated as he heard the hushed giggles of Charlie Brown.

Placing hands on hips she said haughtily, "I don't believe everything you tell me. You know that?"

Stamping off angrily, she wandered the road leading to the bridge. The day was warm, and promising to be warmer, as grasshoppers and butterflies courted brief devotions. Having plucked a Black-Eyed Susan growing wild along the roadside, Janie peered at the bright yellow petals surrounding the brown felt center. Putting it to her nose, she concluded that it had no fragrant smell. The sound of laughter met her, before she rounded the curve to the bridge. When she saw Rosie and Lewis she rushed forward shouting to be heard over the din of crashing water, "Hello there!" and hurriedly joined them. "Did you see the wrecked car at the bottom of the falls? G-Daddy and Charlie are talking about salvaging it."

Rosie said, "Let's go ask if we can help."

They were met on the roadway by the now happy puppy known to all as Teddy. The puppy loped in high spirits to Janie. The little girl knelt and allowed the excited canine to express his affections for her by nuzzling into her long unruly hair, and gently chewing on her fingers. When they reached the overlook area where Charlie had parked, the two men were returning to the truck, ready to leave.

Lewis asked, "You need any help?" The expression on the older man's face amused Lewis, who added, "Janie said you and Charlie are salvaging the wreck."

Bert Noble looked at his granddaughter with interest, "I'm not used to having a stool pigeon in my midst." Extending his hand in a warmhearted handshake he said, "It's an idea right now, anyway." Bert stepped back from the handshake and tapped Janie on the head. "Let's take a lesson from this, Little One. From now on, you don't blabber every little thing you know, and that specifically means to your grandmother."

Rosie said to Charlie, "You have a fine dog there."

Charlie observed the puppy with amusement, "I take him to church with me. Sometimes he sings *The Old Rugged Cross*." Charlie bent over and scooped the puppy up from the dirt road.

Bert watched ruefully as Charlie showed his affection for the puppy and answered Lewis, "If you're not busy this afternoon, I could use another man to stay with the wrecker as we snake that thing up the embankment. Can you make it?"

"Sure can."

Slapping Lewis on the back in a good natured dismissal, Bert got into the truck calling, "Janie, come on now, time to go!"

Dropping the odorless flower, Janie ran to the driver's side of the truck and took her place next to Bert on the tattered old truck seat. She shouted goodbyes and accepted the puppy when Charlie set him up onto the seat. The old truck rolled slowly over the roadway, around the curve, over the bridge, and out of sight, with the engine noise completely lost within the din of the waterfall.

Yearning to know about his evening with Shelley, Rosie leaned toward a previous conversation, "So, Darby is going to play drums for your new band, huh? Do you think he's a good drummer?"

"I think Darby is a great drummer, and a really good singer. Darby has a special style. People," he paused to wave his hand through the air for sincere effect, "people just love Darby Gray. All ages, all races, all different kinds of people praise Darby's talents." Passionate about his music, Lewis appreciated the talents of other musicians equally. "He has this awesome light touch on cymbal and snare. Then he has a powerful solo, playing double kicks that sound like rapid gun fire."

With a gulp of air, she took the plunge of diverting the conversation's attention from Darby Gray to Shelley Noble. "How did Shelley do?"

If he was surprised with her knowledge of Shelley singing in his band, he didn't show it. "She does have talent." Then he continued, "I think her voice is edged, and sweet. Good for country and southern rock, but I don't see her getting away with any Dusty Springfield stuff like Heather can." Winded from the uphill walk he panted, "The thing about Shelley's voice is that she's a good background vocalist, but she could never hold her own on stage the way that you can."

Accepting the compliment with a short laugh she asked, "So is that why you didn't ask me to sing with your band, because I would steal your limelight?"

"No. Not really. We never even thought of using female vocals before. But, Bert asked if I could let Shelley sing with my band, just to give her something to keep her occupied this summer." Pausing to catch his breath, he continued talking, "It just turns out that she sounds really good with our group."

Rosie changed the course of the conversation again. "Heather and Barron aren't entering the competition, and I think they should! Especially now, with Zeke playing bass for them. He's awesome!"

"I'd love to play with Zeke. He's as good on bass guitar as Paul McCartney."

Unaware of the deep underlying distrust he held for Kid, she asked, "Have you thought about asking Kid to play with you?"

"I don't know if he could fit in with the mountain boys. You know they don't talk about sex all the time, and fidget with their genitals the way Kid does. It might be a big mistake, like tossing a cobra into a community of mongoose." Mockingly, he asked, "Do I want that responsibility?"

Jostling his hand in hers she commented as she laughed, "I can understand that!" They reached the clearing at the top of the hillside. "I do thank you, Lewis." She continued quickly when she saw the puzzled expression on his face, "For the driving lessons, and," she pulled him to a stop and threw her arms around his neck. "For the swimming lessons, and all the other lessons I get from you." She pushed her face into his neck, and kissed the moist salty skin below his ear. Her mind raced with jealous thoughts of Shelley, and insecurity flooded her. Still holding his hand, she pulled him along to the truck.

Charlie Brown's old pickup left a cloud of dust coloring the trail of Bert's driveway. Holding Teddy securely in her lap so he could tilt his head back and sniff the dusty air, Janie wondered what odor could cause him such sneezing seizures. "My goodness, Teddy, did you smell a cat?" The little dog appeared to be smiling as his mouth gapped open.

Kid sat on the porch playing his guitar, while Maggie sat with him on the swing listening to her grandson's music. As Janie raced to the porch ahead of the men, Teddy struggled to keep pace with her. She joined her cousin sitting on the edge of the porch. Unable to resist talking, she said, "We saw the wrecked car! It's upside down in the water. I saw Lewis and Rosie at the waterfall, too." An ugly screech peeled from the guitar strings.

Kid sat stunned as he remembered the rainy day he had spent at Rocky Falls with Rosie. A flashback of her standing in the rain with her wet t-shirt clinging to her body assaulted his memory. Without thinking he said, "Damn it!" Suddenly, he stood and entered the house.

Bert approached, saying, "Where is that boy going? I needed to talk to him." He stopped short and asked Janie, "Have you been watching your mouth?"

"Guess not," she murmured guiltily.

Bert stepped closer, "Did you say something that Kid didn't like, and is that what made him go inside the house?" With narrowed eyes he asked, "Did you tell him you saw Rosie?"

Slowly she said, "Yes, G-Daddy I did."

Bert ruffled her hair and said, "You've got to stop telling everything you know, child." Then he carried himself slowly across the porch and into the house. The door closed behind him, leaving Janie in the outside world, watching her grandmother embroidery butterflies onto the back pockets Shelley's jeans.

Standing closer to observe the needlework, she asked, "Can you do that to my jeans, too?"

Maggie sighed, and rolling her eyes said, "I just don't know, Janie. I have so much to do. I don't know when I can ever find the time for it." Taking note of the hurt look that washed across her granddaughter's face, she clipped her needle free from the thread saying, "I'll try, okay?"

Silence fell across the porch. Large white head bumble bees swooped into the rose bushes, heavy with blooms. A blue tail lizard sauntered sluggishly along the porch wall. Birds orchestrated summertime songs, and the breeze blew large fluffy clouds across a pale blue sky. Janie sat in her state of boredom, and she thought about her mother alone in Gulf Port. Memories from that morning, before the suicide, flooded her thoughts. She could remember the sea scent filling the air as she woke. She remembered the crackly sound of the cereal, and how it looked later splashed across the floor. The imaginings were punishing with clouded feelings of being unwanted, and unloved. From somewhere dark and unknown, deep anxiety sprouted and grew. She cupped her hands to her mouth, making a conscious effort to breathe calmly to thwart anxiety.

Maggie noticed Janie's unusual behavior, and avoided the situation by collecting her sewing box and retreating into the house. Now she was all alone with only Teddy, who ran around the lawn snapping at bumble bees and butterflies. A few minutes passed, and Charlie whistled in the distance. The puppy abandoned the idea of catching bees and ran off with his ears flopping.

Janie lay back on the porch and watched the clouds parade along the sky. Her sadness gave her ideas to ponder about the intricate details of heaven. What kind of music was there? Why were the streets gold? What did the roses in heaven smell like? Could people commit suicide and still go to heaven? Some days the depression caused by her father's death could overwhelm her, sending her to bed early with a headache. The memory of the blood flow spreading around the pack of cigarettes on the table often intruded at the most unusual times, turning her mood foul.

The same nagging questions began racing through her mind. Why did my daddy want to die? Why does my mommy want to continue living in the apartment haunted by the terrible memory of her husband's suicide? A dark fatigue swallowed her, and she sat there for the longest time, lost to her dark and tired thoughts.

Later that afternoon, Janie rested on the porch swing and lazily read a mystery novel. Her attention was distracted by Lewis riding his bicycle into the yard. She sat upright and waited for him to join her on the swing. Remembering Bert's warnings, she carefully chose her words. "Hey Lewie, where's Angel?"

"She's spending the weekend with our Mom." Noticing the book he smiled, "I've read that one. Guess what?"

Her eyes widened and she asked, "What?"

"The butler didn't do it," he snickered at her disappointed expression. "Bert called me to come on down here. He needs me to help with the salvage operation."

"I'll let him know you're here." She left Lewis on the porch and went inside the farmhouse. Bert was in the small room that he called his office, but hardly ever used. She could hear her grandfather saying to her cousin, "You are a young man with your whole life ahead of you. Don't let some girl take you off track. Just stay on track, son. There's plenty of time for love, later."

Janie caught their attention when she pushed the door open and stepped into the room, "G-Daddy? Lewis is here. He said you called him." She noticed the reddened look of anger darkening Kid's face, and concluded that whatever the conversation with their grandfather had been about, her cousin was not happy with their grandfather's recommendations. "What do you want me to do with him?"

Bert snapped, "Tell him we'll be right there!" Then he turned to Kid and said, "Let's go. It's time to meet Kenneth Edwards with his wrecker." Bert left the room.

Janie looked at Kid and watched him rub his hands over his face with a look of frustration clouding his expression. "Are you getting lectured because of Rosie?" she asked.

Inhaling deeply, he said, "As a matter of fact, I was. But, how about you and I just keep that between us?"

"I'm learning to stop talking recklessly, Kid," she smiled as he tousled her hair. "Can I go with you to Rocky Falls? I promise to stay out of the way. I can sit on the bridge."

Taking her hand in his, he said, "Well, let's go see." Bert and Lewis were making small talk when Janie and Kid interrupted them. "I told Janie she could go along if she stays on the bridge and out of the way."

Bert looked at Kid with dissatisfaction, "You and Lewis get onto the back of the truck when Charlie gets here. Me, and Meanie Mouth will ride in the cab with Charlie."

The clucking sound of Charlie's truck engine slowly approached from the driveway that led to his cabin. Picking Teddy up from the passenger side seat, Janie took her place between Charlie and Bert. As the truck moved slowly along she could hear bits of the conversation going on between the two young men in the back of the truck.

"So, are you and Shelley getting it on, or what?" Kid deliberately antagonized Lewis with his crass vocabulary.

Janie heard Lewis say, "You and me are a lot alike you know, because I don't kiss and tell, either."

"Other than being mesmerized by the lovely Sunshine Rose, I don't think we have a thing in common."

Riled by Kid's remarks, he curtly remarked, "We're not friends here, and I'm not talking about my feelings for Rosie with you."

"No, we're not friends. But we can damn sure be enemies real fast if you think you're going to come between me and Sunny."

"Let's just talk about something else, okay?" asked Lewis with a softer tone.

Kid's eyes gleamed black in the filtered light of the forest. "Let's not talk at all since you're so pansy assed sensitive."

Lewis replied quietly, "Okay, so it's agreed. We won't talk."

The sound of their voices got lost as the truck hit the main road and picked up speed. Charlie came in from the top of the mountain, and crossed the bridge at Rocky Falls. He stopped his truck and let off Janie, Lewis and Kid at the bridge. Bert instructed her to stay at the bridge, and for the two young men to offer help to the wrecker driver. Bert and Charlie headed off down the mountain with Teddy bouncing on the seat between them. Each young man draped a coil of rope over a shoulder as they started down the trail, just off the main road.

Kid sauntered along behind Lewis on the trail, making rude comments. Enjoying the look of annoyance on his rival's face, he made several more remarks tinged with dark humor and obscenity. Finally, he said the one thing that snapped Lewis' attention into a boiling rage. "You best give up hope on Sunshine. That girl's going to be my wife!"

Lewis stopped, blocking the pathway, and turned with squinted eyes shouting, "You will never lay a finger on her!"

Overcome with impulsive anger, Kid shoved Lewis. The rich soil covered with tender moss broke loose beneath Lewis' feet, and the unexpected jolt propelled him off balance. Losing his footing, he began falling. Sliding, and rolling he tumbled toward the rocky cliff overhanging the waterfall. Janie watched from the bridge, but her screams for help were lost in the roar of the water. Lewis tumbled over the edge, and appeared to be lost.

Racing to the ledge, Kid peered over, and saw Lewis grasping to an exposed tree root, dangling above a thirty foot ravine, gushing with white water. He disappeared, but returned holding to a rope he had tied to a tree, and looped around his waist. He gripped the end of another rope tied to the same tree. Lying on his stomach he leaned far over the edge and tied it around Lewis at his chest then inched his way back from the rough stone ledge. Kid returned holding the opposite end of the rope he had tied to Lewis, shouting, "I'm going to pull you up. Just walk up the side of the cliff. Ready? Let's go!" Using his weight, he dragged Lewis up the face of the cliff.

When Lewis regained his footing on the wooded path, he was breathless from the physical exertion, and mental distress. Kid whooped in glee over his success, and reaching down, he extended his hand in an offer to help Lewis to his feet. Instead of accepting his hand, Lewis pushed it aside, stood to his feet, and threw a punch that landed directly on Kid's jaw.

Staggered by the unexpected blow, Kid retaliated with a punch to Lewis' stomach, and the two men engaged in a bloody wrestling match. They exchanged blows with angry fists, and rolled about stirring up dust on the trail. Janie raced down the roadway to the wrecker truck, searching for help. Lewis was on top, pounding his fists into Kid's face when Janie returned with the truck driver.

The driver stepped to the fighting men, pushing them apart. "Just settle down, now! There's going to be no more of this. Just stop!"

Kid spewed at Lewis, "What the hell, man? I just saved your life!" He calmed down a bit, before he noticed his lip was bleeding. "You hillbilly fucker!" he screamed, "You busted my lip, you bastard!" Pulling away from the driver who controlled him he said calmly, "It's alright, man. I'm through with this!" He started back up the path turned to Janie and said, "Tell G-Daddy you all didn't need me after all." Then he walked away.

Janie looked to Lewis and, with uncertain candor she asked, "Was this about Rosie?"

"What do you know about him," he nodded his head in Kid's direction, "and Rosie?"

They had begun to walk along with the truck driver after retrieving the ropes from the tree when Janie replied honestly, "G-Daddy was lecturing Kid this morning about not falling in love until he was finished with college. I'm not sure, but I think they were talking about Rosie." She reached out and took his hand, "I'm sorry, but I might have caused your fight with Kid today." With a resigned sigh, she confessed, "G-Daddy says I always talk too much. I guess he's right about that. I sure set Kid off when I told him that I saw you and Rosie together at the falls. I don't know for sure, but he does act like he's crazy about her."

Expelling a breath of stale air, she continued, "I don't see a whole lot of love in my family. In my family nobody loves anybody but themselves!" she remarked bitterly.

"My people are so selfish, you never know who's going to wake up and say, 'Hey! I think I'll just blow my brains out today, and not worry about who's watching.'" Those words, once spoken, held a heaviness of dark memories clinging coldly in the air. Shaking herself loose of self pity, she sighed heavily, saying confidently, "Things will be okay, Lewis. Kid will go home. Shelley and me, uh I mean that Shelley and *I* will go home, too." She patted him lightly on the hand, before pulling away to peer at the upside down car, now with cables attached, readied to be hoisted up out of the ravine.

Bert and Charlie stood at the bottom of the ravine with another workman, while Lewis worked with the wrecker driver, keeping an eye on the little girl with her unruly hair pinned back. He peered over the edge as the car was pulled up, and he wondered why this work fascinated her so. Leaning down he asked her, "Would you like to go to the movies with me and Angel next Friday? We go to the drive-in and sit on lawn chairs in the back of the truck."

Sad eyes peered up at him from the pale face with pink cheeks. Without emotion she answered him, "I'd like that." With a deep sigh she asked, "You aren't inviting Shelley are you, because if she's going I'm not."

"No, we won't invite her. We can invite Rosie."

A gleeful look lighted the child's face, "Oh, yes! That would be fun!" Just the thought of spending time with Rosie had vanquished her darkness.

Chapter Eight
Sugar and Spice

Janie rode her bicycle around the large magnolia tree in her grandparent's front yard. Shelley lounged in the sun on a reclining lawn chair, wearing a new white swimsuit. Thick gray clouds gathered in the sky above, threatening to block the sun's rays. Kid stood in the doorway looking out through the storm door glass. Each time she rounded the tree and pedaled past her sister, Shelley screamed at her to go away. He watched with amusement as Janie rounded the tree and pedaled past her sister again. This time Shelley leaned up and kicked the back bicycle tire, sending Janie into a sprawl across the lawn. He raced out to pick her up. Insisting that she wasn't hurt, she wiped at her grass stained knees, and looked up at Kid saying, "See, she hates me."

Furious with Shelley, he walked over and jerked the lawn chair over, tilting her out onto the grass.

She yelled, "Hey! Who do you think you are? You've stained my new swimsuit!"

Kid folded the chair and walked away with it, leaving Shelley lying in the grass.

"You've got to try to understand the emotional upheaval that girl has been through," Maggie explained after Kid told her of Shelley's attack on Janie.

"What about Janie? Hasn't she been through just as much? You don't see her hurting other people because of it!" he persisted.

"Now, you don't know how you would react if you had a younger sister pestering you all the time, do you?" Tossing the jeans aside, Maggie growled, "Janie is a pain in the neck, and you know it!"

A sound from the doorway drew their attention to the young girl they were arguing about. Janie stood silently as she looked at the jeans Maggie was adorning with shooting stars with gold and silver thread, "G-Mama? Can you embroider my jeans with stars, too?"

Maggie answered with annoyance, "I will if I ever get time, Janie."

Giving her grandmother an unforgiving stare she said coldly, "Well, you have time to do it for Shelley. Why don't you have time for me?" When her grandmother tossed the jeans aside and left the room in a huff of exasperation, Janie looked to Kid and asked, "Oh, dear! The old girl seems upset. Was it something I said?"

"Let's go see Sunshine, and pet the horses," he suggested, scheming for an excuse to see Rosie.

"What are you going to tell her about that bruise on your cheek? Does she know about you and Lewis having that fight?" With a scolding tone of voice, she reprimanded her cousin, "I heard some of those things you were saying to make Lewis angry, and they were ugly. Kid, God don't like ugly." She scooted herself off the counter. "You don't have to worry about me telling Rosie anything. I'm learning to keep my mouth shut."

The summer day was gloomy as a rain shower teased the mountain air. Janie adored riding in her cousin's convertible with the top down. She looked up into the cloudy sky as the car rolled along, noting that the sun was completely hidden behind the cloud cover.

When they reached Rosie's house, Janie rushed ahead to the screen door as Mike Douglas' talk show bellowed from the television set. Eva came to the door and pushed it open in a welcoming gesture. She instructed them to go into the kitchen where Rosie was working.

Rosie stepped from the kitchen as they entered the dining room, her face smiling at them in surprise. She wore an ill fitting faded dress with two buttons opened at the bodice. Her hair was pulled back with a ribbon, and sweat moistened her forehead. Janie rushed forward and threw her arms around her in a delighted hug.

After hugging her little cousin, Rosie straightened to look at Kid who was completely captivated by the unfastened buttons on her dress. She broke the silence by saying, "Kid, you're just in time to help me with all that muscle you've got hidden beneath your shirt." She then poked her finger into his bicep, "I've got some heavy boxes that I need moved into the storage room." She pointed at some boxes sitting on the floor filled with glass jars of canned produce and jelly.

"Be glad to help," he said, as he bent forward and lifted a box.

Rosie warned, "Hold it at the bottom. I worked too hard for that stuff to fall out and break on the floor." She turned and led the way down the hallway to an unused bedroom that held storage.

Walking ahead and chattering about coming to see the horses, and how gloomy the sky was, Janie led the way down the corridor. Kid watched the sway of Rosie's hips as she walked ahead of him. She opened the door and instructed him where to set the box. He set it down and went back to the kitchen for the others, as Janie began snooping around the room and asking questions. When he returned, Janie had a sketch pad in her hands and was imploring Rosie to 'write' another book with her. He looked into Rosie's eyes and smiled at her patience with the child.

"Well, let me slip on some jeans, and we'll go see the horses," said Rosie. Caressing his shoulder as she passed by, she whispered at his ear, "Thanks for the help."

He responded by grasping her hand and pulling it to his lips, "Anytime."

She slowly extracted her hand and disappeared into her room. Later, she emerged wearing her old worn jeans that fit too snugly, a faded pink t-shirt, and canvas tennis shoes. Her hair was still secured by the ribbon, with strands fraying about her face. "Let's go!" she said cheerily.

The sky was cloudy, and the atmosphere was humid. Sugar and Spice could be seen grazing near the pond. Rosie whistled to call them up. Spice came walking toward the barn as Sugar continued to graze. After coaxing Spice into her stall with some sweet feed, she slipped a halter onto the horse, and asked Janie if she would like to have a ride. Overjoyed with the suggestion, Janie couldn't wait to sit atop the beautiful Palomino. Kid brought the saddle from the tack room, and watched as Rosie cinched the saddle in place. The bridle was slipped on, and Rosie walked the horse into the breezeway of the barn before letting Janie mount up.

Once Janie was positioned in the saddle, she handed her the reins explaining, "You're not going to need to do anything with these, except hold them. I've got control of Spice with this lead. So just sit tight, and hang loose."

Walking beside Rosie as she led the horse down a well worn path, Kid chatted about lighthearted subjects until they reached the shade of a clump of trees growing along the fishpond. The sun was still shrouded by clouds that dulled the day, but it didn't appear to be an immediate threat of rain. The conversation grew more serious as Kid mentioned the bruise on his cheek.

"Oh, yes, I see it. What happened? Did you get hurt salvaging the wrecked car?" her words falling dangerously close to the truth.

Looking off into the distance, then up at Janie who sat quietly on the horse, her hair frizzing in the humidity, he sighed heavily and answered, "You could say that, Sun. But, the truth is, I got into a fight with Lewis." The sound of the words as they rolled off his lips caused him to cringe.

"Fight!" she exclaimed like the breath had been snatched from her. "Why ever on earth for?"

He closed his eyes as shame flooded through him. "I don't know!" He saw the dark expression on her face and explained, "I said something stupid that made him yell at me."

"What did you say that made him yell at you?" Her face was beginning to show immense anger.

Rubbing a hand across the back of his neck as though to chase away some tension building there, he explained, "I said I was going to marry you!"

"Is that all?" she asked, putting a hand to her mouth as though to help squelch the laughter that lurked there.

Kid wasn't smiling when he answered, "Well, no. See, when he yelled at me for saying that, I shoved him." He stopped to watch her expression. He continued speaking as her blank expression glared at him. "He lost his balance and fell down the hill from the path along Rocky Falls." Pausing for a moment he blurted, "He rolled over the edge! He could have died!" He watched the look of shock cross over her face. "But I saved him, Sunshine! He caught hold of a tree root, and I tied ropes to a tree, and I went over the edge and got him!"

"Oh, my God!" she paced back and forth in front of Spice, holding the lead rope with a grip so tight her knuckles turned white.

"So, even though I saved him, he was still mad, and he punched me." In an effort to calm her emotions, he said, "He wasn't hurt, Sunny, just pissed off. Hell, he doesn't even have a scratch on him!" Kid grasped her by both shoulders and held her firmly. "I love you, Sunny. I would never hurt your friend." He watched as tears welled in her chocolate brown eyes and spilled from the thick black lashes that framed them. "I'm sorry, Sunny, so sorry."

Rosie unsnapped the lead rope and thrust it at Kid. Then, she pushed Janie's foot from the stirrup, inserted her own and mounted the horse herself. Without a parting word she kicked the steed into motion, and they disappeared along the wooded trail. They rode in a smooth gallop alongside the roadway until they reached the Shirey farm. As Rosie dismounted and tied Spice to a tree branch, she asked Janie, "Do you need help in getting down?"

Janie slid sideways until her foot was firm in the stirrup, "Nope," she said, and dismounted easily.

Rosie stepped back, impressed with the young girl's equestrian skill. "Let's go see Lewis," she said, and started toward the house.

Janie caught up with her and said, "Slow down, Rosie. Try to calm down a little. You don't want to go in there and let everyone know how upset you are with Kid. Try to act like this is just a visit."

Rosie came to a standstill, saying, "Yeah, Mamie and Angel probably don't know anything about it, do they?"

"Angel might still be with her mom, and you better just bet that Lewis didn't go telling his grandmother that he almost took a leap off of Rocky Falls."

With a nod, she continued walking toward the house. Rob's old blue pickup truck was in the backyard, and Mamie's Oldsmobile was parked in the car shed. Rosie was sure to find Lewis at home. She knocked on the door, and Mamie opened it.

The sweet face of the elder woman smiled at the two girls, "Come in, girls! What a nice surprise!"

Janie spoke politely, "Hello, Mrs. Shirey. Has Angel returned from her visit with her mother yet?" She folded her hands together in front of her and stood straight as she awaited the older woman's answer.

Mamie smiled down at the sweet child with such gracious manners. "Well, yes, she has, dear." Then she turned and called for Angel. "You know where her room is. Just go on in and see her." Mamie turned back to Rosie as Janie left the foyer, "How are you, Rosie?"

She could hardly keep her breathing quieted as her pulse raced with emotion. "I'm fine. Is Lewis here?" Her eyes darted past Mamie for a glimpse of him in the hallway.

Mamie answered, while noticing the nervousness in Rosie's manner. "Is everything okay? Lewis is at the barn putting away hay."

Stepping to the door, she asked, "Do you mind if Janie visits with Angel just a few minutes while I go see him?"

Mamie waved her on, "Not a bit. You go ahead and see Lewis. She'll be fine here with me." Mamie caught hold of the door and held it while Rosie dashed back to the horse tethered to the tree.

She mounted Spice and took off in a gallop, as Mamie watched from the front door. Spice was in a full run as they crossed the freshly cut hayfield, and sped toward the large barn looming in the distance at the edge of the field near the woods. She slowed to a trot as they neared the barn, and Rosie dismounted before Spice came to a complete halt. Holding the reins and pulling the horse behind her, she entered the barn. The gloomy day made the darkness of the barn thick with shadows, as if twilight had fallen. "Lewis?" she called out into the dim light of the large building. "Are you in here?" Trying to adjust her eyesight to the dim light, she peered through squinted eyes.

The horse snorted while shaking her head, rattling the chains on her bridle, as Rosie tied her with a slip knot to the railing of a catch pen. She turned to look for Lewis when her breath sharply caught in her throat. He was standing right before her. "Oh!" She exclaimed, "You scared me!" Then she laughed tensely, and brushed back the hair which had come loose from the ribbon, and now sprawled wildly across her shoulders and back.

He pushed the long mass of dark curling tendrils from her neck and pulled her close. Kissing her sweetly, he asked, "Are you looking for me? Why? Do we have a date I forgot about?" He kissed her again softly on the forehead.

With closed eyes, she tried to calm her labored breathing, "Oh, no. I mean, yes. I mean, damn it!" She couldn't follow Janie's suggestion to be calm and blurted, "Kid just told me about what happened at the falls."

Shaking his head and smiling, he said, "It was nothing, really. You know how guys are? They lose their temper, they fight. They get over it. That's all that happened with us. Now, we're over it."

Stepping into his body, she submerged her face into his chest. "I know how close you came to falling off the cliffs! I know how you could have died!" Hot tears stung her eyes and streamed down her cheeks, soaking into his dusty shirt.

Thrusting her away, he warned, "Rosie, I'm so dirty. You'll get dust in your eyes." He pulled a worn red bandana from his back pocket and said, "Here, use this to dry your face." He watched as Rosie did as he instructed. Then he clutched her hand and walked her to the flatbed trailer that still held some hay bales waiting to be unloaded and stacked. He reached up, taking a thick yellow rain coat hanging from a peg. He spread it across the hay bales he had been stacking. "Now," he said. "Sit here with me, and let's get this over with." He peeled off the dust covered long sleeved denim shirt, and sat down beside her. He put his arm around her shoulders and hugged her close to his sweaty bare chest. "Everything is okay, now. Don't be upset. Just think of it as ancient history." He rocked her side to side as she wept into the bandana.

Rosie sniffed and said, "I'm so sorry to have caused all this."

Using his index finger, Lewis tilted he face up until she looked him in the eye. "Just look at me, now!" he commanded. "This was not your fault! It was just silly bullshit between me and Kid. He likes being a pain in the ass, and I let him get to me, and it's over!" He laughed as he thought about the ridiculous events that led to the near death situation, giving her pause, and drying her tears. "I really wish you could have been there. It was all so funny. Especially the expression on his face when he realized his lip was bleeding." Laughing harder he explained, "He called me a 'hillbilly fucker!'"

Softly, she smiled, "I'm so glad you're okay, Lewis. I don't know what I would do without you." Impulsively, she leaned in and kissed him forcefully on the lips. She felt his arms close around her and they fell backward onto the rain coat covered hay as heavy drops of rain began falling on the tin roof.

Janie stood looking out the window in Angel's bedroom at the rainfall. She had not told her friend of the drama between Rosie, Kid and Lewis. Being true to her word, as she had promised her grandfather, she was learning to keep her mouth shut. As the sky darkened and the driving rain pelted the ground with wind driven gusts, she silently hoped Rosie and Spice was inside the barn with Lewis.

Over an hour later, Janie and Angel were sitting at the kitchen table playing a game of 'Go Fish' when Lewis and Rosie entered the house through the back door. Rosie's hair was sprawled across her shoulders and back, with curling tendrils sprouting from the mass. Looking at the faces of Mamie and Angel, Janie could see that they didn't notice the change in them, but she did, and it made her smile.

Lewis and Angel both walked with them outside to the horse, and stood in the yard watching them ride away in a swift canter, with Janie riding behind Rosie. Once they had left sight of the Shirey farm, Janie reached up and pulled a sprig of straw from Rosie's hair and asked, "How was your roll in the hay?" Janie giggled wickedly as Rosie snatched the straw from her and flung it into the wind.

She prodded Spice into a gallop, causing Janie to grasp her around the waist tightly. The blonde Palomino carried them back to Mr. Reyes' barn with a swift cantor, and Rosie began unsaddling the horse. Janie raced across the roadway to tell Kid they had returned. She slipped on the wet grass in the front yard, falling down on one knee. After collecting herself, she walked the rest of the way across the lawn and onto the porch. An old weathered rocking chair with peeling paint and splintered wood sat eerily with a potted fern sitting on the seat, and she eyed it suspiciously as she walked past it. The sound of the television had been lowered, and Janie could hear Eva talking to Kid about his music before she opened the door and walked in without knocking.

Kid looked at her with relief showing across his face. "How was the horseback ride? I hope you didn't get rained on." He was speaking to Janie, but looking past her as though he were hoping Rosie would walk in next.

Knowing to say as little as possible, she replied guardedly, "Oh, it was wonderful! We found a barn when the rain started. Spice is the best horse in the whole world!" She swiped at her wet knee. "I slipped just now in the wet grass," she explained, before anyone asked. "I'm just a natural born klutz." Janie stood straight and asked, "You weren't worried about us, were you?"

Kid stood and walked to the door. Janie noticed the way Eva followed him with her eyes. Pity flooded through her for what he must have had to endure with the over-sexed housewife. She walked over and stood next to her cousin. "Rosie is still in the barn with Spice. Go over and see if you can help her. I'll stay here with Eva," Janie glanced over at the blonde woman smoking a long slender cigarette, and took note of the unhappy look she gave her with slit eyes, so she quickly added, "That is if Eva doesn't mind."

Taking a drag of cigarette smoke, Eva held it for a moment before saying, "I don't mind at all." The smoke escaped her lungs with each word she spoke.

Looking as though he was uncertain of what to do, he opened the door and stepped out, closing it behind him gently. Janie stood and watched him jump across the ditch to cross the roadway to the barn. She turned back to Eva and asked, "So, do you like *Dark Shadows*?"

Eva snuffed out her cigarette and answered, "I never miss it."

Taking a seat on the other end of the couch, Janie said, "Oh, good! It's almost time for it to come on. Do you mind if I watch it with you? I haven't seen it at all this week. The last episode I watched was when Laura Collins came back to town to take the children, and Quinton had just killed his wife, Jenny." She folded her hands in her lap as Eva took control of the conversation.

"Well, Quinton's wife was the gypsy's sister, Magda. So, when Magda and Sandor discovered that Jenny had been strangled, they found the button Jenny had clutched in her cold, dead fist. Then they knew Quinton had killed her. So, they worked up a curse and made a potion that they put into some wine, and they tricked Quinton into drinking it. So now, he's a werewolf." Eva sat back, satisfied that she had filled the child in on the gothic drama.

Janie sat back and relaxed, feeling more at ease with the ill tempered woman. They discussed favorite characters and episodes until the show came on. Then they both fell silent and watched as the huge Collin's mansion filled the screen with eerie music playing as the voice of Grayson Hall explained to the audience that the time was 1897, and Barnabas had traveled back in time to save the two children at Collinwood. The scene went to the graveyard to find Laura Collins and Dirk Wilkins digging up the grave of Ben Stokes, searching for the secret of Barnabas Collins. Just as Dirk had pried open the casket, and found the diary Ben Stokes had been buried with, their attention was drawn away by violent lightning and thunder. In the wooded distance watching them was Barnabas, illuminated by flashes of lightening. The music throbbed with suspense as the scene went to the ocean sending pounding white waves crashing upon the rocks below Collinwood.

Janie said, "Oh, this is going to be good!" To which Eva nodded her head in agreement, and reached for another cigarette.

Kid found Rosie removing the halter from Spice as he entered the barn. Her hair was tousled by the wind, and gave her a wild romantic look. He longed to hold her against him, but he was afraid of her reaction if he tried. She looked up at him without smiling, and slapped Spice on the rump to get her out of the barn and back into the pasture. He stood speechless as he watched her take the halter to the tack room. She hung the halter on the designated peg, and then latched the door.

Smoothing her hair, she finally gave him a smile, "I know what you must be thinking."

He watched unblinking as he could only see the sweet beauty of her untidiness, "What's that?"

She laughed self-consciously, "That I look a mess!"

Unable to resist his temptations any longer, he rushed forward and caught her in his arms. "Oh, Sunny, you look nothing less than beautiful!"

Pushing herself away from his embrace she said, "Kid, please. You've got to understand that I care for Lewis, and not you."

Taking a step forward, he wrapped his arms around her, holding her against him as he spoke, "I know you have a crush for Lew, Sunshine, but you don't know how much I love you. If you could just reach inside my chest, and hold my heart for one minute, you would see how I feel for you. And I know, if I only had half a chance, I could prove my love to you." He pushed his face into her tousled hair.

A feeling of exasperation was washing over her, so she turned on one heel and stood face to face with her adoring cousin. "Kid," she began softly. "I know you must have a dozen girls waiting for you to get back home. Why do you want to make such a big deal out of this summer", she paused as she faltered for the right word, "Flirtation?" she exclaimed with a wave of her hands. She didn't push him away as he wrapped his arms around her and clutched her body close to his. The expensive cologne he wore was a pleasure, and filled her with a dreamy emotion.

"I know that's how things started, Sun. But I've changed. I'm so crazy for you. If I can't have you, I think I'll die!" his voice cracked with his confession.

Putting her hands to his neck, she caressed the hair that hung past his collar. "No, Kid. You'll forget about me, when summer's over." She let her hands follow the shape of his shoulders down to his chest. The necklace glittered in the gap left from unfastened buttons on his shirt. She couldn't resist tracing the gold with her right index finger. "You're devastatingly handsome. And, so talented! You can't make me believe you don't have a girl, or maybe more, pining for you back home."

She held still as he cupped her face between his hands and stared into her dark brown eyes. She didn't protest when he placed a heated kiss on her lips, but she didn't respond, either. "Are you not even going to give me a chance?" he asks his breath warm and moist against her lips.

She didn't want to injure his feelings. "This is just a phase that's going to pass. After summer is gone, everything will be just as it was before." She placed her hand gently on his cheek.

Stepping away from her caress, he wet his lips and said, "I will never be the same, Sunny. You just don't know how deep I'm in!" He walked to the other side of the barn, kicking sawdust as he stepped.

She watched him fight with his emotions, and she longed for a way to make him feel better. But, she had committed herself to Lewis this rainy afternoon, and no one was going to sway her from that love. "Let's go inside and have a glass of tea," she suggested kindly.

He swung around, angrily, "I've been drinking tea with that sex fiend stepmother of yours all afternoon!" A low chuckle escaped his lips, "The nasty old broad kept trying to rub her hand into my crotch. Oh, man! Did I get a lesson in dodging the sour pussy?"

She responded with unbridled laughter. His face brightened at the sound, and he smiled. "Let's go have some more tea, Sunshine. I'd drink horse piss if it meant I could spend time with you." They walked back to the farmhouse hand in hand, as Rosie giggled over his raucous remark of her stepmother.

Chapter Nine
Hey Jude

The lazy days of summer passed over Ben Johnson Ridge with farm work, and undiluted pleasures. Lewis had stayed true to his promise and taken Janie and Angel to the drive-in movies, with Rosie joining them. The movie they watched was *Butch Cassidy and the Sundance Kid* with the handsome blue eyed Paul Newman, and the sexy Robert Redford. As Paul Newman rode the pretty Katherine Ross on his bicycle, and the song 'Raindrops Keep Falling on My Head' played, Lewis leaned into Rosie's ear and said, "Just hearing a song about rain does naughty things to me." Then, to answer the question in her eyes, he pulled her hand to the hardness hidden beneath the denim jeans at his crotch. She smiled and looked away, trying not to let him see her blush. They were sitting in lawn chairs on the back of Rob's pickup truck, facing the large outdoor screen, with Janie and Angel sitting on blankets in front of them. Allowing her hand to rest on the private area, that rainy afternoon in the barn swelled back to mind.

The movie gave the girls something to talk about for the rest of the week, and Rosie organized a backyard sleepover for them at her house, as she had promised Janie earlier in the summer. Lewis spent more and more of his free time practicing with the band for the Independence Day festival. Kid took advantage of his adversary's absence by spending all the time he could with Rosie. She had still not convinced him that he could not make her fall in love with him.

One afternoon, Rosie returned home after taking a drive with Kid and Janie. As soon as they entered the back door, Eva called from the living room, "Rosie! That friend of yours, Heather, has called three times. You better call her back. I told her you would as soon as you got back home."

Rosie retrieved a pitcher of lemonade from the refrigerator and set it on the table. She took two trays of ice from the refrigerator freezer and handed them to Kid saying, "Wash your hands, please." Then, she instructed Janie to take the glasses from the cupboard, as she reached for the black phone hanging on the kitchen wall with the long curling cord hanging to the floor. Using the rotary dial, she spun off the phone number. Heather answered after the first ring.

"Hey! It's me, Rosie. Eva said you called." With wide eyes, she listened to Heather's excited conversation, and watched Kid fill the glasses Janie had taken from the cupboard with ice. Rosie motioned for him to pour the drinks as she answered Heather with an occasional "Yes" and "Uh huh." Kid and Janie sat across from one another, as he poured three glasses of lemonade. "Kid is here with me now. This is so cool, please come on over. I'm so excited about this. Do you think she's for real, though? Aren't those kinds of people a little kooky?" Rosie's last words captivated both Kid and Janie's attention. "Do we need black candles or an Ouija board?" This question was followed by a giggle, "Okay, then! We'll be waiting for you. See you soon, bye."

Janie could not contain her interest, "What do we need an Ouija board for, Rosie?" She drained her glass, rattling the ice as the last of the lemonade disappeared in her mouth.

Looking at Rosie with interest as well, Kid asked, "What's up, Sun?"

Taking up her glass, Rosie spoke, before taking the first sip. "Well, Kid. You remember what happened the last time Heather was here with her Ouija board?"

He leaned forward, more interested than ever. "Yeah, but what's she up to today, another séance in broad daylight?" He used his index finger to swipe a line through the moisture beaded on the outside of his glass as he waited for her to answer his question.

Taking a long sip from her drink, she relaxed with a long sigh. "No, no! She wants to bring her mother and her mother's friend over here. It seems that this friend of her mother's is supposed to be a psychic, and when Heather told her about our séance, the lady asked if she could come over and 'read' my house," making quotation marks in the air with her fingers as she said the word 'read.'

Looking about for lurking ghosts, Janie asked, "Oh, Rosie! Is your house haunted?"

Kid answered the question before Rosie could, "We don't know, yet. That's what the psychic is coming to tell us, Kiddo."

Eva could be heard greeting guests from the living room, and Rosie hurried to greet Heather and her mother, "Oh, Mrs. Tillman! How nice to see you. Please come in and have a seat. How are you today?" Rosie asked as politely as she could, while observing the red haired lady who entered the house with Heather and her mother.

Teresa Tillman answered, "I'm fine, dear. And how are you? Heather tells us that you had an unusual experience here, not so long ago. My friend Althea is very interested in your story." Teresa then turned to Eva, saying, "Can I introduce you to an old friend of mine from high school? Althea Phelps, this is Eva Moon. Eva is Rosie's stepmother."

Heather caught Althea by the hand, "This way, Thea." And she began pulling her toward the kitchen, with Rosie following behind. The conversation of Heather's mother explaining to Eva the purpose of their visit resonated into the kitchen. She hadn't bothered to inform Eva of anything about her strange experience, or the fact that guests were coming for a visit. She could hear the irritation in Eva's voice when she answered to Teresa that she had no idea of any such supernatural experience taking place in her own house.

Althea Phelps entered the kitchen, oblivious to any common activity, as she focused on the spiritual energies of the dwelling. The woman had long red hair, parted down the middle of her scalp, and hanging straight down her back. She wore large hoop earrings and hippie love beads around her neck. The blue jeans she wore were faded and torn at the back pocket. Embroidery and patches adorned the jeans, and her white peasant blouse hung off one shoulder, leaving the impression that she wore no bra underneath. She walked to the table and asked Heather, "Where was the boy sitting when he became possessed?"

Heather hurried over to the table, and withdrew the chair that Kid had just used to eat lunch. Althea sat in the chair, and placed her folded hands onto the table in front of her. She closed her eyes, tilting her head back.

Janie looked up at Kid, "Possessed?" She asked in a harsh whisper, "Who was possessed?" Janie didn't get an answer from her cousin. He only shushed her into silence, and pulled her against him, holding her by the shoulders in an effort to keep her quiet.

Althea breathed in deeply and expelled her breath slowly. She opened her eyes and gazed at the ceiling. Without speaking, she stood and began walking through the house. She walked from the kitchen into the hallway. Everyone followed at a safe distance. The red haired lady dressed in gypsy clothing walked down the hallway, past the bedroom Sturgill shared with Eva, and past the bathroom. She entered the living room, and continued walking out onto the front porch. Rosie and Heather crowded into the front doorway, and watched through the screen door as Althea stood beside the weathered old rocking chair holding the potted fern. She ran her hands over the splintered wood on the back of the chair. Then she straightened and stood motionless with her hands raised in front of her, palms up. Her head fell back, her face staring skyward. Invisible images jolted through her, and her body quivered. Everyone gathered in the living room stayed deathly quiet, as Althea completed her reading. They watched in amazement as Althea stumbled to a chair and collapsed into it, exhausted.

Still no one spoke. Rosie asked softly, "Miss Phelps, are you alright?" Kneeling down next to the red haired woman, she asked, "Can I get you anything, a glass of tea, or lemonade, or water?" The woman's face, painted with bright blue eye shadow and pink rouge, fascinated her. Her lips sported red lipstick, and her eyes were framed by thick mascara and eye liner.

Althea Phelps waved her hand in front of her face as though she had been overcome by heat, "Yes please, just some cold water." She leaned forward in the chair holding her face between her hands, staring at the weathered old rug beneath her feet.

Rosie turned to Janie, "Please have Kid help you prepare Miss Phelps a glass of ice water."

Mesmerized by the red haired lady with the strange jewelry, Janie, for the first time in her whole life, wasn't anxious to dash off and complete a domestic chore. Kid said to her, "Never mind, I can do it myself. You just stay here, and stay quiet."

Silence held reign in the room until Kid retuned with the glass filled with fresh ice cubes and cold water from the refrigerator. As a courtesy he asked, "Does anyone else need something to drink?" He caught the hungry look Eva gave him as she reached for her own glass of tea with half melted ice.

Mrs. Tillman responded to his question, "Not for me, thank you, young man." Then she prodded her friend to explain her reading, "Althea, what did you see? You were shaking when you came back from the porch." Teresa Tillman leaned forward on the sofa, "You did see something! I can tell." Then she shifted sideways as her daughter came and perched on the arm of the sofa next to her.

Althea sipped the water slowly at first, but then gulped it thirstily. When the water was drained from the glass, and only the ice remained, she handed it back. He asked, "Do you need more?" Althea answered by shaking her head no.

Everyone was on edge to hear Althea's account of her reading. Kid sat the glass on a doily covered end table, and propped himself against the wall behind Janie as he waited to hear the red haired lady talk. Althea raised her head and looked about the room at all the faces accompanying her. She rose from her chair, and stood as though she were a professor in a class room, about to give a lecture. She reached for the beads that hung haphazardly around her neck, clutching them as she spoke.

"Many years ago, a man lived in this house." She looked to make sure everyone was listening to her with intent. "He had many, many friends here in this community. Many people loved him, but one person hated him." Althea released her hold on the beads and stood behind the chair she had been sitting in, grasping onto the back of it as if for support, in case she swooned. "The person who hated him came here to this house one day, and killed the man so loved by many." Althea raised her head back and looked to the ceiling, as though she was looking past it into another realm. "The loved man's spirit still walks through this house, looking to complete his unfinished business. A type of business that was very important to him, and to the people who loved him. He cannot rest until he realizes that he is dead, and that his business can never be finished here in this house, or on this earth." Althea walked around the chair and slumped into it once more.

Rosie looked to Eva for clarification to Althea's tale. Eva took note and said, "Well, don't look at me! I don't know anything about this. I came to live here in the fall of 1957, just after Rosie had turned five years old. No one has told me any history of this house." Eva anxiously lit one of her long slender cigarettes, and puffed on it furiously.

Speaking from his stance against the wall, Kid said, "I know who can tell us about this house." Everyone in the room turned to look at him. He uncrossed his arms, and stood straight as he explained, "My grandfather was related to Dorothy's mother. G-Daddy would know if a murder had ever taken place here."

Heather stood from her perch beside her mother. "Let's go see your grandfather, Kid!" she exclaimed with enthusiasm. "If this house has always been in the Campbell family, he will surely know about a murder, even if it happened as long ago as the Civil War." Heather turned to her mother, "Can I go with Kid to see his grandfather? He can drive me home later." Then she turned to Kid and asked, "Can't you?"

"Sure I can. But, I'd like for Sunshine to come, too." He turned a charming grin on Eva. "That's alright with you, isn't it, Eva?" The stepmother placed her cigarette in her mouth and nodded as she devoured the young man with her eyes. Kid pretended not to notice the ravenous look Eva gave him as he took a step toward the door. "Okay, then. We'll go see the old man, and let you ladies know what he has to say, later." Kid held the door open as Janie scampered out first, followed by Heather, and then Rosie.

Albert Campbell was sitting beneath the magnolia tree with FCharlie Brown and Teddy when the young people pulled into the drive. The group of young people had discussed the approach they would make. They all agreed not to mention the psychic's reading. Kid gathered lawn chairs from the front porch for Heather and Rosie to sit in, while he and Janie sat on the grass near their grandfather.

After making some small talk, Kid asked his grandfather about his own house, to which Bert replied, "This house was built in 1924, just after the birth of your uncle Ruben." Bert spoke of his first born son, who was killed in WWII, and continued talking. "I built this house with my own two hands, and of course with the help of some paid labor. Your grandmother drew out the floor plan she wanted, and I built it for her."

"What about Sunny's house? Was it built before the Civil War?" Kid didn't take his eyes from his grandfather as his questions were being answered.

Bert rubbed a hand across the back of his neck as he said, "I'm not rightly sure of the year that house was built, but I know it was around the time of the war." Bert paused a moment, "Sunshine, your house was built by your Great-Grandfather's brother. His name was Doc Campbell. Well, that's what everyone called him anyway. He was a medical doctor who practiced right here on Ben Johnson Ridge. As a matter of fact, he saw most of his patients in his own house, at all hours of the day and night."

Bert's memories drifted through the mid-day heat as he recalled stories told by his own father. "I know about Doc, because he was my granddaddy's cousin. I never got to meet him, because he died before I was ever born, but I heard all about him. How the people depended on him for medical care, and back then people couldn't afford to pay with money. They had to pay with services and livestock. Like chickens, goats and blacksmithing." His features grew serious. "Old Doc suffered a tragic end, though. It seems that he had gotten himself involved with a rich man's daughter, and the girl got herself addicted to a drug called Laudanum. It was sold at drug stores in bottles. The stuff was liquid, and was supposed to help all sorts of ailments and pain."

Bert saw that he had awoke the curiosity of the young people gathered with him, and he continued, "Well, that rich man discovered his girl was on dope, you know. Her mother could smell the chemicals on her breath, and everyone could tell she was high as a kite when she was using the stuff. So, her old man decided to blame her drug abuse on the good doctor who was courting her. That arrogant old fool went to Doc's house one day, and shot him dead in cold blood as he sat in his rocking chair on the front porch." Bert paused when he noticed the shocked look on Rosie's face. Then he continued, "The rich old bastard didn't even get hung for his crime. The judge called it justifiable homicide! Then the rich old codger had his daughter locked away in a mental hospital. I guess he felt like it was her fault he had shamed his family with the killing of Doc. That poor girl spent the rest of her life in that institution. She died some five or six years later, when the hospital caught fire. Even after death the family still shunned her. She was buried in the sanitarium graveyard, not her own family's cemetery."

A quite hush fell over the young group. Without his knowing it, Bert had answered the mystery. Kid said, "What a story. Did you ever see a picture of Doc? I was just wondering if he had brown eyes like Sunshine, or blue eyes like me."

"Good Lord, boy! Don't you know they didn't have color photographs back then? But I'm guessing the old boy had brown eyes, considering his mother was a pure blooded Cherokee Indian." Bert turned and walked into the house with Charlie.

Kid rose from the grass and said, "Janie, you stay here while I take Sunshine and Heather home. We've got a lot to talk about, right girls?" He held his hand out for Rosie to take.

Gripping his hand, she stood saying, "Oh, yeah, that's right, Kid." To Janie she said, "I'll tell you all about it someday."

Stroking the puppy in her lap as she watched the car drive away with the teenagers, a silent wish stirred through Janie that she could be the same age as them, and never be left out of their outings. She picked up the puppy and carried him with her to the porch swing. Together, they rocked to and fro as the honey bees buzzed around her grandmother's rosebushes.

Kid drove along slowly so they could discuss the events of the day. Heather hovered between them from the backseat. "I can't wait to tell Althea the story we got from Kid's grandpa. She is going to be so thrilled with herself!" she declared, her hair windblown and wild. "Gosh, I feel like celebrating. Does anyone have a joint?"

Rosie said, "My plants are too young. Don't even ask me to top them."

Kid looked at Rosie, "Holy shit! Are you growing pot?" He laughed with a broad smile covering his face. "Well, we can always get some beer." He looked at Heather through the rearview mirror, "I'm old enough to buy."

Heather reared her head back and hooted, "Yahoo!" They rolled along the roadway, discussing how they could find some marijuana. When they approached a young man with long brown hair hitchhiking, Heather said, "Stop and ask that guy if he has a joint. If he does, we'll give him a ride."

"We can't do that! He could be a hatchet killer," Rosie cautioned.

Kid stared at Heather in the rearview mirror and said, "You do the talking." He slowed for the hitchhiker.

The young man approached the convertible and replied, "Sweet ride, dude. Where are you headed?" He clutched the straps of a pack he carried on his back.

Heather looked the handsome young man up and down, "That depends on you, man. You got a joint to share?"

The young man laughed lightly, "Does a bear shit in the woods?" He looked at Kid who said nothing then he looked at Rosie, who took no notice at all. "What's up with you guys today? Just looking for a buzz? Well, I got one for you, if you got a ride for me." He stepped back from the car as he waited for an invitation.

Heather looked at Kid, who looked at Rosie. With silence as an agreement, Heather smiled sweetly and said, "Hop on in here. My name is Heather. These are my friends, Kid and Rosie." She slid over so the handsome young stranger could get into the backseat with her.

The young man entered the backseat beside Heather, holding his backpack in his lap. "My friends call me Jude, but my real name is Julian Jones. I live in Lake City, Florida."

Heather sing sang, "*Hey Jude*!"

Jude chuckled at her, and continued, "I'm on my way north to New York. I intend to be there for the Woodstock concert." He shifted his backpack while explaining, "I wanted to ride my motorcycle up there, but after seeing the movie *Easy Rider* my old man took the keys, and refused to let me. So, I could either go by bus or hitchhike. I figured hitching would be more adventurous." The young man watched Rosie with interest, "Have you guys heard about it?"

Heather said, "You'd have to live in a cave not to know about Woodstock. But, we just solved a great ghost mystery, and we want to get high. Where's the joint?"

Jude laughed, "I like a lady who gets right to the point." He began digging into his backpack.

Kid said, "Wait till I get us some beer." He wheeled into a gas station, and left the radio playing while he went into the store.

Turning to face Jude, Rosie asked, "So, your parents aren't concerned with you hitchhiking across country like this?" He had soft brown eyes, and feathered straight brown hair, and he smiled a silly grin which made her smile back.

"No way, they think I'm on a Greyhound Bus to visit a cousin in South Carolina. They would shit a brick if they thought I was on the road hitchhiking." He chuckled at his own words. Then he asked Rosie, "Is this dude your old man?"

"I don't have an old man. Kid is sort of a cousin." Then she said absent mindedly, "But he's always trying to kiss me." Rosie realized she had said too much by the gaped mouth look on Heather's face, so she turned back in her seat.

Jude looked at Heather and asked, "Are you Indian?" Then, self consciously, he said, "I mean you look dark and exotic, like a Native American."

Heather smirked and said, "Well, I ain't from India!" Then she smiled seductively, "I like you, dude! Can you play music?"

Kid returned to the car with a case of beer under his arm, and a bag of ice. "I think this should take care of the afternoon." He settled the beer into a cooler he had in the trunk of his car.

Jude offered his help, which Kid declined. When Kid returned to the car he said, "Let's go sit at the lake for a while." Looking to Rosie he asked, "Which way?"

They parked beneath a tree on the side of a road on the back water side of the lake. Kid passed out beer, as Jude cautioned them about the joint he removed from his tote. "Toke on this easy. It's pretty stout, some Redbud Sensimilla from Mexico. It can really toast your brain, man." He handed it to Rosie, "Light it up, my dear."

Kid snatched it saying, "Let me light it up, my dear!" He lit the hand rolled cigarette, and passed it over to Rosie.

She puffed lightly, remembering Jude's warning, while Kid burst into a fit of coughing. A smile formed on her lips for Jude as she turned to hand him the joint. Softly, he caressed her hand as he took the cigarette. Expelling the smoke from her lungs, she said to Jude, "I guess he didn't take your warning very seriously."

Irritated by the attention Jude was showing Rosie, Kid said, "Let's get out of the car and sit on the bank." He opened his door, taking the joint with him.

They finished the cigarette and the first beer sitting by the lake. Jude said he could camp there for the night, and Kid suggested he stay with him at his grandfather's farm. The effects of the marijuana eased everyone's mood, and mellowed the hot summer afternoon. Jude invited the three new friends to come with him to New York for the concert. Kid was taken with the idea.

"Stay with me tonight, and we'll talk about it, dude", Kid told Jude. "If I go, I'm driving my car."

Heather said, "If I go, I'll have to make up one hell of a lie to tell my mom."

"I'm not sure I can think of a good enough lie to tell my dad," said Rosie.

Chapter Ten
GI Joe

When the neighbors on Ben Johnson Ridge heard that Edward Shirey was returning from Vietnam, gladness overflowed conversations that were usually drab and casual. On the night of his welcome home party, the Shirey farmhouse glowed brightly, as it appeared every electric light was turned on. The entire neighborhood seemed to be present for Ed's homecoming. Rosie had helped Mamie prepare food for the party, and the kitchen smelled like Thanksgiving had come to the mountain early.

Foot stooping music pierced the solemn summer night, drowning out the songs of desperation from the tree frogs and cicadas. A bon fire blazed in the back yard, lighting the faces of guests as it carried sparks into the atmosphere. The Mountaineers played *Rose of Old Kentucky* and several couples danced to the rhythm of the banjo and fiddle.

Heather was dressed in a pretty pink dress, and performed occasional songs with the band. Her strong voice with the unusual forlorn edge blended well with the bluegrass lyrics. Rosie smiled when she noticed the exaggerated southern accent Heather threw into the country songs. Shelley clung to Lewis, and Janie was having fun hanging out with Angel. To Rosie's relief, Kid was nowhere in sight.

She greeted her Uncle Bert and Aunt Maggie with a quick hug, and then squealed with delight to see her favorite neighbor, Miss Willene Reyes. She rushed to her reclusive neighbor, blubbering delight at seeing her. Willene calmly reminded her that she and her sister were taking turns sitting with Minnie Mama so everyone had a chance to welcome the handsome young Edward home.

Stepping closer to Willene she asked, "So how are you doing these days?"

A nonchalant expression crossed over the forty-something woman's face. Rosie was painfully aware of the lonely existence her neighbor had in caring for her homebound mother. "There's not much for me to do anymore. I watch soap operas and game shows during the day, and then I watch whatever is on for the night." Her voice trailed off as if boredom had moved in, "What have you been doing these days?"

"I've been busier than a beaver trying to get my garden produce put up. I'm almost out of canning jars, so I'll be freezing stuff next week." With a nod in the direction of her stepmother, she continued, "I don't get any help, if you know what I mean." As she stared in the direction of Eva, she saw Shelley approach her stepmother and chat up an easy conversation.

Disgust crossed Willene's face when a man boldly walked up behind Eva and pinched her on the backside. She hissed, "That no account Bonzie Leak! He's been a scoundrel his whole life." Willene noticed Rosie's surprised expression and explained, "Well, I should know. I've known him his whole life." She watched the man intently as he flirted with Eva. Suddenly, Willene smiled sweetly and confessed, "When we were kids, Bonzie and I were good friends. Then we grew up, and he got married. Then he got divorced, but he got married again. And, that went on until he hit his marriage limit."

"How did he manage to get so many wives? Is he rich, or something?" Rosie gazed at the tall lean man who held a slender cigar clenched in his teeth. A vague memory of Eva pushing his hand away from her knee just as Rosie entered the room came to mind.

"Ha! He's certainly not rich, I can tell you that much." Willene rocked back on her heels, and pulled a short menthol cigarette from a flowered package. She lit it with a petite Zippo lighter. Her face looked younger in the glow of the flame as she puffed her cigarette into life. Willene inhaled a deep drag and then she began, "He's something of an itinerant barber, going to his customer's homes to give haircuts. He was always the most handsome and most popular boy in school. But, he just never did anything with his life!" Scowling in his direction, she continued, "He could have been anything he wanted. Luck was always falling on him. The state of Alabama allows a person to get legally married seven times, and Bonzie's been married eight."

"If the law only allows you seven, how do you get eight?" asked Rosie.

"In the state of Alabama you can legally be married seven times, but you may remarry one of your ex-wives and it's not counted. So, Bonzie's fifth wife was also his eighth." Willene shook her head slowly. "I don't understand her thinking. She knew it was a bad marriage the first time. It's like going to the refrigerator and discovering the milk has soured. So, you put the soured milk back in the refrigerator, and come back later thinking it might not still be spoiled." Willene spoke with wise consideration. Her eyes flashed as she observed Bonzie enjoying the party. "I say just get rid of spoiled milk, and don't give it any more chances."

Rosie focused on a different subject, "Did you hear the *Smothers Brothers Show* has been cancelled?"

With eyebrows drawn in cross contemplation, Willene said, "Well! All they wanted to do was make jokes about hippies and marijuana. They weren't at all funny. They just had fun with themselves while those women wiggled around half dressed. Most everybody watches *Bonanza* anyway. Nobody's going to miss that silly show."

Suppressing a giggle, Rosie said, "My dad never misses the *Johnny Cash Show*. Do you ever watch it?"

"Oh, yes! That man is incredible! I don't always care for some of those new young singers he has on, but it's usually a good show. Did you know that man never did any time in jail? Everyone thinks he did because of his songs, but he never did."

Seeing that Lewis was preparing to sing, Rosie excused herself. "It was good to see you. I'll drop by soon and bring you some apples."

She found a quiet place to observe, but be unobserved, and settled into a dark corner. The crowd grew quiet as Lewis took the stage, announcing that he had prepared a special song for his brother's homecoming, and that it was sure to be a hit with all the returning GIs. He began strumming a fast happy beat on his guitar. Then just as everyone began jigging to the music he cut loose with his lyrics.

GI Joe, GI Joe
Where the blazes did you go?
You've ran off with Uncle Sam,
And, now your ass is in Vietnam.
Was this your clever way,
To get out of baling hay?

The crowd roared with laughter, and Ed held a big smile on his face. Lewis finished his happy tune with a chorus of GI Joe's sexual prowess.

Look at all the girls you got,
They don't care if you're smoking pot.
Why don't you go back to Vietnam?
GI Joe, that's my girl in your hand!
Hey! Somebody give me a grenade!
I'm gonna blast his ass back to Hanoi!

He finished the song with some fancy strumming on the guitar, and the applause was incredulous. The crowd hadn't calmed when another voice came over the speakers announcing a song for the GI's homecoming. Most of the people in the crowd didn't recognize the young lean blonde haired man from Michigan, but they applauded him anyway.

Kid gave some directions to the band and he began picking his guitar with a fast melody that held a vague recognition for the gathering. As the band chimed in, the song was fully recognized by everyone in the crowd who listened to the popular top forty music stations. He sang into the microphone the lyrics made famous by Credence Clearwater Revival, and Heather climbed the stage to back him up with *Who's Gonna Stop the Rain.* Jude found Rosie and stayed by her side like a lost puppy. The mood of celebration was contagious, as Sturgill shared his homemade blackberry wine with those in the crowd that he knew to imbibe.

Sneaking from the shadows, Kid grabbed Rosie around the waist. She almost squealed at the surprise, but squelched herself just in time for the band to fall silent. "Kid!" she exclaimed in a low tone. "What are doing? Don't scare me like that! Look at all the people here. I don't want any gossip going on about me and my cousin."

He sniffed her hair saying light heartedly, "Hell, this is Alabama. What's to gossip about?"

Rosie noticed Bert standing with Charlie Brown, but his gaze was on her, and the exchange between her and his grandson had not gone unnoticed. She watched Bert approach young Ed who was wearing his army dress for the occasion. Ed listened intently. She knew with certainty that Bert was speaking about her, but couldn't grasp a reason why.

Heather sang loud and strong with the band, and when it was time to take a break, Lewis would take the stage and she would sing with him. During one of the band's breaks he called Shelley up to sing a song they had practiced for the occasion. At the conclusion of the song, emotion overtook her and Shelley threw her arms around his neck planting a wet kiss on his cheek. Smiling sheepishly at the crowd, he declared, "These darn girls just can't keep their lips off of me!" Then he strummed violently on his guitar, creating another ripple of giggles. He noticed Rosie's folks driving away without her.

Kid had found some new friends in the band members and enjoyed trying out their instruments, and talking about music. At midnight the band wrapped up the party, and everyone was expected to go home. Bert and Maggie left before the midnight hour, and Bert nodded to Ed as they made their way to his car.

"You take good care of things around here, Eddie," Bert said as he walked by, giving Ed a playful slap on the back.

Rosie stood with Jude at her elbow, but the parting remark between Ed and Bert caught her attention. Ed answered back, "You can count on me, Bert, don't worry." Bert could be heard making explanations to his wife as they walked away. Shelley and Janie were rounded up, and hustled into their grandfather's car. They drove slowly away from the crowd waving their goodnights.

Ed headed for his brother who had taken a stance next to Rosie, while Bert's grandson stood on the other side. Jude held back like a loyal body guard. Ed approached Rosie and took her arm. She smiled into the handsome soldier's face, her brown eyes bright, but fatigued from the evening's celebration. "Rosie, I told your Uncle Bert I would drive you home tonight."

Her smile fell into an instant frown. "Well, Ed. That's nice of you, but I don't need your assistance."

Lewis spoke up, "Ed, I've got the keys to Pop's truck, so I can drive her home."

Kid pulled Rosie a step backward as he objected, "Nobody needs either one of you to drive Sunny home. I already told her daddy I would get her home safe and sound."

Lewis scoffed, "Oh, yeah. When, tomorrow?"

Rosie looked at the ground, the smile gone from her face.

Ed held up a hand for silence, "You two just get over yourselves. I got this one under control. I will be driving the young lady home tonight." He took a step sideways pulling Rosie along with him.

Kid stepped up to the muscular soldier, "I don't think so, Bro, like I told you. I'm taking Sunny with me."

In a smooth expert move, Ed reached out and grabbed Kid by his right arm. Before anyone knew what had happened, Ed had Kid's arm twisted behind him with his face pushed flat onto a picnic table. "Excuse me, Bro," Ed mimicked. "But it's gonna be like I said, and there ain't nothing you can do about it." Still holding Kid down on the table, Ed said to Rosie, "Looks like it's time for us to go, Sunshine."

Infuriation coursed through her, "You suck!" She hissed at Ed, "What makes you think I'd go anywhere with you?"

Jude stepped forward, "Everything's cool, man! There's no need for violence."

Ed released Kid with a warning. "You really don't want to mess with me, slick. Think long and hard before you give it a try." Then as a second thought Ed looked at his younger brother and added, "Neither one of you want to mess with me. That's for damn sure!" He turned to Rosie and said, "Will you just let me take you home like I promised Bert?"

Anger raged through her as she turned and marched to Ed's car. He followed, with the emblems on his uniform glittering in the darkness.

"That asshole survived Vietnam, but he's got a lot of catching up to do here at home," said Lewis before walking into the house with the screen door banging sharply behind him.

Jude stood next to Kid as though to show his loyalty. Kid's face was colored with emotion as he said, "This night ain't over, my friend. We still got Heather's party to go to at the falls." With a clever smile he asked, "Ready to go?" With a slight nudge, Jude followed him to the red convertible.

Without looking back at the admirers she left behind, Rosie slid down into the black leather bucket seat and gazed intently at Ed. His face was serious. "I guess you got a lot of stories you could tell about the war, huh?"

She could see his calm expression from the glow of the dashboard as he said, "Yeah, but none I would want to share with you. It was awful, and I'd never want you to even have to think about it."

Wanting to insult him, she asked nonchalantly, "Did you really kill babies over there?"

Ed slammed on his brakes, throwing her into the dashboard hard. "What the hell is wrong with you?" He shouted, "Are you stupid or something?"

Tears began to flow and she cried, "I'm so sorry, Ed. Really, I don't know why I asked you that, please forgive me. I am stupid, so stupid!" Hot drops of tears spilled down her cheeks. Mortified that she had so easily offended the soldier just returned from foreign soil, she took a deep breath and explained, "I just wanted to insult you for insisting you drive me home. You have no right to ask anything of me, and you know that."

Ed put a hand on her shoulder, "Yeah, you're right, but like I said. I was following Bert's instructions, and trying to avoid a situation between Kid and Lewis. They've already been fighting over you." Silence overcame them for a few moments. "And, you're not stupid!" The irritation was evident in his voice.

"I don't know what Bert's all freaked about, I'm not in love with Kid. I have my own plans, and they don't include him, or you."

Ed wheeled his '65 Mustang into Rosie's driveway. He killed the ignition and turned to her. Softly he said, "I hope all your dreams come true for you. Really I do. But if you're not careful, life can get a choke hold on you, and leave you without any choices."

Rosie snapped, "I'm too smart to get pregnant, if that's what you mean."

Ed exited his side of the car, and walked around to open her door. She took the hand he offered, letting him pull her out of the car. He followed her to the front porch. Once she stepped up onto the first step, she turned and said, "You know, Ed. We don't have to be friends, but I refuse to be enemies."

"I learned a thing or two in 'Nam. One thing is to keep your friends close, but keep your enemies closer." The moon was almost full, and a warm breeze blew through the trees twisting the limbs angrily. "I don't know about you, but I think there's a storm brewing. And, I damn sure think there is a storm brewing between Lewis and Kid. Maybe I do need to take your attention off them for a while. At least till Kid gets his ass back to Michigan."

She snorted a little laugh saying derisively, "You don't have what it takes to get my attention anymore, Ed."

With a dark look he asked, "And, just what does it take to get your attention, Sunshine?"

With a twisted smile she replied, "Integrity." Then she turned and went inside her house without giving the solider a farewell.

Later, Rosie lay awake in bed unable to stop thinking of Ed. She twisted the knob on her bedside lamp and reached for her diary. After filling two pages, a sharp tap at her window startled her. Shoving the diary beneath her pillow, she crawled across her bed to the window, and shoved it upward. Looking out, she saw Kid standing in the shadows holding the coin he had used to get her attention.

"Kid!" she whispered. "What are you trying to do? Get me grounded for life!"

He pushed her back and crawled inside. "Shhh, be quiet!" When he got a good look at her standing before him with her hair twisted up in rag curls he exclaimed, "What the hell is this?"

"I always curl my hair," she explained blushing. "And, I want to look especially nice at church tomorrow," she added defiantly.

With narrowed eyes he asked, "Why, because Ed Shirey will be there?"

His invidiousness provoked her, "That is my business not yours!"

Coolly brushing her comments aside he said, "Come on and get dressed. Heather has a party starting up at the falls. Let's go and have some fun," he said as he tossed her the same jeans she had worn to the barn dance. "Jude is waiting in the car."

Rosie began to get dressed, pulling the jeans on beneath her gown saying, "What if Lewis and Shelley are there?"

Kid grimaced, "They *are* going to be there, but that's not going to stop us from dropping some acid and having a groovy time."

She said, "Well, let's go already. And, I'm not dropping any acid tonight."

Turning up the volume on the radio prevented any conversation Kid wasn't interested in. The top was down on his convertible and he drove slowly with Jude sitting in the middle of the back seat. The stars glittered against the black velvet sky with the huge moon looming in its midst. Unraveling her hair from the curlers, the tendrils spilled down her back in coffee colored waves. Kid could not resist the temptation to reach out and drag his fingers through the chestnut mane. She didn't push his hand away, but he seemed to sense that his action was detested, and he withdrew his hand. They continued driving with deliberate slowness, as the car winded around unpaved mountain roads where the mountain laurel had long since lost the beautiful spring blooms that had weighed their boughs and perfumed the air. Now, only the vague scent of honeysuckle clung to the dusty air, and rabbits skipped in and out of the glare of the headlights in the summer night.

They parked at the end of a line of cars, and using a flashlight, followed the sound of a radio. A group of kids gathered around a small campfire on the road to the bridge above the falls. The occasional snap of a beer can being opened resonated in the hills.

"Well, look who's here?" Shelley cried out, "The kissing cousins and the lost boy from Orangeville!"

Kid pinched her arm saying, "Shut your pie hole! Nobody wants to hear anything you've got to say." They continued to entertain the crowd by exchanging comical insults.

Lewis eyed Rosie from across the campfire. When she caught his gaze, he motioned for her to come to him. After walking around the circle of people, she came to stand next to him. He nodded his head toward the bridge and said, "Something's up with Heather. I saw her over there crying, but she wouldn't talk to me. Maybe you should go see about her."

Noticing the pale pink dress, almost concealed in the darkness, Rosie walked to the bridge and called out, "What's up, Heather?"

Heather didn't look up. She had her face pillowed upon her arms as she held tight to the iron railing of the bridge with her legs dangling off the side. "Rosie, why is life so unfair? I know I'm not beautiful, but neither is she. Hell, she hasn't even got no tits! But, she sure has the attention of all the boys."

Rosie had noticed the popularity of her cousin from Mississippi with the boys. "Yeah," she said as she dangled her legs from the bridge. "Her nose is crooked, so is her teeth, and her chest is flat. She has ugly, frizzy, mousey brown hair, and she uses a ton of makeup trying to cover those awful freckles."

"Well, I guess when you put out the boys don't mind what you look like," Heather's voice couldn't conceal the contempt she felt for her rival. "You know the old saying; a hard dick has no conscience."

Rosie wasn't familiar with that saying, but didn't say so. The moon reflected pale watery shadows from the moving stream that stretched below them. "So, what's Shelley done to upset you?"

Heather snorted, "Well, let's see. Where do I begin? Oh, I know where to begin. Let's begin with the fact that she stole my boyfriend tonight. Right here of all places! I think she wanted me to catch them at it. She's evil!"

"Boyfriend?" asked Rosie.

Heather continued raving her discontent, "Okay, so Joey isn't my boyfriend. But I wanted him to be, and now all he can do is sniff after her." She threw a sideways glance toward the group at the campfire, "My God, she's such a slut!"

"Let's go back to the campfire. Don't let her spoil the party."

The two girls returned to the group of youths gathered around the fire. Shelley, her eyes glassy from beer and conquests consummated, spoke up for all to hear. "Hey, look! Our sweet Sunshine is not only a cousin fucker she's a lesbian, too!"

The crowd roared with brutal laughter. Rosie looked at Heather, who stood immobilized with humiliation. Unwilling to indulge the cruel relative with nasty exchanges, she said to Heather, "Let's get out of here. It reeks!" Taking Heather by the hand, she pulled her away.

Unable to contain his annoyance, Kid walked over to Shelley and shoved her. She fell over onto the ground from her cross legged sitting position. "Hey!" She wailed, "Don't shove me, Kid! I've got a cyst on my ovary."

To everyone's amusement, Kid exploded, "Cyst, hell! That's not a cyst on your ovary. That's some man's wedding ring!"

Laughter erupted from the group.

Motioning for Kid and Jude to follow her and Heather, Rosie left the light of the campfire. Heather was still giggling over Kid's amusing remark when he came along the road with his flashlight. "Hey, Kid." Heather began, "Do you mind giving me a ride home? Shelley was hell bent on messing up my date with Joey." Heather spread both hands palm up in the air, and explained, "I just can't let him drive me home now."

"Girl, I would be honored to drive you home. Has anybody ever told you that you can sing, I mean really sing?" asked Kid sincerely.

Heather smiled, "Coming from someone as talented as you, I'll believe it. Like they say, it takes one to know one."

Rosie and Jude walked side by side along the dusty road, with Kid and Heather leading the way with the flashlight. As they drove Heather home, the radio was turned off so they could talk, and make insulting remarks about Shelley. Heather was dropped off with good nights, and a date to make plans for Woodstock. When they approached Rosie's house, she began gathering the rag rollers she had had in her hair earlier.

"I see," Kid remarked with sarcasm. "You've got to make yourself beautiful for church tomorrow. Next thing we'll be hearing is how you and Ed ducked the sermon to get in on in the parking lot."

Looking at him with revulsion she reached for the door handle saying, "You really know how to make me sick."

He snapped back, "And you really know how to be a little bitch, don't you?"

"Yeah, well the more time I spend with you, the better I get at it!" she fired back, and marched away. Jude's amused chuckle carried across the early morning hours.

Kid made a final remark loud enough for Rosie to hear, before he drove away. She stepped to her bedroom window hearing his words swimming through her brain, *"I'm going to marry that girl someday!"*

Chapter Eleven
Independence Day

Rosie lay awake in bed during the wee morning hours following her return home from the party at the falls. Angry frustration wouldn't allow her to sleep. Memories of the humiliating way Ed had broken her heart wouldn't leave her alone. Even when she tried to focus on her feelings for Lewis, her thoughts skipped back to Ed. Sometime before dawn she found restless sleep, impeded by sinister dreams. Just as dawn broke over the horizon, she awoke in a state of terror from a paralyzing dream that left her heart pounding. As the day progressed, she tried vainly to remember what it was in her dreams that had frightened her so.

The last days of June passed, and Rosie's birthday approached with the first day of July. Kid called her on the telephone, "Do you know what tomorrow is?"

"Yes, July 2, 1969."

He responded to her humor with a chuckle, "Your birthday, Sunshine. Remember?"

She adored his attention, "I do remember, Kid. It's your birthday, too."

"I've got a surprise for you."

"What would that be?"

"Jude, Heather and I are going to show you a really good time."

His mention of Jude reminded her of the plans they had for the weekend concert in upstate New York. She looked around to make sure Eva wasn't close enough to eavesdrop. "Kid, do you really think this camping trip story is going to work with my dad? You know how protective he is."

Answering with confidence he reasoned, "You're underestimating your old man, Sunny. He knows you're of age now, and he's going to loosen up. Trust me."

Rosie's birthday came as any other day. She arose early and prepared breakfast for her father. She packed his lunch while he sipped hot coffee with sleepy eyes. She said, "You know that Kid and Heather are taking me out for my birthday today, right?" Sturgill Moon set his cup down on the table and picked up his fork. Prodding her father for a response, she asked, "You do remember that today is my birthday, don't you?"

Stabbing at his plate he said, "I will never forget your birthday, Sunshine Rose."

Leaning down she kissed his cheek, "I didn't think you would." She placed his lunch pail on the table beside him, and started to walk away.

Sturgill reached out and took his daughter by the hand. Reaching into his shirt pocket he pulled forth a folded twenty dollar bill, "Happy birthday sweetheart."

"Oh, Daddy!" she gushed, "Thank you!"

White fluffy clouds floated through the pale blue sky that loomed above as Rosie drove Kid's car along the highway leading away from Byron Town into the larger city of Jones Port. Her hair whipped around her face, but she seemed oblivious to the nuisance of it. Kid sat in the passenger seat, and Heather sat in back with Jude. The radio blared out The 5th Dimension's, *Aquarius*, and Heather sang along. Obeying directions, Rosie turned into the parking lot of a tattoo parlor.

Heather piped from the backseat, "Okay, who's the dope getting a tat?"

Kid opened his door and got out of the car. "Let's go inside and look around."

The shop had walls filled with pictures of tattoos available by the artist. A muscular man greeted the group and offered assistance. Surprised to hear Kid ask about ear piercing, Rosie asked, "Are you really going to get your ear pierced, Kid?"

Turning his head from the display of earrings he smiled through slit eyes, catlike, "It's my birthday, ain't it?" Then he returned his gaze to the jewelry and reminded her, "It's your birthday, too. We're both getting pierced."

Rosie was speechless. Heather said, "Oh! Yes, Rosie. It's about time you get your ears pierced. I've had mine since fourth grade."

Jude joined the group saying, "The gold studs are the way to go. See?" he pushed back his soft brown hair and wiggled a gold earring in his own earlobe.

Kid said to the shop owner, "I want the gold studs. And, I'm buying whatever my Sunshine wants, too."

Feeling nervous Rosie stammered, "I'll take the same."

Kid was happy, "Alright!" He clapped his hands together saying, "Ladies first!" and pointed to the chair where the manager did his work.

Sitting in the chair, as the others gathered about to watch Rosie asked timidly, "Will I bleed?"

The handsome man prepared his tray for the procedure and answered, "Maybe, and maybe not." He swabbed her earlobes with antiseptic then using a marker he drew dots. Unhappy with his first attempt, he wiped away the marks with the antiseptic, and drew them again. This time he was satisfied, and picked up the device he would use for the job. "Okay, relax and breathe calmly."

Rosie winced when she heard the flesh give way to the needle. "Wow! That didn't even hurt."

"You've got to be careful, and clean your ears several times a day." He handed her a bottle of antiseptic and a pamphlet with instructions.

Stepping from the chair Rosie said, "Next!"

Kid took her place. Everyone burst into laughter when he yelled, "Ouch! Damn, that does hurt!"

The handsome man with rippling muscles made a sound with his tongue pressed behind his teeth, "Tsk, tsk. Now, look who's being a big old baby?" He dropped the second earring into a tiny plastic bag and handed it to Kid. "Sorry, but we only sell earrings in pairs, so you have an extra. Don't just toss it out, it's gold."

Snatching the earring from the broad shouldered man Kid mumbled, "Yeah, yeah! What do I owe?"

While Rosie admired her earrings in an oval shaped mirror sitting on the glass counter Heather asked, "What's your secret?"

"Secret?"

"You've got all the guys in the palm of your hand. How the hell do you do it?"

With knitted eyebrows Rosie asked, "What do you mean? Kid is just a summer infatuation. He'll get over me soon enough." To emphasize the lightness of the situation, she waved her hand in the air saying, "And, Jude hasn't even looked at me. Don't be giving me credit when there's no credit due."

Heather fumbled in her handbag. She produced a small note pad and pen, and franticly wrote down a few words. "I like that 'credit due' remark. I'm putting together a song, and I think I can use that phrase."

Friday, July 4, 1969 came with all the excitement a holiday offers to the young and old alike. Janie scampered around her grandparent's house looking for the canvas sneakers she had worn the day before. Kid and his friend Jude sat on the front porch, while Kid strummed the guitar. Stepping onto the porch barefooted, she waited for Kid to break from his guitar strumming before speaking.

"Don't you think my cousin is talented, Jude? Too bad he's not going to be in the Battle of the Bands today."

"I think he can go far with his music." Jude slumped lazily into the lawn chair and stared into the distance of the corn field. "So, Janie, you're going back home seaside next month, huh? I live in Florida, but I'm not near the ocean like you are. I envy you for that."

Confusion wrinkled her nose, "Envy? What does that mean?"

Her answer came with the rude sound of screeching guitar strings. Kid sighed in exasperation, "It means he's jealous that you get to live on the beach. Maybe you need to practice using the dictionary instead of hounding the dickens out of us." He tickled his fingers across the strings, smiling wickedly.

Jumping to her feet Janie announced, "I've got to find my shoes. G-Mama says I have to ride with you and Jude to the lake today." She snatched open the storm door and disappeared inside.

Rosie sat with Heather at the picnic table Teresa Tillman had coveted by making a six am appearance at the park, and claiming the one nearest the restrooms. The smell of food grilling crawled through the air with tantalizing consequences for Heather. She rummaged through her mother's picnic supplies.

Teresa approached with a rather short unremarkable man at her side. "What are you doing?" she asked her daughter.

Heather looked up and said, "Oh, hi! This is my friend, Rosie. And, Rosie, this is Mom's friend, Harry." Heather sidestepped her mother's question by saying, "I thought Althea was going to join us today." Then she deftly popped open a bag of chips.

Teresa said, "She is later. I wish you wouldn't eat so much of that stuff. Don't you know it all goes straight to your ass?" She picked up a bag of carrots and shook them at her daughter, "This is what you should be eating."

Teresa tossed the carrots, and they landed on the table next to the man she was dating. He seemed to be a little feminine, with his hair cut bluntly shot and straight bangs lying across his forehead. A little gray peppered his raven hair, and a gold ring adorned his pinky finger. His voice was soft and courteous as he spoke against his girlfriend's remarks. "Teresa! Heather is a young girl. You shouldn't say things like that. I'm sure she'll lose that baby fat soon enough." His face faltered with harmless expression as he realized he had only added insult to injury.

Heather crumble the potato chip bag closed and slammed it on the table, before standing and stomping away. Watching the wrinkled bag unfold Rosie said to the adults, "I'll just go with her." And she followed her friend to the lake shore.

Squatting at the water's edge, Heather plucked tiny mussel shells from the sandy bottom. Her reflection waved in the ripples of the water. Without looking up, she spoke, "I hate when she says stuff about my weight! Am I really that fat? I must be. None of the guys look at me as anything but just a friend. I want to be one of the girls, not one of the guys!" Leaning back, she stared out across the smooth water rippling with soft waves. "Rosie, you just don't know how lucky you are to be pretty. It sucks being ugly, like me." She stood and returned the shells she had collected to the lake bottom, by slinging them with a harsh spin of the wrist.

Rosie didn't indulge her friend's self pity. She watched the motorboats in the distance towing skiers at a furious speed. "Wouldn't it be cool to run into someone we know with a boat, so we could go out on the water to watch the fireworks tonight?"

Heather stood and placed one hand on her hip, "Why does it have to be someone we know. All you have to do is bat your thick eyelashes, and you can have any man on the lake!" Her tone had turned angry.

"Don't be silly!" Rosie fired back. Her attention was called away by the shrill voice of a child calling her name. She turned to see Janie standing at the picnic table with Kid and Jude introducing their selves to Harry. Looking back at Heather she said, "If you really want Jude's attention, now is a good time to go for it." Then she curtly walked away.

During the concert, Rosie wore a large brimmed hat she borrowed from Teresa. Musicians performing hit songs of the '50s compelled Janie to occasionally break into the twist. Rosie's attention was drawn by the cool touch of something wet against her arm. She looked sideways and saw Jude smiling at her, holding out a plastic cup. Taking the cup, she looked into the amber colored liquid that floated half melted ice and realized it was bourbon and Sprite. After taking a few sips, she handed the cup back to Jude. Her attention was caught by the know-it-all look Heather tossed. Rosie was pulled back against Kid so that he could speak into her ear. He said a little too loudly, "Let's go to my car and mix us a drink." Then he motioned for Jude and Heather to follow.

Taking Janie by the hand, Rosie pulled her along through the crowd. Tugging her hand away, Janie pointed toward a group of young people near the stage. "It's Shelley and Lewis!" she exclaimed, waving at them.

Rosie waved her greeting as well, then took Janie's hand again, and continued to follow Kid. Once they had gotten out away from the din of amplified music, Janie began her chattering questions, to which Rosie mostly ignored.

The day waned and the hour for Lewis to perform grew close. Harry drank beer from a plastic cup, and got silly from the alcohol. Althea had joined the group with a man of her own. As the group of young people approached the adults sitting at the picnic table, Althea motioned for Heather to come closer. She leaned down to the red haired woman wearing extravagant hippie jewelry, shaking her head up and down in frantic agreement.

Janie helped herself to a hot dog, and spread mustard on it with a plastic knife jutting from a small jar. Kid and Jude excused themselves, and disappeared. Heather pulled Rosie aside, "Your wish has just come true. Althea's date has a pontoon boat, and we've been invited to go with them tonight to watch the fireworks. A concerned look crossed Heather's face, "I wonder if there will be enough room for Kid and Jude."

"Who cares, just as long as there is room for us!" laughed Rosie. Kid walked up reeking of marijuana.

With mustard staining her upper lip, Janie nagged, "Rosie! We can't miss Shelley and Lewis! Isn't it time for their band yet?"

Heather agreed, "Yeah, let's try to get closer to the stage." Then as an afterthought she said, "I wish Lewis had wanted me to sing backup for his group, and not Shelley."

Quick to answer, Kid said, "Well, hell, Heather! He doesn't want anybody up there who can sing better than him."

Smiling from the compliment, Heather stepped into place next to Jude as they walked back to the concert. Janie tagged along, without bothering anyone with questions about what made firecrackers explode, or what hotdogs were made of. The sun was beginning to descend, and it cast a lucid orange glow across the smooth water. Once they pushed their way back into the crowd, Janie joined Angel, who was with her mother, Ed and some friends.

Workmen puttered about on stage, plugging in instruments, and checking the sound. When the crew left the stage, a man walked on to announce the next band. "Ladies and gentlemen!" he began, as a way to quiet the crowd and hold their attention. "Tonight, we are truly blessed by our local talent. We've already heard some good sounds today, but let me tell you, it only gets better." The announcer paused as the crowd broke into applause. When the cheers had died down, he yelled into the microphone, "Let's please welcome, Lewis Shirey and the Mountaineers!"

Rosie and Heather screamed and clapped with the crowd as Lewis and his band took the stage, with Shelley and another girl standing to the side behind microphones on stands. The twilight of the day was filled with the beautiful sound of guitars and drum as the tinkling rattle of Shelley's tambourine blended with the uplifting music. Rosie didn't recognize the first song, but the catchy tune with the dancing rhythm delighted her. Lewis sang about being a rolling stone whose ambition was to find a rich woman to fund his happiness. She noticed Opal and her friends poke one another, obviously delighted by the lyrics, and caught Ed looking at her. She stared back unsmiling. The next song was *Heard It through the Grapevine*, and the entire crowd began to bob with the music. When the song was finished, Angel could be heard above the crowd, yelling and pointing at the stage, "That's my brother!"

Lewis stepped back and Shelley, with the other girl, stepped forward to join him at the microphone. The band began playing *California Dreamin*. Rosie watched with envy as Shelley sang with Lewis. Her sweet voice carried over the music with smooth clarity, blending beautifully with the other female vocalist. The crowd whooped appreciation at the end of the song. Lewis played the keyboard, and the music bleated through the darkening evening as the band started up *Hello, I Love You*.

After the band's rendition of the Doors song, Lewis stepped to the microphone, "I'd like to send out a special greeting to my girl, Rosie." He paused as the crowd cheered him, "And this little ditty is just for her." He stepped back as the band played the song made famous by Steam, *Kiss Him Goodbye*.

Pushing her way to the front of the crowd as the band ended the song, Rosie took the hat and sailed it onto the stage. The hat sailed like a Frisbee, and just missed hitting Lewis in the head. He ducked and smiled, but then his expression changed into a scowl as Rosie was propelled up onto Kid's shoulder. Kissing his right hand as he held her in place on his left shoulder, Kid blew the kiss toward Lewis. Leaning into the microphone Lewis growled, "Yeah! Back at ya' Kid!"

Then he began strumming furiously on his guitar as the band went into their last song. The crowd swayed with the sound of *Twist and Shout*. Kid carried Rosie on his shoulder back to where they had stood earlier. He slid her off his shoulder against his side then held her in place while he pressed a painfully hard kiss against her lips. She tried to pound him with her fists, but he caught hold of her hands, laughing at her efforts.

Tuning away, Rosie noticed that Opal Shirey had witnessed the entire exhibition, and shame flooded her. Janie and Angel stared at Rosie with gaping mouths. Rosie finally found the courage to look at Ed, who stood staring at her with his arms folded across his chest. When the song was over, the announcer came back on stage, encouraging the crowd to give the band another round of applause. The band members lined up and took a final bow. Rosie and Heather pushed their way through the crowd to get to Lewis at the side of the stage. Some sweaty stage crew put up their hands and told them they couldn't cross the barricade. Side stepping the sweaty men, Rosie yelled, waving at Lewis frantically. Shelley stepped into Rosie's view with a smirking smile, but was briskly pushed aside as Lewis hurried to the barrier.

"What do you think?" he asked, handing Rosie the hat.

Heather gushed, "Lewis, you were *so* good!" Pounding her hands on the metal railing she said, "Your band is definitely going to win!"

He acknowledged Heather's compliments before leaning over the rail and kissing Rosie. "I wish I could join you, but the bands have to wait backstage for the final announcement. Whichever band wins has to play six more songs!" He gave her a semi-sympathetic look saying, "I'm sorry."

Rosie's gaze fell past him to Shelley, who stood watching. A rush of jealousy surged through her, but she mustered a smile and said, "We're going out on Althea's boat to watch the fireworks. I wish you could come, too."

Lewis looked from Rosie to Heather and asked, "Althea, the gypsy woman?"

Heather laughed, "Just get ready to play those other six songs." Then she turned and pulled Rosie along as they made their way back through the crowd. When they reached Kid and Jude, Heather said, "Let's go find Althea."

As they followed Heather, Kid aggravated Rosie by putting his hand on her shoulder. She pushed his hand off, but he just replaced it as they walked through the crowd. Once they broke free of the crowd Rosie turned on him with a vengeance. "Do you have any idea how badly you embarrassed me in front of Lewis' mother?"

Giving Jude a mischievous grin, they both laughed out loud. "Sunshine, what are you complaining about? I just made you the talk of the town." Kid tossed his head back and bellowed. Suddenly he stopped laughing and drew up in breathless pain.

Instant regret rushed through her when she saw the pained expression on his face. "Oh, Kid. I'm sorry. I didn't really want to hurt you."

Blowing out a harsh breath as though it contained the agony of the small fisted punch to the stomach, he spat, "Damn, Sunny! Don't you know how to fight fair? That's a sucker punch from hell!"

Jude and Heather pretended concern as they suppressed giggles. Heather said, "Gee, Kid. Is there anything I can do? Maybe hoist you up on my shoulder, or something?"

Jude broke in on the teasing, "Dang, Sunshine. Maybe you better kiss him goodbye." Then Jude and Heather succumbed to vile laughter.

Kid walked away disheartened. They followed him back to the picnic table where Althea and Teresa sat with an inebriated Harry. Heather asked Althea, "What did you do with your man?" as she reached for a slice of banana cake.

Althea smiled and answered, "My man's name is Dennis, and he's bringing his boat around for us."

"Will there be room for Jude and Kid?" Heather asked as she walked to the cooler and removed a can of soda.

Teresa said, "Heather, sweetheart, water is so much better for your complexion."

Heather turned the can toward her mother and ripped the tap off violently. A light spray of carbonation shot through the air in Teresa's direction. Then, Heather turned up the can and guzzled the drink. Althea answered Heather's question, "Of course we have room for the boys."

Heather responded with a rude belch.

Everyone boarded the boat, and once Dennis positioned the craft among other boaters, he tossed the anchor overboard. The vessel drifted around in a small circle. Rosie sat staring into the starlit night.

Heather said, "Hey look! It's Barron with his cousin, Mack."

"Why didn't your band play today?" Kid asked Heather after hearing Barron's name.

With a sour look she replied, "Don't even ask."

Althea said to no one in particular, "This reminds me of the movie *Clam Bake*. Seeing those speed boats out there makes me think of Elvis and his boat race."

Teresa cut loose with singing, "*Mama's little baby loves clam bake, clam bake.*"

Heather spoke up, "That movie has got to be the worst I've ever seen!" She stood and walked to the front of the boat. "The only good scene in it was when Elvis sang *You Don't Know Me*."

Jude joined the conversation by singing, "*You give your hand to me, and then you say hello.*"

Kid joined in, "*And I can hardly speak, my heart is beating so.*"

Althea joined in as well, "*And anyone can tell, you think you know me well, but you don't know me.*"

Harry interrupted the song, "Well, he might be doing bad movies, but Elvis always gets the girl!"

A rocket bursting vividly colors into the night sky ended the conversation. An occasional "Ohh," or "Ahh," was all that could be heard as everyone sat with their heads tilted skyward. While staring at the colored designs left in the blackness of the night sky Rosie didn't even notice that Kid had slid his arm behind her neck. The grand finale of multiple explosions filled the atmosphere with electric anticipation for the last big boom.

Darkness fell across the water instantly, and silence echoed from the waves. Taking her gaze from the empty sky, Rosie was ambushed by a passionate kiss. And for a moment it was nice. With an abrupt shove she freed herself.

Smoky blue eyes devoured her, and she whispered, "That's not fair, Kid! You know I've got a buzz." She pushed herself away and went to join Heather at the front of the boat.

Harry had noticed the heated display and laughed sarcastically, "Ha, looks like she shot you down, boy!" He tipped his cup for another drink, but spilled beer on himself when Dennis pushed the throttle into full speed. Kid caught Harry's attention and flashed him his middle finger, to which Harry laughed in drunken hilarity.

Rosie and Heather jumped from the boat onto the grassy shore, falling forward as they raced toward the stage. Without waiting for the boys, they pushed their way through the thinning crowd. The announcer who had been on stage earlier was speaking into a microphone expressing gratitude to sponsors who had made the festival possible. Then he began announcing winners of *The Battle of the Bands*. He announced the third place winner, and the band took the stage to accept the trophy, and bow to the crowd. When that band had left, he announced the second place winner. Heather gripped Rosie's arm painfully. The girls waited with abated breath. When the announcer called out Lewis Shirey and The Mountaineers as the first place winners, the two girls jumped up and down screaming approval. While the band accepted the trophy, stage crew scampered to reset their equipment.

Rosie became aware that Kid and Jude had located her and Heather when Kid put his arm around her, pulling her backwards into him. She was so happy with the band's success that she didn't mind his aggravation.

The band started up with Shelley singing lead in a rendition of Mary Wells *My Guy*. A definitive snarl pursed Heather's lips. The next song was Lewis and two of the other guys singing their mountain version of Herman's Hermits, *I'm into something Good*. The crowd roared as the band rolled directly into *Time of the Season*, which was a new song released by The Zombies. After the band quieted to regroup, and after counting off the beat, they played *Spooky* by The Classic IV.

Opal smiled proudly at her son as friends flashed blinding lights from their cameras. Janie stayed at Angel's side hooting cheers at the end of each song. Beginning Manfred Man's, *Do Wah Diddy Diddy* the band members danced with the rhythm. When that song was wrapped Lewis stepped to the microphone and said, "This one's for Rosie."

The band began playing *Brown Eyed Girl* which was Rosie's favorite Van Morrison song. Shelley and the other girl sang back up with their arms waving above their heads. When the song was over, he yelled into the microphone, "Thank you, everybody! Good night!" The band took bows and waved farewell before exiting at the back of the stage. The lights came on, and the crowd began dispersing, while the two girls rushed to the barricade. They found Lewis wiping his face with a towel and waiting to see them. Noticing the unhappy expression on his face as he looked past her, Rosie turned to see Kid at her back.

Kid yelled, "Congratulations!"

"I need you to take Shelley home with you. I've got a lot of work here packing up the gear. Do you mind?" asked Lewis.

Scowling at his detestable cousin Kid barked, "Hell, yeah! I mind." Then to Shelley he said, "Well, come on! Get your ass out here."

Shelley ducked under the railing and stepped close to Jude, "Thanks, Kid." She was speaking to her cousin, but her eyes were on his friend.

Heather spoke up, "Jude, do you want to ride to my house with me and Rosie?" She cut her eyes at Rosie with a cunning look.

With a step toward Heather, he answered, "Oh yes! That sounds great." Then he waved at Kid, "See you later, dude."

Giving Lewis a quick kiss, Rosie asked, "Will I see you tomorrow?"

"You bet, tomorrow."

With ire marring his face, Kid jutted his thumb at Shelley asking Jude, "Dude, are you leaving me stuck with her all by myself?"

Jude reached out his arms, encircling Heather and Rosie as he answered with a question of his own, "What do you think?" He turned his back and walked away with the two girls holding his arms over their shoulders.

Kicking dust toward Jude he bellowed, "Oh, yeah? Well, you suck!" Then he said to Shelley, "Come on, Broom Hilda!" and walked away, cursing under his breath.

Chapter Twelve
Indiscretion

Stepping along the winding concrete pathway to the home of Willene Reyes, Rosie strolled by a beautiful rose bush laden with lush yellow blooms. Pausing for a moment, she bent and inhaled the summer sweetened perfume. The scent was intoxicating, and conjured imaginings of opulent royal gardens. She was most impressed by the artfully planted violent bellflowers and purple irises embracing the golden roses.

Holding a basket of apples, she knocked at the back door. Noise came from the kitchen, a television or radio, and the scraping of a chair against the floor. A long minute passed before Willene opened the door. A big smile spread across the woman's face when she saw that Rosie had come to visit. Holding her basket higher she said, "I brought you some apples from my tree."

Willene unlatched the screen door, and pushed it open for Rosie to step inside the kitchen. A window air conditioning unit hummed as it spewed its frosty breeze into the room. Willene took the basket, saying, "You are just the sweetest girl I know." She waved toward the living room, "Please, come in and say hello to Minnie Mama. She can't talk, but she loves to have visitors."

Placing the basket on her small kitchen table, Willene led the way into the living room. "Mama!" she called out cheerfully to the white haired woman sitting in a soft reclining chair. "Rosie came to visit us, and she brought us a basket full of beautiful apples. You remember Sturgill Moon's girl?" She picked up the corner of a handkerchief that was pinned to her mother's nightgown, and wiped saliva from the corner of the elderly woman's mouth.

Rosie took notice of a lovely floral arrangement of the yellow roses she had just admired. "My tree has lots more apples that aren't ready to be picked. So, I can bring you more in a couple of weeks." An odd smell of stale cigar smoke caught her attention. Looking to the side table near the sofa, she saw two crumpled skinny cigar stubs in an ashtray. "Your yellow roses are so very lovely," she continued pleasantly.

Willene seemed to notice Rosie's attention to the ashtray, because she walked over and picked it up from the table. "Yellow roses are Mama's favorite. Billy bought her that rose bush several years ago for Mother's Day. It's called Sutter's Gold, and she has really pampered it." She turned to a trash can and dumped the butts.

"Would it be alright if I take a cutting from your rose bush, just to see if I can start it in my garden?"

"Not at all, here take one of these. I just cut them this morning," Willene said as she plucked a lovely long stemmed rose from the vase.

"Oh, thank you!"

"You should come over and watch Lawrence Welk with us. Mamie comes almost every week. Mama loves the *Lawrence Welk Show*. I especially like to see Bobby and Sissy dance. They wear the prettiest costumes!"

Readied to depart, Rosie answered, "Yes, I'd like that. Well, goodbye. I'll be seeing you."

After making a stop at her own house to place her rose cutting in a pot of wet sand, Rosie arrived at the Shirey farm. Albert Campbell's car was parked in the driveway. There was nothing unusual about Bert visiting with his old friend, except that Rob's car was missing from the car shed. She knocked at the front door, and Angel opened it. "Rosie!" she exclaimed. "Come in, Janie's here, too."

Holding out the basket she said, "I've brought Mamie some of my backyard apples."

Janie raced into the room holding a Barbie doll with frayed blonde hair. "Mamie and Rob aren't here, Rosie. Can I have one of your apples?" She asked while snatching one off the top, before actually receiving permission.

Rosie cautioned, "You should wash it. It might have some bug spit on it."

Angel laughed, "You can call it spit if you want to, but around here it's called worse than that."

"Where's Lewis?"

There was a look exchanged between Angel and Janie, before Angel answered, "He's at the barn feeding his new calf. We have an old mean cow that won't let her baby suck. So, Lewis is having to bottle feed him." Angel smiled and said, "He's a handsome little bull, and I named him Lucky."

"Janie, have you seen the baby bull?" asked Rosie, hoping to catch a clue to the secretive look.

Biting into the juicy apple Janie nodded her head up and down in answer to the question. "He's so sweet. He likes to suck on your finger!" Then she noticed Spice tethered to the tree outside. "Oh Rosie, you're riding Spice! Can you please give me a ride, too? Can I feed her my apple core?"

Rolling her eyes, Rosie answered, "Yes, and yes." Then reached out and ruffled Janie's bangs that hung straight across her forehead. "I'll be back in just a few minutes."

While mounting Spice, she noticed Bert's car again, and decided that he must be at the barn with Lewis feeding the calf. They rode across the hay field that was thick with new growth. The horse was tempted by the lush, green grass, and it took muscle to keep her gait up. After tying Spice in a shaded area outside of the barn, she walked into the large darkened building.

Not seeing Lewis or Bert, she noticed the empty calf bottle sitting inside an empty pail. The baby bull was lying lazily on his haunches in a hay filled pen. Upon seeing Rosie, he stumbled to his unsteady little legs, as though he expected her to provide some milk. Hearing voices at the other end of the barn, she followed them expecting to find both men together. Silence greeted her as she rounded the large stack of hay Lewis had been working on that sweet rainy afternoon she had shared with him in the barn. The light was dim, yet she could see that it wasn't Bert Lewis was entertaining, but Shelley Noble.

Speechless shock rushed through her as she watched Lewis clutch Shelley close to him. Their passion was all consuming for they were oblivious to her presence. Silently she whirled around and hurried out of the barn. With labored breath she walked the horse half way across the hay field.

Fury built within her, as the memory of their embrace played over and over in her mind. Mounting the horse with determination, she nudged her into a furious gallop across the field. Janie and Angel stood in the yard awaiting her return, and were taken aback when Rosie rode up, jerking Spice to a vicious halt.

Angel called out, "Did you see the baby?"

Still breathless with emotion Rosie answered, "Yes, I saw him."

Holding the apple for Spice, Janie asked, "Did you see Lewis?" She jerked her hand away as the horse chewed the apple, and drooled globs of saliva.

Rosie closed her eyes and inhaled slowly, "No, I didn't see him," she lied uneasily. Then to answer the silent questions lurking on both girls' faces she said, "I decided I'd talk with him later, when he isn't so busy. I have a lot to do today." Seeing that her remark seemed to intrigue the girls she quickly added, "Tell Mamie I will have more apples in a couple of weeks, okay." And she started away.

Janie called, "Can I ride back to your house with you, Rosie?" She stood wiping her hand against the back of her pants.

A dark look fell across Rosie's face, then with flared nostrils conveying her pent up anger she answered, "How about if I ride you home to your grandfather's house?"

Placing her foot in the stirrup, Janie clutched Rosie's arm. In a single smooth motion Rosie pulled Janie onto the saddle as Spice pranced around in a circle of impatience. Janie said to Angel, "Tell Shelley I found another ride home." Then with a streak of meanness in her voice she added, "A better ride!" With a huge smile covering her face, she gripped Rosie around the waist as Spice lurched into a gallop, throwing tufts of grass behind them.

Spice carried her riders with enduring spirit past the farms with gawking horses and barking dogs. The lazy cows that grazed dazedly in the smooth green pastures didn't seem to notice the riders galloping by in a frenzied pace. They galloped past the pond floating green scum and croaking frogs. Spice carefully slowed to pace her way along the dusty graveled drive that lead to Albert Campbell's farm. Rosie urged her to gather speed once they reached the smoothly trimmed lawn, and they raced into the yard with the oversized Magnolia tree casting a cool shade for Jude and Kid to lounge under.

The mare pranced with heated spirit when they reached their destination, as though she was not yet ready to discontinue her run. "Anyone else want to ride?" asked Rosie as she helped Janie swing down from the saddle.

Kid gazed at the perspiring horse with quivering muscles, and his eyes quickly fell on the shapely sun kissed legs hanging from the cut off jeans that Rosie wore. Her thin white cotton blouse was rolled at the sleeves and partly unbuttoned as it was rolled up from the waist and tied beneath her breasts revealing a smooth flat stomach. Sitting astride the impatient horse that snorted and pranced, shaking her mane and rattling the chains of her bridle, Rosie was a vision of loveliness. Drinking in her sullen beauty, the two young men each rose. Kid pushed Jude back into his chair. Without speaking, he approached the horse cautiously, and slipped his foot into the stirrup. Just as he was about to hoist himself up he asked, "Where exactly do I sit?"

Reaching back, Rosie patted the blanket covered rump of the horse behind the saddle. "Don't worry, you won't fall off." Teasingly she said, "I'll let you hold onto me," then she narrowed her eyes and added, "Real tight!"

Taking hold of the saddle horn with one hand, he pushed himself up with the stirrup, and settled behind the saddle onto the broad backside of the horse's rump. Awkwardly he asked, "What if this horse doesn't like me?" He leaned into her, wrapping both arms around her small waist.

Loosening the reins, she let Spice choose the direction to ride. "Spice likes everybody." They began a slow walk through the wooded field where Bert's new pond waited at the edge of the forest.

Spice walked with her riders swaying with the motion of her painfully slow cantor. Janie plopped down in the lawn chair opposite Jude and asked, "So, you want to play Go Fish?"

Kid began a conversation on planning the camping trip as they rode along. "We've got to start getting ready for Woodstock, you know." He nuzzled his face into her neck, and continued even though she didn't return his conversation. "So far, I've only got one tent, and we need two." When Rosie still didn't speak he said, "Don't you think we should make a check list so we don't forget anything?" To get her attention, he brushed the hair away from her neck and leaned forward making a raspberry sound against the delicate skin he exposed.

She tensed irritably at the tickling sensation, "Yes, that's a good idea."

Pursuing the subject he continued, "We need a first aid kit, canteens for water and firewood." He added, "You've got to take your own firewood, you know." When she didn't inject any of her own ideas, he said, "And lots of extra underwear."

He smiled when she responded, "What the hell do we need lots of extra underwear for?" Rosie couldn't keep her thoughts from drifting back to the barn.

"I just said that to see if you were paying attention." He leaned in close, and stretching out his arm, ran his hand gently down her thigh, and then back up. A scowl crossed her face as she reached down and clutched his hand. He chuckled and blew gently against her ear.

Pulling away from his breath she said, "I should never have let you get this close to me." With a sharp nudge, Spice took off with spirit.

Sliding sideways he clutched Rosie firmly. "Hey!" he exclaimed, "If I fall off, you're going with me!" Regaining his balance, he rode with a straight back until she reined the horse to a stop at the edge of the pond.

Looking over her shoulder, she said impatiently, "What are you waiting for? Get off!"

Placing his foot into the stirrup, he swung himself off the horse's back and stood looking up at Rosie. His face was tender with concern as he asked, "What's eating you, Sun?"

Expelling a quick puff of breath she mumbled, "Nothing!"

He walked over to the large rock jutting from the water and stepped onto it. The sun was beginning to descend, and the tall pines were spreading cooling shade across the pond. He shoved his hands in the back pockets of his jeans, and watched her pat the horse and coo in a voice most people would reserve for infants. He could see the pained expression cross her face as her thoughts drifted somewhere else. "You may as well tell me now, Sunshine. You know I won't give up until you tell me what's got you so bugged?" When Rosie didn't answer he asked, "Where did you pick up Janie? She and Shelley were going into town on an errand for G-Mama."

With closed eyes she answered, and the truth began to filter from her guarded words. "I gave her a ride from the Shirey farm." Rosie leaned over and tied the reins to the branch of a fallen tree lying in the tall grass. She left Spice grazing as she hopped onto the rock with Kid. The quiet water reminded her of the day Lewis had rode her on his bicycle for a swimming lesson. Remembering that day pained her. That was the day Shelley had come to stay for the summer.

Reaching out, Kid fondled her hair like a lover. "Turn around," he told her. "I want to braid your hair." When she turned her back he began dividing her hair into three equal sections. "So, was Shelley at the Shirey farm, too?" he asked a little too nonchalantly.

"I guess so," she answered simply. Hearing Shelley's name had a wounding effect on her heart, and she clenched her eyes shut as she tried to chase away the memory of the passionate embrace she had witnessed.

Kid twisted the coffee colored locks into a single braid. "You guess? Didn't you see her?" He wrapped a slender strand of hair around the bottom to keep the braid from unraveling.

"Damn! Can't you see I don't want to talk about her?" Folding her arms across her chest, she watched the horse take big bites of grass from the field.

"Did you see Shelley and Lewis together?" he asked bluntly as he tossed the braided hair over her right shoulder. "Something's upset you. Was it them?"

She gazed at the long braid reaching almost to her breast while trying to contain her emotions. It was impossible. Hot tears stung her eyes, and they rolled silently down her face. Her silence was enough to answer his question. He took her by the shoulders and turned her toward him. Gently he wiped away her tears. "Well," he began, "I'm not surprised." He attempted to soften his words, "I mean they've been spending so much time together. It just figures that something was bound to happen sooner or later."

Rosie rolled her eyes heavenward and brought her hands up, knocking Kid's away. Roughly, she wiped the wetness from her cheeks and said, "Sooner or later, yeah." Slumping down on the rock, she reached a hand into the water, making small ripples as she gently swirled her index finger in a circular motion.

He sat next to her, "Face it, Sun. Girls like Shelley will always get the guy." Then he added, "At least for a little while." He watched her stare at the ripples in the water, as the pond reflected billowy white clouds floating above. "Guys marry girls like you, but they fuck girls like Shelley."

His words seemed to have backfired when she furiously slapped her fist against the water cursing, "Damn it! Don't say that!"

Stammering to correct his flaw he whispered, "Oh, come on, Sunny. You know what I'm saying." He watched her draw her knees to her chest and wrap her arms around her legs. "Young guys are always on the make, and girls like you just don't put out." Rosie's face crumpled with anguish. She pressed her face into the hollow of her arms and cried openly. "Oh no, Sunny, you didn't?" She dissolved into shoulder racking sobs.

Rubbing his hand against the back of his neck he cleared his throat. "Okay, Sunny. Everything is going to be alright. This is just a lesson in life, and we all have to live through them. You can't beat yourself up for trusting the wrong person." He was surprised when she threw herself sobbing against his chest. Comforting words were elusive when she was in his arms.

As her tears subsided she pushed away seething, "I want him to pay. I want to see them both suffer." Her gaze crossed the pond and into the dense woods as she said almost absent mindedly, "Come on, Kid. Let's go back and work on the list for our trip." She delved into his captivating blue eyes, and said with a sinister smile, "I want this trip to be so much fun that we'll remember it for as long as we live!"

Suddenly, the sun beamed brighter as he assured, "It will be, Sunshine. It will be."

Sitting across from Jude with an upside down five-gallon bucket between them, Janie looked carefully at the cards she held and cunningly asked, "Got any twos?" The handsome young man narrowed his eyes before handing over two of his cards.

Jude hesitated before he asked, "Got any sevens?" He sat back with frustration as he watched the impish little girl mime someone casting out a fishing rod. Janie smiled with delight as she taunted, "Go fish!" Her giggles carried across the light breeze as Rosie and Kid rode slowly into the yard.

Rosie tethered Spice to a tree limb at a shady corner of the yard, and joined the others beneath the Magnolia tree. Kid disappeared into the house while Rosie watched Janie display her memory skill in the card game. Jude grumbled some inaudible words of ire as he handed over more of his cards. Smiling at the impish child, she said, "Looks like you might just be the Go Fish champion of the county." A burst of laughter exploded from her when Janie inspected her knuckles, blew a hot breath on them, and polished them against her sleeve.

When Kid returned with a note pad he sat on the grass near Jude, and began his list of necessary camping supplies for the anticipated weekend. "Okay, now we've got one tent and two sleeping bags. Sunny, do you have a sleeping bag?" He scribbled on the note pad his items of needs and haves.

Janie asked, "Are you going camping? Can I go, too?"

Kid snapped, "Yes, and no! But keep your face shut, nobody needs to know all our business." He peered over his notepad and asked her forcefully, "Got it?" With a serious look on his face he held the child's gaze until she meekly answered him by nodding her head.

"Excuse me!" Rosie scowled at Kid. "But I happen to know Janie is excellent at keeping secrets." Bracing herself against Jude's chair she looked down at his cards, and silently stuck out three fingers.

Janie leaned forward, guarding her cards protectively, and asked, "Got any threes?"

Pressing his cards against his chest, Jude suspiciously looked at Rosie, "Hey! You wouldn't be cheating would you?"

Taking his cards Janie answered, "Are you saying I look like a cheat?"

Jude took the bait and said, "Well, now that you mention it, you do have a shady look about you, little girl." While waving his fingers at Rosie, Jude said "Do you mind standing over there somewhere?" He only shrugged his shoulders when she pursed her lips, feigning insult.

The sound of an automobile approaching drew everyone's attention to Bert's car driving along the long dusty driveway from the main road. Rosie said, "Well, time for me to ride." She then walked slowly to where she had tied Spice in the shade of the tree.

Kid slammed the notepad on the ground, "We haven't finished our list yet!"

Holding Spice steady, she teased, "Oh, don't get your panties in a wad. We've got time. Call me later, and I'll tell you what I've found in my attic." Leading the horse away she said as an afterthought, "You know if you ever need me Kid, all you have to do is whistle." She mounted the horse and waited to catch Janie's attention, then flashed five fingers.

Taking note, Janie carried on, "Yeah, Kid you know how to whistle, don't you? You just put your lips together and blow." Then to Jude she asked, "Got any fives?"

Jude handed over his cards amid Janie's gleeful giggles. With flared nostrils he shouted at Rosie, "Why don't you go already, cheater!"

Nudging Spice into a trot, she rode the spirited horse down the steep embankment at the edge of the yard, and into the corn field across the driveway. Everyone watched her ride away as her braided hair bounced against her back. Kid pushed his hair from his face saying, "God! I love that girl." Then as if he hadn't intended to make the confession, he snatched his notepad and went inside the house.

"I don't understand him," the little girl pondered, "He knows Rosie is in love with Lewis. Is he just plain stupid?" When Jude asked her for tens she squealed, with a devilish gleam in her bright blue eyes, "Go fish!"

Chapter Thirteen
A Little Help from My Friends

Retrieving the morning paper, Rosie gasped in horror over the headline news. A gruesome murder in Los Angeles had taken the lives of Hollywood movie starlet, Sharon Tate as well as four others at her California home. Fearing her father's protective reaction to the news, she rolled the paper up tightly and placed it on the edge of the coffee table. She prepared her father's favorite meal of barbequed pulled-pork and French fried potatoes in hopes of making him more favorable of her camping request.

That evening, as her father sat finishing his dinner, she left the table saying, "I made you a peach pie, Daddy."

Sturgill's face alighted with suspicion, "A pie? It's not even Sunday, and you made me a pie? What's wrong? Are you in trouble? Do I look like I'm dying?"

Smiling, she placed the pie on the table saying, "I'm not in trouble and you look fine! But, I do have a favor to ask."

"Yep, I knew something was up. Well, spit it out! What do you want?"

Settling back at the table, Rosie glanced at her step-mother who watched her keenly while dragging on a long cigarette with the ash threatening to fall into her plate. "I've been invited to go with Heather on a camping trip, that's all."

Sturgill sliced the pie asking, "Where to?"

"The Smokey Mountains," she lied, rather easily.

Sturgill considered the request as he chewed the dessert. "Well, the Smokies are beautiful this time of year. Hell, I wish I could go, too! Yeah, you go ahead and tell Heather you can go. Just, don't be a nuisance to Mrs. Tillman, now."

Throwing her arms around her father's neck she gushed happily, "Oh, thank you, Daddy! Do you mind if I use some of the camping gear stored in the attic?"

With a wave of his fork Sturgill said, "Help yourself to anything you find."

"I'm going to check it out right now." Looking at her step-mother she said with a hint of sarcasm, "Don't worry with the dishes, Eva. I'll get them later."

Answering crassly Eva replied, "Oh, I won't!"

Kid's '61 Lincoln convertible rolled along the highway beneath the

August heat as they traveled the one thousand plus miles from Ben Johnson Ridge to Bethel, New York. The foursome worked in pairs to get the driving done. Heather and Jude teamed together, while Kid and Rosie were the other. Together they traveled nonstop, and reached their destination three days before the concert was to begin.

They were lucky enough to find a camping spot near the lake, squeezing in between a psychedelic painted school bus and a VW camper van. Making camp with two tents and the fewest essentials necessary, the group settled in for some much needed rest and relaxation. Jude stretched a hammock between two trees, and proceeded to take a nap. Heather helped Rosie set up a kitchen area, while Kid collected rocks to outline a fire pit. For their first night's meal, the girls prepared fried apples with pancakes and country ham. The aroma from their campsite attracted the three guys from the VW van.

"Hello, there," said a young man with wavy dark hair. "My name is Denny. These are my friends, Chad and Brandon. We thought maybe we could sit around together, and maybe share some of our wine for some of your food. It really smells appetizing."

Smiling cleverly Rosie asked, "How much wine do you have, Denny?"

Laughingly he replied, "Plenty!"

Passing around tin plates, Heather said to the three young men, "Welcome to our campsite, boys. The forks are over there on the table, and we have mugs for the wine right here." She pointed to a laundry basket filled with dishes.

During the meal, the group of young people discussed expectations for the upcoming music festival, as well as plans for their futures. Bottle upon bottle of wine was consumed, and the campfire burned low as the night waned past the midnight hour. Kid played soft melodies on his guitar, with Brandon accompanying him on his own guitar. Jude took advantage of Kid's preoccupation with his music to settle close to Rosie. The wine loosened his inhibitions to the point that he languidly caressed her arm with his fingertips. Flattered by his attention, Rosie leaned close and asked, "What are you doing?"

"Trying to tickle your fancy," he moaned seductively.

With an inebriated giggle she declared, "Tickle your own fancy, hitchhiker!"

The morning arrived with a soft sunrise across the still waters of the lake, lying like folds of shimmering rosy satin beneath the dawn. A nagging headache greeted Rosie with the coming of the new day. She rolled over in her sleeping bag expecting to find Heather in the tent with her. A startled cry escaped her when she came face to face with Jude. Rudely, she shook him awake.

"No, no, no," he mumbled.

"Why are you in my tent?"

Peering at her through one opened eye he answered, "Because you invited me. Don't you remember?"

Checking to see if she still had all of her clothes intact she responded to his question, "No, I don't remember."

He feigned insult. "You don't remember last night?"

Slowly she pondered his question. "Did I seduce you, Jude?"

A leisurely laugh built until it became a side splitting chortle. With tears he responded, "Maybe I shouldn't tell."

Pouncing on top, she held him trapped inside his sleeping bag. "Okay, bud! Don't tell. But, get this straight right now. We're not telling anyone that you and I spent last night together. Got it?"

With humor in his voice he agreed, "Okay, whatever you say. But, you've got to let me up, 'cause I've got to piss like a Russian race horse."

This gave her cause to quickly release him, and crawl cautiously from the tent. The campground was still, so she carefully placed a kettle of water on the smoldering coals for instant coffee. When Jude returned she told him quietly, "Go sleep in the hammock."

Jude groaned, "Oh, come on. Why can't I sleep in the tent?"

"Where did Heather sleep last night?"

Jude answered with ire, "In the bus with Sadie and Trevor."

A vague memory crept into Rosie's memory. "What happened to Kid?"

"Hell if I know! You're bumming me out with all the questions. Just cool it, Rosie. You're uptight over nothing."

She realized her absurdity. "Oh, Jude, please forgive me. It's just that I've never drank so much. You're welcome to sleep in my tent."

With a smile he said, "I'd rather just sit here with you, if you don't mind."

"Great," she said, reaching for the jar of instant coffee. "How do you take your java, black or white?"

The farmhouse was eerily silent when Janie returned from her hike in the woods. Boredom consumed her as she repeatedly opened and closed the refrigerator door. She eventually wandered into the living room and turned on the television set. Game shows and soap operas didn't interest her. The Alabama Public Television station was broadcasting a lesson on cursive handwriting. Exasperation filled her, and she switched the set off. Twisting the radio on, she resumed reading a *Hardy Boys* mystery. After having read a chapter of *The Secret of the Caves*, her attention was drawn to the tapping at the front door. Carefully, she marked the page, and went to the door. Lewis Shirey stood beyond the glass, looking pathetically sad.

"Shelley's not here," Janie declared, just before closing the inside door. Again, she responded to the tapping by swinging the door open wide. "What?" she demanded rudely.

Pressing his nose to the glass, he begged, "Please, talk to me, Janie."

The little girl pushed open the glass door and stepped out onto the sun warmed porch. "Why? What do we have to talk to about?"

"You know why Rosie won't return my calls."

A sly smile crossed her face, "Oh, like you don't." Watching his face contort with confusion, she asked cruelly, "Maybe Shelley can explain it for you. After all, it was because Rosie saw the two of you misbehaving in the barn that upset her."

Slapping his hand to his forehead he asked, "Are you talking about the day she brought the basket of apples, and you rode home with her on the horse?"

Plopping down on the porch swing, Janie pushed back and kicked her feet high saying, "Oh, now you remember!"

Lewis bent down and abruptly halted the swing. "Is this the reason she ran off to the Smokey Mountains with Kid?" As he watched the expressions play across Janie's face, he asked, "What's wrong? Didn't they go to the Smokies?"

Expelling a sigh of relief, she confessed, "Well, since they're already gone, I guess I can tell you." Pushing him away so she could resume swinging she asked, "Have you heard about the big music festival in New York called Woodstock?"

A look of staggering surprise crossed his face. "They went to Woodstock? Are you sure?"

A small giggle escaped as she answered, "Oh, I'm sure. And, I wouldn't be surprised if she left this hillbilly mountain to go home with Kid when they get back."

Pacing the concrete, he exclaimed, "Over my dead body!" Then, he turned on his heel and hurried away.

"Wait! Where are you going?" she asked.

"To Woodstock," he called over his shoulder.

"Don't be stupid!" she chastised, "You'll never find her! Don't you know there's going to be like a thousand people there?" Glowering at Lewis as she watched him drive away in his grandfather's farm truck, she muttered to herself, "Stupidity just burns my ass!" Swinging the door open wide, she re-entered the house to continue her adventure with Frank and Joe Hardy.

The days at the lake gave birth to new friendships with the neighboring campers. The young men in the VW van were from Pensacola, Florida and offered to give Jude a ride back with them after the concert. Trevor and Sadie had traveled from Atlanta, Georgia. They were classic flower children who believed in karma and mind altering drugs. Heather and Denny fell into a furious infatuation with one another, while Kid became fast friends with the guitar strumming Brandon. They spent their first day languidly relaxing on the lake in swimsuits and suntan lotion. Jude made a spectacle of himself wearing the inflated Donald Duck swim toy around the campground. He relished in the ridicule he received. Heather sang to the instrumentals Kid and Brandon produced, while Rosie took on the domestic duties of cooking and cleaning. As the afternoon sun climbed to its peak, the group sought refuge beneath the shaded campsite. Trevor and Sadie joined them from the bus, with Sadie holding a ceramic canister.

"Okay, beautiful people," Trevor said. "It's time to enlighten ourselves."

Sadie explained, "It's tea time. Stoke up the fire, boys. We need to boil some water."

Chad leaned closer from his canvas stool asking, "You got 'shrooms?"

Sadie tilted the canister so everyone could see the mass of shriveled mushrooms. Smiling sadistically, she said, "Who wants to take a little trip?"

"You go ahead and make your mushroom tea," Kid said, as he reached for Rosie's hand. "But, neither me nor my Sunshine will be drinking or eating anything that grows out of cow shit."

Rosie followed him. They hiked around the festival grounds, which was nothing more than a farm field, enjoying the comical sight of people making fools of themselves. The crowd was massive, but friendly and cooperative when they paused to ask questions. When they returned, everyone was in the throes of false perceptions.

Approaching the group who sat glued to the lake, Kid asked, "What are you all looking at?"

Heather pointed to the lake, "Don't you see it? It's the most beautiful rainbow ever!"

Denny agreed, "The colors are alive! It's the most beautiful thing I've ever seen."

Wrinkling his forehead Kid declared sarcastically, "Of course I see the rainbow! After all, it is shining out of *my* ass!"

Jude rushed to Rosie looking ridiculous with the inflated Donald Duck float wrapped around his belly like a ten year old. Placing his hands on her shoulders he said, "Thank God you're back! Listen to me Rosie, nobody else will believe me, but I know you will. Come over here." She stepped to the back of the bus with Jude. "Look! Don't you see it?"

"See what?"

"Rosie, look! It's right there."

"What is it, Jude?"

With a glazed look of awe Jude answered, "It's a peppermint dog!"

Rosie rolled her eyes heavenward and snapped, "Damn it Jude! How much of that shit did you drink?"

Looking like a chastised child he mumbled, "Too much, I reckon."

Feeling repulsed by his overindulgent drug use, Rosie reached out and angrily squeezed the toy duck's head, creating a shrill sound. Jude jumped back and whined, "Easy on the Donald, Sunshine!" Stepping away in trepidation, he mumbled, "Ducks are people, too." Then as if the sound of his last word was fascinating, he wandered away repeating, "To, two, too."

The most acclaimed music festival of the century began with Richie Havens performing just before sundown. Rosie and Heather stood side by side amid the rest of the group of campsite friends. It became painfully apparent that Jude took every opportunity to inch closer to Rosie during the concert. Heather paired off with Denny, leaving Rosie sandwiched between Kid and Jude during John Sebastian's performance. A hard rain set in before midnight, halting the music. During the chaos of people leaving the open field to find shelter, Rosie got separated from her group. She fought against a rising panic as she became confused and disoriented in the crowd of people trudging along in darkness.

"Kid!" she called, alarmed by the thought of being lost in the dark field of unfamiliar faces. Fumbling her way along in the throng of humanity as rain pelted her painfully, panic ensued. "Kid! Heather!" she cried, as the downpour drenched her. She found herself being jostled along as people pushed against her, some with flashlights, and some without. With blurred vision from tears and rain she saw a familiar face reaching for her through the crowd. Relief swept through her. "Jude! Thank God, I found you!" she yelled, reaching for his outstretched hand.

Wrapping his arm around her, he pulled her along, saying, "I've got you. You're okay, now."

The crowd grew thinner as people dispersed. Catching up with the rest of their group, they hiked through the downpour together, culminating the slog by crowding onto the bus to escape the driving rain. Rosie sank into a seat dripping wet, trying without success to wipe the water from her face. Sadie began handing out towels, while Trevor brought out a half gallon bottle of Jack Daniels. While drying her hair with the towel, Rosie felt a sensation of being watched. She turned to find Jude staring at her with dripping hair plastered around his face. Sliding closer to the wall, she motioned for him to sit next to her. When he settled beside her, she handed him her damp towel.

"Thanks," he said softly, taking the towel and wiping his face. "What happened to you back there?"

Feeling juvenile, she admitted, "I got all turned around. I didn't know which way I was going, or which way I was supposed to be going." She closed her eyes and admitted, "I was petrified!" She opened her eyes to find Jude smiling, "Thanks for helping me find my way."

Turning to take a cup of whiskey he replied, "Well, that's what friends are for. Helping you find your way when you get lost." Pausing to sip the liquor he added, "Kind of like Jesus."

Rosie and Sadie stayed on the bus while the rest of the group trudged back through the rain soaked muddy fields to rejoin the concert. They awoke early the next morning to prepare breakfast for the group, who didn't return until just before nine. After breakfast, everyone besides Rosie and Sadie crashed for a few hours before heading back to the concert field. Like dutiful mothers, the girls awoke everyone in time for a quick lunch. And then it was back in the field in time for Santana's performance. Kid was enthralled by Credence Clearwater Revival, just as Heather was spellbound by Janis Joplin. The group staggered back to camp after seeing The Who perform in the late night morning hours.

At dawn, Denny shouted everyone awake who wanted to catch Jefferson Airplane's morning show. Breakfast consisted of instant coffee, dried fruit and peanuts. The girls in the group helped one another with shampoos, using a garden watering can. Sadie braided Rosie's long damp hair into two French braids that fell down her back in pig tails. Heather let her own raven hair dry long and straight.

Because of the shampoos, the group was a little late getting to the field, and missed the opening performance of Jefferson Airplane. They snacked on peanut butter with saltine crackers, and shared wine and water. That afternoon Joe Cocker took the stage with his band, and after playing *With A Little Help from My Friends* he took a break to make a special announcement. "I'd like to explain to you all how true this song really is. You see, I have a borrowed keyboard player in my band at the moment. But, my usual keyboardist has finally made it to the show. So, let me thank my young friend who came from Alabama, and literally saved my ass. Ladies and gentlemen, please give a warm welcome to Lewis Shirey!"

A scream escaped Rosie as those words fell upon her ears. She and Heather grabbed hold of one another and jumped up and down in exhilaration. "Now, my friend only had one request of payment for his participation today. His only wish is for a very special girl named Rosie to meet him at the information booth. So, Rosie, if you're out there, please don't disappoint us. Thank you!"

The entire group of campsite friends helped Rosie push through the crowd to meet Lewis. A large group of curiosity seekers had already milled around the information booth when Rosie and her friends got there. When they located him, Kid and Jude rushed in and held him aloft on their shoulders, as if he were a football player who had scored the winning touchdown. Heather leaned in to slap Lewis a high five, while Rosie stood close, reaching for his hand. A photographer with *The New York Times* snapped pictures of the happy group, and yelled out instructions for more photos. The guilty girls shrank from the photographer, while Kid and Jude smiled happily for the camera.

Janie stood at the window, watching for the car that Angel and her mother would be picking her up in. Shelley sauntered into the living room and curled up on the sofa, drenching it with her *Sweet Honesty* Avon cologne. Sneering in her sister's direction she said, "You don't have to take a bath in that stuff, you know. What are trying to cover up, the stench of your ass?"

Taking up the mystery novel Janie had been reading, Shelley slung it at her little sister. "You suck!" she screeched, as the book went sailing through the air.

Retrieving her beloved *Hardy Boys* novel, Janie sneered, "Oh, yeah, well, after all the sucking you've done you still didn't steal Lewis from Rosie. He's gone off to find her right now, and to tell her that he doesn't care spit for you."

"Chatter on, empty head. You don't know anything." Shelley stretched her legs across the sofa and began buffing her nails into a glossy shine.

The car Janie had been waiting for pulled into the driveway. Grabbing her overnight bag she started for the door, pausing just long enough to taunt her older sister with one last offensive comment. "Yeah, well, I know that if you had all the dicks sticking out of you that you've had stuck in you, you'd look like a dick tree." A smile danced across Janie's lips as a skin slicing scowl twisted Shelley's expression. Swinging the door open, Janie stepped out and held it wide before letting loose, so that it would slam loudly behind her.

After Joe Cocker's performance, the group hiked back to camp for a hearty meal. The others rested with full stomachs in anticipation of the evening music. Rosie and Lewis strolled through the crowd of love happy people. The fashions were often lavish. Colorful flowing silks, loose fitting denims, and even bare skin were accentuated with fresh flower garlands and body paint. Many made their own brand of happy music with guitars, tambourines, flutes and cowbells.

"I can't believe my good luck in finding you, Rosie. Janie told me it was impossible, and it would have been if I hadn't caught a ride with one of the crew members in Joe's band."

"I'm surprised you're not angry with me for not telling you I was coming," she admitted.

"How could I be, knowing that you saw me and Shelley in the barn?"

A deep hurt washed through her. "Yeah, that was painful. But, still, I should have given you the chance to explain."

"And that's why I'm here, to explain." Taking her face between his hands, he looked lovingly into her dark eyes. "I was stupid to ever be alone with her, Rosie. I mean, we all know how she is. And, from the minute she got here this summer, she's been trying to seduce me." He tilted his face back as the memory of the afternoon in the barn haunted him. "It was just a kiss, nothing else, and I regret it so very much. Please forgive me, Rosie."

Reaching her arms around his neck she said, "Forgiven, but not forgotten."

Opal had dropped Janie back home on her way to return Angel to her grandparent's. When she entered the front door of her grandparent's home, Janie found them glued to a news report on television predicting a strong hurricane for the Gulf Coast. Maggie fretted to Bert, "Elizabeth said she would call us today to let us know what her evacuation plans are."

"Well, don't worry," Bert said in a haze of pipe tobacco smoke. "She's been through these things before. She knows what to do."

"Why doesn't Mommy just come here?" Janie asked her grandparents.

The sound of the phone ringing in the kitchen took everyone's attention. Shelley called out, "G-Mama! It's Mom on the phone."

Maggie jumped to her feet, with Janie right behind her. Taking the phone she called out, "Elizabeth! Where are you now?" Silence fell as Maggie listened to her daughter across the wire. "The kids want you to come here." Shelley pleaded with Maggie to give her the phone. "That's good dear, but you shouldn't take any chances. Listen, Shelley wants to have a word with you."

Maggie handed the phone to her granddaughter, who cried into the receiver, "Mom, please come here! I miss you so much." She grew quiet as she seemed to find comfort in her mother's words. "Are you sure it is far enough from the storm? But, when will that be?" Shelley turned to Maggie saying, "Yes, okay. Here she is."

Taking the phone, Maggie appeared to be calm, "Yes, dear? Of course, we will. Just you stay safe."

Tugging at her grandmother's arm Janie urged, "Let me talk to her."

Maggie appeared flustered, "Alright, then, call just as soon as you get there so we'll know you're safe." She placed the phone on its cradle.

Wounding hurt coursed through the little girl. "Why didn't you let me talk to her?" she demanded of her grandmother.

Looking away Maggie said, "She was in a hurry. Someone was waiting to use the phone."

"So what, didn't she even ask about me? Doesn't she love me anymore?" When no one attempted to answer, Janie stomped from the room in hot tears.

The final day of the concert dawned with a beautiful sunrise glowing across the lake. Many of the concert seekers had left the previous day, which gave the group of friends an opportunity to inch closer for the electrifying performance promised by Hendrix fans. The sun poured its unrelenting rays upon the field, and when the group filed away with the last of the concert goers, the heat was insufferable. Rosie splashed in the cooling lake with Lewis, Heather and Jude while the others packed up the campsite.

When it was time to tell Jude goodbye a solemn mood fell over the Alabama group. Tears stung Rosie's eyes as she tenderly kissed his cheek farewell. "Stay in touch and keep away from those peppermint dogs!"

He clutched her in a gentle embrace, whispering in her ear, "Don't worry I will! I'll write. Write me back." Then he boarded the van bound for Florida. Soon, the van disappeared among the hoard of other departing vehicles.

Kid stood beside Rosie and waved his final farewell to Jude. "There goes one hell of a nice guy." To everyone else he said, "Are we ready to face the music?"

Misty eyed from Jude's departure, Rosie asked, "What music?"

Looking past her to Lewis he scoffed, "You don't think hillbilly Lew is going to play Woodstock, and nobody back in the sticks is going to know about it, do you?"

They traveled with the top of the convertible shielding them from the searing sun's rays. As they past quiet neighborhoods following the line of traffic, people stood outside their homes gawking at them, relieved to see the swarm of young people leave. They traveled nonstop long past nightfall, through torrential rain at times, and finally stopped for food at an interstate truck stop. After placing his order, Kid left the table to buy a newspaper from an outside stand. When he returned to the table he spread the pages out to reveal the devastating news of hurricane Camille.

"Oh my God," Rosie exclaimed. "This affects Elizabeth and Janie!"

Heather added, "I hope this doesn't mean Shelley's going to stay with her grandparents!"

Folding out pages excitedly Kid exclaimed, "Look at this!"

All eyes fell onto an entertainment item featuring the rock concert known to the world as Woodstock. In a large black and white print photo was the snapshot taken by the *New York Times* photographer of Lewis being greeted by his friends after his performance with Joe Cocker. The caption read: *Alabama Teen Plays Woodstock!*

Staring at her own face in the photo, Heather moaned, "We're busted."

Chapter Fourteen
Camille

Night had fallen over Ben Johnson Ridge when Rosie returned home. Tiredly, she sauntered into the old farmhouse from the back door and followed the flickering television lights into the living room. "Daddy, I'm home!"

"Come on in here, honey!" Sturgill called from the living room. "How was your trip?"

Sinking onto the sofa she said, "I'm just glad to be home. I'm so tired. We didn't get much sleep."

"Uh, huh," he patted her knee in a comforting way. "Well, you just go on and get you some rest. We can talk about everything tomorrow."

With cobwebs clouding her thoughts, she wandered off to her room. She flipped the light switch and stood awestruck at what greeted her. Pages and pages of newspaper articles showing the photograph from the music festival were plastered all over her room. Everywhere she looked were various articles with the same picture snapped by the *New York Times* photographer. Even her bed had been layered with newspapers. A soft chuckle began within her, and built into elated laughter. Shoving the papers from her bed onto the floor, she turned in for the night.

Sleep came almost instantaneously for the fatigued Rosie, and she slumbered peacefully until the dark hour before dawn. A terrifying crash of thunder jerked her from sleep, and she sat bolt upright in bed. Laughter drifted through the old farmhouse. Slowly, she left her room to investigate the noise of clinking coins and glass being knocked against glass. Dim light fogged by a haze of cigar smoke beckoned her toward the commotion in the kitchen. Lightning flashes illuminated her journey down the hallway. She bravely stepped from the corridor to find several men dressed in eighteenth century clothing, sitting around an antique wooden table playing a lively game of poker. None of whom seemed to notice Rosie's presence. A lovely young woman dressed in a flattering gown of the period moved fluidly about the room, as if she were gliding on ice. The young woman fascinated Rosie, with her beautifully coifed chestnut hair loosely pinned and curling tendrils falling about her face. Like watching a movie, she observed the pretty woman sail across the room and reach out to one of the players. The pale delicate hand was reaching out to a man wearing a white hat with a black band. A gasp of disbelief escaped Rosie, capturing his attention. He raised his face and peered threateningly through her.

Embarrassed by her state of undress, a hot flush of humiliation tinged her cheeks pink. "Why are you here?" she demanded. Making no effort to answer, the apparitional man retuned his attention to the game at hand. Attempting to be bold, she leaned on the table and repeated, "Why are you here?"

The poker game continued as if Rosie were invisible. Coins clanked into a pile in the center of the table, while the attractive young woman served amber colored ale in antiquated mugs. Feeling annoyed for being ignored, she pounded the table with her fists, only to be disregarded by the card holding men. Audaciously she reached out and scooped a fistful of coins from the pile. Clutching them above the mound on the table, she repeated, "Why are you here?"

Like an amazing magician's trick, the players vanished from sight, leaving only one man sitting at the table beneath his handsome white hat. Immobilizing fear overcame her when he raised his head to confront her. She immediately released her grasp on the coins, and was amazed when only sand fell from her unclenched fist. Unbelievingly, he tossed back his head and roared with laughter. Stumbling backward with apologies tumbling from her lips, Rosie was assaulted by the echoes of his jovial amusement.

She retreated until pressed against a wall, and there she waited for the demonic presence to exact his revenge. The handsome specter ceased laughing, and stood from the table. Turning away from Rosie, he reached to the pantry door and said, "Come with me." Twisting the knob silently, he pulled open the door to reveal a sunlit garden filled with magnificent blooming flowers. The phantom man descended concrete steps, walking into the fairy tale vision.

Bright sunlight infiltrated the kitchen from the opened door, while crashing lightening boomed beyond the darkened windows of the house. With the same confounding curiosity of Alice and Goldilocks, Rosie followed. Instantly she felt warmed by the sun and lulled by the scent of lilac. Lush green mimosa trees decorated the landscape, perfuming the atmosphere with its fuzzy pink blossoms. A carpet of luxuriant emerald grass cushioned her bare feet.

Awestruck from the breathtaking beauty, she tilted her face heavenward and noted a cloudless azure sky. Wind song danced with a light breeze, rustling through magnolia branches. Picturesque splendor lay in every direction. Flat green meadows surrounded by distant jade mountains beaconed like a foreign mystery. A winding stream of crystal clear water crawled across the landscape lazily, inviting a barefoot romp. She rushed to follow the man who had crossed the stream via a small wooden foot bridge and was sitting peacefully upon an ornate white wrought iron bench.

"Is this where you live?" she asked. "It's magnificent!"

With a raised face the handsome man said, "I want all of this to be yours."

Giddiness overwhelmed Rosie and she giggled, "Oh! Thank you! But, where are we?"

A hard gust of wind blew against the elegant man, and he reached quickly to hold onto his hat. Standing against the wind he looked down at Rosie and replied, "All you need is in the pharmacy." He then turned his back and began walking along a path worn to the bare earth among grapevines and apple trees.

Rosie stood and called after him, "Wait! Don't go! Are you Doc Campbell?" She watched as he retreated slowly along the path, and the wind gusts picked up in strength. The sunshine dimmed, and thunder rumbled in the distance.

Fearful of the brewing storm, she retraced her steps across the wooden bridge, pausing to look down into the babbling water as it flowed across a streambed strewn with quartz pebbles. Strong gusts of wind warned her to move on. She rushed barefoot across the carpet of lush grass back to the concrete steps leading to the open doorway of her home. Moments earlier the sky had been a canvas of the deepest blue, but now was swirling with dark angry storm clouds. She retreated into her home as harsh winds blew against her, whipping her hair and tugging at her nightgown.

Once inside the safety of her kitchen she closed the pantry door against the ravaging winds. Standing against the door panting from exertion she heard a clicking noise followed by the sudden glow of electric light. "Rosie? What are you doing up so early?"

She whirled to face her father in his bathrobe.

Sturgill Moon stared at his daughter, "My God! You look like you've been out in the storm. How did your hair get so tangled?"

Rosie's hand flew to her hair, "I think I was sleepwalking, Daddy."

"Well, go back to bed, sweetheart. You haven't had enough rest." He walked to the refrigerator and took out the milk jug. "Maybe you should have some milk with me. It always helps me sleep."

With the garden still vivid in her mind, she opened the pantry door and stared into the darkened closet of shelves. "I just had the most incredible dream."

Drinking the milk with large thirsty gulps, Sturgill sighed and asked, "You're not having flashbacks from that brown acid are you?"

With a sharp snap, Rosie closed the pantry door. "I didn't take any brown acid, Daddy! Why don't you pay attention when I talk to you? I'm being haunted by a ghost in this house, and it's not just any ghost, its Doc Campbell's ghost."

A peculiar look played across her father's face as he faltered for something to say. "Well, I . . . How do you know? I mean, are you sure?"

"You don't even care. You don't even believe me. You just want to make excuses, because you don't want to face the truth." Glaring at her father she said, "But if it was you Doc Campbell were bothering, you'd want someone to believe you!" She turned and ran back to her bedroom.

A soft rain pelted against her window as a pale dawn broke across the day casting a watery luminosity over the mountain. Rosie lay in bed staring through the rain spattered windowpane into the water colored morning. Memories of the vivid dream plagued her with a gut feeling that the fairy tale garden truly existed, and was in fact a destination, not a dreamed illusion.

The fading storm left Janie awake with worry for her mother. She had suffered fitful sleep throughout the night, and was relieved dawn had finally broken. Slipping quietly from her bed she went to her desk and pulled paper and pencils from the drawer. The sketch began as a mindless doodle to while away time. Somehow, the pencil marks became a turbulent ocean with crashing waves. Angry storm clouds choked the sky above the sea, and in the far distance a tornado formed in the air. Janie shoved the drawing to the back of her paper and began again. She focused on drawing something cheerful and bright. Taking a yellow pencil she formed a brilliant sun shining yellow rays of light from the sky. With a green pencil she sketched a spring meadow with lively colors of spring flowers. Furiously, she sketched trees and mountains. Her drawing became a garden of tranquil beauty with a sparkling aqua stream flowing beneath a foot bridge. Grapevines and Mimosa trees outlined the boundaries, and butterflies floated above fragrant spring flowers. The drawing filled her with a sense of peace. She signed her name at the bottom corner as would any aspiring artist, then propped it against her mirror.

Slipping silently from her room, she tiptoed through the living room and into her grandfather's study. Crossing through, she entered the guestroom where Kid lay sleeping. The room was darkened, as heavy drapes were pulled against the dawning sunlight. She stepped gingerly to the bed and listened to the slow steady breathing of her cousin. Gently, she shook his shoulder. "Kid," she called softly, "please, wake up." His soft slumbering breath became interrupted as he turned away from her. Again, she could hear the sounds of his sleeping breath. Shaking him a little harder she called out, "Kid, wake up!"

He awoke with a start, "What? What?"

"I need to talk to you."

"Janie," he groaned. "Go back to bed."

Tearfully she said, "While you were gone a hurricane hit Gulf Port. My mother still hasn't called us. I'm afraid for her!"

The sudden memory of the news from the paper flooded his memory. Sitting upright, he pulled the little girl onto the bed with him. "I know about the hurricane."

Wrapping her arms around his neck she asked, "Will you go look for her, Kid? Will you go to Mississippi and find my mommy?"

He pushed back the hair from his face and answered, "Sure, I will. If that's what you want me to do."

"Did you bring me a t-shirt?"

Shoving the child aside, he turned on the bedside lamp. Soft yellow light chased the rainy shadows from the room. "I said I would, didn't I?"

"But, did you?"

With a puff of breath, he slung the bedcovers aside and leapt from bed. He rummaged through a duffle bag and withdrew a t-shirt emblazoned with a drawing of a hand with balanced fingers upon the neck of a guitar. A small bird sat perched at the top, and the shape of a television set surrounded the drawing. "I love it!" she exclaimed, and pulled it over top of her nightgown. The oversized garment fell almost to her knees. "I can't wait for Shelley to see me wear this. She'll be oh so jealous!"

"Don't be starting trouble with that witch of a sister you got. I can't take much more of her. G-Mama will be pissed off bad if I punch her one, like she really deserves." Picking up his jeans from a chair, he slid them on over his baggy boxer shorts.

"I never start things with her, you know that. She just hates me." Admiring the t-shirt in the reflection of a mirror, she asked innocently, "So, when will you leave for Gulf Port? Can I go with you?"

Swinging open the bedroom door Kid answered, "You know you can't go."

Running to catch up with the cousin she openly adored, Janie asked, "When will you go?" He did not answer, but continued walking mutely toward the kitchen, and the smell of freshly brewed coffee.

Maggie and Bert were still sitting at the breakfast table when they walked in. "Our wandering grandson has finally made his way back home," Maggie mused.

"Let's just not ask any questions about that hippie festival he went to," Bert remarked, as if Kid couldn't hear.

"Kid is going to Gulf Port to find my mommy!" Janie proudly announced.

Without speaking, Kid poured himself a cup of coffee. Heavy silence clung to the room after the stunning announcement. It seemed no one even dared to breathe. Taking his cup to the table, Kid sat opposite his grandfather. All eyes were on him as the silence continued to loom like a loud deafness. He broke the quiet by slurping his coffee. With acute attention focused on him, Kid finally stated, "I'll be going to Gulf Port tomorrow. I need to do all I can to find Aunt Elizabeth."

Bert dropped his fork onto his plate with a startling clatter. "I'm afraid it'll just be a wasted trip, but it will make me feel better, too. We'll both go. The National Guard will turn us back, and the Red Cross will be very little help, but at least we can say we tried."

White towels and bed sheets swayed slowly in the soft mountain breeze beneath a hazy August sun as Rosie hung out the wash. The vivid dream clung to her waking thoughts the way cobwebs cling to dark, undisturbed corners. Looking about, she could see nothing that resembled the lush garden of Doc Campbell's promise. The rolling meadows of her father's farm were scorched from the summer's heat, bearing ugly bitter weeds and thistles. Even the orchard in the distance seemed exhausted, except for the loaded pear tree still waiting to ripen.

Using the empty clothes basket as a shield from the sun, she studied the horizon carefully. There were no mystic jaded mountains to be seen in the distance, and the sky was a hazy blue. Nowhere could she find the slightest trace of the enchanting garden. Even the wind song was absent from the mountain on this scorched day of fading summer. The feeling that the garden was indeed a real place was unshakable, and her desire to find it overwhelming.

She returned to the house, grateful to be out of the sweltering heat. Upon hearing the slamming of the back door, Eva called out, "Come see the *Mike Douglas Show*!"

The rumble of the old black and white television set echoed within the pine board walls of the living room, while Eva polluted the air with cigarette smoke that clung like smog to the knotty pine ceiling. Rosie leaned against the doorframe peering sharply at the set and asked, "Who is it?"

"Don't you recognize her? That's Joan Bennett from *Dark Shadows*. She's a famous movie star. She's been in more than seventy films."

The sight of Kid's car pulling into the driveway caught Rosie's attention. She stepped onto the front porch to welcome him and Janie inside. The fragrant Wisteria had faded, and the old rocking chair sat innocently still in the shadows of the gnarled winding vines. Racing up the steps Janie exclaimed, "Kid is going to Gulf Port to find my mommy, just like Lewis went to New York to find you!"

Kid appeared behind her with an unsure look on his face. Trying to speak for him, Rosie said, "Yes, well that's a very brave thing for him to do, Janie. But it might be a little harder than you think."

Words of reason fell upon unreasonable little ears. "I just know that Kid and G-Daddy are going to find my mommy. And, when they bring her back here, she's going to want to stay in Alabama, and never go back to Gulf Port."

Slumped against the porch railing, Kid stared blindly at the brittle lawn and politely asked, "Sunny, can you fix me something cold to drink?"

"Yes, come on in."

Hurrying ahead, Janie joined Eva in front of the television, while Rosie and Kid wandered into the kitchen. As Rosie prepared the beverage, she took the opportunity of Janie being out of the room to question Kid, "Do you really think she's alright?"

"I don't feel good about it, that's all I know." He took the glass she offered with tinkling ice cubes, and put it to his temple. "I just don't get it; first her father, now her mother!"

After tilting the electric fan Rosie joined him at the table. The air blew against them, tossing their hair gently. "Well, just making the trip has already made her very happy."

Sipping lightly he replied, "I really love that child, Sunny. It pisses me off to no end the way Shelley treats her. What's wrong with people, anyway? Committing suicide and staying in the path of a hurricane! It's all just too crazy." Looking up to the ceiling he asked, "Have you had any more strange happenings since the séance?"

Images of the sun warmed garden rushed through her as she answered, "No, nothing at all."

Janie entered asking, "Can we go somewhere?"

"Like where?" asked Kid gruffly.

"Maybe we can go down to the lake. It would be a nice drive, and we can skip some rocks and just mess around," suggested Janie.

Seeing that the child's proposal was pleasing to Kid, Rosie agreed as well. "We could drive to Heather's house. She lives near the lake."

"Let's go! Let's go!" Janie cheered.

The house Heather lived in was surrounded by tall hardwood trees. A shaded path led to the lake behind her house. A floral patterned sofa with two matching wing chairs dominated the living room. The floor was covered with a soft pastel pink carpet. A large painting of a vase filled with pink roses hung above the fireplace, and was complimented by pink candles in brass sconces on each side. Rock and roll music played softly from a stereo in the corner of the room.

"I'm so glad you came to see me!" Heather exclaimed. "Did you catch any flack about our trip to Woodstock?"

Rosie giggled lightly, "My room was plastered with newspapers showing our photo, and my daddy thinks I took brown acid."

"Why does he think that?" Heather asked.

Not wanting to discuss the haunting dreams, she answered simply, "He just likes to tease."

"Can we walk down to the lake?" Janie asked impatiently.

Grabbing the child up off the floor, Kid turned her upside down and said, "Yes! And, I'm going to throw you in head first."

"No! No!" giggled Janie.

Heather and Rosie followed behind Kid as he carried Janie perched on his shoulders along the shaded path to the lake. When they left the wooded path and came to the shore of the lake, he deposited her in the sand. She kicked off her shoes and stepped into the shallow water. "Oh, look tiny little shells!"

"They're mussel shells. Sometimes you can find a pearl in the big ones," Heather explained.

"Where are the big ones?" The little girl asked in awe.

Pointing across the lake Heather replied, "In the deep water."

Still impressed with the idea of finding a pearl Janie asked, "How can you get to the bottom of the deep water?"

Heather removed her shoes and joined her. "You have to use diving equipment to go deep enough. Look out there at the little boat with the red flag waving from it. That's a diver's boat. They harvest the mussel shells."

"Why?" Janie asked, with squint eyes against the hazy sunshine to see the tiny boat with the red flag.

Heather laughed, "It's a little crazy, really. But the shells are sold to Japan. In Japan the shells are ground into tiny smooth beads. Then the little beads are put inside oysters. The oysters coat the little beads with oyster spit, and they become cultured pearls. The Japanese string the cultured pearls into necklaces, and sells them back to the Americans for a lot of money."

The little girl stared with wonderment. "How do you know all that?"

"I read a lot," remarked Heather. Walking from the water she said, "Come on. I'll show you my neighbor's boathouse. He doesn't mind."

They followed Heather around the lakeshore to a pier leading to a boathouse. A diving board sat perched at the end of the pier, along with patio furniture and floatation toys. Heather opened the door and they entered where a ski boat floated in the center. The lapping water lulled the atmosphere with a calming ambiance. Rosie sank into a comforting wicker chair with posh cushions, while Janie hopped into a hammock and commanded Kid to give her a push.

"Anybody for a rum and coke?" asked Heather holding up a bottle of *Bacardi*. "Justin won't mind, really."

"Sure," he said, "as long as no one is going to come out here with a shotgun."

"Don't worry. Justin has a thing for my mom," Heather said, as she poured up the drinks. "Besides, I'm always cleaning up from his parties out here, so he owes me."

As she passed out the drinks, Heather asked Rosie, "So, how's the supernatural phenomenon going at your house?"

Again, Rosie was tempted to talk of her dreams, but decided against it. "I just let sleeping ghosts lie. What else can I say?"

"Very wise," Heather replied, as she sipped her drink.

"Kid is going with my G-Daddy to Gulf Port tomorrow," Janie declared as she sipped her soda. "My mom still hasn't called after the hurricane, so Kid is going to find her for me, like Lewis found ya'll at Woodstock."

Noticing the look of admiration from Heather, Kid quickly said to his younger cousin, "I'm going to try my best to find Aunt Elizabeth. But, sweetheart, you're scaring me the way you think I can just go down there and find her. I'm not Superman, you know."

"I know," Janie remarked. "You're better, because you're my cousin."

Heather snickered, "Yeah, Superman doesn't have any cousins, at least not on earth." She flounced down into a matching wicker chair saying, "Too bad we didn't bring our swimsuits, huh? The water is really deep here, and the diving board is a blast."

"I don't think I can swim well enough to go off a diving board," Rosie admitted.

"This is by far the nicest part of the lake I've seen yet," Kid remarked.

Leaping from the hammock, Janie interjected, "I'd rather ride in the boat!"

"And we would," Heather said, "if Justin were here."

What had begun as a hazy summer day became cloudy with seasonal storm clouds. When Rosie returned home she hurried to retrieve the laundry she had pinned to the clothesline earlier. The smell of roast beef baked with onions greeted her as she entered the backdoor, and the ringing telephone halted her task, "Hello?"

"Sunshine Rose Moon, what's up?" asked Lewis.

"Nothing really, I just got home from Heather's house at the lake. She entertained Janie, Kid and me at her neighbor's boathouse."

"I wonder if that's the guy she's been sneaking around with?"

"What do you mean?"

"Jed told me that she was fooling around with some guy a lot older than her, a neighbor."

"How would he know something like that if I don't?"

"I don't know, and I don't care. I called to talk about you and me."

"Okay."

"Opal wants us to come over for dinner Saturday, and I was thinking maybe just the two of us could catch a movie Friday. Jon Voight has a new movie out called *Midnight Cowboy*. Want to see it with me?"

"Oh, yes! I adore Jon Voight."

"I thought I'd better get a jump start on the weekend, before Kid has a chance to make plans with you."

A sad feeling overcame her as she explained, "Kid is going to Gulf Port with Bert tomorrow. They're going to look for Elizabeth."

"Do you think she's dead?"

"Well, what else could it be? After Tom blew his brains out like he did, maybe she just let the hurricane take her. It must be terrifying to be washed out to sea."

"Yeah, just ask Mary Jo Kopechne."

Rosie frowned, "That's not funny!"

His laughter carried lightly across the line, "Gotta go!"

With furrowed brows she said impulsively, "The Devil's gonna get you, Lewis Shirey!" She slammed down the phone with his satirical words twisting her lips into a giggling smile.

Chapter Fifteen
Dark Dreams and Nixon

Dawn edged closer, chasing away the moon and plunging the mountain into its darkest hour. A banging noise awoke Rosie from a dreamless slumber. She left her bed to search out the disturbing sound. Standing in the living room she peered out the picture window to see a hanging flower pot being knocked against the house by a ravaging wind. Stepping impulsively into the windstorm to rescue the plant, her attention was diverted to the old rocking chair in the corner of the porch. He sat there with his hat pulled low across the brow, and the wind seemed to have no effect on him. Crossing the planked porch in bare feet, she took the hanging plant from its hook and placed it safely on the floor, then turned to the man who had become a familiar face in her dreams.

Her hair whipped about her face, and she shouted to be heard above the howling force, "What do you want?"

The illusive man sat rocking slowly in the now painted, new chair. His suit appeared pressed and hardly worn, his jacket was a leisurely bolero, the kind a Spanish cowboy would wear to a Mexican canteen. Stepping closer, her bare feet growing cold in the wind, she watched him intently. The man did not look at her, but kept his head low so that all she could see was the perfectly straight nose and styled mustache. The wind grew ferocious, and her hair was thrashed violently across her eyes.

A black funnel cloud caught her attention in the distance. The twister was speeding toward them. Frozen with fear, she shouted at the man again, "What do you want?" To her astonishment he lifted his head and looked at her with those dark pleading brown eyes. His irrefutable beauty soothed her and she reached out shouting, "We must get inside!"

The apparition struggled against the wind. He raised his hand, now willing to accept help. The force of the wind pushed Rosie farther inside, and the tornado drew closer. Doc shouted communications, but his words were drowned in the wind, and he was drawn backward toward the approaching funnel.

Rosie was thrust violently to the living room floor as debris flew about the room. Suddenly, the storm faded, leaving a sunlit morning behind. Regaining her feet, she stepped out onto the porch again. The rocking chair was no longer painted and new, but old with cracked paint. "Are you here?" she shouted to no one, "Are you here?"

She awoke with Sturgill shaking her. "Sunshine Rose!" he shouted. "Wake up, Rosie!"

"Daddy!" she exclaimed. "It was a tornado!" Looking about her dimly lit room she realized it was not yet daylight.

"No, you were just having a bad dream." He released her saying, "Maybe you should have some milk before you go back to sleep." At the doorway he paused to ask, "Who were you looking for?"

She stared at her father with confusion, "What was I saying?"

"You were saying, 'Are you here?' like you were looking for someone." He watched an expression of remembrance cross his daughter's face.

"Oh, yes," she remembered. "I was thinking someone was lost in the storm." She smiled at her father, "Go back to bed, Daddy. It's Saturday, and you should sleep in. I'll be okay." Sturgill left, quietly closing the door behind him.

Soon thereafter Rosie carefully left her room, stepping through the living room and out the front door. Her bare feet retraced the steps from her dream. The old rocking chair still held the potted fern, and the sun was glowing rosy hues across the Eastern horizon. Turning to go inside she gasped loudly. The hanging plant was sitting on the porch floor, rather than hanging from its familiar hook.

When Sturgill and Eva aroused for Saturday morning breakfast, Rosie had blueberry muffins and fresh brewed coffee waiting for them. Eva reached for her pack of cigarettes as soon as she got seated at the table. Sturgill brought her a cup of coffee, and she promptly began spooning one teaspoon of sugar after another into it, while Rosie sat making out her shopping list.

Sturgill sipped his coffee, "Were you able to go back to sleep this morning?"

Rosie answered, "No. I didn't want to." She made a note on her paper and asked, "What would you like for lunch next week?"

Considering his daughter's request he said, "I liked that tuna salad you put together a couple of weeks ago." He sipped his coffee and continued, "Those BLT's on toast were heavenly."

To her stepmother she asked, "Is there anything special you want me to pick up at the market?"

Eva sipped her coffee then exhaled her smoke before speaking. "Yes, a new magazine."

"You can go to the market by yourself today, Rosie, since Lewis taught you to drive a stick." Sturgill bit into a muffin as his wife began to protest.

"Sturgill, you can't let her loose with my car! How do you know she can even drive it?" Eva spoke in her usual style, as though Rosie wasn't present.

Sturgill narrowed his eyes. "I think if Rosie can drive Rob's old farm truck, she can drive *our* car!" His tone of voice silenced Eva, but she cast Rosie a scathing glance.

"Don't worry Eva. I'll be careful." Then to her father Rosie said, "Daddy, do you remember me telling you about Teresa's friend, Althea? You know I told you she came here one day and said that we have a ghost in the house."

He furrowed his brows as he remembered. "I told you, Rosie. You can't believe all that gypsy hogwash!"

Putting down her pencil sharply she confronted her father, "That man keeps coming to me in my dreams, Daddy. He wants me to know something!" Rosie watched her father roll his eyes in disdain, and she scowled at Eva for giggling.

Sturgill sighed heavily, "Rosie, those dreams are from the stress of your trip. When you get rested up they will go away."

Staring at her list, she causally asked, "Did either one of you take my spider plant from its hook?"

"What the hell is a spider plant?" asked Sturgill as he sipped his coffee.

Eva didn't answer. Asking directly, she said, "What about you, Eva? Did you take my spider plant from its hook?"

Eva exclaimed, "Heaven's no! I haven't bothered any of your plants."

Rosie looked at Sturgill, "Can I ask Althea to come here and hold a séance?"

His face fell into an expression of mirth, "A what? You mean one of those spells that gypsies use to conjure up dead people?" He laughed out loud, "Oh, Rosie! Please tell me you're not serious."

Frustrated with her father's indifference she exclaimed as she rose from the table, "Well! *Somebody* took my spider plant from its hook." Taking up her list, she left the room irritated even more by her father's echoing chuckles.

When Rosie wheeled the yellow bug into the library parking lot the heat of the midday sun was wilting. She crossed the blistering asphalt to enter the air conditioned building. Approaching the card catalogue file, she was not really sure where to begin, and looked under the subject cards for county history. From there she began collecting books. Hours slipped by as she poured over the pages. Finally, she found a section dedicated to medical professionals who practiced at the turn of the century. Her mouth gaped open as her finger traced along a list of names beneath photographs. There she found the name of Jonathon Austin 'Doc' Campbell beneath a black and white photo of a dark haired man with a stylish curled mustache.

She shoved the open book aside as she searched through more. Another hour passed before she found the article she needed. It told of a scandalous crime against a reputable doctor by a man of wealth and honor. There were photos of the wealthy man and his daughter, on whose behalf the crime was committed, and the doctor whom the crime was committed against. Doc Campbell sported a Mexican styled bolero jacket and a white gentleman's hat with a black band. Only his handsome dark eyes, straight nose and mustache could be seen below the brim. She marked the places in the books with a torn piece of paper and returned the others.

That afternoon when she returned home, Rosie approached her father with the books. "I have proof of the man who is haunting my dreams, Daddy." She opened the two books and placed them one on top of the other in her father's lap, then left the room to prepare the evening meal, before Lewis came to pick her up for dinner with his mother.

Snuggling close to Lewis as they drove to Ennis, the town where his mother shared an apartment with a woman from work, Rosie explained her day at the library. The sun was sinking beyond the horizon, but daylight still clung stubbornly to the day when they arrived at Opal's. Turning off the car ignition, he kissed her gently and said, "Let's not think about it anymore, and the next time Heather wants to have a séance, don't!"

Waiting at the top of the stairway were Janie and Angel. "Come in!" Angel shouted, "We have something to show you!"

Lewis smiled and said, "Uh oh!"

Janie clutched Rosie by the hand as Angel led Lewis into the living room. "Look at our book!" Janie exclaimed before Angel could.

Sinking into a comfortable sofa, Rosie pulled Lewis down next to her. Opal entered from the kitchen wiping her hands on a dish towel and said, "These girls have been working like bees to finish this project, so you two had better appreciate it."

Robina, Opal's roommate entered from the hallway. "Lewis!" she exclaimed, "You've got to tell me all about Joe Cocker!"

Opal interrupted her roommate by saying, "Later, Robina." She then gestured for Lewis to pay attention to his sister.

The little girls displayed a large poster board folded in half with sketch pages in between. The book cover had a drawing of a man playing a keyboard on a stage in front of a large audience. The title read *Woodstock* with the authors listed at the bottom as Angel Shirey and Janie Noble. Rosie exclaimed with surprise, "Oh, my goodness! This must have taken you days to make."

Both girls agreed by furiously nodding their heads. "Open it up and read it, Lewis." Opal encouraged her son to appreciate his little sister, "These girls have worked hard on this book. And, it's all for you!"

Rosie began, *"Once upon a time."* She nudged Lewis to continue reading.

Continuing as everyone expected him too, he read, *"There was a handsome young musician named Prince Lewie,"* he rolled his eyes at the name.

Rosie turned the page and read aloud, *"One day Prince Lewie went to a music festival called Woodstock, and there he met a beautiful young Princess named Rose."*

With a looked of affection for his little sister, Lewis continued reading, *"A rock star asked for help."*

Rosie turned the page and they both burst into laughter at the drawing of Joe Cocker. Reading from the book she said, *"Joe Cocker needed someone to play his keyboard, because his own player was lost in rural New York."*

Lewis enjoyed the story, smiling as he turned each page. *"The princess said to Joe Cocker, 'Prince Lewie can play for you, Joe.'"* He tossed back his head and laughed at the drawings.

Rosie read, *"So, Joe said, 'Play little prince, play.' And, Lewie played with all his heart."* They turned the page together, and she continued to read, *"After the concert, Prince Lewie and Princess Rose were married by the lake."*

Lewis giggled at the picture of Princess Rose in her wedding gown. He read the last page, *"And they lived happily ever after, the end."*

Opal and Robina clapped their hands in applause. Angel and Janie were very proud of their creation and said so. "We worked hard on that book for you, Lewis," Angel explained. "You better take good care of it."

Leaning against Rosie, Janie said, "I'm so excited about seeing my mommy, again."

The expression on Rosie's face prompted Opal to ask, "Is something wrong?"

Brushing away haunting thoughts, she answered, "No."

Sunday morning dawned, and Rosie prepared for church. Sturgill and Eva were settled on the sofa in front of the television set drinking coffee when she emerged from her room. The night had passed with Rosie having no memorable dreams. She stepped to the door and stared at the horses grazing the meadow across the street.

The history books she had brought home from the library sat on the coffee table. She asked her father, "What did you think of the article about the murdered doctor?" and watched intently as Sturgill made no effort to answer her question. "Daddy, you do know that Doc Campbell was shot dead right out here on this very porch don't you?"

Sturgill sighed and sat back against the couch. "What do you want me to say, Rosie?" he asked her softly. "Do you want me to tell you I believe the doctor's ghost is roaming around this house?" Sturgill looked away for a moment, but continued, "For God's sake, there could be a dozen ghosts living here with us! But what are we supposed to do about it?" With a soft-hearted look he soothed, "You're young, and maybe you have some extra sensory perceptions that old farts like me don't have. Honey, please don't let these dreams, and historical facts drive you crazy."

Rosie closed her eyes. "I just wanted you to know about the events that took place here, Daddy. I'm not worried about any ghosts." She turned back to the doorway and stared at the old rocking chair sitting still in the morning light. "I just think it's odd I dreamed about him, and then I find out he was a real person who lived here. And, he is a blood relation. I just wanted you to understand me." Several chimney sweeps flew through the air with darting aviation maneuvers. The birds held her attention as she said, "I wanted you to see that what I'm telling you is real."

Sturgill was disturbed by his daughter's revelations. "Rosie, whatever you want to do is alright by me." When she didn't respond to his comment he continued explaining, "If you want to have that gypsy woman come back over here, I'm all for it." He rubbed his hand across the back of his neck. "Rosie, look at me," he commanded.

She turned her gaze from the clear blue morning sky. "You can always tell me anything. I will always be on your side, no matter what."

The church was humid, and becoming too warm for comfort as the choir sang *A Little Talk with Jesus.* Rosie stood next to Ed with her hymn book open to the song, but she didn't sing. She could hear Ed singing in a very low tone. Lewis stood with the choir. The heat seemed to have a depressing effect on her as she remembered the sweetness of her father's words from earlier that morning, and tears threatened to fall.

Later, as Rosie helped Mamie prepare lunch when they returned to the Shirey home, she wandered about the kitchen. A *Life* magazine lying on top of a stack of others caught her attention. The cover of the magazine was a photo of the Cuyahoga River in Ohio that had caught fire on June 22, 1969. Peeling open the magazine she peered at the article all the while vaguely remembering a discontented conversation between Lewis and Kid at the lake. The reporter had written: *Some river! Chocolate-brown, oily, bubbling with surface gases, it oozes rather than flows.* Her brows furrowed as she read: *Anyone who falls into the Cuyahoga does not drown (Cleveland citizens joke grimly) he decays!* Putting the disturbing article aside, she busied herself with the chore of chopping cabbage and onion for coleslaw.

Taking the bowl of chopped cabbage and onion Mamie said, "Why don't you go see what Lewis is doing. I'll finish up here."

Leaving the older woman in the kitchen, Rosie wandered toward Lewis' bedroom. Music from his stereo wafted through his door. The sound of Jimi Hendrix's guitar blended with Lewis' attempt to play in unison seeped through the cracks. She was suddenly caught off guard when Ed grasped her hand. Holding a finger to his lips, he shushed her into silence and pulled her into Angel's bedroom, closing the door behind them.

Taking notice of how sweetly the room was decorated with stuffed animals and dolls cluttering the shelves meant for books, she asked in a serious tone, "What do you want?"

Ed smiled at her and said, "Aren't you the suspicious one?" He pulled a silver flask from his back pocket and twisted the lid off. Mockingly he tilted the flask up and drank from it. With closed eyes he released a satisfied sigh. "Don't you want some?"

Putting the flask to her lips she sipped the rum it contained. "So that's what we've become, rum drinkers after Sunday service?"

He took the flask asking, "Is this thing between you and Lewis real?"

Picking up a teddy bear dressed in blue gingham she replied, "Angel has the cutest things."

A low chuckle escaped Ed, "I knew it. You're just carrying on with him to punish me."

Tossing the teddy bear aside she whirled to face him. "How arrogant you are! To think I would even waste my time to punish you." Rushing past she put her hand on the door knob, but Ed quickly leaned against it to stop her exit.

He tilted his flask for another drink. Again, he held it out to her, but she turned away. "Look, I need to tell you some things." When she gave him a sardonic look he explained, "Just to get it off my chest. Okay?"

She still refused to answer, but he had her attention. Ed put his hands together and said, "I know I did you wrong. Hell! Everybody knows I did you wrong."

In a cold calm voice she said, "I'm listening."

Reaching for her hand he said, "I had a lot of time to think while I was in 'Nam. And, a lot of my thinking was about you." She rolled her dark eyes and pulled to take her hand from his. "I realized a long time ago what a fool I was to hurt you. And, I promised God that if he let me come back I would make amends."

Rosie was growing tired with his speech and said, "There's nothing to amend, Ed. Just accept that I'm with Lewis and everything will be fine."

Blowing out a heated breath he replied, "That's going to be real hard, Rosie. Seeing you with him, while I want to be with you so bad it hurts. I don't know how I'm going to do it. I'll have to leave. Move away."

Nodding her head she said simply, "Okay, leave. Move away." She again reached for the door knob, but he wouldn't budge.

With shimmering eyes Ed said, "I wish with all my heart you could give me one more chance."

She laughed lightly and said, "Fool me once, shame on you. Fool me twice, and well you know. Face it Ed. There's going to be no shame on me." She pushed at him to open the door. Neither of them noticed the music from Lewis' room had ceased.

Ed caught her into a strong embrace and forced her into an intimate kiss. With her hand to her bruised lips she exclaimed, "Damn it, Ed! Why did you do that?"

He put his fingers in his hair and proclaimed, "Because I love you, and you drive me crazy!"

Angrily she hissed, "I should slap you silly! Now move out of my way." When he moved away from the door she swung it open to reveal Lewis leaning against the wall in the hallway. "Lewis!" she exclaimed. "What are you doing?"

Calmly, he looked from Rosie to Ed and replied, "I thought I was going to have to kick the door down, and rescue you from my brother."

She could feel Ed's breath in her hair as he growled, "Yeah, like you even could." She stepped out of the room taking Lewis by the hand.

He pushed her away asking, "What did you do, Ed? Survive Vietnam just to get smeared on the mountain?"

Vile laughter escaped Ed as he warned his brother, "Think about what you're saying little brother. I might take it as a threat, and that wouldn't be good for you."

Impulsively, Lewis threw a punch at Ed. The older brother deflected the blow and twisted Lewis' arm behind him shoving his face into the wall.

Pushing at Ed, she almost shouted, "Stop, you idiot! You'll hurt his fingers!" Her next remark was a shriek, "He's got to play tomorrow night!"

Lewis said, "Stay out of this, Rosie."

"Yeah, yeah, we don't want to hurt sissy boy's fingers." Ed released his brother, and Lewis spun to face him.

Stepping between them she said to Lewis, "Please don't embarrass me in front of your grandmother."

Ed stepped away and said, "Get over your pathetic little self, Lewis. This ain't pansy assed Kid you're messing with." He then sauntered away.

Making an effort to embrace Lewis, he pushed her away and asked, "What are you doing to me, Rosie? Do you want to be with him?"

With shock in her voice she answered breathlessly, "No."

"Then stay out of locked rooms with him," he stated coldly, and followed Ed into the kitchen.

As the Shirey family gathered for Sunday lunch, Rosie couldn't help but catch Ed's gaze across the table. She avoided conversation, even though Mamie tried to draw her into a discussion of the liberal ways of the youth movement. Sitting next to Lewis, she let her knee rub against his thigh, but he showed no distraction, and obliged his grandmother by entering into her conversation.

Ed spread butter on a homemade yeast roll and said sardonically, "The young people coming out of high school today are just not prepared to deal with the society that awaits them." His out of the blue comment brought silence to the table. Taking note of the silence he continued, "It seems to me that all the young people today are wrapped up in television and music. They're all getting fat and lazy, sitting in air conditioned living rooms watching ludicrous television shows." He looked directly at Rosie as he took a bite of the buttered bread.

When no one added to his comment Rosie asked with sarcasm, "What are you saying, Ed? That you don't like to watch *Laugh In*?" She held his gaze, and watched him stop chewing as he considered her question.

Ed sipped his glass of iced tea, and swallowed before he responded. "Yeah, I like to watch *Laugh In,* but I get a little concerned when I travel across the ocean, and see a whole population of people who don't know what television is, or what it's like to see a doctor for medicine."

Rosie responded quickly, "Half of America is protesting the war."

Ed's eyes held a glow of hatred as memories flooded him. "Those so called protestors are the same sons of bitches that stood at the airport to scream obscenities at us soldiers as we disembarked from the airplane, just trying to get back home. The Army had to erect barricades of chicken wire at the airport for the soldiers to walk behind, because fanatical freaks were calling us *baby killers,* and throwing paper bags of human feces at us." Ed finally looked away and sat back as if he had expended a great amount of energy.

The dining table fell into silence as everyone tried to process the indisputable atrocity Ed had just described. Feeling the sting of injustice Lewis asked, "What did you see in Vietnam?"

Ed relaxed and answered in a calm tone. "You'll see when you get there little brother." He put his fork down on his plate as if the food had suddenly become repulsive.

Rob snapped, "Lewis will not be going to Vietnam, Ed!" He put his own fork down and folded his hands together as he rested his elbows on the table. "This family sacrificed enough by sending you over there. No more of our boys will be going."

Mamie spoke hopefully saying, "The war is almost over. By the time Lewis is out of school, all of our boys will be home, where they belong."

Ed pushed himself from the table laughing, "And, Nixon will be run out of the White House on a rail. And, a coal mine will be discovered on our land. And, solid gold turds will fall from my ass!" Ed laughed sadistically as he stepped out the front door, away from Sunday dinner.

Chapter Sixteen
We All Scream

Monday morning dawned on Ben Johnson Ridge and Janie awoke with her best friend at her side. "Wake up Angel! We're going to the farmer's market with Shelley today."

During the drive Shelley did her best to drown out the two younger girl's chatter from the back seat by turning up the volume on the radio. To confound her sister even more, Janie encouraged Angel to sing along with her to the radio. Janie's aggravation must have worked, because her sister twisted the radio knob furiously, ending the music.

Feeling brave in the presence of her friend, Janie spoke to the back of her sister's head. "What's wrong, Shelley?" she asked sarcastically. "Don't you appreciate good company?"

Angel smiled wickedly at Janie and joined the teasing game, "Oh, Shelley? I was wondering if sometime you might let me ski down your nose." Winking wickedly at Janie, Angel said, "All I need is a bucket of water to fall into."

Never being one to let well enough alone, Janie giggled fiendishly, "Yeah, Shell. All my friends ask me if I charge admission for the Shelley Noble nose slide."

As the two happy little girls giggled Shelley cut the car wheel sharply to the left, and then back to the right. The giggles disappeared as they were tossed from one side of the backseat to the other.

"Hey!" Janie shouted, "You're just a big, ugly butt!"

"You really need to learn how to take a joke," Angel told Shelley, holding tight to the armrest.

The two girls fell silent in the backseat for a long moment. With one look at one another they burst out singing the song Shelley had switched off on the radio,

Nothing you can say can tear me away,
From my guy!

They continued singing until the car wheeled across the loose gravel of the Farmer's Market parking area. The girls crawled from the backseat quickly waving the one dollar bill they each clutched tightly in their hand.

"I scream, you scream, we all scream for ice cream!" They sang as they readied themselves to cross the two lane highway to reach the Frosty Freeze that sat on the opposite side. Shelley went straight to the vendor to purchase the vegetables needed to make Mamie's recipe for Chow-Chow. When she returned she could see the two girls across the street. "Let's go, *now*!" called Shelley, motioning for the girls to return.

The girls stood from the outdoor café table, and tossed away the messy used napkins. Cradling the stub of their cones in a fresh napkin they prepared to cross back across the highway. Janie ran across the street first. She turned and saw Angel struggling to peel melted chewing gum from the bottom of her shoe, using the napkin she'd just wrapped around her ice cream cone. A car was approaching slowly, and judging that she could cross the street ahead of it, Angel jogged into the highway. From the other side of the highway Janie could see a red sports car coming up fast behind the slower one. Realizing the fast car was intending to bypass the slower car she called out, "Angel, wait!"

In a slow motioned blur Janie watched Angel look up at the speeding car with terror. The sound of screaming tires ripped the quiet of the morning. Janie screamed with every inch of breath inside her as she watched Angel's small body be lifted up onto the hood of the car and smash into the windshield. The sound of breaking glass and shouts from bystanders brought Janie to her senses. The two approaching cars had stopped, and Angel's lifeless body lay upon the blistering asphalt beneath the summer sun.

Dropping her ice cream cone, Janie ran to her friend crying, "Angel, Angel! Get up! You're alright, get up!"

A pool of blood spread beneath Angel's head. The blood oozed dark and shiny against the black top as her blonde hair soaked up the liquid, extinguishing its true color. Strong hands griped Janie's shoulders and pulled her aside. She watched in a buzz of stunned silence as a man remove his white t-shirt, wrapping it around Angel's head. She could see people moving their lips and shouting orders, but none of the sound penetrated her ears. Shelley appeared, her lips moving, but the words disappeared without being heard. A surge of adrenaline rushed through Janie, and she pulled away, rushing to kneel beside Angel's body, twisted and grotesque upon the highway. A kind woman was applying pressure to Angel's head in an attempt to slow the bleeding. Reaching out, Janie peeled a blood soaked tendril from Angel's face. Something warm bounced onto her arm, and she brushed it away.

When more bits of substance popped about, landing on Janie leaving tiny specks of blood she asked, "What is that?"

The woman seemed to be losing her composure as she answered the traumatized child, "I don't know, honey. I think it's her brains."

Once again, Janie tumbled into a world of stunned silence where no sound could penetrate. She looked about at the faces with moving mouths, but no sound could reach her. The last thing she saw, before succumbing to unconsciousness, was Shelley's face speaking silent communications.

Sometime later, Janie became aware of lying on the ground while a man held a black umbrella above her, shielding her from the sun. She felt herself floating upward and over her body. Like a helium filled balloon anchored by a string she hung in the air, observing the traumatic chaos.

Angel's lifeless body was now cloaked in a pink blood stained blanket. Hearing no sound, Janie could only witness a silent moving picture of anguish. She saw the police cars arrive and block both sides of the highway. Moments later an ambulance sped up with flashing lights. Two men dressed in paramedic uniforms jumped from the vehicle, carrying what appeared to be plastic tool boxes. Quickly, one man injected Angel with some liquid he pulled from a vial with a syringe. The other wrapped her head in gauze that quickly stained with blood. They attached a tube to her small arm and taped it in place. She was then placed on the stretcher and slid into the back of the ambulance. The large automobile sped silently away.

Janie felt her floating self being tugged back into the fragile body lying crumbled on the ground like a discarded tissue. Soon, she was swallowed up by deafening silence, realizing without fear that she was dying.

Rosie was inside the barn with Sugar and Spice when she heard Eva's frantic calls for her. She left the horses inside their stalls as she ran out into the brilliance of the sunlit morning. Eva stood on the front porch, yelling for her to hurry home. Climbing over the metal gate, she raced to the front porch shouting at her stepmother, "What's wrong?"

"I just talked to Maggie." Eva's face was colorless, "Something bad has happened to Lewis' little sister." She turned to walk into the house.

Bounding up the porch steps behind her stepmother, Rosie placed her hand above Eva's, and slapped the screen door closed demanding, "What happened, Eva? What happened to Angel?"

Slowly she turned to look at her stepdaughter with an unbelieving look, "She's dead, Rosie. Angel was just killed crossing highway 79 at the farmer's market." With quivering lips that displayed her shock she whispered, "I'm so sorry."

The world began to spin wildly and Rosie screamed, "No!" before falling into a dead faint.

Some time later, Rosie entered the hospital emergency entrance and asked for Janie. The receptionist shuffled through some papers, and Rosie snapped at her impatiently. "She was just brought in!" Glaring at the middle aged woman on the other side of the counter she explained, "She witnessed her friend's death out on the highway." Saying the words made the truth real, and her tears began to flow again.

The additional information allowed the woman to direct her to Janie who was still being held in triage. Rushing to the cubical exam room, she drew back the curtain to find Janie sitting all alone on a triage gurney. Rosie embraced the little girl, and together they cried until their tears ran dry.

Later, Rosie was sitting beside Janie in a hospital room when Maggie and Shelley came in. Shelley seemed to be distracted, and Maggie was clearly shaken. Janie looked to her grandmother and said, "I want my mommy." When Maggie didn't respond she repeated herself. "I want my mommy!" her demands became loud and desperate.

Stepping closer, Rosie put her arm around the little girl as they both stared at Janie's grandmother for help. Maggie put her hand to her mouth and sniffled, "Janie, dear." She began to speak, but halted as her own tears choked her words.

Kid stepped in and rushed to his little cousin. He sat beside her and cradled her in his arms. "Janie, Janie," he said rocking her to and fro like an infant. "I'm so sorry, sweetheart." He buried his face into her hair, muffling his voice.

Feeling panic growing within her, Rosie asked, "Kid, did you find Elizabeth?" Her dry reddened eyes held no more tears as Kid responded to her question.

"I'm so sorry. We couldn't find your mother, Janie." He summoned the strength to pull back and look at the little girl. "That doesn't mean anything though!" he declared. "That only means she could be farther away from Gulf Port than we looked. She may be calling us any minute."

With a desperate look toward her grandmother Janie began to scream, "I want my mommy!" Her desperate pleas were heart shattering, and she continued to scream until medical personnel rushed in and demanded everyone leave.

After a few minutes of lingering in the hallway a nurse emerged and asked the family to follow her to a small waiting area. The tiny windowless room was sparsely furnished with hard plastic chairs, and a single side table with magazines spread haphazardly across it. The nurse clasped her hands together in front of her, her face marred with a typical cold expression of someone who had seen too much tragedy. "Dr. Martin is the MD on call, and he will be here shortly to speak with you about the little girl's condition." Betty unclasped her hands and moved toward the door. "I don't know what just now upset Janie, but I take it no one has told her the news of her young friend."

Suddenly alarmed to think Janie might be unaware of Angel's death, Rosie asked, "Does Janie think Angel survived the accident?"

The nurse looked seriously concerned, "To my knowledge she has not asked any staff about the status of the other little girl, and if none of you have discussed it with her," Betty crossed her arms across her chest and shook her head expressively. "Shock can be a dangerous thing for anyone to experience. But, that is something for you to discuss with Dr. Martin." The nurse turned and swung the door open, quickly departing.

Maggie announced in a commanding tone of voice, "There's nothing we can do, but wait for the doctor." Her voice held a steel edge, and the room fell silent.

Finally, the door opened and a kind faced doctor entered. "Well, let's see here. I understand that you are Janie's family." The doctor looked at the silent faces. "I'm very concerned for this child, and she will be staying here tonight. I want her monitored closely." The middle aged doctor looked at Maggie and spoke directly to her. "Have you decided how to tell her about the other child's death?"

Maggie's eyes became wide with tears threatening to spill over her lashes. "Oh, doctor!" she exclaimed. "I just thought she knew already. I mean, she was there when it happened."

Dr. Martin cautioned the family, "Shock can be a dreadful thing, and people can react differently to it. I don't want to panic you, but it is important for you to know that the next forty-eight to seventy-two hours are critical for this child's health." When Maggie inhaled sharply at the doctor's words he quickly continued, "Now, don't work yourselves up into a panic. But, please be advised to use every bit of caution when you see Janie. I ask that you remain calm and quiet. She should sleep as much as possible." Dr. Martin looked around the room and said, "You may visit her in pairs of two. Which of you would like to go first?"

Maggie stood and took Shelley by the hand, "We will go first." They took a step toward the door, but Dr. Martin still barred the way.

He looked sharply at the two anxious women and warned, "Keep your visit brief, and if she is asleep, don't wake her." He stepped aside and let Maggie and Shelley pass.

When his grandmother had left the room, Kid said to Dr. Martin, "My grandfather and I just returned from the Mississippi coast this afternoon. It appears Janie's mother may have been lost in the hurricane."

Dr. Martin furrowed his brows and said, "Don't tell her. Keep her optimistic about her mother." The doctor looked at Kid sternly and said, "Lie if you have to, but don't tell that little girl any more bad news." Dr. Martin stepped to the door and said, "I'll be making my rounds tomorrow morning, if you need to see me make sure to be here before eight." He paused for a moment expecting more questions. When none were forthcoming he left the room.

Cradling her face in both hands, Rosie succumbed to tears, "Oh, Kid! I don't know what to do. I know Lewis and Opal are hurting so bad, but I feel like I should stay with Janie."

"You go to Lewis. I will stay here," instructed Kid. "I'll be here with her when you get back." With a glanced at his wrist watch he said, "Take as much time as you need." When she hesitated he urged, "You go on, now. Go see about Lewis and his mother."

Her voice escaped as a hoarse whisper, "Tell Janie I'll be back soon."

Rosie drove to the apartment Opal shared with Robina. Ed opened the door before she could knock. They stood looking at one another for a long awkward moment. Finally, she found her voice and said in a barely audible tone, "How's your mother, Ed?"

He reached out and pulled Rosie into a desperate embrace. He closed the door, and slowly shook his head to express his uncertainty. "She's not good, Rosie."

"Where's Lewis?"

"He's home. I came here right away." He began to pace restlessly. "To tell you the truth, Rosie," he paused as he searched for the words to describe his feelings. "I feel so closed in here. I'm not sure how much more I can take." He walked to the window, peering out blindly into the fading sunlight.

Following him, she looked to see what was beyond the dingy window panes. The street below was quiet, only an occasional car passed by in the fading light of day. Needing to comfort the grieving brother she said, "Let's go for a walk, Ed. Maybe that will make you feel better."

Taking her hand he pulled it to his chest. "You must be the sweetest girl on this earth, Sunshine Rose Moon."

"You're family feels like my family, Ed. I love each and every one of you." Tears flooded her eyes and she sobbed without shame, "I would have given my own life to save her. I really would have."

He stared at her without smiling and said, "I know you would, Rosie. Angel told me about the close call you two had earlier this summer, at the lake."

She turned from Ed and stepped to a box of tissue. Cleaning her face, she turned to him saying, "Let's take a walk, Ed. We can get something to eat at the hotel up the street."

They walked side by side watching the sidewalk disappear beneath their slow steps. The evening grew darker, and eventually they arrived at the hotel. Seated at a table near a window with a candle burning in a red glass, Rosie stared at the flame, thinking about the séance that had awakened the spirit in her home. "Do you believe in ghosts?" Without speaking he took a bottle of prescription pills from his pocket. She watched him take one pill and pop it into his mouth. He washed it down with beer then replaced the lid. She asked, "What's that you're taking?"

He sawed off a slice of bread from the small loaf they had been served saying, "Yes, I believe in ghosts, and it's none of your business about my medicine."

"I have a ghost in my house, and he haunts my dreams."

Ed motioned the waitress over and ordered another beer. "He isn't haunting you, Rosie. He's just attracted to your goodness and beauty. I know about being haunted. I know about seeing people die." Ed looked away quickly as the waitress brought his meal and beer to set before him.

Rosie sat back as the waitress set her food before her. "Ed, what do you think the ghost wants from me?"

"He wants to help you," he said gulping his beer and waving for the waitress.

"How much are you going to drink?"

Ed glared at her angrily, "Don't worry, I'm a big boy. I can look out for myself." He lit a cigarette, inhaling the first breath of smoke with relish.

Confounded with his egotistical behavior she snapped, "Are you really going to get intoxicated? How can you be so selfish?"

The sweet faced waitress returned to their table smiling. Ed ordered, "One more beer and the check, please."

Pushing her chair from the table Rosie said, "Well, I don't have to sit here, and watch you drown in beer."

He drained the beer with fast gulps.

She stood from her chair and turned to go, but Ed stepped in front of her. She allowed him to guide her out of the restaurant, determined to change the mood. "Tell me a joke, Ed."

They walked along the sidewalk, now bathed in street light as night had fallen. He tilted his head back, and looked through the branches of the trees they were passing under as he considered her request. "Okay, I'll tell you the joke Angel told me the other day." He looked at her sweetly and asked, "Why was six afraid of seven?"

With an amused smile she asked, "I don't know."

With a big smile Ed answered, "Because seven ate nine." His smile turned to a soft chuckle as Rosie's light laughter carried across the quiet street. Ed's chuckle soon became a thunderous laugh that evolved into heartbreaking tears. He doubled over with painful shoulder racking sobs.

Without thought she quickly embraced him, "Its okay, Ed. You go ahead and cry."

Through clenched teeth he spat angrily, "Haven't I seen enough tragedy? Haven't I been hurt enough already?" He stumbled to a bench, cradling his face in his hands. "I thought nothing could hurt worse than losing little Le Quan, but this is going to kill me." Tears ran down his strong handsome face, contorted with anguish.

She wrapped herself around him, "Talk to me Ed. Tell me how I can help you?"

He took her hands in his. Leaning back against the bench, he looked into the distance as though he were somewhere else. "Can I tell you about Le Quan?"

"Yes, please do."

His face softened with a sweet memory. "In Vietnam there are so many orphans." His gaze held to the infinite obscurity of the night. "These kids take up with the GI's, because the soldiers give them candy, and take time with them. Le Quan was about eight years old, or maybe older. He just seemed younger maybe, because he was so small." Ed seemed to relax as he remembered his little companion from the war. "That kid attached himself to me like a lost puppy. He was nothing but loyal, I mean we were tight!" Ed laughed from unspoken memories. "He even saved my life once. I was sleeping, and a gook was sneaking up behind me. Le Quan jumped up and threw a knife at that bastard, and the gook ran away." Ed laughed lightly.

Rosie laughed, too. "Well, he was a brave little booger wasn't he?" She pulled her hands free, and began rubbing the back of Ed's neck. "So, whatever happened to Le Quan? Did he find a family to live with in Vietnam?"

A dark look overcame the soldier's face as he answered, "No. Le Quan was killed. He was in a market square when a bomb blast ripped it apart." Ed's voice was cold and calm. "When I found him I tried to pick him up for one last hug. But, his tiny little body was so riddled it was like trying to pick up a rotting rag doll."

Her heart sank. "Oh, Ed," she said softly. "That's so sad. You have been wounded, terribly." Pressing her face against his neck she soothed, "Come on now. We need to see about your mother. She's hurting, too."

But, he sat heavily in place without making any attempt to rise, "What you said in the restaurant is true. I am selfish."

She soothed, "You're hurting, Ed. It's hard to help others when you're in so much pain yourself."

Ed turned to her, and in a moment of anguish pulled her close and kissed her deeply. For a long moment they sat embraced with the pain, and passion blurring all reason of right, or wrong. It was the sound of a familiar voice that disrupted their delirium.

"Hey!" Lewis shouted, "Don't let us get in your way here!" He stood beside his father on the sidewalk, just short of the bench Rosie and Ed shared in such a scandalous embrace. The look on his face was lethal, and Bob stood between his two sons speechless.

Pushing herself from Ed, Rosie stood trembling beneath the street lamp, "My God!" Clasping her hand to her mouth, tears glistened in her injured brown eyes. "I'm so sorry, Lewis." With a sorrowful look at Ed, she cried, "Oh, Ed, I'm so sorry!"

Lewis lunged for his brother, and Ed stood to defend himself. Bob grabbed Lewis, pulling him back from the altercation. "Stop this!" he shouted to his sons. "This just ain't going to happen tonight." He stood with his outstretched arms holding the two brothers from one another. Bob looked at Rosie and said, "You go on back and see about Opal, while I take care of this situation."

With a curt nod, she began walking briskly away. She found Opal sitting on the sofa holding a cup of tea. "Is Ed okay?"

Sitting opposite Opal she answered gently. "Bob and Lewis are with him."

Opal pulled back at the mention of her ex-husband's name, placing her teacup and saucer harshly on the coffee table. "Yes," she said dryly, "I've got to work out the preparations for the memorial service with Bob." She dropped her face into her hands and sobbed, "I'd do anything to make all of this not true!"

Rosie held her composure and responded to the bereaved mother. "Yes, I know you would, and so would I."

The sound of footsteps entering pulled their attention to the door. Ed and Bob stood shoulder to shoulder looking at the two grief stricken women sitting across from one another. Rosie asked, "Where is Lewis?" Her eyes darted past the father and son to the empty doorway.

Bob's gaze fell to his ex-wife's face as he said, "Lewis won't make it back tonight, but he'll see you tomorrow, Opal."

Rosie looked to Ed. He stood staring across the room at a family portrait hanging in an embellished silver frame. Softly she said, "I've got to be going now, Opal. I'll be close, so if you think of something that I can do to help," her voice trailed off as she considered how empty her words must sound.

Once again, she looked to the photo. There the Shirey family sat posed for the camera, dressed as if they had just come from church. Heartache seared her, and she left the apartment without saying goodbye.

Chapter Seventeen
The Late Night Side of Morning

The hospital room was dim and quiet as Rosie slept with her head pillowed against Kid's chest. The dream came before dawn in its usual fashion. She stepped from her front door onto the porch where the handsome man, in the white gentleman's hat, sat rocking in the chair. Feeling as though she was welcoming an old friend she smiled. Doc Campbell rose and approached the door, his hand closing over hers.

She pushed the door open asking, "Won't you please come inside?"

He stepped past her and removed his hat, showing dark hair with traces of gray. Walking toward the kitchen, he beseeched her to follow him with hand motion. Rosie followed him to the pantry door. He opened the door and instantly the sunlit garden appeared. She followed, stepping down the concrete steps with bare feet. She walked slowly, admiring the azure sky stretching beyond the bottle green landscape of grassy meadows. When she turned to face Doc his face was down turned and only the top of his hat was visible.

She stepped closer saying, "Excuse me, Doc." Astonishingly, he tilted his head to reveal the sweet handsome face of Lewis. "Oh! It's you." Stepping into his arms she closed her eyes as the scent of jasmine and brandy encircled her senses.

The morning sun radiated golden light across his smooth youthful face, and his voice was honeyed, "I didn't want to die. I never wanted to leave you."

Her pulse quickened, "You didn't die!" she exclaimed. "You never left me!" The wind became a quiet fury, blowing her hair and whipping her nightgown. The garden grew dark as the fluffy white clouds were now gray, suffocating the sun's rays. Flowers were cruelly blown to and fro, and the trees twisted grotesquely in the impending storm. She stretched out her hand, "Let's go inside!"

Bending his head forward he replaced the hat. When he raised his face again he was no longer the handsome young Lewis, but the older gentleman of a previous century. "You will find what you need in the pharmacy," he said. Then he turned and began to walk away through the garden, and into the oncoming storm.

She screamed against the wind, "Come back! Come back!"

Awakened by Kid softly shaking her shoulder, Rosie opened her eyes to the unfamiliar darkened hospital room. Pushing herself upright in the oversized chair she shared with him, she looked about. Blinking, she focused on the small form of a child's body sitting upright in the hospital bed. To no one in particular Rosie asked, "What time is it?"

From the darkness came the cold emotionless voice of a shattered heart, "The late night side of morning." LED lights from a switchboard wall panel surrounded the small bed-bound form, casting her in an eerie halo.

Rosie said, "Yes, the late night side of morning seems to greet me more and more often these days." Closing her eyes, a new fear crept in; threatening to extinguish the very air she needed to breathe. September was coming nearer with each passing day, and Kid would be leaving for school. What would she do without his strength to carry her? She caught a ragged breath and asked, "How are you feeling?"

From obscure darkness Janie answered, "Numb; I'm feeling nothing." The rustle of stiff sheets rippled through the shadows as the little girl wiggled restlessly. "I think they must have given me some zombie medicine, so I can't feel or think or sleep."

Kid spoke softly, "Are you thirsty, Janie? I can get you a soda, or some milk."

Through the darkness Janie asked, "Have the Shirey's made the arrangements yet?"

"What arrangements?" Kid responded, carefully.

"For Angel's funereal," replied the child simply.

Rosie went to stand at the window where the neon's glow profiled her delicate features against the gray skyline. An electric sign glowed from the pharmacy next door, advertising a coffee shop opened for business at daybreak. Standing as an outline, she listened to his gentle voice.

"I suppose they are in the process of all that, but who told you Angel died?"

The room radiated frost as Janie replied, "Nobody had to tell me anything. I was there." A deep breath was inhaled and expelled as she asked, "When will I get to leave this place, Kid?"

Reaching out he caressed her hand saying gently, "Soon, baby doll, real soon."

Dr. Martin came in a little past seven o'clock. He looked over her chart, asking questions. "How did you sleep last night, Janie?"

In a mature manner she answered, "I didn't. I slept all afternoon." Her attention was diverted to the opening door.

Maggie and Shelley stepped inside. Maggie carried a vase with pink carnations, "Good morning sweet heart!"

With a beseeching look Janie asked, "Did my mother call?"

Maggie looked away and cautiously answered, "No, dear. Not yet."

Dr. Martin said, "Now, Janie, I want you to eat breakfast even if you don't feel like it. The nurse will be in later. If you have any more stress related incidents you may have to stay another night. Do you understand that it is important for you to remain calm?" He waited patiently until his patient nodded her head in understanding before leaving the room.

Shelley approached her little sister cautiously, "Do you like the flowers?"

"Yes, thank you." Janie smiled as she asked mischievously, "What would America be if everyone drove a pink car?" When no one had an answer she explained, "A pink car nation."

Light laughter filled the room with Maggie asking, "Do you know about Angel's condition?"

"What condition? She's dead." Janie's face was pale and serious.

Maggie dropped her face as her composure crumbled. Leaning toward Janie, Shelley cried, "Oh! Janie, why weren't you holding her hand? You might have saved her!"

To everyone's incredible shock, Maggie agreed sobbing, "Why didn't you hold her hand?"

"Do you hear what you're saying?" asked Kid, his voice angry. "How can you say that?" His teary eyes sparkled like sapphires, "Thank God you were on the other side of the road! Don't you see God was looking out for you?"

Her anger exploded. "Where was God when my daddy put a gun to his head? And, where was God when he let that hurricane take my home away, and leave my mommy lost in Mississippi?" Kid tried to console her, but it was useless as Janie wailed piteously, "It's my fault Angel was killed, and there is no God!"

Moments passed silently following Janie's outburst. Hospital service personnel entered with a breakfast tray. Speaking cheerfully as she set the tray in front of the little girl, she lifted the dome cover revealing scrambled eggs, bacon, toast and grits. Janie looked at the food, snarling her displeasure at the sight of it.

Kid offered to help prepare her meal by putting some butter on her toast, but she only grimaced and said it didn't matter, because she wasn't hungry. Rosie reminded her that Dr. Martin had said it was important she eat in order to be released from the hospital. Taking up the fork, the little girl prepared to take a bite of the unappetizing food.

With her fork posed, unable to go any further, Maggie snapped from across the room, "Eat your breakfast, Janie!"

Glaring angrily at her grandmother she dropped the fork onto the plate with a loud clatter. "Why don't you eat it!" she yelled at Maggie, and shoved the entire tray from the table onto the floor at Maggie's feet.

A nurse entered the room just in time to witness the outburst, and she said to everyone in the room, "Clear this room now, everybody out!"

Maggie and Shelley rushed past Rosie and out the door. She stayed until Kid pulled her away while Janie screamed at the nurse, "Stop! Stop! Leave me alone! I just want to die! Please, let me die!" Her words were heartbreaking, and Rosie wilted into sobs of despair. As Kid helped her through the door and into the hallway, they could hear Janie crying to the nurse, "I could have saved her! If only I had been holding her hand, I could have saved her! It's my fault she's gone!"

They found Maggie and Shelley in the large waiting area at the entrance of the hospital facing the parking lot. Kid approached his grandmother and said, "If you can't be any more help to Janie than you were just now, then you should go home and not come back."

Maggie's face fell with shock at his words. Anger crept into her as she spit back, "How dare you speak to me like that! Don't you know I will slap you?" She drew her hand back in a threatening gesture.

Kid crossed his arms across his chest, and continued his attack. "All summer long I watched the two of you push that little girl aside, as though she were no more important than an old shoe, constantly getting under your feet." His eyes narrowed as he looked from Shelley to Maggie.

"What do you mean?" Maggie demanded.

"I mean the way you are always doing embroidery for Shelley, or one thing or another, and when Janie asks for the same attention you tell her you haven't got enough time." He turned on Shelley, pointing his finger in her face, "I know how that kid got the scar across her arm, and I saw you deliberately shove her off her bicycle. Do you have any idea of what I'd like to do you?" He pursed his lips in contempt and threatened, "If you were a man I'd just show you!"

Shelley responded venomously, "Yeah, Kid. You know, that might actually scare me. If *you* were a man," she reached for Maggie's hand, and pulled her grandmother away.

Rosie stepped toward the exit as others looked on in curiosity. "Let's go next door and have some breakfast, Kid."

He followed along. The August morning was awash in humid stillness, leaving the air void of any breeze. The pharmacy was buzzing with conversation and clattering coffee cups, and it offered very little air conditioning. She stepped inside and gazed around the familiar store. Echoed words from the haunting dream followed her as shelves of pharmaceuticals caught her eye.

Sliding into a booth, Rosie motioned for Kid to do likewise. A waitress brought small glasses of ice water, and laid a menu before each of them. After gulping from the glass she gushed, "I'm being haunted by a ghost that's a hundred years dead."

The waitress returned and a deafening quiet fell between them. Rosie continued once the waitress was past hearing range, "It all started after that séance. I've been dreaming about this man, and I researched some of the county history books. And, I found him."

Tossing the hair back from his face he asked, "Who, Sunny? Who did you find?"

Her bottom lip trembled, "The man I've been dreaming about is Doc Campbell."

"The same ghost that possessed me at the séance?"

She nodded her head yes.

"Well," he said simply, "That's why you should come home with me." Looking about the small crowded pharmacy, and judging it to be inferior to those back home, Kid announced, "We can be married before the month is over, and you can be free from all your ghosts and demons."

Sitting back she gazed at her handsome relation across the table while logic closed around her like prison bars. "How could I leave? You know Janie needs me."

"Go ahead and say it, Sunshine," he taunted mildly, "Lewis needs you, too."

The mention of his name pained her. "Oh, Kid! After last night I don't know if Lewis will ever want to see me again." During breakfast she confessed every detail of the previous evening.

He listened intently, and when she had finished simply said, "So, doesn't Lewis know he has nothing to worry about from Ed?"

Intrigued she asked, "What do you mean?"

"Ed has some medical problems. He can't get an erection."

"How would you know?" she asked, rather alarmed.

"Well, one night when me and Jude ran into Ed at a bar, and well, we were drinking and talking." Kid paused then blurted "Ed told me and Jude that he was under a doctor's care, and he explained some of his problems." Picking up his toast he held it in mid air to take a bite, but decided to finish his comment first, "That's how I know."

Slumping in her seat Rosie said, "No, I don't think Lewis knows."

Around mid-day, Rosie returned home and walked up the plank steps to the back door. When she stepped into the kitchen and found Eva working with an apron on, she asked with furrowed brows, "Did Lewis call?"

Eva rustled through some papers and held one out for Rosie. "No, but Ed called, and some others."

Silently impressed that Eva had written down the date and time of each call, she said, "Thank you, Eva." She turned to leave the kitchen, but was taken with inquisitiveness upon seeing the pantry door partly ajar.

Swinging open the door she stepped inside. A string hung from the bare bulb above, and she pulled it on. Reaching her hand out to the shelf with the extraordinary coldness she pondered the curiosity. As she turned to leave a small shaker jar of cinnamon was knocked over, falling to the floor. Reaching down to retrieve the bottle of spice, a cobweb caught her attention. The grey fluffy mass shivered as a draft of air was expelled from the other side of the wall. Straightening, she looked at the wall of shelves and pushed against it, but it stood fast. Using a fly swat, she stooped and inserted the wire handle through the cobweb into the drafty space between the walls. To her surprise, the wire handle went through the crack all the way to the flat plastic flap. Baffled, she wiggled the wire furiously. There appeared to be nothing but dead space behind the wall.

Eva's voice abruptly took her attention, "Would you like for me to fix you a sandwich, Rosie?"

She straightened to face her stepmother who had a long cigarette hanging from the corner of her mouth. "No, thank you. I just had breakfast at the drug store. Do you know of the arrangements for Angel's memorial?" She pulled the light off with the string, replaced the fly swat, and stepped out of the pantry, closing the door.

"Yes. The viewing will be tonight from six to eight, and burial is scheduled for tomorrow at two." Eva stepped to the counter where she dumped the ash from her cigarette into a crystal ashtray. "I called and ordered flowers. I asked for pink carnations and white roses."

Rosie's lips curled into a soft smile as she remembered the pink car nation joke. "I need to take a nap," she said dryly.

Wandering from the kitchen into the living room, she stepped out onto the porch. The spider plant was hanging from its hook and the old weathered rocker still held the potted fern. Leafy wisteria vines cast a soothing shade where the rocking chair sat motionless in the shadows. She stepped back inside and closed the front door softly just as a soothing breeze picked up from the East and sailed across the porch, causing the spider plant to sway gently and the forlorn old chair to slowly rock.

Kid returned to Janie's hospital room to find his grandfather with her. "How are you feeling, kiddo?"

"My mother still hasn't called," she answered. "She didn't want to talk with me the last time she called, anyway." Janie smoothed the hospital gown across her knees and explained, "Maybe she doesn't love me anymore; maybe she never did."

Bert scoffed, "What do you mean?" He leaned over and tousled her uncombed hair. "Everybody loves you, especially your mother!"

Reaching into his shirt pocket Bert withdrew a letter addressed to Kid. He looked inside the envelope and found an airplane ticket. "Dad wants me to fly home?"

"You must be home by the twenty-eighth to register for school." He slapped his grandson playfully on the back, "summer is spent, son."

Chapter Eighteen
Beware of Those You Love

The funeral home parking lot was full. Crowds milled about on the lawn of the mortuary, and those crowded inside were speaking within a roar of hushed voices. Sturgill and Rosie signed the guest register before entering the chapel. Once inside she searched the crowd of faces for Lewis without finding him present. Stepping into the chapel she could see almost every seat was filled. Opal stood at the head of Angel's casket, greeting those who came to pay condolence.

Her voice was hoarse and raspy from her endless flow of tears, "Oh, Rosie! How can this be?" Opal sobbed in a voice barely louder than a whisper, "She was only a baby!"

Ed stepped alongside his mother and clasped hands with Sturgill. They exchanged greetings as Rosie stepped to the casket to view her lost friend. Angel's long smooth blonde hair had been combed into a flat wave that lay across each shoulder. Her bangs lay flat across her brow, just as they always had. She was dressed in a soft flowing pink dress of sheer organza over satin. The smocked bodice was adorned with pink daisies and green stems sprouting ivy leaves, and the cuffs were smocked likewise at the wrist; her fingernails buffed to a shimmering shine.

Taking a breath Rosie stepped back and closed her eyes in prayer. Unable to hold her composure any longer, she threw herself into her father's arms and cried miserably. Sturgill slowly pulled his daughter away from the casket, with Ed following.

Consoling his daughter with soft words, Sturgill rocked her in his arms as he did in years long past. When she was dry of tears he said, while rubbing a hand edgily up his arm, "I just saw Kid come in. Will it be alright if I ask him to drive you home?"

Understanding his anxiety she nodded in agreement, "I don't know when I'll be home, because we'll be going to the hospital."

"You do whatever you need to do, darling," agreed Sturgill just before going in search of Kid.

Facing Ed, shame swept through her, "How's Lewis?"

Ed exhaled softly, "Lew is a total wreck. He won't talk to anybody." He shoved his hands inside his trouser pockets and said, "I think he's still around here, somewhere. But he's so angry with me." Ed cut off his sentence, saying, "I want you to know how sorry I am for my behavior last night. I was completely out of line."

She looked about to see if her words might be overheard. "I, too, am guilty." It was airless in the stifling corridor, and she turned to make her exit coming face to face with Lewis.

He was silent and pale. She waited without breath for him to speak, but he didn't. He walked past, entered the chapel and disappeared beyond a wall of floral arrangements. Heartache blurred her vision as she walked through the crowd of people gathered in the parlor. A soft hand closed around hers and she turned to see her cloistered neighbor sitting in an upholstered chair. Rosie sank to the chair's arm asking tearfully, "How can life go on?"

Willene pushed Rosie's hair from her face with a kind touch and said, "Nobody says it will be easy."

A tall slender man approached speaking a soft greeting to Willene. She only gave the man a silent nod in return. "Who is that man?" asked Rosie. "He looks familiar."

"Yes, he should. I believe he's one of Eva's friends," retorted Willene sarcastically, "Bonzie Leak."

"Oh, yes. I remember him." Absent mindedly she watched the man circulate through the room and remarked casually, "He smokes those skinny cigars."

Kid arrived saying gently, "Sturgill said you need a ride."

Willene spoke encouragingly, "Go ahead, Rosie. Go see about Janie."

"Yes, I should go now," she mumbled tiredly, "Goodbye, Willene."

They rode together in silent darkness to the hospital. Kid didn't speak, as Rosie twisted the dial on the radio searching for some heart mending music. Clutching her hair against her shoulder to keep it from tangling in the wind, she watched the starlit sky hang above them as they rolled along the smooth highway. After parking in the designated area, she waited for Kid to put the rag-top up before they entered the hospital.

"I want you to pay attention to me, Sunshine. You will need to know how to put the top up and down when I'm gone."

"What do you mean?"

"I'll be flying home in a couple of days, and I'm leaving you my car." He walked around and joined her. "My dad sent a plane ticket. I have to leave the day after tomorrow."

She rushed into his arms crying, "Oh, Kid! I'll miss you so much." Peeling from him she said, "You made this summer magic. I had the best time of my life, thanks to you."

Clasping her hand in his, he tugged her along. When they reached Janie's room she looked at him, eyes shining from suppressed tears, and confessed, "I love you, Kid." Then, without waiting for a response, she pushed open the door and stepped inside.

Maggie was seated in the large chair beside the bed, as Janie sat propped up watching TV. When they entered the room the child's eyes sparkled with questions, "Hello, you two! Did you visit Angel? How does she look?"

Kid sat on the edge of her bed saying, "She is more beautiful than I've ever seen her."

Maggie stood and said, "Well, since you two are here, I think I'll stretch my legs for a minute, and get myself a cup of tea." The strain of worry showed on the elder woman's face as she departed the room with slow, painful steps.

"Kid," asked Janie, "Can I go with you to the airport when you have to leave?"

"As a matter of fact, I would like for Rosie and you to both see me off." He watched Rosie's eyes twinkle from withheld tears. "Because you two are my favorite people in this whole world, and I want it to be your faces that I see last when I have to leave Alabama."

The night before Angel's funeral was a sleepless one for the girls. Darkness engulfed the rooms where they attempted to rest, but a cruel anxiety kept sleep at bay. Just as dawn approached, Rosie succumbed to a fitful dream. She looked down to see the cold concrete steps below her feet, and knew she was at the threshold of the pharmacy. Through the shadows she could see the dismal dark room of rock walls and stone floor alighted by a single hurricane lamp. The man with the white hat sat in the rocking chair holding a dark leather covered box, his jacket folded and resting on the back of the chair. Slowly he raised his head to reveal the handsome face with dark eyes and fashionable mustache. He raised his hand and motioned for her to come closer.

Suddenly, she became startled. Her feet were unable to move from the concrete steps, she was paralyzed! Frightened, she asked, "What do you want?"

He stood from the chair saying, "Everything you need is in the pharmacy." Placing the box on a shelf, he took his jacket and slipped into it. After smoothing wrinkles from the sleeves, he turned to leave.

Franticly she searched for the correct words to say, but when she opened her mouth she couldn't speak! As the phantom man prepared to walk away she desperately searched for her voice. "Dr. Campbell!" she shouted, and was astonished when he turned to face her. "Where are you going?"

The handsome doctor answered, "I'm going to save you." Then he turned and stepped through the stone walls, vanishing like a vapor. Rosie turned from the pharmacy and stepped away. When she decided to turn back and enter she was confronted by the shelves of her own pantry. She pushed against the shelves, but the wooden structure didn't yield.

Stepping from the food closet into the kitchen Rosie was awash in a soft white light. There bathed in a heavenly glow stood Angel dressed in her burial shroud. Tears of joy traveled down Rosie's cheeks, "Angel! I'm so happy to see you!" Oddly, her voice echoed through the room as if she stood at the precipice of a great hollow divide.

The radiant child responded, "I've come to say goodbye."

"No, don't go!"

"I'm so sorry, Rosie. Can you forgive me? I didn't mean to die. I'm so very, very sorry." With a glance heavenward she said with a look of joyous anticipation, "I'm going to be very happy, Rosie. You must be happy, too." Having delivered her message, she turned to walk away on the fluffy cloud-like path. With one last message she turned and said, "Beware of those you love. They can hurt you. Follow your heart, and you will find happiness." She continued walking into the radiant clouds.

"Don't go! Don't go!" cried Rosie.

Uncontrollable sobs awoke her, with tears soaking her pillow. The ache of watching Angel go into the clouds pained her with depressing sorrow. She clung to her pillow and cried until she could cry no more. Sleep would not come again, and in the darkness she stepped lightly into the kitchen, looking for any sign of ghostly apparitions. None was to be found.

Daylight came slowly over the horizon as Rosie sat at the kitchen table with her second cup of herb tea. The vivid dream was played over and over in her mind. She heard the alarm clock ringing in her father's room, bringing awareness of how little she'd slept since the disturbing dreams had begun.

Eva entered and seemed surprised to find Rosie there. "Are you alright, Rosie?"

"I just couldn't sleep." She went to the sink and placed her teacup. "Eva, do you have a black dress that I can borrow for the funeral?"

Eva answered slowly, "I'm not sure." She pulled a skillet from the bottom drawer of the stove and said, "You'll just have to look through my closet." As she positioned the skillet she added, "Feel free to help yourself to anything you can find, dear."

"Thank you, Eva." Rosie left to sit on the porch.

The battered rocking chair lurked in gray shadows as the sun continued to rise in the hazy morning sky. She removed the potted fern, brushed the dust from the seat and slowly sank into the chair. Resting her head against the tall back she closed her eyes and drifted into a peaceful slumber, where images flashed in comforting fragments of memory. Only a few minutes had passed when she awakened with a start, her heart pounding. Anxiety crept over her and she wondered how she would ever survive the day.

Dressed in a black dress that belonged to Eva, Rosie stood before a mirror. The skirt was full and the waist was tight. The bodice was lace covered satin and the short sleeves were of delicate black lace. The dress zipped along the side, and the fit was perfect. The time neared noon and she hurriedly pinned her hair into a twist. With the gold studs glistening in her earlobes, she smudged makeup under her eyes to hide the dark circles.

Eva appeared at her bedroom door holding a small black clutch purse, "I thought you might like to use this today."

"Thank you, Eva."

"I put a ladies handkerchief inside for you. I thought you might need that, considering the sad occasion." Eva turned to leave, "Don't forget to take the cake to the Shirey's house on your way out."

"Yes, I won't forget."

Bert stood at the nurse's desk signing papers for his granddaughter's discharge. His attention was diverted as a nurse pushed Janie from her hospital room in a wheel chair. Maggie followed carrying the pink carnations and colorful balloons. "Well, now!" Bert declared as he stuffed the folded papers into his shirt pocket. "I think ole' Charlie and Teddy will be happy to see you get back home."

The nurse wheeled Janie outside the entrance doors to Bert's car, and she happily settled into the back seat, taking possession of the balloons. Once they were driving away from the hospital, Janie broke the silence with a childish question. "Is Angel already in heaven?"

The grandmother looked tiredly at her husband and answered, "I don't know, dear."

"She came to say goodbye to me this morning, and I saw her walk the path back to heaven," explained Janie while watching the balloons bob against the roof of the car, missing the worried exchange between her grandparents.

Rosie stood at the back door of the Shirey farmhouse. She had knocked twice, but no one had responded. She tried the door knob, and it turned. Pushing open the back door she called into the house, "Hello! It's me, Rosie." She stepped inside and set the cake plate on the counter along with other food items brought in by friends and neighbors.

The house appeared empty, and only Bob's car sat alone in the driveway. Stepping to the corridor, she peered toward Lewis' room. A sad melancholy piano tune wafted from the other side of the door. Slowly she stepped to the door and knocked upon it. There was no answer. She turned the knob and the door swung open. Lewis sat on the edge of his bed staring at the book Janie and Angel had made for him after his adventure at Woodstock. It was propped on a chest of drawers, with newspaper photos of the famous *Alabama Teen* framed on the wall behind it.

"Lewis, didn't you hear me calling?" He sat unyielding, staring at the childish art work of his little sister. Gingerly she stepped around the bed. "Lewis, will you please answer me?"

His eyes blinked at her touch, as though lost in catatonia. Sinking onto the bed next to him she clasped his hand within hers. "Do you need a ride to the chapel?" Suddenly, she felt uncomfortably out of place. Leaning her head over to rest on his shoulder she became aware of the strange scent of lilac and brandy. Looking around the room she noticed an air freshener that was responsible for the floral scent. Pulling back she asked, "Have you been drinking?" But he said nothing. The memory of the eerie dream overpowered her with alarming déjà vu.

Taking her hands from his she said, "I'm going now. I'll see you at the chapel." She started to rise, but he caught her with a steely grip.

Looking down at the white knuckles gripping her wrist, panic stirred, but she calmly looked him in the eye. The dark coldness of his expression was terrifying, and her effort to stay calm, valiant. He stood and purposely went to his bedroom door, bolting it closed. Rosie stood from the bed as Lewis approached her, saying with a quiver to her tone, "Would you say something, please! You're acting like someone I've never seen!"

When he stepped into the filtered sunlight of window sheers, she could see his face clearly, the eyes red rimmed and rheumy, dark sunken shadows behind the lids, lashes matted and pupils as large as the iris. Absent was all reason, for he was demonized by pain, enraged by betrayal and hell bent on retribution. In a petrified whisper she pleaded, "Please, Lewis, I should go!"

The sound of his name on her lips sent him into a fury. Grabbing her hair he spat hot words with breath that felt like steam, "Who's going to save you now? Where's Ed? Where's your hero?"

Bracing against him with both arms she found courage and voiced it. "I need no one to save me! Not from you!"

He abruptly jerked her hair upward, pulling her on tip toes. A chilling giggle escaped him as she whimpered, and he rasped in a voice heated by brandy, "Where's your hero, Ed?"

Anger, fear, disbelief and survival swam through her, choking her breath and squelching her speech into a rasp of winded words, "Please, stop! Let go of me!"

When he clutched her close for a forceful kiss, she pulled back only to slam her forehead into the bridge of his nose. He staggered from the blow, his pupils eclipsing the iris. Steely black coal glowed within sunken eye sockets. She screamed when he forcefully flung her upon the bed. Bouncing off the other side she jumped for the bolted door. Before she could open it he had his arms around her from behind. He picked her up and fell onto the bed, with her beneath him. Face down in a pillow she struggled to get free, but he held her arms pinned above her head. Her cries of protest were muffled, and she began to panic, thinking of suffocation.

He lifted her skirt, tearing at her underwear. Unthinkable imaginings raced through her mind and she fought desperately. Weak from the fight and inability to breathe, he penetrated her from behind. The savage act blinded her with hot mortification. Upon his satisfaction, he released her. She heard the bedroom door open and close as she sobbed into the pillow. The sound of a car's engine driving away floated through the stillness of the empty house. Long minutes passed before she could pull herself together. She retrieved the torn panties from the floor, and standing in the doorway, looked at the wrinkled bedcovers showing evidence of the violation. Shame besieged her and she ran from the house crying.

She sat weeping inside the car. Catching a glimpse of herself in the rearview mirror she observed her hair spilling from the carefully styled twist. Looking a disheveled mess, Rosie opened the small beaded purse and stuffed the torn panties into it, then used the delicate handkerchief to wipe her swollen eyes and clear her nose. Looking about the deserted driveway she remembered Angel's warning from the dream, "Beware of those you love. They may hurt you."

The television noise drowned out the sound of her coming into the back door. Quickly, she rushed to the bathroom and undressed. Pushing her hair into a shower cap, she stepped into a warm rush of water. Tears of degradation escaped as she remembered every moment of his brutal attack. Over and over she wondered, "How could he hate me so?" Suds circled the drain, and then disappeared, taking evidence of the violation with them.

After the shower she stood before the steam fogged mirror, and wiped away a space large enough to look into her own eyes. Vengeance reflected from the glass. Never had she felt such hatred. Vowing to herself, she swore to make Lewis pay dearly for his brutality.

The browning corn field stretched for acres as Janie stared out the glass door into the distance. Kid entered, breaking into her thoughts. "You look like a real lady in that dress."

"Angel came to say goodbye to me this morning," said Janie simply. "She was so beautiful, dressed in a billowy pink gown with pink daisies embroidered into the tiny little ruffles across her gown here," motioning to her own bodice. "And here," she pointed to her wrists. "She asked me to forgive her. She said that she didn't mean to die. And, then she walked away on a path of clouds into the sky, toward a beautiful bright light." Falling quiet she turned to look beyond the cornfield again.

Stunned into silence, Kid knew that neither he nor Rosie had discussed Angel's burial shroud with Janie, and neither of his grandparents or Shelley had attended the viewing. Befuddled by her uncanny wisdom, he followed her gaze to the fatigued field of sun-bleached withering maze.

Deliberately waiting until the hour of the service, Rosie approached the church, her heels clicking on the asphalt parking lot. She had dressed in a sleek gray skirt, with a thin white cotton blouse. Beneath, she wore a lace slip, barely covering the bra that she had tightened to hold her breast upward and ready to spill from the cups. With hair loosely pinned and ample make up to cover the dark circles, she looked like a fashion model. Artistically, she had enhanced her eyes with sultry charcoal eyeliner, and her lips glistened with pink tinted gloss. Her vengeful goal was to torture Lewis with something that would never be his again.

The chapel was spilling over. Rosie stepped in past some men standing outside on the steps. The hazy gray sky offered no relief from the suffocating heat. Inching her way inside the foyer she could hear the minister's voice echoing across the chapel in an incoherent rumble. She stepped back outside as the wind began to pick up and dry leaves, dehydrated from the August heat, were blown about with tiny whirlwinds of dust.

In the distance thunder rumbled, sending mutters through the men who stood outside with her. The choir could be heard singing *Amazing Grace,* and the pall bearers emerged with the small white casket adorned by a large floral spray accentuated with pink and white roses. The Shirey family followed the casket, standing steady as the pall bearers placed it inside a hearse, to be driven into the cemetery.

Anxious eyes looked skyward to the darkening clouds. Rosie deliberately fell into step beside Ed. Numbed by his grief, Ed took no notice. She walked hand-in-hand with him behind the hearse to the cemetery.

The tent covering the gravesite waved in the angry wind as if it might at any moment take flight. Many of the mourners didn't follow, due to the impending storm. Rosie stood close to Ed as the preacher gave the final prayer. The wind began to buffet the family and the funeral home personnel. Ed led Rosie to his car as big drops of rain began to fall around them. By the time they reached his car the stinging rain was upon them like enraged bees.

He sat back and pounded his fist on the steering wheel in frustration. "Hand me that flask in the glove compartment." Reaching in, she removed his ever present flagon. After three gulps he sighed loudly, "Ah! That's better. Here have some."

Remembering the potent rum, she sipped it carefully. Handing over the container, she noticed his attention transfixed on something in the cemetery. Following his gaze, she saw Robert and Bob struggling to pull Lewis from the tent covered gravesite. The wind driven rain soaked the men as they overtook Lewis with physical force, dragging him away as he resisted in screaming hysteria.

"Dear God!" Ed proclaimed, "He's gone mad!"

"He's been drinking," she said as a matter of fact.

Ed sighed, "Yeah, and that's not all. I gave him two Quaaludes." Ed shook his head sadly, "I never would have done it if I had known he was going to empty Mamie's brandy decanter." Ed took another sip of rum, "The poor bastard won't remember any of this tomorrow. He doesn't even remember how he got two black eyes today."

Her heart lunged, "You mean to tell me Lewis is acting crazy because he's overdosed on your medicine?"

Ed tipped his flask saying, "I just know he's stoned as hell, and that's the way I'm gonna be in about five more minutes."

The rain slacked to a drizzle. Specks of water accumulated on the windshield, and for a long moment no one spoke. In an anesthetized state of mind Rosie emerged, walking blindly to Eva's car. She searched in the back floorboard until she found an old umbrella. Opening the umbrella above her, she started back to the tent covered grave. She lifted her head as Bob drove by with Lewis and Robert seated in back. Through the rain speckled window she saw Lewis, his face blank and emotionless. As the car got nearer she could see the bruises beneath both eyes. Lewis recognized her, and dove across his grandfather, pounding on the car window and screaming her name in anguish.

Blinded by tears she stumbled back to the car, and sat inside while the rain sprinkles once again became a raging torrent. Clinching her eyes shut, she thought of the peaceful white light that pacified her the day she was drowning. If the bright calming light had been imminent death, than she wished to succumb to the brilliance. Thunder rolled off the mountainside, tumbling away within seconds of time, leaving Rosie behind with nothing but her grief.

Chapter Nineteen
Ticket to Ride

Kid's car was in the driveway at the Moon farmhouse when Rosie returned from the funeral. She entered the house through the back door. Eva was removing a meat loaf from the oven, and the kitchen smelled of sautéed onions and freshly baked bread. "Oh, good, you're home," she said. "Kid and Janie are staying for dinner. Would you help me set the table?"

Stepping to the cupboard, Rosie began to remove place settings for the dining table. Eva stopped her by saying, "Let's use the good china tonight. After all, Kid is leaving us tomorrow."

Her eyes grew wide in surprise at her stepmother's hospitality. She walked into the dining room, and took the special occasion dishes from the china cabinet. After setting the table, she wandered into the living room where her guests sat with Sturgill.

Janie rushed into her arms and embraced her. "I didn't see you at the church today."

"Yes, that's because I got there late." Her eyes fell on Kid across the room, and she spoke directly to him, "I hope you know Eva has gone all out for your last supper here in Alabama." Taking a deep breath she turned to her father, "How was your day, Daddy?"

A look of consternation crossed his face. "It come a toad strangler down on the river, just as it was time for us to come home. How was your day, sweetheart?"

Memories of Lewis and the event that took place in his bedroom flooded her. She closed her eyes tightly, trying to push aside the recollection, and hold back the tears.

Sturgill put his arm around his daughter and pulled her close to him, "Now, that's okay." He patted her gently, "Just try to forget all about it now. We're having a special meal, and Kid and Janie are spending the whole night with you. You can stay up as late as you want. This is Kid's last night, and we're going to have some fun!" Sturgill reached for a box of tissues.

Accepting the tissue Rosie dabbed her eyes. Suddenly something jogged her memory. "Daddy, what's behind the pantry in the kitchen?"

Sturgill shrugged his shoulders, "I don't know. Why?"

"When I was cleaning out a cob web I pushed the wire end of the fly swat into a crack. And, there's some open space back there."

"I guess that's the closet where the hot water heater is next to the laundry room."

"Yes that must be it," she reasoned.

The family enjoyed a pleasant dinner with animated conversation. It became apparent that Eva had made special efforts to show her domestic side to Kid, as a way to convey a message to his father. She said, "Now, Kid, when you get back home you be sure to tell your folks that we fed you, and treated you just like one of us."

"Okay, I certainly will," said Kid kindly.

After the dinner dishes were cleared, Rosie helped Janie set up her *Dark Shadows* board game. As each player attempted to complete the skeleton to win the game, Kid kept cracking jokes. "Who knows why the skeleton wouldn't cross the road?"

Looking at each other tiredly the girls asked in unison, "Why?"

"Because, he didn't have the guts!" exclaimed Kid, joyously.

After winning the game, he pulled the plastic vampire teeth from the cardboard casket. "Oh!" he exclaimed fiendishly with the plastic teeth protruding from his lips. "Who do I want to bite first?" He grabbed Janie and exclaimed, "You!" He pulled her against him as she struggled and squealed.

Taking the plastic teeth from his mouth, he went to the sink to rinse them off. Walking back to the table he dried them with a paper towel, and replaced them in the game box. He asked with a silly tone, "Now do you want me to entertain you by lighting my farts on fire?"

Janie said wryly, "If you don't stop doing that you're going to make an ash of yourself." They all burst into laughter.

Feeling the exhaustion of the day catch up with her, Rosie said, "I think I want to put on something comfortable, and settle down in front of the television for a while." She turned to Janie and asked, "Do you know if anything good is coming on?"

"Elvis is on tonight!" When Janie noted the sour look between the two she said encouragingly, "It's one of his better movies."

Still dressed in the skirt and sheer blouse, Rosie asked, "Well, do you want to put on your night clothes before we watch it?"

"Yeah, I'm sleeping in the t-shirt Kid brought me from Woodstock." Then she looked to him and asked, "What are you wearing to sleep in?"

With a devilish grin he said, "I sleep in the nude."

Rosie gave him a shove saying, "Not tonight you don't!"

Janie scolded, "Stop acting like a boy!" and burst into peels of giggles when Kid grabbed her, and holding her upside down, carried her to Rosie's room where he tossed her on the bed. Bouncing from the bed, Janie ran to Kid, who grabbed her up and tossed her onto the bed again. Meanwhile, Rosie took her nightgown, and retreated to the bathroom.

While stripping off the clothing she had worn to the funeral, depression crawled into her heart like an insidious shadow, clouding her thoughts and darkening her emotions. The reflection in the mirror showed dark eyes with a stranger's wisdom. Heart sickness overcame her, with the realization that this day had changed her, forever.

Entering her room dressed for the night, she found Kid and Janie waiting for her patiently. Wearing her oversized Woodstock souvenir, Janie was obviously comfortable. Dressed in gym shorts and a white t-shirt, Kid sat cross legged on the bed while Janie wove a string across her fingers in an intricate pattern. Instructed to put his hand inside the puzzle web, she trapped his hand, but then with only one small move, the string fell away leaving him unshackled.

"Great, you're ready to watch the movie," said Janie to Rosie, tossing her circle of string onto the bedside table, and jumping to her feet.

Rosie walked over and stretched out on the bed, "It's not time yet." She rolled onto her side, "Have you guys got tonight's sleeping arrangement all worked out?"

Enthusiastically Janie said, "Let's not sleep at all. Let's just stay up all night!"

Kid winked, "Yeah, Sunny, let's just stay up all night."

With just as much enthusiasm she said, "Let's not!" Then she said without thinking, "We're going to miss you, Kid."

Later, the threesome sat on the sofa and watched the movie credits roll while Elvis sang, *Follow That Dream*. The late news came next with the lead story focused on the hurricane ravaged Mississippi coast. Television footage was harrowing, as the appalling damage was shown in the wake of Camille. The number of deaths was noted, as was the number of people still missing.

Kid quickly turned the channel. Janie sat with a dull look staring at the screen and said, "You didn't have to do that, you know."

"What do you mean?" he asked. "We don't want to watch news."

"You can't shield me from the truth. I know what's going on, and I don't care. It doesn't bother me. It did at first, but not anymore."

"What truth, Janie?" asked Rosie.

With little forethought the child blurted out, "Mama isn't dead, but she's going to pretend to be, just so she doesn't have to be bothered with Shelley and me." She abruptly stood and walked across the room to peer beyond the screen door into the velvety darkness of nightfall where the fading season was filled with desperate calls of nocturnal life.

Carefully, Kid said, "I don't think she's dead, either."

Janie whirled to face him, anger staining her face, "She's not dead! And, she will come back someday, begging for forgiveness because she left me. And, I'm going to laugh in her face. Just like this, ha, ha, ha!" Her anger turned sharply inward, and became grief. She fell to the floor weeping.

Kid rushed to scoop her from the rug, "It's alright."

Rosie said, "Let's just go to my room, and read some stories. I think that will make us all feel better." After closing the front door, she turned off the television set and followed Kid, carrying Janie along the corridor.

Turning on the bedside lamp, she positioned herself next to Janie with a large hardcover book of children's stories and read until the child fell asleep. Putting the book aside, she and Kid lay awake, with Janie sleeping between them. They softly talked about plans to spend the next summer together. Their conversation ranged from everything they had done during the summer, to everything they would do the following summer. When silence filled the room, the sound of a soft summer rain lulled them into slumber.

A loud clap of thunder and rain blowing through the window awoke Rosie. She jumped to her feet and pushed it closed. Returning to bed she realized Janie was missing. Shaking Kid she exclaimed, "Wake up and help me find Janie!"

He sprang from the bed, and rushed into the hallway. The front door was ajar, and Kid rushed to it, with Rosie close behind. A lamp burned on the television, casting vague light through the window and onto the porch. Kid stared transfixed through the screen and pushing him aside, Rosie also stared. Janie sat cross legged on the planked floor peering intently at the old rocking chair.

Putting his hand over her mouth, Kid signaled Rosie to remain quiet as Janie's voice carried along the breeze. The blowing rain, blinding flashes of lightening and deafening thunder bothered her none, and her manner was serious. Rosie pushed past Kid, stepping out her gaze fell instinctively on the old chair. A startled cry escaped as she saw the rocker engulfed in translucent fog, floating about in stringy wisps, shredded by the wind and rain. Stepping out behind her, Kid saw the ghostly vapor and gasped audibly.

"What are you two doing out here?" asked Janie angrily.

Rosie swiftly pulled the child to her feet, "Let's go inside!"

Protesting, Janie demanded, "No, leave me alone!" But Rosie rushed her inside anyway.

Kid followed asking aggressively, "What were you doing out there, Janie?"

The child pursed her lips, and wrinkled her nose as she considered the question. Her answer followed a deliberate pause, "He's in love with Rosie, and wants her to have something."

Sinking onto one knee he asked, "Who?"

Janie rolled her eyes, "He doesn't like you being here!"

Losing patience Kid almost shouted, "Who?"

"You know who! Doc Campbell," Janie looked from Kid to Rosie. "You know you disturbed him with that séance, and now he can't rest until he delivers the promise he made."

"What promise?" asked Rosie, enthralled.

Shrugging her shoulders Janie answered, "Don't you know? He made it to you!"

Rosie's memory was flooded with images from the haunting dreams. She finally said, "I had a dream about Doc, and he told me that he was going to save me." Locking eyes with Kid she continued, "He told me I could find everything I need in the pharmacy, and he walked through the panty door into a garden."

"Then we should begin by looking at the pantry," suggested Janie.

"Let's go have a look," said Kid.

With eyes wide in anticipation the little girl sprang from the sofa and rushed to the kitchen. Rosie asked Kid, "Do you really think some kind of clue could be there, just waiting for us?"

He lowered his voice, "I don't know, but Janie has really been freaking me out lately." He glanced toward the doorway, "Before the memorial service, she told me that Angel had visited to say good bye. And, that she walked away on a path of fluffy clouds into Heaven wearing a pretty pink gown with embroidered pink daises here, and here." He motioned with his hand to his chest and wrists.

"Oh, I see," Rosie said softly.

Compelled by her easy acceptance, he intently gazed at her; his indigo eyes bore through hers until he glimpsed the tenure of her insight. Grasping her hand he explained, "There's one thing I never told you. That first night Janie was in the hospital, she said something that totally blew us away. She said while she was lying unconscious on the side of the road after the accident, she watched someone cover Angel in a pink blanket. Shelley swears there is no way Janie could know that happened, because she was unconscious." He stood and pulled her to her feet. "I think she has some kind of extrasensory perception. Maybe she did speak with Angel this morning."

"I, myself, had a dream like that. She was wearing the pink gown, and she walked into the clouds toward a heavenly light." Recalling her own dream made Rosie's face flush pink, then pale, and her eyes filled as she whispered painfully, "She told me she was sorry for dying, that she didn't mean too!"

His voice condensed to a whisper as he declared, "Oh, my God! Janie had the same dream."

They followed Janie into the kitchen and found her standing inside the pantry. The overhead bulb spilled wavering luminosity as Janie scrutinized the walls board by board. Rosie stepped in pulling Kid with her. "There's a cold spot here," she explained, placing his hand to inspect the chilly draft.

He began removing the bottles of spice. With the shelf cleared, he leaned closer to examine the boards. A splintered slat caught his attention. Reaching in, he grasped it with his fingertips. The panel was loose. He gripped one of the nails and pulled it from the loosened cavity. Slowly, he removed four nails, and the board came free.

He asked, "Do you have a flashlight?"

Rosie handed him a box of matches. Striking one into a blaze he held it to the back of the shelf, the flame flickering in the currant of air. He exclaimed, "Oh, yes!" Then a snapping sound was heard as he unbolted a latch hidden behind the loose plank. Stepping back, he tugged at the wall of shelves. The wall swung open with rusty hinges groaning eerily.

Withheld breaths were expelled when the door was opened, revealing a secret room behind the pantry wall. Striking another match, Kid stepped into the cold musky room. He descended some steps and faltered with his lighted match until it burned out. Lighting another, the surreptitious space soon glowed with beams from a dusty old oil lamp.

Bare feet met cold stone as the girls tip-toed into the darkness of the chilled room. In the center was a small round table, the kind that would be perfect for card games. The walls were lined with dust covered rough hewn timber shelves.

A lump rose in Rosie's throat while Kid moved about casting light into darkened corners. "I had a dream and Doc told me that I would find what I need in the pharmacy." She keenly watched the movement of the lamp focusing sharply on every object it brought into view, and speculated "This is the pharmacy."

Holding the lamp aloft, Kid slowly moved it along the shelves where dust covered jars of bandages and bottles of medicine sat patiently waiting. When a dusty leather box came into view Rosie gasped loudly. Taking it from the shelf Kid offered it to her, keeping the lamp close. Slowly she lifted the lid as the flickering flame drenched the box with shadowy yellow light. Once the lid was opened, they gasped in unison at the sight of shimmering silver coins.

"These are the coins the men were playing poker with in my dreams," Rosie whispered.

"Yeah, well from the looks of this pile of silver Doc Campbell must have been one hell of a poker player."

A slight tug on his sleeve drew Kid's attention downward where Janie stared up at him, her face angelic in the wavering flame. "Can I see?"

Robotically, he handed the box over saying cautiously, "We shouldn't tell anyone about this. These coins might be very valuable. I mean, like so valuable that if someone found out about them they would rob you." He took two coins from the top saying, "I'm going to take these with me. When I get home I'll have them appraised."

Janie exclaimed, "We could be rich!" Exhilaration overcame her, and she twirled around with her arms spread wide knocking over a cardboard box. The sound of tinkling glass echoed against the stone walls as the box landed upside down onto the brick floor.

Kneeling to inspect the spilled contents, Kid placed the lamp closer to the floor, illuminating dozens of tiny glass vials filled with amber liquid. He grasped one gently and held it closer to the lamp. A look of wonderment crossed his face, and just as quickly an expression of alarm. He began scooping the vials back into the small box.

"What is that stuff?" Janie asked as he dropped some of the vials into the pocket of his t-shirt.

He answered apprehensively, "It's just some kind of old medicine, I guess." Taking up the lamp he said, "Let's get out of here before we find a skeleton, or a ghost." Putting his hand on Rosie's shoulder, he gently shoved her toward the doorway while she guided Janie ahead of her. Blowing out the flame, he left the oil lamp sitting near the box on the table.

Once they had stepped from the secret alcove, Rosie and Janie lingered as Kid secured the latch, and replaced the plank in the wall. After replacing some of the spice bottles, he switched the light off. The threesome stood in the dimly lit kitchen.

Rosie inhaled slowly and asked, "Is anyone thirsty? I've got lemonade."

"Yeah, I'd love some," responded Kid.

Janie sat down and looked at Kid suspiciously, "Don't get any ideas about keeping secrets."

He answered with a chuckle, "What kind of secret would I try to keep?"

Janie's nostrils flared, "That medicine, what do you think it is?"

Closing his eyes tiredly, he rubbed a hand over his face, "Okay, Janie. Remember, I don't want you to talk about the coins?" He watched her nod her head. "Well, if the medicine is what I think it is, it could be more valuable than the money."

Serving lemonade, Rosie asked, "What do you think it could be, Kid?"

He lowered his eyes as if needing a cautious moment to weigh words, "Morphine," quickly adding, "And on the street that stuff is worth more than gold." He tugged on each girl's hand as he emphasized his words, "We must tell no one about any of this. Not the coins and not the medicine."

"I won't tell a soul, Kid. I cross my heart and hope to die," pledged Janie.

Consumed by exhaustion, Rosie's eyes grew heavy, and her neck ached with stress. "Can we please get some rest now?"

The storm had faded from the mountain, leaving behind only an occasional distant rumble of thunder. A weak flash of lightening attempted to illuminate the night sky among diminishing rain clouds. Janie snuggled between Rosie and Kid as the storm faded. In a mixed emotional exhaustion, they fell asleep.

The morning's dawn warmed the room with cozy sunshine. A tickling sensation against Rosie's nose awakened her. She attempted to brush it away, but it returned vengefully. Wrinkling her nose, she blew at the pestering nuisance. A soft chuckle awoke her completely. Kid was propped on one elbow as he used a strand of her own hair to annoy her, his wide grin exposing glee. Rolling off her side of the bed, she whispered, "I smell coffee," quietly leaving the room with Kid following.

The kitchen smelled of bacon, sweet bread and coffee. Sturgill had already left the house for work, and Eva was in her usual place on the sofa in front of the television. After pouring herself a cup of coffee, she stood at the counter gazing at the pantry door. Kid entered and followed her gaze. He smiled as he reached for a mug and the coffee pot. "Doc really came through for you."

"As far as I'm concerned it belongs to you and Janie, as much as it does to me."

"Oh! Well, good morning," Eva's voice caught them by surprise. She stood in the doorway holding an empty coffee mug. "I have bacon and muffins. I'll be happy to fix some eggs if you like."

"Thanks, Eva, but this is fine," smiled Rosie.

Eva took her refreshed cup of coffee back to the living room, leaving them alone in the kitchen. "She really tries hard to impress you," mentioned Rosie.

"Why do you say that?" he asked taking the plate.

"You just don't know Eva. She never cooks or cleans or does anything domestic. But here she is pretending to be the dutiful housewife, like she wants you to go home and brag to your parents about what a great cook she is, or something. I'm sorry. I shouldn't have said that about her. I should just be glad she's finally making an effort."

Kid swallowed and said, "You know something I've noticed about here in the South? You can say anything about anybody, and it's alright as long as you say 'Bless their heart!' or 'Poor thing!' So go ahead and talk about Eva all you want, just be sure to add a pity phrase afterward, you know, so you won't go to hell." He sipped his coffee then said, "You know Shelley sure has turned out to be a whore, poor thing."

Tossing her head back, Rosie laughed spiritedly.

When they were ready to leave Kid said, "I want to stop by and say goodbye to Lewis on our way out." He noticed Rosie's startled look and asked, "Is there something wrong between you and Lewis? I mean besides that little thing with Ed?"

Looking at the ceiling she contemplated telling Kid the truth about the attack. Fear of what he would do kept her from it. "Lewis was atrociously rude, and I'm not over it," she answered in a barely audible whisper.

Leaning down, he kissed her softly on the cheek. "Maybe his loss can be my gain."

Rosie and Janie sat in the living room of Bert's house while Kid gathered his bags and gave his farewells. Shelley ranted a tireless tirade against her cousin, "I hate your guts, Kid Campbell!" She screamed, "You have no right to leave your car with Rosie! She's not even you're real cousin!" Then she stormed through the house, slamming doors.

Maggie cast a worried glance toward Rosie, "I don't understand why she is so upset. Her grandfather and Charlie are using the motor from the crashed car to build her a nice one."

Slumped against Rosie, Janie kept her gaze focused on Maggie. The lines around the elder woman's face had deepened through the summer. Oddly, she felt detached from her grandmother, and had no sympathy for her. The memory of her mother's last phone call came flooding to mind. Maggie and Shelley were the only people Elizabeth had wished to talk with. The child's guts wretched painfully as her mother's rejection were remembered.

Kid hugged his grandparents goodbye, "Okay, girls! I'm ready." He left the house without a parting word to his detestable cousin.

Outside the bright August sunlight scorched the looming acres of corn, now wilted and yellowed from summer's dog days. Rosie stepped to the passenger side of the car, but Kid stopped her. "What do you think you're doing? You're driving me, remember?" He tossed his car keys into a high arch and they fell perfectly into her palm.

"Yes," she replied. "What was I thinking?"

As they drove along the long dusty drive away from Bert's farm Janie said, "Shelley was madder than an old wet hen. She's so ugly when she pitches those fits. She scrunches her face up like the Grinch who stole Christmas."

Kid and Rosie looked at one another and said in unison, "Poor thing!"

With rising anxiety, Rosie drove to the Shirey farm, where Rosie asked Janie to stay in the car with her while Kid said his farewells. A few moments later Ed came walking back to the car with Kid. Rosie noticed how the handsome soldier seemed to be adjusting to civilian life. His hair had grown shaggy, along with a trace of sideburns.

Kid said to Ed, "Well, dude. I hate that I missed saying goodbye to your brother, be sure to let him know I came by."

Ed walked around to the driver's side of the car, "How are you, Rosie?"

She forced a stiff smile, "I'm good, and you?"

Straightening he replied, "I think I'll survive." He nodded his head toward Kid and said, "Have a safe trip, man."

Giving Ed a friendly salute, Kid got in the car and Rosie started the engine. Ed leaned in again saying, "Hey, how about giving me a call sometime soon."

With a nod she answered, "Okay."

As they drove along Kid said, "We have to take one last hike to Rocky Falls."

The waterfall had slowed its rushing waters of early summer. Now the creek flowed slow and easy, as did the waterfall. They stood on the bridge while Janie splashed in the cold shallows.

"I'll miss you so much," said Rosie.

"I would stay if you asked me too," said Kid.

Negatively shaking her head she reasoned, "I'll not be responsible for getting you drafted!" She looked skyward and noticed the clear blue sky beyond the tree tops. "I'll just keep dreaming of next summer."

Janie appeared kicking water from her feet, "Let's go already, and let's eat barbeque for lunch."

They stopped to eat, lingering over the meal with dreams and promises. The radio played loud during the drive. As Rosie helped Kid carry his bags across the parking deck, she began to sing sweetly a song made famous by the Beetles. *"I think I'm gonna be sad. I think it's today. The boy that's driving me mad is going away. He's got a ticket to ride, he's got a ticket to ride, he's got a ticket to ride, and he don't care."*

With heavy hearts, they awaited the boarding call. Kid said to Janie, "If you ever need me, just call. I'll always be here for you. See," he pointed to the waiting plane on the tarmac, "I'm just a plane ride away." Cradling her in a soft warm hug, he reached to embrace Rosie as well. Impulsively he took the heavy gold chain from his neck and clasped it around Rosie's. "There! That'll let Ed and Lewis both know you belong to me."

With teary eyes she said, "Don't worry. I'm waiting for you, and next summer." She pressed her lips to his in a desperate attempt to squelch her desire to shed tears.

The time came for him to board, but he lingered until the last minute. "I want you to catalogue each and every coin. Send me a copy of your list. I'll find out the value, and then you will have a rough estimate of how much money you have." He delayed boarding the plane, "God, I don't want to leave!"

The setting sun spread rosy waves of pink across the blue horizon. Rosie cheerfully exclaimed, "Look, Kid! You'll be flying through your favorite color, sky blue-pink!"

With a sorrowful smile he sighed, "Well, who could resist that?" He walked away backwards shouting, "I love you!"

They watched until he was gone from sight then waited for the plane to taxi down the runway and take flight. Later, on the way home, they rode without conversation through the darkening shadows, with only the radio playing low. Rosie fondled the gold chain around her neck, fantasizing of next summer.

Looking skyward and wishing she could be flying away, too, Janie switched off the radio and began singing, *"I think I'm gonna be sad, I think it's today."*

Rosie joined in and sang with her. They sang *Ticket to Ride* over and over, and when she let Janie off at her grandparent's house the little girl knew the song by heart. Slowly she crossed the lawn looking into the night sky where glittering stars lighted the pathway to heaven. This would be the first night back at her grandparent's house since the terrible accident that took her best friend's life. Tonight she would sleep in her familiar bed knowing that she was fatherless, motherless, and except for Rosie and Kid, friendless. Softly she began humming *Ticket to Ride* and entered the door of her now permanent home.

Yellow light glowed from the windows as Rosie wheeled into the driveway. After parking the car, she sauntered around the house to the front porch. Eyeing the old weathered rocking chair, searching for any sign of Doc's presence she said, "Just because you gave me your coins doesn't mean a thing. So, just get it straight right now. I don't owe you anything." The old battered chair sat mockingly still.

The front door opened and Sturgill stepped out, "Sunshine Rose? Who are you talking to out here?"

Feeling ridiculous, she said, "Nobody."

"So you were just now talking to yourself?"

"Yeah, I guess so."

Sturgill stepped aside, letting his daughter enter the house. "Well, you know what they say about talking to yourself, don't you?"

Passing by the clamor of the television set she asked, "What's that, Daddy?"

"It's been said talking to your self is the first sign of madness. Are you going crazy, or is this just more flashbacks from that brown acid?"

She retorted angrily, "I didn't take any damn acid. Call me certifiable if you want too, but stop saying I took brown acid!"

His laughter sent her fleeing in irritation. As he turned to close the door, something caught his peripheral vision. Stepping back onto the porch he eyed the old rocking chair that had abruptly halted motion.

Chapter Twenty
Piss Ants

Labor Day came with Rosie and Janie horseback riding along wooded trails to Rocky Falls. The two matching Palominos made a striking pose as the girls crossed mirror smooth streambeds and dense wooded trails. There was a comfort in the forest, a soothing serenity the troubled girls were hungry for.

After a short visit with Willene and Minnie Mama, they rode side by side back toward Mr. Reyes' barn. Fall hung heavy in the air. Spent corn fields spread across neighboring farms, along with wilted gardens, browning from lack of rain. A car pulled alongside causing Spice to prance sideways. It was Ed.

Silencing the engine, he stepped out of the car, "You girls having a good day?"

Janie eyed him suspiciously. "We were about to put the horses away."

Ed looked to Rosie, "Every time I ring your house your stepmother tells me you're not home. I've just about decided to give up trying to talk to you."

A pang of guilt touched her, "I'm sorry, Ed." She sighed heavily, "Why don't you come with us to the barn? After we get the horses put away, we can talk."

"Okay," he said and climbed back into his car.

"You can't lead him on, Rosie," cautioned Janie. "Don't forget you're going to be with Kid."

Just the mention of his name brought a smile to Rosie's lips. "Yeah, and when you're old enough you can come live with us."

"Oh yeah, I can hardly wait for the day!" agreed Janie.

When the tack was put away and the horses released back to pasture Ed suggested Rosie join him for a ride. She agreed saying, "Okay, but we have to drop Janie off at her grandparents house."

Holding his seat forward, Ed allowed Janie into the backseat of his car. Helping herself to the radio, Rosie found a station playing Tommy James & The Shondells *Crystal Blue Persuasion.* After dropping Janie off, they started along the long dusty driveway to the main road.

Janie walked inside the house to find her grandmother and Shelley watching the Labor Day Telethon. Maggie asked, "Did you have a nice ride with Rosie?"

"Yes, it was very nice."

Sneering at Janie, Shelley said to Maggie, "I don't know why you let her spend time with that low class Rosie."

Janie replied calmly, "Well, you know what they say, Shelley. It takes low class to recognize low class." The dull drone from the television grew louder in the silence following her coldly calculated comment.

Shelley shot her a daggered scowl while Maggie simultaneously exhibited a harsh expression. The little girl who never got attention was suddenly at the center of it, and it wasn't pleasant. Janie said, "I think I'll just go to my room now." She left feeling angry stares chill her spine.

Ed turned the radio off as they took the main road and picked up speed. She could feel his eyes on her, so she asked, "How's Opal?"

"Not good." He maneuvered the car down the mountain, and carefully steered into twisting curves. "She's taken leave from work, so Dad and I are paying her rent."

Driving through dense forest they approached a small concrete bridge spanning a wide creek. Pulling to the side on the bridge, he turned off the ignition. A pale blue sky with dingy clouds floated above, and the tree lined roadway framed the view with a leafy border. "I was hoping to ask you a few questions about Lewis."

Memories flooded her mind when she just wanted to forget. "Listen, Ed, I can't do anything for him." Rosie placed her arms across her chest, and continued, "Besides, I've made plans with Kid for next summer."

He said agreeably, "Okay fine, but today let's focus on Lewis."

With annoyance she exclaimed, "Don't you get it, Ed? I'm not interested in you, or your brother!"

Softly he said, "I want you to be completely honest with me. Did you and Lewis have a physical altercation the day of Angel's service? Was it you that gave him two black eyes?"

Impulsively she opened the door and stepped out. Silvery minnows swam in the shallow water below the bridge, reflecting glints of sunlight. Ed joined her with his flask, clutching it like a security blanket. Tipping it to his lips he drank carefully and said, "Lew's in bad shape, Rosie. "But, so it seems are you."

"Don't waste your time worrying about me, Ed."

After a long moment of silence he said, "Happy Labor Day," and offered up his silver flask.

. They drove back to Ben Johnson Ridge with heavy silence between them. Astonishingly, Ed pulled into the driveway at the Shirey farm calmly commanding, "I'd like for you to come inside, and say hello to Mamie."

She icily replied, "I'd love to see Mamie."

Taking the concrete path to the backyard, Rosie noticed a motorcycle parked at the back door. Ed said, "Dad got that motorcycle for Lewis."

Refraining from comment, she followed him quietly through the kitchen door. Mamie was pleasantly surprised to see Rosie, and reached an arm around her asking, "How are you doing, dear? Did your cousin get home safe?"

"I'm doing well. Kid is home, and registered for his fall classes." She smiled slightly asking, "How are you?"

"Well, to tell you the truth, some days I just don't know if I'm coming or going. But today has been fair to middling." Mamie tilted her head and said, "Oh, but you're here to see Lewis! Go on and knock on his door."

Ed stepped closer saying, "Rosie's here to visit you, Mamie, not Lewis."

Mamie nodded slightly, "Oh, I see."

Ed sensed Rosie's uneasiness, "Ready for me to drive you home?"

Smiling with cynicism she said, "Yes, thank you!"

Mamie said with concern, "Rosie dear, would you like for me to talk with Lewis?"

Inhaling a deep breath, Rosie released it slowly saying, "I've got to deal with Lewis on my own. Goodbye, Mamie."

Ed pulled the front door open and Rosie started down the steps. Suddenly, Lewis rounded the house in a fast jog. To avert a collision they instinctively reached out, steadying one another.

"Dang brother, be careful with my company there!" Taking Rosie by the hand, Ed began leading her away.

Glaring, Lewis asked, "What's this, Ed? You took my girl, and now you want to rub my nose in it?" Perspiration plastered his hair against his face, and he sucked in long heavy breaths, "Well, maybe I don't give a flying rat's ass about neither one of you! What do you think of that?" As he watched Ed open the door for Rosie, and close it back again, jealousy boiled. Lewis stepped to the passenger side window and stared at his brother as he looked past Rosie, "If you want to know what I think of the two of you together, let me tell you now. I think you are both insignificant little piss ants!"

Ed cranked the car and said, "Why don't you go ahead and apologize to Rosie for whatever it was you did to her the day of the funeral."

Looking confused he asked, "Why? What happened?"

The pain turned sharp as she heard Lewis deny remembering his attack. Refusing to return angry looks or words, Rosie said, "Home, please."

Lewis finally said, "Maybe we should just talk, Rosie."

"I have nothing to say to you, Lewis."

Anger flooded him and he spat, "Then to hell with you!" He turned and rushed into the house slamming the door behind him.

Ed inhaled and sighed deeply. He drove Rosie home in silence. Before she got out of the car he said, "Call me."

Without speaking a farewell, she left him. Just as she was about to go inside she caught sight of the old rocking chair. Noticing the potted fern still resting on the floor she took seat. Gently she rocked to and fro, daydreaming of the coins and the wealth they could bring. As she dreamed a cool breeze stirred, and the touch of a hand lightly caressed her cheek. Startled, she looked about anxiously, but no one was in sight. Rosie left the chair, and went to her room. There she spent hours writing down every painful detail of her experience with Lewis and her hopes for a happy future with Kid.

School began, and Janie spent more and more time with Rosie at the Moon farm. She supervised Janie's homework, and let her take part in the household chores. But, Rosie seemed to be more alone than usual as the school days stretched into weeks. Senior year was extremely stressful for Heather, and she became withdrawn. Rosie kept in touch with Kid regularly. His cards and letters were all she looked forward to. She had opened a checking account with the check from one of the coins he sold. The coin brought almost two thousand dollars, and the other was appraised at a higher value. He explained the coins shouldn't be sold unless necessary, because they would only increase in value over time.

On late night weekends the girls worked together to catalog the coins. They talked in hushed tones about plans to buy a house of their own, and live happily ever after with Kid. Fall came, painting the landscape with warm autumn color. The days became cooler, and the nights held a refreshing chill. Life had changed on the mountain for Rosie. It had become richer with Janie and Kid's involvement, but the absence of Lewis and Angel delivered melancholia.

One late September afternoon, while gathering pears in her orchard, a particular blushing yellow pear called seductively as it hung from the limb. Rosie plucked it, and as she impulsively bit into the soft juicy flesh a soft voice startled her.

"I always thought you were supposed to wash fruit before you ate it." Lewis stood silently beneath a gnarly peach tree, watching her.

Taking the fruit from her mouth she said, "That's only for significant people. Insignificant piss ants don't bother with protocol." Opening wide she sank her teeth into the pear ruthlessly, taking a large sloppy bite.

Dropping his chin, he looked at the ground. A long moment passed before he spoke again. Looking up as Rosie drew back and hurled the core into the pasture he watched the half eaten pear sail through the air, landing on the grazed field. "I don't know how to make right whatever I did wrong," he said honestly.

Indignant pride rushed through her. How dare he not remember his attack! "There is no *right* that can undo your wrong!"

"What did I do, Rosie? I remember what you and Ed did, but I don't remember doing anything to you." He raised his eyes skyward and said, "If you want me to know, and make it right," he caught her eyes with a steadfast gaze, "well, you're just going to have to tell me."

Her nostrils flared. "I have nothing to say to you, Lewis." Taking up the basket of pears, she began walking away.

Without moving from the tree he called behind her, "I'm willing to work this out, Rosie."

Quickening her pace, she walked away as her mind raced. She wanted him to remember! He should be punished with the memory, just as she was!

Thanksgiving came and went on Ben Johnson Ridge. Preparations for Christmas were laborious, and painstakingly executed. The city park became a living Christmas card with multicolored lights and festive decorations. Byron Town School was housed in a single building for grades K thru twelve. The annual talent show contestants had been practicing for the Christmas show since October, and the final dress rehearsals were winding down. The dance line was much more difficult than the year before, and the football players, who were forced to participate, grumbled about the challenge.

During a dress rehearsal contestants dwindled as some were dismissed. Rosie noticed she had fallen into a handful of students still practicing. The group included herself, three other girls, one football player and Lewis. She strove to make excellent steps and stay in rhythm with the other dancers. By the time she was dismissed Rosie was damp with perspiration, and jogged to the locker room.

The water was warm and soothing as she stood beneath the spray working shampoo through her hair. Just as she shut off the water she was frightfully taken aback by the shower curtain being jerked open. A towel clad Rosie was exposed to the intruder. Lewis stood gripping the shower curtain as he gazed at her with spiteful, smoldering hazel eyes. He stepped inside with her and slid the curtain closed behind him growling, "Why do you wear that damn necklace like it's some kind of goddamned engagement ring?"

Shrinking away she gasped, "I will scream if you touch me!"

"What do I have to do to win you back?" he whispered near tears.

She cringed from his pain, "I'm with Kid now." The words fell from her lips like chips of ice.

He tilted his head back and laughed cruelly, "I don't get it! You're all hot for my brother one week then you're committed to Kid the next." Menacingly he asked, "What happened to my sweet little Rosie? Where did she go?"

Clutching the towel she cried, "Just stay away from me!" As she pushed past she wrenched the shower faucet on and raced to the toilet stalls grabbing her clothes along the way. Hurriedly, she dressed as she heard his footsteps nearing the stall. Rosie slipped her shoes on and gasped sharply when she heard his voice from above.

Leaning over the stall divider he stared down at her. "I insist you talk to me!" She unlatched the door and rush to the exit. He caught hold of her just as she had her hands on the push bar. "Damn it!" he cursed, "What in God's name did I do to you?"

Tossing damp tendrils defiantly from her face she declared, "You broke me, okay! Like a dry twig, you snapped me in tiny pieces! Now, leave me alone!"

Lewis melted with pent up anguish. His face crumbled as he gave in to tears. "I've just really messed everything up, Rosie! I used the pills and drank the booze, and just spun out of control. I'm so ashamed of the degrading things I've done! What would Angel think?"

She attempted to pull away, but he held her pinned to the wall. Voices from the other girls alerted them of their approach, so he reached over and pushed the door open, shoving her out ahead of him. Once outside, Rosie seethed, "Stop it you jerk!"

Tears blinded him as he cried, "Please forgive me, Rosie! Whatever I did, I'll make up for it a thousand times over."

With closed eyes she stipulated sternly, "Leave me alone, Lewis." Her voice was steely jagged, and her expression lethal. As if burned by hot coals he quickly stepped aside and she ran to Kid's car, locking the doors once inside.

Rosie was impressed with a new girl at school named Sally Cook. She was pretty and smart, and like Rosie, Sally's school attire was often exhausted hand-me-downs. Perhaps it was due to Rosie's true friendship with Sally that the new girl became ridiculed in vile whispers and threatened with isolation by a miserably unhappy Shelley Noble. Sally's father was a disabled Vietnam Vet; he'd lost both legs, but stayed active. He could drive independently, transfer from automobile to wheelchair effortlessly, but despite excellent credentials gainful employment eluded him, forcing his wife into a minimum wage job to supplement the humiliatingly low military disability pension. Rosie witnessed Sally being ridiculed behind her back by a venomous Shelley, who whispered snide criticisms, citing rumors that Sally's father's alcoholism kept their family in poverty.

Speaking up for Sally, Rosie would interject logic and independent reasoning, telling Shelley in front of others that she had no proof of what she was saying and should not be believed. Suddenly, it was Rosie who became isolated, ignored, provoked and scorned by Shelley's supporters.

Heather had become more and more detached. She side stepped every effort Rosie made to continue the friendship they had shared for so many years. It was impossible for her to determine if Heather felt jealousy over Rosie's new friendship with Sally, or if there was another reason for her odd behavior. Since the summer days of Woodstock, Rosie's dark haired friend had put on weight, staying isolated and perpetually sad. Thus giving cause for Rosie to spend more time with Janie and Sally.

They attended the fall fair together, spending money recklessly. Whether it be collecting insects for a science project or browsing the library for new books, the three girls became adventurous friends. Janie and Rosie rode horses at least once a week. And on occasion Sally would join them with Sugar as her steed, and Janie doubling with Rosie on Spice.

Chronic depression seemed to plague Ben Johnson Ridge that winter, and the evidence was visible. Janie had developed dark circles beneath her eyes, and for some inexplicable reason her hair began to fall out. Once, when Rosie questioned her about being tired, the little girl broke down and sobbed against her breast, "I can't sleep, Rosie! I just can't sleep!"

Deeply concerned for the child, Rosie spoke with Bert and Maggie, and they assured her that Janie was working through her anxieties. But when Dr. Martin prescribed medicine that sometimes caused Janie to sleepwalk, Rosie was convinced Janie's guardians were failing to protect her.

Following the final dress rehearsal, Rosie was surprised to find Shelley's car parked in the Moon driveway. Carefully, she carried a pink evening gown, acquired especially for the show, draped across her arm. Eva and Shelley were sitting perched on the living room couch talking seriously when she entered the room.

Rosie said plastically pleasant, "Hello, Shelley." When Shelley made no reply, Rosie said cheerfully, "Well, you're obviously not here to see me, so I'll just excuse myself."

"You got mail today, another letter from Kid," Eva said as she busied herself preparing a cigarette by tapping it lightly upside down on the coffee table.

A smile crossed Rosie's face as she recognized the large bold writing. Turning to leave the room, her gaze locked with Shelley's. Putting the envelope to her nose for a whiff of his extravagant cologne, Rosie closed her eyes dreamily. Smiling wickedly, she replied, "Thank you, Eva," and departed with the letter still resting at her nose.

Safely inside her room, she inhaled the scented letter deeply before ripping it open. Immediately, Rosie sensed dire news. Kid was beside himself with anger and regret. He told her of how he had gotten himself in trouble with a college girl who had become obsessed with him as a musician, and how he had awoken one morning in her dorm room. The physical appearance of the girl was described as *homely*, and then he explained who her father was. Kid's written words disclosed that he had obviously been drugged, and made to think he had spent a romantic night with her. The pages pleaded for Rosie to believe him. He implored her to stand by him as the girl was now saying she was with child, and demanding marriage. He openly worried that because the girl's father was a State Legislator he could become a victim of political clout. Asking for time to work out his problem, he vowed to be with her by summertime.

Safely coveting the letter inside her diary, bitter tears fell as she contemplated life without Kid. She imagined seeing him with a wife and children, and the image tortured her. Taking out her stationary box she began writing him a letter filled with hopeful expectations. She dabbed *Chanel No 5* on each folded page, before sliding them inside the envelope addressed to: Mr. J. E. Campbell

The night of the contest came, and Rosie prepared to leave after carefully applying make-up and wig to imitate Marilyn Monroe. She wore the strapless pink satin gown with matching wrap and long pink gloves. The reflection from the mirror dazzled her. Looking like a movie star from the past was intoxicating. She began searching for her purse.

Sturgill sat half awake on the sofa in front of the couch, "Daddy?" Rosie called to him, "Daddy!"

He looked at his daughter with glazed eyes, "What?"

"Where is Eva? Have you seen my purse?" Frantically she tossed pillows from the sofa onto the floor as she searched.

Sturgill said sleepily, "I don't know where she's at. Isn't it time for you to go, sweetheart?"

Rosie felt like crying, "Yes, Daddy! It is time for me to go, but Eva's not here and I can't find my purse with the car keys in it." Closing her eyes in defeat she exclaimed, "All this work for nothing!"

Sturgill held up his index finger saying sternly, "Now wait one minute! I'll take care of this with one phone call." He sauntered sideways toward the kitchen. Seconds later he returned beaming triumphantly, "You're chariot is on its way my lady!"

A few minutes later a car horn honked from the driveway. Quickly she raced down the steps to find Ed Shirey in his '65 Mustang.

The drama teacher was relieved to see Rosie arrive. "Glad you could make it, Marilyn. Now break a leg!"

"Look for me after the show," Ed told Rosie. He then sauntered away, wearing his tight jeans, long sleeve Wrangler shirt, and leather jacket slung over his shoulder. Turning to face the stage Rosie noticed Lewis scowling disapproval.

The show opened with a group of football players performing a comedy musical sketch. Individual performers followed. Many of the students performed with extreme talent, but poor showmanship. Lewis performed Elvis Presley's *Jail House Rock* with the football players dancing a background show. His performance received enthusiastic applause. Heather sang *Somewhere over the Rainbow* with gut wrenching talent and heart melting emotion. Shelley did a tired performance of *Tammy,* without even making an effort to look like Debbie Reynolds.

Butterflies nauseated Rosie when her turn to perform came. She took the stage lightheaded with nerves. Four of the football players positioned themselves behind her in costume for her portrayal of Marilyn Monroe's *Diamonds Are a Girl's Best Friend.* When she sang into the microphone, the audience froze in rapt attention. She made every dance step perfectly, and for the finale, fell deftly into the arms of two football players. She sang passionately, mimicking the soft sexy voice of Marilyn Monroe, "*Diamonds! I don't mean rhinestones. But, diamonds are a girl's best friend!*" The spotlight rested on Rosie as the lights dimmed and the recorded orchestra music played on to a dramatic finish.

Exiting the stage breathlessly, Rosie inched her way down a few steps, past other contestants. Breaking free of the side entrance she stepped into the auditorium where she found Ed waiting. Searching the crowd for a glimpse of Janie, she allowed Ed to seat her. Rosie finally noticed Janie in the distant shadows waving frantically at her. Standing on tip toes she returned the gesture.

The show ended, and the judges made final selections for third, second and first place in two divisions, male performance and female performance. A two minute spotlight dance wound take place with the winners, followed by a group dance that had been painstakingly choreographed.

It was a thorough surprised when Shelley was given third place. Heather was called to collect the second place trophy and when it was announced the first place female performance went to Rosie Moon, she leapt to her feet with joy exclaiming over and over, "It's me! It's me!" She smiled sweetly as she was given the trophy, and congratulated. Retreating to the stage mark with her trophy, she waited for the final announcements.

For the male decisions third place was given to Zeke Tidmore for his portrayal of Jack Lemmon as the character *Honey* from *Some like It Hot.* He had wowed the audience with his talent on the bass fiddle, dressed in drag and smiling like a silly girl. Second place was given to Barron Webster for his Gene Kelley performance of *Singing in the Rain.* When Lewis Shirey was announced as the male performance first place winner, the audience exploded with ovation.

The winning contestants took the stage to sing the farewell song from the *Lawrence Welk Show.* When the song ended the performers bowed and waited for the curtain to close. Rosie left the stage hurriedly, tugging the blonde wig from her head. She broke free from the backstage door and rushing to Ed, flung herself into his arms, laughing wickedly.

Later, as they sat in his car, she relaxed against the passenger side seat holding the small trophy like a weapon. Softly she said, "If you hadn't driven me here tonight, I wouldn't have won. Now, I'll be scheduled to appear with your brother in about a half dozen more performances." She focused her attention on the gathering crowd of people in the parking lot and began pulling pins from her hair as people milled about. Flash bulbs from active cameras occasionally illuminated the darkness. When she noticed Janie wandering around aimlessly Rosie left the car and called to her.

"Thank goodness I found you!" Janie exclaimed. "If I can't find another ride home, Shelley is going to make me go with her and Lewis to a band practice." Rolling her eyes, she blew a spring of hair from her face. "Do you mind giving me a ride?"

Ed nodded, "Not at all."

"Great!" Janie whirled and disappeared in the crowd.

They watched Janie catch up with her sister who milled in a group with Lewis. After hearing Janie's explanations, they both stared in Rosie's direction. Deliberately ignoring the evil twosome, Rosie chatted easily with Ed until her attention was diverted by the sound of an idling car engine. When she turned toward the automobile Lewis was glaring at her from the front seat of Shelley's car. He blew a cloud of marijuana smoke her way. "Piss ants!" he sneered. They pulled away fast, squealing tires with the sound of his mocking laugh hanging disrespectfully in midair.

"That little bastard!" exclaimed Ed. "I swear to God I'm going to rip his head off, and shit down his neck one of these days!"

Janie quickly approached, calling out with a huge smile, "All's settled." With a questioning expression she asked, "Are you okay, Rosie?"

With a wry smirk Rosie replied dryly, "Well, now that you mention it, I am feeling a bit insignificant right now. Sort of like a piss ant."

Chapter Twenty-One
Everybody's Got Enemies

School was in winter break, and Rosie had awakened to a frosty morning on the mountain. Fronds of fern frost garnished the windowpanes and beneath the thick layer of quilts she shivered. Pulling on a robe, she slipped her feet into comfy house shoes then hurried to the fire place. After adding kindling to the ebbing embers, she teased the sparks to flame. The morning was quiet, and her parents were still sleeping. Pondering Kid's circumstances with the legislator's daughter, Rosie felt desperately sad. Returning to her chilled bedroom, she took her diary with special letters from Kid and returned to the warmth of the hearth where she browsed information concerning value of the silver coins, and letters of remorse.

The letters explained only time would tell if the elected official's daughter was indeed not pregnant, but he was terrified. Because of her weight, she could hide a non-existent pregnancy for months! And what if she were impregnated, but by another man? What kind of pickle would he be in? Having become so despondent over his situation, Rosie no longer attended church, and if not for Janie and Sally, would have become a total recluse.

Christmas came and went with no one questioning Rosie how she could afford the gifts she bestowed. One afternoon, she and Sally sneaked away for an after Christmas shopping spree. With great pleasure she bought Sally three new outfits, complete with shoes and handbag.

Despite the bank account, Rosie became reserved and only went out once during the holidays. Barron Webster invited her to a New Year Eve's party. Without enthusiasm, she agreed to go. Stepping from her bedroom on New Year's Eve, she silently wondered why her parents never said anything about the new clothes. Janie only bought one Christmas present, a gift for Rosie. She had asked Rosie to take her to a locally celebrated jewelry store. Now, on New Year's Eve, Rosie had cause to sport the expensive jewelry, and she stood before the hallway mirror admiring the ruby earrings dancing with fire in the lamp light.

When she emerged from the shadowed corridor Sturgill roused enough to acknowledge his daughter's loveliness, as his wife sat quietly smoking a cigarette, making no comment at all. Wearing a red leather mini skirt with black patent leather boots and tight black sweater, Rosie draped a ridiculously expensive trench coat over herself, and stood waiting for Barron to come knocking at the door. Sturgill sat dosing on the sofa, his chin on his chest. Eva was in stone statue mode, silent and glassy-eyed from imbibing whiskey.

Taking advantage of her father's absence, as it was, Rosie deliberately provoked her stepmother, "That was a most unusual thing that happened to me the night of the talent show." She waited for Eva to look at her, but Eva would not. "I never leave my purse in your car, ever. So how do you suppose that happened?" Leaning against the wall patiently, she watched Eva twirl the ashes off the tip of her cigarette into a crystal ashtray, obviously agitated. Remembering Shelley's visit the day before the show, Rosie's imagination rushed with ideas of possible blackmail scenarios, but found no sympathy for her stepmother.

Finally, Eva looked at Rosie evenly and said, "I guess everybody's got enemies." Putting the cigarette to her mouth she took a monstrous drag. The resulting cloud of exhaled smoke shrouded the room like blight.

With a sudden rush of boldness Rosie reached down and took up Eva's package of cigarettes. Slowly she removed one of the grotesquely long thin cigarettes and placed it beneath her nose inhaling the tobacco's scent leisurely. Dryly she asked, "Yes, but who has enemies in their own home?"

Eva's eyes widened, and without saying a word she took another hard drag. Locking eyes with Eva's, Rosie said, "If that happens to be my problem, then either me or my enemy will have to go." She tossed the cigarette onto the table next to the ashtray still clutching the package. "So, here's something for you to think about." Calmly, she took the cigarette package with both hands and twisted it so as to crush each fragile tube within.

A gasp of shock resonated from Eva, but still she said nothing. Rosie tossed the package of crushed cigarettes onto the table just as the sound of Barron's van caught her attention. Stepping to the door she called cattily, "Happy New Year, Eva."

Rushing outside to meet Barron ensured not having to introduce her nodding father and shameless stepmother. He smiled handsomely, his long sleek brown hair was pulled into a ponytail, and he was dressed in black jeans with an expensive black leather jacket. Taking her hand he exclaimed, "You look great! This party is going to be fun. You'll be glad you came."

They drove to a huge house on the outskirts of the small town. From the road, the impressive home loomed eerily beyond dark silhouettes of leafless trees. He drove through a gated entrance and along a winding paved driveway. Rosie mused, "Your aunt must be loaded!"

He snickered, "Yeah, usually with vodka."

Apprehension crept up as she noticed the cars parked along the circle drive. "Damn it! Shelley is here, really?"

"She's part of the band, remember? The Mountaineers won the talent festival. Aunt Helen and Uncle Andy always have the winner of the talent festival play their New Year's Eve shindig. It's a tradition." After parking the van Barron said, "I do need to warn you about someone, though."

"Someone?"

"Yeah, my cousin Mack," greeted by a blank stare he explained, "He sort of fell in love with you at the talent show."

"Well, that's sweet. How old is he?"

"Nineteen." They made their way to the grand house alight with Christmas decorations, and the sound of rock and roll music. "Be careful not to hurt his feelings. He fancies himself a cowboy, and takes the profession very seriously."

Entering through the double doors she slipped off her coat, hanging it in the foyer closet. A crowd was gathered in a large sunken living room where people of all ages were dancing on shag carpeting. Lewis sang into a microphone while the band created electrifying music.

Pulling her into the dancing crowd, Barron's long chestnut ponytail swayed with the rhythm of his moves. The music was infectious, and she danced with abandon. When the song ended a slow dance tune began, Barron pulled her close and murmured, "Want to get high after this tune?"

"High on what, may I ask?"

Dancing her around in a complete circle he dipped her back so dramatically her ponytail pooled onto the floor. "On me, baby!" He skillfully pulled her back upright, and swung her outward on his arm, then rolled her back with a dancer's embrace.

She enjoyed dancing with Barron, and never took notice of the dark scowl Lewis had on his face. When the song ended, they walked about the crowd, and he introduced her to people she had never met. A large young man wearing dark blue wrangler jeans, a wrangler western style shirt, and cowboy boots with extraordinary silver pointed tips, interrupted him. "Dang, Barron! You're dancing with the girl of my dreams!"

Giving her a sly wink he said, "Hey, Mack, let me introduce you to my date, Sunshine Rose Moon."

Extending her hand Rosie said, "It's a pleasure to meet you." Suddenly, she was taken completely off guard when the hefty Mack swept her off her feet, swinging her around in a complete mid-air circle. She staggered sideways and grabbed onto Barron saying, "I've seen this movie before! It's called *Bus Stop,* but someone needs to tell Mack I'm not really Marilyn."

Barron chortled as he saved her from Mack, "Excuse us for just a little while, Buddy. We'll be back in a few."

Holding hands, they stepped onto the patio where candles floated in the swimming pool, and people milled about in the frosty night air. He tugged her past ladies wearing extravagant jewelry and expensive furs; accompanied by men dressed in polyester leisure suits, in odious checks and stripes. They mumbled greetings in passing while following a shadowed path to the pool house. Stepping inside, Rosie rubbed her arms briskly to chase away the chill. The pool house was just slightly warmer than the patio outside. Barron led her to a huge mirrored bathroom, and closed the door before flipping a switch, illuminating the excessive lavatory with walls covered in luxurious cobalt-blue satin wallpaper. Expensive cut crystal fixtures shone brilliant beams directly onto decorative brass faucets, gleaming above indigo porcelain sinks.

Barron bolted the door, and flipped another switch, engaging an exhaust fan. "This is a disgusting display of wealth!" Rosie giggled.

Brushing aside his sleek ponytail, Barron slid a cigarette box from his shirt pocket. Retrieving a vial of white powder from the box he explained, "A little blow for a lift." Next he revealed a hand rolled cigarette, "A little smoke for a buzz." Then he held up a narrow strip of paper with tiny square pictures smiling lewdly, "And a little blotter for a blast!" He handed the strip of paper over saying, "Check it out, tadpoles!"

Looking closely at the tiny cubes of paper she said, "No, Barron. These aren't tadpoles, they're sperm cells."

"No shit?" Sheepishly he confessed, "Damn, I feel stupid."

A half hour later, they returned to the party just as the band stopped for a break. Rosie waited with apprehension as band members filed past, destination patio. With perspiration beading his forehead Lewis stopped and said, "Happy New Year, Rosie." Then he continued on into the chilled night as if he didn't expect a response.

She was startled by a voice in her ear. Whirling to face the rude intruder she found Mack smiled childishly at her. "Well, hello again."

"I can mix you a drink that will warm you all the way down to your toes." He winked flirtatiously, "Want to try me?"

"Yeah," she said taking his proffered arm.

He accompanied her to an extravagant bar with crystal champagne glasses, and bottles upon bottles of sparkling white wine. Taking one of the glasses filled with the bubbly brew, she sipped while Mack mixed a number of different liquors into a tall glass filled with chipped ice. He topped it off with a bit of cola and stirred it thoroughly.

Coming from behind the bar, he held out the glass explaining, "This is called Long Island Tea."

She sipped it cautiously, quickly becoming hypnotized by rainbows reflected against cut crystal from melting ice shards. The desire to giggle was irresistible, and she snickered girlishly under the influence of paper sperm cells. There was a puzzled look on Mack's face and she apologized. "Oh, I'm sorry. I'm not laughing at you." Recklessly she tipped the glass and gulped it. "Ah!" she exclaimed, "You make one hell of a drink!"

Mack beamed at her; his sandy blonde hair trimmed and combed to feathery perfection. "Want another one, just like the other one?"

With her head tossed back she laughed charmingly, "Yes, please!"

"Coffee, milk or Long Island Tea?" he asked holding out the glass with a boyish smile teasing his face. "Hey, do you know the Texas Two-Step?"

Taking Rosie in tow, Barron interrupted his cousin, "Hey Mack! See that skinny girl with frizzy hair singing with the band?"

The band was back from break and playing loud. Mack peered critically at Shelley mumbling, "Yeah, I see her."

"I overheard her say she's got the hots for you, man!" Barron lied easily.

With a squinted eye Mack took a closer look-see saying, "Oh, yeah? Well, she kind of looks like she could have the hots for just about anybody."

Rosie melted into tear welling laughter, and Barron pulled her into the crowd of dancers. The sparkling wine flowed and the party drew closer to midnight. Lewis appeared to be a bit unsteady on his feet as he played a foot stomping tune on his harmonica accompanying the band.

"What's Lewis drinking?" she asked.

Shaking his head disapprovingly, Barron replied, "Same thing as the rest of the boys, rocket fuel!"

They danced energetically as the band wound down the song. During a brief intermission, Mack broke in asking, "Rosie, can I have this dance?" In the next instant she was whisked away, clutched in his bulky embrace.

As the band started into Hank William's *I'm So Lonesome I Could Cry,* Mack instructed, "Now this dance is real simple. Just follow me. Step right, step-step left. See? Step, step-step, you're doing it! Now turn and you'll be going backward, just keep making the same steps, only backward."

Gliding past Barron, Mack gave him an exaggerated wink with a nod. The room was filled with the honeyed sound of Lewis Shirey's sweet voice. Singing the tune like a bereft soul, he belted out the lyrics as if the ghost of Hank stood by his side. Spellbound by the tune, Rosie danced in a haze of emotions. Where was the hatred? She needed that odium! Somehow the past was dulled in memory, cooling the fury of injustice. The music stopped, the waltz was ended, and Rosie was painfully empty.

The microphone squeaked as Zeke Tidmore began an announcement, "Okay folks! The end of 1969 inches nearer, so I'm going to give this mic over to our host and hostess. They are going to count down the end of the year for us, so ladies and gentlemen may I please introduce Helen and Andy Martin!"

The party goers applauded as the couple stepped to the microphone and began giving thanks to everyone who had come to celebrate the season. The crowd began the count down, "Five, four, three, two, one, happy New Year!" Darby went into a feral drum solo as the crowd cheered. Somewhere mixed in the roar of noise was a chilling sound of breaking glass. Hysterical screams stunned the crowd into silence.

Everyone rushed to the scene of broken glass where Shelley stood ghostly pale and transfixed before the shattered picture window. Beyond the splintered glass, crawling about on the lawn was an out of control Lewis. Barron and Zeke tried vainly to calm him. It was hard to tell if he was laughing or crying.

Helen raced into the room. "Good lord!" she exclaimed. "What kind of dope is that boy on?"

Mack said, "I don't know, Mom. But if you fetch me my lariat I'll rope and tie him for you." He sauntered out the door, proceeding to help his cousin get the unruly musician under control.

Rosie followed, devastated to see Lewis so wounded and wild. Cobwebs of abhorrence clung to memory while the cocktail of drugs and alcohol unleashed concern. "Lewis! Lewis!" She rushed to him crying, "Please don't be hurt!"

For an instant, he stopped his wild behavior and focused on Rosie. He welcomed her with outspread arms, and she cried against his shoulder. Leaning down he said in her ear softly, "I'd do anything to make you notice me. Don't you know that?"

Unexpectedly, she could see clearly through the haze.

A look of rage crossed his face, and murder glinted in his wild-eye expression. "See!" he screamed obscenely, "See what a fool I am for you? See!"

Terror gripped her, and she tried to pull away, but he wouldn't let go. "What do you mean?" Her voice was determined, and she twisted free while demanding, "That this is my fault? Are you saying that broken window is my fault?"

Lewis stepped toward Rosie only to be pulled back into a firm grip by Mack. "Let go of me!" he shouted, as Mack now had him in a choke hold that left the drunken musician's arms waving loosely in the air.

Barron rushed to grab him by the legs, and, because he kicked like a wounded deer, Zeke had to help pin him down. With makeup running down her face, Rosie watched the guys carry Lewis into the shadows, away from the house. Mack's mother put a sympathetic arm around her shoulders.

Shelley brushed past glaring with hatred. "Happy now, Sunshine?" she hissed.

Helen said soothingly, "You can't take the blame for a boy's idiotic antics. He wanted attention, and he got it. If he had just wanted your attention, he would never have done something like this!" With sincere sympathy she added, "Just come on inside, dear. If Barron can't take you home tonight, Mack can."

Stumbling back into the house with bleary perception, Rosie sank into a comfortable armchair blinded by the drugs, the booze and the tears. With closed eyes she sat in a quiet corner and contemplated the year that had just slipped past. Memories of sunlit summer days spent with Lewis and Angel flooded the dimmed corners of her mind. She yearned to return to the simple days of strawberry polished teeth and bicycle rides. Barron found her sitting near the foyer and gently helped her to her feet. Without talking, he led her out the door and down the steep imported brick steps. Together they wandered the asphalt drive to his parked van. After seating her inside, he glanced back at the big house. There in the shadows of the front entrance he saw the lanky form of his cousin, Mack. With a final wave farewell, he climbed in and drove away.

A frosty meadow crunched beneath the horse's shoes as Rosie and Janie rode the two palominos along worn cattle trails through the pastures. Warm breaths made tiny clouds in the wintry air. They rode in silence, defeated by disappointment. Just the day before came news of Kid's upcoming nuptials to the legislator's daughter.

The bridle chains rattled, ringing out into the silent wood as the horses labored over the muddy half-frozen turf. Meandering down a rock strewn path with deft sure footedness, the blonde ponies took sloping trails. Rosie instructed her charge to lean backwards, therefore assisting the balance of the steed. With short quick steps the equine plodded along the mountainous trail until they came to the edge of the Moon farm. Another hour of riding pushed the girls to an abandoned rutted logging road leading through the woods to Rocky Falls.

With casual slowness Rosie took a path along the ridge of the falls. The brisk air blowing off the falling water chilled them through warm layers. Carefully, Spice cantered along kicking up an occasional pebble that bounced down the side of the cliff and landed with a soft *plop* into the water below. Riding the trail along the cliffs was exhilarating to say the least, and at times frightening. Reluctantly, the ride ended with the girls arriving at the Campbell farm in good time to meet Janie's curfew.

The young girl looked up at Rosie seated astride Spice. A listless sigh escaped her as she searched for something to say. Shadows rimmed her eyes, and without speaking a word, the little girl patted Sugar on the neck then turned to enter the house. Stopping at the front door, Janie waited to see their departure. Nudging Spice into action, Rosie rode slowly away with Sugar following.

As she worked to groom the horses, a dark mood lingered. Rosie settled the horses inside their stalls wearing blankets. And, with a hearty helping of hay and grain with fresh water they were in for the cold winter's evening.

Returning home, she became acutely aware of the vacant plants, and blooming wisteria of summertime. Staring at the old rocking chair she wondered if the ghost of Doc Campbell was now satisfied that Kid would in no way be sharing in his treasure. The tiny vials of liquid morphine all remained in the pharmacy. Recalling stories of extreme drug addiction following the Civil War, she presumed that explained why Doc had such a quantity.

Entering the house, she found her parents in their usual Saturday activities. Sturgill had cleaned the fireplace of ashes earlier, and now had a warming fire burning seasoned wood in the hearth. Eva sat with her attention immersed in a true crime magazine, while Sturgill watched sports on television. No one bothered to speak as Rosie made her way through the house and into her bedroom. Pulling a quilt around her shoulders, she took a cross legged position on the bed to journal in her diary.

The last entry had been made at the beginning of the month when she had been upset over Lewis' destructive behavior following the New Year's Eve party. She read the last passage of that day's event. *Amazingly, not a drop of blood was lost with the shattered glass. Invisible shards of a young man's broken heart mingled with the debris of his own self destruction. Other than his own self-hatred, I only know that it was his screaming fury that frightened me so terribly.*

Rosie inhaled deeply. Lewis now avoided her at school. Barron seldom spoke, and Heather seemed to be spaced out beyond comprehension. She no longer wore Kid's gold chain. And, now that his wedding plans had been cemented on expensive stationary, she made plans to package the necklace and return it to him. With loneliness closing in, she wrote these plans in her diary.

Janie wandered about her grandparent's farmhouse aimlessly. No one was home, and isolation overwhelmed her. She hadn't made friends at school, therefore having no one to talk with on the phone. Standing at the refrigerator she opened and closed the door, not really hungry, just bored. She settled at the table and began doodling pictures to convey her utter despair. She drew a picture of Doc Campbell sitting in his rocking chair. The area surrounding him was shaded in dark blue and overlaid with deep purple. His hat covered all of his face except for the tip of his nose, and the mouth adorned by the fashionable moustache of his era. She drew the thin ribbon tie and depicted his Spanish style jacket as casually unbuttoned. Just as the picture seemed complete, she impulsively sketched a bullet hole on the left side of Doc's jacket, and finished her picture with blood staining the professional man's attire. At the bottom of the page she wrote in block letters, *The Murder of Doc Campbell.* Then she wandered away leaving the crayons and pad littering the table. A smile played wickedly across her lips as she imagined the astonished look on Maggie's face upon seeing the darkly fashioned portrayal of an ancestor's demise.

Chapter Twenty-Two
Cowboys and Indians

Rosie waited with the group of talent show winners, observing how introverted and withdrawn her old friend Heather had become. Mrs. Brown entered the auditorium and announced the plan of rehearsal they would be following for the upcoming two weeks. The Byron Town School did an annual fundraiser for the athletic department on Valentine's Day each year. Shelley hovered near Lewis, apparently not minding the way he ignored her. Zeke approached Rosie and said, "I wish Mrs. Brown would pair us together for a skit." He narrowed his eyes at Shelley saying, "That skinny little bitch unnerves me with her stupid Prima Donna demands."

With a shrug of the shoulders she replied, "I'd like that, Zeke." Peering at Lewis she added, "At least I can trust you to keep your head, and not go jumping through windows."

"Gee, Rosie. You know, I don't think he can be held responsible for that." She cut her eyes toward him, and he stammered, "I mean, damn it to hell! The poor fool was already on prescribed medication. Then the Martin's were plying the band with that cheap champagne knock-off. And, then along comes Jed with his blotter acid and cocaine." Zeke shook his head slowly, "We all know Lew has had some hard times. The combination of drugs and alcohol just pushed him over the edge." He stepped closer and said softly, "Just imagine losing your little sister?"

Impulsively she responded, "Angel was like my own sister, and I loved her, too." Staring at Lewis across the room she spat, "I would never use my grief as an excuse to hurt another person."

Zeke seemed confused, "What do you mean, Rosie?" With closed eyes she exhaled deeply, and sensing her unease, Zeke excused himself and walked away.

As the days wound down to the Valentine fundraiser, Rosie began to suffer unprovoked attacks from Shelley during school hours. The cruel intentions of the unhappy cousin didn't really bother her. It was the old friends who sided with her that caused Rosie bitter feelings of betrayal. Heather had begun to snub her and spend time with the increasingly popular Shelley. So, Rosie remained isolated and gifted herself with a new outfit each month. Fashion consumed her with stacks of magazines and catalogues. But, her obsession came with a painful price. She became the subject of envy, and ridicule. Bully boys began calling her *Hollywood* and envious girls spoke of her in third person, *The Princess*.

For the final dress rehearsal Rosie appeared wearing a classic red evening gown, strapless and adorned with tiny glass beads sewn into extravagant swirls across the bodice. The work-out was grueling. After showering, Rosie was leaving the locker room and bumped into Heather. Her old friend looked at her with dulled eyes, her complexion splotched from an outbreak of acne. Rosie said sweetly, "Your song is perfect for your voice. I can't wait to hear the applause you get." Heather didn't return an attempt at conversation. Feeling uncomfortable Rosie said, "Well, I'll see you later, Heather. Bye."

Brushing back strands of oily dark hair, Heather said, "Bye," and sauntered away.

Fighting a desire to cry, Rosie crossed the parking lot. She blinked unbelievingly as she watched Barron and Lewis approach her car. She spoke first to Barron. "Jed! Just the person I was looking for," calling him by his nickname.

A confident smile crossed his face, "Why me?"

"I was wondering if Heather is still part of your band."

Fidgeting he answered, "Well, she could be if she would show up for rehearsals."

"Yeah, well we used to be good friends, but now she avoids me," said Rosie.

Barron said enthusiastically, "She wrote a kick ass song! I've got it on tape, you should hear it."

"I'd love too. Did you guys need a ride home or something?" asked Rosie.

"We just wanted to talk," said Barron.

"That sounds friendly," retorted Rosie

Lewis said, "We *are* friends, Sunshine."

The sound of her name on his lips softened her heart. "What made you jump through that window like a lunatic? Are you still blaming me?"

Closing his eyes at the memory he said, "When you're full of 'ludes and booze you should never drop acid and snort coke. What else can I say?" He smiled slightly and asked the question he had been getting around too. "So, are you going to be attending Kid's wedding?"

She answered abruptly, feeling provoked, "No. What about Shelley? Is she going?"

At that moment, Shelley and another girl exited the girl's dressing room. Watching her like a hawk Lewis explained, "I don't talk to Shelley. It was Janie who told me." Taking hold of her hand he said, "Look, Rosie. I want us to be friends again."

With a blissful bicycle ride remembrance warming her heart she responded, "I'd like that, Lew. I'd really like that."

The day of the show arrived and the football players who doubled as dancers opened the act by dancing around a huge cardboard sign reading: *The Valentine Day Revue*. The entire group of performers took the stage and performed a medley of songs from the fifties. Then the performers broke away and did solos. Rosie changed costumes and donned her bedazzling red gown for her solo of *My Funny Valentine*. She was spotlighted on stage as she leaned against a prop piano for dramatic effect. Lewis took the spotlight after her performance and sang *It Had to Be You*. His performance drew loud applause, and then he and Rosie stepped into the spotlight together to perform *Stormy Weather*. After all scheduled performances, Rosie and Lewis stood front and center with the rest of the singers to execute a number to *Putting on the Ritz*. The finish was flamboyant as the girls were swept up with great flare by the boys while the curtain closed and the lights dimmed amid jovial ovation.

Having danced and sang the last three songs nonstop, Lewis was sweating and red faced from exertion when he caught up with Rosie at the girl's locker room. Deftly unfastening his bow tie he caught her hand saying, "Come on! Let's get out of here!"

"I need to change!" she protested.

He pulled her along, stopping just outside of the auditorium doors, where he hoisted her onto his hip as he had done many times when dancing. Tripping down the steps like Fred Astaire, he danced to the bottom and twirled her onto her feet with flamboyance, her gown flowing gracefully. They twirled and danced to the convertible never noticing the scathing look from Shelley Noble as they drove away.

Janie celebrated her eleventh birthday the week following Valentine's Day. Bert purchased a four year-old gelding mustang for his granddaughter's gift, and Rosie had been asked to help her break in the present. Impressed by the animal's magnificent beauty, but troubled by the horse's age, Rosie pointed out to Bert that youth was simply absence of experience and training. The animal would need a lot of attention.

Charlie approached with Teddy at his heels. "Happy butt-day, Janie!" he called in a sing-song.

She politely said, "Thank you, Charlie."

The older man climbed between the fence rails and joined the frisky young horse in the lot. Rosie sang softly, so Charlie couldn't hear, "*Happy butt-day to you.*"

"Oh, stop it. You're not funny," scowled Janie.

The ending days of March were blustery on the mountain. Keeping in touch with Rosie, Kid disclosed plans regarding his new band. He never mentioned the woman he shared an upscale home with. Her father provided everything the spoiled girl needed to be happy, and that included a locally popular musician for a husband. Mentioning he had uncovered a way to get money for his band without cashing in any of the coins, he hinted at the vials of morphine in the secret room. Filled with uncertainty, Rosie agreed to ship one of the small boxes to him at a post office box address.

Her parents were asleep, and it was drizzling cold rain when she sneaked into the forlorn alcove. Slippers covered her feet, yet she shivered remembering the cold stone underfoot. Hurrying inside with a flashlight she scooped up one of the boxes from a dusty shelf, and hurried out. The spirit of Doc Campbell hadn't intruded upon her dreams in weeks, and she hoped to keep it that way.

Addressing the package settled cold dread through her. She could only pray they never had to take this chance again. The urge to write down her adventure of the dark room was strong, but she didn't dare journal those actions.

The spring days of April dawned with the two girls riding on a regular basis. Happily, the sleek black mustang fulfilled Janie's desire for friendship. And, having restored a casual relationship with Lewis, Rosie was happier, too. Sturgill surprised his daughter one cold April Saturday when his buddy arrived with a trailer hauling the glass walls and roof to a small greenhouse. Anticipation consumed her as she marked the area at the edge of her garden for the planting house. The day lingered on as the men assembled the small conservatory, and Rosie was the first to enter through the glass paned door when it was complete.

"It's the coolest thing I've ever had! Now I'll be able to grow lettuce, onions, radishes and spinach during winter months! Imagine, a garden fresh salad in winter?" The small hothouse consumed her energy just as the horse named Wildfire consumed Janie's.

On a cold April night Kid called Rosie. In cryptic code he asked for more of the product she had hoped he would never need again. Following along with his request, Rosie only answered in simple words, and quickly got off the phone with him. She had been shocked when her handsome cousin mailed her a receipt from where he had deposited a generous amount of cash into the banking account she had opened after he sold the coin. Once again, she complied with his request and addressed the small box to the post office, but addressed a personal letter to his father's residence.

Being careful not to acknowledge any wrong doing, Rosie expressed concerns she was feeling. She ended her letter in a coded way to tell Kid she was nervous, and wanted to stop the game they had been playing. Several days past, and she received a card in the mail. The card had enclosed another deposit receipt for her bank account, and a detailed letter in which he expressed regrets for how things had worked out in his life. He wrote over and over of his plans to be free of his wife, and his only desire was to be with her. He promised to send a demo tape of his band, writing, "Once you hear the sound my boys can make, you'll agree that the risk was worth it."

The last Saturday in April dawned with a beautiful layer of white snow, and Rosie fretted over the weight of the substance littering the glass hothouse roof as she worked preparing cups of soil with lettuce seed sprouts. Preparing to leave, she paused at the entrance, admiring her progress. Suddenly, a sharp snapping noise startled her, drawing her attention upward. She screamed when someone grabbed her from behind, jerking her from the glass building.

A thunderous crash occurred just as Rosie cleared the danger. She heard Lewis's exclaim, "Dear God! How did that happen? I thought Sturgill knew what he was doing when he built this!"

Breathless, she stared at a ceiling pane that had given way and crashed where she had been standing earlier. Impulsively, she pulled away, "What brings you here just in time for my rescue?" Taking in the mess of broken glass and mounds of snow littering her work bench she announced, "You have a knack for showing up just in the nick of time to save me."

He looked over the accident asking, "Is it just a coincidence the glass pane broke right over where you work?" He stepped inside and stared at the windy hole in the glass roof.

Poking her head inside cautiously, she asked, "Want some hot tea, or something?"

Raising a hand he pointed with his index finger, "That glass is smoothly cut." He touched his hand to his chin and said, "Like it was scored with a cutting tool."

"Who would gain anything from hurting me, or my property?" she asked.

"Do you have enemies?"

Remembering her stepmother's words, she replied, "Of course, don't you?"

Later that night Kid called. Sounding slightly desperate he asked, "Can you send me more?" He let the line go silent for a long moment before saying, "This should be the last time."

"Yes, well the supply isn't exactly unlimited, you know?" Rosie agreed begrudgingly.

The following day was Sunday. She packaged the box, hoping the venture was ended with this last shipment. It was ready for the postman on Monday, and just as she was beginning to journal, the phone rang in the kitchen.

Eva called to Rosie. "Hold on, Maggie, I hear her coming."

"Is something wrong?" asked Rosie through the phone.

Maggie began explaining hurriedly, "Janie went out forty minutes ago on Wildfire. Now, Wildfire is here without her." Franticly she asked, "What should I do?"

Panic surged through Rosie as she imagined hazards on the trails. "Just keep Wildfire right there. And get me one of Bert's ropes," she commanded, "I'm on my way."

Maggie was cloaked in warm wool and holding tight to Wildfire when Rosie arrived. Worry wrinkled the woman's brow, "I hope she's okay, Rosie. I don't know if I can take any more tragedy." Maggie seemed short of breath as she said, "I don't think I've ever felt this scared!" She covered her face with her hands and attempted to console herself, but tears flowed miserably.

A slender rope was coiled onto the saddle horn. Rosie said, "I'm sure she's fine, but go ahead and send someone down to check on us at the falls. Call Lewis and have him find Charlie."

Apprehension grew as Wildfire neared the final path to the falls. The horse took the steep trails easily, and Rosie watched diligently for signs. Occasionally she would stop and call out Janie's name, holding her breath each time as she strained to hear the child respond. Wildfire traveled a treacherous path winding slowly down a steep cliff along the trail to the falls. Trees held tiny green buds and wild crocus bloomed among tender green ferns along the trail. The sound of an engine greeted her as she and Wildfire crossed the bridge. Old Charlie's truck came around the bend and jerked to a halt. The passenger door opened and Teddy bounced from the truck followed by Lewis.

While Lewis and Charlie began descending the cliffs on the opposite side, Rosie urged Wildfire over the slippery wet paths that he had crossed earlier. Hoof prints were embedded into the moist soil and moss from his earlier trek. Rounding a sharp curve in the trail, Rosie was taken aback by the sight of Janie sprawled over a fallen tree, half in and half out of the icy water.

Dismounting Wildfire, she led him into the piercing cold creek toward the lifeless child. With every ounce of her strength, she pushed the unconscious child over the saddle. Holding her securely with one hand and leading the horse with the other, Rosie started out of the bitterly cold water. Settling Wildfire into a level area she mounted, pulling the child against her in the saddle and allowed Wildfire to ascend the trail at his own pace, which became quick and sure.

They broke from the trail just below the bridge. Wildfire was beaded in perspiration, and his muscles quivered from strenuous exertion. Prodding the beast to Charlie's truck, she dismounted and placed Janie inside. After wrapping Janie in her own coat, Rosie leaned on the steering wheel sounding long on the horn.

The child's face was colorless; her breathing shallow. Again, Rosie leaned over and sounded the horn. Rosie cried, "Wake up! Wake up!" Putting her face against the chilled cheeks she wept, "You'll be okay!"

Suddenly, Charlie jumped into the truck. Sliding Janie over the seat, Rosie climbed inside just as Lewis appeared at her elbow. He closed the truck door and led Wildfire away from the bridge, with Teddy at his heels. Charlie cranked the engine and the old truck lunged into life as it rolled across the bridge, headed into town.

Later, Rosie sat at the hospital with Maggie, Bert, Charlie and Shelley as they waited for hospital staff to inform them of Janie's condition. Maggie was suffering from dizziness and Shelley clung to her grandmother's every word. Bert and Charlie stood at opposite sides of the small waiting area while Rosie sat near a window, peering out into the aging day.

Shelley's shrill voice alarmed everyone when she cried, "G-Mama needs help!"

Maggie collapsed into the floor, sliding gently from the chair. In only a moment the waiting area was infiltrated by hospital staff as they assessed Maggie's condition. Two orderlies rushed in with a gurney, placed the limp body on it then rushed to ER.

Shelley and Bert hurried away with Maggie. During a baffling moment of silence Rosie became aware Lewis had arrived. Looking about the almost vacant lobby she noticed that Charlie had taken her prior position, and now sat looking out into the gathering dusk.

Evening fell and the mountain was cloaked in satin darkness. Finally, a young male hospital employee stepped into the room announcing that Janie had regained consciousness, and they could see her.

Rushing to Janie's room, they gathered around her protectively. She was conscious, and had an intravenous tube taped in place on her hand. The circles beneath her eyes had intensified and she seemed very sleepy.

Rosie perched beside her and asked, "Do you remember what happened this morning?"

Her eyes darted about as she tried to recall events. In a weak voice she answered, "I tried to cross the creek where you never would let me before." Tears welled in her pale blue eyes, "Wildfire stepped in a deep hole, and got spooked. I fell off while he was jumping around trying to get out of the cold water." Her eyes closed with exhaustion. "I'm sorry for disobeying you, Rosie."

"Just rest," she said, pulling the blanket to her chin. The younger girl closed her eyes and fell asleep.

Leaving the room, Rosie followed the corridor to the hospital exit behind Lewis to his grandmother's car. Charlie left in his truck alone. The ride home was mostly silent. When they came within sight of Rosie's house he said, "I hope Maggie recovers from her stroke quickly." He maneuvered the car into the drive way. "But, I need to tell you about something I overheard at the hospital today." Without looking at her, he said, "Dr. Martin seems to have convinced Bert that Janie's problem is mental, and not accidental."

With disbelief she sighed, "Thanks, I'll look out for her."

Rushing to her bedroom, she found a message from Kid taped to her door asking her to call, regardless of time. She ached from stress and tension, so she soaked in a warm bubble bath till the water got chilled.

After having dressed for bed, Rosie settled next to the phone and called Kid long distance. Listening to the ringing of the phone, her imagination raced to a formal day when he wore a tuxedo, and brushed rice from his shoulders. When Kid answered the phone, she was lost in a racing imagination, "Hey, there. You left a message with Eva for me to call when I got home."

"I've made an enemy, Sun." His voice sounded a little desperate as he said, "My enemy could be your enemy. Get it?"

"I doubt it," she said. "But just in case, go ahead and tell me what this villain looks like."

"Two of 'em; one with a snake tattooed on his neck, and another with a scar across the back of his right hand." He fell quiet then he said, "If you see either one of those guys I want you to run. Got it?"

"Run where?"

He answered with sarcasm, "You might not want me to know." Sounding despondent he said, "Hey, listen. I don't like doing this, but I'm being pressured for more." He seemed on the edge of tears, "I want it to be finished just as much as you do." Clearing his throat he said, "Good news, though! We're getting more dough this time around."

"Great. Maybe we'll live to spend it." The dry humor she used unnerved him, so he sat silently on his end of the phone. Taking a deep breath she said, "Well, I've got some disturbing news. Dr. Martin has told Bert he thinks Janie's accident was more or less a suicide attempt."

A long audible sigh came over the phone. "G-Dad is already blaming the child for G-Mama's stroke."

In a moment of weakness Rosie gushed, "Oh, Kid, I wish I had never let you leave last summer. If you were still here none of this would be happening." Then with resignation she said, "I'm going to bed now."

He sounded off, saying, "Sweet dreams, Sunshine."

Janie pulled through her precarious ordeal with flying colors. Maggie, however, would need months of nursing to see her through her debilitating stroke. A cruel twist of fate brought Opal Shirey to the Campbell farmhouse as Maggie's nursemaid. Each time she looked at her friend's mother, Janie felt guilt for Angel's death. So, she avoided Opal when she could.

One Saturday morning Janie was surprised by a visit from Rosie. The younger girl stood in the warm sunshine of May, throwing a hunting knife at a large chunk of firewood. Rosie sat on an old garden bench, "I've got to do grocery shopping. Would you like to go with me?"

Carefully sliding the knife into a leather sheath, Janie replaced it safely in the tool shed, before taking the trip with her older cousin. Maneuvering the car along the winding country roads, Rosie talked to Janie about the ludicrous things Kid had warned her about. They were to beware of a man with a snake tattooed on his neck and a man with a scar across the back of his right hand. Janie asked some childish, yet important questions. "Okay, so if I see a big ugly man with a snake tattooed on his neck, I can't just say, 'Oh, my God! There's a man with a snake on his neck!' So, we got to get us a code word." After a moment of silence, she exclaimed, "Cowboys and Indians!"

Rosie burst into giggles, "Cowboys and Indians! That's your code word?"

"Do you have a better one?"

"Cowboys and Indians is the perfect code word!" laughed Rosie.

"I keep having dreams of living in the seaside apartment." The younger girl announced, as if Rosie had been waiting for such a confession.

"Are they good dreams, or bad dreams?"

"Neither, really." The little girl's words lingered heavily in the air.

"Well, the good news is if you're dreaming it means you're sleeping." The country roadway had led them onto Byron Town's main street, and Rosie drove slowly as she chatted. "So, what will you do if I say, 'Cowboys and Indians?'"

"Run out the back door?" Janie asked mockingly. "How did all this get started anyway?"

Rosie explained she had gotten involved with trafficking narcotic drugs with Kid in a long drawn-out story. With a contemptuous look Janie responded, "That's so stupid! Why didn't you just sell some coins?"

"Because I am stupid," moaned Rosie.

"How much money do we have?"

"Enough."

The school year was drawing to a close, and expectations were high as the students in the one building schoolhouse stressed over final exams, and graduation. Rosie was putting books away in her locker when Lewis approached.

"May I carry your books for you?" He shifted them under his arm with a flirtatious smile.

Shelley appeared next to him and asked, "Aren't you riding with me to band practice?"

"Did I ask you for a ride?" Tossing her an aggravated look he snapped, "No! The answer is no!"

"Oh! So I get my head bit off just for trying to be nice?" She stepped back and crossed her arms with a disdainful look. "Well, thanks for nothing!" The tall slender girl stormed away.

Feeling embarrassed for him, Rosie asked, "So, are you okay after that?"

"Damn! She is so pathetic, you know? She's always like 'Look at me!' when we're practicing. I'm just so tired of her attitude." He grumbled as they walked away together.

As they rounded the corner, Shelley was talking with Heather at the exit. When she noticed Rosie and Lewis walking toward them, Shelley ended the conversation and called out loudly, "I'll call you tonight." She then left the building.

Heather stood waiting for them. Rosie said, "Hello, Heather. How are you?"

Tilting her head sideways she said, "Good. How are you?"

"Very well, thanks." She started to walk by, but Heather stopped her.

"Hey, Rosie, would you like to come to my house for a sleep over next weekend? I'm just having a little party, and some of the girls are going to sleep over."

The idea wasn't pleasing to Rosie, but she didn't want to hurt her old friend's feelings. "Well sure, if you want me to."

"Great!"

Opal Shirey had stepped out onto the porch to greet Ed as he pulled into the Campbell driveway. Teddy's playful barking had drawn her attention to a pile of pillows and cushions on the lawn at the front of the porch. Stepping from the porch, she followed Teddy's gaze upward to the roof. There, silhouetted by the afternoon sun, she saw Janie standing with an open umbrella readied to jump. Opal stumbled backward and yelled, "No! No! Janie, don't!"

Her words were spoken just a split second too late, as Janie had already begun a twenty-foot drop. Opal heard herself scream when the umbrella fold backward uselessly and she fell into a dead faint just as Ed ran in at the precise moment, catching Janie in midair.

Clutching onto Ed while still holding to the crippled umbrella, she tossed aside the broken gadget while shouting, "Damn it!"

Ed set her down gently then rushed to check on his mother. Looking up to the roof from whence she had just leapt Janie announced, "If I had only had a good umbrella I know I could have floated down." She reasoned, "I don't weigh as much as the flying nun, so surely I can float."

Ed helped Opal to her feet and said dryly, "Nuns can't fly, people can't float and don't call me Shirley."

The little girl laughed, "Why would I ever call you Shirley?" She began picking up pillows and cushions meant to break her fall as Ed walked his mother safely into the house.

Teddy lay in the grass watching intently. A low growl escaped the interested canine as he yawned and panted sleepy-eyed. "Tattletale!" scolded Janie.

Chapter Twenty-Three
Graduation and Betrayal

The lake sparkled beneath the setting sun, reflecting kaleidoscope rays like wavering rainbows. Lewis and Rosie stood side by side at the bon fire in Heather's back yard. Music blared from stereo speakers placed strategically in the windows from inside the house, and teenagers discretely drank beer from Dixie cups. Shelley approached, a smirking smile played across her lips. "Rosie, your hair looks especially lovely this evening." Using her index finger to twirl a fizzy lock of her own hair, she asked, "Is that what attracts you to her, Lewis, her hair?"

Taking Rosie by the hand he said in her ear, "Let's go see what Shotgun Jed has in his pockets tonight." He tugged her away while nudging Shelley rudely aside with his shoulder.

She shot him an angry glance as he and Rosie walked away. Resentment raged, staining her neck with splotches of red, and she stomped into the house in search of Heather.

"Something about that girl scares me," admitted Rosie. "It's like she's demon possessed. She hates me so much."

Standing next to Barron, Lewis said, "Well, Jed here ain't scared of her. Are ya Jed?"

With narrowed eyes Barron growled, "I eat bitches like her for breakfast."

They laughed and wandered the trail to the lake. "Why do they call you Jed?" asked Rosie.

"Barron always brings a shotgun with him when we go hunting, instead of a rifle. So we just started calling him Jed. Because that's how Jed Clampett discovered oil on his land, by shooting at game with a shotgun," explained Lewis.

Dusk was growing across the mountain lake, and bats flitted along the shoreline drawn by mosquitoes. At the water's edge Barron removed a cigarette box from his shirt pocket and began inspecting his goods. "Okay," he said, "What can I interest you in?"

Back at the campfire night had fallen and wind from the lake was chilled. Rosie slipped on a denim jacket and Lewis slipped an arm around her shoulders. She hadn't forgotten the violence that still scarred her, but she had somehow made peace with it. Heather stood in the midst of young people, quiet and obscure.

Barron said loudly, "Hey, Heather! Get your guitar and do that song for us."

"No, Jed!" She waved her hands in the air dismissing the idea.

Voices from the crowd rang out, "Sing, Heather!"

With a little more hesitation Heather gave in and said, "Okay, Jed! You go get my guitar, and I'll do the damn song."

Heather held an apprehensive look on her face when Barron returned. She took the instrument while he began quieting the crowd. Settled on a bench, she began strumming soft mournful cords. The minor chords infiltrated the cool evening, building crescendo until she sang out with powerful vocals blending smoothly with the guitar harmony.

"It's hard to make the teenage scene,
When all you've learned is from movie screens.
And, no one cares if you've had a chance,
To sing the song, or dance the dance.
As long as you're beautiful,

Oh, those of us with lovely faces,
Play the game and win the races.
While those of us without fine graces,
Find life's empty places,
When you're just a teen."

She paused for a long instrumental, keeping her head low, focusing all attention on guitar chords. A smooth breeze fanned the fire, which sent sparks flying beyond the tree tops to die among the glittering stars.

"So those of us with rags to wear,
Stay at home playing solitaire.
While the pretty girls play truth or dare,
And, live their lives without a care.
Feel the pain of the tragic few,
Giving credit when no credit's due;

Oh, to have an ugly face,
To never play the game, or win the race,
Living without simple grace,
Just to find its empty place,
Is simple hell, when you're just a teen.
It's hard to make the teenage scene,
When all you've learned is from movie screens.
And, you're just a teen."

With a soft strum of chords the song ended. Applause erupted and Heather dropped her head, as if embarrassed by the praise.

In the moment of quiet following the applause, Shelley stepped forward and said, "Great song, Heather!" Then she held her plastic cup up and said, "Here's to Heather and all other song writers!" Everyone cheered to the toast. After sipping from her cup Shelley narrowed her eyes at Rosie, and pushing back frizzy hair said, "Hey, everybody! Did you know John Prine wrote a song about Rosie's father! It's called there's a hole in Daddy's arm where all the money goes."

The crowd fell silent and Rosie's heart sank with humiliation. Zeke yelled, "Oh shut your pie hole!"

The crowd agreed with likewise shouts of, "Shut your pie hole!" then erupted with laughter and conversation.

Lewis quickly stepped next to Shelley and taking her elbow pulled her from the fire. They shared brutal words before she stomped away. When he returned Rosie said, "Good thing you're friends with my worst enemy. No telling what she would have told next, maybe about the ghost on my porch."

Heather approached with a blended drink. "I mixed you a special drink, Rosie. It's called a White Russian."

Rosie sipped the drink, "Thanks!" A short time later she grew suddenly sleepy. Approaching Heather she said, "I think I'm just going to go home. I'm so tired."

Heather said, "Please don't go. You can lie down in my bed. Most of the girls are going to crash in the living room anyway."

Rosie tried to focus across the fire, but her vision doubled, causing her head to spin. "Damn!" she declared, "How did I get so drunk?"

"It's okay. Just come along with me." Heather led Rosie to her bedroom, and pulled back the bedcovers for her.

Snuggled beneath the blankets with all her clothes on, she said with a weak voice, "Thanks, Heather, for being so nice."

Sunrise brought a golden glow through the windows and Rosie stirred beneath the covers. An odd smell caught her attention, and she rolled onto her back, gazing at the ceiling with efforts to recall the previous evening. Absently minded, she combed fingers through her hair, but they became entangled in a hard substance. Bewildered, she roused and peered into the dresser mirror. Dark streaks of glossy strands reflected from the glass. She touched her hair again, gasping in horror. Long tresses of coffee colored hair were ruined with hardened glue.

Rosie rushed through the house to find Heather, who was sleeping on the sofa. As she passed through the kitchen, she picked up a pair of scissors lying on the counter, and awakened her friend frantically. Heather protested, "I'm sleeping!"

Leaping on top of her, Rosie held Heather pinned to the sofa with her knees demanding, "What did you do to my hair?"

Sleepily, Heather said, "It's only honey, it'll wash out."

"Like hell it's only honey! This is glue!" Rosie shouted angrily.

Heather focused on the scissors glinting in the morning rays and grew frantic. "But, Shelley said it was honey!" The betrayal struck both girls simultaneously.

Rosie's eyes welled with tears, "Shelley said!"

Heather whispered with teary eyes, "Oh Rosie, I'm so sorry. I'll do anything you want, but *please* don't cut my hair!"

Still gripping the threatening scissors Rosie seethed, "What was in that drink you gave me?"

"I put two of my mother's sleeping pills in it so you wouldn't wake up when I was pouring the honey on your hair." Heather's confession fell shamefully from her lips, and she clung to the blanket, trembling.

"Shelley will be very proud of you. But our friendship is over!" Raising the scissors Rosie pointed the sharp tip at Heather saying, "Don't even try to talk to me again, ever!" With the ultimatum announced, she savagely plunged the scissors into the pillow next to Heather's head. While tiny feathers floated in midair the door slammed from Rosie's departure, rattling windows.

A few minutes later, she was knocking at the door of her neighbor, Willene Reyes. Willene came to the door in her nightgown and showed surprise. "Rosie! Why are you up so early on a Saturday morning?"

Stepping inside the familiar farmhouse she said, "I'm so sorry to trouble you, Willene, but something terrible has happen." Putting her hand to her hair she frowned, "A little prank got out of hand. You see, one of my friends thought she was putting honey in my hair last night at a slumber party, but in fact it was glue." Huge tears hung in her eyes. "I'm afraid the only thing I can do is cut my hair."

Willene put her hand to Rosie's hair and said, "Oh, dear! This is a mess. Come sit down. Let me fix some coffee."

The older woman began preparing the percolator while Rosie sat slumped at the kitchen table. "You know, even if I do have to cut my hair, I don't care. I've been looking for a change anyway."

Willene smiled at her young neighbor's comment. "That's a good attitude. And, I think I know just the person who can help you." She poured two cups of coffee. "I'd like it if we kept this just between us."

"Of course," agreed Rosie.

"Do you remember me talking about an old friend of mine, Bonzie Leak?"

"Yes, you said he was a barber."

"Yes, that's right." Willene smiled sweetly before saying, "He's here right now. I'm sure he won't mind helping you. Just wait here."

While Willene was out of the room the painful memory of Shelley complimenting Rosie's hair the night before caused her to cringe. A slow steaming hatred began. As revenge plots coursed through her mind, she touched her ruined hair miserably. The sound of soft footsteps caught her attention as a tall lanky man stepped into the kitchen.

He nodded his head and said, "Good morning, Miss Moon. I hear you've got a problem. Willene thinks I can help. I'll give it a try if you want."

With a thankful smile she responded, "Yes, thank you so much."

Hours later, she sat in her room with the plastic cap of an electric hair dryer over her head as she wrote Kid a letter explaining what Shelley had accomplished. Putting the letter aside, she went to stand before the mirror. Uncurling the short mass of hair from the rag rollers, her hair sprang into soft curls.

Rummaging through her makeup bag, she began darkening her eyes with a deep charcoal gray eye pencil. She enhanced the arch of her eyebrows with the same shade, and applied blue eye shadow across the lids. The image reflecting from the mirror was startling. With a dark shade of lipstick staining her lips, she left her room and went to face her biggest critic.

Saturday sports shows played in the Moon household as usual. She walked into the living room to be ignored by her parents, as they always did. To gain their full attention, she went and stood in front of the television set. When her father took notice of her his mouth dropped open. "Sunshine Rose!" he exclaimed. "What have you done to your hair?"

Eva looked up at her and said, "Oh! It's beautiful. I wish I could get my hair to style like that."

Sturgill scowled, "Whatever caused you to do such a thing?"

She couldn't tell her father the truth for fear of the scene he would cause with Bert, and his granddaughter. "I just wanted a change, Daddy."

"Change my ass! You don't even look the same." Sturgill dragged his fingers through his own thick hair and said, "You look like you stepped out of some movie magazine."

Eva smiled, "It really becomes you, Rosie."

Shocked at the flattery from her stepmother Rosie asked disbelievingly, "Do you really like it, Eva?"

"Oh hell, she don't know nothing!" Sturgill snapped.

Giving her husband a hateful glare Eva said, "I adore your new hairstyle, and I can just bet you all the other girls in school will be following your lead, and cut their hair short, too."

Incredulously, Sturgill shook his head, "You look like that movie actress who played in that movie where she had the devil's baby."

"Do you think so?" asked Rosie enthusiastically.

Sturgill leaned back, propping his feet on the coffee table. "I didn't mean it as a compliment. But, to tell you the truth," he hesitated a moment and said, "Well, you look damn cute!"

Monday morning came and Rosie walked through the hallways of school wearing an off the shoulder peasant blouse with hip hugging flare legged jeans and big hoop earrings. Other students stopped to stare as if she were a new student. While looking through her locker she was confronted by a startled Lewis. "Oh, hello Lewis," she started past him.

He followed saying, "Wow, Rosie! What did you do to your hair? It's totally cool!"

She noticed Shelley standing with one of her friends and they appeared to be laughing. "This is what happens to you when a jealous bitch named Shelley cons her dip shit friend, Heather, into pouring what she said was honey on my hair while I was knocked out at the party." Seeing the look of confusion on his face she explained, "You see the White Russian Heather gave me was really a Mickey. She dosed it with some of Teresa's sleeping pills." She turned, caught his gaze and completed her story. "And, the honey turned out to be glue."

With anger darkening his face he cursed, "That bitch! Damn her!"

Putting out her hand, Rosie pushed him gently back saying, "Just give me some space, huh? I mean, if you keep on making her jealous my whole greenhouse is going to fall on top of me." With purposeful intent, she turned and walked away.

Janie sat with her grandfather in the doctor's waiting area nervously kicking her feet beneath her as she sat in an orange plastic chair. She looked at Bert and asked, "Why do you want me to see a new doctor G-Daddy? Don't you like Dr. Martin anymore?"

Bert looked down at his granddaughter. "This new doctor is going to help you with your problems, Janie."

"What problems?"

"Like how you want to float off roofs, and how you torture your poor teacher, and what about that picture you drew of your daddy committing suicide?"

"What about it? He did commit suicide."

Bert shifted in his chair. "This doctor is going to help you forget those bad memories."

"Well, the only way I could ever forget bad memories is if that part of my brain were to be cut out." She looked seriously at her grandfather and asked, "Are you going to ask this doctor to cut part of my brain out?"

"Heavens no child!" exclaimed Bert. "He's just going to talk to you, and that's all."

A nurse called from a swinging door, "Janie Noble."

Suffocating apprehension swelled within Janie. Focusing a dizzy gaze at the nurse, the confused child followed her into the doctor's examining room.

It was high school graduation night and Janie sat with her grandfather as they watched Shelley, Lewis and Rosie take the walk for the prized diploma. Bert nudged her asking, "Aren't you happy for your sister? She's graduating, and you know what that means?"

"What?"

Bert leaned closer and said, "It means she'll be looking for a husband, or going off to college." He winked and said, "Either way, you'll be rid of her!"

Her eyes grew wide and she smiled at his suggestions. "Nothing could make me happier!"

Following the crowd outdoors, and intending to get to her car and go home, someone sneaked behind Rosie and goosed her ribcage by poking a finger on each side. She jumped, and whirled to see the culprit. Ed Shirey stood smiling as if he were about to burst into laughter.

"You scared the shit out of me!" With a scowling look she turned away and continued walking.

Ed grabbed her by the hand, "Wait a minute. I want to talk to you."

Inhaling deeply she said, "Let's get out of here first then we can talk." And, they made their way out of the crowded gymnasium.

Once outside she took a deep breath of the clean evening air. "Finally!" she exclaimed, "I hate to be caught in a crowd like that."

Ed teased, "Oh, yeah. Well, Woodstock must have been a real drag for you then." He chuckled when she rolled her eyes and waved his comment away. "But, look! You've got to see the graduation present I got here for Lew."

He held a Joe Cocker album titled *Mad Dogs and Englishmen,* but Ed had cleverly crossed through the word *Englishmen* with a single line from a black marker and written above it *Hillbillies.* Breaking into a gentle laugh she said, "That's adorable!"

"Hey! You want to go to Jed's party with me?"

She had heard Barron's aunt was giving him a party at her big country house. "Well, I don't know. I didn't bring my swimsuit with me."

"Are you kidding? It's a skinny dipping party!"

Driving along with the radio playing softly, Ed held out his clenched fist, "Here you go, Sunshine."

He dropped a pill into her palm. Staring at the large round tablet she asked, "What's this?"

Taking the ever present flask from his jacket he said simply, "A Quaalude."

"Isn't this what made Lew freak out the day of Angel's funeral? And, isn't this what contributed to him jumping through the window on New Year's Eve?"

Ed sighed heavily, "Just take it, you'll mellow out, that's all."

"No, thank you. If I let myself pass out at another party with Shelley around I'm likely to wake up dead."

"I'll take care of you, don't worry."

"Thanks, but no thanks." And she dropped the tablet back into his hand.

A short time later, while standing inside the familiar foyer of the grand house Rosie smiled when Mack took notice and rushed to greet her, "Hey there! How are you, Rosie? Gosh, I just love your hair!" Turning to Ed he said, "Don't think we're holding a grudge against your brother." He shifted his weight and tipped his cowboy hat saying, "We just wanted Barron's band tonight."

"Do you know if Heather is playing with the band?" asked Rosie.

Mack closed one eye and said, "No, I don't know." He turned on his heel and walked away with his silver tipped cowboy boots gleaming.

Looking at Rosie, Ed asked, "Well, now that *Hoss* has left us alone, how's about us taking a stroll around the swimming pool?"

She tried to suppress a smile against his cruel humor, "Okay."

Janie returned home from the graduation ceremony and joined her grandmother in the living room. Maggie had been left reclining in a chair with Charlie Brown as her sitter. Charlie teased by asking, "You been jumping off woofs lately?"

With a sour look Janie answered, "No. But next time I jump I'm going to have a real good umbrella and a windy day."

Maggie mumbled, shaking her head at the child's remark. Charlie chuckled and said, "Now, don't worry. We won't 'et her jump off any more woofs."

Bert entered the room and said, "Janie, don't forget your bedtime medicine. I think it's about time you be taking it."

Furrowing her eyebrows she declared, "G-Daddy! That medicine makes me feel loopy. I don't think I should take it anymore."

Bert said gruffly, "You will take it, because the doctor said too!"

Janie looked at her grandmother and asked, "Will Shelley be getting married now or going away to college?"

Maggie looked at Charlie and mumbled something unintelligible. Bert asked, "What do you think, Charlie? Will Shelley be getting married?"

Charlie shook his head negatively and said, "Who wants to buy de tow when he tan det de milk for fee?"

Bert said gruffly, "Damn, Charlie! You weren't supposed to say that." He looked at Janie sternly, "Go on now! Take your medicine and get ready for bed."

While Barron's band played, Shelley danced with Mack Martin and Rosie stood next to Ed, appreciating the music. Suddenly, he put his arms around her waist and pulled her against him seductively. Following his gaze to the foyer, she saw Lewis walking in with a familiar looking girl. Immediately, he noticed Rosie and his brother. Putting a protective arm around his date, he walked her to the middle of the floor where the others were dancing.

Rosie asked, "Who's the girl?"

"She's a cheerleader from Ennis." With his mouth to her ear he said, "He's trying to make you jealous."

With squint eyes she said, "You're silly."

Laughing lightly he hugged her closer. With his mouth still at her ear he said, "You really should have taken that 'lude you know?"

"Oh, I'm just fine without it."

Heather appeared looking sad, as though she had been crying, and joined the band. She sang with Barron while tapping a tambourine against her hip. Rosie suspected Heather deliberately avoided eye contact as she quickly took leave when it was announced Lewis and Shelley would perform a song. Everyone applauded, except Rosie and Ed.

During the transition Barron approached, "Hey, hey! You guys having fun yet?" He slapped Ed on the back and shook his hand. "You'll have to excuse me I need to take a little stroll to the pool house." Turning to walk away he asked, "You two want to come with me?" He put his finger to his nose, "Have a little blow?"

Ed shook his head slowly.

Rosie smiled, "Not this time, Jed."

Barron smiled and walked away through the glass patio doors.

Shelley and Lewis were still singing, but the loathing Rosie felt for Shelley wouldn't allow her to enjoy the song. All she could think was how badly she wanted to jerk the girl's stringy mass of hair from her head.

The song ended and Shelley left Lewis's side as he began singing with another band member. The girl who had come to the party with him stood close. Four unfamiliar boys entered the grand living room from the foyer. One of them walked to the girl and pulled her away. They began to argue. The girl shook her head in disagreement and returned to the place where she had been standing near the band.

"Looks like trouble's brewing," said Ed. "Those guys are football players from Ennis, and from the looks of it that big one must be the cheerleader's boyfriend."

The broad shouldered young man began taking menacing steps toward the band. Stepping away from the microphone, Lewis braced to defend himself.

Screams and shouts were heard from the patio as Helen Martin and her husband rushed in. Lewis was protecting himself against unprovoked blows as Helen rushed for the telephone to call police. Shouts of encouragement were coming from the gathered crowd as they watched the fight. The larger man lost his balance and fell backward. Lewis jumped on top of him and was delivering one blow after another. The girl who had come to the party with Lewis screamed obscenities, and jumped onto his back beating him with her fists.

Shelley sprang into action, pulling her away from Lewis. The two girls began fighting, and it seemed to unleash a dam of hostility. The three other boys rushed into the scene meeting opposition from Mack, Ed and Zeke. Porcelain lamps shattered against the hardwood floors as tables were knocked against during the scuffle. The room exploded into screams, curses and bloody punches. Men from the patio rushed in to help. Finally, the three boys broke and ran when someone yelled, "The police are here!"

Only Lewis and the burly football player continued to throw punches. Andy Martin shouted for them to stop. Lewis attempted to stop, but the robust stranger pushed him over a chair, landing on top of him. It appeared Lewis was in dire trouble, but using his feet, he pushed the heavier man over in a midair flip that left the football player sprawled on his back.

Two police officers entered the room and grabbed Lewis off the other man. "You're under arrest, both of you!" The officers handcuffed both men.

Helen followed the officer saying, "It was self defense! He was attacked!"

Rosie saw Ed across the room, a bruise turning dark under his left eye. Stepping gingerly over the broken glass and around the overturned furniture she reached to touch the swelling eye.

He winced and pulled away, "Don't do that! It hurts."

With worry she asked, "What are we going to do now? The police are taking Lewis to jail."

Knitting his brows together, he said, "Let Lewis worry about himself! Maybe he'll think twice before he dates around with another man's girlfriend." She replied with such a scathing look that Ed inhaled deeply and said, "I can call Dad."

Barron walked in from the patio. "Holy hell, what happened?"

She rushed to him, "Jed! Four Ennis football players came in and started a big fight, and the police took Lewis into custody."

Barron swayed, "Damn! Why do I always miss the fun?"

Mack approached his cousin, "I'll go with you to fetch your buddy out of the pokey if you want me too."

Barron tossed his long sleek hair over his shoulder and said, "Let's go, but you do the talking."

Ed stepped forward and asked, "Do you mind if I ride to the station with you, Jed?" With a look at Rosie he added, "After all, he is my brother."

The three young men walked away from the shattered lamps and overturned furniture while Rosie wandered into the kitchen where she found Andy and Helen. "Oh, excuse me. I was going to offer my help in cleaning up out there."

Helen smiled and said, "Oh, yes! Thank you dear." She proceeded to hand over a broom and dustpan. "We'll be right out to help."

She went back into the large living room, now mostly deserted. Only a couple of the band members were still there, and they had begun to pack their equipment and carry it away. She began picking up large shards of porcelain when she heard Zeke say, "Well, aren't you just a sweetheart?" He stooped down next to her and took the dustpan filled with broken glass saying, "Seems to me you're always cleaning up someone else's mess."

"Why do you say that, Zeke?"

The wavy haired boy blew a stray lock from his face and answered, "I know more about you than you think I do. Lewis and I have gotten pretty tight."

"Well, you should never believe everything you hear."

"I've seen you this past year stay to yourself, and never go out." He hesitated when she gave him a nonchalant scowl. "And, I know how you got that pretty new hairstyle, too."

She shook her head casually, "It's just hair, Zeke. It'll grow back."

"Damn all that, Rosie! You should kick her ass, and good for what she did."

Looking beyond the glass patio doors she asked, "Who do you mean, Zeke?"

Feeling as though he'd said too much he sighed, "Forget it. It's none of my business anyway."

"Do you need a ride home?"

Zeke clamped his lips closed. "Well, as a matter of fact, I really do."

They left the big house and started down the brick steps. A breeze ruffled the leaves on the maple trees lining the drive. She stopped to gaze up at the starlit sky. Pale moonlight cast a sallow glow over her upturned face. "Isn't it funny how small you feel when you look at the stars?"

Zeke followed her gaze heavenward. "You should never feel small. You're the biggest person I know."

The comment flattered her. Soft giggles became intertwined laughter as the two high school graduates walked side by side away from the grand house.

Chapter Twenty-Four
Red touches yellow

Janie walked away from the mental health clinic behind her grandfather. The June day basked in bright sunshine, inviting butterflies that floated about the brilliant colored dahlias growing along the sidewalk. She took seat in her grandfather's car carefully, because the sun had left the leather seats hot enough to burn tender flesh. Bert cranked the car and asked, "You want to stop at the Frosty Freeze for an ice cream?"

Just the mention of the restaurant caused her to wince, "No, thank you."

Her grandfather prodded, "Well, then how about a milkshake?"

She watched out the window as they drove past city businesses. Pigeons walked lazily about the sidewalks in front of the courthouse. In a manic moment, she thought of jumping from the speeding automobile. "I'd really just like some cold water with ice, and we can get that at home."

Bert drove along silently for a while then he casually asked, "So, what did you and the therapist talk about today."

Wrinkling her nose in disdain she sighed, "Same as always, she always talks about Daddy."

A worry winkle furrowed the gray eyebrows of Albert Campbell, "Do you feel better after you talk to her?"

Shifting in her seat she responded, "I don't feel anything. I don't feel happy, or sad. I just feel numb and I'm gonna go on feeling numb, because of that medicine you make me take." She turned her face away and confessed, "Sometimes it make me throw up, and sometimes it makes me sleep too long, and sometimes it makes me think crazy things."

Bert felt alarmed and asked, "What kind of crazy things?"

Janie confessed, "Sometimes I think about slapping the therapist for no reason, or screaming ugly words out in church."

"How do you know it's the medicine that makes you feel this way?"

"I never felt like that before I started the medicine."

Bert frowned, "We'll talk to the doc about it."

The garden at the Moon residence was picture perfect with clean straight rows, mulched free of weeds with thick mounds of pine straw. Kneeling on the straw blanketed ground, Rosie plucked succulent strawberries from the vines, and dropped them into a basket. The summer sun shone across her pale skin, baking it into a red tint. The sound of a motorcycle approaching was the only sound in the still day. Lewis drove into the yard and parked his motorcycle next to her window.

With a chuckle she watched him go to her window, calling her name. "Out here, in the garden!" she yelled, waving to catch his attention.

He jogged to the strawberry patch, "Hey! There you are. I called a while ago and Eva said she wasn't sure where you were, but she knew you were here somewhere." He leaned down and took a berry from her basket.

Swatting his hand away she commanded, "Pick your own!"

He flashed a brilliant white smile. "Why didn't you come to Zeke's party? He said he called you twice about it."

"I just didn't feel like it," she said while holding out the basket for him to help himself to more of the berries.

Biting the fruit clear of the stem, he tossed the stem aside. "I thought maybe you'd like to take a ride with me over to Coppertone."

"What's so great about Coppertone?"

"The covered bridge, don't you remember?"

The mention flooded her with nostalgia. "Yes, I remember."

Taking another berry from the basket he said, "It's a great day for a ride."

"Will you teach me to drive your bike?" she asked devilishly.

A clouded look of apprehension crossed his face as he thought about it. Then with a smile tugging his lips slowly upward he answered, "Sure, why not?"

When they returned home from the clinic, Janie and her grandfather found Shelley sitting in the sun, her skin glossed with oil. As they walked past Shelley called out cruelly, "How's the little psychopath doing?"

Janie ignored her while Bert chastised his hateful granddaughter for her treatment of her little sister. Then he preceded to beret her for sitting in the sun, warning her of all the hazards of UV rays. When Janie walked into the living room, Opal was helping Maggie from her wheelchair to a recliner. For some inexplicable reason, the little girl leaned against a wall and stood staring at Opal, as if in a fixed trance.

"Well, how did your session with the therapist go, dear?" Opal asked. When the child didn't respond Opal said, "You don't have to talk about it if you don't want to."

Stepping to the goldfish bowl, Janie began sprinkling food flakes while unreasonable thoughts swirled dangerously. "Maybe you should see a therapist, Opal," she said in a cold flat voice. "Maybe you should talk about your daughter's death, and your husband's leaving you for another woman. Maybe talking about the same horrible things over and over will help you like it's helping me." Her words became dagger cold and frozen sharp as she continued sprinkling the fish food into the bowl until the flakes floated on top of the stagnant water like an island. "Then, when you feel better, you can get your job back at the factory and be the hell out of my way."

An audible gasp from the doorway caused her to stop sprinkling the fish food, and set the container down on the table. Bert said, "I think you should just go to your room, and think about what you just said to Opal. And, don't come back in here until you're ready to apologize and behave yourself!"

Impulsively, Janie reached over and shoved the fish bowl from the table, sending it crashing to the floor. The goldfish flopped helplessly against the carpet. With a cruel smile on her lips she said, "I'll never apologize, and I'll never behave the way you want me to." Her voice rose into an almost incoherent scream as she yelled into the room, "Because I'm psycho! Crazy! Flipped! Can't you see? Can't you see?" When the tirade within her quelled, she looked wild-eyed at Bert; holding his gaze for a long, hard moment, before running through the house and out the back door.

Bert scooped the fish from the floor and returned it to the shallow water still in the fish bowl. Opal turned and spoke soothingly to Maggie, "Now, don't you worry about her, Mrs. Campbell. I'm sure this behavior is normal for all she's been through."

Letting the clutch out too quickly caused the motorcycle to pop the front wheel off the ground and the engine to die. "Easy with the clutch, try again," instructed Lewis as he clung tightly to Rosie.

She let go of the clutch smoothly, accelerating slowly. The motorcycle began a smooth motion and he called out over the engine noise, "Second gear, Rosie." She shifted gears, and smoothly released the clutch. After the gears were wound out she increased the speed to forty-five miles an hour then slowed to a stop at an intersection. Managing to release the clutch smoothly, she kept the front tire grounded. Pulling into a parking lot, she let him take control.

"You did great! I'm really impressed, I didn't think you could catch on so easy," said Lewis while taking over. Slipping the clutch, he started off fast.

When they reached the covered bridge, she removed her sneakers and rolled up her jeans. Towering hardwoods cast long shadows across the creek as she tiptoed about the slippery bottom. Joining her with his own jeans rolled up, Lewis held out his hand. With a suspicious look she took it. He leaned forward intending a kiss, but she turned away. With a step back he asked, "So that's how it's going to be with us, just friends?"

Still without looking at him she said, "I thought we understood that a long time ago."

"You haven't found anyone else, and Kid is married. Why can't you give me another chance?"

"Why are you still interested? You can have your pick of girls."

He shook his head saying, "Well, that's obviously not true, now is it?" With honest turmoil he asked, "What was it I did? I can't remember much of what happened the days following Angel's death. I took the pills, and drank anything I could get my hands on, just to escape the pain. It was so bad, Rosie. I don't know how I ever lived through it."

Dryly she said, "Try not to think of it. Everything's okay now."

Janie led Wildfire from the barn, saddled and bridled. The spirited animal stomped with impatience, shaking his head and pulling back from the reins. "Easy, Wildfire!" she chastised. Once they were clear of the barn he broke into a feisty sprint across the pasture toward the pond, and she leaned into the wind, giving him free reign. The magnificent animal threw sod tufts airborne as his powerful hooves pounded the grassy meadow.

The sleek Mustang raced along the rolling field oblivious to the child lightly tugging the reigns to slow his pace. Unreleased energy urged him on despite the stinging jerks of the bit. Finally, he slowed as they neared the wooded path at the edge of the pond. Just as they rounded a fallen oak a quail flew from the tall grass. The horse bolted with fear. Wildfire skidded to a halt, and reared against the imagined assault. Clinging to the saddle, Janie held her seat until the horse whirled, racing back toward the barn. With the unsteady turn she lost her balance and was thrown hard to the ground.

A distinctive crunch sounded when she hit the soil. She lay in stunned shock, watching the horse momentarily prance above her, before taking off in a hard gallop. A searing pain in her arm gave evidence it was broken. Fear and pain blinded her as she sat crying.

Her crying had stopped by the time she reached the house, but her face remained pasty white. Janie stepped into the house calling for her grandfather. No one answered, and she remembered that her grandmother had an afternoon doctor's appointment. Opal always accompanied Bert with Maggie to the doctor's office. Peering out the window she saw Shelley's car was missing from the driveway.

She left the house and walked slowly down the path to Charlie's cabin, but stopped before leaving the wooded trail. Charlie's truck was not in his driveway. She walked painfully back into the house where she dialed Rosie's phone number. Eva answered. When she explained that Rosie had gone riding with Lewis on his motorcycle, Janie burst into tears.

Eva asked, "What's wrong, honey? Are you okay?"

Janie cried, "No! I fell off my horse and broke my arm, and there's no one here to take me to the hospital."

"Okay, Janie, I'll be right there. Don't worry I'm on my way right now." And the phone line went silent.

After putting the phone back into its cradle the little girl went to the living room to wait for Eva. Seeing the goldfish swimming happily in his bowl caused guilt to flood her and she burst into miserable tears, "I'm sorry little Goldie. I'm so sorry for hurting you this morning."

The farmhouse was quiet and empty when they returned from the covered bridge. They entered through the backdoor, and Rosie was immediately drawn to a note taped to the refrigerator. She took the note and said, "Oh, no! Not again."

Lewis asked, "What's wrong?"

"Eva had to take Janie to the hospital. She fell from Wildfire and broke her arm. I've got to go check on her!"

While the ER doctor examined x-rays, the frightened little girl sat in triage and listened to him very carefully. "You see the break here?" Pointing with an ink pen at the film, the doctor explained, "It's a clean break. Just like snapping a twig in half." He watched the child draw her eyebrows together with concern. "That's not such a bad thing. We won't even have to cast your arm. All we have to do is immobilize it by strapping it to your side. It will heal perfectly."

"How long before it's healed? I need to get back on my horse. G-Daddy says when a horse throws you off you have to get back on him."

The doctor chuckled at her and said, "Now that's between you, your grandpa and the horse, isn't it?"

Lewis and Rosie found Bert with Eva at the ER. Rosie asked, "How bad is it?"

Bert shifted in his chair and said, "Well, it's broke. But they don't have to put her in one of those hard casts, so I guess it's not to awful bad."

Stepping from the ER exam room with her arm strapped down across her abdomen, Janie's face alighted at the sight of Rosie and Lewis together. "Rosie!" she exclaimed, "I broke my arm, see."

"Oh, I'm so sorry. What happened?" asked Rosie sympathetically.

"Wildfire is so silly. A dumb old quail flew up from the grass, and you'd think it was the devil himself the way that horse acted."

"What happened to Wildfire after you fell off?" asked Lewis.

With worry clouding her face she answered, "He's running around the pasture with his saddle and bridle still on. Do you think he's alright?"

Brushing the little girl's hair back Rosie said, "Don't worry. Lewis and I will take care of him. Does your arm hurt very much?"

"Oh, yes. But the doctor gave me a prescription for some medicine that's supposed to make it feel better."

Holding Bert's gaze as she spoke to Janie, Rosie suggested, "Well, maybe you need to spend a few days with me, so I can take care of you while your arm is hurting."

"Oh, yes. Please, G-Daddy. Can I stay with Rosie?"

Bert looked at Eva and asked, "Do you mind Mrs. Moon? She's liable to fuss a good bit with that arm. I don't want her to put you out any."

Eva replied smiling, "I don't mind. Rosie is very good with the little girl. And besides, you're just a few minutes away if anything comes up."

Bert looked down at his granddaughter and said, "You go ahead with Rosie. I'll get this prescription filled, and bring you some clothes and your medicine a little later."

Janie smiled meekly, "Thanks, G-Daddy. I'm awfully sorry about what I did to the fish this morning."

Bert looked away and said, "Well, all that don't matter now. Let's be sure it never happens again, though."

"It won't ever," replied Janie meekly, uncertain if she could keep the promise.

The next few days passed without incident on Ben Johnson Ridge. Janie suffered terribly with her arm, and Rosie had to prop pillows around her to ease her pain so she could sleep. Because the little girl insisted the medicine from the mental health clinic made her feel irritable and bad, Rosie decreased the dosage each night until Janie stopped it all together.

"I don't think you should tell your grandfather about not taking the medicine for a while. He's got enough to worry about right now." She said while washing the child's long thick hair.

The little girl sat in the bath tub holding her injured arm gingerly against her ribs. "I won't tell him, Rosie. But, I feel so much better now that I'm not taking those pills." She fell silent momentarily then felt the need to confide her thoughts. "I just can't explain it. Before, when I was taking the pills, I just felt crazy sometimes. I even thought about jumping from the car while G-Daddy was driving along the highway. Rosie, do you think if you jumped from a speeding car that the other cars behind you would run over you?"

"Probably!" she gasped.

When Janie returned home she began to fake taking her nighttime medicine. A vase holding an array of peacock feathers on her dresser hid the deceit. She escaped the side effects of the mental health medication, and began to feel happy again.

One morning after an hour with the therapist, she waited in the lobby for her grandfather to return from an errand. Her attention was drawn to a man who sauntered into the clinic and sat down as though he were waiting for someone. He picked up a magazine and pretended to be interested, as he looked around the room peering over the top. His eyes came to rest on her, and she quickly looked away. Janie walked to the bathroom. When she stepped behind the grimy man, her breath caught in her throat. There on his neck, in living color, was the tattoo of a coral snake. Once inside the restroom she pondered the scary looking man and how she could escape without him seeing her. Pushing open a window, she jumped from the ledge onto soft grass and waited, crouched behind some shrubbery, until she saw her grandfather approach the clinic parking lot. When Bert pulled into a marked parking space, she jumped into the automobile and snapped the door closed.

"Let's go, G-Daddy. I'm all finished for the day."

Bert engaged the car in reverse and began backing from the sidewalk. "Did you have a good session with the therapist?"

Using her uninjured arm, she pushed herself against the car seat so she could look back. "Oh, not really," she answered. "It was just the same old stuff. I don't know why you want me to come here. If you ask me, it's just a waste of time."

Bert pulled from the parking lot saying, "I'm beginning to agree with you, sweetheart. I want to talk to Dr. Martin. I'm going to ask him to discharge the orders for this counseling. You seem to be doing just fine."

Watching the clinic doors, as if she expected the ugly man to come running out and start chasing behind them like a rabid dog, she responded, "Good."

When they returned home, Opal was helping Maggie perform range of motion exercises, and she looked apprehensively at Janie. Taking notice of the wary look Janie said sweetly, "Don't worry, Opal. I'm not psycho today. Isn't that nice?"

Opal raised her eyebrows and said, "Yes, it certainly is."

She wandered aimlessly into the kitchen where Shelley was making a milkshake in the electric blender. Janie watched her sister plop scoops of vanilla ice cream into the mixture of milk. "Make enough for me, too," she said.

Shelley scowled, "Make your own!" Then she placed the lid over the pitcher and turned to replace the ice cream in the freezer.

As Shelley turned her back, Janie quickly stepped to the blender and loosened the lid. Swiftly she stepped away saying, "Why do you have to be such a stinking ass? It wouldn't kill you to do something nice every once in a while."

Shelley smirked at her little sister as she returned to the counter and pressed the button on the blender. The blades whirled the ice cream violently and pushed the lid from the pitcher, sending milk and ice cream splattering across the countertop and Shelley. Janie laughed joyfully.

Fire danced in Shelley's eyes as she leaned over and punched Janie on her broken arm. "Ouch!" she cried with tears falling freely from the pain. When Shelley laughed heinously, Janie let loose with a string of the most fetid words in her vocabulary, "You ugly whore! I'm never going to be rid of you, because you're too stupid for college, and no man's ever going to marry a dirty slut like you!"

Shelley's face turned dark with fury and she started toward the child with menacing intent. "You little retarded twerp," Shelley began with a deadly calmness. "I'm going to break your other arm, and then you won't even be able to wipe your ass!"

Janie backed away yelling, "G-Daddy! G-Daddy! Help!"

Opal rushed into the room saying, "What is going on in here? Do you want to send your grandmother back to the hospital?"

Shelley retreated a few steps. Running to the safety of her grandfather's office, Janie locked the door. She picked up the phone to call Rosie. Eva answered, and had to step outside to call her from the greenhouse. Rosie hurried to the phone. "Hello, Janie. Is everything okay?"

Janie held her tears back explaining, "I wish I could be there with you, Rosie. Shelley punched me in my hurt arm, and I yelled bad words at her. Then Opal said I was going to send G-Mama back to the hospital."

With an aching heart for the troubled child Rosie asked, "Do you need me to come and get you?"

"No, you don't have to do that. I just needed to tell you about a man I saw."

"Okay, what about the man?"

"What kind of snake is it when red touches yellow it kills a fellow?"

Lost in confusion Rosie asked, "Snake? Oh yeah, the king snake and the coral snake. If red touches black, he's a friend to Jack. But if red touches yellow, he can kill a fellow. Why are you asking about those snakes? We don't have those around here."

"Maybe not the real ones, but I saw a man today with a coral snake tattoo on his neck."

The phone line held silence for a long moment. "Where?" asked Rosie, "Where did you see a man like that?"

"At the mental health clinic," answered Janie. "He had black shaggy hair, and he was broad shouldered, but kind of short. Like one of those wrestlers on TV."

Instantly alarmed, yet needing to stay calm, Rosie said, "Okay, maybe that's just a popular tattoo these days. But, to be on the safe side I'm going to call Kid tonight and tell him about it."

When Rosie called Kid's house his wife answered the phone, "Hello, Valerie. This is Rosie. Is Kid at home?"

"Not at the moment. Can I give him a message?"

Feeling apprehensive she asked, "Do you know when he will be home?"

"I really don't, but I can tell him you called."

"Please do. I need to talk to him about Janie."

"Okay."

"Goodbye, Valerie."

The female voice on the other end of the line answered, "Goodbye."

She put the phone down and wandered into her room. Pulling the diary from beneath the mattress, she began writing about Lewis. When the phone rang Rosie sprang from her bed. "Hello?" she answered breathlessly.

"Hey there, what are you doing?" Lewis asked.

"Nothing really," she answered trying to hide her disappointment that it wasn't Kid calling.

"Well, go out with me."

"Now?"

"The band is playing at Darby's house, and they asked me to come."

With closed eyes she said, "That means Shelley will be there."

"No, Shelley was not invited, Darby detests her," he explained.

"She punched Janie's broken arm today." Then with a chuckle she added, "But I think Janie told her off pretty good."

"Damn! I wouldn't be surprised if Janie set her bed on fire some night while she sleeps."

"And, who could blame her?"

Returning home just after eleven o'clock, Rosie found no message that Kid had returned her call, so Rosie picked up the phone and dialed his number. When he answered, she said, "Hey! Did you call me back?"

"Was I supposed too?"

"I had a feeling she wouldn't tell you I called."

"If you mean Valerie, well she kind of hates my guts these days. She's not going to do anything for me. So, what's up?"

"I need you to talk to Janie as soon as you can. She claims she saw a man with a snake tattoo at the mental health clinic today."

The line was silent for a long moment. "Holy shit, this ain't good."

"Are you really worried?"

Moaning anxiety he explained, "Someone broke into the house last week. The whole place was ransacked, but the only thing missing was a box of letters and cards from you and Janie." He fell silent for a moment and said, "That means they have your addresses."

"Who?"

"Those bastards I was doing business with. You know, when I needed the money for my band a while back. I mean they are a rough bunch of characters, and they've threatened me to keep supplying them with the, uh, you know."

"This kind of stuff only happens in movies. No one is going to travel all this way to harass your friends," Rosie reasoned.

"I don't know, Sunny. Was there anything in those letters that could have given them a clue about you being involved with my business?"

Rosie thought carefully. "I was very cautious, using vague words when I mentioned that. But, why would they bother with us anyway."

"Kidnap, extortion, ransom, I can only imagine!"

"I refuse to be frightened, Kid. This can't be a real threat."

"I'm going to send you the title to my car, so you can trade it in."

"Oh, Kid. Don't you want your car back?"

He scoffed and said, "You should only see what I'm driving now. My father-in-law is loaded, and he got me a part time job paying an outrageous salary." He laughed and admitted, "But, I still won't get his daughter pregnant."

"I don't need details." She opened the pantry door and looked inside at the shelves of food. "Call me after you talk to Janie."

"If this is a real threat, you and Janie are going to have to come here for the summer. You can stay with Mom and Dad, but you'll have to get away from there."

"How am I going to explain this to my dad?"

"I'll explain things to him. I'll take the blame for it all. He'll agree with me, he's a rational man."

"I'm going to bed now, and when I wake up tomorrow none of this is going to be serious. I refuse to believe drug traffickers want to kidnap me or Janie."

"Go to sleep, Sunny. But this will still be serious when you wake up tomorrow. I promise," Kid remarked.

Rosie snapped, "Aren't you even ashamed of yourself for getting us into this situation?"

He answered, "I'm very ashamed of myself, for a lot of things. But my biggest regret is not staying with you last summer. You'll never know how my heart aches, because I'm not with you."

Feeling a terrible urge to cry she said, "Goodnight," and hung up the phone.

The pale light of dawn crept into Rosie's bedroom, and the ghost of Doc Campbell infiltrated her sleeping mind. She found herself looking through the panty door at the sunlit garden, awash with green plants and colorful flowers, while the gentleman doctor entertain the pretty daughter of a wealthy man. They sat at a whitewashed wrought iron café table on matching iron chairs with red checked cushions. He poured sparkling wine into delicate long stemmed crystal goblets. Her laughter floated across the garden like music. Their happiness was contagious, their love intoxicating. A well dressed servant appeared with a violin and began playing a sweet melody. The doctor stood and took the girl's hand. He pulled her to her feet and began waltzing around the garden with her held tightly against him. She tossed her head back and laughed at something he said against her ear, and he laughed with her.

The wind picked up and began blowing against them, and the sky turned dark, but still they danced. The rain fell in pelting droplets and they danced about getting drenched in the downpour. The violinist continued producing the animated music in the rainstorm while the lovers danced with delirium. In a frightening twist, Rosie felt herself drawn into the realm of her own dream, as it suddenly became herself dancing beneath the deluge of rainfall in the arms of the handsome doctor from a past century. The warmth of his fingertips penetrated the wet fabric of her dress. Beginning to succumb with passion, she opened her eyes and discovered she was no longer dancing with the doctor, but Lewis.

Rosie awoke with the dream a vivid memory. She turned to face the window and watched the curtains flutter from a gentle mountain breeze. The conversation with Kid began to seep back into her thoughts, and she felt a headache growing in the back of her neck.

Janie was helping Opal remove the sheets from her bed. It was wash day, time to put fresh linens on her mattress. Opal began replacing the fitted sheet and Janie gathered the linens to be washed. As she walked past the dresser with the bundle in her arms, she brushed against the vase holding the peacock feathers. The vase toppled to the floor and crashed with a thunderous sound. The hidden pills now lay scattered on the floor amid the broken glass.

Opal stepped forward, "Oh, dear let me help you clean that up."

Tossing aside the linens Janie exclaimed, "Oh, no! Don't bother. I can do it." Falling to her knees she tried to cover the secret of her hidden medicine.

Opal called out, "Careful! You're going to get cut." Then she stopped and gasped at the sight of the pills. "You haven't been taking your medicine?" she accused.

Bert had heard the crash and entered the room. "What happened?"

Opal turned to him and said, "Bert! Just look. See what Janie has been doing? She's been hiding her medicine, and not taking it."

Anger at Opal grew into a resentful fire as Janie listened to the woman talk to her grandfather. She crossed her arms against her chest and remained stubbornly quiet.

Bert asked his granddaughter, "What were you planning on doing with all those pills?" When he got no response from the child he gruffly demanded, "Answer me!"

With a scowl at her grandfather Janie asked bitterly, "Well, what do you think I was going to do? Go ahead and make up your own story, you never listen to me anyway!"

Opal interrupted by saying, "Now, Janie. You weren't planning on doing anything drastic were you?"

Flames rushed through the child's veins as her anger burned. "Oh, I get it. You're trying to push the suicide theory again. Well, go ahead. Tell whatever story you want. There's nothing I can do about it anyway! I'm just a kid, and no one believes me, ever!" She bolted from the room and ran outside, across the back yard and through the pasture. After crossing the fence, she continued running along the riding trail until she could run no more. Then she walked through the woods to Rosie's house.

Rosie was pulling weeds from the flower bed next to the porch when Janie arrived. "Well! Where did you come from?"

Perched on the side of the porch she answered, "I walked."

Brushing the soil from her hands, Rosie said, "If you had called I would have picked you up. Is something wrong?"

Janie burst out, "I wish Opal would go away! She's always getting me in trouble."

"Why do you say that?"

Pouting, she explained, "She found the pills I haven't been taking, and right now she's trying to convince G-Daddy that I was saving the pills up to kill myself."

Gasping at the thought, Rosie said, "Oh, no! I'll go inside and call Bert. I'll explain how I helped you to stop using them."

With misery contorting her face the little girl asked, "What makes you think they will believe you, when all they want to do is blame me for everything?"

Rosie slumped back onto the grass, "Well, maybe Bert will let you just stay with me for the rest of the summer. After all, you and Shelley don't get along. And, you feel uncomfortable being with Opal. I think he should let you stay with me. But, first we have to ask." She then went to use the phone.

Opal answered at the Campbell house.

"Opal, its Rosie, Janie is here. Was anyone looking for her?"

Opal whined, "I should say so! Poor old Bert has been out calling and calling for that child. Oh, Rosie! You just don't know how disturbed she is. I found medicine she has been saving up. And, only God knows why!"

Rosie quickly said, "Look, Opal. It was my idea for her to stop taking the medicine. It was giving her bad side effects, and I helped her decrease her dose until she could stop taking it completely."

"Now, why on earth would you do such a thing? Sunshine Rose Moon, are you lying for that child just to keep her from getting punished?"

"I'm not lying, Opal. It was my idea for her to stop the medicine," she explained crossly.

Opal said with sincere worry in her voice, "Oh, Rosie. I don't know how Bert will take this news. I really don't!"

"Opal, try to talk Bert into letting Janie spend the rest of the summer with me. I'll watch out for her, and she won't be in your way."

"She is not in my way!" snapped Opal.

Inhaling deeply Rosie said in a very calm voice, "Now, Opal. You know that I know you have your hands full taking care of Maggie." She reasoned with the older woman, "How can it hurt anyone if she stays here with me?"

Opal answered, "Yes, well. You're right. She's just a minute away, and it might be good for her. I will talk to Bert about it. I'll have him call you when he gets back inside. Okay?"

"Okay, then. I'll talk with you later."

When she stepped back to the porch Janie was sitting in the old weathered rocking chair. "I've got Opal asking Bert if you can stay the rest of the summer with me. Would you like that?"

"You know I would." The child rocked steadily in the chair. "Do you suppose this is the same chair Doc Campbell died in?"

"I have no idea. What does it matter anyway?"

"Oh, it doesn't. I was just wondering."

Rosie leaned back against the porch railing. "Kid is supposed to call you this evening. I told him about the man with the snake tattoo, and he wants to talk to you about him."

Janie's interest intensified, "Oh, really?" Standing from the rocker she asked, "What are we supposed to do if that thug comes after us? I mean we can't just shoot him! That would be an awful mess to explain." Pacing around in a complete circle an idea came to her. "Kid has already told you what to do. Hasn't he?"

"He wants us to come to Michigan and stay with his parents."

"Well, we may as well face it."

"Face what?"

"That our dearest cousin ain't the sharpest tool in the shed. Why should we leave here and go there, where the thug lives!" Janie paced around saying, "We're going to have to go somewhere away from here, and away from Kid." She thought and asked, "How much money do we have?"

"Quite a lot actually," admitted Rosie.

"Can we buy a new car?"

Astonished that Janie was thinking like Kid she answered, "Sure."

A huge smile lit up the little girl's face. "Let's get a VW camper van! We can travel all summer long. We can go to the Smokey Mountains, and even the Grand Canyon! We can go white water rafting, and horseback riding. We can have so much fun!"

"There's no way Bert will let you go with me on a cross country camping trip."

The sound of the phone ringing sent Rosie rushing inside. She answered the phone to hear Opal say, "Rosie. Tell Janie I'm packing her clothes. She has permission to stay with you this summer. But, Bert is still working with Dr. Martin about her mental health appointments. So, he'll let you know what's going on with that."

When Rosie emerged smiling, Janie yelled, "Whoopee! Now we've just got to talk the old man into letting us take that camping trip."

"I don't see that happening, Janie."

"Where's your sense of adventure?" The little girl scolded. "Haven't you ever heard of running away?"

"I can't do that! I could be prosecuted for kidnapping."

"Nobody's going to prosecute you when Kid fesses up, and explains we had to hit the road for our own safety."

Rosie sank onto the porch step and said, "Let's just take this one day at a time, okay?"

"Sure, as long as it's not one day too many," Janie replied and reseated herself in the haunted rocking chair.

Chapter Twenty-Five
Our very own fairy

Shelley was honking in the driveway. Janie said to Rosie, "Well, the witch is finally here. I'll see you after the doctor's appointment." She walked out to the car, slowly.

Rushing to the phone Rosie called Lewis. "Are you ready?"

"I was born ready."

"I'll be right there." She ran to her room, and grabbed her beach bag packed with towels and suntan lotion. Then she hurried to Kid's car and started off for the Shirey farm.

Waiting in the driveway, Lewis jumped in demanding, "Let's ride, Clyde!" He twisted on the radio and immediately began singing along with Roy Orbison's *Pretty Woman*. As they drove to the lake he pulled some round tablets from his shirt pocket wrapped in cellophane.

With disdain Rosie asked, "Is this going to be another Quaalude day?"

"Don't you want one?"

Without giving him an answer she stared at the roadway and said, "You know those things just get you in trouble."

Slapping one in his mouth he chewed while saying, "I like trouble."

They arrived at the Martin's lake house to find Barron and Mack waiting for them in the Martin's new speed boat. Barron introduced the two bikini clad girls joining them, and took off speeding across the smooth water. Mack drove the boat fast, jumping over the wake of other boats crossing his path. When they reached a quite area, Barron donned a single water ski and slipped into the deep water. Rosie watched in disappointment as Lewis chewed another Quaalude, swallowing it down with beer. Stumbling, he made his way to the nose of the boat for another beer.

Mack said, "Damn, man! How many have you had?"

Lewis answered, "Not that many, dude. I just took a couple of 'ludes."

Mack shook his head, "No more skiing for you, my friend."

"I can ski! Hell, right now I can fly."

"Listen, Bud!" said Mack. "I've cleaned up your messes before. Today I'm telling you. Don't make a mess."

While making his way back, a wave rocked the boat causing Lewis to stumble into the lap of one of the girls. Giggling, she put her arms around his waist.

Mack said with pity, "How do you put up with that, Rosie?"

Moaning her discontent she said, "Thank goodness there are no windows on this boat."

Mack chimed in, "Or jealous football players."

Leering at one of the bikini clad girls Lewis said, "Don't listen to anything they say about me." He turned up his beer and drained it.

When Barron returned to the boat he asked Rosie while slipping off the ski, "What would you like to do?"

She shook her head, "Nothing, really."

Lewis said, "You're asking the wrong person there, Jed. Ask me."

Tiredly, Barron sighed and asked, "What would you like to do?"

Pointing at the Lazy Creek Bridge, he exclaimed "I want to ski under that bridge!"

Mack whooped his encouragement, "Yeah, let's do it!"

"Oh shit!" groaned Barron, "Why did I ask?"

As she listened to the doctor explain how her arm would be painful to use, Janie gingerly attempted to raise her arm out to her side, but couldn't bear to lift it higher than her shoulder. A nurse caught hold of her arm and pushed it just slightly higher. Janie gasped from the pain and her knees buckled.

The nurse crooned, "Now, now! Just do it slowly."

With a moan Janie said, "I'll never be able to use my arm again."

The doctor smiled. "Oh, sure you will. You'll be back on that wild horse before you can say Ticonderoga."

Looking at the doctor perplexed she asked, "Why would anyone say Ticonderoga?"

The young doctor said, "The Three Stooges do."

"Yes, I know, but they're stupid."

With a smile the doctor asked, "Do you even know what Ticonderoga is?"

Becoming bored she sighed, "A place where stooges live?"

"It was a fort built in New York by the settlers against the Indians."

"What became of it?"

"The Indians took it."

Janie looked disgustedly at the doctor and said, "That sucks."

The doctor laughed. "You go along now, Miss Noble. Use your arm, ride your horse and have a very good day."

Lewis bobbed in the water holding to the ski rope. Barron asked Mack, "What'll we do if he kills himself?"

Mack replied, "What the hell do you think we'll do? We'll pull him out of the water and take him down to the coroner."

The speed boat raced toward the bridge with Lewis on the ski. Rosie cringed as they neared the concrete structure. Momentarily, the boat was shrouded in the shaded tunnel beneath the bridge as they passed beneath it. Not until the boat cleared the danger, amid shouts of praise, did she expel her breath.

Motioning for the boat to stop, Lewis dropped the rope and Mack slowed to turn and pick him up. Taking a towel Lewis dried himself while flirting shamelessly with the two girls. Rolling her eyes Rosie said to Barron, "You'd think he's never seen a girl in a bikini before."

Inside the Campbell farmhouse, Janie showed her grandmother how her arm was healed. Holding out her arm she said, "Look G-Mama? This is only as far as I can raise it."

Shelley came up behind and pulled it upward. "No, it isn't," she sneered. "You can raise your arm this high."

Janie screamed with pain. When she heard Shelley's malicious laughter she flew into a blind rage. Jumping to her feet she grabbed a pair of scissors from a sewing basket and ran at Shelley with them poised as a lethal weapon.

From nowhere appeared Charlie, who grabbed Janie around the waist and stopped her just short of her sister. "Now, 'top dat!" he ordered. Taking the scissors, he handed them to Opal. "Ou don't want to hut ou tista!"

"I want to cut her ugly head off!" she screeched.

Opal was shaken from the incident. "Janie!" she said harshly to the little girl. "I want you to go to your room."

Indignant at the thought of being punished she protested, "But this was all Shelley's fault. You saw what she did to my arm."

Opal said firmly, "Go to your room young lady."

Righteous anger turned her face crimson. "You're so unfair to me!" she screamed. "Someday you'll regret it. Just wait and see!" She then ran from the room crying.

The boat was tied at the dock, and Rosie helped collect wet towels and trash. Giggles and laughter could be heard coming from the backyard of the lake house, as Lewis entertained the bikini girls. Barron asked, "You are staying aren't you? Mack is grilling for us."

"Well, I'm supposed to pick up Janie at her grandparents house." She closed her eyes in disgust as the laughter intensified. "And, I really don't know how much more of this I can take."

Barron smiled, "Oh, you mean Lewis. Ah, he's just having fun."

"Well, I need to go home, shower and change into some dry clothes. Okay, I'm sure he'll want to stay if you've still got some beer."

Mack said, "He doesn't need more beer."

Rosie approached the backyard just in time to see Lewis attempting to pinch one of the girls breast as she slapped his hand away. Clearing her throat to get his attention she asked, "Are you coming with me?"

Drunkenly, he asked, "Where?

"Home," she said, "to get dressed for the cookout."

"Oh no, I can't go home like this. Mamie would piss her pants if she saw me this drunk. I'll just hang out here."

"Yeah, okay," she said, and turned to go.

When Rosie returned home, she called the Campbell house to speak with Janie. Opal answered and began explaining how Janie was being punished in her room. After listening patiently she explained that she and Lewis were going to eat at the lake house. Opal assured her Janie would be fine until she came to pick her up. When Rosie put the phone down a feeling of dread crept over her.

The sun was sinking low when she pulled into the driveway of the lake house. Music from a stereo came from the back yard. Following the music, she walked around the house and found Mack standing over a brick barbecue pit turning steaks. Barron came out of the house and smiled when he saw Rosie, "Wow, you look nice."

She asked, "Where is everyone?"

"Inside," answered Barron, then he asked, "How do you like your steak?"

Rosie looked at Mack and answered, "Well done, please."

Mack cast a wry smile. "Your wish is my command."

"There are sodas in the fridge," Barron told her.

She went into the house through the kitchen. A television was playing a game show in the living room, but everything else was quiet. Taking a cola from the refrigerator she meandered into the living room. One of the girls was asleep on the sofa, wearing an oversized t-shirt over her bikini. Growing suspicious, she walked toward the hallway listening for voices of Lewis and the other girl. Nearing the bathroom she could hear muffled voices amid running water. She put her hand on the door knob and turned it. Using her foot to give the door a slight kick, she released the door knob and the door swung open.

Two bodies were visible through the shower curtain, and the sound of the girl's giggles sent shivers through Rosie. Walking closer, she took hold of the shower curtain and jerked it open. They both gasped in shock. Merciless heartache washed through her as she stared at the spectacle. Stepping away from the naked girl, Lewis reached for a towel to cover himself.

"Rosie!" he exclaimed drunkenly, "I know this looks bad, but nothing happened. We were just fooling around, but nothing happened."

Without a word, Rosie turned and walked away. He jumped from the shower dripping water, and chased after her. "Listen to me!" he shouted.

She whirled and shouted back, "I will *never* listen to anything you have to say again!" He stepped back, almost cowering. Her fury raged. "How could you do this to me? Why did I ever trust you again?" She jerked away when he tried to embrace her seething, "I *hate* you, Lewis!" Turning a jagged glare on him she said with a voice as splintered as her heart, "And, if hatred could kill," she paused to lick her lips sadistically, "you'd be dusty bones right now!"

Setting the unopened soda on the kitchen counter she stepped into the backyard. Walking past Barron and Mack she said, "I'm not staying. I can't take anymore of Lewis and his stupid shit. I'm going home, and you can tell him that I hope I never see his sorry ass again."

Barron caught her arm and pulled her back. "What's wrong now? What's he in there doing?"

"Nothing really, just taking a shower with that Candy girl; they seemed to be having fun until I interrupted them." Rosie said, "This doesn't matter to me anymore. I'm through with Lewis for good." She walked away into the gathering dusk.

Rosie pulled into the Campbell drive with her headlights on, and caught sight of Ed's car parked next to Bert's old farm truck. When she rapped on the storm door, Janie rushed to open it.

"Guess what?" Janie exclaimed. "G-Daddy talked to Kid today, and he said I can go with you to visit him. Isn't that great?"

Fear rushed through Rosie as she caught the expression on Bert's face. Trying to cover her fear she said to Janie, "Yeah, that's wonderful."

Bert said, "Sunshine, I'd like to talk to you, alone."

Directing her voice at Janie, Rosie said, "You'll have to excuse me," and followed Bert into his study.

Bert settled himself behind his desk and folded his hands together. "Janie had a long talk with Kid this evening. Then he had a long talk with me." The old man's eyes blinked with seriousness. "I understand my grandson has gotten himself into some trouble, with your help."

"Yes," she said meekly. "I helped him."

"Well, I've just come from your house. Your father and I had a long conversation over this, and he agrees that you and Janie need to take this vacation. I've urged Kid to go to the authorities to get this settled. I believe my grandson will do the right thing. Are you willing to do the right thing?" Bert looked at her with his gray eyebrows drawn together.

"Yes, of course."

"You must get rid of the rest of those drugs," Bert demanded.

"There's none left to get rid of," she lied. "That's why those goons are after Kid, because he can't supply them with more."

Slamming his fist onto the desk Bert declared, "They are not only after him!" He shouted, "But you and Janie as well!" His eyes were dark with angry fear. "I want this to end favorably, Sunshine Rose. If there are more drugs in that doctor's house I want them destroyed."

Rosie felt speechless, but she lied, "There are no more."

Bert rose from his chair. "You and Janie are leaving tonight. Kid assured me that you have enough money to make this trip." When Rosie said nothing, Bert shouted, "Well, do you?"

Flinching from the verbal assault she answered meekly, "Yes."

Bert said, "Janie has her things packed. I'm sending Shelley to stay with one of her aunts in Louisiana. And, Kid will be working with undercover agents to get this problem taken care of in Michigan." The elder man looked at her with concern, "Keep in touch, call me collect. Just let us know you two are alright."

Rosie stood to leave saying tearfully, "I'm so sorry, Bert. I knew it was wrong."

"You're not the first person to regret a mistake, and you won't be the last." Bert said, "Just learn from this."

She followed him out of the study. Opal and Ed sat with Maggie in the living room. Ed approached asking, "Do you need me to go with you, Rosie?"

Janie reappeared from retrieving the double blade hunting knife she was so fond of, and carried it concealed beneath her t-shirt. Seeing her struggle to tote a heavy suitcase, Rosie reached down and took the bag saying to Ed, "Oh, no. We'll only be gone for a little while, and you have your job to think about."

Taking the case, Ed said, "Job be damned if you need me."

Seeing Opal's anxious face Rosie said, "No, Ed. We're just fine. Don't worry." She walked across the room and hugged Opal around the neck. Then she hugged Maggie and turned to hug Bert. "Don't any of you worry, we will be fine."

Following Rosie's lead, Janie hugged everyone goodbye, then she followed Rosie and Ed out the door to the car. Rosie hugged Ed goodbye. He pulled her back against him when she started to turn away, "I want to help, Rosie. Let me go with you."

"We're just going to Michigan for a few weeks."

Ed expelled a long breath and asked, "What are you going to tell Lewis?"

She laughed dryly, "The last time I saw him, he was standing naked in the shower with a girl he just met." Turning to go she replied, "I don't plan to tell Lewis a damn thing."

Ed pulled her close saying, "He's a fool, Rosie, just like I was."

Pulling away she sighed lightly, "Too little, too late." She then got into the car and drove away.

When the girls got to the Moon house, Sturgill was waiting worriedly. "Well, we packed for you. You're all set to go." Anguish rippled across his face as he cursed, "Damn that Kid! I knew he was sending you money, but I never dreamed he was using you to sell drugs." Sturgill paced back and forth, "Jesus Christ, Rosie! How could you be so foolish?"

Tears streamed down her face, "I'm so sorry, Daddy!"

"Rosie, you might need this," said Eva who stood holding an envelope.

Reaching for it she asked, "What is it?"

Sturgill said, "Kid sent you the title to the car. He wants you to get rid of it." Rubbing his hand across his face Sturgill said, "You just do what you need to." He went to Rosie's bedroom, and began taking luggage to her car.

Recognizing the luggage as the set Eva earned from last year's Tupperware party she exclaimed, "Oh, Eva! You don't mind if I use your luggage?"

With a sardonic smile Eva replied, "Where am I going anyway?"

Embracing the stepmother who had resented her so terribly, she said, "Thank you, Eva." Pulling away she explained, "Well there are a few things I need to get. Janie, will you help me?"

She took the pillows from her bed, two hand stitched quilts, some records and tapes, and her diary. Impulsively, she snatched the red sequined gown, and put her cosmetic bag inside her purse. She left the room after switching the light off. "Okay, we're ready. But I still think Kid is all uptight over nothing."

Sturgill said, "That boy knows what he's talking about, Rosie. Now when he gets this business straightened out, it'll be safe for you to come home." Sturgill hugged his daughter saying, "Call me as often as you want."

She walked out of the house with Janie following her, and tossed the quilts on the back seat. "Well, time to hit the road."

Janie smiled, "Yeah, let's make like a tree, and leaf."

Waving goodbye to Sturgill and Eva, who stood on the porch watching them, Rosie took the driver's seat and cranked the car. She backed from the drive, and slowly drove away from the farm on Ben Johnson Ridge. "We won't be gone long. Things will settle down soon," said Rosie hopefully.

"What are you talking about? We're never coming back."

A cold shiver traversed Rosie's spine as she heard the serious tone of the little girl. The child sat with her face turned toward the window and watched the summer countryside cloaked in darkness glide past them.

They drove according to Kid's directions until the wee hours of the morning when Rosie decided to stop at a rest area in Kentucky, and sleep in the car. Janie slept on the front seat, while Rosie slept in the back. They awoke to the sound of an eighteen wheeler driving past them in the parking lot. After using the restroom to wash up and brush their teeth, they scoured the lobby for pamphlets on attractions in the area. An advertisement for a local flea market intrigued Janie.

Waving the pamphlet in the air she asked, "Oh, can we go?"

Rosie remarked sarcastically, "Gum Pond Flea Market. Oh, this sounds glamorous!"

While she was getting directions to the flea market, Janie browsed through other pamphlets advertising historic sites in Kentucky. Rosie returned and said, "Well, let's go. I think I can find it."

The market place was crowded. Rosie found a shaded area to park between two buildings next to a scum covered lagoon that appeared to be a run off of Gum Pond. A haphazard chain link fence surrounded the property housing the slimy green body of stagnant water. She put the pillows and quilts inside the trunk, and left the top down.

Janie was thrilled by the carnival like atmosphere, and she became especially interested in the booths that displayed knives and guns. When she came across a vintage German WWII sword, she insisted she be allowed to have it. Placing an old army helmet on her head she said, "This, too!" Rosie counted out the cash while Janie strapped the weapon around her waist. The case of the sword almost touched the ground as the child hurried from one booth to another. Rosie caught up with her peering through a glass case at a snub nosed pistol.

Tired and hungry Rosie said, "Let's go already."

Janie pointed at the gun. "That's a Saturday night special. I want it."

"What? Are you crazy?"

Janie captured Rosie's gaze with staid eyes, "We need it."

Knowing the child's insight, Rosie inquired about the gun. The young man attending the booth took the gun from the glass case for her. Paying the man his asking price, she placed it in a bag of other purchases. When the man asked if she would need bullets, Rosie shook her head no, and walked away.

Passing by a produce stand with cut watermelon on display, Rosie's mouth watered. They were near the car, and Janie was wearing the old helmet while drawing the sword from its sheath, as if practicing for battle. Rosie said, "Go ahead to the car and wait for me. I'll get us a watermelon."

A descending summer sun dipped below the exalted pines, casting long shadows that draped across the wooded inlet. A steady buzz of nocturnal life was already ringing out in resounding tympani. When Janie reached the car, she continued past it, the frantic song of summer's promise beckoned her closer to the woods. She stopped at the drooping fence that encircled the scum filled lagoon. Her attention was drawn to a private roadway on the other side of the pond. She observed some angry men who exited the cab of a pickup truck cursing and punching livid fists into a young Native American man. The two men took turns punching the young man about the body and face until he fell to his knees. She could hear one man say to the other, "Get those blocks and rope off the back of the truck. We're gonna give this Injun some concrete boots."

The sagging fence allowed her to cross over, and make her way around the green water toward the altercation. One of the men had left to do the bidding of the other when she reached the area of the assault. The remaining man said as he flicked out a switch blade knife, "I'm going to cut you boy, from ear to ear."

The young man pleaded, "Please don't hurt me. I brought your daughter home safe. I never touched her!"

Angrily, the man kicked the young man in his ribs, "You filthy Indian! I ought to cut your lying heart out, and shove it down your throat!"

Stepping from the brush Janie boldly put her sword to the grimy man's neck, saying loudly in a gruff voice, "Drop that blade!" The man was taken aback by surprise and quickly dropped the knife. He put his hands in the air as if Janie held a gun on him.

Rosie returned to the car and put the watermelon on the back seat. She looked around for her little cousin, and noticed the sagging fence. As she stepped closer, she heard voices from the other side. Disbelief took her breath as she saw Janie pointing the vintage weapon at a stranger. Clutching the plastic bag close she leapt across the sagging fence.

When the other man returned from the pickup truck with two concrete blocks and rope, he found his partner held at sword point by a little girl. "What the hell?" the grubby man asked. "Well, it's just a little girl, Delbert! Are you going to let a kid cut your stupid head off?"

The man named Delbert reached down and grasped the sword. Janie jerked the blade backward, slicing the man's fingers. "Holy hell," Delbert cursed, "She just about cut my damn fingers off!"

Stumbling backward and tripping over a root, Janie fell against the hard ground. The other man rushed over and grabbed her sword. "Now we got to kill two of 'em!"

The clicking of a gun hammer stopped him, and he looked up at Rosie holding the pistol. "Look away!" She ordered for fear he could see there were no bullets in the gun. "Drop the sword and lay face down, now!"

The man and his friend named Delbert lay face down, side by side on the ground. The young man who had been beaten jumped to his feet. "Come on, let's go!"

"No!" objected Janie. "We can't just leave them here so they can come after us. We have to tie them up."

Steadily holding the gun pointed at the men, Rosie barked at the young man with the bloodied face, "You do it. Tie them up with that rope."

Grabbing the rope, he tied the men's hands behind their backs one to the other. "There, that'll hold them for a while."

"Not good enough. Give me that duct tape you just bought," said Janie holding her hand out palm up.

Rosie handed her the plastic bag and Janie fished the tape out. "Tape their feet so they can't walk, then put some over their mouths so they can't yell for help."

The weary young man followed Janie instructions. As everyone prepared to leave Janie said, "Wait a minute. Pull their pants down so their asses are shining for everybody to see."

Rosie exclaimed, "Oh, you've got to be kidding!"

The young man smiled and stepped back over the men. He unbelted their trousers and pulled them down to their knees. Stepping back, he laughed at his handy work. Janie stepped closer and put her foot on one of the men's naked buttocks. "I hope skitters eat your asses off!" she yelled. Then giving the man's butt a shove with her foot, she turned and raced to the truck.

"Come on. Let's take their truck so no one will find them right off when they start looking for them." Opening the door Janie said, "The keys are here."

Rosie rushed and took the driver's seat, while the young man took the passenger seat. Leaving the private drive, they took the main road and drove back into the flea market parking area. Grabbing his backpack as they scrambled from the vehicle, the young man ran with the girls to the car. "Get in." Rosie said, "We'll drop you somewhere."

Driving away from the flea market, Janie shouted victorious whoops from their conquest. She removed her army helmet and sword case. Turning in her seat, she asked the bruised and beaten young man, "What did you do to make them so mad?"

Looking up, he could see Rosie watching him in the rearview mirror. "I helped that man's daughter get home, and he thought I was the reason she ran away, I guess. But I didn't even know her! I just met her at a fair, and I talked her into going back home. I swear that's all that happened. We hitch-hiked here from Indiana, that's where I live." He put a finger to his bloodied and swollen lip as he realized that talking caused him pain.

Wrinkling her nose, Janie said, "Let's find a service station so he can wash up. He's starting to make my face hurt."

While Rosie waited in the car, a service station attendant filled the gas tank and cleaned her windshield. Janie sauntered out of the store with colas and a large bag of potato chips. After handing off the drinks she tossed the chips aside, and leaned against the car as she drank from her soda bottle. Both of the girls were drawn to the handsome figure of the young shirtless man who emerged from the gentlemen's restroom. His black feathery hair blew away from his face as he walked, and his muscles rippled with the sun shining on his bronze skin.

Taking the bottle from her lips Janie said breathlessly, "Ooh, la la! Have you ever seen a beef cake like that before?"

Rosie stared at the young man with her mouth gaped open. "What are you talking about? So, he's cute, big deal."

"Excuse me! I'm cute. He is fine!" She rushed to the passenger side of the car and opened the door just as the young man approached with his shirt slung over his shoulder. She pushed the passenger seat forward, and took a seat in the back.

He sat down and said, "I swear on my life, I'm going to pay you back, someway, somehow."

Janie said, "Rainwater. What kind of name is that?"

"It's Native American. You see, I'm Cherokee."

Janie said, "Yeah, I can tell. Are you a full bloodied Indian?"

Embarrassed by the child's brash question Rosie warned, "We shouldn't get personal."

The young man smiled a brilliant white smile from his bruised and swollen lips. "It's okay. To answer your question, my father is only one sixteenth Cherokee, but he's considered Native American. And, my mother is Cherokee; all the way."

Janie said to Rosie, "Just like Doc."

"Who is Doc?" Randy asked.

Cranking the car, Rosie pulled the gear shift into drive, "He's an ancestor of ours who was murdered by his girlfriend's father." She drove away saying, "I think we may have just experience an ancestral déjà vu."

Randy said, "You can let me off anywhere. I can hitchhike home."

Janie was looking at the atlas Sturgill had sent with them. "We're going to Michigan, and Indiana is like on the way. Why don't you just ride with us?"

Unable to keep her eyes from Randy's shirtless state of dress, Rosie replied, "You can stay with us if you like. I don't mind." Then after wetting her lips she added, "Maybe we can have some fun along the way."

Randy slid down in the seat, physically spent, and said, "Yeah, okay."

They zigzagged through the small town until they found a café. Rosie rubbed the stiffness from her neck as they took a seat at a booth with a window. "Maybe we should find a room and stay here for the night," she suggested.

Janie perked up, "Yeah, a place with a swimming pool." Then to tease Randy she asked, "Can Indians swim, Randy Rainwater?"

Randy looked at her with ire and answered, "This one can."

After the child left the table for the juke box, Rosie smiled sweetly at Randy, "She likes you."

With authentic interest Randy asked, "How old are you?"

Without looking up from her purse she answered, "Eighteen." Taking out a compact mirror she asked, "And you?"

Wincing from the pain of bruised lips, Randy answered, "Eighteen."

Feeling more comfortable with the young man, Rosie gently asked, "Why are you out hitchhiking like this?"

Randy raked his fingers through his hair. "I had a fight with my parents, because they wouldn't let me take the car, you know. So I could drive this girl home. You know; the one I was telling you about earlier today. And so, we just took off hitchhiking."

Music from the juke box filtered through the café as Janie made her selections. "Have you called your parents since you've been gone?"

The handsome young man locked his deep brown eyes with hers. "I guess I should. They are awfully protective with me." He looked away and said, "You see. I'm their only child. My father is the DA in Winston County. My mother was a teacher, but she's retired now, and they have big plans for my future." He looked up at the young girl as she returned to the booth. "I'm supposed to follow my father into the law practice, if you know what I mean?"

Janie took her seat next to Rosie as the waitress brought their plates, and began eating with a ravenous appetite. Looking up from her plate she asked, "Rosie, are you going to eat that pickle?"

Rosie pushed her plate over for Janie. Catching him gazing at her, she asked, "Is your food okay, Randy?"

He nodded his head yes. Slapping her hand on the table Janie declared, "I think we should go shopping for a new car. What about you, Randy? We were thinking of buying a VW camper van, you know with the pop up roof. Like the hippies drive. Want to go along with us?"

He smiled painfully, "Are you a hippie?"

Holding up the three middle fingers of her right hand, Janie asked, "Can you read between the lines?"

Tossing his head back he chortled, "You two just made my summer!"

Janie's face grew animated, "Hey, why don't you go to the Grand Canyon with us before we take you home?"

His laughter vanished, "Are you girls rich?"

Rosie interjected, "We're going to trade the convertible. We're not rich, but we do have some vacation money."

With his fork poised he said, "Okay, count me in."

After eating the threesome made their way to a motel on the edge of town. Sitting in the parking lot Rosie explained the situation. "So, to save money, we'll just get one room with double beds. Is that agreeable to everyone?"

Randy said, "Sure."

Janie called from the back seat, "Okay." She ogled the swimming pool, shimmering blue and tempting. "Oh! I can't wait to jump in that pool."

Leaving Janie with Randy in the car, Rosie went inside the motel. Leaning forward, Janie asked, "You think Rosie's pretty, don't you Randy Rainwater?"

With a heavy sigh he said, "You don't have to keep using my first and last name. Can't you just call me Randy?"

"Can't you just answer my question?"

He turned and looked at her incredulously, "Well, what do you think? I'm not blind, and neither are you. We both know she's pretty."

"Do you want her to be your girlfriend?" Pulling the sword from its sheath she waved it before her face like a samurai warrior.

Randy mumbled, "That would be nice."

Janie said loudly, "Speak up boy! Don't be shy."

His patience was beginning to wane, "Yes!" he shouted back.

Peels of childish giggles came from the back seat as she relished provoking his dander. Very seriously she said, "Well, just be patient. I can tell she likes you. And, I predict the two of you will be very good friends." Then to make her point she repeated, "Very, very good friends."

With drawn eyebrows he asked, "Are you clairvoyant?"

"No," she answered honestly. "I just have ESP."

Returning with the key to their room, Rosie said enthusiastically, "I got us a room close to the pool." Looking at Randy she asked, "I do hope you have swim shorts."

Without smiling he said, "I do."

The pool was clean and cool with only a few people gathered during the mid-day heat. Janie walked to the deep end and dove in fearlessly, and their handsome new friend followed her lead. Rosie preferred to ease in slowly, still not confident in her swimming ability. She walked down the concrete steps. Goose bumps rose as she entered the cool water. Randy swam to her and exclaimed, "Damn, Rosie! Are you cold?"

With a perplexed look she asked, "Why do you ask that?" Then she followed his gaze to her chest, noticing the tell tale protrusions from her bathing suit top. She gasped with embarrassment, and quickly submerged herself in the water to hide the erect nipples. Randy laughed and swam away, escaping her scolding look.

A little boy was quick to strike up a friendship with Janie, and soon they were hounding Randy and Rosie to play a game of chicken. Janie called, "Girls against boys! Come on Rosie."

After checking her chest and seeing the earlier embarrassment had subsided, Rosie agreed. With Janie on Rosie's shoulders, and the little boy on Randy's, the game began. Rosie couldn't help but appreciate the lean muscular body of her opponent, yet grew irritable that he was looking at her as well. When she lost her balance, falling backward into the water with Janie, Rosie surfaced gasping for breath.

"This is not fair!" Rosie complained to Randy. "What do you do? Lift weights?"

He chuckled, "Yes, I do. And, what do you do to build those, um, muscles on your chest?"

"Why don't you just stop looking at my chest?" she asked hatefully.

Randy returned her annoyed tone, "Well, why don't you stop looking at my chest?"

Angrily, she reached out and shoved against his muscular upper body. In return he placed his hand on her breast, and gave her a shove. With a gasp of indignation, she gave him a smart slap on the cheek. He mocked her gasp and returned the slap. Her eyes narrowed with fury, "Just what do you think you're doing?"

Randy replied, "Just the same thing you're doing."

Calmly she said, "You're a pig." And, she turned to leave the pool.

Randy called after her, "Oh, yeah. Well there's a word for this. It's called double standards."

With a cross look over her shoulder Rosie wisely replied, "'Double standards' is two words. You know, Randy. There are three kinds of people in this world, those who can count and those who can't."

Standing confused Randy said, "Those are just two kinds of people."

Perching in a chair she looked down at Randy and said, "Congratulations, you *can* count."

Aggravation crossed his face. Janie spoke to her new friend, "Rats! This is happening sooner than I thought it would."

The little boy asked, "What is?"

Shaking her head Janie said, "Never mind. You wouldn't understand."

The motel room was quiet as Rosie dried her hair. A knocking at the door alerted her that Janie or Randy was finished with the pool. She opened the door to find both of them waiting to be let in. She said to Janie, "Go straight to the bathroom and wash the pool water out of your hair." She eyed Randy suspiciously as he stepped in with a towel covering his chest.

"Do I have, too?" Janie protested.

"Just do it," commanded Rosie.

The little girl rummaged in a suitcase for proper attire. "Will you take a walk with me after I get out of the shower, Rosie? There's a shop near here that Tommy told me about. I want to get a necklace like he was wearing."

"Sure," agreed Rosie. After the child disappeared into the bathroom she turned to Randy. "We need to get some things straight between us, mister."

Drawing the towel closer he said confrontationally, "Yes, we certainly do! I want you to know that you make me feel very uncomfortable the way you stare at my body."

Her mouth dropped open in dismay. "What!"

"And, just because you're paying for everything doesn't mean I owe you any special favors." He waved his fingers daintily saying, "You know what I mean. Just because I'm a guy doesn't mean you can take advantage of me."

Infuriated, Rosie stammered for something to say against his arrogance. "Who do you think you are?"

Stepping away he continued, "I know things are all hip these days with free love, and dope. But, I don't think like that." Pointing his finger at her he said indignantly, "I don't smoke grass, and I don't sleep around!"

His conceit incensed her. Unwilling to continue the discussion, she shrieked with annoyance and left the room, slamming the door behind her.

Pacing around the deserted swimming pool, she waited for Janie to emerge from the motel room. When she appeared, Rosie shouted her name. The little girl rushed out to the pool with her damp hair bouncing about her face. "What are you doing out here without Randy?"

Just the sound of his name caused her to flinch, and she snapped rudely, "I really wish you hadn't invited that asshole to accompany us."

The little girl giggled, "What do you mean? He's a lot of fun, and it makes me feel safe having a man with us."

"Some man!" she sneered.

With a bewildered look Janie asked, "Why do you say that?"

"Well, he acts like a virgin," Rosie answered carelessly.

Giggles erupted from the child, "So? Who cares?" Then with a devilish gleam in her eye she asked, "What have you been thinking?"

"Well, not *that*!" declared Rosie contemptuously.

"Yeah, right!" the impetuous girl exclaimed. "We'll just see how long you can go without thinking about *that*!"

When they returned to the room, they found Randy standing before the mirror wearing one of Rosie's prettiest dresses with her favorite pair of heels. The girls gasped in amazement at the sight of the beefy handsome young man dressed in drag. He turned to face them, saying "Oh, hi! You have some beautiful clothes, Rosie!" Taking up a scarf he tossed it around his neck with a feminine flourish.

They stood like stone in utter dismay, speechless. After a long five seconds of silence Janie chimed in cheerfully, "Looks like we found our very own fairy!"

Chapter Twenty-Six
Damn the Pusher Man

The sight of Randy wearing her clothing stunned Rosie. "Dude, that's my best dress!"

He ran his hands across the fabric and enthusiastically agreed, "Yes, it's fabulous! Would you zip me up?"

Infuriation plagued her, making her dangerously calm. "No, I will not!" she hissed at his reflection. "I want you to take my clothes off right now."

Randy gave her a look with raised eyebrows. "You want me to help you off with your clothes? Why?"

"Oh, this is too funny!" Janie giggled.

Taking a deep breath Rosie calmly replied, "You know what I mean, Randy. I want you to take my dress off, and put it back where you found it."

Rushing to Randy's side, Janie surveyed him top to bottom saying, "Hey, you don't look bad as a girl. Are you one of those funny boys who like to kiss other boys?"

With eyebrows drawn sternly together he answered, "Heavens no!" Then he looked into the mirror and said softly, "I just like to wear girl's clothes, sometimes."

With anger brimming at the point of eruption Rosie yelled, "Just give me back my clothes!"

Randy asked, "Why? Were you planning to wear this tonight?"

"That doesn't matter!" she snapped.

Janie sniffed at their guest, "Hey! You even smell like a girl."

With a closer look Rosie asked, "Are you wearing mascara?"

"Looks good doesn't it? It took a lot of practice to get my eye makeup to look this good," he replied with a pleased smile.

A gut wrenching emotion churned inside, staining her with guilt for the immediate response of anger. With a show of complete defeat, she threw up her hands and declared, "I give up! " Crawling across a bed, she fluffed the pillows saying, "Go ahead and wear the stupid dress if it means so much to you. You're right. I wasn't planning to wear it anyway." With a tired sigh she asked Janie, "Hey, kiddo. Will you twist the TV on for me?"

Racing to turn the set on, Janie bounced onto the bed and settled next to her favorite relative. The local station was broadcasting a news segment. The female journalist sitting at the anchor desk reported, "Police were called to Gum Pond today, when two men were discovered bound and gagged. The two men told police they were accosted by three long haired men. The men stole their pickup truck, which was found hours later at the parking grounds. Police are asking anyone with information regarding these three assailants to call the local police department."

Shouts of laughter echoed through the room as all three burst into hilarity. Randy joined the girls on the bed and asked with humor, "Those ignorant hillbillies couldn't come up with a better story than that?" He adjusted his fake breasts as he teased Janie, "I wish she had told us if they had mosquito bites on their asses."

"Don't you know they did?" giggled the little girl.

Randy asked no one in particular, "Do you think I have too much stuffing in my bra?"

With an angry look Rosie yelled, "You better not be wearing one of my bras!"

"Oh come on, how many do you need at one time anyway?" he whined.

Janie leaned toward Randy and asked, "What do you think of my necklace? Cool, huh?"

Looking at the necklace made of braided hemp with tiny ocean shells Randy said, "I don't know. It's too unisex. A girl or a boy could wear it."

With a confrontational tone Janie asked, "So, what's your point?"

"Well, I just like to be one or the other, you know."

"How long have you been this way?" asked Rosie, a hint of fascination reflected in her tone.

"What way?" he asked with knitted brows. "I've always liked girl stuff," then he quickly added, "And boy stuff, too." He fidgeted on the bed to get more comfortable. "When I was a little boy I played with army men and Barbie dolls. My mother insisted. I think it was her way of trying to make me sensitive to women's issues."

Patting Randy on the knee supportively Janie said, "Well, she did a good job." Turning to Rosie, and abandoning any remaining encouragements she had to offer, Janie asked, "Can we go roller skating at the skating rink we passed down the street?"

With a listless attitude Rosie answered, "Yes, anything to get out of here." She looked at Randy asking, "What about you twinkle-toes? Want to go skating?"

Kicking his feet up he wiggled his high heeled shoes and answered, "Yes! I love skating, and I'm very good at it." He jumped from the bed saying, "Give me a minute to change."

Very snidely Rosie remarked, "Please do."

The skating rink was crowded and Janie skated with confidence across the polished floor. Randy zipped up to Rosie asking, "May I have this skate?"

"My patience is wearing thin with you," she warned. Then as one girl would say to another Rosie motioned with her finger, "You still have some mascara smudges."

He circled her on his skates and said, "Won't you give me a chance to show you that I'm not a bad person?"

"I don't think you're a bad person, Randy."

"I don't believe you," he remarked while circling her like a vulture.

Putting out her hand, she took him by the shoulder saying simply, "Then show me, don't tell me."

Janie skated past waving enthusiastically, like a child seeking attention from her parents. With a smile on her lips for Janie, Rosie confessed, "You're the best looking guy I've ever met, and you like to wear girl's clothes. That kind of freaks me out."

Randy looked at her seductively and said, "You're the prettiest girl I've ever met, and you freak me out a little, too."

With an awestruck look she asked, "But why?"

Randy looked at his feet as if inspecting the skates and answered, "You're just so damn tough. I mean, the way you came after those criminals today, and saved my life." He stopped talking and swallowed hard. "Well, what can I say? We know that I owe you my life." The background music swelled into a new popular song that brought the rink alive with rhythm. Touching her face tenderly Randy felt a twinge of guilt when he saw the confused look on her face. "You are the bravest, most beautiful girl I've ever met."

Taking his hand she followed him to the arena. They skated together and laughed as if they had been friends forever. When the night ended, and they were back at the motel getting ready for bed Rosie said jokingly to Randy, "I have an extra night gown if you'd like to wear it."

Casting a scandalous smile with his battered lips he answered, "That's okay. I always sleep in the nude."

Janie squealed, "Ugh! I don't want to see that!" Taking the pistol from the drawer she threatened, "If I see something ugly, I'm going to shoot it."

Giggling, Rosie asked, "Why did you want that funny looking gun anyway?"

Janie replaced the pistol and taking up her pajamas replied, "Because that's the kind of gun my daddy used to kill himself." She disappeared inside the bathroom.

With a look of pity Randy said, "Gee, that kid has issues."

"You're not allowed to sleep in the nude, you know," said Rosie.

With a malicious grin, he began undressing. When he stripped to his boxer shorts he jumped into bed. Then while moving about under the covers, he removed his boxers and twirled them on his index finger before sending them flying through the air in Rosie's direction.

Slinging them back she said, "You're just a pain in the ass!"

Morning came with a wake-up call from the front desk. After breakfast, Rosie found a car dealership and the threesome looked about the lot at all types of automobiles. An ecstatic squeal escaped Janie when she spotted several VW vans. They inspected them individually, each with a different preference.

Randy argued, "The safari style windshield is the way to go."

"I want the hatchback door, and walk thru seats," interjected Janie.

Standing beside a green and white 1967 Westfalia camper, Rosie declared, "This is the one we're taking. It has the drive away tent, refrigerator, pop-up roof and luggage rack on top."

It took an hour to finish the paperwork for the purchase, but all was complete after the transfer of funds. While unloading the convertible and packing the van, Rosie became aware that her diary was missing. Presuming she must have dropped it when packing the car, she gave up the search.

"We're ready to roll," said Randy observing Rosie's discontent. "Is something wrong?"

Slamming the door she sighed with frustration, "I've lost my diary."

"Was there anything incriminating in that diary, Sunshine?" asked Janie.

Answering with narrowed eyes she snapped, "I'm not that stupid." To Randy she asked, "You want to drive?"

"Sure, but where?"

Janie responded, "Let's find a really cool state park! We can swim, and canoe and cook over a campfire. It'll be a blast!"

The VW camper rolled along the Mountain Parkway toward Natural Bridge State Park. The Kentucky Mountains were breathtaking as they drove along Red River Gorge, with the setting sun casting rays of golden orange hues dancing across the smooth mirror like surface. They made camp near the lake, and Randy went foraging for campfire wood while Rosie lit charcoal briquettes. Night had fallen, submerging the park in velvety darkness when Rosie served barbecued chicken from the grill. The flames from the campfire danced soft illuminations across the faces of the three young travelers.

A fulfilled Janie sighed as she stretched her arms leisurely. "I am so in love with our van. I want to live in it forever!"

A chuckle came from Randy as he said, "You'll change your mind with the first snowfall of winter." He changed the tone of his voice to mock that of a wise old cowboy, "That van will be *colder* than a witch's tit."

With careful consideration over his remark she said, "Not if you're camping in Florida." A look of genius came across her young face, "Or Southern California. Oh, Rosie! Wouldn't it be wonderful to travel the coastlines of California?"

Collecting the trash from their meal she answered, "Stop dreaming, you know we have to go back home at the end of summer."

Knowingly the young girl replied, "I've told you already, Sunshine. We won't be going back to Ben Johnson Ridge for a long, long time. Reaching for her radio, she twisted the dial until the static lifted and Elvis sang *In the Ghetto.*

As she dumped trash in a metal garbage can Rosie said, "Will you use your headphones? That song always makes me cry."

Plugging in the headphone jack to the radio Janie said, "You're just too sensitive, Sunshine. That's going to get you in trouble someday if you aren't careful." Having made that visionary statement, the little girl crawled inside the van with the big black padded earphones covering her ears.

Rosie went to the van and withdrew a sleeping bag. Tossing it at Randy she said, "You're not sleeping in the van with us. You'll have to make yourself a bed here under the tent."

He glared at her wide-eyed, "I can't sleep on the ground! What if a rattlesnake wants to cuddle up with me during the night?"

A slight smile teased her lips. "You really are conceited, aren't you? Take my word for it, not even a rattlesnake would cuddle up with a cross dresser like you."

"Oh very funny," Randy fumed. "Are you really going to make me sleep out here by myself?" He waited for her to answer, and when she remained silent he added, "I'm afraid of the dark."

Placing the dirty utensils in a dishpan of hot soapy water she said, "Keep the fire burning. Then you won't have to worry about snakes, or the dark." She entered the van and closed the door. Incoherent mumbles drifted through the closed doors, as Randy prepared himself a bed.

Soft rays of morning sun filtered through the dense forest canopy awakening Rosie. She lay comfortably in her cot listening to the deep steady breathing of Janie from the upper bunk. The mountain hummed with melodies of birdsong, and a soft rustling breeze titillated the leaves of towering trees, creating whispering wind song within the leafy boughs.

After a few minutes of silent appreciation, she left the bed and reached for her jeans. Emerging silently from the van she found Randy fast asleep inside the sleeping bag on an extended lawn chair. Mischief was born as she reached for a shortened water hose. Taking the cut end she began wiggling in down into Randy's sleeping bag. The young man awoke terror stricken. In an instant he was fighting to get out of the zippered bag. He bolted screaming in fright. The sound of her laughter stopped him in flight. Turning, he faced Rosie laughing so hard that she fell over onto the ground.

Walking quickly back to the tent, Randy snatched the sleeping bag from the chair. "You're not funny! You could have given me a heart attack, you know that?" Stuffing the sleeping bag into a crumpled wad he slung it back onto the chair. Irritation was apparent in his voice as he darkly asked, "How funny would it be to have a dead man on your hands?"

Wiping mirth from her eyes she said, "Now, now Randy. Cross dressers don't die." Pausing with repressed laughter she exclaimed, "They just smell that way!" Then she burst into more exultant giggles.

"That does it! I'm hitchhiking home today. I don't need this kind of abuse." He grabbed his shoes from beneath the chair and started putting them on in a furious flurry.

Janie emerged from the van with sleep tousled hair. "What's going on? Randy, are you mad?"

The young man tied his shoe laces with quick determined action and answered the child curtly, "Your sister thinks she's a comedian!"

"She's not my sister." With eyes slanted angrily the child retorted, "As a matter of fact, she's barely related to me at all. What did she do?"

Randy whined, "She made me sleep out here in the dark by myself, then she woke me up by tricking me into thinking a snake had crawled into my sleeping bag."

Janie gave Rosie a hard determined stare and began spouting rules. "The only time we can joke with Randy about being a girl is when he's dressed like one. At all other times we agree to treat him like a man. Agreed?"

Rosie inspected her fingernails in silence, but jumped with a start when Janie shouted, "Agreed!"

Extending her hand to Randy, Rosie said, "Agreed."

Janie placed her hand over Rosie's, and Randy did likewise. In unison they repeated, "Agreed!" And, giggling, they pulled their hands upward and away, wiggling fingers wildly once pointed skyward.

They spent the day hiking the forest trails, and observing the wildlife in the Kentucky Mountains. Randy carried lunch supplies in his backpack, and each carried water in a canteen. Rosie sported a pair of binoculars that she shared with the others. They came across a small herd of deer feeding in the distance, and a water snake making his way slowly along a narrow creek at the bottom of a cliff. They ate lunch on a huge boulder that jutted out of the mountainside, with a spectacular view of the forested valley below. Tearing crust from her sandwich, Janie tossed it onto a rock beneath them, hoping to attract some birds while they ate quietly. When no birds appeared after a few silent minutes, her usual incessant chatter materialized.

"Rosie's going to be a nurse, and I am going to be an artist. I'm going to draw illustrations for children's books. What are you going to be, Randy?"

With his dark brown eyes conveying certain sadness he explained, "I've got my future all planned out for me by my folks. I'm going to be a lawyer."

Janie asked, "Do you want to be a lawyer?"

Gazing out at the landscape of tree tops he answered, "Sure, why not? After all, there's no future as a drag queen."

When they returned to camp, heated from the hike, the lake beckoned them. The calm cool water sparkled with reflected sunlight. Sitting beneath the sun on a towel, dressed in her favorite swimsuit, Rosie watched the water droplets evaporate from her skin. Randy entertained Janie in the water. His wet chin length raven hair was slicked back from his face, and his muscular body glistened beneath the midday sun. He plucked her from the water and tossed her easily back into the lake with a splash. The little girl's giggles carried across the water like melody.

Finally, the two were exhausted from their play, and they joined Rosie on the grassy bank. Janie took a towel saying, "That was fun. What can we do now?"

Randy sat down next to the little girl and answered, "Rest."

With her nose wrinkled in disdain, the youngster said, "That's no fun. Let's rent a canoe and explore the lake."

"That sounds like a good idea. We're leaving here tomorrow anyway, so if we are going canoeing we'd better do it today," said Rosie.

They gathered their towels and returned to camp. Then they hiked to the General Store, and rented a canoe. Rosie completed the rental agreement while Randy and Janie wandered the store. Sometime later, she found them waiting at the boat pier.

Breathless, Janie climbed into the canoe and asked, "Hey, Randy. Have you ever jumped off a roof with nothing but an open umbrella?"

The handsome young man looked at her as if she had just asked him the silliest question in the world. "No!"

Sitting at the opposite end of the canoe Rosie said, "Randy, let's get closer to the bank so we can be shaded by the trees. It's so hot out here, we're going to bake."

She didn't notice the mischievous smile Randy flashed at Janie as he answered, "I don't know if that's such a good idea. I've heard fisherman talk about snakes falling out of trees into their boats."

Rosie snapped, "That's ludicrous! Let's get out of the sun."

Giving Janie a secret look Randy said, "Okay, okay. You're the boss." He maneuvered the canoe toward the shaded shoreline.

The rocks along the lake had turtles resting lazily in the shade of the trees. As the canoe came closer to them they would retreat back into the water. Long legged cranes browsed about the shallow shoreline for food. Rosie sat twisted as she watched the canoe approach a family of ducks. With her back turned, she didn't see the secret signals between Randy and Janie as they brought their evil plan to fruition.

Suddenly, Randy called out, "Look out, snake!" Janie leapt closer to him, leaving Rosie at the far end of the canoe alone with the rubber snake they had purchased at the General Store.

Rosie quickly turned to see the black snake in the bottom of the canoe. Frightened, she leaped from the canoe into the shallow water. The canoe rocked violently and Randy and Janie burst into side-splitting laughter. She emerged from the murky water sputtering. The laughter from her fellow campers dumbfounded her until she realized that she had been the butt of their evil joke. Randy reached over and plucked the rubber snake from the bottom of the canoe. Holding it in the air he waved it about saying, "Oh, who's afraid of snakes now?"

Infuriated, Rosie grabbed the canoe and pushed down on it with all her weight, causing it to tip them both out into the water. Soon the three were splashing water viciously at one another while laughing with hysteria. Randy put Janie back in the canoe then turned to give Rosie a hand. Suspiciously she asked, "You don't really expect me to trust you?" With a swift move Randy caught her beneath the knees and placed her back in the canoe as easily as he had the little girl.

With rivulets of water dripping from her sodden clothing Rosie asked, "How did you learn to sweep a girl off her feet so easily? Not while you were wearing a dress?"

He gave her a narrow eyed look. "I'll have you know that back home I'm a highly respected man." Randy tilted his head and crossed his arms. "Besides, you agreed to not hassle me about my extracurricular activity."

She tossed her head back and laughed. "Okay! Okay!"

Randy pushed the canoe into water so shallow it almost dragged the bottom of the lake, and stepped back into the boat. "Why don't you just try to focus on me one way or the other? Right now I'm a manly man. Tonight I might be a girly girl. But, when I'm a man I just want you to treat me like a man. And, when I'm a girl I just want you to treat me like a girl."

Janie said, "If you plan on being a girl tonight you'd better be extra careful with yourself. The folks around these parts don't look like the type to appreciate girls with hairy knuckles."

Randy looked at his hands and exclaimed indignantly, "I don't have hairy knuckles!"

They returned the canoe just before dusk, and rushed back to the campsite, ravenous. After changing into dry clothes, Rosie quickly cooked hamburgers and they ate them with potato chips and pickles. Having eaten, they relaxed, and let fatigue overtake them. Randy stretched out on the lawn chair, and Janie perched on the van floor with her legs dangling out. "I'm not in the mood for cleaning up right now," said Rosie with a yawn.

"Let it wait. I thought this was supposed to be a vacation," Randy declared.

Janie cajoled, "Well, let's do something fun. I'm bored," and she followed her statement with a yawn. Then she tilted her head and exclaimed, "Hey! Let's go to the square dance. Can't you hear the music?" She took a few steps in the direction of the bluegrass tunes floating through the still night. "Come on," she urged. "We can clean up later."

With an exhausted sigh Rosie said, "Okay, okay. Let's go."

Some of the campers sported beautiful square dancing garb, with colorful full skirts for the ladies, and western shirts with old fashioned string ties for the men. Janie jumped into the group and began circling around arm in arm from one dancer to another. Randy and Rosie joined her lead, and soon they were perspiring from the efforts of the dance. A titillating sensation rushed through Rosie each time she and Randy joined hands, and she soon realized that her attraction to the young man was beyond her control. When the caller announced the last dance, her heart swelled with regret. She was enjoying the close contact with her partner, and wished the evening never had to end. They walked side by side back to the campsite with Janie leading the way. The young girl chattered nonstop about things she had witnessed during the square dance.

"Oh, my God!" exclaimed the animated child. "Did you notice how the dance caller kept fidgeting with his privates? Even Kid was never that bad. And, what about the lady all dressed in pink? One wrong move and those boobies of hers would have popped right out of that dress!"

When they reached the campsite Janie picked up her radio and settled her headphones over her ears. Randy reached for a towel and headed off for the showers. Submerged in her own fantasies, Rosie motioned for Janie to listen. The little girl removed her headphones. "I want you to stay right here and don't go anywhere," she drilled as she grabbed a bathrobe and towel.

"What are you up too?" asked Janie suspiciously.

"Just don't go anywhere," warned Rosie.

The sign on the men's shower was turned to read *Occupied*. Silently, Rosie entered and removed her clothes. Slipping into the terrycloth robe she walked catlike to the drawn shower curtain and tenderly slid it open. Randy looked up surprised. "Ah!" he exclaimed, embarrassed by his vulnerable state of undress. She pushed the robe from her shoulders and it slid to the floor. With a petrified glance he muttered, "Oh, my!"

Stepping beneath the warm spray of water Rosie asked, "You don't mind sharing this shower with me, do you?" An amused giggle was suppressed when she heard his whimpered response. Reaching for the soap in his hand, Rosie deliberately dropped it. "I'll get it," she said, slowly sinking down. Momentarily, an incoherent moan escaped him as he plunged his face beneath the steaming spray of the showerhead.

When she returned to the campsite dressed in the terrycloth robe and clutching her outerwear under her arm, Janie asked, "What have you done to the poor boy?" When Rosie refused to answer she accused, "You just couldn't keep your hands off the virgin boy, could you?"

Curling up on the bunk at the back of the van Rosie only smiled at the question. Minutes later Randy retuned to the van sniffling and drying his damp hair on a towel. He looked nervous. Answering his unasked question the little girl announced mockingly, "Rosie has enough room for you to sleep on her bunk."

He eyed Rosie hesitantly. She slid to the back of the bed and patted the mattress invitingly. Stepping lightly, he quickly lay down with his back turned against her. Rosie said to Janie, "Put your headphones on and turn the light off."

As soon as Janie was snuggled in bed, Rosie drew the quilt over her and rolled on top of Randy, covering him beneath the quilt with her.

Morning dawned over Natural Bridge State Park awakening the day with soft warming sun rays. Rosie stirred next to Randy. He turned, putting his arm across her as he continued to doze. With a contented smile she brushed her hand along the muscular bronzed limb. When she pushed his arm aside he awoke and asked with a graveled voice, "Where are you going?"

"Go back to sleep."

He rolled over with his face against the pillow and murmured, "You're beautiful."

The day was spent preparing to leave camp. The dark circles had vanished from beneath Janie's eyes, and she had ceased talking about bad dreams or impulsive thoughts. As the sun continued to ascend into the Kentucky skyline, Rosie sat nestled against Randy. Fresh from the shower, Janie began to comb tangles from her wet hair.

Goose bumps rose on Rosie's skin as he lightly traced his fingertips across her arm. "When are you going to call your parents and let them know that you're alright?"

He answered with his mouth against her ear. "I called them when we were at the motel, and I told them all about what happened. They know what you did for me."

"You must have scared them to death with that story."

"Yeah, but I had to tell them." Gazing at the shimmering lake he said, "It's hard to explain how protective they are with me. You see they had me kind of late in life. My mother is sixty-two, and my dad is sixty-four." He chuckled and added, "Growing up, all the other kids thought my parents were my grandparents."

"They must be chomping at the bit to get you back home. How did you ever persuade them to let you stay with us?"

"I just said I was staying, and there was nothing they could do about it. Of course I promised to be home in time for school."

"I'll be starting nursing school this fall."

"Really?' asked Randy with genuine interest. "Well, I'll be a sophomore."

Rosie twisted in his arms asking, "A college sophomore at eighteen? Did you skip a grade?"

"No, I'll be nineteen in September."

"Oh, I see." She stood and raised her arms over her head in a stretch then turned to Janie and asked, "Did you map us out some clever routes to take west?"

Looking up through strands of wet tangled hair the little girl replied, "Trust me. We're taking the scenic route."

Driving away from Natural Bridge State Park, Rosie stopped to call Kid from a pay phone. She held her breath as she hoped for him to answer instead of Valerie. "Hello." It was his voice.

Expelling her breath she said, "Oh, I'm so glad it was you who answered! How's everything?"

"I've been talking to people, you know, about our problem."

The line fell silent momentarily, "And?" she prodded.

"I don't feel comfortable talking on this line. Is there a number where I can call you back later?"

Fidgeting she said, "Not really. You know we're on the road. We're just leaving Kentucky heading west to the Grand Canyon."

He quickly interrupted, "Don't say anything else about where you're at or where you're going. I don't trust this phone line."

A discontented sigh escaped her as she looked through the dingy glass of the telephone booth. "Well, I traded your convertible for a Volkswagon van, and we bought a gun, but no bullets."

"Damn it!" he snapped. "Don't say another word about any of that!" The line fell silent as she recoiled. With a more tender tone he said, "When can you call me back? We'll discuss everything then."

"Will you be home after nine?"

"I'll be waiting by the phone. Nine o'clock, on the dot; don't make me wait."

The metal phone cord scraped against the small metal shelf holding a phone book, as she squirmed inside the claustrophobic cubicle. "Okay, I'll call tonight from a pay phone, and give you the number. Then you can call me back on a phone line that makes you feel more comfortable."

Softly he explained, "I know you don't think there is anything to worry about, but I think differently."

With a slow exhalation she agreed, "Okay."

Before ending the call he said, "You know I love you, Sun. And, I'm so very, very sorry I've caused you this trouble. No matter what I have to do, I will make this up to you. Believe me?"

Imagining his handsome face she smiled, "I believe you."

A sigh of relief rang over the long distance line as he said, "Till tonight then?"

"Till tonight," and she softly placed the phone on the hook.

The sun was rising higher when she climbed back into the van. Randy started the ignition asking, "Is everything good?"

Wishing she could be more optimistic Rosie answered, "I guess so." Then she looked over her shoulder at Janie. "Do you two know which way to go from here?"

Giving Randy a sly look Janie answered, "Oh, yeah. We know."

Later, they stopped at a rest area to lunch on Rosie's homemade pasta salad, with fruit and wheat crackers. After Janie had eaten her fill, she ripped a picture of President Nixon from a life magazine. Pinning it to a rotting stump with bubble gum she proceeded to throw her hunting knife with remarkable accuracy.

The knife flew through the air and pierce Richard Nixon's face with a dull sounding thud. Rosie called, "Hey, squirt! That little trick will come in real handy if you ever meet the President."

The little girl bent over to retrieve her knife, "Go ahead and laugh. You won't be laughing when I cut the head off a rattlesnake that's about to bite your ass."

With large eyes Rosie replied, "I hope to God I have enough sense not to sit on a rattlesnake."

Withdrawing the knife and stepping back for another throw the little girl retorted dryly, "Well, between you and Kid I seriously doubt either of you have enough sense to come in out of the rain; even when it's hailing."

Randy interrupted, "Who wants to see a movie tonight? They've got the documentary on Woodstock playing. I've seen it advertised."

Simultaneously the girls shouted, "Far out!"

When the sun began descending, they stopped at a fast food restaurant for dinner. Randy and Janie consulted locals to get directions to a drive-in theater, and an overnight camping spot. Rosie took advantage of the restroom to wash her face and brush her teeth. She combed her hair that had grown a good two inches since the spiteful haircut. When she returned to the booth, Janie waved a napkin at her with handwritten instructions.

"Ready to go to the show, Sunshine?" she asked.

Fluttering mascara laden lashes Rosie answered, "I was born ready?"

Randy studied her eyes and asked quietly, "Do you mind if I use a bit of your makeup tonight?"

Janie groaned, "Oh, no! Not again."

After the movie they drove to a waffle house, and Rosie made the phone call while Janie curled up on the back bunk with her blanket. Randy stayed in the van, and snooped through Rosie's cosmetic bag.

The phone was abruptly answered in the middle of the second ring, "Hello," said Kid.

"Hey, it's me again," she said energetically.

"Don't say anything, just give me the number, and I'll call you back in five minutes."

Squinting to read the faded numbers, she warned before hanging up, "Don't keep me waiting. This is a public phone you know." With a harsh click, he was gone.

Standing next to the phone, she patiently waited for her call. In less than five minutes it rang. Quickly, she answered, "Sunshine here."

"My only Sunshine," he responded sweetly. "I hope you girls are having a blast with your summer adventures. When do you think you'll be here?"

"Janie doesn't want to come," Rosie replied honestly. "She's talked me into the Grand Canyon, and maybe even the California coast."

"What?" he asked in dismay, "Not come see me? How can you be so heartless?"

"How much time could a married man like you have for us anyway?"

Groaning, he asked, "Must you remind me of that unfortunate fact?"

Smiling fondly she asked, "Have you really managed not to sleep with your chubby bride?"

"I learned something last summer. I know how to fake a medical condition that I learned about from Ed. The doctors call it *erectile dysfunction* and it's really saved my ass," Kid laughed sadistically across the wire.

Rosie giggled, "So, what's the deal with not talking on your phone?"

"I can't trust anyone here. I suspect my phone is bugged. If not by the mob, than by my father-in-law, who by the way is nothing but a criminal with political influence I've discovered."

"Mob!" she exclaimed, "What do you mean, mob?"

"You know, like drug cartel, the smugglers, and the dealers, and the nastiest of them all, the pushers." He inhaled deeply and said, "You know Steppen Wolf were right on with that song *Damn the Pusher Man*. I've been talking to some undercover drug enforcement agents, but the things they want me to do have me scared shitless, you know. Like wearing a wire and doing deals." He exhaled completely before he said, "Sometimes I feel like I sold my soul to get that money to start the band up." Then as if he felt rejuvenated just mentioning music he exclaimed, "But damn we got a good sound! I really think we can do something. And, I've still got enough money for us to cut an album."

Holding the phone cradled to her ear she imagined Kid as a hit music sensation. "Oh, Kid," she said softly, "I have all the confidence in the world that you'll be truly great someday."

"Yeah, if I survive this," he said with dire seriousness. "These guys that I've dealt with, Bud and Ron, well they've found out how important you and Janie are to me, because of the letters you wrote." His voice stopped as if he were considering how to say what he wanted in the most effective way. "Well, you two have been threatened, as have I. But, I'll get us out of this."

A gasp escaped her, "My God! Maybe you should just leave there."

"I wish it were just that easy, Sunny. I'd like nothing more than to be right there with you. No, I've got to work with the task force. I've got to do this right, or I'll never be free of these thugs."

Tears stung her eyes. "What do you need me to do? Just tell me. I'll do anything you say."

A brief silence crossed the wire before he answered, "I think you're doing everything right. Just keep moving, and when you call don't say a word about anything until I can call you back on a safe line. Can you call me on Wednesdays and Sundays? Let's say six o'clock in the evening. Valerie will be out of the house, and I can run to the gas station and call you right back."

Slowly she responded, "Okay, Wednesdays and Sundays at six." She fell quite for a few moments then said sincerely, "Just always remember how very much I love you, and I take as much responsibility for this mess as you. I should have insisted you use the coins for the money you needed." She raised her head and looked at the ceiling as two large drops of tears trickled slowly down her cheeks. "But, I didn't do that, did I?"

Kid's voice was soft and husky when he responded, "I love you, too. So much it hurts sometimes. And, don't even mention the coins. What's done is done, and the coins are for you and Janie. You know that's what Doc wanted."

"No" she said sternly, "Doc wanted me to be happy, and helping you makes me happy."

"Do you think he's still there?"

Looking past the crowded coffee shop she answered, "Yes, I do." Closing her eyes she tried to envision Kid's eyes consuming her with sexual heat. "Oh!" she remembered, "We saw the Woodstock documentary tonight. I saw those same naked people again!"

"You can see me naked anytime you want."

Giggling she said, "Night, night," and hung up the phone.

The parking lot was humid with nighttime closing in. When she crawled into the passenger seat of the van she was surprised to find Randy wearing breathtakingly beautiful eye makeup. With a gasp of approval she said, "Nice smoky eyes." Upon closer scrutiny she asked, "Can you show me how to do that?"

Chapter Twenty-Seven
Fireworks and Farewells

The days of summer passed with Rosie and Janie enjoying the company of Randy, and their travels in the VW camper van. Like children they played in the soft summer rain and splashed through puddles, speckling themselves with mud. They ate water melon from the rind, and stopped on roadsides to pluck wild fruit from the vine. Fun was lurking everywhere, and finding it was the easiest thing to do. They traveled across state lines and camped in beautiful scenic parks. After visiting the Grand Canyon, they traveled on to Las Vegas. Rosie kept in touch with Kid as she had promised. She felt terrible for all the stress he was going through, and deliberately didn't tell him about Randy. When they reached Las Vegas they got a motel room, and prepared to enjoy the city.

The town offered around the clock entertainment, and adventure was only an idea away. "Let's go out tonight dressed real fancy and snoop around one of the casinos," Randy suggested.

The idea intrigued her. "Okay, but what are you wearing?"

He touched his finger to his lip as if in deep thought before saying, "Maybe that little short red leather skirt you have."

"You want me to go out with you dressed like a girl?"

"Why not?"

Janie asked, "What about me? I can't go to no crappy casino."

"All you have to do is keep the door locked tight, and behave yourself. You'll be fine!" explained Randy.

That night when they were ready to leave the motel Janie looked at them in awe. "Geez, Louise! You really do look pretty, Randy."

Rosie was dressed in a snug fitting black spandex sleeveless dress. Glaring at Randy she said, "You actually shaved your legs. Unbelievable!" Looking at the clock she said, "Oh! I almost forgot to call Kid," and rushed to the phone. He answered on the second ring. "Hey! It's me," she said.

"Give me the number," he demanded.

After reading off the motel number, she replaced the phone and waited for the return call. When the phone rang, she quickly picked it up.

"Don't stay there long. If my phone is bugged they will know exactly where you are," he warned."

Disregarding his worry she asked, "Are you any closer to whatever it is you have to do?"

With a tired weariness Kid answered, "Yeah, it's getting close now. I'm not sure, but something's going to happen soon."

Trying to sound nonchalant for the sake of Randy, who knew nothing of the situation, Rosie said, "Well, I just called to let you know we're having a great time. We're not staying here long. So don't worry about us, okay?"

"See that you don't stay there long, like get out of there tomorrow morning," he insisted.

"Okay, will do." After a brief hesitation she sighed, "Till next time, huh?"

A deep sigh came over the line, "I love you so much, and I miss you even more."

Feeling the old familiar sting of tears she said lightly, "I love you, too. And, I miss you just as much." She placed the phone gently on the hook, and turned to face Randy who stood looking at her with a pained expression. "Ready if you are." Looking back she said to Janie, "Put the chain on the door."

Nightfall engulfed the electric city, and with it came a twilight magic infusing the atmosphere with gaiety and ambition. Rosie and Randy strolled into a casino as if they had done it a hundred times before. They helped themselves to drinks offered by scantily clad waitresses. Perched on stools at a Black Jack table, they pretended to know all there was to playing the game of twenty-one. Gambling bored her, so Rosie dragged Randy from game to game until she had all she could stand of the noisy bright casino lights.

They walked along city sidewalks in stiletto heels, and stopped at a coffee shop. As they sat across one from the other, warmed from the consumption of alcoholic beverages, Randy began asking about Kid. "You know I can see from the light in your eyes every time you talk with him how much he means to you."

"Yeah, well once upon a time we had plans to be together. But, that all ended when he got married."

Randy eyed her seriously, and said in a soft voice, "There's this thing called divorce. You could still be together someday."

Impulsively she reached out and grasped his hand. "You look so cute tonight! I'm almost jealous."

A smile crossed his lips. "That's the nicest compliment I've ever had." For a moment he lost himself, and leaned closer for a kiss, but drew back when he heard a man clear his throat.

Looking up, they found a handsome man dressed in elegant clothes standing next to their table. Witnessing the halted moment of passion between the two girls, the gentleman was rendered speechless. He looked from Rosie to Randy. Finally he said, "Uh, never mind!" and hurried away.

Bursting into giggles Randy said, "I think it's time for us to go."

"Oh, I wish we had something more to drink."

Randy said, "All we have to do is pop into a store and buy something."

Inhaling deeply Rosie replied, "We're underage! We can't buy alcohol."

Haughtily, Randy said, "Speak for yourself. I have a fake ID."

"Oh, no you don't? Why didn't you tell me this sooner?" Rose peeled bills from her wallet to pay for the coffee, and stood from the booth pulling Randy along with her.

"Well," he said with a girlish voice, "You never asked me."

When they returned to the motel, Rosie insisted they sit in the van to drink the wine they had purchased, so Janie would not be disturbed by their chatter. Randy twisted off the metal top of the cheap wine, and kicking off his shoes he tucked his legs beneath him as he poured it into plastic cups. "I'd like to make a toast to the best girlfriend a person could have, to my Sunshine Rose."

Rosie giggled and tapped her plastic cup against his saying, "I'd like to toast you, Randy. For being the most fun I've ever had."

With a resounding, "Cheers!" they drank in celebration. "Oh, hey this is pretty good." Randy commented smacking his lips, "A little sweet, but really good. You made a good choice."

She kicked off her shoes. "This is what we used to get back home from the bootlegger." Watching his rhinestone earrings sparkle in the darkness she asked suggestively, "Are you going to be a girl all night?"

With careful consideration he answered, "Nope, after this bottle of wine is finished I intend to be a man."

Taking the bottle, she poured more into the cups saying, "Well, let's drink up then."

Their laughter rang out through the open windows and across the sizzling evening. Flashing neon's and bright street lamps illuminated the van with a soft diluted glow. Danger was a forgotten enemy, and love bloomed in Vegas.

Bright sunshine and sweltering heat awoke Rosie with a perspiring body, and an aching head. She moaned as she turned away from the impeding sunlight, and groaned even louder as she felt the sickness of a hangover grip her stomach. With one eye open she looked over at Randy who still slumbered with smeared mascara, and drool glistening from the corner of his mouth. With a grimace she raised herself from the bunk. Randy roused and asked, "What time is it?"

Pulling the wrinkled black dress over her head, she mumbled, "Time for the walk of shame." She stumbled to the doors and swung them open. Shielding her eyes from the sun, she stepped from the van barefoot, and slung the doors shut behind her. Lightly she crossed the parking lot to the motel room. The sound of the television could be heard coming from inside as she knocked on the door.

"Who's there?"

"The big bad wolf, let me in, or I'll huff and I'll puff and I'll blow your house down."

The door promptly opened with Janie looking past Rosie asking, "Where's Randy? And what happened to your clothes?" She stepped aside as Rosie rushed for the bathroom. "You look a mess!" Closing the door she followed Rosie. "Were you drinking last night?" she asked as Rosie fumbled through her cosmetic bag for aspirin. Before Rosie could answer there was another knock at the door. "Oh, gee! I wonder who that could be," Janie said acrimoniously.

She opened the door to find a pathetic looking Randy with smeared mascara and tousled hair leaning against the door frame. "Did you guys sleep in the van? Why?"

Randy collapsed across a bed, curling into fetal position and clutching a pillow to his chest. Emerging from the bathroom with her hair wrapped in a towel, Rosie wore nothing but an oversized t-shirt. She pulled back the bed covers from the unused bed and disappeared beneath them.

Janie walked to the window and peeked out. The black sedan she had notice earlier was still parked in the same place, but only one man with sunglasses was now sitting in the passenger seat. Silently she wondered where the other man was. The sound of a housekeeper's cart drew her back to the window. Taking a key she quietly slipped from the room. The bright Nevada sun brought tears as she shaded her face from the piercing rays. She stepped into the room with an open door, startling the housekeeper. "Excuse me."

The plump lady with fiery red hair straightened with a gasp, "Oh, my!" She exclaimed, "You frightened me child!"

"I'm sorry, but I was wondering if you would mind walking with me to the vending machines. You see my friends are still sleeping, and I'm very hungry." Seeing the housekeeper wet her lips with a scowl, she hurriedly explained, "It's just that I'm not allowed to go out alone, and I didn't want to disturb them."

The housekeeper's face softened. She stooped to pick up a bundle of bed linens, and waddled to the cart. "Well," she said. "You're in luck. I was heading back to the laundry room anyway. So, come along."

Walking next to the housekeeper toward the vending machines, Janie dared to take an opportunity and glance past the plump woman's shoulder at the black sedan. When she returned to the room she carefully closed the door behind her. Placing the snacks onto a table, she ripped the tabs from the sodas. Putting one to her lips she drank from it with long gulps. Then she took the other to the bed where Randy slept. Shaking him awake, she held out the soda as he glared at her with sleepy eyes. "Be quiet," she told him softly. "Don't wake up Rosie."

He sat up and took the soda. In thirsty gulps he drank half the content before taking it from his lips. Janie motioned for him to follow her into the bathroom. When Randy entered, she closed the door explaining, "I need for you to get dressed. But get this, you need to dress sort of like a girl, you know. You were seen dressed like a girl last night, and it's important for you to look like to a girl this morning."

Randy sat on the toilet looking at her with smeared eye makeup. "What's going on?"

"I've got to do something very important, and you're going to help me. Just get ready as quick as you can, I'll tell you all about it when we get out of here."

Opening the bag of chips he muttered, "Yeah, okay. Let me finish my breakfast, and shower. I'll be out in less than ten minutes."

"Okay, I'll be watching the clock." Then she went to leave Rosie a note.

When Janie returned to the room, Rosie was finishing the packing. "Where's Randy?"

Janie answered, "He's in the lobby, checking us out."

"Where have you two been?"

Taking up her suitcase Janie answered, "Just out for a walk. Randy's waiting for us to drive to the front and pick him up."

Stepping through the door Rosie grimaced against the bright sunlight. "Ugh! Please find my sunglasses."

Janie didn't dare look toward the black sedan until she was inside the van. Peering out the back windshield she noticed the two men from the car standing beneath some trees away from the parking lot. Handing the glasses to Rosie she said, "I hope you're not mad that I took some money from your purse." Propping her right foot on the back of the seat, she explained, "I really wanted these moccasin boots."

"Wow, they're cool." Then with a giggle Rosie said, "Looks like Randy is rubbing off on you, huh?"

With a slight smile Janie answered, "Yeah, I guess so."

Rosie drove the van beneath the concrete canopy of the motel entrance. The van was shielded from the sun, as well as any peering eyes from the parking lot by a brick wall. Randy carefully exited the lobby. He entered the van through the side doors. Janie climbed from the back seat, and sat next to Rosie. Randy quickly lay down on the bunk.

Rosie asked, "Are you feeling okay, Randy?"

"No. That wine gave me one hell of a hangover."

With the road atlas spread over her knees Janie said, "Don't worry, Sunshine. I know which roads to take."

Rosie pulled away from the motel as Janie kept her eye in the side mirror. The black sedan slithered from the motel parking lot, and kept an inconspicuous distance behind them. The radio played softly as Janie chattered, "I hope we see some movie stars when we get to Los Angeles. I just can't wait to see the Pacific Ocean. I've heard the water is very calm and blue. Maybe we could take one of the excursion boats to those little islands off the coast. It looks like Santa Cruz Island is the closest to Los Angeles."

Rosie relaxed as she maneuvered the van along the highway. The wind from the opened windows tossed her shaggy short hair about her face. She glanced in the rearview mirror at Randy, stretched out on the bunk while sweet memories from the adventurous night they spent together in Vegas teased her thoughts.

When they stopped for fuel before crossing the state line into the Mojave Desert, Janie watched the black sedan drive past the gas station. The station attendant filled the tank, while Rosie used the ladies room. Janie called to Randy, "They just drove past. They're probably waiting for us down the road. You should go use the restroom, and get you a cold drink while we've got this opportunity."

Randy rose from the bunk and looked around carefully before stepping from the van. He returned a little later with a brown paper bag containing a six pack of beer. He stashed the beer in the small refrigerator, but kept one out to drink. Rosie looked at him suspiciously, and Randy defended himself by saying, "Just a little hair of the dog that bit me." He guzzled the brew and sighed loudly, "Nothing better for a hangover."

Traffic was sparse along the lonely roadway crossing the desert. Anxiety became so strong within Janie and Randy that Rosie could sense it. Driving along she asked, "Is something wrong?"

The black sedan followed them at a closer distance now. Janie watched with a pounding heart as they drew closer. "It's cowboy and Indian time, Sunshine."

"What!"

"They don't know Randy is with us, he's our trump card, so play it cool."

Rosie's heart leapt to her throat as the black automobile sped up beside her on the two lane highway. Looking over at the car with tinted glass, she watched the passenger window slide down with electric power. A dirty looking man pointed a gun at her and waved for her to pull off the road. "What do I do?" she asked, panicked.

Calmly, Janie replied, "Pull over."

The two men left the car and cautiously approached the van. The men split up as one approached Janie, and one approached Rosie. "You need to get out of the van," the curly haired man standing at the driver's side said. She opened the door and cautiously stepped out into the scorching midday sun.

The balding man who stood next to Janie said, "Don't be afraid, we just want to take your picture. It will be a little souvenir for your cousin, Kid."

Making a show of his revolver, the man next to Rosie hid the gun grasped in his scarred hand inside his jacket pocket. "We're going to walk out to those rocks, see. Then after we take a few pictures, we're all going for a nice long ride in our car, see. And, if Kid comes through for you, we'll set you free in Tijuana."

A scathing laugh came from the tattooed snake man accompanying Janie. "But, if your dear cousin disappoints us, well you don't want to know." He reached out and shoved her to walk faster.

They walked around the boulders, and sat in the shade of the huge stones. The man with the scarred hand said, "Okay, Ron. Take the pictures, now. Make sure you get the desert in the back ground."

The snake on Ron's neck moved with the beat of his pulse as he took a small camera from his back pocket. He began snapping photos while the other man held a gun in front of them. "Now, listen here idiot!" The gunman yelled, "Don't get my damn face in the pictures."

The balding man with the pulsating snake tattoo said irritably, "If you think you can do it better, than get your mangy ass out here, and do it."

Janie sat sideways with her face down, and deftly scooped up two hands full of the desert sand. Bud stuffed his gun into the back of his pants as he stepped to Ron, snatching the camera. "I don't know why I ever trusted you to take the damn picture anyway! It takes at least half a brain to snap a shutter."

Ron thrust the camera at Bud saying, "Why don't you just shut the hell up, Bud. I'm sick of your constant bitching!"

"Put your foot up to the kid's head, like you're fixing to kick her brains out," Bud instructed.

Ron laughed at the suggestion. He stepped closer, and was just about to lift his foot as though to kick Janie, when suddenly she leapt to her feet and slung the sand in his face. Like a wild Indian in the movies, she withdrew the hunting knife from her moccasin boot, and threw it with the precision of a deerstalker at the man holding the camera.

Rosie screamed as she watched Bud drop the camera, the knife protruding from his forehead. Instantly his eyes dimmed and he fell face first into the desert sand, shoving the knife through the back of his skull, spurting blood and brain, leaving the scarred hand twitching in the dust.

Ron danced about rubbing the sand from his eyes. When he looked back for help from his friend, he saw the lifeless man lying in the sand. Rushing over he turned Bud onto his back. "You Bitches!" he screamed. The girls leapt to their feet, prepared to run. Ron jerked the knife from Bud's split skull, and ran after them.

Just as he was about to race around the boulders Ron came to an abrupt halt. There stood Randy with the *Saturday Night Special* pointed in the kidnapper's face. Ron started stepping backward away from the gun. Randy pulled a length of rope from his back pocket and tossed it at the balding criminal. "Tie yourself up and I'll let you live."

With the hunting knife grasped in his hand he stared at the rope lying at his feet. A slow evil laugh came from deep inside his belly. "You want me to be afraid of a gun with no bullets?" Tossing the knife aside, he reached for the gun tucked in his waist band and sneered, "You half breed Indian faggot! You're going to die!" Ron raised his gun with deadly intent. The sound of multiple gunshots tore through the quiet desert stillness. The gun dropped from Ron's hand, and he crumbled to the desert soil, his last breath a guttural moan.

Now, only a slow hot wind moved across the desert sands, tossing about the thin stringy hair on the dead man's head. Randy walked cautiously to him, pushing him over onto his back. When he saw the glazed look in the balding man's eyes, he took up Janie's knife, and stabbed the blade into the sand repeatedly to rid it of blood and brain tissue. Randy almost jumped out of his skin when he heard Janie say, "He's dead."

"What should we do with them?" Randy asked, threatened by nausea.

"Leave 'em here, and let's go," Janie answered simply.

In a breathless voice Rosie agreed, "Yes, leave them here." Turning away from the gruesome sight, she leaned against a boulder and repeated Janie's suggestion, "Let's go."

Taking up the camera, Janie blew the dust away. Together they walked from the shadows of the boulders back across the hot dunes to the van. As they drove away, she popped the roll of film from the camera and ripped the black shiny ribbon from its case. Then she let the exposed film fly out the opened window. Letting it loose, the film flew into the desert like a dark spirit.

Rosie asked, "What just happened? You knew they were following us, didn't you? Where did you get the bullets for the gun?" Looking over at Randy she asked, "How did you know about those men?"

Pushing the raven hair from his eyes he asked, "Don't you remember telling me about everything last night?"

"No, I don't remember." She leaned her head back against the seat and said, "I don't remember anything after we started drinking the wine in the van. Alcohol does that to me. It wrecks my memory." Memories of Lewis in his drunken state of brandy and Quaaludes rushed through her.

The green and white VW van rolled along the desert roadway as the relentless California sun beat down on them. Janie turned the radio on to drown out the overpowering silence. The straight flat road stretched before them with a blurry haze of heat shrouding the distance. Plucking tissues from a box, she began meticulously cleaning specks of remaining blood from her hunting knife.

"We can never tell anyone about what happened here, ever," said Rosie.

Janie remained silent, and Randy said, "I think that's a very good idea." And, they drove in silence for hours.

Sitting on the hotel balcony with the phone pressed to her ear, Rosie watched Janie and Randy play in the surf of the Pacific Ocean. She listened as Kid spoke, "I'm looking at a picture of you walking down a Las Vegas street with a black haired girl. Is she still with you?"

"No," she lied, "We left her in Vegas. She was just someone we met along the way."

"This goes to show how easily those thugs can tail you. I'm surprised they haven't sent more photos. You must have lost them along the way."

"Yes, we must have," she lied casually.

"So, this picture is why I'm not calling you back today. I don't want you giving me a phone number that you can be traced by. I do have some interesting news that's going to have a devastating effect on Janie," he said sadly.

"What?"

"Janie's mother has returned from the dead. She's living with my grandparents, pretending to be concerned with G-Mama's health. But speculation has it that the man she had run off with kicked her out when his wife wanted him back."

Rosie gasped, "Oh, my God! She was right all along. Her mother wasn't dead!"

"Elizabeth used the convenience of the hurricane to disappear, and shun her responsibilities as a mother. It's rumored, between certain members of the family that she would have never returned if the man had continued to keep her up."

Anger raged as memories of all the tragedies the little girl had suffered flooded her. "The horrible bitch, how could she turn her back on that little girl?"

A long silence followed her remark before he asked, "How are you going to tell her?"

"With great reluctance," she sighed heavily. "I'm going now. Bye." Walking from the balcony, she crossed the beach, and joined Randy and Janie who rushed from the water to meet her.

Tugging at her hand Janie said, "Come on! Get in the water, its fun." The look on her face told the child something had happened. "What's wrong? Is Kid okay?"

"Yes, he's fine. But he did tell me some news that's rather shocking." Looking at Janie with pity, she said, "Your mother has come home to Ben Johnson Ridge. She's taking care of Maggie."

The happy expression faded from the child's face instantly. "Well, of course she has. After all, I don't live there anymore, do I?" She fell to her knees and began drawing lines and circles in the sand.

Sinking to her knees beside Janie she explained, "This has nothing to do with you. This all happened because the man she had been living with kicked her out so he could be with his wife again."

"Oh, well! That makes me feel better," Janie said scornfully and took a fistful of sand just to sling in back down. "Whatever she does means nothing to me. I'm never going back there, and if you tell me I have to, I'll go running out into the ocean and disappear right now."

Shock grasped Rosie with cold reality, "I'll never make you go back there! We'll find a place where I can go to school, and work. By the time you're in high school I'll have a good job."

The look on her face was dark and morose as the child replied, "Yeah, that's a good plan." She stood and began walking across the beach dragging her feet in the sand.

Summer was drawing to a sad end, and Randy had to get home. They drove from Los Angeles along the coast to San Diego before heading straight on to Indiana, making as few stops as possible. Randy and Rosie took turns sleeping so they could travel night and day.

Janie fell into a dark place after hearing the news of her mother. Sitting next to Randy as he drove across Arizona, she noticed a roadside fireworks stand ahead. "Let's stop," she said with the first hint of joy since hearing the news of her mother.

With an uncertain look Randy said, "I don't like fireworks. They're noisy, smelly and dangerous."

"That's okay, because they're not for." She turned and looked back at Rosie who slept on the back bunk.

Randy pulled the van over at the fireworks stand and got out to browse with Janie. He was appalled at the amount of fireworks she collected. "Okay, I can go along with the bottle rockets and firecrackers, but I can't approve of the M-80s."

With a hard look she asked rhetorically, "Did I ask for your approval?"

Deciding to be assertive Randy said, "I'm saying you can't have them."

Taking a step back she declared, "I *will* have them." Then with an impulsive gesture of her middle finger she hauled off and kicked him in the shin.

He inhaled a gasp as the pain spread down his leg, then turned and limped back to the van, slamming the door angrily as he got inside. He watched her pay the amused vendor. When she got inside Randy said to her, "If you blow your damned arm off, don't say I didn't try to warn you."

The little girl withdrew one of the cherry bombs and inspected it closely. With a devilish smile she replied, "Oh, don't worry. What I blow up with this baby won't be connected to me."

It was late afternoon when Rosie roused and asked Randy to stop at a place to eat. She took a cold soda from the small refrigerator and removed the tab. After taking a few drinks she handed the soda to Randy, who took it from her and drank it with big noisy gulps. Seeing Janie take the fireworks from the paper sack and place them inside her hobo bag she asked, "Where did you get those?"

Janie answered simply, "From a roadside stand."

A sense of dread began to grow in Rosie's gut as she cautioned, "Well, don't get yourself into trouble with them."

Smiling devilishly she asked mockingly, "What fun would that be?"

It was nearing dusk when Randy pulled off the highway into the parking lot of a quiet little café. They wandered in, weary from the road, and sank into a cushioned booth. Apprehension gripped Rosie, as she noticed a greasy haired man give instructions to a meek skinny waitress with yellow hair. The waitress approached their booth and said apologetically, "I'm very sorry, but we can't serve you."

"Are you closing?" asked Rosie.

The waitress dropped her head and looked at the floor as she answered, "No, you see, uh, we only serve whites."

Rosie's hand instinctively flew to the beaded headband she wore, as she looked at Randy with pathetic embarrassment. "Oh, I see," she said, looking around at the rough unclean men with crew cuts. Standing to depart, she said, "We'll just go then."

Janie looked sweetly at the waitress and asked, "Is it okay if I use the restroom before I go?"

The waitress smiled and said, "Well, sure *you* can."

Slinging the bag over her shoulder she stepped alongside the waitress saying to her companions with a smirk, "Go ahead and start the car. I'll be right out."

The approaching nightfall had cooled the sweltering day, and Rosie closed her arms around herself as they left the café. "Do what she said, and start the van."

Sliding under the wheel he asked, "Why waste the fuel? She's going to be in there for a while."

Shaking her head slowly Rosie replied with logic, "I think we should be ready to roll as soon as she gets her vindictive little ass back out here."

While inside the ladies room, Janie opened her packages of firecrackers and twisted the fuses together. She used the rubber band from her hair to hold them all together in a bundle. The bottle rockets were bound together in a similar way, with the ribbon from her ponytail. She placed the two bundles back into her hobo bag, and peeked out just as the owner entered the men's room. Carefully, she stepped out of the ladies room to the men's room door. She turned the door knob and pushed the door open just slightly. From beneath the toilet stall she could see the man's feet with his pants bunched around his ankles. Returning to the ladies room, she took a Zippo lighter from the hobo bag, and lighting the fuse to one of the *M-80s,* she flushed it down the toilet.

Hurrying back to the men's room, she looked around cautiously. She turned the knob on the door, but before pushing it open she lit the fuse to the other explosive, then sent it rolling across the floor toward the man's feet. Nonchalantly, she began walking to the exit, and stopped at a newspaper stand, where she took the bundle of bottle rockets from her bag. The blonde waitress was shocked to hear a frightened cry come from the men's room, and stopped short when her boss came running from the john with his pants around his ankles.

After lighting the fuse to the bottle rockets that she had propped next to the newspaper stand, Janie quickly stepped outside, but paused long enough to put flame to the fuse on the bundle of firecrackers, which she unhurriedly tossed just inside the café door. She ran fast calling frantically, "Let's go! Let's go!" The popping of the firecrackers blended with the whistling of the bottle rockets as she raced across the parking lot. Just as she reached the van the loud explosions of the *M-80s* could be heard.

Rosie stood with the passenger door open and shoved Janie inside as she followed, slamming the door shut, "Oh, my God! Oh, my God! What did you do?" She and Janie sat twisted on the seat watching out the back windshield as people ran from the café through a cloud of smoke.

Laughter erupted from the child as she whooped from her success. She turned away from the disruption gripping her arms around her waist, laughing. Finally, she calmed and said, "Ah ha, that was priceless." Looking up at Randy she scowled, "And, you didn't want me to get any fireworks."

Winston County, Indiana was an agricultural area quickly becoming residential rural in the southwestern part of the state. The neighborhood Randy lived in was calm streets with lush green landscaped lawns, lined with large expensive homes. When they reached Randy's house, Rosie gazed at the large two story home with awe. "You never bothered to tell us you were a spoiled rich kid," she said to tease.

With a heavy heart Randy said, "And, you forgot to tell me not to fall for a girl who was just going to leave at the end of summer."

The front door of the magnificent house opened, and Randy's parents stepped out to greet him. "You have to meet them," he said.

Randy's father embraced him with tears in his dark eyes. "Welcome home, son. Did you enjoy your journey across country? Tell me about the Grand Canyon. Did you see any movie stars in Los Angeles?"

Randy smiled, "We saw Linda Evans sitting at a traffic light, and she was driving herself. I thought big stars had chauffeurs."

Trudy said, "Sunshine, sweetheart. I have a room all ready for you girls. You don't mind sharing a room do you?" She put her arms out, cradling Rosie and Janie against herself. "We're going out for dinner tonight, so go ahead and make yourselves at home. Your room has a full bath, and you'll be able to soak in a tub or take a shower, whichever you prefer. Just be ready to go at six."

That evening they sat in a beautiful dining room at a private country club among many of their friends. Rosie looked elegant in an off shoulder white summer dress, and Janie was dressed sweetly in a yellow dress with mint green polka dots, and a matching green ribbon holding her hair back.

Trudy wore a stylish red dinner dress with a glimmering beaded bodice. Her raven hair was swept up and held in place by two silver combs, and her dark Indian skin glistened with a dewy shine. Randy and his father were both dressed in starched white shirts with sports jackets, and no tie.

Dale Rainwater said, "I understand you intend to be a nurse, dear."

Rosie answered, "Oh, yes. That's my dream."

"Well, if you're interested I might be able to help." He picked up his wine glass and took a sip. "I have a friend who is a doctor with his own clinic. I've spoke to him about you, and he has agreed to give you a job while you attend school. Would you be interested?"

Her heart leapt with hopeful excitement, "Oh, yes! Where is his clinic?"

"Ft. Lauderdale, Florida." Taking notice of the disagreeable look clouding Rosie's face, he quickly added, "A beautiful place indeed."

"Oh, but that's so far from here," she commented sadly. "I was hoping to study close to Randy."

"Randy will be going to state university, dear," announced Dale.

Rosie said softly, "It's such a long distance from Florida."

The older man smiled charm in her direction, remarking, "You can still spend holidays together. That's the magic of air travel you see."

"Well, then!" Trudy exclaimed, "It's settled. Let's plan our first holiday together right now. Let's see, Thanksgiving, hum?"

Dale waved for the waiter to bring him more wine. "Yes, we'll send you airline tickets for Thanksgiving weekend. Would you like that?"

With heaviness in her heart Rosie mustered a smile and answered, "Yes, I would like that very much." She reached for her glass of water and tried to swallow the lump of loneliness growing in her throat.

Sitting politely quite, the little girl only uttered a response when she was spoken too. When they returned home, Trudy and Dale begged the young people to play a game of Monopoly with them. Janie was obviously uninterested in the game. When Trudy pressed her to explain her doldrums, she simply answered that she was sad to be leaving Randy.

Feeling touched by the child's despondency Trudy said, "I'm so glad Randy had you and Sunshine to spend his summer with. Thanksgiving will be here in no time."

Janie looked at Randy's mother with complete skepticism, "Yes, I know." Falling back into silence, the only noise she made was the sound of rolling dice.

Later, as Janie lay in bed waiting for Rosie to turn off the lights, she closed her eyes and relived the events of the desert deaths. Something about remembering the destruction of those evil men gave her satisfaction. There was a light tapping at the patio windows. Tip toeing from the bed, she pulled back the heavy draperies and peered outside. There was Randy standing on the small balcony. Unlatching the French doors she pushed them open, smiling brightly.

He stepped inside and said, "I don't think I can sleep without you girls."

When Rosie emerged from the bathroom, he crossed the floor swiftly and kissed her. Kneeling down on one knee he stretched his arms out to Janie, who ran across the room and threw herself into his embrace. With her face pressed against his neck Janie said, "You're the best friend in the whole world, Randy Rainwater."

A soft rapping on the door awoke them the next morning. Randy crawled from bed, putting his finger to his lips as Janie awoke. Waving goodbye, he stepped to the balcony and disappeared. The knock at the door came louder, and Rosie went to open it. Trudy Rainwater stood completely dressed. "Good morning, dear! I thought I would wake you early, so you and Janie could go shopping with me. Dale insists that I take you shopping as a reward for bringing our son home safely."

Janie asked, rubbing sleep heavy eyes and smoothing bed tousled hair, "Is Randy going with us?"

Trudy looked at the little girl bewildered. "Well, he isn't usually interested in shopping. But we can ask him if you like."

Janie frankly replied, "Yes, I'd like to ask him very much."

The day was spent going from one extravagant store to another, with Trudy pressuring Rosie and Janie into accepting gifts while Randy watched with amusement. Nightfall came, and for their last night together, Trudy invited two of Randy's closest friends over for dinner. When the friends left just after midnight, Rosie slumped tiredly against the foyer wall as Randy closed the door behind them. He turned, and she fell into his arms. Pulling back, he produced a small box covered with blue velvet. "I picked this up today while we were out shopping. I hope you like it."

"Oh, Randy!" she whispered with a tear in her voice. "It's beautiful."

He withdrew the necklace, and opened the tiny locket to reveal a miniature picture of him, "Just something for you to remember me."

Taking the locket, she gazed at the picture for a long moment before snapping it shut. "Will you help me put it on?"

From the huge oval mirror in the foyer, she gazed at the locket hanging around her neck. Tiny diamonds in the shape of a heart sparkled. Throwing her arms around his neck she declared, "I love it! And, I love you."

Randy pulled her close to him and confessed, "I love you too, Sunshine. So much I can hardly bear to see you leave."

She kissed him deeply then said, "We've still got tonight." Taking his hand in hers she led him upstairs.

Indiana had glorious mornings, Rosie decided as she stood looking across the neighborhood from the balcony of the room she had shared with Janie. The beautiful manicured lawns were drenched in soft morning light. Hummingbirds flitted from flower to flower, and songbirds chirped musical lyrics. She stroked the gold locket around her neck, and watched Randy carry luggage to the van. Prepared to leave, the girls descended the stairs. Rosie's heart lurched when she saw Randy step inside the front door holding a long stemmed red rose.

"It's okay, you can take it. I pinched all the thorns off," he said.

She took the rose and put it to her nose, "Oh, Randy! It's beautiful, thank you."

Trudy said, "I don't mean to rush you, dear. But you do have a long trip ahead."

"That's okay," Rosie said, "It is a long trip."

Trudy stepped forward holding out an envelope, "This is just a little thank you note from Dale. He felt awful that he couldn't say goodbye to you this morning."

Taking the envelope, she smiled, "Tell him I said thank you and goodbye." Rosie placed the envelope inside her purse and said reluctantly, "Well, goodbye Mrs. Rainwater. It's been a pleasure meeting you."

"Goodbye dear. And, do take good care of yourself," said Trudy.

Randy followed the girls to the van, and opened the door for Rosie. Rushing into his arms Janie let her tears flow freely, "I miss you already, Randy Rainwater!"

He wiped a tear from his eye saying, "I miss you, too. But, don't forget about Thanksgiving, and I'll write."

She peeled herself away and crawled into the van. Rosie held her breath, refusing to let him see her cry. "Well, good bye twinkle toes."

He leaned closer and said, "I'll remember every second of our last night together."

"Yeah, me too," she sighed and started the engine. Lifting the rose to her nose, she waved a final farewell. Randy walked slowly away until he stood at the edge of his lawn, then he waved goodbye once more and turned away. Tears streamed down Janie's cheeks as she watched him disappear inside his beautiful home. Placing the rose on the dashboard Rosie pulled away, never knowing that inside the affluent home she had left behind a heartbroken Randy, crying in his mother's arms. Once she had driven out of sight of the posh neighborhood, she paused at a stop sign, and resting her head against the steering wheel, sobbed miserably.

Chapter Twenty-Eight
He's Found Us

After having traveled only a few miles from Randy's home, the VW van passed by a serene lake, reflecting golden rays of sunlight beneath the Indiana sky. Janie watched the calm water pass beneath them as they crossed a bridge. Suddenly, she turned to Rosie and said, "I want to stop here." Without questioning the child, Rosie slowed and pulled over onto the side of the road. "Go back to the bridge," instructed Janie.

Rosie turned the van around, and drove back to the bridge. She parked off the road beneath a grove of trees, and they walked along the rocky lake shore to the shadows of the bridge above them. Without speaking, Rosie sat perched upon a boulder and watched small brim swim along the craggy rocks lining the shore. Janie collected small stones that she skipped along the smooth surface of the calm water. Silence consumed them for long depressing minutes. Rosie evoked the sweet summer romance she had shared with Randy, while Janie sank even deeper into misery as she pondered her mother's betrayal.

Finally, Rosie asked, "Shouldn't we be going?"

Janie answered by slinging another rock. "Six times," the child said. "That pebble skipped six times."

Trying to lighten the mood Rosie said, "Look at this sweet necklace Randy gave me last night."

Slinging another pebble at the mirrored surface she said without emotion, "I noticed it already."

"What's bothering you?" asked Rosie as if she didn't know.

Janie sat back and sighed, "I'm not sure." The little girl drew her knees to her chest. "I feel like I'm supposed to do something, you know what I mean; like I'm supposed to wait here for something to happen."

Rosie sighed as she prepared herself to wait out the little girl's whim. A few more pebbles skipped across the water, before the sound of a car stopping on the bridge caught their attention. With a finger to her lip, Janie motioned to be quiet. They sat silently, and listened to car doors open and close. The sound of a trunk lid being slammed shut followed with muffled voices. An unexpected splash took them completely by surprise. They watched as a quilted bundled bobbed, and began to sink beneath the surface of the greenish lake. Suddenly a small hand reached out and flailed about in the water as it sank.

In a state of shock, Rosie watched as Janie dove into the water. Edging closer to the water's edge Rosie crouched, and when the bundle broke the surface, she snagged it. After pulling the sodden lump from the water, she waited with rising panic for Janie to swim out.

Together they untied the rope coiled around the wet quilt. Rosie gasped as they uncovered a tiny Hispanic girl about five years of age. She pulled the child to her ear and listened, and when she heard no breathing from the child, she quickly administered mouth to mouth resuscitation.

Janie knelt next to Rosie, watching the efforts made to breathe life back into the unresponsive child. A coughing sputter came and when the child seemed to be breathing without difficulty, Rosie pulled her into her arms, cradling her. With large frightened eyes the child looked from Rosie to Janie, but didn't speak.

Quietly, Janie said, "Maybe she doesn't speak English."

Rosie asked the tiny girl, "Are you alright, now?"

With eyes as brown as Rosie's, and dark wavy hair surrounding an angelic face, the little girl answered, "I'm okay."

Simultaneously, Janie and Rosie expelled a deep sigh of relief. "Do you know what happened to you?" asked Janie.

Looking upward at the bottom side of the bridge, the little girl answered, "They threw me off the bridge."

"Who did?" Rosie asked.

With pure honesty the child replied, "My Daddy did."

Rosie asked, "Why did your daddy throw you from the bridge."

The child looked miserably sad and said with chattering teeth, "I don't know."

"Well, let's get you out of those wet clothes," said Rosie. The child wrapped her arms around Rosie's neck, and held tight as Rosie carried her to the van.

Examining the quilt carefully, Janie found that gym weights had been wrapped inside the quilt with the child. She rolled the quilt back around the weights and tossed it into the lake. As the quilt sank, a dark feeling came over her. Knowing a man had attempted to murder his own child permitted a vengeful anger to brew. To dispel her fury, Janie closed her eyes and relieved the moment when her knife had found its target. A sadistic smile twisted her lips as she dreamed of doing the same exact thing to this hideous excuse of a father.

When she returned to the van, Janie found the girl dressed in one of her t-shirts. A warm blanket was around her as she sat comfortably on the back bunk. Janie crawled into the van, and sat dripping on the floor. Taking a towel from a storage bin beneath the table seat, she began drying her hair. "Let's get something warm to drink."

Peering into the soft brown eyes of the child Rosie asked, "Would you like some hot cocoa?" She smiled when the little girl nodded her head yes. "Let's just go and get some right now." When she was settled into the driver's seat Rosie asked, "What's your name little girl?"

The child looked timid, barked a hoarse cough and answered, "Andrea."

"Oh, that's a lovely name," she said as she started the engine and continued talking to the child, "My name is Sunshine, and her name is Janie."

Janie said, "Not anymore. From now on my name is Jane."

Rosie corrected herself, "Oh, I beg your pardon, *Jane*." She drove from the shaded grove of trees, and back across the bridge. They continued following the directions Dale Rainwater had written for them, but stopped at the first restaurant they came to.

Rosie stood at the counter placing her order. When she reached for the money to pay, her hand brushed against the envelope Trudy had given her from Dale. After paying for the order, she sat on a bench to wait. Taking the envelope from her purse, she carefully peeled it open. Seeing cash money in one hundred dollar bills inside, she quickly closed the envelope. Carefully, she withdrew the letter, and stuffed the envelope with the cash back inside her purse. The letter was typewritten and formal.

Dear Miss Moon,

As you know by now, my son means the world to my wife and me. No amount of money or words can ever repay you for what you have done for Randy. However, you must understand that Randy's future has no room for a girl like you. It is with sincere appreciation that I ask you to accept this money, and opportunity to work with Dr. Thayer in Florida as a small token of our gratitude. Randy will be calling and writing in the near future, but understand it is only in his best interest if you ignore his attempts to contact you. In time he will get over his infatuation with you, and this past summer you shared will fade into history. If you can abide by my wishes, I will continue to support you in any way needed.

Sincerely,

Dale Rainwater

Her fist clenched around the letter. Tears spilled over her eyelids, and rolled freely down her face. She had hoped to contact Dale for advice about Andrea, but now she didn't dare. Wiping her face dry she gazed about the restaurant as couples dined together, some with children and some without. An empty ache filled her.

Returning to the van she handed the food across the seat to Janie who placed it on the table for Andrea, asking, "What are you eating, Sunshine?"

Rosie closed her eyes hoping to hold back the flood of tears threatening to unleash and answered, "I'm just having coffee right now."

Janie prepared a hamburger for Andrea and poured out French fries alongside of it. She removed the lid from the hot cocoa and pushed it toward the little girl. Andrea took the cup and drank from it as if she were extremely thirsty. Then she ate the food ravenously. Janie asked, "When was the last time you ate anything, Andrea?"

The forsaken child answered with her mouth full of food, "I don't know."

Taking note of Andrea's sniffles and cough, Janie asked, "Are you sick?"

Wiping away a sniffle with the back of her hand Andrea answered, "Uh huh."

Rosie sipped the strong black coffee, and jealously watched couples come and go from the restaurant. The afternoon was slipping away, and they had hundreds of miles to travel. "Tell me something, Jane. What are we going to do with Andrea?"

Janie questioned the girl, "Do you want us to take you home?"

With large fearful eyes the child shook her head. "No, no, Daddy don't want me there! He's mean! He makes me take bad medicine!" Her eyes welled and she began to cry.

Drinking from her cup of cocoa Janie watched the child carefully. She then asked, "Do you have a grandmother you can live with?"

Andrea sat back and wiped her eyes saying, "Oh, no. She's mean. She never lets me eat anything. She said the bologna was for the dog. She never lets me eat anything!" The tears flowed freely, as if speaking the truth were more painful than the little girl could bear.

"Where's your mother, Andrea?" asked Rosie.

Looking down at her tiny hands lying folded in her lap the child replied, "Mama's in jail. I visit her sometimes with my grandma. She loves me, but she can't take care of me, because she's in jail." Her tears subsided. "When my mommy gets out of jail I'm going to live with her." A whisper of a smile crossed her lips before a painful memory ripped it away, leaving more tears in its wake.

Shutting her eyes tight against the vision of a child visiting her mother in jail, Rosie said, "Well, in a case like this, Social Services will find you a better home."

Andrea's head shot up and she asked, "You mean the welfare lady? Oh, no! The welfare lady is bad. She just wants me to stay with my daddy."

With her face buried in her hands as the true horror of the little girl's life began to sink in. A dull headache began to grow in the back of her neck, and a sickness churned inside her stomach. Rosie asked, "What do you want to do, Andrea?"

The child looked at Janie fearfully and asked, "Can I stay with you?"

With a tender smile Janie said, "I would like that. I always wanted a little sister. Would you like to be my little sister?"

With a sparkle in her eye Andrea nodded her head and answered, "Oh, yes! I'd like to be your little sister."

Sliding into the passenger seat Janie said, "We have no other choice, Sun. Her father thinks she's dead anyway."

With a blank stare, Rosie pulled the letter from her purse. "Read this," she said with sadness tarnishing her voice.

While reading the letter, Janie's brows furrowed. Upon finishing the letter she opened the envelope and counted the money. "Two thousand dollars," she sneered completely baffled. "And, I thought he was a nice man."

Tears stung Rosie's eyes as she replied, "We have no other choice, but to take the money, and abide by the terms."

Sadly Janie shook her head, "Poor Randy. He'll be heartbroken when you don't write or call. I'd be willing to bet every cent of this money there will be a letter waiting for you at the clinic when we get there."

Andrea approached from the back of the van and patted Rosie tenderly on the shoulder. "Please, don't cry," the child said comfortingly.

Sniffing back more tears, Rosie said to the sweet little girl, "Oh, you are just an angel." Then she suddenly succumbed to shoulder racking sobs.

Before leaving Winston County, Indiana, Rosie stopped at a pay phone and stole the phone book. Janie looked at her with a questioning gaze, to which Rosie replied, "Just a souvenir."

They traveled for as far as Rosie could drive, before stopping at a motel for sleep. Finally, they got to Ft Lauderdale, exhausted and grimy from the road. They found a motel where she bathed and rested before going to meet Dr. Thayer. Standing before a mirror with the reflections of Andrea and Janie looking at her, she felt a panic building within. Andrea's cough had not gotten any better, and Rosie knew she must seek treatment from Dr. Thayer. "I think we made a big mistake in bringing Andrea with us."

Andrea and Janie looked at one another, and then back at Rosie. Janie said, "Well, it's not like we kidnapped her."

"But, legally we did." Rosie looked down at the little girl who stared back at her with large fearful eyes. "We can get in big trouble over this. I just know it."

Janie reasoned, "Who will ever know where she came from? It's not like there's a manhunt going on for her back in Indiana."

Rosie's eyes widened at the suggestion, "Maybe not yet. But her father is going to concoct a story of how she was kidnapped, don't you know? He's not going to tell the law that he threw her away like a sack of garbage. We very well could be charged with kidnapping." Then looking at Janie she said, "Well, not you, but me."

A coughing spasm gripped Andrea, and she gagged tearfully.

"Andrea told us no one wanted her back in Indiana. What else could we do but take her in? Don't you see? The whole nation would agree with us."

Rosie whispered with fear, "And, that may very well be what happens."

Dr. Thayer's clinic was not what Rosie had expected. It was located on the poorer side of town, and most of the patients waiting in the lobby were impoverished Cuban immigrants. When she introduced herself, the receptionist seemed to know all about her. "I am Carlotta Hampton," smiled the pretty thirty-something African American woman. "Let me show you to Doc's office."

Rosie recoiled at the name, "Doc?"

"He doesn't like formalities, he usually asks everyone to just call him Doc or Dr. Al," said Carlotta as Rosie followed her to a small office, with a sparsely filled bookcase, and metal desk. "Just take a seat and I will let him know you're waiting." The receptionist was a pretty woman with chiseled cheekbones, short ethnic hair and smooth mocha skin.

It was a long time before Dr. Thayer made his appearance, and when he did he appeared to be hurried. He was a tall, thin Caucasian man, with white hair and black rimmed glasses. Seating himself behind the desk he shuffled papers mixed with mail into a disorganized pile. Without extending his hand for a formal hand shake, he simply nodded his head and began talking. "I've discussed you're education with Dale Rainwater, Miss Moon. If you apply yourself, and work hard you can have your RN degree in two short years."

"Yes," she agreed.

"You'll need to get registered with the community college. I'm willing to let you work for me part time while you attend school full time. Please understand that you will be given some school credit for your experience in working here at the clinic. As you progress further in your education, you will be given more skilled duties to perform. As for now, you will only work at the front desk, doing clerical duties." Dr. Thayer picked up a type written letter and said, "I understand you have money to get yourself settled.

"Yes, I do."

"Very well, I expect you to present me with a fall schedule ASAP."

Feeling dismissed, she stood. "Thank you, for this opportunity. I promise to work hard."

The doctor motioned for her to exit the tiny office ahead of him. "Carlotta will be in charge of your training for the front. Do you have any questions?" He stood tapping his foot impatiently.

Taking not of the dusty unpolished shoes he wore she answered, "Yes, sir."

His foot immediately stopped tapping. Dr. Thayer said harshly, "Don't call me sir! I find it subservient, and I deplore hearing people say it. You may call me Doc or Dr. Al, but never call me sir."

"Yes, s- I mean, doctor."

Squinting through his bushy eyebrows he growled, "What is it?"

"I'd like you to treat my housekeeper's granddaughter. She has a terrible case of bronchitis, I think," she spilled a little too quickly.

"Of course, bring her in first thing tomorrow morning," he barked, and left without a goodbye.

Using a pay phone inside a laundry mat, Rosie explained to Kid the way Janie felt about her mother, and the child's refusal to go back to Ben Johnson Ridge. "So, I've talked to Daddy, and he's agreeing with my plans. Now, you've got to get Uncle Bert to send me Janie's school records, so I can get her enrolled for fifth grade here."

He chuckled across the line, "No problem. G-Daddy is so wrapped up in taking care of G-Mama that he'll be glad to let you take care of Janie."

"Oh, one thing though. Next time you talk to her, you have to call her Jane. She's outgrown *Janie*."

"You don't say. Well, what brought that about?"

Remembering the death scene from the desert, and the hilarity of the café incident in Arizona, Rosie could only reply, "She's just decided to grow up I guess."

"I'm coming to spend some time with you as soon as I can," said Kid. "You could say I've decided to grow up, too." He hesitated a moment, "I wore the wire for the Feds, and they got the big guy they were after. It's a funny thing, though. I expected to get hounded by those sleaze balls, Ron and Bud. But I haven't seen anything of them. Anyway, I've consulted a lawyer, and I'm filing for divorce."

Optimism ran through her like electricity. "That is good news!"

A tired sigh came other the line, "I've waited too long to be with you, Sunny."

Feeling guilty for not telling Kid about Andrea, she began her confession, "Well, something happened that I haven't told you." The line went silent. "I guess you could say that Jane and I sort of took in an orphaned child."

"What?" he gasped. "How do you sort of take in an orphan?"

She blurted, "We kidnapped her."

"You what!" he yelled.

In a rush of words she explained, "The little girl is only five years old, and her stepmother thought she had killed her with an overdose of cough medicine. So, the father and stepmother wrapped her in a quilt with weights, and threw her off a bridge." She paused long enough for him to fully comprehend the situation.

Hurrying to conclude the story she gushed, "We just happened to be sitting under the bridge, and Jane jumped in and pulled her out. We didn't know what to do, the child begged to stay with us. I've subscribed to the town newspaper so I can keep up with what goes on about her disappearance." With a shaky voice she said, "Now, you can't breathe a word about this."

A deep sigh was followed by him agreeing, "You can count on me. We'll deal with this together, don't worry."

Inhaling deeply she said, "I knew I could count on you, Kid. I've got to go now. I'll stay in touch."

With a hurried sound in his voice he said, "Take care, I love you."

"Love you, too." A thought crossed her mind and she quickly asked, "Oh, hey? Do you still have the picture of me and the girl in Vegas?" When he answered that he did, she made a gentle request, "Send it to me, okay?"

The last days of summer slipped into fall. Rosie stayed so busy with nursing school and afternoon work at the clinic that she left most of the child care and house work to Lillian Cox. Lillian lived with Rosie in the tiny house she had rented near the clinic. She was a tiny woman with short black hair flecked with gray. The little displaced woman was happy to take the job caring for the girls. She had a sweet southern accent, and an easy going personality.

As a cook, Lillian possessed the golden touch. Aromatic breads, baked delicately brown, often adorned the kitchen counters, glistening beneath a melted layer of butter. And waiting patiently on the counter were jars of homemade jellies and jams. Andrea loved warm bread with jam more than anything, and the little girl was becoming quite plump.

As a caregiver, Lillian possessed golden knowledge of homeopathic remedies that she used to treat Andrea's bronchitis. She fermented Oregano leaves and flower stalks to create miraculous oil. She called this powerful medicine *Liquid Gold.* Using age old recipes she created germ fighting hand creams and medicines. Using a few drops of *Liquid Gold* in a humidifier made a remarkable difference in Andrea's health. The bronchitis and asthma all but disappeared.

Extremely happy with Lillian as a surrogate mother, the two little girls stayed on very good behavior, not wanting to disappoint their newly adopted mom. In turn, Lillian seemed to appreciate the family who valued her dedication capaciously. Never having had children of her own, she doted on the girls. To Rosie's great delight, the household thrived with the care and guidance of the sweet natured Lillian.

News from Ben Johnson Ridge came via the telephone as Rosie kept in touch with her father. Janie never wanted to call her grandparents or her mother, and Rosie never did more than gently suggest it once in a while.

Thanksgiving came with a wholesome traditional meal prepared by Lillian, but a letter from Randy had yet to arrive. Had she had misjudged him, and the affection he truly seemed to have had for her? As the Christmas holiday neared, she became so melancholy that she removed the locket Randy had given her, and put it away.

Newspapers arrived bi-weekly from the little town Randy was from. The town had begun to look for the child the week following their departure. At first the father had declared the child was missing, but as time went on he confessed to his crime. A search crew of divers scoured the lake bottom near the bridge, but only found the quilt Andrea had been wrapped in. Andrea's father and stepmother had been incarcerated pending a murder trial. Rosie shared all of this news with Andrea and Janie, showing them the pictures from the newspaper. Andrea seemed to understand all that she was told her, yet at the same time appeared ambiguous and disinterested. The child flourished in her new environment, and she loved *Sesame Street.*

Late one afternoon, as Rosie returned home from a long grueling day, Andrea raced to her with a drawing, "Sunshine! Today's letter was *S* for Sunshine." Andrea handed her the childish drawing of a sun with a smiling face.

Cradling the little girl Rosie exclaimed, "It's absolutely beautiful!" Looking across the room she saw Lillian smiling warmly at them. Rosie often wondered what Lillian thought of the unusual family they made, but the little woman never asked a question. "This belongs on the refrigerator. Don't you agree, Lillian?" asked Rosie as she attached the drawing with magnets.

Janie appeared at the edge of the kitchen. "I've got a problem."

Rosie stood back admiring the drawing and asked, "What is it?"

Leaning against the wall Janie said, "A bully has decided to pick on me."

Concern swept Rosie's face, "What has he done?"

Looking up at the ceiling, Janie described the torture she had endured the past few days. "He hangs around and waits for me just a little way from school. And, when he sees me walking home, he starts walking in the opposite direction. Then when he gets close, he tries to spit on me."

Gasps resonated through the room. "That's disgusting!" Lillian exclaimed.

"Why would he do such a thing?" asked Rosie.

With a look of anger Janie exclaimed, "I don't know! He just has moved here, and I haven't so much as said hello to the creep!"

A dull headache crept into her neck. "Just stay away from him. Cross the street, whatever you have to do. But, stay away from him. He sounds depraved." Looking down at her books Rosie said, "I have some work to finish."

She entered her room, and closed the door. Dropping the books, she reached for a bottle of aspirin on her dresser. Stepping into the tiny bathroom Rosie bent forward at the sink and drank water from her cupped hand to swallow the tablets. After drying her hands she stepped to her closet and opened the door. The dress that Randy had worn the first night they were together was hanging on the inside of the door. She had pinned the photo of herself and Randy walking the streets of Vegas above it. With tears welling she whispered, "Do you ever think of me?" Stepping away she closed the door, and allowed the tears to unleash.

On one particular sunny day in December, Dr. Thayer sent Rosie on an errand. The clinic's only bottle of tetanus vaccine had expired, so she visited the local health department. As she exited the clinic, with the vaccine tucked safely inside her handbag, her attention was caught by a mother's frantic screams. Drawn to the commotion, Rosie saw a toddling child chasing a shiny red ball as it rolled out of the parking area, toward a busy highway.

Without thinking, she stepped out of her shoes and hiked her dress. Thrusting her purse and shoes at a man leaving the clinic Rosie exclaimed, "Hold this!"

With swift confident moves she raced after the toddler. Beyond the curve, a thundering tractor truck approached, towing an enclosed semi trailer. Rosie looked the opposite direction, seeing the road clear of oncoming traffic. The sound of the engine from the approaching truck became louder as she ran into the road. She scooped up the baby as the sound of air brakes and downshifting gears echoed across the asphalt. When she cleared the highway her body was in full speed.

The sound of screaming brakes resonated through the air, followed by a crash with breaking glass. An automobile following the truck had been unable to stop before rear ending the trailer. Now that her feet had touched grassy earth, she began the struggle of a safe landing. When Rosie took charge of her feet again, she turned and began retracing her steps back up the hill, handing off the toddler to his mother.

Traffic had come to a standstill. The truck sat in an almost jack knife position. The unfortunate driver of the automobile was unharmed, but his car suffered major damage. Helpful citizens rushed to help. The mother of the child clutched the baby close to her bosom crying gratefully.

Taking a man's hand, Rosie pulled herself up the embankment. Placing her feet upon the asphalt she looked to see the handsome face of the man holding her purse and shoes. "Thank you," she said. Taking the purse, she turned and disappeared with the dispersing crowd.

The last day of school came before the Christmas break, and Janie walked cautiously home. As usual, Todd Weeks was waiting to ambush her. She crossed the street to avoid him. To her angst, he crossed the street as well. Upon seeing his ploy, she crossed the street again. Anxiety crept into her as she watched Todd cross the street and step next to her. Just as they were side by side she heard the noise of him spitting. Looking down, she saw a glob of saliva rolling down her sleeve. Consumed by fury, she tossed her book bag to the ground and turned on the cruel, sandy haired boy. Grabbing him by the collar she thrust him into the street. He fell to his knees and slid face down on the roadway. Todd turned and looked up at her with tear filled eyes, radiating cowardice as she stepped over him and put her foot on his chest holding him down.

"You pig!" she screamed. "Has anyone ever told you why your name is Weeks? It's because you *are* weak. Weak and pathetic! I'll bet your own grandmother hates you!" Then she drew her head back and spit in his face.

Todd wiped the saliva from his cheek crying, "I'm going to tell my mama!"

Removing her foot from his chest she screamed, "Go tell your mama, you big pansy assed baby, I'll spit on her, too!"

Todd jumped to his feet and ran away as if he were being chased by a pack of wild dogs. Janie stood staring after him so enraged that her knees were knocking. After picking up her book bag and continuing on her way home, she began to see hilarity in the chicken-hearted tormentor's terror. Before long, she was holding her sides as she was racked by insane laughter.

Christmas in Ft Lauderdale was empty compared to the frosty mountain Christmas of Ben Johnson Ridge. Lillian did all she could to make the season festive with decorations and baking. The night before Christmas, Rosie slept in her room with the door closed to the rest of the house. An old familiar dream crept into her subconscious during the early morning hours of Christmas day. Thinking she was fully awake, she left her bed to investigate a clinking noise. She entered the dining room to find a group of men gathered around the table playing poker. The room was hazy with thick cigar smoke, and the muffled voices carried on animated conversations. Recognizing one of the men as Doc Campbell, she stepped closer to him and asked, "What are you doing here?"

He raised his face and looked at her from beneath the gentleman's white hat with the black band, and he smiled. Feeling he was mocking her she yelled, "Answer me!"

The room fell silent as the men ceased their conversation and laughter. The smile faded from Doc's face, and he lowered his head till his face was hidden beneath the hat.

She pounded her fist on the table, "Why are you here?"

A familiar voice called out, "It's because of me, Sunshine."

Turning to the voice she was elated to see Randy sitting among the poker players wearing the same outdated fashion. "Oh, Randy, I'm so glad you're here!"

"Better not touch that Indian scum!" an angry voice cried out.

Whirling to face the intruder who spoke against her beloved Randy, she found Lewis dressed in army fatigues holding tightly to an assault rifle. With dismay she exclaimed, "Lewis!"

Terror consumed her as she watched him rise from the chair and point the gun toward Randy. Looking back at Randy she could see all the other players had disappeared, and Randy sat all alone dressed in his modern day clothing. Spinning back to face Lewis, Rosie screamed, "No!" Attempting to move she found that she couldn't. Her feet were heavy, as if tied to concrete. Again, she screamed out as she watched Lewis put the rifle near his face to set the sight on Randy. Covering her eyes she screamed one last frantic cry, but the sound of the deafening rifle shot rang out.

Grief consumed her as she saw Randy lying lifeless upon her dining room floor, blood spilling from the bullet hole in his chest. She awoke crying out, "No, no, no!"

The bedroom door swung open and Janie rushed inside. The soft glow of a bedside lamp cast a gentle radiance across the room. Smoothing Rosie's hair from her eyes Janie consoled her. "I know, I know," she said. Crawling into bed next to Rosie, "He's found us."

The bedside alarm clock showed the time to be a few minutes before four am. "It's always this time of night when he haunts me." Rosie whispered as if he could hear, "I wonder why?"

Pulling her knees to her chest Janie reasoned, "There must be something about this time of morning that gives him strength. Do you really think he's evil? I mean in the past his visits always brought about something good, like the coins."

"What about the drugs? That wasn't good."

"That wasn't his fault. That was your and Kid's decision, not his."

With a shiver, Rosie pulled her blanket closer. "Is he really angry about that? Everything worked out all right."

Janie's jaw dropped, "Need I remind you two men died in the desert? You can hardly say everything worked out all right."

Tears streamed down Rosie's cheeks. "I miss Randy so much. I didn't even know then how much I loved him, and now I can never tell him."

"Let's go back to sleep. We'll sleep together. Remember how Doc didn't bother us after Kid left?"

Thinking of Kid reminded her of the shattered dreams they had shared, and she felt even more abandoned, "Oh, Jane. I feel so alone, and I want so badly for someone to love me."

Reaching over to the bedside lamp, Janie switched it off. "You'll soon find that you have more love than you know what to do with." She snuggled under the blanket.

Lying down beside her, Rosie said, "Merry Christmas, Jane."

With a disgruntled groan Janie responded, "Bah humbug!"

A few days after Christmas, Rosie was shopping at a local grocery store. It was near closing time. The store's manager was a husky good looking man in his mid-twenties, and he always tried to impress her with small talk and helpfulness. She had developed a dislike for the man, because of the subservient way he treated his personnel. Especially melancholy this evening, the sound of his humiliating tone riled her ire. He was berating a young high school boy for not having placed a particular display to his liking. When Rosie walked past he stepped eagerly to her asking, "Can I help you find anything?"

Without smiling she answered, "No, thank you," and continued shopping. The young girl working the cash register hurriedly put aside a broom she was working with to ring up Rosie's purchase. A handsome young man, about Rosie's age, began placing the items in a brown paper bag. He wasn't especially good looking, but his long hair and sparse beard was attractive, reminding her of David Cassidy. She paid for her groceries and was about to take them from the young man when the manager barged in, snatching the bag.

"I'll take this out for you, Miss," he said with an arrogant smile.

"That's alright. I can take it myself," and Rosie pulled back.

The manager rocked back on his heel smiling ignorantly, "No, I'll take it for you."

Rosie sighed, "That's alright."

"It's no trouble," he insisted.

Reaching for the bag she tugged on it hard saying, "I'll take it." To her surprise the bag ripped, and the groceries fell back onto the counter.

The manager looked at the bag boy angrily, "You overfilled the bag, numb skull!"

Rosie snapped, "The bag was not overfilled. It was just fine. Now, will you please let this young man do his job? I don't want you to carry my groceries, or help me shop or walk my dog. I want you to leave me alone!"

Silence consumed the store. Stepping back she crossed her arms and waited for the manager to make a rude comment. But he said nothing. He simply walked away.

The young man replaced her spilled items into another bag, and stood holding them. "I'll be happy to help you out with this," he said politely.

"Yes, I'd appreciate that." His eyes were soft brown with tiny flecks of cocoa floating within. The parking lot was almost empty of vehicles. Pointing to the van she said, "There I am."

"Oh man! A Westfalia camper, my friend has one. We use it to haul equipment for our band. It's a sweet little ride."

Opening the side door she said, "My name is Sunshine. I'm new to the area, and I haven't made any real friends yet." Looking toward the grocery store she sighed, "But it seems like I may have made me an enemy tonight."

"I'm Billy Ray, nice to meet you." He followed her gaze. "Don't worry about ole Dan. He does enjoy being an asshole."

She could see the manager looking across the parking lot at them. "Why is he watching us?"

"He's a funny one. Think nothing of him."

An idea brewed. "Well if he wants to see something interesting out here, maybe we should just give him something to gawk at." Having made that statement she placed her hands on Billy Ray's face and abruptly kissed him. Seeing the look of shock on his face she asked softly, "I didn't hurt you, did I?"

With a barely audible voice he answered, "No, no, not at all."

"Oh dear, did I just get you in trouble? Is that your girlfriend in there?"

With a laugh Billy Ray said, "No."

A look of devilish glee sparkled in Rosie's eyes. "Oh, well. In that case," she threw her arms around the young man's neck and pressed her lips to his again. He stumbled backward until he was pressed against the van where he became trapped, and succumbed to her kisses. When she pulled away from him he seemed to be disoriented and weak. "Thanks, Billy Ray," she said sweetly.

Putting a finger to his lips as if she had left them bruised, he asked, "Hey, would you like to come to my house, and listen to my band practice?"

A swift smile stole across her face. "Sure, when?"

He ran his fingers through his hair. "Tonight, just as soon as I get off work. The guys are already there playing without me."

Thrilled with the idea, she said, "Okay. What time do you get off?"

Holding a finger in the air he said, "Just as soon as I go clock out. Can you wait here a few minutes?"

"Wild horses couldn't drag me away." Left alone in the deserted parking lot, she watched him jog back into the store.

The outside lights were turned off, leaving only a street lamp to light the parking area. Rosie stood leaning against the van as she watched the grocery store crew exit, with Dan locking the door behind them. Billy Ray jogged back across the parking lot suggesting, "Why don't I just ride with you to my house? I'll come back for my car later."

"Sounds groovy, you want to drive?" she asked holding out the keys.

"You trust me?"

"No, not really."

They drove to a middle class neighborhood with rows of brick houses and clean cut lawns. He wheeled into a driveway littered with cars and alive with electric lights. "This is it, home sweet home."

She followed him into a garage that was nothing like a garage. It was more of a finished room with a garage door. The room held furniture and carpeting. There was no evidence of a car ever having been parked there. "Would you like to meet my Mom?" He pulled her past the crowd of people to the back door leading into the kitchen. Stepping into a lovely home with polished tile floors and handsome furnishings, he called, "Mom, hey, Mom!"

A voice came from the hallway, "I'm in bed, Billy Ray!"

He shook his head sadly, "Her back has been bothering her, again."

The bedroom door was opened. Her room was quietly illuminated by television light. "Hey, Mama," he said softly, pulling Rosie along with him to the side of her bed. "Is your back still not any better?"

Looking curiously at Rosie she answered, "Oh, a little."

"I brought someone to meet you. Mama, this is Sunshine. Sunshine, this is my wonderful mother, Dolly."

With extended hand Rosie said, "It's a pleasure to meet you, Dolly. Your son is awfully sweet to invite me over."

The woman smiled and said, "He is a sweet boy. But don't let him fool you. He can get into mischief if I don't keep a close eye on him."

With a chuckle Billy Ray pulled Rosie from his mother's room saying, "The guys are waiting for me. I got to go play."

"Even rock stars have to eat, son. Your dinner is in the oven," called Dolly.

Leading her down the hallway he said, "Right here is the bathroom." He stopped long enough to flip on the light and turn it back off. "And, here is my room." He pushed open the door and switched on the light.

"Oh yeah, I owe you something," he said closing the door. Pushing her against the wall he covered her mouth with his and kissed her with youthful passion. His tongue probed between her parted lips, dancing with hers. When he pulled himself away, Billy Ray was weak in the knees. Hesitantly he opened the door. "My fans are waiting."

Clamping her lips together, as if to hold back words that shouldn't be spoken, she said, "We must not disappoint the fans."

The music Billy Ray's band played was impressive. The other band members were older than him but Billy Ray was the one holding the talent when it came to playing lead guitar. Rosie was equally impressed when he later showed his skill with the harmonica. The music style of the band was Deep South and hard rock, blended together in a unique fashion. Some of the songs they played made it hard to sit still, the rhythm was so moving. After a half dozen songs one of the guys said, "We've got to practice those songs for the New Year's gig."

Another member quipped, "Those songs suck."

This comment brought about a quick remark from an older gentleman, who was balding with long frizzy hair, "Those songs pay!"

The band practiced Marvin Gaye's *It Takes Two*, Crosby, Stills, Nash and Young's, *Teach Your Children*, and Credence Clearwater Revival's, *Suzy Q*.

The band took a break from rehearsing, and conversations regarding the music list began. "I can't stand doing Chubby Checker's *The Twist*. What do these old folks want from us anyway?" complained Bobby.

"They want what they want, and that's why they pay us. So stop complaining," Billy Ray stated.

"I'm tired of singing Elvis. Can't somebody else please sing Elvis instead of me?" Bobby whined.

"Oh good Lord, if you could really sing Elvis you wouldn't be here in this garage band, now would you?" grunted Ted.

"Where's the love? I'm not feeling the love," Billy Ray declared.

"Oh yeah, well love this!" The older man named Ted held up his middle finger.

Billy Ray called out, "Hey, everybody! I'd like to introduce my new friend. Please say hi to Sunshine." The crowd murmured a hello to Rosie, and she waved her hand in the air as a salutation. Billy Ray continued, "So, I would appreciate it if some certain guys in the band would try to behave, and not chase my new friend away." This remark earned him groans and chuckles from the band.

A chubby band member with long blonde hair replied, "You're the one who needs to behave, Billy Ray. She'll split the first time she sees you pitch a hissy fit."

Billy Ray held up his hand and called out, "Hold up right there, Jeff. Didn't I promise to do better?" When no one responded to his question he repeated in a louder tone, "And, haven't I done better already?"

The guys mumbled agreement to his questions. "All right then," Billy Ray said. "I happen to be working on my New Year's resolution early."

"To hell with resolutions," Ted interjected. "We've got to be ready for the gig. An important producer is going to be at this party, and we've got to be more than ready. This could be a break for us."

A roar of conversations followed Ted's remark as Billy Ray turned to Rosie and said, "Come to this party with us. You'll get to meet a lot of rich uppity people, and you can bring in the New Year with me."

With a smile she answered, "Nothing could make me happier."

Billy Ray focused on the spinning blades of a ceiling fan as he said, "All you need to do is perform two chick songs."

"I'm not sure I get you? You want me to sing? But you're gig is only three days off!"

Billy Ray said reassuringly, "We need a girl to sing *Band of Gold* and a sad ballad called *Lonely*. Any girl with a strong voice can do both these songs with no problem." With a sweet smile he put his arm across her shoulders. "The most important thing is to look good. If you look good, no one even pays attention to your talent. But if you look good, and display genuine talent, you're a star."

She asked, "Billy Ray, why didn't you have someone by now to sing these songs?"

With a tinge of guilt he replied, "We did have a girl. But, she got mad and broke up with me."

"So, you really need a girl to sing?"

"You can sing, can't you?"

"I can, but I'm not sure I can be ready in three days."

Billy Ray licked his lips and said, "Oh, sure you can."

"Okay. So, when are you going to break it to the band? Aren't they going to be surprised?"

Taking hold of her hand, he placed it over his heart, saying, "They'll be relieved."

Chapter Twenty-Nine
Part of the Band Now

The garage was too warm, and Rosie was becoming apprehensive by the way Billy Ray's girlfriend, Jackie, was looking at her. She was practicing *Band of Gold,* and her confidence was failing. At the end of the song, she was relieved to hear Ted call out, "Perfect!"

Stepping away, Rosie noticed Jackie following her. Jackie was a dark haired beauty who had Billy Ray wrapped around her little finger. With dancing eyes she said, "I'm so glad the guys found you. Your voice is perfect for the band." Seeing Rosie reach for a glass of water, Jackie seductively traced her fingertips along Rosie's arm until they reached the glass. "Let me get you some fresh water."

When Jackie left the room Billy Ray asked, "How does it feel?"

"How does what feel?" Rosie asked, showing her confusion.

He answered, "How does it feel to be adored by a beautiful girl?"

"You mean Jackie?"

With pathetic wisdom Billy Ray announced, "If I could get Jackie to look at me like that I'd be the happiest guy in the world." He stepped a few feet away as Jackie returned, holding a glass of water with plump cubes of ice.

A sweet smile danced across her lips as she handed off the glass to Rosie. "I really love the way you do your eyes! Do you think you could show me how to do my eyes like that sometime?"

"I'd love that, Jackie. Just hang out, and share some girl secrets." Rosie couldn't help but detect the disapproving look Billy Ray shot her.

Jackie threw her arms around Rosie's neck and drew her into an excited hug. "I'm so thrilled!" she giggled. Gently, she pushed Rosie toward the band. "We'll be great friends, okay?"

"Okay," answered Rosie, tentatively.

On New Year's Eve, Rosie stood before the dresser mirror wearing the same gown she had worn for the high school Valentine's performance. Her hair had grown longer and was styled in a layered cut. The ruby earrings glittered on her earlobes, and her eye makeup was done well enough to impress Randy Rainwater. Janie whistled from the doorway, as Andrea and Lillian pushed in closer.

A devilish whoop came from Lillian as she teased using her unique blend of Arkansas country dialect, and Deep South charm. "Somebody's going home with heartache tonight."

Rosie smiled at her family from the mirror. "Tonight I'm only interested in Billy Ray." Turning to the others she said smugly, "And, I think tonight is the night I'm going to reach right out there and take him."

Janie said, "Get off of Billy Ray already. He's small stuff. Tonight you have the opportunity to reach out and take an important man, one with power and money."

Narrowing her eyes Rosie asked, "What makes you say something like that?"

Feigning insult the child replied, "You, yourself said an important music producer is supposed to be there. So, then! Reach out and grab him why don't you?"

Shaking her head Rosie said, "You scare me sometimes." Then she turned to Andrea and dabbed cologne on the little girl's neck. Looking back at Janie she said, "I wouldn't even know how to talk to a rich man anyway."

Entering the room with swaying hips Janie said, "That's when you use body language." She pushed herself up next to Rosie and portrayed a seductress acting coy. With a soft breathless voice she mimicked Ginger from *Gilligan's Island.* "I've always admired creative men." Then with a comic flare she batted her eyelashes seductively.

Stepping back from the impish child Rosie retorted, "If I can't say anything more intelligent than that, I'll just keep my mouth shut."

As Rosie left the room Janie followed her down the hallway declaring, "Hey! That's not a bad line. I saw it in a movie!"

Peering down at Andrea, who stood looking up at her with admiration, Rosie suggested, "Why don't you put one of those *Happily Ever After* books together with Andrea. It would be a project that can keep you two busy for a couple of hours."

A devilish smile crossed Janie's lips. "Okay, but just you remember, you asked for it."

Gripped by apprehension, Rosie entered the beautiful Ft Lauderdale country club. The opulence of wealth filled her with trepidation. Whispering to Billy Ray she confessed, "I feel so out of place with these rich people."

Billy Ray kissed her on the cheek. "Don't feel like that, Sunshine. You're going to be the prettiest thing here tonight."

"Would you like to spend the night with me?" she asked out of the blue.

Billy Ray dropped a portion of the drum set he was carrying, and it fell to the floor with a loud clatter. "Yes!" he exclaimed. "But there's a little problem. You see Jackie's at my house right now. Hoping to spend time with you, I presume."

Rosie gently caressed his cheek, before pushing him away. "I don't know how to deal with female crushes." She left Billy Ray with the band and wandered around the ballroom.

Very promptly, at eight o'clock, people began to arrive, noisy with excitement. Mingling with the guests as they grazed on hors d'oeuvres, and drank sparkling white wine, Rosie hung back to observed the crowd's reaction to the music. Very few people seemed to be moved to dance by the requested songs.

She drifted away from the bar, and stood near the band, listening to the music. Dressed in the stunning red evening gown, she caught someone's attention. Two older gentlemen approached her. The men were forty-something gentlemen who seemed very at ease with one another. "I beg your pardon, my dear. But I was just wondering who you are?"

Facing the chubby balding man, Rosie answered, "I'm Sunshine Rose. I'm with the band." Extending her hand she asked, "Might you be one of the music producers?"

The handsome tall man with dark thick wavy hair, and thick mustache smiled warmly. "So, then you're with the band?"

With feigned confidence she affirmed, "Yes, just one of the guys."

A deep chuckle escaped him, "Have we met before?"

"You do look familiar. I work at the Eastside Clinic, for Dr. Thayer."

A look of remembrance crossed the man's face. "Oh, yes. I remember now. You were the young lady who rescued the child from the highway in front of the health department."

With a sparkle of recognition she replied, "Yes, you held my things for me!"

The balding man introduced himself, "Well, now to be up and up with you I think it is only fair to tell you that I am the music producer who's looking over your band." Bowing dramatically he said, "Frank Ryder, at your service."

The handsome man quickly added, "Of *Ryder/Hart Strings Music Studio*. Have you ever heard of our company?"

Cautiously, she shook her head demurely. Frank said, "Don't take Victor so seriously, he's usually a very good sport."

Victor said with a serious tone, "Well, all that's about to be over. My new year's resolution is to become an absolute asshole."

Giving a light laugh she asked, "When do you plan to actually listen to the band?" Seeming to catch the two men off guard she continued, "It's their original music you want to hear."

Looking at one another Frank and Victor agreed that was a favorable idea. "I gave your group a certain song I wrote myself. They are supposed to be performing it tonight?" asked Victor.

"If you're talking about *Lonely,* I do know that they are performing it tonight."

Terribly interested, Victor asked, "Who will sing it?"

With a glance at her empty wine glass Rosie answered, "I will."

As if reading one another's mind the two men hooked their arms around hers and picking her up, walked with her hanging between them. They placed her next to the microphone, and then stepped back, crossing their arms.

Soon the familiar music had caught the attention of the audience, and Rosie began singing *Band of Gold.* When the song ended applause erupted from the guests. Turning to Ted she said, "Play *Ghost Riders in the Sky* and follow up with some of your own music. Forget about the list." Taking up a tambourine she began playing along. When the band had the audience's attention with the foot stomping music, Rosie took a cowboy hat hanging from a microphone stand and donned it. She left the area marked off for the stage, and began dancing about the floor. Keeping beat with the tambourine, she danced as if she were riding a horse. Guests drawn to the invigorating music approached the floor to dance. After Ted finished the vocals for the song the rest of the band exploded into a wild electrifying instrumental. When the song ended, Rosie waved the cowboy hat to encourage applause from the guests.

Replacing the hat, she turned back to the dance floor only to find Frank and Victor waiting for her. Victor held out his hand. Holding to his hand, she wandered back to the bar as they listened politely to Frank's analysis of the band. When placing an order at the bar, Victor asked, "What does Sunshine Rose like to drink?"

Feeling devilish Rosie said, "I'm a tequila kind of girl. Want me to show you how to shoot tequila?" Reaching over she banged on the bar with her open hand, and called for the bartender to bring them shots of tequila. Reaching for the salt shaker she said, "First a little salt." She licked the back of her hand and sprinkled salt there. Picking up a slice of lime with her salted hand, she said to Victor, "I'd like to toast the bee that stung the bull." She licked the salt from the back of her hand and downed the tequila, following it with the lime.

Victor mimicked her moves and grimaced from the sour fruit. "Tell me more about the bee and the bull," he asked seductively.

With a wicked smile she said, "I can only tell that story in a toast." Pushing the glasses toward the bartender she called out, "Another, please." When they had the spirit in hand Rosie resumed the toast. "Here's to the bee that stung the bull that started the bull to bucking. And, here's to Adam who stuck it to Eve and started the world to - uh, well, you know." Licking the salt with a lewd expression, she swallowed the alcohol in one gulp.

Victor Hart burst into giggles at her brashness. "How can you even say that with a straight face? You're a movie actress, too?"

Waving the suggestion away, "No, no, I'm not much more than office help right now."

"You mean you're a secretary?"

"Yeah, pretty much."

Mischievously he said, "Oh, I get it! You're a *sex-atary*."

With a calm and serious face she said, "Oh, no I could never be a *sex-atary*."

"Why not?"

Fluttering her eye lashes suggestively she responded, "Because, I don't take *dictation*."

The melodic laughter of Victor Hart floated along the air waves with the harmony of chiseled singers and guitar chords. Not knowing when or why, Victor and Rosie found they had fallen into a drinking game, which they called *Last One Standing*. Walking arm in arm they stepped out for a breath of fresh air.

Whistling wolfishly at a shining new Harley Davidson Motorcycle parked at the curb, Rosie exclaimed, "What a beauty!"

"Do you ride, Sunshine?" he asked slyly.

She lied, "Oh, yes." Catching the look of doubt on his face she added, "All the time," and shrugged her shoulders slightly as if there was nothing more to be said on the subject.

Victor's voice sounded soft but commanding as he said, "So, do it, ride."

Whirling to search for clarification, she faced Victor holding out keys for her to take. Pretending to be calm, she took the keys and gazed at them lying in her hand. "You actually trust me to ride your bike?"

The perfectly groomed Victor Hart rocked back on one heel. "You don't really ride, do you?"

Her fingers closed around the keys. "I would be honored to ride your hog. But due to my manner of dress, I cannot do the driving. Why don't you drive, and I'll ride side saddle." She tossed the keys back.

They fell easily against his palm. "Well, well, well. Aren't you the Cinderella of the evening, getting whisked away on a steel steed just before midnight? I do hope that unlike Cinderella, you do not change after midnight."

Remembering Janie's pep talk, instead of taking a seat behind Victor, she sat sideways in front of him. Throwing her arms around his neck, she seated herself with her chest pressed next to his. The bike began smoothly rolling across the tree lined concrete drive.

They rode to a nearby park where he put down the kickstand, and turned the ignition off. Drawing a heavy breath he said, "I'd like to say how honored I am to have made your acquaintance tonight, my dear Sunshine. I've only just met you, yet I feel as though I've known you forever. Do you by chance feel that *thing* between us? It's like a sexual attraction, blended with a mutual affection." Expelling his breath he exclaimed, "Wow! It's just something different for me. I don't like people easily."

Rosie smirked, "Me either!"

Victor burst into laughter, "It's time for another drink, Sunny girl. I still intend to be the last one standing tonight." Removing himself from the motorcycle he added a command, "Okay, your turn to drive."

Reaching down, Rosie grasped the hem of her dress, and began drawing it upward higher and higher, until she had the dress above the matching red panties she wore beneath it. Victor appeared to be spellbound by her partial nudity. Pushing the kickstand up, she switched on the ignition and sat astride the Harley as it rumbled beneath her.

Victor seated himself behind her, and perched his feet on the pegs tensely. She released the clutch just a bit too quickly, and the bike started off with a slight jolt. With giggles consuming her, she performed all the remaining gear changes smoothly.

They returned to the country club with Rosie maneuvering the big bike easily. She disembarked from the motorcycle, after giving Victor time to get free, and tossed him the keys. "What a ride!" she giggled, tugging her dress into place.

She followed Victor to the bar, as he ordered more tequila. Taking up the shot glass she said, "You know Victor, there's a reason they call this stuff *to kill ya*, because it will." She tossed back the drink, and sucked deeply on a lime.

With simple wisdom he replied, "Nothing can kill you, Sunshine. You're gold dust and moonbeams. You're indestructible." He twisted in the bar stool and looked around the room. With a slight wave of his finger he said, "Of all the people under this roof tonight, I doubt I could find one loyal friend among them." With a despondently serious expression he continued, "Friends are more precious than gold, you know." The undertone of sadness swept Rosie up into the rhythm of his voice, and she sat spellbound by the handsome man who was known primarily for his money. Peering into her eyes Victor said, "Cherish your friendships. Don't give them up easily, lest you be lonely like me."

As the disco lights swirled across the ceiling with multicolored hues, she used her sweetest Marilyn Monroe voice to tantalize her aficionado, "Oh no, I refuse to be lonely. Life's just too short!"

He pointed his finger at her. "You have another song to sing." A soft expression crossed his face, "I wrote that song myself you know. Some say it is a self portrait."

Taking her hand he pulled her back into the ballroom. When she took the microphone, standing center stage, Rosie focused double-vision eyes on Victor, and sang as if he were the only person in the room. The music lulled the listener into an intense state of sorrow, and Rosie brought life to the words of tender sadness. Uninhibited by the tequila, the lyrics rolled off her tongue, dripping with emotion and brimming with passion. Fueled by her pulsating blood, washed in her tears and caressed by her pain, the song filtered through the heart and settled in the bone.

Filled with emotion, as her voice carried out the melancholy tone necessary for its success, Victor stared immobilized. Her voice was strong, yet fragile as she sang the story of a man lost within his own success, making choices to be rich rather than choices to be loved. The simple lonesome words expressed a mountain of feelings, and with tears blinding her, she sang out the expression depicting Victor's life with chilling emotion, "*And, he wakes up lonely.*"

Dancers pulled apart to applaud. Victor shook away the emotion holding him mesmerized by the strength of his words in her voice. Walking thru the crowd of guests, he took her hand. They walked back through the party goers as the countdown to midnight began. And, when the New Year dawned, they danced gracefully with *Auld Lange Syne*. The evening ended with Victor Hart standing with the band as they prepared to leave. He stood unsteadily with his friend Frank. At parting time Victor took up Rosie's hand and placed a gallant kiss upon it as a farewell.

"Good night, my dear. And, thank you for an enchanting evening." As Frank helped Victor walk away, Victor could be heard saying, "Enchanting evening. That sounds like a good name for a song. Don't you think so, Frank?"

Turning to Billy Ray, Rosie asked, "Is he gone, yet?"

Looking past her shoulder he could see Victor Hart being half carried by his friend away from the ballroom. "Yes, he's gone." As if on cue, Rosie took a step toward Billy Ray and collapsed into his arms.

The sound of a telephone ringing awoke Rosie sometime around noon. Grimacing from the pain of her hangover, she turned away from the daylight filtering through the pulled drapes. The motion of someone in bed beside her caused her to open her eyes. The familiar posters told her she was waking up in Billy Ray's room. She rolled over and found herself face to face with a slumbering Jackie. Dolly's voice carried softly from the doorway, "Sunshine? You have a phone call."

Wincing as she raised her head from the pillow Rosie called, "Okay, coming." Looking past Jackie, she could see Billy Ray sleeping soundly.

Jackie awoke and stretched catlike next to her. Sliding from the bed Rosie became aware of her mostly nude state of dress. Picking up the red sequined gown from the floor she wrapped it around her, and tip toed to the telephone.

Janie's voice called out cheerfully across the line, "Happy New Year, Sunshine! Can you come home? We need the wheels."

Looking down the hallway toward Billy Ray's bedroom she watched Jackie, wearing only panties and a bra, linger within the doorway. "I'll be right there."

Dolly said cheerfully, "I overheard you talking to the little girl on the phone. Is she your sister?"

Blinking back a pounding headache Rosie answered, "No, she's a cousin."

"How did you make such fast friends with Billy Ray?" asked Dolly. "He's usually standoffish when he meets someone new."

"Really?"

Dolly continued, "That sweet little Jackie just adores you!"

Holding the dress closer to her bosom Rosie asked, "You don't mind if I just step back in Billy Ray's room and get dressed?"

Dolly answered with a light tinkling laughter, "Oh, honey! Just go ahead and put your dress back on standing right there."

Gathering the dress into a bunched circle, Rosie dropped it over her head, and the red sequined fabric slithered around her. With a smile for Dolly she said, "Thanks, so much. Tell everyone I'll call later." Scooping her purse from the counter she headed out the door.

Jackie's voice stopped her just as she was about to step out into the light of day. "Bye, Sunshine. I hope to see you soon."

Turning back Rosie responded, "Thank you, Jackie. Goodbye."

Suddenly, Jackie rushed forward and placed a desperate kiss upon Rosie's lips.

Pulling away Rosie said, "Bye." She turned and quickly walked away from the house. Once having seated herself inside the van, she glanced at her appearance in the rearview mirror. Seeing herself with smeared makeup, and tousled hair made her wonder how anyone could find her appealing, especially another girl. Leaning heavily against the seat Rosie heard her name being called.

Jackie ran from the house, dressed in an oversized t-shirt and faded jeans, shouting, "Wait Sunshine, wait!" Racing to the driver's side of the van she waited patiently for the window to come down, "You were forgetting your earrings!"

Holding out her hand for the jewelry Rosie said sweetly, "Thank you, Jackie." Looking down at the ruby earrings brought back a melancholy memory of Christmas. "These have a special place in my heart."

Taking Rosie by the hand as she released the earrings into her palm seductively, Jackie said, "How very interesting. I was just thinking the same thing about you." With a tilt of her head and a wave of her fingers, Jackie turned and ran back inside.

Janie came out to the driveway to greet Rosie still wearing the now wilted, red sequined gown. With a turned up nose she declared, "You look like shit!"

At a snail's pace, Rosie walked the path to her house. "You're so sweet, Jane. You always know how to say just the right thing to make a person feel better."

"Just do something with yourself, because you've got to eat black eyed peas and greens today," Janie asserted.

"What?" Just the mention of food caused her to wince.

"Don't act like you don't know we have to eat that crap for good luck and all for the New Year," Janie rambled on.

"Yeah, yeah," Rosie said as she held up her hand to ward off any other nauseating words.

Tossing her shoes and bag aside, Rosie rushed to the refrigerator and removed a carton of orange juice, and a half bottle of white wine. Quickly, she mixed the two together and sipped it slowly. Sitting at the table with a slow slump, Rosie sipped her cocktail as she watched Lillian busy herself in the kitchen. Gently, she asked, "Have you ever had a crush on a girl?"

With arched brows she answered, "No. And you?"

"No," she snorted. Then she explained, "There's a girl who has a crush on me."

"Well, don't worry. It'll pass just like any other crush, don't you know?"

Andrea entered the room holding a half poster size book she and Janie had created. "Here's your book, Sunshine."

The way Andrea pronounced her name was enduring. With a true look of surprise Rosie asked, "Is that for me?"

As if she were too timid to speak, the little girl nodded her head yes. Reaching her arms wide open, Andrea toddled into them, allowing Rosie to scoop her into a cuddle.

The cover page depicted a princess stepping into a convertible limousine as a hand, with an unseen face, helps the princess into the car. Awed by the colored pencil artwork, her heart swelled with appreciation, as she recognized full well the sacrifice of time the artists' gave for their masterpiece. The second page was a drawing of the princess sitting in her VW van, which gave the strongest clue yet that Rosie and the princess were one and the same. The third page was a cutout newspaper picture of her riding Victor Hart on his Harley Davidson.

"Where did you find the newspaper picture?"

Andrea wriggled free of Rosie's arms and hustled away, only to return just as quickly waving a newspaper. Taking the paper, she could see is was from the gossip column page. A hole was left in the paper where the photograph of Rosie riding into the country club with Victor Hart as her passenger had been front and center. The caption beneath it read, "*Hart heart-throb, meets dream girl.*"

With eyes narrowed as she absorbed the words of the columnist. "Rumor has it that *Ryder/Hart Strings Music Studio* has its heart set on new comer Sunshine Rose to record Hart's personal favorite *Lonely*. Frank Ryder had this comment: *Victor and I were extremely impressed with Miss Rose's talent. And, we look forward to working* with *her in the future.* Recording is expected to begin in early spring."

Tossing the paper aside she asked, "These gossip articles? Do they usually tell the truth?"

Lillian tilted her head as she considered the question, then looking Rosie squarely in the face answered, "Yes."

Pushing from the table Rosie mumbled, "I've got to have a shower. I just can't think without a shower."

Lillian agreed, "One always feels better with clean skin." And, then as if nothing had been said at all, she resumed her cheerful cleaning.

Throughout her reminiscing of the events from the previous evening, Victor Hart remained foremost in her mind. He seemed surreal, yet solid and intimidating. Looking at the reflection of cleansed skin through a steam fogged mirror, Rosie mused at the oddity of being attractive to such opposites as Victor and Jackie. Stepping into a terry cloth robe she slung open the bathroom door, releasing a fog of steam into the hallway. She went directly to the telephone and called her father. Eva answered the line, and Rosie made polite small talk with her. News from home hadn't changed much, and luckily, the newspapers around Ben Johnson Ridge didn't carry gossip columns from Ft Lauderdale.

"There's some news that may set uneasy with you sweetheart," Sturgill began cautiously.

"What's that Daddy?"

"Well, the good news is Shelley finally got herself engaged to that fat Martin boy. I guess small town money is good enough for her. And, the bad news is that Lewis tossed his scholarship away and joined the Army. He dropped out of school in the middle of the quarter, and no one, not even his grandparents understand why."

Fear caught in her throat as recollections of a dream came to memory. "The Army, oh why did he do that? He could get killed!"

Sturgill softened his voice and said, "He's in the Lord's hands now, sweetheart."

"Oh, Daddy this just upsets me so much. I'll call you back later."

"Now darling, you just stay calm and don't worry about that boy. He's a soldier in the US armed forces now, and can take care of himself."

"Goodbye, Daddy." And she hung up without hearing her father's farewell.

Slowly she made her way to her room where she dressed and dried her hair. The tidy bed with the ruffled bedspread called to her invitingly, and she stretched across it languidly. Sleep overtook her, and she dozed with fretful dreams of the Vietnam War plaguing her slumber.

Rosie awoke with Janie standing in the doorway saying, "Time to eat for your luck." The smell of fresh baked bread pulled her from bed. Lillian had a table filled with wonderful tasty foods.

"Now, where I come from," Lillian began her story, "we always ate black eyed peas cooked with ham hock, and turnip greens on New Year's Day. It's meant to bring you good luck with health and money in the new year."

A knock at the front door drew Janie from the table. With her usual caution, she strode to the window and took a quick glance out to see who stood at the other side. With a piqued look of curiosity, she stepped to the door and swung it open. Billy Ray and Ted stood with animated expressions. Making an effort to be polite, Billy Ray asked, "Well, hello Jane. How do you like school?"

She answered dryly, "Closed."

Chuckling at her remark, Billy Ray stepped past Janie, "The damnedest thing just happened." He made his way to the dining table, and standing beside Rosie said triumphantly, "Frank Ryder has asked us to cut a record. How about that, huh? And, guess what else Frank wants? He wants you, Sunshine. He wants you to sing *Lonely*. What do you think of that?"

Ted spoke up and said, "I suppose this makes you a member of the group."

"A member of the group," she repeated.

Billy Ray said, "You'll have to record a song for the flip side you know."

"Maybe we could do one of your songs," she suggested.

Ted fell into a conversation with Lillian as he helped himself to some of her greens and peas, but he kept one ear on the conversation Billy Ray shared with Rosie.

Standing from the table, she took Billy Ray by the hand, and led him into her bedroom. Once inside she closed and latched the door. She turned to Billy Ray and threw her arms around his neck. "Was I the last one standing last night?"

With his lips to her neck he answered, "Yes, you were."

"We did spend the night together, didn't we?"

Billy Ray pushed her down onto her bed and began smothering her face with kisses. Laughing and gasping for breath, she got him under control by kissing him forcefully with fervent passion. He fell limply against her when she finished her kiss with a low moan, and a noisy snapping apart of lips.

Lying in a silent embrace, Billy Ray whispered, "If it hadn't been for you, Victor Hart would never have taken notice of our band."

A wicked smile tickled across her lips as she asked, "Did you see my picture in the gossip column? I was driving Victor's hog."

Billy Ray's eyes shot open wide, "A Harley? You drove his Harley?" Staring at her with astonishment he said, "It must be love! Victor Hart is in love with you." Billy Ray began waving his arms about as he rationalized. "No matter how you face it, when a man lets a woman drive his Harley, he's blind crazy in love."

"Why, he's so rich he could have any woman in the world!"

Billy Ray stared at her nodding his head, "Exactly."

The first weeks of January slipped past as Rosie stayed busy with school and work. School had become such drudgery she looked forward to the afternoons at the clinic. One afternoon Rosie covered the desk so Carlotta could leave early, and found herself locking up the clinic with Dr. Thayer.

She stepped inside the open door of his office and asked, "Is there anything I can do, before I go?"

The aging doctor awkwardly reached out and snatched up a letter from the pile of mail that Carlotta had placed on his desk. Holding the letter to his chest, Dr. Tucker crossed the room and opened a file drawer labeled *Personnel*. He deposited the letter and snapped the drawer closed, pressing the locking mechanism on the cabinet. "Everything is taken care of, you can go now."

Billy Ray's car was parked in the driveway when Rosie got home. She silently wished for him to be alone, without Jackie. The door sprang open before she could turn the door knob, and Billy Ray stood staring at her with an odd look on his face.

Janie appeared announcing, "You're part of the band now, Sunny! You're going to record their first record with them!"

Gripped with apprehension, for a long minute, Rosie said nothing. Finding breath enough for voice she asked, "For real?"

Billy Ray said quickly, "Frank Ryder insists you sing *Lonely*, and that makes you a member of the band."

Throwing her arms around him she pledged, "Oh, I'll work so hard to make the band look good. I promise I won't let you down."

Chapter Thirty
Yellow Roses for Minnie Mama

There was much dissention within the band as preparations were made for the recording. Ted and the other guys spent a week at the studio in Boca Raton laying down music tracks, while Rosie went about her usual business of classes and work. One afternoon at the clinic, Carlotta tossed a folded newspaper at Rosie. It was a section of the classifieds, with a big circle drawn around one ad in particular. After reading the advertisement Rosie asked, "Five hundred dollars a week is a lot of money to offer a nursing student, don't you think?"

Carlotta wagged her finger at Rosie, "Don't be looking a gift horse in the mouth young lady. You be sure to mail in your resume to that rich lady's address, you hear?"

"I'll do it." Rosie smiled as she said, "A fat lot of good it will do."

Carlotta placed her hand on her hip and said, "You just address the envelope, and let me mail it for you."

Laughing forthright Rosie exclaimed, "Carlotta! You don't trust me?"

The tall, thin woman smiled back at Rosie and said, "I trust you." With mischief in her voice Carlotta added, "About as far as I can throw you."

The small cottage style house was aglow with electric light, beckoning Rosie a warm welcome home. Entering the foyer, she put aside her books and purse on the bench sitting near the door. The television could be heard playing the theme song to *The Partridge Family*. She entered the living room singing along with the television.

Lillian said, "Sunshine, your daddy called. I told him I would have you call back when you came in. I put you a plate from supper in the oven, dear." When the commercial ended and the show came back on, Lillian became as engrossed in it as the two little girls were. With a girlish gleam in her eye Lillian said, "Oh, David Cassidy is even more handsome than his father."

Rosie wandered into the kitchen and took the plate from the oven. She smiled at the country style food Lillian had prepared. Lillian had fried strips of chicken breast golden brown, and prepared fluffy mashed potatoes and green peas. Rosie sat down with the plate of food and reached for the phone. She dialed off the numbers to her father's house, and he answered sounding groggy as usual for early evening.

"Daddy, it's me. Lillian said you called."

"I just wanted to hear your voice, Rosie. I miss you something awful around here. Sometimes I worry you will never come back to Ben Johnson Ridge."

"Of course I will, Daddy! Why are you so down in the dumps tonight?"

Sturgill Moon cleared his voice again and said, "Well, I hate to tell you this, but-"

Rosie's heart jumped at the thought of hearing bad news. "Is it Lewis? Has he been hurt in the war?"

A long sigh sounded over the phone line before Sturgill said, "No, honey. My God! Are you not ever going to get over that boy?"

Relief swept through Rosie as she said, "I can't help it, Daddy. I guess I just love him as much as I hate him."

With wisdom Sturgill said, "And, there's a very fine line between love and hate, my child." He cleared his voice, "Now what I was going to say is that poor old Mrs. Reyes finally passed away."

Rosie pressed her fingers to her temples with the realization her headaches were beginning to precede bad news. Could she really be having premonition headaches? "Oh, Daddy, I wish I were there," she moaned. "You've got to send flowers! Yellow roses were Minnie Mama's favorite. I'll send Willene a card with a long letter."

"Yes, Rosie. I'll do that." His voice sounded more tired than groggy.

"Are you feeling okay, Daddy? You sound so tired."

With a graveled voice he said, "Oh, I haven't been sleeping too well. I've been having strange dreams that wake me up. Then I can't go back to sleep afterwards."

Rosie's curiosity was piqued, "What time of the night do you have these dreams, Daddy?"

Sturgill sighed and answered, "Usually just a short time before dawn."

"That's called the late night side of morning, Dad."

"Oh, is it? Nobody ever told me."

"Jane had to tell me."

"That child is," he paused and added, "different."

Hesitantly Rosie asked, "Is it Doc Campbell?"

Gruffly, Sturgill responded, "I'm not going to let your ghost stories bother me."

Wanting to change the subject Rosie said, "I sent in my resume for a private sitting job in Boca Raton today."

A soft whistle came over the phone. "Those people down there are rich. I wish you luck if that's what you want to do."

Thinking of the money she said, "It pays five hundred a week plus room and board."

Sturgill asked, "What are you going to do with the rest of your hoard?"

Remembering she had told her father Andrea was Lillian's granddaughter Rosie said, "Things will work out. I don't really expect to get the job anyway. I've hardly had the experience to earn that kind of money." Rosie fidgeted with her fork as she maneuvered a pea around on her plate, and decided not to mention the recording for Victor Hart just yet. "I love you, Daddy. How's Eva?"

Sturgill replied, "I love you, too, Sunshine Rose, and she's a bitch."

Again Rosie laughed. "You be sweet, I've got homework to do."

"You be sweet, too." And, he hung up the phone.

Listening to the receiver click into silence, Rosie was filled with home sickness. She replaced the phone in the cradle and fought to hold back tears. Pushing back the plate, Rosie took the phone back up and dialed Kid's number. Valerie answered the phone, and Rosie asked to speak with Kid. Without saying a word to Rosie, Valerie put the phone down and yelled for Kid to take the call.

With irritation in his voice Kid said, "Hello."

"Gee, did I call at a bad time?"

With a softer tone he said, "There's never a bad time for you to call, Sunny. How are you?"

"Oh, just a little down. How's the divorce thing?"

A low groan came across the wire as he confessed, "The bitch refuses to grant me the divorce!"

Rosie was confused, "You mean she can say no?"

Moaning softly he said, "That's exactly what she's doing!" Then he said in a low tone, "And, having a father-in-law who's a damned legislator doesn't help."

Disappointment consumed Rosie as she listened to Kid's unsettling news. "Damn it, Kid! I miss you. Jane misses you. Do you know her mother has not called all this time we've been gone? Jane refuses to even talk about Elizabeth. She tells her friends she's an orphan, and that Lillian is her guardian!"

"I wish I could do something, Sunny. You'll never know how bad it's been. Living with Valerie, and wearing the wire for the Feds. If I can just get out of this marriage, life will be good again, for all of us!"

Closing her eyes Rosie said, "I've got to record a song with this local band. We'll be doing the vocals week after next, down in Boca Raton."

He exclaimed, "Holy shit! How did you get so lucky?"

Rosie explained about going to the New Years Eve party and meeting Victor Hart and Frank Ryder. "I sang Victor's song at the party and he fell for me. And, guess what? I drove his Harley! Billy Ray says a man only let's a woman drive his hog if he's in love with her."

With an edge to his voice Kid asked, "Who is Billy Ray?"

Rosie smiled, feeling pleased that he might be jealous. "He's the lead guitarist for the band, and the guy that's been keeping my juices flowing. If you know what I mean."

"Damn it! Why do you tell me things like that?"

Laughing, Rosie said blatantly, "Well, you asked! And besides, what do you expect me to do? Dry up while I'm waiting for you?"

She could imagine Kid nodding his head in aggravation as he said, "Well, don't get attached to him, because I'll be there before you even know it."

"Love ya, bye."

"Bye," he said and softly hung up the phone.

Looking at the resting receiver Rosie remembered the last day she and Janie shared with Kid in Alabama. Memories flooded her mind of getting caught in the summer rain, and camping at Woodstock. Taking the plate to the sink Rosie stumbled over Andrea's shoes. She kicked them out of her way, and thanked God she was at the bridge that fateful day to rescue the forsaken child.

The days of January passed briskly by. Rosie traveled with the band to Boca Raton and did the vocal recording. The technology of the studio intrigued her as she listened to the playbacks, hardly recognizing her own voice on tape. The session was grueling. Frank insisted on perfection, demanding a strong rhythm section and perfectly blended vocals, prompting Rosie to develop an intense dislike for the man. When she finished, she left unhappy, secretly hoping Victor's song would be a flop.

Janie's twelfth birthday was celebrated with a meal at a family restaurant. When the meal was finished, she was surprised with a small cake and a group of staff clapping and singing *Happy, Happy Birthday*. The gift Rosie gave was a beautiful silver handle dagger in a gift case. Lillian gave a record album by the Archies. Andrea's gift was a smiley face t-shirt. With a beaming face she thanked everyone and declared that as a twelve year old she was ready to take on more responsibilities.

Rosie looked at Lillian with a raised eyebrow, "What do you mean?"

Janie announced, "I'm talking about the responsibility of taking care of a pet. I want a dog."

Groans escaped both, Lillian and Rosie, as the thought passed over. Defending her desire Janie reasoned, "A dog is good security for a family. They bark when strangers come around, and when the house catches on fire."

The only time during the drive home that Janie and Andrea didn't chatter about getting a dog was when the Archies came on the radio with their hit song *Sugar Sugar*. The two little girls hushed talking long enough to sing along.

The following day Rosie arrived at work to find Carlotta smiling brightly. "Doctor Al says he wants to see you ASAP. He's in his office."

"Am I in trouble?"

Carlotta smiled a big toothy grin saying, "Not exactly."

Rosie wandered down the quiet hallway to Dr. Thayer's office. She didn't need to knock at the door, because he had left it open. Peering inside, she saw the aging doctor pouring over a patient's chart. Softly she asked, "Dr. Thayer, you wanted to see me?"

He looked up and gazed over the rim of his reading glasses, "Oh, yes. Come in. Have a seat."

Rosie sat in the familiar steel framed padded chair. Folding her hands in her lap she looked at Dr. Thayer with a slight look of dread crossing her face. "Is there a problem?"

Making notes in the chart he said, "Not really. I think you're going to be very excited when I tell you that the lady in Boca Raton has requested an interview with you."

With shock Rosie declared, "I'm surprised! I never thought I had a chance."

"I can shed some light on that perhaps. You see, Edwina Morgan owns a cosmetic company. Anyone in her employ must look a certain way. In other words, she surrounds herself with *beautiful* people." Dr. Thayer used his fingers to make quotations marks in the air.

Rosie shook her head in confusion, "But she doesn't know what I look like."

Dr. Thayer answered, "Evidently she does. She mentioned a newspaper photo of you driving a motorcycle?"

Rosie's face flushed as she realized Mrs. Morgan had been able to connect her resume with that article. Closing her eyes Rosie realized a rich socialite such as Edwina Morgan could easily get evidence on any number of applicants to her advertisement. Placing her hands over her face Rosie said, "Oh, I'm so embarrassed."

With a chuckle Dr. Thayer said, "Don't be! If that picture is what got you this opportunity, be proud of it."

Carlotta tapped on the open door, "I brought you the mail."

Motioning for her to bring it in, Carlotta stepped in and laid the stack of mail on his desk. A dark expression clouded Dr. Thayer's face as he reached out and snatched an envelope from the top. He slid it to the bottom of the stack. With a cross look at Carlotta he said, "You may go, now."

Trying not to show curiosity, Rosie looked down at her folded hands. Pushing the stack of mail aside, he continued, "I agreed for Mrs. Morgan to send her legal aide to interview you Friday afternoon. Is that okay with you?"

"Yes. That's fine."

Dr. Thayer sighed, "Good. Now, today I will need for you to go through the supply closet. Make a list of what Carlotta needs to order." Having given Rosie her instructions for the day's work, he began to sift through the stack of mail, tossing away certain correspondences without opening the envelopes.

When she got home from work, Rosie was greeted by two little girls excitedly waving around a section of the classified ads. Andrea exclaimed, "We found a puppy in the paper!"

Janie followed by saying, "His family has to move, and can't take him along. He needs a new home."

Before having time to set her things aside, the phone rang and Lillian called out, "Sunshine! Billy Ray is on the phone."

Closing her eyes and taking a deep breath Rosie said, "He's got to be a little dog you know?"

With delight in her voice Janie responded, "He's a terrier."

Rosie went to the phone and said, "Hey, there! What's up?"

His voice was cheerful and light, "Jackie asked me to call and invite you over to her house for a Marilyn Monroe flick. Have you ever seen *Some like It Hot?*"

A sweet feeling rushed through Rosie as she said, "You know what? I haven't seen that one yet. When should I come over?"

"Eight o'clock doll face, and don't be late." Billy Ray hung up the phone with a sharp click.

Shaking her head at his remark she returned the phone to the cradle and turned around to see both children staring at her with crossed arms. Holding out her hand she said, "Let me see the ad." After reading the ad she said, "I've never heard of a Jack Russell Terrier. And, this creature's hardly a puppy. He's almost a year old."

With pleading faces the girls said in unison, "Please!"

Turning to Lillian she said, "Will you please call these people and see if they still have the dog? Be sure to ask if he's healthy and well behaved."

Smiling sweetly Lillian rushed forth and took the paper from Janie. "Don't worry about a thing. I know just the right questions to ask."

Without thinking Rosie looked at Janie, and they locked eyes briefly. Looking away Rosie said, "If you want the dog, just go get him." Pointing at the girls she said, "You will be responsible for him you know."

The younger girls nodded their head and said in unison, "Uh huh."

Waving away their response as if she didn't totally believe them Rosie mocked, "Uh huh! That doesn't sound very convincing."

Lillian called behind Rosie, "Don't worry, Sunshine. I'll help the girls look after the little guy."

Standing before the bathroom mirror, Rosie combed out her hair and applied a thin coat of lipstick. The sound of voices entering the house told her that Janie had returned with Lillian and Andrea from their puppy expedition. Rosie left the bathroom and walked down the hallway into the living room. She was greeted by a happy little Andrea with a big smile.

"See, Sunshine! He is a puppy." The dark eyed little girl pushed back her thick long dark hair. "And, he likes me!"

Janie approached with the little dog cradled in her arms. Cautiously, Rosie stretched out her hand to caress the little head with tall ears. "He's not going to bite me is he?" Before the words had left her mouth the little guy bared his teeth and growled menacingly. Withdrawing her hand Rosie said, "Uh oh! This is not good."

Lillian giggled, "He's just bluffing you. That little guy is just a pussy cat." To prove her point she reached out and grabbed his nose playfully.

With a narrowed look Rosie said, "I think he's the devil."

Janie pleaded, "Oh, give him another chance. Watch him play fetch." She put the dog down and taking a small rubber ball from her pocket, bounced it across the floor. The dog raced after it. He then trotted back to Janie, and sat at her feet holding the ball in his mouth. She knelt down and ran her hand across the smooth sleek short haired white coat decorated with liver spots, and brown freckles. "See how loving he is?"

Rosie decided to try again to pet the little dog. She knelt down along side of Janie, and reached out her hand to pet the small canine. Before her fingers could touch him, he again snarled and growled. Retreating from the threat Rosie said, "To hell with him. He hates me!" Rosie took up her purse and walked to the front door.

Andrea sweetly interjected as she patted the dog's head, "No, Randy don't hate you."

Rosie repeated, "Randy?"

Lillian chuckled, "I thought it was an odd name for a dog, too. But that's what the family named him, and the girls say they don't want to change it."

With closed eyes Rosie shook her head slowly, "Jane? What do you think of his name?"

Janie answered, "I think it's the nicest name in the whole world." She pushed her cheek against the top of the dog's head.

Andrea became overly excited and exclaimed, "He's the best dog in the whole world!" Then she too pushed her cheek against the dog's face.

Taking up the car keys Rosie walked away saying, "I'll be home after ten, so leave the light on for me." Seeing the girls stroke the contented dog she added, "Make that mutt a bed on the floor. I don't want him sleeping with you, and I mean it."

Returning home, Rosie opened the front door with her key and stepped quietly inside. She could hear the click-click of tiny toenails against the hardwood floor. Turning to face her foe, Rosie was completely caught off guard when the pint size canine began barking at her like a guard dog. She tried to calm him, but his barking only intensified as she shushed at him. Lights turned on as everyone was awakened by his commotion.

Andrea stood rubbing sleep from her eyes as Janie scooped him into her arms and reentered their bedroom. Rosie looked at Lillian who stood in her doorway dressed in an old fashioned flannel nightgown, with a smirk on her face. Sleepily she said to Rosie, "It'll be okay, Sunshine. He just has to get to know you." She then turned and went back into her room.

The dawn of Friday morning awoke Rosie who needed much more sleep. She made her way through the day of classes, and was finally alert for her afternoon of work at the clinic.

Carlotta smiled her gap toothed smile when Rosie entered the office and said, "Your interviewer is in Al's office. He's really nice!"

Rosie felt a sudden jolt of nerves. "Oh my God!" she exclaimed breathlessly. "I forgot all about that!"

"You'll be fine, don't worry."

"Oh to hell with it, I'm not going to get the job anyway!"

Placing her hands on Rosie's shoulders Carlotta said, "Now, what do you mean? You gather up your guts, and go in there with confidence."

Rosie inhaled deeply through her nose, and began the slow torturous walk to Dr. Thayer's office. She stepped inside expecting to see Dr. Thayer with the interviewer, but she only found a tall young man sitting all alone at Dr. Thayer's desk.

"Hello, I'm Sunshine Moon," she said extending her hand.

He rose quickly to his feet, "I'm Ollie Onstott. I work for Mrs. Edwina Morgan. Please have a seat and we'll get started with the interview."

Sitting upon the hard upholstered chair Rosie smiled at the young man and asked, "How long have you worked for Mrs. Morgan?"

Brushing back his perfectly combed dark hair, Ollie answered, "Not long, hardly a year, yet. So forgive me if I can't answer all your questions."

Feeling more at ease with the young inexperienced man Rosie asked, "Why does Mrs. Morgan want a nursing student and not a nurse?"

Ollie sat in Dr. Thayer's chair and responded, "She wants to mold her own private nurse. She believes the best way to do that is when the nurse in still in training." Reading from a printed form he asked, "Why are you here when your family is in Alabama."

Rosie answered cautiously, "A friend arranged this employment with Dr. Thayer while I attend school."

Ollie wrote furiously. "How many people are in your household?"

"Four."

"If you are chosen for this job you will be required to live on the estate."

"That's okay if my family can come with me."

The young man kept his head down as he wrote. "How soon could you start work should you be chosen for the job?"

Rosie shook her head slightly at the thought. "Well, the winter quarter has just begun. But, if I am chosen for the job, I would gladly transfer to a new school."

With a slight smile on his lips the dark haired young man with the black rimmed glasses sat back and said, "Well, I thank you for your time, Miss Moon. I would like to tell you in confidence you should be making preparations to accept Mrs. Morgan's advertised position, because I think you are just exactly what she is looking for."

Rosie could hardly believe her ears. "Are you sure? I mean, I'm so inexperienced."

Ollie smiled and said, "Trust me. You're exactly what Mrs. Morgan is looking for." He stood and extended his hand as he shoved the notebook into a briefcase.

Rosie took his hand in a firm handshake and said, "Okay, then, from your lips to God's ears, huh?"

Chapter Thirty-One
To the Bee

The fifth grade class room was overheated and smelly, as if someone couldn't control a case of flatulence. Janie watched miserably as the tall skinny teacher made irritating noises with the chalk against the black board. The science book was opened to a page depicting the planets in orbit, and she stared at how small earth was in comparison to most of the other planets. Acting out of boredom, she took a clean sheet of writing paper and began drawing a skeleton dressed in the prudish looking suit her teacher wore. To make it even more personal, Janie added the round wire rim glasses and severely short hairstyle. Beneath the drawing of the skeleton teacher standing at a chalkboard she wrote in bold print *BONES*. Turning to the girl sitting behind her she passed the drawing and immediately heard a slight giggle from her classmate. The girl quickly handed off the drawing to another classmate who also giggled.

The stern faced teacher looked around the classroom and asked, "What's so funny class?" No one said a word. Narrowing her eyes at Janie, Mrs. Skelton said, "Jane, would you stand up please?"

Worry crossed her face, "Why, I didn't do anything?"

Mrs. Skelton's voice held a sharp edge of irritation as she answered, "I didn't say you were in trouble, I just asked you to stand."

Glancing around, Janie slowly stood. The frail looking teacher began lecturing the class. "Now class, I have drawn the planets in orbit just as they are depicted in your books. I want you to tell me without looking at your book which planet is the largest."

Her eyes widened as she realized she didn't know the names of all the planets, and therefore could not answer the question. She stood silently looking at her teacher without attempting an answer.

"It's okay to take a guess if you don't know," said Mrs. Skelton.

Janie stammered, "Well, uh I know it's not earth." Some of the students laughed at her remark. The feeling that she was entertaining her class emboldened her, and she bravely spoke up, "Is it Pluto?" Again, the class hummed with giggles. "Oh, I know, its Dumbo." A smile twisted her lips when the class erupted in laughter.

Mrs. Skelton remarked smartly, "I'll ignore that answer, Jane, this time." She turned back to the board and made an unnerving scratching noise as she underlined the largest planet in orbit. "Uranus is the biggest."

Unable to resist the temptation Janie exclaimed, "No, yours is!" The classroom erupted in uproarious laughter.

Mrs. Skelton stared at Janie with sharp piercing eyes. "That's it!" she exclaimed as she placed the chalk into the tray with a loud snapping noise. "I want you to go to the principal's office right now young lady, and I will meet you there shortly."

The classroom grew silent, "But why, Mrs. Skelton? Mr. Johnson already knows Uranus is the biggest."

Again, the classroom erupted in uncontrolled laughter. Mrs. Skelton held her arm in the air as she pointed toward the door. "Go!" She commanded with her pale pencil thin lips pursed angrily.

With a deep desire to keep the class entertained Janie said, "Well, I guess I need to take my book. Mr. Johnson will probably want to look at Uranus."

When the class again burst into laughter, Mrs. Skelton hastily strode across the room. Grasping her by the upper arm, she tugged Janie along. "Gee whiz! You sure do have boney fingers, Mrs. Skelton," said Janie as she was drug from the classroom causing the rest of the fifth grade class to erupt into chaotic hilarity.

The teacher released her arm and commanded, "Walk."

With a sad look of defeat Janie continued until she reached the office. "Oh, gee!" she quipped, "Mr. Clod has his door closed. I guess he's busy right now." She twisted on her heel and took a big step away.

Mrs. Skelton reached out and caught her by the arm. "That's okay. We'll interrupt him."

Stepping into the small office, Janie was greeted by a scowling principle. Mr. Clod cleared his throat, "You again? Let me guess. You've been spreading rumors that the girl's bathroom is infested with crab lice."

Sardonically she mocked, "I'm fine thank you, and how are you today?" Janie flounced down in the old familiar chair against the wall, and tapped her fingers annoyingly against the wooden arms.

Mrs. Skelton said, "The class clown can't answer a simple question with a simple answer. She insists on taking every opportunity to disrupt the class by making clever remarks that make the other children laugh."

Leaning back in his leather chair caused a disturbing sound to reverberate in the office. Janie grimaced disgustingly and dramatically pinched her nose together. He frowned and said, "Now, don't start with me young lady."

Pacing the room Mrs. Skelton said, "Miss Noble seems to find humor with the planet Uranus. And, because of her comments I can't even mention the word without stirring up the entire classroom."

Mr. Clod asked, "What do you have to say for yourself, Miss Noble?"

Janie stammered, "Uh, I'm a kid?"

Mr. Clod said, "Well, I guess we're going to have to call in your guardian, again. Is that what you want?"

With a deep sigh Janie answered, "Well that would be better than the National Guard wouldn't it? I mean they just shoot students!"

With a gaping mouth Mrs. Skelton exclaimed, "Jane Noble! That is not true! My husband is a Guardsman."

Janie perked up and asked, "Really? How many kids has he shot? Maybe a rock band will write a song about him, like Crosby, Stills, Nash & Young did. Have you heard it? It's called *Four Dead in Ohio*."

With a red face and lips pressed into nonexistence Mrs. Skelton pleaded with the principle. "Please! Can't you do something?"

Mr. Clod barked, "I'm calling your house, Jane. I think maybe some punishment from home might be what you need."

Rolling her eyes Janie moaned, "Wouldn't it be better if you just sent me home for the rest of the week?"

With a serious look he asked, "And, just how would that help?"

She answered cautiously, "Well, it would give Mrs. Skelton enough time to talk about how big Uranus is."

He sat back, creating the irksome noise again. "Well, then. I have no choice but to call your guardian."

Making a note on his desktop calendar, Mr. Clod said, "You may return to class now. Keep your clever remarks to yourself. Disrupting the class is uncalled for."

She stood and stepped to the door. Mrs. Skelton reached over and opened it. They strode side by side down the hallway. A low roar of chaos quickly ebbed as they stepped back into the classroom. Janie and Mrs. Skelton both stood motionless as their attention was drawn to the sketch of the skeleton teacher someone had taped to the blackboard.

Hurriedly, Janie found her desk. Mrs. Skelton jerked the drawing from the board screeching, "I want to know who is responsible for this!"

The classroom had gone from a chaotic roar to complete silence. Looking at the ceiling with pursed lips, Janie remained mute. Using marginal vision she watched her teacher take slow deliberate steps around the room holding the drawing out from her in disgust. When Mrs. Skelton came to a stop at her desk, Janie's face fell into a frown. Looking up at her teacher she sneered, "Oh, right. Go ahead and blame me. That's just typical for you isn't it?"

The next thing Janie knew, the teacher was shoving her desk, with Janie in it, out into the hallway. Mrs. Skelton returned inside her classroom slamming the door closed, leaving Janie all alone in the empty corridor.

After having spent about ten minutes in the hallway, Todd Weeks came along on his way to the boy's bathroom. He stopped still when he saw Janie in his path.

"Well! What a coincidence," she said to him boldly. "I was just thinking about you."

"You were?"

"Yeah, I had a pain in my ass," she retorted caustically. "And, now that you're here, I've got a little something for you to do, weak boy."

When school was dismissed for the day, Mrs. Skelton opened the classroom door to find her disruptive student sitting hostage in a mass of clear tape and toilet paper. The entire fifth grade class erupted into hysterical laughter at the sight. The exasperated teacher began tearing at the tissue and tape. "Who did this to you?"

Janie responded with a mumble as her mouth had been crisscrossed with tape. When Mrs. Skelton ripped the tape form her mouth Janie exclaimed, "Ouch!" which caused another outburst from her classmates.

Mrs. Skelton demanded, "Who did this to you?"

Janie's response was, "One of those sixteen year olds in the sixth grade."

Mrs. Skelton continued ripping tape and toilet paper from Janie's bound arms and body saying, "We don't have any sixteen year olds in the sixth grade."

Janie replied, "Oh, then he must be in the seventh grade." Again, her classmates erupted into laughter.

Mrs. Skelton turned and dismissed the class before she released Janie from her bondage. "I suppose you're going to use this against me."

Standing from the desk and pushing away the toilet paper and tape Janie replied, "Now, would I do that?"

Rosie entered the clinic after a hard day at school. The difficult courses were beginning to make her doubt her ability to become a nurse. She approached the desk she shared with Carlotta only to notice a large yellow ribbon on a poster board with the words *Congratulations Sunshine!* written in black marker. Looking at Carlotta she asked, "What's the poster talking about?"

Carlotta leaped to her feet and clasped her hands together. "Mrs. Edwina Morgan chose you for the nursing assistant job! Ollie Onstott will be calling this afternoon to confirm your acceptance of the position." Carlotta brought her clasped hands to her chin as she asked, "You will accept, won't you?"

Rosie answered, "Oh, yes! How could I not?"

A big toothy grin emerged from Carlotta as she answered, "Exactly!"

When Rosie returned home with her good news, Janie interjected with her own that wasn't good. "You've got to talk with the principle again. Mrs. Skelton is just hell bent on seeing me kicked out of that school." She asked Lillian, "What's wrong with having a sense of humor anyway?"

Lillian consoled Janie, "Don't you worry! Sunshine will go in there and set him straight."

Looking at her little cousin with narrowed eyes Rosie exclaimed, "The hell I will! What have you done this time? Posted another drawing of Richard Nixon roasting in hell on the hall bulletin board?"

Janie defended herself by saying, "Richard Nixon will roast in hell," she paused and added, "someday."

Lillian put her hands to her ears. "Let's not talk about hell, please."

Ignoring Lillian's request, Rosie said, "I don't understand why you do some of the things you do. Remember how upset you made your grandfather when you drew a picture of Bear Bryant roasting in hell?"

Janie said nothing.

Andrea sat quietly on the sofa stroking the little dog named Randy. "My daddy's in the newspaper again," she said pointing to the front page of the small Indiana town newspaper.

Rosie snatched the paper from the coffee table and read the headline, "*Parents Found Not Guilty in Child's Murder.*" Her eyes went quickly to Lillian who stood close looking at the paper.

As if reading Rosie's mind, Lillian said, "I know all about it, Sunshine. Andrea told me everything, and Janie showed me the scrapbook."

Looking back at the paper Rosie explained to Andrea, "Your daddy and your stepmother are being released from jail, because the jury only found them guilty of child abuse. The penalty for that charge has been reduced to time they've already spent in jail." Trembling with anger Rosie slung the paper toward Janie saying, "Cut out the article for Andrea's scrapbook. She'll need to read all this again when she's older, and can understand."

Lillian exclaimed, "Understand! These people abused their child to the point they thought they had killed her. Then they threw her lifeless body from a bridge! How can they not be guilty of attempted murder?"

Janie sat down next to Andrea with scissors and began clipping the article from the paper saying, "I guess that old saying is true. No body, no crime." Holding up the picture of her father and stepmother Janie said to Andrea, "Wow, your folks sure look happy."

The little dark haired girl shrank from the photo. Holding to the dog she asked, "I don't have to go back and live with them, do I?"

Lillian rush over and sat next to the child, "No, no! You're staying with us till you get all grown up." Looking to Rosie for encouragement Lillian asked, "Isn't that right, girls?"

Rosie sank to her knees by the coffee table and reassured Andrea. "You will stay with us, as long as you want too, forever and a day."

Janie began singing, "*Those were the days my friend, we thought they'd never end. We'd sing and dance forever and a day. We'd live the life we chose, we'd fight and never lose. Those were the days, oh yes! Those were the days.*" Soon everyone, including Andrea joined in singing.

The ringing of the telephone took Rosie's attention, and she answered to hear Billy Ray say, "Hello, Sunshine! How's life?"

A smile crossed her face just at the sound of his voice, "I'm moving to Boca Raton to be a nursing assistant for a rich old lady."

Silence clung to the phone line momentarily, "You're shittin' me! Boca Raton?"

"It's not that far, Billy Ray. We can still get together."

"What about the band?" Billy Ray sounded worried.

Rosie had already dwelled on that question herself. "I can still be a part of the band, if you need me."

"Need you!" Billy Ray shouted, "You know as well as the rest of us that Victor's song is going to be a hit record. Of course we're going to need you. We'll be touring all over the United States when that song hits the air. Don't you know anything about being a famous recording star? There will be television shows, and magazine interviews. How can you possibly hold that job?"

With a sigh Rosie answered, "Well, I explained all of this to her personal secretary, and he promised I would be given all the time I need if our song does well."

His voice softened, "We'll just have to cross that bridge when we come to it. Can you come over and practice with us this evening? My mom is fixing hamburgers."

"Of course!" she exclaimed.

The familiar music of the band drifted through the air as Rosie emerged from her van. A delicious smell of meat grilling delighted her senses, making her realize how hungry she was. Jackie rushed out to greet her. Taking Rosie's hand in hers, Jackie pulled her toward the garage. "Have you heard your song yet?"

"No, I haven't."

With the excited look of a child giving a Christmas gift, Jackie pulled Rosie along faster. "Oh, hurry! Frank Ryder sent a copy to Billy Ray. Do you know what they put on the flip side? The duet you did with Teddy, *I'm Coming Home*. Oh, Sunshine! Both songs are wonderful!"

Rushing along side of Jackie, Rosie only smiled at Dolly as they hurried past her standing at the grill. When Rosie entered the garage all the band members greeted her. Teddy rushed forward and grasped her by the shoulders. "You are not going to believe how good we sound together on *I'm Coming Home*, it even blew my mind."

Bobby sidled up next to Rosie and said, "Despite Victor's efforts, *Lonely* can't measure up to *I'm Coming Home*."

Rosie was smiling from all the attention, but when Billy Ray put the record on the hi-fi and it began playing the old familiar music, the smile vanished into an expression of awe. The studio had isolated band instruments, and blended them with studio musicians playing background harmonies, layering them underneath with right-out-front vocals. The melody was moving, and the storyline strong. Jackie danced around the room in Billy Ray's arms, and Rosie's eyes filled with tears. When the song was over she wiped at her eyes, "Oh, Bobby! I think you're right."

Billy Ray spoke up and said, "Well, now, wait a minute. You haven't heard your studio sound on *Lonely* yet." He turned the record over and placed the needle down with a slight skip. The sad melancholy music echoed through the room, moving Rosie to immediate sadness. Her voice was clear and deep as she sang the moving words. She stood leaning against a dining table as she listened to the story of a man who forsook love for success and money told with her own vocals. Tears sparkled in her eyes as the song came to its conclusion.

Looking at Teddy she declared, "The studio really does make magic, doesn't it?"

Teddy beamed a self-confident smile and disagreed, "No, sweetheart. We make magic. We're going to be famous, Sunshine. Get ready for it!"

A bright smile illuminated Billy Ray's face as he pulled Rosie into a sincere embrace. "You are our angel!"

Clinching her eyes shut, Rosie wondered how long it would take for the mention of Angel's name not to cause her anguish.

The end of February neared and Ollie Onstott arranged for Rosie to move her family to Boca Raton. She went to her guidance counselor and explained her reason for dropping out of nursing school. The counselor was supportive, and offered good future advice. Lillian, with the help of Andrea and Janie, had the household packed for moving. They would be living in a two bedroom apartment on the estate of Edwina Morgan.

Thrilled that she would be escaping her dull and dim witted teacher, and knowing her days were numbered in Mrs. Skelton's class, Janie began her own terror campaign against the rouge educator. On the Monday of her last week at the Ft Lauderdale School, Mrs. Skelton made the mistake of talking too much about herself.

While discussing *The Wizard of Oz* Mrs. Skelton said, "Well children, I grew up in Kansas, and being that my name is Dorothy, I got lots of teasing in school."

With her head resting in her hand to show her boredom, Janie chimed out, "So, Dorothy, why don't you click your heels together three times and go back to Kansas?" When the class erupted into laughter, Janie felt her courage rise.

Looking at Janie with narrowed eyes, Mrs. Skelton said, "Well, Jane. Why don't you stand up and tell the class what you're favorite part of *The Wizard of Oz* is."

Looking around the room at the smiling faces of her classmates, who seemed to think that Mrs. Skelton had put her on the spot, she rose from the desk. "Well, I liked the part when the wicked witch set the scarecrow on fire." The gasps of astonishment her classmates provided only fueled her desire to say more shocking things. "And, I liked when the tin man rusted in the snow." Taking a moment to indulge in the miserable moans from the class, she continued. "But, I'd have to say my most favorite scene from the movie was when the evil old school teacher put Toto in her bicycle basket and rode away with him." Janie smiled wickedly as more gasps sounded from her class.

The teacher said, "Okay, that's enough. Sit down!" After Janie returned to her seat, Mrs. Skelton called on Jimmy Henderson.

The pudgy little blonde haired boy stood and said, "I especially liked when the Munchkins sang the lollipop song."

Janie feigned a yawn and said, "Poor boy, if he only had a brain." The class burst forth with laughter, and she fought to keep a smile from her face.

Jimmy shouted at Janie, "You shut up!"

Mimicking the classmate Janie echoed, "You shut up!" Then with a toss of her head she remarked, "Munchkin lover!" More laughter filled the class room as Mrs. Skelton attempted to bring order to the chaos.

"Children please!" she exclaimed. "Keep the noise down, and don't encourage Miss Noble. Her comments are unnecessary and ruthless." Standing, the teacher went to step around to the front of her desk, but tripped as the toe of her shoe caught the desk leg.

Janie quickly took the opportunity to say, "What's wrong, Dorothy? Did you sit on your brain too long?" This time a big grin crossed Janie's face as the class laughed out right at their teacher.

With a red face Mrs. Skelton said, "Go to the Principal's office right now young lady. I've had about as much of you as I can take!"

Janie stood from her desk and took a couple of steps toward the door. Turning to her teacher she said, "Don't bother telling me the way; I'll just follow the yellow brick road."

One of her classmates called out, "Pay no attention to the man behind the curtain." And, more laughter followed as she stepped out into the hallway.

When she walked into Mr. Clod's office, he looked up at her through his bushy red eye brows. "What's going on now?"

Slumping into the old familiar chair she sighed, "Ah! There's no place like home."

Ollie Onstott accompanied Rosie and her family on their drive to Boca Raton. A large van and moving men were bringing the rest of their belongings later in the day. Janie and Andrea entertained Ollie with tales of Randy's canine achievements. The little dog sat stoically next to them as if he dared Ollie to get too close to the girls. Rosie sat next to Ollie and watched Lillian try to keep the girls settled. To her surprise, Ollie displayed a clever sense of humor, and played along with all of Janie's clever remarks. Andrea remained quiet and only giggled occasionally.

When the limousine arrived at the Wildwood estate, Janie fell into a silence and stared at the magnificent house with wide eyes. The driver stopped to punch in an electronic code on a panel that made the iron gates slide open. Once the gates were opened, the driver drove the luxury car along a picturesque cobblestone driveway toward a towering house, resembling a grand hotel. The driver pulled the car along an entrance on the side of the great house, away from the circled cobblestone drive that went directly to the front of the house where a grand fountain adorned the center of the circle. Lillian's face held a mixture of awe and fear, while the young girls gaped at the house with opened mouths.

Even Rosie wasn't prepared for this extravagant wealth. She turned to Ollie and asked, "How many rooms does this house have?"

Without hesitation he answered, "Forty-two rooms, and the staff apartments out back. Six of those," he added as an afterthought. "Then there are the stables. That has a small apartment for the grounds keeper." He leaned forward and pointed to a large building with a red tin roof. "Over there is the garage for the cars," he sat back and answered Rosie's next question before she could ask it. "The estate has eighty acres of beautiful trails for horseback riding. There's also a tennis court and swimming pool."
Looking at Lillian he said, "Miss Lillian, I'll bet you will be most impressed with Mrs. Morgan's rose garden. It's truly amazing."

Lillian said to Ollie, "I'm impressed already."

Rosie looked at the girls and said, "Well, I know someone who's going to be excited to see horses again."

With a big smile Janie said, "Oh, yeah. I can't wait to see those horses. What kind are they?"

Ollie turned to exit the car as the driver opened the door, looking over his shoulder at Janie he replied simply, "Thoroughbreds, what else?"

Rosie and her family followed Ollie through the side entrance of the grand house. He pointed out the corridor that led to the kitchen as they stepped into the grand dining. Exquisite artwork decorated the walls. Pointing toward the polished dining table he said, "I'll have to tell you later about some of the people who have sat there." Leading the way along tiled corridors, Ollie stopped occasionally to explain what certain rooms were used for. He showed them the library holding a fabulous display of handsome leather bound books, and more art. The foyer at the front entrance was dominated by a beautiful crystal chandelier. He then led them into an enormous drawing room where a uniformed maid served a cocktail to a lean older woman wearing a dark wig styled into a beautiful coif. She was dressed in a bright orange silk dress with burnt orange paisley print, and huge teardrop shaped diamonds dangled from her earlobes.

Having noticed the intrusion, Edwina Morgan looked at Rosie with her family in tow and only slightly smiled. "Well, I see my new nurse has arrived with her family." Looking at the middle aged maid she said, "Hazel, please offer my guests refreshments."

Turning her attention to the newcomers, Hazel asked, "May I get you something cold to drink?"

Lillian smiled and said, "It might be easier if we just follow you to the kitchen."

With a glance back at Edwina, Hazel got her boss's approval through a silent nod and agreed, "Yes, follow me."

"One moment please, Hazel. I'd like to be introduced before you go." Edwina looked sharply at Ollie who stepped forth immediately and began the introductions.

"Mrs. Morgan, please allow me to introduce Sunshine Moon and her family, Lillian Cox, Jane Noble and Andrea Chavez. Miss Lillian is the acting Grandmother to the younger girls, and assistant to Miss Moon."

Rosie felt the need to elaborate, "Lillian has adopted us, you might say. I don't know how I would manage without her."

Edwina eyed the motley crew of a family with suspicion saying, "How very nice."

Janie spoke up, "Oh, and this is Randy. He's new to the family, but we love him very much." She pointed to the little dog Andrea carried like an infant.

With a look of irritation Edwina said, "Yes, well let's just keep him away from Elvis, and we'll be fine."

With her usual dry sense of humor Janie asked, "Who's Elvis, your hound dog?"

Not missing Janie's humorous remark Mrs. Morgan replied tartly, "Elvis is my white Persian." She motioned with a flick of her wrist toward a large snowy fluff ball lounging leisurely on an antique settee, languishing contently in a puddle of filtered sunlight. "He's very delicate and mustn't be traumatized by your dog." As if understanding the conversation, Randy bared his teeth and stared menacingly at Edwina Morgan. The lady of the house remarked with hostility, "He's snarling at me."

Andrea bounced the dog gently in her arms, "Oh, no. He's smiling at you." At that moment the feisty canine wrestled free of the little girl's embrace and rushed to the sleeping kitty, barking passionately.

The exquisite feline simply curled his tail inward daintily, waited for the dog to get within paw's reach, and *smack!* Elvis sent the little dog flying into a backward somersault.

Randy yelped from the blow then, with tail tucked, ran from the room yelping.

Edwina drew a ragged breath and declared, "Well, that was certainly unfortunate."

The girls ran after Randy, followed by Lillian and Hazel.

Ollie motioned for Rosie to take a seat in a butterscotch colored leather chair. Rosie sank into the most comfortable chair she had ever sat in.

With a cutting look Edwina asked, "Is the contract signed?"

Ollie patted his briefcase and replied, "All's done, Mrs. Morgan."

With a satisfied smile Edwina said to Rosie, "Perhaps you would be interested in my son's music room. He has won many awards for his music productions."

Mentioning music captured Rosie's attention immediately, "He's a producer?"

Still holding her smile, Edwina said, "Oh, yes. Didn't Ollie tell you about my son? You met him in Ft Lauderdale at a New Year's Eve party. I saw your picture with him in the gossip column."

Disbelief consumed Rosie. "You mean, Victor Hart?"

Letting loose with a light laugh Edwina declared, "Yes, isn't this just wonderful? To have you here with me, so I can spare you the time you need to work for Victor."

Now she understood why she was chosen for the job. Rosie stared at Ollie who looked away from her probing gaze. Knowing she had signed a year-long contract made Rosie feel even more manipulated. Trying to hide her anger she asked, "Does Victor know?"

Edwina's smile vanished, "Well, no. But he's going to be thrilled, trust me." Standing from the recliner she stepped to a polished Mahogany bar that held a silver tray with spotless crystal glasses, and a crystal decanter of brandy. Taking up the carafe she poured herself a drink. "I suspect that we will all be very happy with this arrangement." She easily drained the glass and said, "Come, dear. Let me show you Victor's music room."

She led Rosie through a heavy oak door explaining, "This room is where Victor spends most of his time when he's home. Of course he is a busy man, trying to continue his father's contracting business, and follow his music dreams. I always dreamed of Victor being a concert pianist, and he could have easily. But, Charles insisted on pushing him into the contractor's business." Edwina flipped the light switch, giving artificial illumination to the glass enclosed shelves of awards and collectible memorabilia. She practically waltzed across the room to take seat at a white baby grand piano. "After all, it was the contractor's business that made us rich. Tall buildings and resorts have been very good to us. It even allowed me to start up my own cosmetics business." Placing her fingers expertly, she played across the keys expertly, producing tender melody.

Rosie was drawn to the trophy case with sparkling awards and photos of Victor with famous people. One snapshot in particular caught her attention, and she gasped, "Is this Victor with Marilyn Monroe?"

Edwina chuckled, "Yes, he was just breaking into the music business at that time. As you can see, he was much younger there." With a melancholy sound to her voice Edwina said, "Unfortunately, Victor wasn't allowed to pursue his music dreams until after his father's untimely death."

Edwina finished her playing, and turned away from the piano, "I think it's time for Ollie to show you the rest of the house." She paused for a moment and added sternly, "I will expect you to take your meals with me in the dining room, and your bedroom is right next to mine, in case I need you during the night. We will go over your schedule tomorrow. Tonight Victor will be joining us for dinner." Smiling as if coveting a dark secret, she said, "I had a special dress purchased for you to wear. You will find it in your closet. Maria will help you. See that you are ready by seven. Ollie will escort you from your room. There will be a few additional guests tonight, including that repulsive man, Frank Ryder."

Rosie simply said, "Yes, Mrs. Morgan." She turned and walked away with Ollie.

Ollie said, "Let me show you to your bedroom first, then we will go see how the rest of your group are doing with Hazel at their apartment."

Rosie followed up the magnificent staircase and commented, "I never dreamed I would have a room in the main house."

"Your room is here," he turned to a white painted door with a gleaming brass door knob and let it swing open.

Rosie stood awestruck as she let her eyes play across the beautiful room with white carpet. A white loveseat sat near a glass topped coffee table with a brass frame, and a beautiful brass bed dominated the room. She stepped inside and gasped at the crystal vase holding a huge bouquet of fresh white gladiolas. Ollie followed Rosie into the room and pointed to a door. "Your bathroom is in there, and here we have your closet." He pushed open the folding doors to reveal a beautiful ivory colored cocktail dress hanging in the closet.

She rushed to inspect the garment. The dress was sleeveless with gold piping around the neckline and armholes. The hem was decorated with ivory lace embellished with gold thread. A pair of gold colored stilettos sat on the shelf above. Rosie said, "This is the most beautiful dress I've ever seen." Looking at the tag inside she asked, "How did Edwina know what size I would need?"

Ollie admired the reflection from the mirror. "Mrs. Morgan has worked with models for many years. I would think she could guess the size of anyone."

Closing her eyes Rosie said, "I almost feel like I've stepped into a dream, but then I fear it may actually be a nightmare."

Ollie said confidently, "You'll do just fine."

That evening Rosie allowed Maria to style her hair into an up-do that was held in place by gleaming gold combs embellished with sparkling rhinestones. As she stood before the mirror wearing the beautiful dress, Rosie was shocked when Maria held out a velvet box for her to open. Her mouth fell into gaping astonishment when she opened the box to reveal lovely pearl earrings hanging from a gold studded post on a tiny gold chain. When she put the earrings on Rosie starred at her reflection.

The dark skinned Cuban girl said with a thick accent, "Aye, you look beautiful."

Taking note of Maria's loveliness, Rosie could only remember what Dr. Thayer had said about Edwina Morgan, and how she chose to be surrounded with beautiful people. Maria picked up a small bottle of perfume from the makeup table and dabbed a tiny amount on Rosie's neck, "Just a wee bit. You must never wear too much perfume in Mrs. Morgan's presence." Maria replaced the perfume bottle and said, "However, she does like just the slightest hint of scent. She calls it an illusion of perfume."

Pursing her lips with the subtle color of shimmering pink lip gloss Rosie asked, "What time is it, Maria?"

Taking Rosie by the shoulders, Maria said, "It is time to go."

At the bottom of the staircase, Ollie was waiting. Holding out his arm he said, "Edwina gave me strict orders to not let you enter the dining room alone."

Taking his arm Rosie asked, "Is Victor here yet?"

Looking at her briefly he answered, "Yes."

The dinner guests sitting at the table fell silent when Rosie entered the room. Victor stood near a tea cart with Frank pouring scotch whiskey from a bottle. Edwina sat at the head of the table and said, "Ollie, dear. Bring my new assistant to sit here beside me."

Rosie smiled when she heard Edwina call to her son, "Victor, I have a surprise for you. Let me introduce my new nursing assistant, Miss Sunshine Rose Moon. And, for those of you who don't know it yet, Sunshine Rose has recorded a beautiful ballad Victor wrote and composed himself. I have no doubt that it will be on the radio airwaves any day now."

Victor replaced the bottle of scotch and carried his glass back to the table where he was placed opposite Rosie. "What a wonderful surprise, Sunshine. I'm almost at a loss for words, but let me say welcome."

With a blush Rosie answered, "Thank you, Victor."

Sensing the presence at his side Victor asked, "And, you remember Frank?" Rosie nodded a greeting to the silent Frank Ryder. "So let's introduce you to the rest of our friends and guests."

Rosie greeted gossip columnist Ritzie Watkins along with a handsome elder gentleman named Brock Bailey. Also, there were two of Victor's studio musicians named Glen Thompson and Terry Fields. Glen was a handsome rosy cheeked man with perfectly combed golden blonde hair, enhanced by expertly groomed sideburns. Terry was a small man with wavy dark hair.

Victor remarked, "I think it's obvious that we have the makings of a sensational singing star. Take her exceptional beauty and couple that with her extraordinary voice, and walla! A star is born."

Holding a champagne glass to her lips Ritzie asked, "Can we hear you sing after dinner, Sunshine? After all, we have plenty of musicians to accompany you."

Glen and Terry agreed with Ritzie, and Edwina prodded, "Oh, please say you will, dear."

Catching a searching gaze from Victor, Rosie smiled sweetly and nodded with close eyes as she said meekly, "Okay, if you insist."

Victor raised his glass and toasted, "To our brightest new star, Sunshine Rose, and to the bee!"

Rosie raised her glass and said, "To the bee!"

Chapter Thirty-Two
Blackmail, Marriage and Perfume

The weeks at Wildwood catapulted into months as Rosie was thrown into her nursing duties and recording sessions. Luckily she was able to do vocals for the album without the band, as the technicians magically added her tracks to the music and vocals of other singers without her physical presence. Only on occasion did she share the sound booth with Teddy and Billy Ray. The single, *Lonely* had still not gotten any on air play in Florida, or any other state.

Victor arranged for Ollie to be the band's manager, and it was Ollie who secured high profile events for publicity. It seemed that whatever Victor Hart wanted, Victor Hart got. He had caused an angry uproar with the band months earlier, when Victor insisted the name of the band be changed from Dixie Dirt Devils to what he considered the more sophisticated, mysterious name of Gemini Rain. And, so the band, Gemini Rain, was scheduled to perform popular favorites along with some of their own music at state fairs, various musical events and the most popular nightclubs in the South.

Suddenly, Rosie was thrust onto a bus for weeks at a time. The bus was none other than a rolling motel room, and because she was the only female, her room was secluded at the back with a private bath. The male members had to sleep in bunks stacked three high, with a narrow hallway between them that led to Rosie's room.

Under the fashion influence of Edwina, Victor insisted Rosie wear modest, yet chic outfits for her appearances. The rest of the band was allowed to wear ragged jeans and denim shirts topped with fringed vests. Teddy even wore a tired floppy hat to hide his thinning scalp. But she always stepped out in sequined jeans, and floral silk blouses with flowing sleeves. Her hair and makeup was always done to Victor's (or rather, Edwina's) instructions.

As always, after a performance the band would sit at a table to meet fans. They would autograph t-shirts and programs, as well as the single of *Lonely* with *I'm Coming Home* on the flip side. After playing at a festival in Orlando, Rosie was surprised at the interest the festival goers paid her. One young girl asked for her autograph on a Gemini Rain t-shirt, and then began plying her with personal questions.

The teenager pulled her own long hair to one side and asked, "What's the name of your hairstyle, Sunshine Rose?"

At a loss for an honest answer Rosie quipped, "I call it the Gemini Gypsy."

The following month, Rosie opened a fashion magazine and discovered a new fad hairstyle called *Gemini Gypsy*.

The band's promotions were grueling, making Rosie regret her complaints of nursing school. They seldom slept in a motel, mostly sleeping on the bus and showering in dressing rooms. She began to lose weight, as well as sleep. They posed for professional photos dressed in their concert fashions with Rosie always out front as Bobby, Teddy, Billy Ray and Jeff shadowed her.

The bus rolled on, and the band continued to play the scheduled dates, and the days flew off the calendar. When Rosie came home for a short break she was truly surprised by the friendship that had blossomed between Edwina and Janie. They were extremely comfortable with one another, playing cards and board games together. Edwina seemed to bask in the youth of her friend. Janie's sense of humor had not waned a bit, as she continued to draw cartoon caricatures of the President and other newsworthy people of the day. Edwina laughed at her art, exclaiming they were worthy of publishing. She even insisted Janie sit with her for her casual meals.

During one such meal Edwina asked, "Victor, dear. When do you plan to announce your plans to run for senate?"

Frank coughed as if the idea literally choked him. With an almost closed eyed squint at his mother, Victor said, "Whenever you insist, Mother."

The meal remained painfully hushed, with only tiny bits of small talk. Finally, Edwina dropped her fork noisily against her plate. "This dinner is completely boring! Jane should tell us all a joke, right Jane?"

Janie mumbled, "Well, I don't know."

Victor said, "Yes! Young Jane, tell us a joke, please."

She responded with a bored tone, "Well, I did hear Tony Orlando was kidnapped."

Victor picked up his wine glass, "Oh, really?"

Janie answered, "Yes, the police searched all night for him, and finally found him at the crack of dawn."

Choking on his wine, Victor wound up spitting into his napkin. Edwina laughed until she had tears. When the chuckles ebbed, Edwina looked to Victor and said, "I think you should announce your senate run next week. I've had Ollie researching the opponents, and I've decided the time is right."

Victor carefully put his fork to the side of his plate. "So, you have all the little details ironed out do you?" He tossed his napkin on the table next to his unfinished meal, and left the room. Frank excused himself, and followed Victor's path.

After the meal Edwina dismissed Janie to her room while she instructed Rosie to join her in the drawing room. Taking up her glass of wine Rosie followed the lady of the manor. Edwina took seat, and reaching to a side table, withdrew a folded newspaper clipping and handed it to Rosie. It revealed a newspaper photo of Andrea as a missing child the year before.

Without softening her words Rosie asked, "Did you steal this from me, or did you have Hazel do it for you?"

Edwina smiled confidently, "There's no need for hostility, dear."

Slinging the newspaper article onto the coffee table Rosie asked, "What are you planning to do with this information?"

Edwina's smile vanished, "I intend to tell you exactly what I expect from you for my silence."

Rosie's heart fell. "*Your* silence?" she asked in a harsh whisper. "You're going to blackmail me?"

With a soft chuckle Edwina said, "Oh, please! I simply want to make an arrangement with you, my dear. Your contract as my nursing assistant is nothing, now that you are an up and coming recording star. I have a much better plan for you." Edwina chose her words carefully as Rosie stared with skepticism. "I think you would make a perfect wife for a state senator."

The room began to spin. "Victor?" She asked in disbelief, "You want me to marry Victor?"

Edwina smiled wickedly, "That's exactly what I want of you, Sunshine. So from now on, Ollie will accompany you on all of your tours to see that you remain pristine for the upcoming nuptials."

Shaking her head slowly Rosie asked, "But, why me? Knowing what you know, why would you want me associated with Victor and his campaign?"

Edwina inhaled slowly and said, "It's because I know what I know that will keep you in check my dear. As long as I have this information, you will walk the line, and be a perfect asset to my son's campaign. You see, Sunshine. Today he is running for senate, but tomorrow he will be running for the White House." Edwina sat back and grinned like the Cheshire cat saying prophetically, "You, my dear, will make Jackie Kennedy look like Little Orphan Annie."

Shock settled over Rosie as she comprehended Edwina's plan. Ever since that photograph had appeared in the newspaper proclaiming Victor Hart had found a new love, Edwina had schemed until she got Rosie locked tight in her web. Rosie was nothing more than Edwina Morgan's puppet, and so, it seemed, was Victor.

Spring was blossoming into summer across the lush gardens of Wildwood. The band was scheduled for dates in Nashville, Atlanta and Charlotte. It was during a hot afternoon when Rosie relaxed beside the pool that Maria came running onto the patio holding a transistor radio and babbling excitedly in Spanish, "Su cancion esta en la radio! Escucha su musica!"

Rosie was dumbfounded until she heard the song *I'm Coming Home* playing. With gusto they danced around the pool, and screamed joy when the disc jockey announced the name of the band as Gemini Rain.

Janie rushed out saying, "Sunshine! I heard your song on the radio!"

The band embarked on a two week stint. Their songs were to be audience-tested before studio sessions began. When Rosie returned to Wildwood, Victor Hart was waiting for her with champagne and roses. Maria was given orders to put away Rosie's luggage as Victor ushered her into the drawing room where Edwina waited. As Rosie entered she locked eyes with the smug Mrs. Morgan, offering a cold smile.

Victor put a glass of champagne in Rosie's hand. "Mother has confided to me that you have agreed to a marriage, and I thought this would be an opportune time to sit back and make some arrangements."

Tired from the road, Rosie downed the champagne and motioned for more. Victor hastily refilled her glass as he spoke, "We can be married in a small intimate ceremony, before you leave for your next tour. I've announced my bid for the senate seat, and if it's okay with you, I'll have Ritzie announce our engagement in tomorrow's edition." He smiled with confidence, "I do hope you will be able to handle the pressures of politics, my dear."

Edwina interrupted, "Oh, Victor! Sunshine is a hardy farm girl, who's handled her celebrity status amazingly well. Of course she will be a perfect political wife."

Victor sank into a chair opposite Rosie and held his glass high, "Very well, Sunshine. Let's toast to a successful marriage and political career."

Putting her lips to the rim of the glass, Rosie did not drink, but boldly asked, "And, what if you don't get elected, Victor? What will become of the marriage then?"

The handsome man wiped the wine from his mustache with the back of his index finger, and tossed his head back, laughing. Edwina joined him, and they laughed until Rosie began to feel uneasy. Her thoughts rushed to Kid, and the extortion marriage he had fallen into. How ironic, she thought. That both of them had befallen the same ultimate fate of arranged marriages through blackmail.

The band had a four week break for rehearsing and recording, before going back on the road. Edwina arranged a small ceremony in the rose garden with a handful of famous and important attendees. Rosie was dressed in an extravagant ivory gown glistening with tiny seed pearls sewn across the bodice. The veil was short and simple, and her hair was styled up. With a heavy heart she went through the ceremony robotically. Certain members of the paparazzi were invited to snap photos for newspapers and magazines, but it was the professional wedding photographer working for Edwina that was given complete access to the famous couple. A five piece band played waltz medleys. When the time came for Rosie to dance with her husband, she let her feet follow his lead, when they really wanted to run.

Janie was present, dressed in a beautiful yellow dress with puffed short sleeves. The yellow satin sash tied into a big bow around her waist, and her hair was styled smooth and straight. Rosie caught Janie looking at her with empathy, and wondered if she had a clue as to the reality of their predicament.

When the time came for Victor to walk away with his new bride, the guest lined up to catch the bouquet and to throw rice. Rosie got a quick glance at the scowl on Frank's face as she tossed the wedding bouquet to a small gathering of single women. Victor made a sling shot of her garter belt toward the eligible bachelors, with the garter falling at Frank's feet. They ran through the traditional rain storm of rice out of the garden and back into the mansion.

Victor took her by the hand, "Your room in is my suite now." He pulled her along beside him up the staircase and down the hall. Opening the door he stopped and said, "Oh, wait. We have to do this right, don't we?" He scooped her into his arms and carried her across the threshold. Once inside he set her feet onto plush carpet. "This is your room," he said and walked to double doors, swinging them open. "You see there is your closet to the right, and your bathroom to the left."

Confused, she asked, "But, where is your bedroom?"

Victor smiled and pivoted on his heel as he pointed at double doors across the sitting room. "There," he said simply. "Why don't you relax in a bubble bath, and get dressed for our night out." He stepped away, but then stopped to say, "You understand that we have to hit all the posh night spots, just to have our picture splashed in the papers about our marriage." Smiling he turned and went into his own bedroom and closed the door.

Victor and Rosie dined with influential people at a posh resort in Boca Raton. She was treated like a celebrity, often blinded by flashbulbs. The evening ended in the wee hours of the morning after she and Victor had made appearances at three elite local gathering spots for the wealthy and famous. When the evening ended, and they returned to their suite at the mansion, Rosie was silently thankful when Victor disappeared into his own room, after saying an exhausted goodnight.

When the short break for the band was over, and Rosie boarded the bus with Ollie to make the next tour, she was greeted with hostility. Teddy said, "If you were going to marry the producer, the least you could have done was invite us to the wedding." His tone of voice was nothing short of lethal.

Billy Ray stared at her with glistening eyes, "I'm in shock, Sunshine, absolute shock."

Tears sprang to her eyes as she shot back, "Well, I wasn't exactly in control of the guest list you know." Anguish engulfed her as she saw the blank stares of cynicism from the group. With a stifled cry she ran to her room and closed herself in.

She lay on her bunk as the bus rolled across the smooth miles of highway. Ollie knocked at her door to offer food, but she sent him away. Never before had she felt so imprisoned and helpless. The realization of the energy she was expected to produce for Victor in his campaign, and the hours of time she would have to spend in the recording studio, coupled with the weeks of touring, left her in hopeless tears.

While waiting backstage to perform, Ted and Bobby glared at Rosie crossly while Jeff stood next to her supportively. Ted made the remark, "Marriage for money never makes anyone happy." Ted turned to Jeff and asked, "What's the wager this farce of a marriage will fall apart in less than twelve months?"

Jeff sadly answered, "That's a cruel wager, and I want no part of it."

Facing her foe, Rosie stepped up to Ted. "This marriage has nothing to do with money. And, I would appreciate it if you leave my personal life out of this public one."

With cold piercing eyes Ted glared at her, "Nothing to do with money?" He stepped back and began to laugh.

The cruel actions of Ted didn't go unnoticed by Billy Ray. He put an arm around Rosie, "He's just angry that he didn't get to come to the wedding and rub elbows with some of those high profile celebrities. He'll get over it."

"I hope I can," she sighed while fat drops of tears rolled down her cheeks. She wanted so badly to confide to someone her misery. Desperately, she wanted to talk with Kid and unload her tale of misfortune and bad luck. But, her busy schedule had left her little time for a long telephone conversation. She had only managed a short call to her father to explain to him her newly married state.

Billy Ray tenderly wiped the tear drops from her face. He whispered, "I can see you're not happy. I don't know why you married Victor, but I think you did it without wanting too."

A movement in the backstage shadows drew her attention to Ollie. Rosie quelled her emotions at the notice of him. The roadies cleared the stage and announced it was time for the band to take their positions. She turned her back as the rest of the group filed past to take up their instruments. Lingering a long moment, she finally stepped onstage and took her spot next to Ted. As the lights came up, she glanced at Ted whose face was plastered with a plastic smile for the audience, and even though she tried, she was too disheartened to fake a smile of her own.

With a whirlwind summer of concert tours, and television and radio guest appearances, Rosie was also faced with the campaign tour of Victor Hart. The husband that she had yet to share an intimate night with was always careful to appear loving and affectionate with his wife during speaking engagements, and televised promotions. Rosie had gained a full time employee named Amber who took care of her wardrobe and hairstyling. One evening before a campaign dinner, Rosie emerged from her bathroom, her pale skin blotched and red from some nerve induced rash. Amber rushed to find a dress that would hide the blotched skin, and hurriedly added layers of makeup to her face.

While apologizing to her assistant, Amber sweetly shushed Rosie, "Everything is going to be just fine. You don't really think you're the only person this has ever happen to, do you?" Amber smiled and slung back her long blonde hair. Her blue eyes danced within the radiance of her youthful face as she said soothingly, "This, too, shall pass."

With Amber's help, Rosie endured the grueling labor of the campaign trail, and managed to do vocals for the album. On more than one occasion she rushed from a campaign fund raiser to catch the bus for a performance hundreds of miles away. To make matters worse, Edwina had her chemistry department create a signature fragrance called *Sunshine*. Rosie was flown to Aruba to shoot photo ads for the product. When time was extremely tight, she was flown on Victor's private jet to concert destinations. The friction between Rosie and the band grew worse, as she was often too exhausted to rehearse.

One sultry night in late August, Billy Ray tapped on Rosie's door as she lay quietly in her bunk. She opened the door and peeked out to see him looking tired and haggard. Letting the door swing wide, she threw her arms around his neck and pulled him inside. "Billy Ray! How did life get so hard?" she cried against his neck.

Peeling her arms away, Billy Ray pushed her to sit on the bench at her dressing table. "I can't for the life of me understand how you manage it, Sunshine. Just look at yourself! This life of politician's wife and music star is killing you, and you don't even know it."

Looking into the mirror Rosie could see the cheekbones protruding from what had once been a healthy, nurtured face. "Oh, Billy Ray!" she exclaimed as she put her hands to her face. "I do look awful don't I?"

Taking her hands in his Billy Ray asked, "Why did you do this to yourself, Sunshine? Why on earth did you marry Victor?"

With a harsh whisper she replied, "Ted's right. I didn't marry him for love." Then she quickly added, "But it wasn't for money either!"

Unable to understand, Billy Ray shook his head. "Well, whatever it is, I'm sure you know what you're doing." He sighed heavily, "I've got some bad news that's going to shake up the band, but I wanted to tell you first." His eyes locked with hers, "I've been drafted."

A dull pain gripped her stomach, and for a moment Rosie was unable to breathe. Feeling hot tears she cried, "No!" With the universe spinning around her she crumpled into his arms, sobbing. Soon there was knocking at the door as Ollie and Amber begged to be let in.

"What happened here?" Ollie demanded as Amber soothed Rosie's tear stained face.

Billy Ray shrugged as Bobby, Jeff and Ted crowded the corridor, saying, "I told her about getting my draft notice, and she took it harder than I thought she would."

Ted exploded, "Holy hell! What are we going to do without you, Billy Ray? That's the end of the band! We're finished!"

Something about Ted's ranting sparked hope in Rosie. The ruin of the band could mean only one thing for her. Rest, much needed rest. Ollie put a glass of water to her lips. Holding out his palm with two white tablets he instructed her to take the medicine. She swallowed them down with a few gulps of water, and then nestled back into the downy soft pillows. Amber comforted her as Ollie pushed everyone away from Rosie's door.

With a quivering voice Rosie asked, "Do you think the war is near the end?"

Placing a cool cloth to her forehead Amber answered, "No, I don't. But, Billy Ray will be fine. Perhaps Victor can do something to get him placed in a safer position."

Rosie calmed at the mention of Victor's influence. "Yes!" she whispered with hope, "Victor can keep him safe."

Closing her eyes, she fell into a lulled trance with the humming tires of the bus. Somewhere during her drug induced sleep she dreamed of Doc Campbell and Kid. They were playing cards, tossing the unique coins into a heap on the old battered table. The oil burning lamp cast a golden light throughout the room. Rosie approached with happiness to see them again. She sat at the table beside Kid, and poured a shot glass of whiskey for herself. With the glass to her lips she asked the doctor, "You're not really dead, are you?"

During the following weeks Rosie became more fragile despite the efforts of Amber's constant mothering. She ate the fresh fruit and nutritious meals Amber put before her. The vitamins and other nutrition supplements were downed with unpleasantness. Janie was often comforting. The tomboy now wore skirts with white blouses, while her hair was ironed and restrained with exquisite satin ribbons, tortoise combs and jeweled pins. Andrea blossomed in the care of Maria and her son Eduardo. Andrea and Eduardo were bosom buddies, and shared a governess with Janie.

On a warm August morning, Rosie sat on the balcony in the suite she shared with Victor. She contemplated why Victor never showed her any interest as a wife, and what would become of the band without Billy Ray. Suddenly, hope flared inside her as she saw a life altering possibility. She reached for the phone and dialed off the number to Victor's office. The receptionist answered and Rosie asked to speak with Victor.

Victor picked up the phone saying, "Sunshine? Are you all right?"

Trying to sound cheerful she said, "Yes, why wouldn't I be?"

"You never call me at the office."

"Oh, I've just been thinking about Billy Ray's replacement. I know you said Glen or Terry could fill in here and there, but I know just the musician we need, my cousin from Michigan. Remember when I gave you some music of my friends from back home? His band was one of them."

Victor sighed, "Why don't you give me his number, and I'll call him for an interview."

"I was hoping you could send Frank to meet him."

The phone line was silent for a moment, and Victor replied, "I'll send Glen to interview him, how's that?"

Hope soared within, "Oh! He sings, too."

"Let's not upset Teddy, now. You know how sensitive he is."

With a tone of sarcasm she retorted, "Don't you mean *insecure*?"

Chuckling from her comment Victor said, "Listen, if you want your cousin, you can have him. I'll send Glen to pitch him a contract."

Smiling for the first time in weeks, Rosie said, "Thank you, Victor."

The week before Billy Ray left, Kid came to Boca Raton to meet the band. He was welcomed into the mansion, and settled into a guest room next to Janie's. He and Billy Ray struck up an instant friendship, while Ted seemed to hold a distrust of the Michigan musician. Rosie felt renewed when Kid held her close, whispering encouragement. She had told him all about her extortion marriage over the phone one night when she called him from her hotel room in Nashville.

That fateful night when Rosie had divulged her secret to Kid, she was sedated with medication and wine. "Oh, Kid!" she had cried, "How will we ever be together if I'm a senator's wife?"

With soft words he soothed, "Don't worry about that, Sunny. We'll find a way."

Watching her beloved Kid play rehearsals with the band enthralled her. Just having him close enough to touch brought her manic happiness. Victor worked hard to get Billy Ray a safer assignment during his tour of duty. The night before his departure, Rosie managed to pull Billy Ray aside and tell him from her heart how she adored him, and only wanted him to stay safe.

"When you get back from your tour you will be part of the band again," Rosie told him insistently.

The band returned to the grueling task of touring while they squeezed precious moments into the studio to finish the album. And, while the disc jockeys continued to ignore *Lonely* they frequently played *I'm Coming Home.* As the weeks faded the song charted on billboard's pop chart at number twenty-two. Ted was extremely proud, because he had written the lyrics, and he and Billy Ray had composed the music. A new enthusiasm was born, as the festival crowds recognized the song at concerts and cheered wildly for it. By the end of September, Rosie was having roses thrown onstage while Ted was bombarded with soft teddy bears. By the end of November the album was finished, and would be hitting the record shops in mid December. The album photographs had been redone with Kid standing beside Billy Ray.

Billboard magazine rated *I'm Coming Home* with four and one-half bullets. A magazine reviewer wrote: *Gemini Rain is THE band to hear!* Fans had begun hounding radio stations with requests for the popular song. By the end of the New Year's first month the band's first album, titled *I'm Coming Home,* had sold over one hundred thousand copies. Bobby and Ted received screams from enthusiastic young girls when they performed the album's title song, and in March *I'm Coming Home* reached number twelve on the charts.

In the spring of 1972, Gemini Rain appeared on a national television talk show with celebrity Doris Davidson. Doris spoke of the single *I'm Coming Home* that had now reached number seven on the charts. The studio audience cheers became a roar of ovation when the lights came up to reveal the band playing introduction to the popular song. After the performance, Rosie was called onstage for a personal interview.

The scrutiny on her private life left her a quivering mass of nerves. When she joined the band backstage she was still shaking. Kid put his arm around her. "Why are you so nervous?"

Giving him a curt look she asked, "Well, why don't you try explaining how you became a senator's wife and rock star in the same year, and see if you get nervous?"

Pulling her close he said, "Guess what I got in the mail yesterday?" Looking down at her with a happy smile he exclaimed, "My divorce papers, I'm free at last!" He grabbed her in a solid embrace and swirled her into a flying circle, her feet dancing on air.

Suddenly they were confronted by Ollie. He looked all about, as if paparazzi were hiding around the corners. Pushing herself free of Kid's embrace Rosie laughed, "I'm so happy for you!"

The following day, Rosie joined Kid and Janie for horseback riding on the estate. As the sleek thoroughbreds carried the riders smoothly along the trails, Janie asked a sudden question, "Why did you marry Victor, knowing that he's a fag?"

Kid indulged his little cousin, asking cattily, "Yes, Sunny, why did you marry a fag?"

Rosie asked with consternation, "How can you say that about Victor, after all he's done for us?"

With a puzzled look Janie said, "Uh, because it's true."

Kid laughed and said, "Oh, come on. Don't act like you didn't know."

She put her hand in the air to silence him, "Answer my question, Jane. Why would you say such a thing?"

Squirming in her saddle Janie replied reluctantly, "Like I said, it's true. I saw Frank and Victor in the barn one day doing the *no pants dance*. I wouldn't make up stuff about people. You know me better than that."

Feeling a sick panic stir within her, Rosie exclaimed, "My God! Are you sure?"

Her reign loosened and the horse pranced restlessly in place. "I peeked through the crack to see what the grunting was all about. I'm sure."

"Which one was, oh never mind, I don't even want to know," mumbled Kid.

Taking his lead Janie said, "I saw Victor with his face pushed down in the hay, while Frank did the dancing."

Kid exclaimed, "Dang! You'd think with all his money Victor would get to be the man."

Finding it difficult to breathe Rosie said, "Go ahead without me. I'm going back."

Grabbing her horse's bridle, Kid said, "Now, look. There's no reason we can't continue our trail ride." Looking to Janie he asked, "Right?"

She agreed brightly, "Right."

Dizzying tears welled in Rosie's eyes as she whispered, "Let me go, Kid." When he didn't release the bridle she took the reins and slapped him across his forearm. Then she snapped the reigns backward across her horse's flank. The steed sprang into motion and was off and running toward the barn.

Jerking his hand back he cursed, "Damn it to hell! That hurt."

With a dry look Janie replied, "No doubt."

He narrowed his eyes in the direction of the retreating equine and said, "You wait. I'm going to get her."

Pulling her long smooth ponytail from her back, Janie inspected it carefully as she said, "Go ahead, but I'm riding on."

With a disapproving look he asked, "Why?"

She smiled slyly and answered, "Because, Sunshine has a fascination for barns, and I'm not wasting time sitting around waiting for her to show you the tack room."

Tossing her a look of confusion, Kid took pursuit of Rosie. He rode into the barn as she was unsaddling her horse. "Stop that right now," he ordered. "You agreed to a trail ride, so just get back on that horse and let's go."

Blinding tears streamed down her face as she spat, "Just leave me alone!"

Dismounting, Kid let the reigns fall into the sawdust. He walked to Rosie, taking her forcefully by the shoulders, "Damn it, Sunny. You really didn't know? How is that possible?"

Her face contorted painfully as she gasped, "I'm just so stupid!"

Caressing her shoulder tenderly he softly said, "Don't ever say you're stupid."

Allowing him to comfort her, she sobbed with anguish, "Why didn't I see?"

Feeling her pain he asked, "He's never made love to you, has he?"

She could only shake her head no, and wiped her face with the backs of her hands. "I just thought it was medical. You know? Like Ed." Again, she broke into tears.

Kid tilted her face to look at him and said softly, "We're together now. We will make everything right, just like we always planned." He kissed her cheek lovingly. Then he kissed her forehead, only to kiss her other cheek. Soon he was kissing her lips, and she responded.

With a furious passion they became entangled in one another. Feeling a wild abandon that had been absent in her life for many months, she fumbled with his belt buckle, while he pulled at her blouse. Blindly she led him into the tack room where fresh bales of hay lined the wall.

Chapter Thirty-Three
If Love Were Flowers

Victor's face turned dark with anger as he listened to Rosie's livid ranting. "This schedule is ludicrous! How can you let Ollie book us for so many concerts? I'll never have time for anything!"

"He is your production manager," Victor explained calmly. "That's the nature of the business, Sunny. Fame is fleeting. You have to take it while you can."

"But, I don't want it! I never wanted it!"

With a cold hard look Victor asked, "What *do* you want?"

Trying to control her conflicting emotions she said, "I want my family."

Loosening his tie Victor asked, "And, what can I do about that?"

"I just think that my entire family should live in the mansion with me. Andrea and Lillian are still in the apartment, and I want Kid to be a permanent resident."

Victor smiled and reached for a cigarette. "I have no objections, but it does seem that Andrea is very happy in the apartments with Maria and Eduardo. And, I have no qualms whatsoever about Kid staying where he is right now. In the room next to Jane is just fine." With narrowed eyes he said, "You know, I often wonder just exactly what my mother has on you, to keep you blackmailed into this marriage."

Feeling uncomfortable with his twist in conversation she replied, "Well, I'm a firm believer that some secrets should remain secret."

Victor said smugly, "Yes, indeed. Some secrets should never be shared. Still I can't help but think that you must have committed murder, or something."

With a cruel laugh she retorted, "Yes, or something."

Grinding out the unfinished cigarette Victor shot back, "Have your family with you anywhere you choose, Sunshine." He stood and glared at her with his dark eyes shining like chunks of coal. "Just be sure that you don't get pregnant by your cousin."

Anger flared through her with his stinging remark. She stepped inside her bedroom slamming the door harshly behind her. Shaking with rage Rosie wondered how Victor could so easily see through her, when it took so long to see through him.

On a stormy afternoon in May, Victor called Rosie at Wildwood from his office. "Sunny, I've been called away on urgent senate business, and I need for you and Ollie to oversee a new group at the studio." His voice was edgy and stressed as he asked, "You can handle this for me, can't you my darling?"

His sentimental words stroked her heart with fondness, "Why do you need me? Where's Frank?"

"He's at home with bronchitis."

"I'm not sure of how much help I can be, but I'll go."

Victor's voice sounded relieved as he said, "Thank you, my dear. I promise to reward you for this. I know I don't tell you often enough how very much I appreciate you."

Responding to his kindness she replied, "It's not necessary to say it, Victor. We both know that we love each other."

A long silence clung to the wire between them, and Rosie was beginning to feel that she had said the wrong thing. Victor finally said, "Yes, Sunny. I do love you. More than you will ever know." With those words being said, he hung up.

Rain continued to fall through the night and into the following morning. The studio reception office seemed unusually quiet as Rosie and Ollie filed through. Glen worked with the technicians while the band played instrumentals. Stepping next to Glen she peered at the band playing familiar music. Her heart leapt when she saw Lewis on lead guitar and Darby on drums. Overwhelmed with joy, she searched the other faces for familiarity. When she saw Heather on keyboard with Zeke playing bass, and Barron on acoustic guitar, she gasped in astonished happiness. Rosie laughed, "I know these guys! We all grew up together in Alabama!"

With a big smile Glen waited for the instrumental to be recorded before breaking in to announce Rosie's presence, "Okay, great job! Listen folks, I understand you all know this young lady here by my side. And, if any of you don't remember her, then let me refresh your memory. Here is our hottest new female vocalist. The lovely Sunshine Rose!"

Rosie leaned into the microphone. "Hey, guys!"

There was a lot of commotion in the booth as her old friends recognized her and shouted out greetings. But Rosie only had eyes for one, Lewis. His hair was still short from military service. He looked tan and healthy. His eyes locked with hers, and he smiled. Still standing at the microphone, she said, "Welcome to *Ryder/Hart-Strings Music Studio*. I'm so happy to see you! Thanks for coming."

More excited shouts and greetings came from the group, while Lewis stood quietly holding his guitar with a disbelieving look. She stepped back, letting Glen take control, and joined Ollie. Reaching across Ollie's workspace, she turned his notebook so she could read his notations. Ollie's notes read: *Purple Sage band at studio #1, Tuesday - nine o'clock.* Rosie said out loud, "Purple Sage." Looking at Ollie she replied, "Sound's rather homegrown."

Glen instructed Lewis and Heather to enter the booth for vocals. It was excruciatingly hard for Rosie to see Heather struggle to sing the duet. Rosie knew the song well, because Glen had attempted to record it with her and Ted. But, being the perfectionist he was, Glen scratched their attempt. Showing his disgust with Heather, he called for a cut, "Okay, Heather. I want you to take a short break while Sunshine sings this with Lewis. And, pay close attention, because she's very familiar with how I want it done."

Nodding in agreement, Heather left the booth. Stunned at Glen's instructions, Rosie slowly stood and removed the gray silk blazer she wore with matching skirt. "Well, give me a moment to get ready." She unpinned her chestnut mane and shook it loose. Unbuttoning her sleeves, she rolled them up, and stepped into the booth. He stared at her with his soft hazel eyes reflecting particles of citrine, and Rosie felt an old familiar connection with him. Smiling with closed lips she reached out and gave him a slight embrace. "Welcome home, soldier."

He blinked as if dazed, "Thank you, Rosie." He turned to Glen with a thumbs-up sign.

The music played and Lewis took the lead in the soft ballad of love lost and yearned for. His voice was sweet and clear, and he devoured Rosie with his eyes as he sang the phrase, "*The love we had before, could be ours once more.*"

Moved by the melody, she stepped to the microphone to sing, but he didn't step aside. With her mouth just inches away from his, she sang, "*No matter what I do, I just can't stop loving you.*" Her eyes widened in surprise when he put his hand on hers, holding it captive around the microphone stand.

An undeniable emotion swept through her. Just as her father had said, she wasn't over Lewis. Blending together their voices for the final stanza, they locked eyes and sang with trembling emotion. When the music ended, and Glen shouted his approval, they still stood clinging to one another, their hands entwined on the microphone stand.

Finally, he swallowed hard and stepped away with a little laugh. "It's been a long time since you and I sang together."

Glen said, "Take five. Lewis, drink some of that hot lemonade for your vocal cords. I've got a call to make."

Rosie led the way from the booth to the urn with Glen's special hot lemonade. She asked Heather, "How's your mom?"

"Real good," she answered. "And congratulations on your success with Gemini Rain. You've got a lot to tell me, huh?"

Feeling like nothing had ever come between them Rosie said, "Yes. I really do."

The rest of the day was spent with Glen putting the band through grueling paces. He even insisted on having lunch brought in to save time for the session. By six o'clock Rosie was exhausted, and so was the band. Glen called a wrap with instructions to be back at the studio by eight the next morning. Rosie collected her things, and called out a good night to the group as she and Ollie prepared to leave. Standing alone in the foyer waiting for Ollie, she was taken by complete surprise when Lewis suddenly came up behind her. He grasped her by the hand, and with a big smile pulled her outdoors onto the sidewalk.

"Hurry," he exclaimed, "Let's get out of here before the rest of that motley crew come along!"

Laughing like a misbehaving child, Rosie ran away with him. The rain clouds had cleared, and the evening sun was mild. They ducked into a small café giggling and holding hands. Sipping wine, they talked of all the things they had been through the past two years. He spoke briefly of some things he'd seen in Vietnam, and happily unbuttoned his shirt to show her the tattoos he'd gotten while overseas.

"You'll have to come around behind me to get a good look at them," he advised with a devilish smile.

Stepping around the table she gazed at his bare back, and gasped at the sight. On his left shoulder was a modest tattoo in black ink of a heavenly angel, and on the right was a menacing Satan in black ink enhanced by red. "Oh! They're just like the drawing you did years ago."

Reclaiming her seat, while Lewis buttoned his shirt she asked, "How's Opal and Bob? Are your grandparents doing well?"

"Well, I know you heard about the assassination attempt on George Wallace. That certainly upset Granddaddy. But, other than that everyone's okay." He folded and unfolded a paper napkin restlessly. After folding the napkin into the tiniest square possible, he tossed it at her. The paper napkin hit her chest and fell unfolding into her lap.

Unsmiling, she asked, "What's bothering you?"

Sitting back he drained his wine, and then refilled the glass from the carafe. Unable to look her in the eye he sighed heavily and said, "When you left the mountain, I thought it would kill me." Twisting in his seat, Lewis put his chin in his hand and said, "I know I treated you awful, and I'll never be able to explain why, to you or even myself. But, when I joined the army I was hoping I would never come back." He finally raised his eyes to hers. "The day after you left I went to see you at your house, and there in the dust of your driveway I found your diary."

Breathless, she asked him, "Did you read it?"

Tears glistened in his eyes. "I know now what I did that hurt you so bad the day of the funeral and I would never blame you for not forgiving me." He inhaled a ragged breath and said, "I cannot believe I could hurt you like that. The Devil does live deep inside me. I don't know if I'll ever forgive myself." He looked away and exhaled a deep cleansing breath before he continued. "I hoped the war would be enough to punish the guilt out of me, but it wasn't."

Silently, Rosie took up her glass and drank it empty. She watched as he refilled it and motioned for the waitress to bring another carafe. Suddenly, she felt numbly exhausted as she blinked dry eyes at the café ceiling. "I don't know what to say, Lewis. I forgave you for that so long ago. It's nothing we need to talk about."

They sat silently as the waitress removed the empty wine carafe and replace it with a full one. With an emotion filled voice he said, "I prayed everyday for God to give you back to me, and seeing you today was like having a prayer answered." Tears rolled down his face as raw grief showed through. "I would give my life to right my wrongs."

With a rush of pity, she reached across the table and clasped his hands in hers, "It's all over. There is nothing to make up to me. I'm just so thankful to have you back." Sniffling away her own tears she said cheerfully, "We've got so much to talk about. Look where our future is going. Did you ever once think you'd see my picture in a *Teen Beat* magazine?"

Pressing his lips together as if suppressing a smile he answered, "I never thought about it, but it certainly didn't surprised me."

"So, is Ollie going to be the manager for Purple Sage?"

Taking up his glass of wine he asked, before drinking from it, "Sure, why not?"

It was after midnight before Rosie got back to the mansion, and Kid was waiting to ambush her before she reached her suite. "What the hell, Sun? Dinner was a little tense not having you there. Edwina was tight lipped, and Victor must be off somewhere with Frank."

Holding open her door, she shushed and ushered him into her sitting room. "Please, Kid. I'm exhausted, and I have to be up early tomorrow for another day at the studio."

Nodding his head agreeably he said, "Okay, I'll get out of your way. It must be some band to keep you burning the midnight oil. Tell me a little about them."

Peeling off her clothing she sighed, "The name of the group is Purple Sage, and you know each and every one of them." She paused a moment and added, "Its Lewis and Heather from back home."

His face fell into a dark expression, "You've been out with them?"

"No," she answered, "just Lewis."

Taking her by the shoulders he forced her to look at him. "I thought you were through with him. What about us?"

Putting her face in her hands she explained, "I had no idea I was going to see him today. We just sat down for some wine and conversation. And," her voice halted as she faltered for words.

Kid's voice was angry, "And, you just wound up in bed with him didn't you?" Roughly he shoved her away. "If you didn't want to be with me, why didn't you say so a long time ago?"

Feeling too tired for tears Rosie said, "Stop putting me on your level. I have some scruples you know. Do you want to start a fight with me? You know Lewis and I have a lot of history between us. We could talk for a week and still not have enough time to say everything. And, I did not go to bed with him!"

Pacing the carpeted floor and nodding his head in aggravation Kid said poisonously, "Maybe not, but I'll bet you had time to say how much you still love each other, didn't you?"

Slinging her pearls into the jewelry box she asked dryly, "What's wrong with that?"

He looked at her broken heartedly, "Because, I only want you to love me, Sunny. Now, can you tell me what's wrong with that?" Taking her forcefully by the shoulders he planted a harsh kiss on her lips, and left the room abruptly.

Sinking onto the loveseat, Rosie stared blankly at the door he had just left by, and wondered how she would smooth out the mess she had created. Knowing that Kid and Lewis had parted as friends three years earlier sent guilt pangs through her as she realized she was about to reinstate the old rivalry. But worst of all, what if the press got news of her dalliance with either one of the men she cared for. The Senator's wife would be hot tabloid news, and she just couldn't allow that to happen.

Rosie arrived at the studio alone the following morning. Ollie jumped to his feet after stuffing documents into his briefcase when she entered the reception area. "Sunshine," he called after her as she walked by. "Sunny," Ollie repeated as he rushed to catch up with her. "Mrs. Hart!"

Turning to face him, she snapped, "I'm not feeling well this morning, Ollie. What do you want?"

He whispered harshly, "You were supposed to ride home with me yesterday."

"I just spent the evening with an old friend, that's all," she simply explained.

Paranoia gripped Ollie as he sputtered, "You can't be out and about without a chaperone. You know that, Sunny. The paparazzi could have a field day with something like that."

With fingers to her temples she asked, "How long have you known that Victor and Frank are lovers?"

Without expression Ollie replied, "Never ask me that question again."

"Why do you say that, because some secrets should remain secret?"

"That's one way of putting it."

Unable to argue she said, "It won't happen again. I promise." Standing on tiptoes, she softly kissed him on the cheek.

He reached over and opened the door. "Today you let me see you home, deal?" he asked. She agreed with a nod of her head.

The members of the Purple Sage band stood gathered around the piano as Glen explained his plans for the recordings they were working on. When they entered the studio Glen welcomed them with showmanship. "Here we are folks. Our backbone has arrived and we're ready to begin the day."

Heather spoke up and said, "I thought we were going to be working with Sonny Hart. Is he going to be here today?"

Rosie's mouth fell open. Glen laughed outright and asked, "What? You mean you don't know who Sunny Hart is?"

With her eyes focused on the puzzled expression Lewis held, Rosie watched his face when Glen explained, "This is Sunny Hart, none other than Gemini Rain's Sunshine Rose. She's one and the same person, only she just has two jobs." Then with a chuckle he added, "Well, I guess it's more like three." His handsome face beamed with mirth.

Lewis asked, "You're Sunny Hart?"

Heather said, "I thought Sonny Hart was someone related to the producer, Victor Hart."

Glen laughed, "Oh, yeah she's that all right. May I introduce you to Mrs. Victor Hart," he swept his hand toward Rosie saying, "Better known here in the studio as Sunny." Having fun with his introductions he continued, "Most importantly known in this state as Senator Hart's wife."

Rosie felt the room begin to spin. "I thought you knew."

Heather said, "Oh? That must be what this is." She held Rosie's hand up for all to see the extravagant antique diamond band. Then letting her hand drop she said cattily, "Well congratulations for hitting the jackpot, *Sunny*!"

Suddenly, Rosie felt like she was back in school during the days of Heather's betrayal. Her eyes rested on Lewis as he appeared to be weak from the revelation. "I'm still the same person," she said as she watched him turn away to hide his shock. To the rest of the band she exclaimed, "I will always be the same person!"

Ollie put a hand on her elbow to show his support while Glen continued speaking. "And, we will always be grateful for that." Turning to the band Glenn held both hands palm up and said, "Right gang?" Silence followed his comment, and anger tinged his voice with his next statement. "If we're going to do this you need to get your asses in the booth already."

Following behind Glen with Ollie guiding her, Rosie watched Lewis for any signs of emotion. He refused to look her way, stepping to the keyboard, he readied to play. The day was torturous as she waited for a sign from him that he held no ill feelings against her. But, the day continued with him avoiding eye contact, and at the end of the workday Lewis quickly disappeared.

When Rosie returned to the mansion, she went looking for Janie. Maria told her Janie was in the garden with Andrea, Eduardo and the canine Randy. Following the sound of happy voices she came upon the children. Andrea and Eduardo busied themselves blowing bubbles, while Randy chased after them with the intent to bite the floating orbs. Stretching onto a cushioned lounge next to Janie, she watched the children play without speaking.

As they sat in the warm sunshine beneath the azure sky with wispy fair weather clouds, butterflies darted about, collecting nectar from the flowers. With a sigh of resignation Rosie said, "This is the garden Doc Campbell showed me in my dreams, long ago. It sounds crazy doesn't it?"

Watching the younger children race across an arched wooden foot bridge that spanned a shallow flowing brook lined with white quartz pebbles she replied, "He shared it with me in my dreams, too. And, yes it does sound crazy."

The garden was peaceful with tranquility. Randy eventually tired of chasing the elusive bubbles, and jumped onto Janie's lap for a snooze. While Andrea and Eduardo continued creating bubbles that floated along with the butterflies, Elvis emerged from the pathway. Quietly, the feline positioned himself in the mulch for a bathroom break. Noticing the cat, Randy leaped from Janie's lap, took a running go, and rolled the cat across the mulch, with Elvis completing his business in mid roll. The incensed feline freed himself from the dog's ambush and ran from the garden. They both burst into side splitting laughter.

When Janie finally caught her breath, she declared, "Now that's what you call getting the shit knocked out of you!"

Touring resumed, and tensions grew as Ted and Bobby overindulged with the free flowing whiskey and champagne. Being an ever present hothead, Ted only got worse with booze. The name Gemini Rain was fast becoming notorious with the barroom brawls those two managed to create while on the road. Even worse for Rosie, were the constant arguments Ted lured her into. He had worked her into such a rage during a performance in Baton Rouge, that she followed him off stage shouting insults. His inebriation was so intense that he turned on Bobby, grabbing him by the throat. "Shut her up!" he screamed at Bobby, "I don't care what it takes, just shut her up!"

Having imbibed of the free whiskey before the concert himself, Bobby turned to Rosie and gave her a sudden shove which sent her crashing over a table supporting a porcelain lamp. Suddenly, she found herself lying on the cold marble floor among broken shards of porcelain, dazed and dumfounded. Jeff rushed to help Rosie to her feet, while Ted turned on Bobby.

"You idiot, I didn't say kill her!" The ensuing fight between Kid, Bobby and Ted had to be broken up by stage crew, as Jeff helped Rosie to her hotel room.

The scheduled tour was hellish for the band. At every concert the group found bottles of liquor and wine waiting to help them unwind before the performance. Once, Bobby got so drunk that he couldn't play. A substitute guitarist was rounded up at the last moment. Ted had become notorious for taking a bottle of whiskey on stage during concerts. The audience loved it when he held the bottle up for all to see, before drinking from it. Kid kept a cautious eye on Rosie's safety, as he and Ted were constantly at odds. Good natured Jeff seemed to be the only member who managed to avoid conflict.

A delightful ghost from Rosie's past came to call one sunny afternoon at the recording studio. Julian Jones sat waiting patiently in the lobby for her arrival. She stood frozen, momentarily shocked to see him, but quickly overcame her surprise and leapt into his arms. "Jude! How nice it is to see you!"

He responded happily, "You are a sight for sore eyes!"

Emerging from the studio behind them, Kid called out, "Jude is interested in joining our crew. He's willing to drive our tour bus, and do his best to keep us sober before the shows."

Rosie's face shone with happiness. "Oh, yes! Where have you been? We've needed you for so long!"

True to his word, Jude took on the responsibility of casing the green rooms at the concert halls for the bottles of free spirits. He managed to get to the room used by the headlining band, before band members did, in order to hide the bottles of liquor and champagne left by promoters. Once the liquor had been cut in half for the band's pre-performance consumption, the shows were more smoothly executed, with fewer hostilities.

After a steamy performance in Frankfort, Kentucky on a sultry July night, Rosie was being escorted to her hotel room by Kid and Amber. While passing Bobby's room a shrill scream shook them with apprehension. Bobby emerged pale faced, and panting, "It's a he-she! It's not a her!"

All eyes were drawn to the beautiful girl who emerged behind him in the doorway, adjusting her bra. Rosie's heart leapt. "Randy!"

His face shone exuberance at the sight of her, "Sunshine!"

Racing across the hallway she threw herself into his arms. "What are you doing with Bobby?"

"Looking for you!" exclaimed Randy.

Embraced and laughing, they stammered and giggled until Rosie clasped his hand in hers and drew him into her room, closing the door on Kid and Amber. "I'm so happy to see you!" She exclaimed over the sound of pounding fists on the door. "I missed you so bad when we had to part!"

Still looking frightened Randy asked, "Are they going to kick me out?"

Pulling him toward the balcony, she grabbed a blonde wig she used to disguise herself when she went out in public. "Come with me."

They rushed to the terrace and stepped over a railing separating the balcony from the one for the room next door. She slid open the glass door and they hurried inside.

When the sound of a key turning in the lock came, she pulled Randy into the bathroom. Kid rushed in with Amber right behind. They ran to the terrace and disappeared. Pulling the blonde wig over her head, Rosie peered into the hallway. She motioned for Randy to follow her as she hurried to the elevator, stuffing her hair up beneath the wig. When they reached the hotel lobby, they ran like school kids to the lounge.

Perching on a bar stool Rosie giggled, "What are you doing here?"

Randy sat next to her adjusting his skirt. "I've been trying to get in touch with you for two years! And, all I ever got in return was an autographed eight by ten glossy from your fan club." With a gleam in his eye he leaned closer, tilting his chin high. "Sniff me."

She leaned into his neck. "You're wearing *Sunshine* perfume!"

"It's my favorite. I even spritz my pillow with it!"

"Oh, Randy, I'm so sorry for not having called you at school, but things just got so complicated." Feeling at a loss for words, she managed a feeble smile.

"Complicated? But, I thought you loved me!"

Throwing her arms around his neck she hugged him saying, "I do love you! But, things happened."

"What things?"

"Your father for one thing, but there's so many other obstacles I've stumbled across over the years." With sparkling teary eyes she said, "I'd really like to tell you everything, someday." Overcome with emotion, she leaned close and kissed his lips.

The blinding light of a flash bulb caught them both off guard. Rosie whirled to see a paparazzi shutter-bug leering at her. In an instant Kid was upon the photographer making demands for the film while Amber coaxed Rosie back to the hotel room. Randy hurriedly wrote his phone number on the back of a cash register receipt, and thrust it at Rosie. She managed to snatch it just as Bobby pulled him off his bar stool.

"Don't hurt him!" she shouted at Bobby, while clutching the receipt.

Ted appeared next to her and plucked the paper from Rosie's fingers. When she whirled to face him, he stuffed it in his mouth and began chewing with a lewd expression. Pounding his chest with her fists she shouted, "Give that back!"

Because of the shouting and chaos, hotel security arrived demanding they leave the bar. Amber ushered Rosie from the lounge, while Kid continued dealing with the photographer. As Rosie looked over her shoulder, she could see Randy being escorted away by security staff, while Ted stood at the bar laughing with Bobby.

"Oh, Amber!" she wailed, "You just don't know what Randy means to me. This is the first time I've seen him in years, and he gets treated like a criminal."

Boarding the elevator Amber said, "Well, he made a spectacle of himself. Showing up dressed like a girl to get in Bobby's hotel room. He's lucky Bobby didn't punch him out!"

Consumed by exhaustion she murmured, "I'm so tired of fighting, Amber. I'm just so tired of everything. Randy's the best thing that's happened to me in months and we didn't even get to finish our conversation."

"You can get up with him later, when you're off the road. Now is not a good time for reunions with old friends. There's too much work to do."

When the doors on the elevator opened, Rosie stepped out ahead of Amber. "If only you knew how miserable I am. I'd do anything to change places with you."

Following the carpeted corridor behind Rosie, she replied, "Nothing could make me happier."

A soft knocking on her door awoke Rosie the next morning. She pulled on a robe and called, "Who is it?"

"Delivery," a voice called back.

Opening the door without removing the chain she peered out. A hotel staff member stood with a huge bouquet of flowers. She closed the door and removed the chain. "Oh! Thank you." Taking the flowers to a table she hurriedly removed the card. Tears welled in her eyes as she read, *"My lovely Sunshine. If love were flowers, I would grow you a garden. Randy."* Cheery chuckles erupted as she gazed at the phone number written beneath his signature.

Chapter Thirty-Four
Marching Soldiers

Summer came to Boca Raton with a vengeance. Gemini Rain gained immense popularity, and *Lonely* finally got air play. Glen hounded Frank to produce another album featuring Gemini Rain, with many of his own songs offered up as temptation. Unfortunately for Rosie, Glen wanted her vocals for most of his songs. This created an ever widening rift between her and Ted. And to exhaust even more of her time, she was commanded to do television commercials to promote *Sunshine* perfume for the holiday season. Victor was so busy with his contracting corporation and senatorial duties that he hardly had time to attend to his beloved work of producing music. Frank was given carte blanche over the studio. Spending more and more time on private jets flying from one engagement to another, there were times when Rosie couldn't even remember the day of the week as she was pressured into appearances as the senator's wife, and as the singing sensation known as Sunshine Rose.

After a long conversation with Amber, Rosie requested that Glen do a few simple recordings in the studio with Amber singing some Gemini Rain songs. With immeasurable pleasure, she noted how Amber sounded very much like herself on the recordings. With this ammunition, Rosie begged Frank to use Amber as a stand in for herself on occasions when she simply could not perform with the band.

Trying to convince her adversary to agree with her, she reasoned, "It's unfair to the others when we reschedule, or cancel shows just because I have to be somewhere else with Victor."

"It's unfair to the ticket holders not to see Sunshine Rose," Frank retorted. Finally, Frank gave in and included Amber in all rehearsals and costume fittings. Amber was ecstatic.

During a late night ride on the tour bus, Rosie and Amber sat about with the guys, drinking beer while they tried out some of Glen's new songs. Growing tired of their rehearsal, Bobby turned on the radio while an Allman Brother's song played. With a big grin he cranked up the volume saying, "I want this song played at my funeral."

Rosie caught a smile from Jude as he drove the bus, enjoying the conversations. Ted laughed, "Why in the hell do you want *Ramblin' Man* played at your funeral?"

Bobby explained, "Because my father was killed by a bullet in Atlanta during a poker game. I can't say I was born on a Greyhound bus, but I can say I was born to a social climbing bitch that has made my life hell."

Amber saw an intriguing story and prodded Bobby to tell more about his life. "There's not a lot to tell. My old lady refuses to acknowledge the success our group has had, or even the fact that her son plays in a rock and roll band. She tells her snobby friends I'm away at school. And, don't even get me started about my stepdad." Bobby turned up his bottle of beer and drained it. Exhaling he continued, "I know the dame that managed to marry old money would never allow such music to be played at my funeral. So, if I die tomorrow you guys make sure that song is played while I lay in my coffin."

Ted laughed and slapped Bobby on the back, "We'll do one better, Bro. We'll sing it ourselves."

Taking up Bobby's hand Amber said, "Let me look at your life line." She announced, "Nobody's going to be singing at your funeral anytime soon."

While the group made light conversation and simple chatter, a new song came on the radio that sent everyone into a complete state of silence. It was Rosie's own voice coming through the speakers, coupled with Lewis Shirey's. Teddy jumped to his feet cursing, "What the hell is that?"

Speechless, she exclaimed "We only did that song once in the studio! I never agreed for it to be released."

Slamming an empty beer bottle into the trash can Ted declared, "Well, obviously since you're the producer's wife, he doesn't need your consent. Does he?"

Feeling indignant anger she could only answer, "I guess not."

The single released as *Loving You* wasted no time in climbing the charts, which put even more pressure on Rosie's limited amount of time as she and Lewis were booked to appear on television variety shows and daytime talk TV. Being thrown together with him in silent limousines and backstage green rooms was unnerving. The agony of his elusive attention strengthened her resolve to hide all emotion. But, she never offered an apology, or explanation of the misunderstanding that befell them upon their reunion.

It was due to the success of *Loving You* that Frank signed a record deal with Purple Sage. The band was scheduled for a grueling recording session as well as promotional performances. In between downtime, Lewis and Rosie were flown to various cities across the country to promote *Loving You.* From their exhaustive promotion appearances, as well as Frank's magic with Disc Jockeys, *Loving You* became a top ten hit by the winter of '72.

During a winter break for the holidays, Rosie sat in the grand dining room between Janie and Kid. Victor sat across from her with Frank at his side. Edwina was overwhelmed with her son's success, and made a toast to all of his achievements. Sitting in the glare of her husband's success, Rosie felt tired and old. Only when Kid pressed his thigh against hers did she feel a rush of adrenaline. Drinking to Edwina's toast, she smiled at Victor as a way of acknowledging her appreciation for his admirable victories, but she couldn't help but relish the jealous stabbing looks she received from Frank, and secretly wished she could seduce Victor just once in an effort to even the score with her spiteful rival.

Later in the evening, she joined Kid in Janie's room for a game of monopoly. As usual, Janie was in entertainment mode as she poked fun of people, and made snide comments to her opponents as they played. "I read an article in *Look* magazine about the Purple Sage band. They described Lewis as *handsome with an innocent sexuality* then they described Heather as *plain as cornbread, resembling a mixture of Janis Joplin and Mama Cass*! Don't you think that's disturbing? In one sentence they call Lewis weak and pretty while they call Heather ugly and fat!"

Kid chuckled, "That's life in the lime light, Jane. You didn't see me get upset when *Rolling Stone* called me rowdy and rebellious did you?"

Looking at him with jaded exasperation Janie dryly replied, "That's because you are rowdy and rebellious!"

The winter days past swiftly at Wildwood, and Rosie found herself assisting Edwina in decorating the Christmas tree. The mother of the future president contemplated each ornament, and told Rosie the boring history behind it. "Oh, look. Victor made me this when he was in the second grade," said Edwina holding up a tired plastic ornament with shedding silver glitter.

Rosie cared nothing for Edwina's nostalgia, and longed for the cold mountain Christmas of Ben Johnson Ridge. She grudgingly followed her mother-in-law's instructions for placement of the tacky decorations. Some declared what year they had originally celebrated. She hung them wondering why 1972 had vanished so quickly. Edwina's incessant prattle became nonsensical after a while, and she simply tuned her out while dutifully placing the ornaments. A long pause in Edwina's chatter passed before Rosie noticed. Walking around the huge tree she found Edwina staring into space moving her lips without uttering a sound.

"Edwina, are you okay? Edwina?"

The ambulance came quickly. Rosie followed with caution lights flashing her distress. As much as she resented Edwina, she held an undeniable fondness for her, and for that she prayed. She prayed for Edwina, she prayed for Victor, and she prayed for herself.

Christmas Eve found Rosie and Victor beside Edwina's bedside in the hospital. Edwina had suffered a stroke, and the doctors couldn't say how severe her disability would be. Extreme pity bruised her heart as she watched Victor weep at his silent mother's bedside.

The hospital became an uncomfortable home for the two of them as they stayed day and night with Edwina. The handsome Victor took on a tired and ragged look, as his beard grew scraggly from lack of attention. Finally, Rosie got him to sit inside the cold stark bathroom so she could shave him. Victor's eyes were bloodshot, and his hand trembled when he reached to grasp hers. "I never deserved you, Sunny. But as God is my witness, I will never take you for granted again."

Gently, she pushed his hand aside and smiled sweetly while she shook the can of shaving cream. Smearing his face with the creamy soap she said, "Now, just relax. This is going to make you feel better." She took up the razor, and kissed him tenderly on the forehead. "She's coming home, Victor. Don't worry." Then she carefully shaved his face as tears rolled down his cheeks.

It was the third week of January 1973 when Edwina Morgan was released from the hospital. The grand drawing room was converted into a makeshift hospital room. Nursing staff was hired to provide around the clock care, and her personal physician remained on call.

Gemini Rain had returned to their scheduled tour with Amber standing in. Victor praised Rosie for having the foresight to insist that Frank allow Amber to train with the group. For a complete month Victor's contracting industry functioned with only his guidance through phone calls. The only time he left his mother's side was for pressing senate business.

Slowly, Edwina improved and was able to speak simple sentences. Occasionally she mixed up her words and became infuriated with herself. Rosie spent as much time as she could, planning Edwina's care, and when she was forced to make appearances Victor took her place.

The tour bus became obsolete for Rosie as she was pressed even more for precious time. She continuously chartered private jets to get to her destinations. Glen and Frank had begun work on Gemini Rain's second album, but she rarely appeared with the band for rehearsal sessions. She listened to the music and rehearsed with Victor, using a pleased Edwina for an audience. The success of Purple Sage had become phenomenal with the popularity of *Loving You*, which was included on their first album. Amber was now performing the song with Lewis during concerts.

The tabloids and teen magazines reported romance between her and Lewis, which Rosie was faced with each time she fumbled through the mail. One day as she sorted the mailman's delivery, she came across a package addressed to her from the Ft Lauderdale clinic. She opened it to find the familiar handwriting of her old friend Carlotta. The letter read:

Dear Sunshine. I regret to inform you of the sudden death of Dr. Thayer. His passing was completely unexpected, and due to his wishes no memorial service was held. As he wished, his ashes were scattered at sea. I came upon these letters while packing away his office. I never understood why he instructed me to keep your personal mail from you. But, now that he is gone, I only think it right that you should now have them. Your faithful friend, Carlotta.

Staring at the bundle of letters Randy had written so faithfully, Rosie felt as though she'd just uncovered treasure. Now, at last, she had in her possession the proclamation of his love, written in ink and sealed with kisses. Coveting the letters away, she read them with great relish and leisure. Many late night conversations with Randy across long distance wires followed the delivery of the letters. She wanted to confess the crime she had committed upon leaving his home state, but she couldn't.

The following weeks were a blur as Rosie made her commitments to the recording studio. Glen was unusually harsh with her, and insisted she join Ted and Kid in the studio for vocal tracks. With a heavy heart she managed to make it through the recordings with Glen's satisfaction. Touring resumed, and she joined the band on the tour bus for a three week stint doing nineteen shows across the southwest. Amber was her usual gentle self as she attended Rosie's hairstyling and clothes. It was during a makeup session that Amber confessed her feelings for Lewis. Having worked through the pain of his rejection, she smiled for Amber and offered her best wishes for the success of the relationship she herself yearned for.

Amber had accompanied Lewis to Ben Johnson Ridge to meet his family. "I saw the farm where you grew up, and Rocky Falls." She said softly as she applied the makeup to Rosie's face. "Oh, and he took me to this sweet little covered bridge. I just love historic things like that, don't you?"

A rueful smile crossed Rosie's lips. "Yes, I do." Trying to sound nonchalant she asked, "Did he take you to the river?"

"Oh, yes. We took a motorboat to a cave where endangered bats inhabit." Stepping back to view her work Amber said, "Those Mountains are beautiful."

Standing before the mirror Rosie studied Amber's creative work. She always managed to make a presentable public image from the simple farm girl Rosie never stopped being. Not wanting to ask if he had explained the past he shared with her, she turned to Amber and said, "I'm glad you and Lewis found each other. I couldn't have picked a better match for either one of you." A knock on the door and a muffled voice announcing the countdown for the show drew her from reminisce, and Rosie walked courageously on stage.

Recording the second album was much more painstaking and difficult than the first. Glen and Terry recorded Rosie and Kid singing background, then dubbed over the background vocals with them singing lyrics with Teddy. The finished song was polished and moving. Glen made magic in the studio, creating perfection - crisp, clean, carefully crafted recordings. He mastered a variety of tricks and sounds to good effect, without overusing them. The second album was created using the strengths and subtleties of unique individuality, which came across as auditory magic.

Dance music was becoming ever more popular, and Frank wanted to cash in on the market by producing southern rock worthy of the dance floor. Becoming disillusioned with the business, Kid wanted to record some of his own songs. Ted agreed with Kid that they should be allowed to record their own songs for the second album. Giving in to their pressure, Frank allowed the recordings, but refused to guarantee any of them would appear on the album.

Bobby and Ted kept in contact with Billy Ray, and updated Rosie with news of his possible homecomings. News of the war continued to be gruesome and disheartening, while the country continued to spiral out of control with protests and demonstrations. When she suggested adding a song of tribute to America's soldiers to the album, she met opposition with Glen. Holding a serious look to his usual smiling flirtatious face, the handsome blonde frowned at her suggestion. "Sunny," he said with a shake of his head. "People listen to our music to escape reality. There's too much of the war on the news, and in the headlines already. A syrupy song about the soldier's sacrifices is the last thing the public wants."

With a hard look she said, "I don't agree. I've got a gut feeling it could be appreciated, not only by the public, but by the soldiers themselves."

Still unsmiling, Glen said, "I'll think about it. Maybe you have a point."

To the amazement of Frank and Victor, Purple Sage was becoming phenomenally popular. Glen had added three female backup singers, and one was another ghost from the past. Janie's eyes widened when Rosie explained that Shelley had joined the Purple Sage band. "Well, we have to admit that she and Lewis always had a good sound together."

Angrily Janie fumed, "Maybe so, but that doesn't change the fact that she's a hateful bitch who doesn't deserve to be part of that band."

"At least we don't have to be around her," sympathized Rosie. Those words would come back to bite her only weeks later, when Frank announced that the two bands would be touring together for eight weeks of grueling shows. And, to make matters worse, Gemini Rain would be opening for Purple Sage.

Ted was furious, "That sucks! We're the top band here."

Frank stood firm, "Purple Sage has two songs in the top ten right now, and that puts you opening for them. You have to remember we work for a fickle public. We could all wake up tomorrow and be forgotten like this," Frank snapped his fingers to make his point.

Reminding Frank of one important fact Kid said, "Well one of those songs Purple Sage has in the top ten is with Sunshine, and she's Gemini Rain."

Frank said, "It's a Purple Sage song, Kid. Now unless we get some air play soon off this second album, Gemini Rain will be lucky to continue opening for Purple Sage."

During the following weeks of touring together, Rosie and Heather regained the friendship that had been left behind. Amber was not only working as Rosie's stylist, but also as one of the backup singers for Purple Sage. The entourage for the two groups had swelled into five buses to haul personnel and stage equipment. Boredom with the business had overcome Rosie, as lack of control had overtaken Ted and Kid with rage.

It was the last week of the tour, when she found herself sharing a dressing room with Heather, that Rosie noticed how painfully thin Heather had become. She exclaimed, "My God girl! What's happened to you? You were always so healthy and plump before."

Heather replied, "Those bastard reporters can't call me fat anymore!"

Stepping closer she could see how the billowy blouse and hip hugging jeans actually hid the emaciated body. "You must be less than a hundred pounds!"

With a smile Heather said, "No, not yet."

Placing herself between Heather and the mirror Rosie stated, "This can't be healthy, Heather. I want you to see a doctor about this weight loss. Maybe you need some vitamins or something."

Laughing lightly she said, "Stop being a worry wart. Bobby likes me thin, and I like Bobby. So there, case closed."

Realizing that she had been so wrapped up in her own life that she had missed what was going on around her, Rosie asked, "You and Bobby are a thing? I didn't even know."

With more laughter Heather quipped, "It's in all the magazines, and tabloids. Don't you ever pick up a paper?"

Thinking of the stack of letters she was still reading from Randy, she replied, "No, I never have time."

Making quick strides across the room Heather snatched up a magazine and thrust it at her saying, "Well, make time."

The article showed Heather and Bobby frolicking on the Florida beaches with the headline reading: *Another couple pair up between Gemini Rain and Purple Sage*. Rosie said, "I guess the other couple they're referring to is Amber and Lewis."

Smudging her eye shadow Heather said, "Or, maybe they mean Shelley and Ted."

"Shelley! But she's married."

Heather replied, "Come on, Rosie. We're talking about Shelley. You don't really think she's changed any."

Pacing across the room and shuffling through the stack of magazines for reports on Ted and Shelley she declared, "If that kind of news gets back to Mack he'll show up at one of our shows and shoot Ted in the heart."

A quick knock at the door was followed by Amber rushing in. "Sunshine, they're calling for you. You've got five minutes."

With an aggravated shrug of her shoulders Rosie slung down the mound of magazines saying, "Give me a look see. Do you think I'm ready?" Amber pulled her to the glare of a lighted mirror and nodded her head in approval. Rosie paused at the door and looked back saying, "See a doctor, Heather. I insist."

Janie was reading poetry to Edwina when Rosie returned from the road. Leaving her tote and purse in the foyer, she joined them in the drawing room. Edwina mumbled her greeting and jerked her left hand in awkward nervousness. Janie placed a notepad beneath Edwina's right hand. She then positioned a ball point pen in the elderly woman's fingers. When Edwina had written her message Janie removed the instruments and handed the notepad to Rosie. "Look, Edwina has a message for you."

"Ask Jane to play."

Edwina began motioning and making incomprehensible sounds. Smiling, Janie stepped behind Edwina's wheelchair and said, "Let's go to the music room, so I can play the piano. Edwina thinks I'm progressing well."

The remainder of the afternoon was spent with Janie playing difficult pieces on the beautiful baby grand piano, while Rosie sipped champagne and Edwina indulged in one brandy.

Hazel returned to the room. "Mr. Campbell is here. May he be allowed in?"

Edwina pounded her fists on the wheelchair arms and mumbled aggravated frustration at her servant, "Yeah!"

Kid entered the room, stepping first to Edwina, where he placed a gallant kiss on the back of her hand asking, "What is Hazel's problem? Sometimes she really acts like a nut."

With her usual candor Janie quipped, "Well, her name is Hazel!" The humorous remark was not wasted on Edwina, who chuckled and clapped her hands in agreement.

Summer changed to fall, and Gemini Rain was still falling behind Purple Sage on the charts. Two of the songs from their second album had received air play and attention, but a single of Heather's song *Teenage Scene* had overshadowed the industry, and made Purple Sage a household name. Frank had called Gemini Rain together at the studio to practice a new song Terry and Glen had collaborated on. It was a warm surprise when Rosie heard the sentimental words, praising the soldiers in Vietnam, set to inspirational music. Ted and Kid were especially happy that one of Kid's songs would be cut for the flip side. Teddy had a true appreciation for Kid's raw rock and roll style, and rejoiced in what he saw as a breakthrough with the stoic Frank.

For some reason, Rosie saw the painstaking recording process as too slow, and complained bitterly. "It's just two songs, Victor. Why are we spending so much time on it?"

They sat with Edwina on a rare occasion in the drawing room. Victor fluffed his mother's pillows while persuading his wife, "I think you should trust Frank, Sunny. He's a brilliant man when it comes to music. And, let's not forget Glen. That man can make magic happen in the studio."

Looking at her son with adoring eyes Edwina mumbled for something. Rosie took up the notepad and pen for Edwina to write out her request. She wanted to hear the song. Victor left the room, and returned a short time later with a reel to reel tape recorder. He played the soldier's tribute song for Edwina then pried her for her suggestions. Quickly, she scribbled her comments on the pad and handed it to Victor. With alighted eyes he told Rosie, "It needs piano and violin."

The song was rerecorded with Victor playing piano, and Terry playing a soulful sound on violin. Edwina had been right. The song was finished. True to Rosie's predictions, radio stations jumped at a chance to play the tribute for America's soldiers, and listeners made repeated radio requests. Gemini Rain was back on top with *Marching Soldiers*. By the end of winter, the song jumped to number eleven, while Kid's song from the flip side was slowly climbing from number forty-eight. Frank was very pleased with himself. The year ended with Gemini Rain standing neck and neck with Purple Sage. Distressingly, Frank paired the two bands for a new concert tour to begin shortly after the seasonal break.

Edwina beamed with pride each time she saw a Christmas commercial for her highly successful *Sunshine* perfume. She managed to rule her cosmetic empire through written commands from her mansion, and the help of a new secretary who worked closely with the company's CEO. Edwina Morgan was not yet ready to retire.

Victor put together a star studded New Year's Eve party at the grandest resort in Boca Raton with members of the two bands being special guests. The year 1974 was expected to be very promising for *Ryder/Hart Strings Music Productions.* Rosie stayed by her husband's side throughout the evening, allowing him to treat her as a true and valued wife. During a visit to the restroom, she came upon Heather sobbing heart wrenching tears.

Concerned, Rosie pressured her to explain her heartache. Heather moaned through a fistful of tissues, "It's Bobby," she cried. "He dumped me for Shelley!" Heather slumped to the floor and wrapped her arms around her knees as she cried wretchedly. "Of all the men she could have, why did she have to take Bobby? Oh, Rosie, I love him so much. Why can't he see what a nasty bitch she is?"

Perched on an ornate stool at the mirrored counter, Rosie laid her arm around her old friend's shoulder, "Oh, Heather! I'm so very sorry. I wish I could help."

Moaning in agony Heather cried, "I think this is going to kill me. I really think I'm going to die. It just hurts so bad!" She then succumbed to incoherent moans of anguish.

Sinking to her knees Rosie crooned, "Now you listen to me. You are ten times prettier than Shelley, and one hundred times more talented. Without you, Purple Sage would be nowhere. Now, you get up from there, and pull yourself together. We are going back out to the party, and you are going to flirt, and have a damn good time despite Bobby's ignorance and Shelley's loose morals." Shaking Heather by the shoulders, Rosie asked, "Do you understand what I'm telling you?"

Heather cleared her nose and wiped her face dry. "Why did we ever grow apart, Rosie? Oh, why did I have to be so jealous of you?"

"Jealous?" asked a bewildered Rosie.

"When Shelley told me about seeing you and Justin out on the town, I was so crushed. Even though I was forbidden to see him, I couldn't stand the thought of you having him. I was so wrong for feeling that way toward you!" Heather's shoulders heaved with sobs.

"Justin?" Rosie asked, still perplexed. "I don't know anyone named Justin."

"Yes you do," insisted Heather. "Remember the day we spent at his boathouse?"

A flicker of remembrance alighted Rosie's face as she answered, "Yes, but we didn't meet Justin that day."

"No, but didn't you figure it out after you started seeing him?"

"But I never saw him, never met him, never remembered the man's name from the boathouse!" insisted Rosie.

Heather's face paled as she suddenly realized she had been victimized by Shelley's lies. "What was it you said to me that day you had glue in your hair?" Inhaling shakily she answered her own question, "Since when do you believe anything Shelley says."

"I do remember telling you that," replied Rosie sadly.

With a tearful sigh Heather said, "I can't escape her. She's like a demon."

"Yes, you can escape her, Heather," said Rosie firmly. "You simply stay away from her, and never listen to anything she says."

Standing slowly, Heather slumped onto the bench at the mirrored counter. Stepping to the door, Rosie motioned for a waiter carrying a tray filled with glasses of champagne. Taking the entire tray, she returned to Heather.

It was on a bright sunny day in March when Kid came to Rosie with sad news from Ben Johnson Ridge. Maggie Campbell had succumbed to a bout of pneumonia and died. Arrangements were made for Amber and Terry to fill in for three shows so they could return home for the memorial service. Sobbing with the desperation of a guilt ridden child Janie wailed, "I should have called her. I should have told her I loved her."

Comforting his young cousin, Kid told her, "She knew you loved her, kiddo. G-Mama was a wise old gal. You know that."

They arrived at the church just half an hour before the service. Shelley had refused to return for the funeral, electing to continue the tour. Taking Rosie by the hand Janie cried, "This reminds me of Angel."

Rosie embraced the child who had grown almost as tall as herself, while Kid walked past them to view his grandmother. Still holding her close, Rosie pushed Janie along the aisle toward the wall of flowers surrounding the open casket. Albert Campbell stood with his son, James, as they embraced Kid near the coffin. Elizabeth stood from the front pew and walked to her youngest daughter. Rosie cringed. Thankfully, Janie remained silent as Elizabeth gushed about how much she had missed her little girl. When the missing mother began to babble empty compliments, the teenage daughter bushed her aside and stepped to the open casket.

With tears contorting her vision she saw her grandmother's frail body, lying as if beneath a window of ice. Folding her hands beneath her chin she bowed in silent prayer. Rosie prayed, too. After the burial, Rosie returned to her father's house, while Janie and Kid went to Bert's home. The old farm house was warm and welcoming from the cold March wind, and it felt good to be back. She wandered through the familiar old house thinking how small it was compared to the mansion at Wildwood. When she opened the door to her old bedroom a smile contorted her face happily. It had remained the same as it was from the day she had left. Tiny details caught her eye as she noted repairs needing to be done. Excusing herself, she left Eva preparing the evening meal while she donned a heavy coat from her old closet, and left the house.

The wind was blustery as she stepped onto the front porch. The old weathered rocking chair was moving with the gusting wind and she searched for signs of Doc's ghost. She crossed the roadway and whistled for Sugar and Spice. Like a loyal old friend Spice came trotting while Sugar continued to graze. Rosie walked around the old farm house making observations, and she strolled through the greenhouse. The small glass building was alive with growing herbs and vegetable plants waiting for the open soil of spring. She crossed the plowed earth of the garden area, and smiled at the patch of turnips she saw growing dark and green. The brown meadow with spots of green grass called to her, and she walked the hundred acres with her cheeks glowing red from the cold.

When she returned to the warm kitchen her fingers were numb from the icy weather. Eva poured her a cup of hot coffee, and she took it with her into the living room where her father watched the old familiar television. Rosie sat beside her father on the old sofa and said, "You know, Daddy, I have quite a lot of money now."

Sturgill turned to face her and said, "Yes, I know dear."

Wanting to protect her father's dignity she asked, "Would you mind if I hired Ed to do some work on the house?"

Sturgill put his arm around his daughter and pulled her close. "This will be your house someday anyway, Rosie. You go ahead and do whatever you want."

The two days on Ben Johnson Ridge passed so quickly. Rosie barely managed to visit her favorite neighbor, Willene. She did manage a lunch with Bob and Ed, to talk over some of the adventures she had enjoyed with Lewis on the road, and to explain the renovations she wanted done to her father's house.

Ed pulled his wallet out and asked, "Would you like to see a picture of my kids?"

She gasped, "You have children? I didn't even know you were married."

Bob and Ed chuckled at her remark. Ed explained, "Well, Sally and I have only been married a few months." He pulled out a photo sleeve to reveal a picture of himself and his wife with two small Asian children.

"Sally!" she happily exclaimed, "She and I became friends my senior year. Well, what a coincidence!" Tears stung her eyes as she asked, "Are these Vietnamese children?"

"Yeah, Sally and I both feel there is a bigger reason for the conflict than just a battle between Communism and Democracy. We hope we're following God's plan, and making a small difference."

Blinking back tears Rosie asked, "Are you doing this for God, or little Le Quan?"

He smiled, and taking the photos casually asked, "Does it even matter?"

When she returned to Wildwood, Janie seemed quieter and more mature. Elizabeth had made a valiant effort to make amends with her youngest daughter. Victor's music room echoed with Janie practicing the difficult classical pieces that Edwina requested. The summer of '74 continued with Gemini Rain headlining concerts with lesser known bands opening for them. Purple Sage was now set on a tour of their own, and working to release a second album. Heather continued to stay in touch with Rosie, and happily called to tell her of a new and exciting romance. She had embarked on a whirlwind romance with a high profile race car driver, and had accepted a proposal of marriage. They had planned to marry in October amid the colorful backdrop of Ben Johnson Ridge, and Rosie sweetly accepted when Heather asked that she be the maid of honor.

October loomed as an exciting month for Rosie and Kid. They would travel back to the mountains of Alabama for Heather's wedding, and she would be able to see firsthand the renovations of the old farmhouse. She met Heather at an upscale bridal shop in Boca Raton to look over wedding dresses. Without knocking, Rosie stepped into the dressing room. A gasp of shock escaped her as she saw Heather's unclad body standing before the mirror. The healthy vivacious girl from Ben Johnson Ridge stood reflecting an image of protruding ribs, and sagging flesh.

Grasping Heather by the wrist, Rosie forced her to the mirror. "Don't you see what I see, Heather? You look like a holocaust victim!"

Heather sighed, "All I need it to tone up with some exercise. You know as well as I do that there just isn't enough time in the day to work out."

Not willing to accept explanations Rosie exclaimed, "You're body can't hold out like this! Don't you understand anything about starvation? The human body is a machine that needs food for fuel. I want you to promise you will see a doctor about this weight loss."

Seeming to feel shamed, Heather meekly promised she would see a doctor. "But, I don't want to be fat at my wedding," she proclaimed.

Clutching her into an embrace Rosie said, "Heather, you're thin. Can't you see that you're too thin?"

Heather said sweetly, "I'm so thankful to have you back as my friend, Rosie. And, don't you worry. I'll get myself on track." Looking at herself dressed in the wedding gown she grinned happily and said, "Right after the wedding."

Chapter Thirty-Five
Friends Left Behind

Victor awoke Rosie from a dead sleep to take a desperate phone call from Heather, who was touring the Northwest with Purple Sage. Rosie could hear her pathetic sobs as soon as she took the phone. "The wedding's off," Heather cried. "Kyle called me after the show. He thinks the wedding would be a mistake, and he doesn't even want to continue the relationship."

Stunned by her admission Rosie asked, "Did he explain why?"

Through sniffles and sobs Heather answered, "He thinks a marriage can't endure the kind of separation we would have to face. Because, I'm on the road so much of the year touring, and his racing commitments. He said he wants a traditional marriage with a stay at home wife to raise his children."

Understanding Kyle's logic Rosie said gently, "Well, look at the bright side. It's better to abort the wedding now than to endure a painful divorce later."

"No," she sobbed. "You don't understand! I offered to give up the band, and be the stay at home wife he wants. But he wouldn't hear any of it. He said he wouldn't be responsible for coming between me and my career."

Rosie fumbled to pour a glass of water while she held the phone to her ear with her shoulder. "Regardless of his motives, you must accept the fact that he wants out of the relationship. All you can do is be strong, and go on with your life."

Anguished cries came across the phone line as Heather sobbed, "Oh, God! I just love him so much. I would do anything to make him happy, but he won't even let me try."

Concern grew and she asked, "Are you alone? I don't want you to be alone. Have Amber come stay with you."

"I can't do that. I don't want anyone to see me like this," Heather moaned.

Bending to Heather's will, Rosie began talking of happier times. She forced Heather to relive moments from the mountain when they were young and carefree. They stayed on the phone talking until dawn. It was only after Heather swore she would be alright that Rosie said her goodbye. For a long time she sat in the silence of her sitting room contemplating the sad irony of how life had become for herself and Heather. More and more Rosie found herself pining for the uncomplicated days of Ben Johnson Ridge.

A correspondence between Janie and her mother was born after Maggie's funeral, but the budding teenager often found it hard to write those letters. A cold bitterness remained, because of the choices her mother had made following the destruction of Gulf Port in the summer of '69.

Rosie was informed of her nomination for a Grammy award for the hit single she had recorded with Lewis. Victor refused to accompany her to the ceremony, saying it just wasn't dignified enough for a senator. Instead, Victor suggested that Ollie escort her, but she defied her husband by insisting that she be escorted by Kid. On the night of the televised award ceremony Rosie sat with Kid, Lewis and Amber awaiting the announcement of the year's winner for the best pop duet. Never expecting to hear her name called as the winner, Rosie was positively flabbergasted by the announcement. They walked onstage to accept the award together.

Stepping to the microphone, Lewis said, "I'd like to thank our producers, and the public for making this night possible. But, I'd mainly like to thank my partner,
Sunshine Rose, for being my truest inspiration since first grade." The crowd cheered as he held the award above his head and stepped back smiling.

Rosie stepped to the microphone overwhelmed, and all she could mutter was a tearful, "Thank you, so very, very much!" She then turned and took Lewis by the arm he offered, and left the stage, leaving thunderous applause behind.

Once they were hidden safely backstage, Lewis embraced Rosie happily. He lifted her off the floor and spun her around. After putting her feet back on the floor, he impulsively kissed her, paying no attention to the flashing camera lights.

The fallout from the photos splashed across the tabloid magazines was an immense annoyance for Victor. "Can't you remember who you are?" He shouted at Rosie, "This is just the kind of publicity that can be used to make me look like a fool!" His handsome face was strained, and his age had begun to show from the emotional turmoil of his mother's failing health. The pressures of politics coupled with the empire his father had left were taking a tremendous toil on the mighty Victor Hart. Rosie tried vainly to offer apologies. The only response from Victor was, "Do not let mother see those headlines." With that being said he stormed out of the suite they shared.

The rigors of the band continued until they finally finished the album that Glen and Frank had polished to his version of perfection. It was scheduled to be released in February of the following year, which turned out to be amazingly appropriate. The album was tilted *Marching Soldiers* and miraculously coincided with the end of the Vietnam War.

Ted gushed with news of Billy Ray's return, "We're going to give him the biggest welcome home party Ft Lauderdale has ever seen!"

"Something tells me we're in for a three day hangover!" exclaimed Bobby.

1974 continued with a flurry of concert appearances, and album promotions. Amber was working full time with Purple Sage, her hairstylist duties were replaced with a feminine man who walked with a wiggle and held his hands in a peculiar little girl fashion when he conversed. Kid and Ted loved making jokes behind his back, sometimes even to his face. But if Carlos was offended by their remarks he never let it show. As with Amber, Rosie became attached to Carlos. They spent time together even when they weren't working. Their friendship irked Kid, but Victor found it amusing.

The band arranged for a festive coming home party at the country club in Ft Lauderdale where Rosie had first met Victor. The guest list ranged from high profile entertainment personalities, to high school friends of Billy Ray's. Jackie and Dolly were instrumental to the success of the celebration. They saw to it that all of Billy Ray's favorite foods would be served. When Rosie arrived for the party she was embraced by an energized Jackie.

While holding her clutched in an embrace, Jackie said to Rosie, "I'm so proud of your success, Sunshine. I tell all my friends I knew you when!"

Everyone welcomed the clean cut Billy Ray home with a resounding chorus of *For He's a Jolly Good Fellow.* Billy Ray wore his army dress to symbolize the soldier's pride. Friends surrounded him with shouts of welcome, while the song played that helped put Gemini Rain back at the top of the charts, *Marching Soldiers.*

When Rosie finally got the chance to speak with Billy Ray she asked how soon he could return to the band. Sounding a little reluctant Billy Ray answered, "Well, right now I just want to rest and be with my family. I appreciate what you're trying to do, but I'm a little stressed out, and I just need some time."

With heartfelt sympathy, Rosie embraced her friend and agreed he should take all the time he needed to recuperate from his ordeal. When the evening came to a close she jotted down all the phone numbers she could think of, and gave them to Jackie for safe keeping. "Call me anytime you need me. I'm only a phone call away." This time it was Rosie who leaned forward and kissed Jackie on the cheek. She left the party with Kid in his new convertible corvette.

As time passed, Rosie saw less and less of Victor. Edwina grew stronger with each passing day, and Janie indulged her with every whim possible. Andrea seemed to have become family with Maria and Eduardo, while Lillian simply vegetated in the apartment watching soap operas, and game shows day after day.

When the band wasn't on the road, Rosie spent her free time with Kid horseback riding along the trails of the estate. She had grown comfortable with her lifestyle, and only dreaded the next senate election. Ironically, Kid was the restless one, always wanting more from the music industry. He wanted a harder rock and roll edge added to the band's music, and he wanted more of his own music recorded on the next album. He and Glen often butted heads in the studio, with Ted always taking sides with Kid. The entire business of being a music star was tiresome work for Rosie as she was always working out to keep her body toned, and enduring beauty regiments that almost seemed like a foreign cult ritual of torture. Seaweed facials and body waxing made her nauseous. Edwina kept Rosie stressed, doing promotions for the astonishingly trendy fragrance called *Sunshine*. Toiling to keep up with her responsibilities, Rosie achingly longed for the day when the popularity of the band would dwindle, and she could live a simple normal life.

Kid's plans for the future were completely opposite. He schemed for ways to be placed more in the public eye, often creating chaos just to have his name plastered on tabloid covers. He managed to get himself arrested for fighting in a bar, and he crashed one of his sports cars while attempting to elude paparazzi. The fan magazines sensationalized each event which only made Kid Campbell's name more recognized.

Rosie worked alongside Glen and Frank in the studio as Purple Sage recorded a single Frank felt strongly about. Lewis had written the song, and Glen had composed the music. Frank wanted to promote the second album while he had the band hard at work on a third cut. He believed this single would lead off the third album for Purple Sage. Rosie sat spellbound by the enduring music of piano and guitar as Lewis began singing his ballad.

Hey, do you remember when
You and I became more than friends.
It was the summer of '69
You said I was the best you could find.

Oh, but I lost my Angel, and you lost your pride.
And, your going left me cold inside.
But, it's no matter where you go, or what you do,
Because, my Angel watches over you.

I know I pushed you away from me,
I read about it in your diary.
Written with the tears I caused.
I still ache from the love I've lost.

No matter where you go, or what you do.
My Angel watches over you.
And, I would travel a thousand times around this world,
To be with my love, the brown eyed girl.

Like the sweet smell of a sun warmed rose,
My heart follows wherever you go.
And, someone up above gives the power to
My Angel, who watches over you.

With tear filled eyes Rosie made excuses and rushed to the ladies room where she succumbed to her tears. Heather followed, "I knew that song would get to you," she said. "Hell, it even gets to me!"

Rosie looked at Heather and cried, "I'll never get over losing her, Heather. It's almost like she was my own little sister, you know?"

Hugging Rosie against her, Heather answered, "Yeah, I know."

Frank was thrilled with the recording, and he pushed hard to get air play for the ballad. With Victor's consent, Frank had paired Gemini Rain with Purple Sage for a two month tour of Europe. This tour was especially grueling, with the band and equipment being flown from one destination to the next. Rosie felt extreme sympathy for Amber, who suffered so badly with fear of flying that she literally had to be sedated for air travel.

After two months in Europe, the band hardly had a break before beginning the same promotion in the states. Tension was still strong between Shelley and Heather, even though Bobby had grown tired of Shelley, dumping her back at the feet of her husband. Ted's temper never diminished, and he continued to pummel Bobby and Kid at the drop of a hat. And both, Bobby and Kid, were hospitalized for a short stay after having two separate automobile crashes. After six weeks of exhaustive travel and work in the states, Rosie was still moved to tears each time Lewis performed the new single titled *My Angel*. He didn't have to tell Rosie the song was written with her in mind. It was just too painfully obvious.

Unfortunately, the demand for Lewis and Rosie to perform their award winning duet had not subsided, and Frank capitalized on it. Several times throughout the tour they were forced to travel separated from the entourage, because Frank had booked them for a television special or talk show. The band was flying out of Bangor to destination Pittsburgh on a rainy morning, after having had only a few hours of rest, while Rosie and Lewis were being flown to New York for a nationally telecast morning show. The flight they had taken left hours before the flight the rest of the crew took. Their equipment and most of the road crew had been flown the night before. Stagehands plied them with coffee, while makeup artists worked magic to hide the tired circles beneath their eyes. Wearing her signature long mane styled with flowing perfection, Rosie joined Lewis onstage beneath the hot glaring lights of the television cameras to perform *Loving You*.

After the performance, they were driven to the airport to catch their next flight to Pittsburgh. They were flying commercial, and had to wait as the flight was delayed due to the weather that had become a dangerous thunderstorm. They waited in the airport restaurant sharing a meal with polite conversation, while the rain pelted against the windows, and the lightening crackled across the sky.

"I'm glad the rest of the crew got out of here sooner. Amber would be completely hysterical flying in this weather," Lewis mused. Thinking for a moment, he reached inside his jacket pocket and withdrew a small red velvet covered box that he placed on the table. "I wanted you to know before anyone else that I'm planning to ask Amber to marry me."

The news was like a punch in the gut for Rosie. She inhaled deeply to alleviate her anguish. Tiredly she replied, "I think she will make you a good wife, Lewis." Rosie reached out and opened the box to reveal a simple marquis cut solitaire diamond. She smiled as she gazed upon it, thinking how she would rather be wearing it than the outrageously expensive band Victor had chosen. "It's perfect," she said before closing the case and sliding it back across the table. "She's going to love it." Forcing a smile Rosie said, "I wish you all the happiness in the world."

Taking the case and returning it to his pocket he replied dryly, "Yeah, well I think Victor is the one with all the happiness in the world."

Reaching over, she put her hand on his, "Lewis, I think I should be honest with you about something." Taking her hand away Rosie sat back and said, "I mean, after all I do trust you, and I know that anything I tell you will remain confidential."

Holding a puzzled expression on his face he agreed, "You can tell me anything, Rosie."

She took a deep breath and confessed, "I know everyone thinks I only married Victor for his money, but that just isn't true."

Giving her his full attention he asked, "Why did you marry a man more than twenty years older than you?"

The truth caught in her throat and she whispered, "I didn't want to."

Pressing for a reason he asked, "Then why did you? Did he force you?"

With closed eyes she weakly responded, "No, he didn't. But," she couldn't find the words to express the truth without confessing to her crime. Finally Rosie said, "It's extremely complicated."

"Was it for the band?" She shook her head no, and tears fell like diamonds over her lashes. "I just don't get it, Rosie!" Agitation consumed him, and he abruptly shoved his plate away, creating a sudden clanking of ceramic against crystal.

The sudden noise startled her, and her lips were pursed to confess the sordid truth about Andrea, and Edwina's extortion when they were suddenly interrupted by an airport employee placing a phone on the table, "Sunny Hart? You have a call on line one." With eyesight blurred by tears she stared at the black telephone with a flashing light next to several push buttons. He took up the receiver and pressed the correct button for her.

"This is Sunny Hart," she said into the receiver as she watched the look of ire on Lewis' face. "Ollie? We're waiting for our plane to be cleared, the weather here is-"

From across the table, Lewis saw the color drain from her face. He sat silent while Rosie remained open mouthed and speechless. "Rosie? What's wrong?" he asked gently. Seeing her fear he demanded, "What's wrong?"

Frozen with shock, her eyelids fluttered and she fell from her chair into a dead faint. He leapt to her side. Unable to revive her, he grasped the phone and shouted, "Ollie? This is Lewis. What happened? Rosie's out cold, she just fainted!"

Ollie explained, "The jet carrying both bands went down in the storm. Rescue crews are on the scene right now, but we don't know all the details yet, just that there are fatalities." Lewis rocked back on his heels from the devastating news. Flashbacks from Vietnam flooded his mind. He dropped the phone, and sinking to his knees, took his head in his hands, rocking himself to and fro, crying like a frightened child.

Airport personnel quickly removed Rosie's lifeless body from the restaurant to a private lounge. Lewis was escorted by two strong security guards who sometimes carried him as he stumbled on weak legs to follow. Once they reached the lounge Lewis was settled into a thick comfortable leather chair, and Rosie was laid upon a sofa.

Before she was roused with smelling salts, Rosie's confused thoughts went back to Ben Johnson Ridge. She was lost in the warm remembrance of a sunlit day, nestled in the comforting arms of Lewis while he pedaled her along a quiet country road. Segments of her life flashed thru memories, and once again she could smell the river as a motor boat carried her with friends to the bat cave. The sound of Lewis's, "I love you!" echoing through the covered bridge, and the tantalizing touch of horseflesh soothed her senses.

Stimulated with smelling salts, Rosie opened her eyes to a brightly lit airport staff lounge. Lewis was holding to her hand, calling her name. She called out in confusion, "Lewis?"

"Rosie? Are you alright?"

"We were waiting for our flight," she whispered, remembering. "You showed me the ring." Rosie let her eyes play across the room as she tried to recall the morning's events. With the remembrance of the terrible news came panic. "Oh, my God, does Victor know about the crash?"

Pressing her back against the sofa he explained all he knew. "He's been informed. Frank is on his way to one of the hospitals now."

"How's the weather?"

"It's still raining, but the storm has passed." Holding to her hand he said calmly, "I saw a breaking news segment on television. The plane went down at approximately eight this morning." Laying his head to her hand he replied tearfully, "We were on the air at eight."

Looking for a clock she asked, "What time is it now?"

He answered with his head still down, "After ten."

Tears burned as she replied, "We should know everything by now." Nudging him with her arm she demanded, "Call Ollie, again."

"I don't need anyone to tell me about Amber." With a shaky sigh he said, "She's gone."

Shocked by his admission Rosie asked, "How can you say that, Lewis? We don't know, yet."

He opened his mouth to explain, but choked on his own words. With tears pooling in his eyes he said simply, "I know."

Rosie closed her eyes and let the tears stream down her cheeks, and Lewis sat holding her hand, and together they cried for all they knew, and for all they feared. They watched news footage of the plane crash on the television in the staff lounge while sipping strong black coffee. Amber was gone, along with the handsome, talented Bobby. Jeff had perished, as well as Shelley, four crew members and both pilots. Some survivors were reported to have life threatening injuries, while others were said to be unharmed.

As soon as they could, they flew to the Pennsylvania town where the victims had been taken for treatment. Heather was waiting with Ted and Zeke in a private lounge. They both appeared shaken from the experience. Rosie embraced Heather asking, "Where's Kid?"

Ted answered, "He's okay, possible collarbone fracture. They got him in x-ray. Jude has a busted knee, and a broke arm." Turning to Lewis he said, "Your buddy Barron took some hard knocks. He and Darby were sent to a different hospital. They've got Barron in surgery right now. I'm not sure about Darby, it might be bad."

Long agonizing minutes passed before hospital personnel delivered the facts of the survivor's condition. Lewis sat down with a blank look on his face, while he listened to incomprehensible news. The voices seemed to be coming from far away as he heard of Barron's severe head injuries, and slim chance for survival. Darby was afflicted with a cervical spine injury and collapsed lung. His right arm was slashed so deeply he was in danger of losing use of it. The backup singer, Terri, was in surgery for a shattered pelvis. Lewis fell into a manic state of shock, realizing his band had been eliminated within a few fateful moments. And, his beautiful Amber was gone forever. He slid from his chair and crumbled onto the floor sobbing.

The following days were a blur for Rosie. The memorial service for the lost members was planned with as much care as a concert production. Kid was with her at Wildwood, recuperating from a dislocated shoulder and some broken ribs. He, Ted and Zeke were heroic in saving the other members. Heather told of how they ripped through the side of the plane to rescue Barron and Darby from a fiery death. Heather and Terri had been sitting together. Their seat had been thrown from the plane through a hole in the fuselage, landing them in a grassy field. After rescuing the survivors, Kid, Ted and Zeke continued to pull their fellow band members from the burning wreckage. All were saved from the fire, but not from death.

Unable to attend all the services together, Victor and Rosie separated, attending services for the lost members alone. Rosie had Kid and Jude with her as they traveled to Ft Lauderdale for Bobby's service. Victor and Frank attended Jeff's that was also in Ft Lauderdale, and Amber's in Miami. Never before had Rosie shed so many tears. She watched the strong soldier, Billy Ray weep uncontrollably for his friend as he stood at Bobby's casket.

It was with curiosity that she searched the pale pinched face of Bobby's mother, who held herself so regal and strong. After the service, as the crowd stood graveside awaiting the burial, they bowed their heads for prayer. When the workman took up shovels to fill in the grave, Ted fell to his knees. He began pushing the loose soil into the opened earth, and he sang. *"Lord I was born a ramblin' man,"* the words rolled off his tongue with the sad resonation of a spiritual slave song. *"Trying to make a living and doing the best I can."*

Following his lead, Billy Ray joined him on his knees, and he too pushed the earth with his hands onto the cement vault. He sang along with Ted in the same sad tone. Soon, other close friends of Bobby's were on their knees shoving the earth into the grave and singing, *"When it's time for leaving I hope you'll understand that I was born a ramblin' man."*

Jackie embraced Rosie, and they stood tearfully watching the heartbreak of so many strong men. It didn't go unnoticed when Bobby's mother turned and coldly left the gravesite while her son's death was brutally mourned.

Following the service for Bobby in Ft Lauderdale, Kid and Rosie were rushed to the airport where they joined Janie to travel by chartered jet to Shelley's service in Alabama. Ironically, Janie spent the time in flight comforting Rosie. Entwined with their arms, they sat together and talked quietly. "I hate that this has happened. We never even liked each other," Janie confessed. "Somehow I always thought things would change. And, now they never can."

Caressing her long smooth golden brown hair, Rosie said to the teenage girl, "Just as long as you know it wasn't your fault that your relationship with your sister was flawed, you'll be alright."

She relished the mothering touch of Rosie's hand and conceded with a heavy sigh, "I know I'll be alright. And, when I cry at her funeral, it won't be because I've lost her. It'll be because I never had her."

The service for Shelley was held in the same small church where Rosie and Janie had said their final farewells to Angel and Maggie. Lewis stood next to Mack offering condolence, while Mack slumped across her wooden casket. The big man shook with sobs, and Lewis spoke encouragement quietly in his ear. Rosie observed from her seated position in the pew, and wondered what Lewis could say to soothe the heart of his large friend. Straightening himself, Mack allowed Lewis to lead him from the casket, and seat him on the front pew with family members.

Following the service, the mourners stood around the grave piled high with aromatic floral arrangements. Slowly, people dispersed until only the family remained. Lewis approached Rosie who stood next to Heather, and gave her a soft kiss on the cheek. Taking his hand in hers Rosie asked, "When will I see you again, Lewis?"

Staring into her tired brown eyes he smiled and said, "Anytime you want, Rosie. Anytime at all," he then walked away with Opal and Ed.

Janie stood embraced by her mother, and together they wept for Shelley. Bert's health was not good, so he had been taken home by his good friends Rob and Mamie Shirey. Kid stood next to Janie with his head hung low, and his arm stretched out across her and his aunt. His father and mother stood behind him, each pressing a hand to Kid's shoulder, thankful for his survival.

Rosie turned to Heather and said, "I'm going home."

With a look of surprise Heather asked, "Back to Florida?"

"No," Rosie answered, "My father's house."

When Rosie drove into the now concrete driveway her eyes widened with delight. The photos Ed had sent didn't prepare her for the reality of the change that had been made to her childhood home. The grounds were landscaped and groomed. The house had been renovated back to its original post civil war state, with everything seemingly new. She entered through the back door, and marveled at the newly refurbished kitchen. Eva raced to greet her, still wearing the black dress she had attended the funeral in. "Come in. Let me fix you a glass of tea."

"Oh, please. Can I have a cup of black coffee, instead?"

Sturgill called from the living room, "Rosie? Is that you?"

"Yes! Just a minute, I want to look at the house." She opened the pantry door and smiled. Only the flooring had been replaced, just as she had instructed. Rosie wandered down the hallway admiring the new hardwood floors, and rich wood paneling. The lighting fixtures had all been replaced with beautiful brass ones. She marveled at the bathroom which had been enlarged with a huge window next to the bathtub, and approached her room with apprehension. Pushing open the door she revealed a cozy room with plush white carpet, pink wallpaper and a sweet canopy bed dressed in pale pink. She stepped to the closet and opened the door to reveal the same clothing she had left behind. She stepped to the floor mirror with the pink strapless gown she'd used for her high school performance. Closing her eyes she could see herself on stage with Lewis, and she longed to relive that night. Happiness then known now eluded her.

Eva was pouring a cup of coffee from a beautiful tea pot when Rosie arrived in the living room. Sitting next to her father on the new leather sofa she accepted the cup Eva offered. "Umm," she said agreeably.

Eva perched on her leather recliner and said, "I can afford the good brands now that I'm working at the hospital."

"Eva files insurance claims, and fights with insurance companies over patient's benefits," Sturgill explained.

Proudly, Eva declared, "And, I'm damn good at it, too."

Taking her cup, Rosie opened the new front door, and stood looking out at the renovated porch through solid glass. Admiring the ornate Cornish molding that had been replaced and smoothly painted, her eyes traveled across the new wood floor, coming to rest on the old rocking chair.

"Who are you looking for, Rosie?" Sturgill asked.

With a devilish smile she answered, "You know who."

The following weeks at Wildwood became months. Kid and Janie passed time horseback riding, and lounging by the pool. Barron and Darby had survived their devastating injuries, and were in rehabilitation centers near their Alabama homes. Rosie stayed in contact with Heather who stayed connected to Terri. The other singer was back in her native state of Tennessee, recovering from bone shattering injuries.

The publicity of the plane crash had sent album sales for both bands skyrocketing, and Frank toiled with Glenn to piece together a third album for the devastated Purple Sage. Radio stations continuously played *My Angel* in tribute to the fallen members. Die hard fans would be forced to pull off the highway in tears when the song played. Edwina especially loved the song, and requested Rosie play it on the expensive stereo, over and over. The frail woman would sit staring across the room with tears in her eyes as she listened to the sweet clear voice of Lewis Shirey singing the heart crushing lyrics that told his own sad story of loss.

The poignant sound of soft piano and tender violin swelled the heart with a knowing pain of someone's loss that was now felt by millions of Purple Sage and Gemini Rain fans. Hearing the song so often only added lesions to Rosie's wounded heart, and she yearned for the day when the song would be forgotten.

Edwina's health improved, and she regained strength. A stair lift was installed so she could enjoy her own second story bedroom. She could now walk with the assistance of a walker, and security of a health care provider. Continuing to dote on Edwina by playing piano and reading her favorite works aloud, Janie found the relationship she'd always longed for with her own grandmother. Rosie was surprised one day when she found Janie snuggled next to Edwina in her large expensive bed watching an old Fred Astaire movie. At the foot of the grand bed, lying together cozily, were bosom buddies, Elvis and Randy.

Because of Edwina's improved health, Victor took Rosie on an extended vacation to Paris, which was just as much a publicity stunt as it was a vacation. The senator and his singing wife made Paris headlines that reverberated back to the states. When they returned to Wildwood they were met by a scowling Frank who pretended to be happy with the news of the third and final album of Purple Sage. The album was scheduled to be released three weeks before Christmas, and was anticipated to be a huge seller.

Sensing Frank's jealousy, Victor suggested the two of them embark on a motorcycle trip like they had done in their younger days. "We can stay low profile, and camp beneath the stars. No one will know who we are. We'll be two ordinary guys on a cross country bike ride." Victor ignored the scowl his mother gave him as he pitched the idea to Frank.

Rosie poured a brandy for Edwina as she listened to Frank's acceptance of the idea. "I've always wanted to see Washington state," Frank mused.

Victor explained, "We'll truck our bikes up, and hit the trail once we get to Washington." He made the expedition seem so simple, saying, "Then after a few days, we'll simply truck the bikes back to Florida."

Edwina motioned frantically for her note pad as she mumbled words of discouragement. Rosie handed Edwina's note to Victor who chuckled as he read. *"Don't ride the bikes. It's beneath a Senator."* With humor dripping from his words he asked, "What's the matter, Mother? Are you afraid I won't be reelected if the public knows I'm a biker?" He laughed even harder when Edwina pointed her finger and mumbled angrily.

The week of Victor and Frank's trip, Ollie called Rosie and Kid into the studio to discuss with Glen efforts to repair the band. They met with Ted in Frank's office, and heard some unfinished tracks of Bobby and Jeff playing with the band. Glen explained, "We just can't use this to complete that song. The music tracks have to be redone, and I think it's time to find replacements for the band." Glen tossed down his silver ball point pen, and leaned back in the plush leather chair. "It's been six months since the plane crash, and it's time to move on. Do you want to choose your own replacements, or do I need to hold auditions?"

Ted spoke up and said, "We need Billy Ray. He was the heart of this band from the beginning."

Kid said, "I think it's best if we choose. It makes for less personality conflicts."

The meeting lasted for hours as Ted and Kid argued with Glen over Frank's selection of songs for the third album. Feeling unnecessary, Rosie paced slowly about the office observing awards and gold records the studio had produced. Signed photographs of top artists that no longer commanded an audience stared at Rosie mockingly. Thinking of a day when Gemini Rain would be just as forgotten gave her solace.

A meeting was set for the next day with Billy Ray and an old member of his garage band by the name of Cody Wells. Glen had them play solo in the studio and did several recordings. Then Glen had Cody and Billy Ray play with Ted and Kid. Glen listened to the tracks later in the presence of the group and announced the problems he detected, and proposed solutions.

Jackie had accompanied Billy Ray to the studio, and she sat next to Rosie as they merely listened. The group fell into an unexpected rehearsal with Rosie and Jackie providing vocals. At the end of the session, Glen announced his impressing views of Jackie's vocal talent. "I think you should consider a future as a singer, Jackie. You have great talent."

The following two days were scheduled as rehearsals in the studio, and Kid was overjoyed to be back at work. He and Ted had strong armed Glen into recording three unapproved songs for Frank's consideration. Rosie had Billy Ray and Jackie stay at Wildwood for the week as her guests. The demands of the studio had them up at dawn, and kept them until after dusk. Edwina was pleased to have fresh faces at the dining table, and encouraged Janie to tell naughty jokes for the guests. Life for Gemini Rain resumed with a ruthless determination as Ollie worked on concert dates and future tours.

Lunch had been catered at the studio for the group who ate while discussing business plans. Everyone fell quiet when Sonja burst into the room in tears, "Oh, my God! Glen take line one. It's Victor and Frank. They've been in an accident."

Glen snatched up the phone and spoke into it, "This is Glen Thompson, I'm Frank Ryder's associate." As he listened, Frank's head snapped back involuntarily. "Yes," he said, "I see." Looking at Sonja he told the caller, "Just stay on the line with me for a moment. I've got to put you on hold while my secretary gets this information." Listening to the caller, Glen said, "Yes, I see. But I've got to have someone else contact you with that information. One moment, please."

Glen pressed the hold button and turned to Sonja, "Get this guy's name and number. Call Ollie and get him on the line with the fellow ASAP. Then have Ollie meet me here. We'll fly out together for Washington." As Sonja started to leave the room Glen called behind her, "Tell Ollie to prepare a statement for the press, and to notify the senate committee of Victor's death."

Standing abruptly to her feet Rosie screamed, "No!" before folding into a dead faint.

Chapter Thirty-Six
What If

The funeral for Victor was a political affair with public officials speaking professionally polished eulogies. A huge historic cathedral contained the swollen crowd of well known mourners. The assembly included neighboring state's governors, as well as the vice-president of the United States. Note worthy stars of Hollywood and Motown joined with lesser known artists from Nashville's music row and Broadway. Rosie was directed with the precision of an actress on how to dress, what to say, and even when to cry. The entire experience left her cold and confused. Poor Edwina was sedated and flanked by her personal physician with two nurses at the funeral. Victor's casket was carried by uniformed members of the National Guard from the cathedral, and placed inside the hearse that carried him slowly to the cemetery where he was buried beside his father.

The weeks following Victor's death were painful and tense, as everyone waited with abated breath for news of Frank's recovery. After six weeks in intensive care, Frank succumbed to a lung infection and died in the hospital. Again, Rosie was prepped for a funeral, and this time she was chosen to speak the eulogy. Edwina was still fragile and did not attend the service, which only attracted a sprinkling of music stars. Frank's passing was sadly overshadowed by the more newsworthy death of Victor Hart. Because Frank had been estranged from his family, Rosie received permission from his closest relative to bury Frank near Victor in the Hart family cemetery. Something she kept secret from Edwina, who despised Frank and blamed him completely for her son's refusal to provide her with grandchildren.

Bitterness set into the frail mother's heart, as her hopes and dreams faded with the absence of her son. Edwina began to drink too much, and would occasionally shout mumbled curses at Rosie for weeks after finding out that she was responsible for the cursed Frank Ryder being planted in her family's plot. Janie and Hazel stayed with Edwina around the clock, trying to comfort her grief.

The loss of Victor and Frank put an indefinite halt to the resurrection of Gemini Rain, and Kid stayed by Rosie's side day and night. "I know you loved him, Sunny. Even though you didn't love him the way a wife loves a husband, I could see the respect and affection you had for him," Kid said to her as they walked the grounds of Wildwood one evening at dusk.

Falling into his arms she sobbed, "I did love him, I really did!"

In true Amber fashion he replied, "This, too, shall pass."

Ollie was constantly at Wildwood having Rosie sign papers and make decisions. "Frank's only beneficiary was Victor, and that means the entire studio is now yours, and your responsibility," he explained. "I suggest you give Glenn more authority, and bring Terry in to assist full-time. Music is a fickle business, Sunshine. It can't survive the least bit of neglect. I advise you allow Glen free reign. He will keep the studio alive." Ollie shuffled his pile of legal papers and eyed Rosie candidly. "After all, that studio is your legacy."

Staring silently at Ollie, Rosie said as a matter of fact, "You know how Edwina blackmailed me into this marriage, don't you?"

Taking up his briefcase he replied, "I thought we decided a long time ago, some things should remain secret." He then left the room.

Following Ollie's advice, Rosie turned the management of the studio over to Glenn. Jackie sat in for her as the band rehearsed and put down instrumental tracks. Despite her efforts to make amends with Edwina, Rosie was still shunned by her frail mother-in-law who drank more and succumbed to more weakness with each passing day. When Dr. Conley pressured Edwina to stop imbibing for her health's sake, the feisty delicate woman became furious, and slung mumbled curses at the doctor that were easily decipherable. It appeared the only person who could calm Edwina was Janie.

The year was 1976 and the month was July when Edwina lost her fight with the condition that weakened her body known to all as old age. Rosie was humbled by the sobs of grief that Janie screamed throughout the great house on the morning she found Edwina, cold and alone within her great bed. Again, Rosie was faced with the dignitaries of a memorial for the rich and powerful Edwina Morgan. Her service was carried out specifically to her written wishes, and she was buried next to her son and his father.

Darkness descended over the estate, and the servants mourned as if they had lost one of their own. Rosie was resigned to allow Ollie to make all the formalities as he was instructed, by provisions of Edwina's last will and testament. Being named the executor, Ollie arranged for the reading of the will in the great drawing room, so loved by Edwina. The room was filled with long serving employees, and the only family Edwina Morgan had, which consisted of Rosie and Janie.

Ollie read off monetary amounts left to various servants that Edwina had employed for many years. He announced certain charities that would be endowed with considerable amounts. To Rosie's astonishment, Edwina had left an extravagant amount of money to Andrea, with express wishes that Maria be made her legal guardian. Icy numbness gripped Rosie as Ollie remarked the remainder of Edwina's fortune would be bestowed upon Janie, and that nothing was left to her daughter-in-law, named as Sunshine Rose Hart.

Following the reading of the will, Ollie asked for a closed conference with Rosie. With just the two of them left in the lonely drawing room, he counseled her as an attorney. "Edwina has made provisions that you be exposed as the kidnapper of Andrea Diaz. There is ample evidence to indict you, and as your friend I advise you to seek out a criminal attorney as soon as possible. It will only take a few days for the Indiana state judicial system to have you arraigned, and extradited on a variety of charges."

Astonished, Rosie sank into the chair most favored by Edwina, and put her face into her hands. "All these years I wasted for nothing," she moaned. Then somewhere deep inside her consciousness, she saw the dark humor of her predicament, and Rosie laughed. Her icy laughter rang out across the desolate room, and through the heavy oak doors, closed against prying eyes.

With defense attorney John Walker at her side, recommended by Randy, Rosie turned herself in to Indiana authorities. After being booked, she was placed in a holding cell while awaiting bond. A soft familiar voice spoke to her through the steel bars, "Sunshine?"

She raised her head, and broke into a big smile. "Randy!"

"I most certainly wish you had confided your crimes to me sooner, my Sunshine, but have no fear. John Walker will keep you in good, gentle hands," said Randy with confidence.

"Confessing sooner would not have changed anything, my Randy," she smiled. "Sooner or later, these prison bars were just waiting for me."

A soft laugh erupted from the handsome young lawyer, dressed impeccably in suit and tie with expensive soft leather shoes. "Prison bars can't hold Sunshine!" he exclaimed. "You belong in the sky amongst the stars, you silly girl!"

While awaiting the decision from the Indiana Grand Jury on whether or not she was to stand trial for her crime, Rosie returned to Boca Raton where she threw herself into studio work. Gemini Rain finished the third album with plans to embark on a strenuous promotional tour. Jackie became Rosie's stand in, and she worked diligently to carry off the smooth soulful sound of Rosie's voice. Kid became Rosie's crutch, and she leaned on him constantly. Kid was appointed Janie's guardian, and they remained at the estate with only a skeleton crew. Jude came to live at Wildwood, taking residence in one of the apartments left empty by retreating staff. Maria had achieved temporary custody as Andrea's guardian, pending further appeals from Andrea's own birth mother. Lillian took over the kitchen duties, and decided to reside in the spooky mansion only if Rosie shared her suite. Victor's old room became Lillian's, and the kitchen became her exclusive domain.

Reporters hounded Rosie, lying in wait outside the gates of Wildwood and the studio. Unable to make any comments on the criminal charges, Rosie swam through the slew of reporters tight lipped. For additional support, Sturgill and Eva flew to Boca Raton, and spent a week with their daughter. They went out in public allowing photographers to snap pictures of a united family. No one was safe from the glare of publicity, not even Janie, who was being declared the nation's richest teen.

Rosie had become a late night telephone addict as she spoke with Heather, Lewis and Randy for hours at a time. During one conversation with Lewis he asked her, "That day at the airport restaurant, you were about to tell me about Andrea weren't you?"

"Yes. I was ready to tell you everything. I was going to tell you Victor was gay, and only married me to further his political career, and how his mother blackmailed me into marrying him." Rosie paused and said, "But, I wasn't going to tell you because you wanted to marry Amber. I was going to tell you because I wanted you to know."

"Well, I'd be lying if I said that I didn't want you to be jealous of my plans to marry Amber. But, I can't say I didn't love her, either."

"We've both lost too much, Lewis. I want you to have happiness, and I know you want the same for me."

"I don't think either one of us know how to be happy."

Glen pushed the band into resuming the tour he had negotiated. Gemini Rain started out doing six shows a week along the East Coast, ending in Vegas doing eight shows in one week. Rosie was delighted to see fans holding signs proclaiming their support for her. At the end of their tour, promoting songs from the new album, Glen set about planning for its release. Ironically, the album was released the same week that the state of Indiana declared a date for a preliminary hearing in Rosie's case. Maria too, had to face courtroom dramas with the birth mother who failed to protect Andrea, and now only wanted her for the money she had inherited.

The hearing date was set for late November, with Rosie being allowed to remain free on bond pending a trial. Ironically, all the bad publicity strengthened Rosie's popularity, which in turn reflected on Gemini Rain. Having the legal woes looming ahead of her, she was forbidden to do interviews with the top ranking journalists who vied for her story.

On a hot late summer afternoon, Heather called gushing over her newly laid wedding plans. "It's for real, Rosie. I've found the love of my life, and we're getting married in September, the Labor Day weekend. You will be my matron of honor won't you?"

"Of course I will!" Rosie proclaimed, "With my uncertain future, this may be my last formal event." She spent hours talking on the phone about the man Heather was to marry, and all her happy plans. Lewis and Heather had revived Purple Sage with the healed Barron and Darby. Terri had returned as a backup singer, and they had painstakingly located two more singers resembling the voices that Amber and Shelley had left silenced. Heather was on top of the world.

Without understanding why, Rosie noticed unhappiness in Kid. Nothing seemed to satisfy him. Everyone gave in to his demands, the producers, the band members, even Rosie herself. Still his discontent was dampening to the spirit of the entire band. He began acting in his old outrageous manner to gain attention from the press. He was hospitalized briefly following a car crash that totaled another one of his prized Porches. Glen became furious with him following an arrest in a Las Vegas nightclub where he punched a drunken heckler out cold. He began to disappear for days at a time, and tabloids reported his dalliance with Hollywood starlets and runway models.

Heartbroken from his behavior Rosie asked, "When did you stop loving me, Kid?" They sat alone in the recording studio.

He came to her and sank to his knees. His astonishing tear filled eyes sparkled breathtaking amethyst as he confessed his feelings. "The public will never forgive us if we marry, Sunny. They only see us as cousins, and we can't change that." He put his head in her lap and cried, "I can't do anything that will damage your public image, my love. It's for you I do this, please believe me." He lifted his face saying painfully, "But I haven't stopped loving you, and I never will."

With tired resignation she asked, "What am I supposed to do without you?"

He pushed away from her with an exhausted effort, and meandered slowly across the room toward the exit. Standing with his hand on the doorknob Kid said without looking at her, "Move on, Sunny. Find someone new." Slowly, he opened the door, and without looking back, left her alone in the studio.

Unable to face the pressures of the press, Rosie didn't attempt to date anyone. Her escorts to public events were usually Glenn, Terry or Ollie. The loneliness of not having Kid with her at Wildwood shoved her into a dark depression, and she began to rely on sleeping pills for rest.

It was on a sun warmed mountain day that Rosie stood beside Heather during the rehearsal for her wedding. The small lake cottage had been transformed into a grand house with the money Heather had given her mother. Only the most intimate friends of the bride and groom had been invited, and Teresa Tillman basked in the happiness of her daughter. Lewis was at the rehearsal dinner with Terri as his date. Rosie was without an escort, as she had at last come to terms with being alone.

The rehearsal dinner was a buffet set up in Teresa's dining room. Tables had been set up outside on the deck with the setting sun reflecting on the lake in the background. Soft music drifted from a stereo system inside the house, and professional photographers snapped roll after roll of film. Not having much of an appetite, Rosie continuously reached for the glasses of champagne. When Heather teased her about drinking her meal Rosie responded with her own criticism, "The last time I saw you eat a meal was the fourth of July 1969." Her comment brought chuckles from the guests gathered at the party.

Lifting her champagne glass to her lips Heather retorted, "Well, I'd rather be thin than drunk." Heather's comment brought even more chuckles.

Later, when the meal was finished, and night had fallen, Rosie stole away to take a quiet walk along the lake shore. She was startled by the presence of a man with the glowing end of a cigarette in his mouth. "Oh! Excuse me."

The dark figure asked, "Is that you, Rosie?"

Hearing his voice was like hearing music. "Lewis, what are you doing?" Stepping nearer, Rosie's question was already answered as she recognized what kind of cigarette he was smoking.

Smiling broadly, Lewis offered her the joint. "Like old times, huh?"

"Not for me," she said. "I decided to give up the smoke when I kept driving around my neighborhood looking for my house."

"Really?" he asked through inhaled smoke. "I'd be like 'Damn, where can I get some more of this shit!'" He laughed lightly, "Can you remember the first joint we smoked together?"

She giggled, "We sat in Ed's car. It was Red Bud and badass!"

"There was snow on the ground, and if anyone had seen they would have thought Ed's car was on fire!"

"We were twelve years old, Lewis!"

"And, I was madly in love with you, even then."

"Of course you were! That's why you shot me in the eye with your water pistol," she giggled. Seriously she asked, "Do you think pot will ever be legal, like alcohol?"

"Only pot brownies will ever be legal," he sighed knowingly.

"What makes you think that?"

"You don't smoke them."

Rosie giggled, "Right, I see your point."

"Did you hear about the kid who overdosed on pot?"

"No!" exclaimed Rosie.

"Me neither," he smiled. "Why didn't Kid come with you?"

She hesitated to answer, but finally said, "Well, I didn't ask him for one thing."

Without any hesitation at all he asked smartly, "Every tabloid in the country has published pictures of him with a string of women. Don't you care?"

"No, I really don't."

Rosie spent the night with Heather, and they stayed up late giggling like the schoolgirl friends they once were. For her sleeping concoction, Rosie broke open a sleeping capsule and sprinkled the powder in a glass of champagne. Using her finger, she stirred the wine until the crystals were dissolved, and then downed it in two big gulps.

Heather groaned, "You can't keep doing that, Rosie. That's how Marilyn Monroe died."

Rosie replied, "Really? I thought she was murdered."

Later, while slumbering in the guest room, Rosie dreamed of Doc Campbell. He sat in the rocking chair shuffling cards. His head was bowed low, and all Rosie could see was the perfectly straight nose and mustache sprinkled with gray. Without fear, she approached him saying, "Deal me in."

Standing from his chair he motioned for her to follow. She followed him. When he opened the pantry door she followed into the sunlit garden. They settled at the wrought iron patio table. Taking a seat, he began dealing cards. Having dealt five cards for each, he waved his hand in a gesture for Rosie to take the chair opposite him.

Taking up the cards she revealed two black aces, and two black eights with the queen of hearts. Discarding the queen she said, "I'll take one card please." Before the card could be dealt a strong gust of wind blew against her, and dark clouds blocked the sun. Pushing hair from her eyes, Rosie looked across the table for Doc, but he was gone. Lying on the table was an old fashioned revolver on top of four cards to prevent them from blowing away. Reaching across the table she took up the cards. They were all red, two aces and two eights with the queen of diamonds.

She awoke with a start, thinking she heard thunder in the distance. Panic stricken, she sprang from bed to look out the window. Sparkling stars shone brilliantly in a cloudless sky. Slipping into her night robe, Rosie left the bedroom and tiptoed downstairs. The clock on the kitchen wall mockingly showed the time to be four o'clock as it loudly ticked off the seconds. Remembering Janie's description of this particular time of day, she sat down and began jotting off lyrics to the first song she had ever attempted to write. She titled it *The Late Night Side of Morning.*

Rosie was drinking her second cup of coffee, and watching the early morning news when Teresa came into the kitchen. "Well, good morning, dear," she called cheerily. "How long have you been up?"

Rosie frowned and said, "Don't ask."

With sympathy Teresa said, "I'm sorry you didn't sleep well." She poured herself a cup of coffee and sat next to Rosie. "I do hope things will work out for you in that ridiculous kidnapping case. And, I'm so proud of you for all you've accomplished. Not to mention the gratitude I feel for the help you've given Heather to realize her dream in the music industry."

"Heather was bound to find success. Her talent is just too big," said Rosie.

"Yes," Teresa smiled. "I believe you." Glancing at the clock she said, "Well, it's time for me to wake her. I'll be back shortly."

Back in her room, Rosie dressed in jeans and t-shirt, pulling her hair back with a jeweled clasp that was a gift from Victor. When she returned to the kitchen, Teresa seemed worried. "I'm afraid Heather is coming down with the flu. She's too tired to get out of bed." Teresa poured a small glass of orange juice and headed back up the stairs. Several minutes passed before Rosie was alarmed by Teresa's shouts for help. Racing up the stairs, Rosie found Heather crumpled on the floor unconscious. She rolled her onto her back and assessed her vitals. Trying to hide her fear, Rosie calmly told Teresa to call for an ambulance, and she began administering CPR. When the paramedics arrived, Rosie was drenched in perspiration from her continuous efforts to revive the nonexistent heartbeat.

She stepped back and embraced the frantic Teresa while they looked on helplessly at the emergency workers efforts to save Heather. The frantic mother collapsed into fearful sobs as she watched her daughter be carried away.

Quickly, Rosie collected Teresa and followed the ambulance. They arrived at the emergency room entrance just in time to see Heather being rushed in. Leaping from the car, Rosie and Teresa ran after the gurney carrying Heather's lifeless body, but hospital personnel stopped them with physical force as they tried to brush past them.

"You can't go in there!" A stern faced nurse shouted. "We're working an emergency, and you're not allowed to interfere."

Reluctantly, Rosie and Teresa allowed themselves to be ushered into a waiting room filled with other people who all faced a crisis. Teresa dissolved into sobs, while Rosie tried to soothe her with encouragement. "I just can't understand what's happened," the tearful mother cried. "She's young, and healthy. She has her whole life ahead of her. What could possibly be wrong?"

Rosie hugged Teresa, and soothed her with words of comfort as the emaciated image from that day in the dressing room haunted her. Instant regret took hold of Rosie, for she felt blame for the state of Heather's health. After all, it was her suggestion to Victor that landed Heather in his studio. It was Rosie who opened the door for Purple Sage to join the ranks of rock stars, making it possible for cruel critics to dub Heather as fat. Guilt gnawed at her.

Only a half hour had passed since Heather had been brought into the ER, when a nurse came to Rosie and Teresa. "The doctor is ready to see you now," she said. They followed her through triage and onto an elevator to the second floor. The nurse brought them into an empty waiting room where one of the attending physicians waited. "This is Dr. Jenkins. He is the doctor who attended your daughter in the ER."

The nurse's tone sent a cold dread over Rosie, and she held her breath while waiting for the doctor to speak. Taking Teresa's hand he gently said, "I'm sorry. She didn't make it."

Pushing the doctor's hands away Teresa dissolved into grief sobbing, "What have you done with my daughter? Where is my baby?"

Feeling faint, Rosie slumped into a hard chair while tears flooded her face.

"I'm so sorry, Mrs. Tillman. It was her heart, and we couldn't save her. She's been sick for a long time. I'm very sorry." Dr. Jenkins spoke quietly to the nurse who quickly left the room and returned with a tray. "I'd like for you to let me give you a sedative, Mrs. Tillman. This will help you cope."

Teresa slid into a chair while staring blankly at the wall as she allowed Dr. Jenkins to give her the injection while tears streamed down her anguished face. Before leaving the room, Dr. Jenkins folded his hands as he looked sadly at Teresa. "Your daughter's heart condition was brought on by malnutrition. I only wish I could have seen her sooner." Without any further words Dr. Jenkins left the room.

It was Teresa's decision that Heather be buried in her wedding gown. The funeral was almost more than Rosie could bear. She leaned heavily on her father as they filed past the casket for a final farewell. A poster size enlargement of the happy couple's engagement photo sat stoically on an ornate easel. Heather was mourned pitifully by her groom to be, and his anguish was felt by everyone in attendance.

Overwhelmed with grief, Rosie rejected the condolence Lewis offered. She turned away from him, and leaned on her father as they made their way from the mausoleum where Heather was laid to rest. Words spoken by Teresa haunted Rosie as Eva drove her and her father from the cemetery. "Ever since she was a little girl, Heather was afraid to be buried in the ground. She made me promise to place her in a mausoleum, and I promised her I would."

The following days left Rosie unable to leave her bed in the newly refurbished room of her father's house. Eva brought trays of food to her room, and begged her to take just the smallest amount of nourishment. A small mountain of phone messages grew on Rosie's dressing table. Finally, after four days of bed confinement, Willene Reyes arrived to comfort her.

Willene said, "Heather is gone now, and you've been through more loss than anyone ever should. But, you've got to take care of yourself. God works in mysterious ways, you know. All that you've been through is meant to make you stronger." Urging Rosie to take a shower and dress Willene said, "Sometimes only the strong can be gentle. I know you, Rosie. You are the strongest, gentlest person I've ever known. You can survive this."

After a shower, Willene dried and styled Rosie's hair as she sipped coffee and stared miserably into the mirror. As she watched her neighbor through the reflection Rosie could see a change in the older woman. Willene appeared younger, and her happiness shone like an inner light had been left burning.

"You are glowing, Willene. What has made you so happy?"

The older woman caught Rosie's gaze in the mirror and held it briefly before answering. "You are observant, aren't you?" She smiled softly, "It is true. I am happy, but I wasn't going to say anything until you were feeling better."

"Tell me now and maybe it will make me feel better."

Willene's gaze went back to the thick russet locks she was working with and replied, "I've decided to enroll in cosmetology school. I want to be a hairstylist now that I'm all grown up."

"You would be great at it," Rosie said with encouragement. "But I don't understand how continuing your education can make you shine with such happiness."

"Well, there is something else."

"Aren't you going to tell me?"

A blush crossed the older woman's cheeks, "I'm getting married."

"Bonzie?"

Willene shook her head yes in response to Rosie's question. Tears welled in her eyes as she replied, "I think he's grown up now, too."

Confusion embraced Rosie and she felt a variety of emotion surge through her. Distrust of the man who had visited with Eva in the past caused Rosie to fear the possibility of her dear friend suffering heartache at his hands. "Wait a minute. I thought Mr. Leak had used up all his marriage opportunities. How can he legally marry again?"

Putting her hand to her mouth to hide girlish exuberance Willene explained, "His first wife has agreed to sign annulment papers for us. After all, the only reason they married was because Bonzie was going off to war. Times were hard when the war broke out, and it was an honorable thing for a man to do at the time. You see if Bonzie had never made it back Effie would have received a pension. But, she filed for divorce while he was still fighting in Italy."

A soft chuckle grew deep inside Rosie until she was laughing happily. She threw her arms around Willene, saying, "Make sure I get an invitation to the wedding, okay."

Returning the hug, Willene answered, "I will, I will."

Willene coaxed Rosie into a simple meal of grilled cheese and tomato soup. After forcing the food down, she went for a walk among the turning leaves. Meandering around her backyard, she came upon the rose bush she'd grown from the cutting Willene had given her from Minnie Mama's garden so long ago. One last tired bloom clung to the thorny bush, and Rosie mused dreamily of Willene carrying a bridal bouquet of the delicious flowers. Carefully she bowed to inhale its fragrance. The aroma of the effervescent rose was intoxicating, awakening memories from an innocent summer, not yet touched by the bitter experience of lost love, lost innocence and lost lives. Remembering the name of the rose, she repeated it out loud, "Sutter's Gold."

While sitting in the old rocking chair on the front porch, Rosie heard a strangely familiar sound, and looked in the direction from which it came. Along the concrete path to the porch rode Lewis on his old rusting bicycle. He smiled boyishly when he came face to face with her. "Hi ya!" he called out while he maneuvered the bike into a halt.

"Hi there," Rosie called. "What are you trying to prove? That you're not an old man, yet?" She stood and descended the steps from her porch to greet him with a hug.

"Well, I'm not!" he proclaimed then added, "Yet." Looking at the rocking chair she had just left empty Lewis asked, "Is that old guy still here?"

Laughing she said, "If you're talking about Doc Campbell the answer is yes." Tilting her head she added, "Or, at least his spirit is."

With a mischievous laugh Lewis asked, "Does he still play cards and drink booze?"

Closing her eyes, Rosie inhaled deeply and replied, "As a matter of fact he does. I even played a hand with him myself not long ago." She became quiet for a moment as she recalled the unusual dream. "It was strange. He dealt us both the same hand. My cards were black, but his cards were red."

With curiosity in his voice Lewis asked, "What were the cards?"

Straddling the bicycle tire, Rosie pulled Lewis closer to her and answered, "Two aces and two eights." Seeing the expression of shock on his face Rosie asked, "Why? What's special about that?"

Lewis blew out a chortled breath. "Rosie, that's the dead man's hand." Seeing her furrowed brows he explained, "That's the cards some old gun slinger had when he got shot down, and ever since it's been called the dead man's hand."

Tilting her head sideways, Rosie realized the importance of the dream as a warning she couldn't understand and said, "Well, how interesting." Stepping back she asked, "Did you come to give me a history lesson, or did you come to give me a ride on your bike?"

Smiling sweetly, he answered, "Willene called me. She thinks you need some distraction." With a motion of his hand to the handlebars Lewis said, "Hop aboard!"

Positioning herself on the handle bars, she leaned back against the familiar scent of fresh soap. As they rolled smoothly from the concrete drive onto the asphalt country road Lewis asked, "Are you worried about the hearing?"

Gliding beneath the autumn colored trees that sent occasional showers of falling leaves into their path Rosie replied, "Not at all."

"Why? How can you be so calm?"

"Oh, I don't know really. Maybe I just inherited old Doc's gambling traits. Let's just say I feel like I have an ever present ace up my sleeve."

"No one thinks you have anything to worry about. There's great confidence that'll you'll be acquitted. *Rolling Stone* even did an article on it, revealing a poll of its readers that considers your actions as heroic, not criminal."

Leaning against his firm body, Rosie asked, "Do you ever sit around and ask yourself *what if* questions?

"My most contemplated *what if* question is, what if Tom Noble hadn't committed suicide? Do you realize how different everything would be right now, if that poor unfortunate soul hadn't put a bullet in his head? Shelley and Janie would never have come to live with Bert. Meaning, Angel could still be alive, and Kid would have stayed in Detroit that summer. I never would have gotten involved with his drug dealing, and I never would have wound up in Florida where I met Victor."

The narrow bicycle tires hummed along the smooth pavement, "Maybe, but maybe not."

"Why? What are you thinking?"

He leaned closer with his lips at her ear and said, "Camille would probably have brought Shelley and Janie here, anyway. And, who's to say how Kid may or may not have come to Ben Johnson Ridge that summer." Lewis put his lips to Rosie's ear lobe and left a delicate kiss, before talking on. "It's hard to accept what happened to Angel, but all in all, I have to make myself believe it was her time to go. If it hadn't been for you, she would have been lost that day at the lake."

Closing her eyes against the sunlight she asked, "What if I go to jail? Will you visit me in prison?"

"Sure," he replied. "Maybe they'll give you a job in the kitchen and you can bake up some of those special brownies for the inmates."

"And, maybe you can be a celebrity advocate for the legalization of marijuana," she suggested.

"Yes, I certainly could," he agreed. "You know it's much less dangerous than alcohol. Drunks run stop signs; stoners wait for it to turn green."

Rosie laughed delightedly as they traveled through a shower of fall foliage. And her laughter became entangled in the cool breeze, carrying it like wind song across the vibrant autumn colored landscape of Ben Johnson Ridge.